The Magnificent Era:

A saga in five parts based on historical characters from the Era OF Suleiman the Magnificent

Part III

IBRAHIM Pasha

From heaven to hell

By
Alexander Garbolas

Part 3: Ibrahim

"Ask an infant with his eyes still closed and trust its words.
There are no other worlds or second lives!
Everything I know is just my own experiences.
You are the hallucinating one!"
(Rumi)

Part 3:
Ibrahim: From Heavens to Hell

TABLE OF CONTENTS

Introduction of the third book of the series

This particular volume is freely based on the historical evidence related to the acts and days of Grand Vizier Ibrahim Pargali during the final period of his illustrious career, after he became "Serasker", i.e. Field Marshal, participating actively in the historic Ottoman victory against the Hungarian Kingdom at Mohacs in 1526, the conquests of Budapest, and the first Ottoman siege of Vienna in 1529 with his friend and Sultan, Suleiman Khan the Magnificent.

His notable military exploits were later continued, as he conquered Tabriz while Suleiman remained ill in Constantinople, and later entered Baghdad in 1534 along with the Sultan who by then had recovered. However, on their return to Constantinople, something unexpected happened that led to his execution during the night of 15/3/1536 according to the existing historical sources. What was the true reason for this execution it has not yet been accurately resolved by historians and the only reliable source of the events, besides unconfirmed rumors, is the Ottoman miniature at the beginning of the last chapter of this volume that depicts Ibrahim's coffin being transported from the Seraglio to the Golden Horn shore by Janissary guards.

Where Ibrahim was buried is still open to wild speculation that was recently further enhanced as an old tomb on the European shores of the Bosporus Straits was supposedly identified. However, this dubious archeological find has not yet been confirmed by reliable archeologists, and the possibility it was an advertising stun related to the popular Turkish TV is at the moment the most probable explanation.

The most common and digestible excuse offered by historians for Ibrahim's execution, namely that he signed a peace treaty using the title "Sultan" Ibrahim under his signature, makes no sense, unless Sultan Suleiman was a mentally disturbed personality with an inferiority complex, insanely fearful of traitors, usurpers and conspirators.

Of course, this sever explanation may be consistent with Suleiman's later murderous decisions to execute two of his sons, the most able ones; however, executing an intimate friend or your male children is an extremely violent choice, demanding many more causes than the remote possibility of treasonous behavior that was never proved or even hinted by first hand witnesses who swear Ibrahim was loyal till the end.

The reader should be finally reminded that all legal wives of Suleiman the Magnificent as well as his mother and sisters were addressed as Sultan! Thus, for Ibrahim signing with this title could be considered even as a private joke related to their intimate relationship.

Even more dubious is the accusation that Ibrahim was supposedly executed, because he had an intimate relationship with an unnamed female slave. During this glorious era, four legal wives were allowed and dozens of concubines residing inside the mansion of every affluent Ottoman sharing his bedroom with his wife. Therefore, this is another travesty conception comparable with blaming the low morals of every Oriental man engaged in homosexual relationships in an era, when any man in the Middle East might be considered a freak, if he didn't appreciate the charms of a young handsome lad. Therefore, the historic texts that are presently available might well be the result of extensive diachronic censorship, erasing all the unacceptable details of a powerful sovereign's life during each subsequent era, as stricter morality standards became gradually the acceptable norm for all the subsequent Sultans.

This trend was fully realized when "democracy" was introduced triumphantly in the Ottoman Empire, the Swiss constitution was adopted, oriental clothes and religious customs changed, and a variation of the formal Latin alphabet replaced the Arabian calligraphy for modern Turkey to make a new start from scratch, without the heavy Ottoman ballast under Mustafa Kemal "Ataturk" leadership. However, no historical editing and beautifying can be expected to be perfect, and the general dismissal of the entire Osmanli dynasty as comprised by sexually degenerate sovereigns is another apparent travesty that unjustly dismisses for political reasons the contributions of many brilliant strategists and capable administrators, like Murat II, Mehmet the Conqueror, Selim the Grim, and Suleiman the Magnificent, Murat IV, or Mahmud II. These exceptional men have turned in few centuries an aging Eastern Roman Empire that had shrank within the walls of a single city into the most powerful empire in the world since the demise of Genghis Khan and Tamerlane.

Another critical piece of information about Ibrahim's personality comes from an unexpected source, Venice. Thus, the Venetians considered Ibrahim as the most handsome man of the Ottoman Empire, which might be an exaggeration; however, the fact they also used the term Ibrahim the "Magnificent" because of his great attention on appearances and glamor for as long as he was alive, is an important clue suggesting jealousies between the two friends. Indeed, "Magnificent" is an adjective used only by European historians for Suleiman many years after his death, while the less flamboyant Ottoman subjects consider him simply as "Kanuni" or the "Lawgiver".

A curious coincidence, "Allah's blessing", or a stroke of luck is the emergence during the Suleiman era of a considerable number of outstanding statesmen, warriors and artists that were almost completely absent during the previous two Sultans, Bayezid II and Selim I. Capable admirals like Barbarossa, Piyale Pasha, Piri and Turgut Reis, brilliant Grand Viziers like Pargali Ibrahim, Rüstem and Sokollu Pasha, inspired architects like Mimar Sinan and his students Devut and Mehmet Aga, notable poets like Baki and Fuzuli, and nameless other artists like calligraphers, ceramic tile iconographers, or Islamic floral decorators appeared for almost one hundred years, creating the Golden Ottoman Century approximately from 1500 to 1600 AD.

Such a notable coincidence naturally poses the cyclical question: "Were these remarkable men responsible for the prosperity of the Ottoman Empire, or was the unusual prosperity of the Ottoman Empire responsible for their emergence?" This is a rhetorical question similar to the doubt about the origin of the chicken and the egg that has been answered recently by paleontology that has proved that both the chicken and the egg are the result of evolution of the egg-laying dinosaurs.

The present author, as explained in greater detail in the introduction of the first volume centered on the deeds of Selim I the Grim, tries hard to create a logical myth based on truthful traditions and customs that encircles unquestionably fixed in time historical facts in a similar way as a string acts in the childish game "cat's cradle", knowing that drastically different shapes may appear using the same string and fingers depending on the skill of the player. Thus, the fundamental questions, seeking answers and playing the role of the string in this novel, are why a remarkable sovereign would decide to execute a devoted friend since childhood.

To seek answers the author had to travel back in time, when the hero's cruel but brilliant father, Selim the Grim, was the Sultan for eight short years. During this period narrated in the first volume, Selim had not only usurped the throne from his father Bayezid and executed his two older brothers and their children; but also two of his own children for obscure reasons.

Similarly appalling crimes occur occasionally also in modern times by so-called "disturbed personalities" or "serial killers", as many mental disturbances are caused by childhood traumas and severe sexual aberrations. Therefore, if a biased author tries to bypass these historic events, he is left with several insolvable puzzles that have no convincing answers worthy of modern more sophisticated and uncompromising forensic minds.

Fortunately, despite isolated cases of modern world leaders, contemporary readers are more liberally oriented than in the Middle Ages. They have seen with their own eyes many "unreasonable" miracles during their lives, like patricides, matricides, infanticides, genocides, etc., so they tend to accept more scientific and refined approaches than simply the medieval assertion "It was Allah's will", or consider "man to man" relationships as an abomination, or the result of viruses and genetic abnormalities.

Another problematic personality that plays an important role in the second and third volume is a female Ukrainian slave who had skillfully manipulated the Sultan Suleiman the Magnificent into commit several atrocious murders. For this particular slave's social status, the author pays special attention and considers as a very important clue another irrefutable historic event, namely a historically real harem brawl, when the Tatar Princess and legitimate wife of Suleiman, Mahidevran Sultan, attacked and battered badly the lower status female slave, Hurrem, calling her names like "sold meat" without her offering any resistance.

This is not a totally surprising behavior, as a slave striking back her master's legal wife might be considered a sufficient reason for a summary execution. However, this is not an easily explainable event, since at the time of this brawl both women had already produced Suleiman offspring, creating an unbreakable blood bond within the House of Osman.

The "official" formal narration of Suleiman's story, accepts the rumor that Hurrem was the daughter of a priest abducted by marauding Tatars, and carried to Constantinople as a virgin to be sold in a slave bazaar for the Sultan's harem. However, considering what happens to captive women even in the "civilized" present era during "religious" or other violent nationalistic wars, as the Yugoslavian crisis, the Islamic revolt in the Middle East, or WW II in the Ukraine and Germany, to mention just a few conflicts, this is a highly unlikely scenario this suspicious author is not willing to accept, because it would mean that the human species in the last five centuries has been transformed from forgiving angels into raping beasts.

On the contrary, it is much easier to presume that the largely dissolved or subtly transformed institution of slavery that extends even today leading women or young men into prostitution, worked equally efficiently in the Balkans during the Middle Ages as it presently does, especially after severe military conflicts, or several political and economic crises.

Traces of our more violent past can be still discovered in many unexpected places. For instance, a very common curse even among modern Greek Orthodox Christians in the Balkans is the despicable for all Christians: "I'll f... your Virgin Mary". If such appalling concepts were so widely spread around in the Middle Ages that have reached modern times, imagine what chances had an attractive virgin daughter of a Christian priest captured by pagan or Muslim Tatars to reach Constantinople slave bazaars unmolested!

The truth is that modern nationalistic states prefer to create perfect national heroes with impeccable characters to serve as inspiring role models for the so-called deplorable masses. During this "noble" process many human faults are swept under the rug with the false notion that, if all these character "weaknesses" became widely known, the historical image would fail to perform as intended, i.e. as a unifying national symbol. A typical example of this tendency in the Balkan Peninsula is Count Dracula the Impeller who was considered a national hero of Rumania under Ceausescu.

For the present writer this trend is fully understandable, but not convincing enough to be accepted at face value in a novel. The author is not a politician or a fanatic nationalist and philosophically he trusts that all world leaders are human beings as faulty as anyone else in a state of continuous evolution from inventive monkeys to benevolent divine entities. Therefore, the fact that if someone manages to unite nations around him and perform unusual deeds despite few uncommon character faults is a notable fact that makes his deeds even more remarkable historical phenomena. For instance, if we decide to present Napoleon Bonaparte as a magnificent male specimen like the classic Apollo, Hermes or Hercules, we are distorting his image so much that he may not have become who he was, if he was a foot taller.

Napoleon was not the only historic figure with drawbacks. Tamerlane was lame, Stalin had his left hand shorter than the right, and Hitler might have few drops of Jewish blood in his veins that spoiled his Aryan "perfect" mixture, science has proved it originally came from the heart of Africa.

At this point the author will simply point out that many times during a war extremely violent behaviors are encountered, and there has to be a reason for it besides the will to survive deeply imbedded in the human unconscious. For this reason the author has adopted the more democratic strategy of accepting morally compromising roles for all his heroes, so no one can ever claim this author is idealizing the ruling class or demote the proletarian slaves!

Finally, it may sound like a truism, but it is a well-documented historical fact that in every royal, imperial, or aristocratic family, secrecy about the past is forcefully enforced, and there is no reason for secrecy, if there are no secrets. On the contrary, it has become a popular motto that absolute power corrupts absolutely!

If powerful dynastic sovereigns do not exist these days, the imaginative reader should carefully observe the lives of movie, rock stars, or politicians instead. Then, before expressing doubts on the author's objectivity, he may discover their careers are not so rigidly based on "democratic" rules, sexual abstinence, or religious values. Thus, it is much more probable that when more secret communications, emails, private confessions, paparazzi photos, selfies, etc. of modern notables are revealed by legal or probably illegal means, all existing myths for the sanctity of the blue bloods of many world leaders, celebrities and aristocrats will collapse.

A summary of historical facts on the main heroes of the third book

1. Selim I the Grim: He was the son of Bayezid II and Aisha Hatun. He was born in Amasya in 1470 and he reigned from 1512 to 1520 until he died. With the help of the Janissary Corps he forced his father to abdicate because he was too benevolent, religious and peaceful. Sultan Bayezid favored as his heir his older son Ahmet, but this son lost favor with the Ottoman clergy, when he followed the heretic sect of Sufism. Immediately after the "coronation" of Sultan Selim I in 1511, on his way to Edirne his deposed father died suddenly, possibly by poisoning. Thereafter, Selim's older brothers Ahmet and Korkut were strangled together with their sons on his orders. Next Selim executed three of his sons too, keeping alive only Suleiman and his six daughters, Hatidge Sultan, Fatma Sultan, Beyhan Sultan, Shah Sultan, Hafsa Sultan, and Hâfize Sultan from two of his wives Ayşe Hatun I and Ayşe Hafsa Hatun II.

Selim was a tall, strongly built man. He was a valiant warrior, expert swordsman and rider, as well as capable archer and wrestler. He was also educated with intense interest in sciences, fine arts, and religion. When he was young, he was posted as governor of the Pontus region in the city of Trabzon. There he became known for his successful raids on horseback against the Christian Georgia.

He had simple manners, didn't seek luxury and ate in wooden plates. As a result of his diplomatic skills he managed to unite the Turcoman and Tatar tribes under his banner. Then, he achieved a decisive victory against the Shah Ismail of Persia in the battle of Chaldiran in 1514, crushing the superior enemy cavalry with his artillery. The victory was so extensive they say Shah Ismail never smiled again. Subsequently, he attacked the second major military power in Middle East, the Mamelukes of Egypt winning several battles, conquering within a year all major cities Aleppo, Damascus, Jerusalem and Gaza. In 1517 he crossed the Sinai Desert in thirteen days, and crushed the Mamelukes at Giza in front of the gates of Cairo, putting an end to the Mameluke dynasties that dominated the Middle East for centuries since the Crusades.

As a result of the Egyptian conquest, Selim became the master of Mecca and Medina, extending his empire all the way to the Yemen border. This way he became the "Protector of Islam", and was awarded the religious title of "Caliph" in Constantinople by the Serif of Mecca, carrying inside Topkapi the holy relics of the Prophet where they still lie. After these conquests the entire trade of silk and spices passed in the hands of the Ottoman Empire, forcing Spain and Portugal to seek new trade routes to the Far East around the Cape of Good Hope and towards America. Gradually the occupation of all major Palestine harbors also led to the decline of Venice, Genoa, Pisa, and Florence as world powers.

Selim died suddenly in 1520 probably because of a rare skin cancer or an anthrax infection developed by his prolonged contact with the saddle. At the time he was preparing a new expedition in the West probably against Belgrade. When Selim became Sultan, the Ottoman Empire occupied an area of 2.4 million square kilometers, and when he died eight years later more than 6.0 km^2. Selim's tomb is in Istanbul inside the courtyard of his mosque built by his son Suleiman on the Fifth Hill of the New Rome, Constantinople.

2. Ayşe Hafsa Hatun: She was Suleiman's mother and favorite legal wife of Selim. She was probably a daughter of the Tatar Khan Mengli Giray of Crimea, but few historians claim she was of Greek origin as Crimea was an ancient Greek colony! Besides Suleiman, she produced three daughters, Hatidge Sultan, Fatma Sultan, and Hafsa Sultan. She had great influence on her son and she was probably the one who supplied Suleiman with concubines of her choice. Eventually she supported Ibrahim Pasha in his quest, but after her early demise, Suleiman gradually fell entirely under the influence of Hurrem Sultan who gradually managed to create conflicts between Suleiman and his intimate friend Ibrahim. She finally died in 1534, 55 years old from an unknown cause. Today her tomb lies ruined by an earthquake in the courtyard of Sultan Selim's mosque next to his tomb. There are plans for a modern restoration of her tomb.

3. Suleiman the Magnificent: He was born in Trabzon in 1494, son of Selim the Grim and Ayşe Hafsa Hatun. He became the tenth Ottoman Sultan, ten being the holy number for Muslims.

Suleiman continued his father's conquests, firstly in the West by conquering Belgrade, occupying the strategic island of Rhodes, and finally entering Budapest twice, and unsuccessfully besieging Vienna. Later in the East, he recaptured the Persian capital of Tabriz as his father had done, and finally Baghdad and Basra. Using the Ottoman fleet and supporting the Barbary corsairs, he effectively occupied the entire northern Africa coast all the way from Egypt and the Sudan to Morocco. He also conquered Yemen, imported coffee into Europe and through Basra extended the Ottoman commerce all the way to India; but there the Ottoman fleet suffered several naval defeats in the hands of the Portuguese.

Another major setback was the unsuccessful Ottoman attempt to wrestle Malta from the Knights of Saint John Suleiman had defeated previously in Rhodes. Despite these failures during the last stages of his reign, the Ottoman Empire achieved its maximum military power in both land and sea, threatening Western Europe either by pirate raids all the way to the Spanish coast, or by major invasions into Austria, leading immense armies of more than 200000 warriors. As a result of his expeditions he succeeded in doubling the empire he inherited from his father who had also doubled his inheritance.

Besides his military conquests, Suleiman had major contributions as a lawmaker and as a prolific builder. He was very fortunate during his reign to be served by great generals and brilliant statesmen, like Ibrahim, and Sokollu Pasha, effective admirals, like Hayrettin Barbarossa, Piyale Pasha, Turgut Reis and Piri Reis, efficient administrators and tax collectors like Rüstem Pasha, and talented architects like Mimar Sinan.

Physically he was tall and slim, with a long neck and an aquiline nose. According to testimonies he was suffering from kidney disease and gout, and especially during the last years of his life, his overall state of health was weak. His disposition was often effected by his environment, and especially by strong personalities as Ibrahim Pasha, Hurrem Sultan and Rüstem Pasha. He was religious and somewhat superstitious. He committed war crimes, executing enemy prisoners, but this kind of behavior was not uncommon during his era. He also executed many of his able and devoted associates like Ibrahim Pasha, Piri Reis, Kara Ahmet Pasha, and two of his own children, Mustafa and Bayezid because of suspicions of conspiracy.

Suleiman's death occurred during the siege of the city of Szigetvar in Hungary on 7/9/1566 possibly of a major stroke, and this news were received with great joy in the rest of the non-Muslim European Continent from the Atlantic Ocean to the Caucuses.

His tomb is in the courtyard of his mosque, Suleimaniye, on the Third Hill in Istanbul.

4. Pargali Ibrahim Pasha: He was born in 1494 and probably he was a son of a Greek fisherman from Parga, but others claim he was Albanian. For his early years nothing is certain as few claim he was a slave of a rich widow who gave him to the then Prince and heir Suleiman as a present. Others claim he was a member of the Janissary Corps, serving in Topkapi under Sultan Selim I after successfully concluding several years of education in the Seraglio School.

Initially during the reign of Sultan Selim he became chief of the falconers, and when Suleiman became Sultan, he served as Hasodabashi (Chambermaid) of the Sultan. Because of his numerous talents, extending from being a skilled string instrument player to diplomacy and military commanding, he was quickly promoted to Pasha (General), Beylerbey (Governor) of Rumelia, Grand Vizier (Prime Minister) and Serasker (Field Marshal) of the Ottoman armies.

According to the prevailing historical evidence, he became

the husband of Suleiman's sister, Hatice (Hatidge) Sultan; but there are other versions of his biography claiming he had three wives and three children. Few notable historians even claim he was a eunuch as traditionally the post of Hasodabashi was given only to White Eunuchs. Although it is very difficult to prove conclusively what he really was, many historians claim his friendship with Suleiman had also erotic dimensions, as they were practically inseparable, eating together and sleeping in adjacent rooms of the Seraglio, or in the same tent during the numerous military expeditions, facts that created considerable gossip at the time.

As a Grand Vizier, Ibrahim had important contributions in several military successes, as in the Battle of Mohacs, the Conquest of Budapest, Tabriz, and Baghdad. Despite his high position in the Ottoman hierarchy, Ibrahim was considered as an atheist by both Muslims and Christians or even worshiper of the Olympian Gods, a rather dubious claim. Nevertheless, they all agreed he was well-educated and extensively cultured; he also spoke many languages and laid the foundations of the Ottoman diplomacy by establishing the Sublime Gate, i.e. an organized ministry corresponding to an Ottoman Foreign Office. Supposedly he also transformed the Seraglio School as the first state university for competent public officials.

His sudden and enigmatic execution was most probably the result of a conspiracy, since he favored the extremely popular Prince Mustafa as Suleiman's heir, coming into conflict with Suleiman's favorite Hurrem Sultan who naturally favored one of her sons as heir of the throne. It occurred inside the Sultan's apartment on 15/3/1536 under mysterious circumstances.

According to the prevailing scenario the Sultan had great doubts about this act and invited his Grand Vizier into his quarters for seven consecutive nights before summoning the Mute executioners. His body was found in the Seraglio gardens and the burial was carried out in great secrecy at night in the garden of a mosque in Galata according to the prevailing myth.

Even though the standard way of execution by the Mutes

were strangulation, it is said that Ibrahim's blood had stained the walls of his bedroom, and the Sultan refused to repaint this room until his own death decades after. From few existing poems of Suleiman it is evident he eventually regretted this act, as there is no evidence Ibrahim ever conspired against his Sultan. However, all things considered, there are rumors Ibrahim had an affair with the son of the Venetian Doge Gritti. It is very difficult to prove beyond the shadow of a doubt, if there is a bit of truth in this rumor. What is a historical fact is that this Venetian diplomat, known also as Beyoğlu (Son of the Bey), was later sent as a governor of Moldovalahia, but for some reason he was also executed. The district of Peran is presently known as Beyoğlu.

Today there is a mosque on the shores of the Golden Horn on Ibrahim's name, but it is a newer construction as the old one was burned to the ground many decades ago.

5. Haseki Hurrem or Roxelana (Russian): She was born between 1502 and 1504 and died on April 15, 1558. She was the favorite wife of Suleiman the Magnificent, and mother of five sons known as Sehzade Mohamed, Sehzade Abdullah, Sehzade Selim, Sehzade Bayezid, and Sehzade Gihangir, and one daughter, Mihrimah Sultan. Three of her sons, Abdullah, Mohamed and Gihangir died prematurely of sicknesses, while Bayezid was executed by his father for treasonable behavior. She was a slave from Ukraine, but Suleiman early on became infatuated by her personality and charm and wrote for her many erotic poems in Persian.

When Mustafa was the dominant heir of the throne, she conspired against Ibrahim Pasha who was supporting him and achieved his execution. Then, she pushed her daughter Mihrimah to marry Rüstem Pasha who became Grand Vizier and her most faithful instrument. With his help she calumniated against Mustafa and convinced Suleiman that his son was trying to usurp the throne prematurely in the same way his father Selim I had dethroned his father Bayezid II.

During the final contest for the throne of Suleiman between his son's Selim and Bayezid she took the part of the second, but when she died, Suleiman supported Selim and executed Bayezid. Hurrem died in Constantinople in 1558 from an unknown cause, and was buried in a separate tomb next to her husband in the court of Suleimaniye Mosque.

6. Mahidevran Sultan: She was Suleiman's first legal wife (Kadin). There are many conflicting stories about her which is not surprising since there are not many details for any Sultan's consorts in the annals of Ottoman history. She is supposedly a Circassian or an Albanian slave, or possibly the daughter of a Tatar Princess wife of a Circassian Prince. She was supposedly married to Suleiman in Constantinople in January 5, 1512. If this date and ceremony are true, then Mahidevran could not be just a concubine slave, but had to have noble ancestors, as marriage of a slave to a Sultan was inconceivable. This opinion is supported by the fact Suleiman's father was also married to at least one Tatar Princess, and Tatars remained trusty allies of Suleiman throughout his reign, and by Mahidevran's proud and rebellious acts unfit for a slave.

Mahidevran was supposedly born in 1498. She bore her husband three children Sehzade Mustafa in 1515, Sehzade Ahmet in 1517 and Raziye Sultana in 1524. In 1521 two sons of Suleiman, Abdullah and Ahmet, died, and Mustafa became the oldest surviving heir. This development led to a series of intrigues and a serious harem rebellion that had as a result the expulsion of Mahidevran from the Topkapi harem by Suleiman's orders.

As her son Mustafa grew older, Mahidevran followed him to all his official transfers and posts to Manisa and Amasya in Anatolia until his execution for treason. Then and until her death by natural causes in 1581, she moved to Bursa where she resided close to her son's mausoleum, where she is also buried next to her son.

7. Mimar Sinan: He was born in 1491 in the town of Ağırnas in Cappadocia and became the greatest architect not only of the Ottoman Empire but possibly of the entire world in terms of number of building projects. Originally he was a Christian, but was recruited in the Janissary Corps, quite possibly taking part in the sieges of Belgrade, Rhodes, Baghdad and Vienna as numerous others.

During his service in the Janissary Corps he probably impressed the Sultan with his bridge building ability and prompt delivery, which made him Chief Architect of the Empire. Sinan eventually served four Sultans, namely Selim I, Suleiman, Selim II and Murad III, completing or repairing 477 buildings among which 159 mosques, 74 schools, 38 palaces, 56 public baths and 31 Caravanserais and numerous bridges considered the most important constructions of the Ottoman Empire of that era.

From all these buildings 204 still exist among which 85 are inside Constantinople. His most important works are the mosques of Sultan Suleiman, Sehzade, Mihrimah Sultan, Hurrem Sultan, Rüstem Pasha, Sokollu Pasha, Nurbanu Sultan and finally Selim Sultan in Edirne which he considered as his masterpiece. He worked hard until 1588 when he died 97 years old from natural causes. He was buried in the courtyard of Suleiman's Mosque in Istanbul; nevertheless his work was continued by his assistants and students who built the Blue Mosque and probably the Taj Mahal too.

Secondary nameless characters

1. Janissary Aga: The military commander of the Janissary Corps, an elite force acting on land and sea comparable to the US Marines, but with even more civil rights and duties. During the Suleiman era members of this corps were ex-Christians mainly from the Balkans and Asia Minor who had been converted to Islam at an early age either willingly or by force. For the selection of a Janissary very strict rules were applied that allowed only gifted individuals to join.

Later on after several centuries, Muslims, mainly Turks, were allowed to join the Janissaries; but this measure quickly deteriorated the Corps to a state of civil servants, protesting more for special privileges rather than fighting as elite soldiers ready to die for their Sultan and faith.

During the nineteenth century the Janissaries became a menace, refusing to fight against the enemies, preferring instead to exert political pressures during the selection of the Grand Viziers and the Sultans. The Corps was finally dissolved with extreme cruelty by Sultan Mahmud the Second during the Greek Revolution killing many thousands by artillery shots. Up to final stage, the Janissaries had revolted innumerous times leading to the execution of two reigning Sultans, Osman II and Selim III and many Grand Viziers and state officials.

2. Kapi Aga (Chief of the White Eunuchs): A Circassian white slave comparable to the Lord Chamberlain of the British Court in charge of the White Eunuchs Corps that served exclusively the Sultan inside the Topkapi Seraglio.

3. Kislar Aga (Chief of the Black Eunuchs): A Nubian slave in charge of the Black Eunuch Corps responsible for keeping order among the concubines in the Sultan's Harem.

4. Bostanjibashi (Head of the Mute Executioners): One of the main aides of the Sultan in charge of the secret execution service of the Sultan responsible for clandestine murders. This service was comprised by mutes who also served as gardeners of the Seraglio and normally executed their distinguished victims by strangulation using silk ropes.

5. Hasodabashi (Chief of the Imperial Valets): Another important aid of the Sultan in charge of his personal service. This page was normally a White Eunuch and among his duties were the organization of the Sultan's daily and night activities in close cooperation with the Chief Black Eunuch. In the case of Suleiman, Ibrahim despite becoming the husband of the Sultan's sister, he served also as his Hasodabashi for many years and spent innumerable nights in an adjacent room, a fact that caused many negative comments in the Ottoman court.

Dates of major historic events described in book 3

1523 Ibrahim Pasha becomes Grand Vizier
1523 Birth of Abdullah second son of Hurrem Sultan
1523 Marriage of Ibrahim and Hatidge Sultan sister of Suleiman
1524 Ibrahim Pasha travels to Egypt
1524 Birth of Selim third son of Hurrem Sultan
1525 Birthday of Raziye Sultan daughter of Mahidevran Sultan
1525 Repression of a Janissary riot by Sultan Suleiman
1525 Birthday of Sehzade Bayezid fourth son of Hurrem Sultan
1526 Victory of Suleiman and Field Marshal Ibrahim Pasha over the Hungarians at Mohacs
1526 Death of Abdullah second son of Hurrem Sultan
1529 Expedition and conquest of Budapest
1529 First siege of Vienna by Suleiman and Field Marshal Ibrahim Pasha
1531 Birthday of Sehzade Gihangir fifth son of Hurrem Sultan
1532 Second expedition against Vienna by Suleiman and his Field Marshal Ibrahim Pasha
1533 Marriage of Suleiman and Hurrem Sultan
1534 Death of Hafsa Hatun mother of Suleiman
1534 Conquest of Tabriz by Field Marshal Ibrahim Pasha
1535 First conquest of Baghdad by Suleiman and Field Marshal Ibrahim Pasha
1535 Military alliance between Ottoman Empire and France
1535 Conquest of Tunis by Andrea Doria
1536 Execution of Grand Vizier Ibrahim Pasha

Chapter 11

In front of the Vienna Gates

"All who believe in Allah fight like Him, while the unfaithful fight like Satan,

Fight fearlessly all the unbelievers because the strategy of Satan is at fault"

(Quran, Sura IV, 76)

Since the days of the Persian Wars in Greece the East had always the manpower advantage, while the West tried hard to overcome with superior technology, extreme canning and supreme valor. The Byzantine Empire for many eons had succeeded in repulsing numerous massive invasions from the East and North using its ultimate weapon, the Greek Fire, especially during sieges and sea battles, but the East hadn't say yet the last word in terms of military technology. And when the crucial moment arrived in 1453, then the East managed to combine overwhelming numbers of capable and discipline soldiers with black powder and artillery, the result was devastating, and the Eastern Roman Empire finally collapsed.

However, every Eastern invention could not remain a military secret for long; so, soon the artillery advantage of the Ottoman armies would evaporate, and only troop numbers would be the only weapon remaining in the Eastern armory to threaten the West.

******

The new Sultan's son by Hurrem, Bayezid, was promptly delivered nine months after the successful recovery from the Janissary rebellion, and its birth was celebrated by a long cannonade from the Sea Walls, proving that the House of Osman was healthy, strong and ready to accomplish a new string of victories over the infidels and heretics.

By the end of the winter the military preparations had already entered their final stages. The best warriors had arrived from the very depths of the Empire as soon as the message had come the Sultan was getting to ready to reach the Red Apple without any hesitation.

Suleiman didn't have to pay big salaries or promise rich rewards. They all knew he and his Serasker were both open-handed to anyone virtuous and brave enough to put his life on the line. The only obligation the Sultan had was to secure food, gunpowder, transportation and arms. Every other necessity would be the involuntary contribution of the enemies.

Many months ago the heralds had started visiting every town and village to make sure that every man capable of carrying arms would be informed that the Great War, the Jihad-el-Akbar against the infidels was about to start again. The town assemblies were carried out inside the mosques. There the Mufti asked their flock to rise and fight again, so that the words of the Prophet could be heard inside the temples of the entire humanity. The goal was always the same, destroy Venice, conquer the Old Rome and turn Saint Peter's Cathedral into a mosque.

Soon enough the first groups of men capable of carrying arms formed long lines behind the leading Pashas for the long walk towards the Bosporus Straits. Along came also many auxiliaries that would take care of the beast of burden and shepherds that could feed the animals to be slaughtered to feed the troops. These were not the only helpers. There were also many farriers, saddlers and tanners, along with tailors, blacksmiths and general builders that comprised the army's logistic support.

As the Ottoman Empire constantly expanded its borders, to achieve absolute discipline, retain the fighting spirit, and keep the molestation of women and young men to a minimum, during this several month-long advance through friendly territories the armies were followed by caravans of all kinds of courtesans, prostitutes, and oriental dancers. Thus, soon enough the small brooks of people turned into mighty rivers converging to the Eternal City.

The Ottoman navy didn't remain isolated from this widespread preparation. Thus, every available vessel from war galley to row boat was used to carry this oriental flood from Asia to the European shores. Additionally, many barges were requisitioned and prepared to carry guns, munitions and supplies up the Black Sea shores to the Delta of the Danube River. Regulating the flow of food and supplies to an army considerably bigger than 100000 fighting men through the Balkans and Asia Minor was a logistical feat no other army in Europe had achieved till then. This was the main reason why many nations like Hungary, Poland, or Russia, could not field armies larger than a couple of myriads of soldiers and knights.

The Muslim army's moral was high. From the first moment

the young Sultan climbed on the throne he had proved he was a worthy son of Selim, the greatest warrior Osman's breed had ever produced. In every big town the army was concentrating, the soldiers didn't fail to stage celebrations, war dances and feasts. The lamb's blood was the first to be shed in torrents.

The main points of focus for the concentration of the troops were the hills in front of the Edirne Gate. In this location half a century ago, Mehmet Fatih had set his tent for the final assault against the capital of the Roman Empire. From this lucky spot the Anatolian Armies, the Anadolu Asker, would now start their march to meet the European Armies, the Rumeli Asker, arriving from Greece, Albania, Thrace and Macedonia before moving north to meet the troops from Serbia, Bulgaria, Moldavia and Valahia along with the Tartars of Crimea and the most distant Caucasus Mountain Range.

On top of these hills the six horse tail banners of the Grand Vizier and the seven horsetails of the Sultan were posted. It was one more great honor for Ibrahim Pasha, as according to the Ottoman tradition a Pasha had the right to have a banner with one tail, a Beylerbey two, a Vizier three and a Grand Vizier only five; but now everyone knew Ibrahim was more powerful than any Grand Vizier and the horsetail banners had to testify to that effect.

Ibrahim Pasha was the Serasker of this new expedition, and everyone was aware of the small difference between the Sultan and him, a single horsetail. Many Turks were angered by this new insult and the high position a slave son of slaves had occupied, but no one dared to complain, because no one wished to take the blame of another riot. The Ottoman Empire was on its way to a holy war, and these crucial hours even a single whisper could be interpreted as treasonous act punishable by death.

These days it was very easy for anyone to lose his head; so all the mouths remained closed shut, as everyone friend or foe of the new Serasker waited patiently to see how Ibrahim Pasha would rise to this historic occasion. If the outcome was disastrous, then no one would object if this audacious and infidel head was cut off. However, if the Serasker came back victorious, what else would he dare to ask from his master after the highest offices, the riches and the hand of his sister? This was a question no one could answer with convincing arguments, as there was not much left but the throne.

That momentous day, on top of the hill covered with the colorful spring wildflowers, the Sultan, Suleiman Khan, Shah and Padishah son of Selim Khan forever victorious, was waiting for the elite troops to walk out of the Eternal City. He was riding a Cappadocian stallion, son of another famous father, Karabulut. Next to him the Grand Vizier and Serasker, Ibrahim Pasha was standing ridding a white Arabian charger sumptuously caparisoned, another magnificent present of his brother-in-law the Sultan to his friend the untried warlord.

Every soldier who passed in front of them admired their gold inlaid armors, their damascene swords and their golden thread knitted quivers, and even they who had complains and hated their guts could not help but admit that since the days of the Roman emperors who had hired first Ottoman troops to fight for their wicket causes, never again two such warriors one Turk and one Roman had cooperated so closely in a war effort. It was a very good sign for these two nations that now shared the same lands. If a Sultan could be friend with a Roman, why was it not possible for these two nations to follow their example?

****

As the last warrior passed in front of them, Suleiman could not hold his tongue and asked the question troubling him for days.

"How do you feel that you, a slave son of a Greek slave and an infidel, are now the Serasker of the army of Allah?"

Ibrahim smiled and replied with pride:

"I will reveal to my master something that Turks and Greeks are still too scared to utter. Your grandfather Mehmet Fatih who conquered the Eternal City had also some Greek blood in his veins. This means our two nations can be united and exceed any other nation in valor and canning, as he did. When the Turks took the City, half of the Romans became Muslims. If the Romans had won the battle back then, then all the Turks would be now Greeks out of shame, because ten thousand Christian warriors would have overwhelmed one hundred thousand Muslims. This is why I never distinguish men as infidel and faithful, white or dark skinned, Turks or Greeks, but only as brave or coward, useless or worthy. Every man who is gathered here today has the same single goal, and he is willing to sacrifice his life to achieve it. We all want to perform great deeds that will glorify our generation for all times around the world. If Allah can help us one day to post our banners in Venice and Old Rome, then the graves of every Greek and Roman who died back then will flower, because we would have taken revenge for all the looting, raping and carnage we've suffered by the Latin Crusaders and Venetian Pirates. I desire nothing more than admire the stolen Greek bronze horses on the Cathedral of Saint Mark galloping on the Hippodrome grounds once more. Changing my faith, clothes and language are very small prices to pay, if I can thus achieve such a historic feat."

Now it was Suleiman's time to smile and say:

"This is what I would have done too, if I were in your shoes. I never had any problem changing my language, if this was the way to make my wishes better understood. I pray to Allah in Arabian, I recite poems to my favorites in Persian, I order my bravest soldiers in Slavish, I speak Jewish when I seek a loan, and I ask my horse to gallop faster in Turkish. Every language is a sea full of pearls, and only a very foolish sovereign would try to force his subjects to lose even one. My ancestors wisely decided to change both their faith and tongue to raise the sword of Allah and conquer the world. Let's just now pray to Allah too, so that He awards us the victory."

"Our swords are so numerous that when they'll rise they will cover the skies. No matter what Allah wishes, the victory is ours!" Ibrahim boosted proud for his preparations.

"Don't be blasphemous! The road is long, hard and crooked, so no one knows what Allah's wishes are," the Sultan said humbly; however, the Grand Vizier's arrogance did not diminish.

Suleiman's pietism always annoyed Ibrahim because it meant his horizons were limited; so, he found a way to stop short this fruitless discussion.

"When we are together, I can dare even Allah to punish my optimism in our victory."

"Bismallah!" the Sultan replied and urged his horse to move forward and follow the army column that advanced north leaving thick clouds of dust behind.

****

When the Anatolian armies reached the city of Edirne and were united with the Rumelia rank and file, the entire column became so long that it would take horseman one hour of riding to trace it from head to toe. First on the line were the lancers, with their yellow and red banners, and then followed the swordsmen and the harquebusiers. Then, the Spahis followed armed with their composite bows and arrows, dressed in lamb skins, followed by the Janissary officers and soldiers. They were carrying besides their arms a small shovel used in making trenches and tunnels under the enemy fortifications.

Behind the army massive oxen with long horns pulled the light cannons, followed by the dervishes who constantly sang and danced to raise the soldiers' moral. Then, the religious judges came with their green flags, the holy relics of the Prophet, and the horsetail banners of the Sultan. Further back, the Grand Vizier and the entire Divan to serve as military council came on horseback and their aids on foot followed by the Spahis from Anatolia on horses with saddles richly caparisoned, shinning armors and shimmering spoors.

Last in the army column came the Sultan with his entire court and slave attendants. He was surrounded by his personal guards in two columns guarding his flanks. The left column was comprised by right-handed archers and the right by left-handed ones, all holding bows and arrows. They were skillful and strong enough to deliver three arrows with deadly accuracy in a distance no bullet from a harquebus could ever reach and even faster than a pair of eyelids could open and shut. Each archer had practiced his skill for many years, and now on a galloping horse they could aim an arrow to pass through the eye slid of an armored knight. If a harquebus had an active range of seventy paces, their arrows could kill a man as far as three hundred.

At the end of the column thousands of beasts of burden followed, horses, camels, and donkeys loaded with supplies and ammunitions, while further back more oxen pulled the heavy guns, the mortars and the other siege machines.

The procession was finally closed by an immense number of irregulars on horseback and on foot that were always the first waves of the attack to tire and confuse the enemy formations, before the main attack was launched by the heavy cavalry, the Spahis, and finally the heavy infantry, the Janissaries, who always tried their luck last.

These irregulars were also useful to carry out raids and sabotages and burn down the crops and isolated farmhouses, demolishing the enemy moral before the battle. All together the troops were more than one hundred thousand, the irregulars forming more than half its force. This was the Ottoman army that was aiming at Europe's heart this blooming spring. Allah willing, the first target was Hungary, the strongest Christian enemy of the Ottoman Empire on land for many generations.

****

The Hungarians had been the worst Ottoman adversaries from the first moment they stepped on European soil at Gallipoli. It was the enemy along with the Albanians who had fought them very hard and won many battles, even when Sultan Fatih was in command.

The Hungarians with the incomparable Janos Hunyadi as a leader had even managed to make him turn tail and run away in panic in front of the Belgrade towers, leaving behind two huge siege guns as spoils of war. However now, this mighty Christian hero was long gone, dead and buried, and in his place the young king Louis the Second had taken his place, trying hard to unite the rebellious Boyar nobility under his banner.

Against this divided nation proud descendants of the Huns, the Ottomans stood united behind a young Sultan who had already proved his worth capturing Belgrade, the South gate of Europe, away from Hungary. Nevertheless, the Ottoman Army was still too far away from Hungary to cause great worries. The Christian god was still in the Hungarians' favor, as the skies opened and heavy rains fell in the Balkans, causing rivers to flood and sweep away the bridges the army had to cross on its way to Belgrade.

Thus, three months took the Sultan's army to reach the Sava River, as the mud made the trip slow, torturous, or even hazardous. Fortunately, Ibrahim had sent during the winter Sinan and a detachment of Janissaries to build the two wooden bridges needed to enter Hungary.

The traveling conditions from Edirne to Belgrade had been extremely stressful and extreme discipline was exerted. Almost daily severe punishments were carried out to anyone who failed to comply with the orders of his superiors. And the orders were for the soldiers not to harm anyone they encountered, because all these Christian lands already belonged to the Sultan. Especially the irregulars had to wait patiently until they reached the domain of Catholic Hungary. Thus, a soldier lost his head for galloping inside cultivated fields, two more because they stole horses, and two riders because they ruined a vegetable garden. Ibrahim's plan was for the army to reach Hungary as a liberator rather than a spoiler and a thief.

After the Sava River, only the fortress of Petrovaradin stood in the way, and it quickly fell, because the Ottomans had by then achieved a high level of competency in sieges. It simply took a combination of mining under the walls and some heavy gun bombing for the resistance to collapse during a determined Janissary attack. Eight hundred enemy soldiers were captured.

Ibrahim wished their lives to be spared, but Mohamed's

law was clear. In every city that resisted, all men had to be executed and all women and children to be sold as slaves.

The Hungarians were religious fanatics, and had cut the noses of the ambassadors the Sultan had sent to negotiate the terms of surrender; so, there was no way they would change faith. The Sultan had not forgotten this outrageous behavior, and Ibrahim didn't waste his time trying to convince him to spare the life of any man. The response to savagery was more savagery. Thus, five hundred heads were cut and three hundred lives were spared only to be sold as slaves and pay for some of the expenses.

Moving northward, the army reached the Drava River, and Ibrahim who was now riding in front of the column was pleasantly surprised. There was no sign of the enemy. As there was no bridge, it would have been impossible for any bridge to be built on the flooded river if the other bank was in enemy hands.

He passed across a small detachment of scouts in a boat, and when they returned they reported that the enemy was concentrating his forces in a wide valley three hours riding away, at a location called the Mohacs Plains. It was a welcomed sign the Hungarians were not ready to fight yet and were still behind in preparations.

He asked Sinan's opinion and he assured him that a stone bridge could be built in three months. They simply couldn't wait that long, because it was already the end of August. His preparations were completed while the Hungarians were still amassing more forces from Austria, Germany and Poland. They were already twenty five thousands, mainly heavy cavalry.

Ibrahim decided that a floating bridge would serve his purpose best and in three days the bridge was ready. In one day the army, the supplies the ammunition and the light artillery had crossed. When the last soldier passed across, Ibrahim ordered the bridge to be set on fire, so that everyone would realize that there was to be no retreat in the oncoming battle.

They had to spend the night on the banks, so Ibrahim ordered a defensive perimeter to be formed by the carriages and the artillery pieces. Then, he had ropes tied between these pieces to form a barrier against the enemy cavalry, so they could rest in peace from any possible Hungarian cavalry raid. Good food, sound sleep and plenty of rest was necessary for the army to recover their strength from all the efforts of this long expedition. The battle plan was already formed on the way there.

The Ottomans had practically used the same battle plan since the days of the Crusades. First the irregular cavalry attacked from a safe distance with their arrows, thinning the enemy cavalry and infantry formations with casualties. If the Ottoman center held, then the battle was usually won for the Sultan, because the light cavalry, the "Akinji" with their greater mobility and long range weaponry, the composite bow could demolish the heavy Christian cavalry from a safe distance as the enemy carried only lances and swords good only for close encounters.

On the right flank of the Ottoman armies the Anatolia Spahis were posted, and in the left, Ibrahim leading the Rumelia troops. The only innovation Ibrahim envisioned was the role of the artillery, and when the plans were finalized, the Sultan asked the Serasker whether he was confident his battle plan would succeed. Ibrahim assured him with his usual cocky style that there was no hope for the enemies to stay alive.

"Even if the Christian god performs another miracle?" Suleiman asked and Ibrahim replied without much thought:

"Since the day the Ottoman guns arrived in front of the Saint Romanos' Gate, the Christian god has stopped performing miracles for his flock, and the last Roman Emperor who put his trust on Christian miracles against Fatih's artillery lost his head. Nevertheless, if Christ performs a miracle today after all these years, then I will be glad to lose my head for putting all my faith to Allah."

"I pray that Allah keeps your head at its place. I will be very sorry if one day I have to cut it off," the Sultan temporized.

He was smiling and his words sounded like a joke, but Ibrahim felt cold sweat running down his spine. This day would be critical for every soldier, but mainly for him. He was playing his entire life in a roll of dice, as every battle could have a surprise ending, simply if a single arrow found its target.

The Hungarians on the other hand, had severe doubts on their best battle plan. Few of them and King Louis would rather retreat and wait for further reinforcements. However, all the opposing views were silenced, when the clergy that comprised the most fanatic portion of the cavalry knights were in favor of an immediate attack that would crush the Ottomans under the weights of the heavy cavalry charge. They considered the help of the German reinforcements and Zapolya, the Boyar of Transylvania, superfluous.

Finally, the clergy and Boyar cockiness and audacity prevailed and immediate attack was chosen rather than caution. The prevailing opinion was that the Muslim barbarians from the East could never defeat the Christ's strong arm. For one more time the god of Christ and Allah were set to fight out and decide who was the stronger. This was the divine message that both fanatical Christian priests and devoted dervishes preached in both enemy camps; however, the truth was different. More than half of the Sultan's army was of Christian descent that had changed faith and they were the bravest of them all. Religion and divine help had nothing to do with victory. Victory was going to be awarded to the most valiant and better trained troops that were supplied with the best leadership and more deadly weapons.

When the decision of the Hungarian leadership was announced and reached more sober ears that knew something about war, they shook their heads with dismay. Tomorrow the Pope would have 20000 more saints to celebrate, they said. The age of the brave cavalry charges and the stone fortifications was gone, and the era of the artillery had commenced.

The battle started exactly at daybreak, as the irregular cavalry of the Ottomans started its audacious sorties wave after wave. It was the provocation, and when this game of nerves took its toll, the Christian heavy cavalry attacked in close formation trying with its momentum, armor and weight to crush the Ottoman irregular army lines. It was actually what happened that day in the right flank; but, in the center the Muslim lines held firm. There the Janissaries and the handpicked personal guards of the Sultan were posted, as usual. This was always the area where the battle was decided and this time even the Sultan was threatened by the enemy's arrow volleys. However, the attack failed to achieve its goal, because the Akinji were very well trained, flexible and retreated in order.

It was a planned retreat aiming to attract the heavy but inflexible Christian cavalry to its doom, even if the right flank of the Ottomans with the Anatolian troops had to retreat somewhat to release the mounting pressure. This delicate strategic maneuver gave the impression the Ottoman lines were pierced, but soon the presence of the Ottoman artillery was revealed at the two flanks sending volley after volley against the Hungarian center creating havoc as its knights in the center found themselves in a cross-fire that forced their retreat in panic with their lines shuttered.

This was the right time for the two Ottoman flanks to reverse course and attack the Hungarian infantry that without the cover and support of the cavalry had no hope of survival against the rain of the Akinji arrows and harquebus bullets by the Janissary infantry.

Within half an hour the outcome of Mohacs battle had been decided and with it the short reign of King Louis who trying to escape with his life had been crushed and drowned under the weight of his horse in a swamp. With him twenty thousand Hungarians lay dead on the plain of Mohacs, and among them almost all of the Boyars, and the clergy including five bishops and two archbishops. It was a decisive battle that became the tomb of the Hungarian nation and its knighthood for many years to come.

****

When the last Hungarian soldiers and knights had been killed or surrendered, the Sultan and his Serasker visited the battle field. The spectacle they saw was horrendous. Everywhere the eye could see mutilated bodies posed in strange positions as death had met them together with pieces of flesh and shuttered bones butchered by pig iron cannonballs. It was the first time their eyes had seen such a bloody battlefield. Until then Death had scythe human lives only with swords, pikes, knives, harquebuses and arrows, not explosives.

Around the dead bodies the triumphant survivors were searching for ornamented weapons, fancy armors, jewels and gold, as the rain started to fall wiping out the bloody shame of the human species, and the fertile fields of Mother Earth sucked eagerly the human blood to nurture her plants. This frantic search soon led to the discovery of the drown king Louis' body was discovered dragged to the bottom by the weight of his shiny armor, when his horse was struck by a musket bullet and fell dead.

Suleiman was very sorry to see his young adversary dead. The king had been forced to follow the dubious advices of his generals and made a valiant but disastrous attack against the death-spitting Ottoman cannons. This was not the kind of inglorious death that fitted such a young and handsome king, before he could have a taste of his royal privileges.

Ibrahim did not hesitate to point out that the success or the failure of any sovereign depended largely on his wisdom to choose the best advisers no matter if they were of noble birth or not, and his ability to judge the correctness of the advices he receives.

Sultan Suleiman ordered once again the execution of all prisoners to satisfy the demands of the most fanatic Janissaries and Muslim Imams. Before the day was over in front of his tent another pyramid of human heads was laid, while Ibrahim preferred to remain silent rather than oppose the entire army hierarchy, even though he considered this new bloodshed a wasteful and cruel practice. He decided that after the battle fervor, it would have been against his interests to argue in favor of these Christian captives. The religious fever of the Catholic Hungarians had not let them see their future as clearly as he had seen his.

These Christian fanatics who had followed as military

leaders into battle archbishops and wooden crosses, would never consider putting their skills in support of a Muslim Sultan. Their sight was severely restricted by absurd religious beliefs, and would never have realized where their blind faith in the power of Christ was leading them.

His opinion was already firmly based on the notion that the Ottomans were not going to simply raid and loot Hungary, and then depart. They were going to stay on its fertile plains for as long as they could. When profound changes like these happened that might last for many generations during a man's life, a wise family man should try to adjust accordingly for the sake of his children, because during his lifespan his previous status would never be achieved.

He had faced the same problem with his future, when the Eternal City after many glorious centuries of being the greatest city in the world, had had eventually declined and fallen to the Ottomans. Now many centuries would have to pass before the New Rome could rise again from its ashes; but his life could not last long enough for him to obtain the portion of power he deserved as a Roman. If as a Roman this was impossible, he did not hesitate to claim it as an Ottoman. Today the entire continent of Europe was discussing his victory as the Sultan's Serasker and no one doubted his abilities, his bravery or strategic canning. Mohacs was now for him what Belgrade and Rhodes had been for his master, the day of vindication.

During the military council after the battle, the Sultan, who was always very conservative on praises for his Pashas, this time he stood up and expressed his pleasure for Ibrahim Pasha's services calling him with poetic disposition "**a leopard of strength and valor**", "**a tiger in the forest of bravery**", and "**a pearl in the ocean of strength.**"

Ibrahim chose to remain silent, as he kneeled deeply in front of his master until his forehead touched the rug. He decided it made no sense to reply or to thank his master for his kind praises. In public, it was better for him to let Suleiman have the last word; but right then the greatest surprise of all was the title the Seih-ul-Islam awarded by naming him "**the lionhearted champion of the Faith**". No one dared to add any nasty comment that day, because it was clear to all that after this victory in Mohacs Ibrahim had earned a special place in the heart of every Ottoman no one had the right to challenge it.

If there was one reason for envy, it was not for his brilliant victory, but for his new allowance as Grand Vizier and Serasker. If everything went well, in a few years Ibrahim was destined to become the richest man in the world, besides his master the Sultan of course.

****

After the Battle of Mohacs, all Hungarian resistance stopped and the gates of Budapest lay wide open. Unfortunately, despite the Sultan's orders the city was pillaged and burned and all its citizens that were not enslaved, mainly women and children, were put to the sword.

The Ottoman revenge for all the years the Hungarians had fought them was cruel and inhumane. The only building that remained standing was the king's palace where the Sultan and the Serasker resided.

It was almost midnight when the Sultan and Ibrahim Pasha finally managed to rest alone in the dead king's palace. They had spent almost the entire day trying to secure a shelter inside the enemy's capital. The Hungarian army may have been buried in its native soil, but there was always the chance that a Christian fanatic could escape through a secret passage the attention of the guards and try to rewrite history with an assassin's dagger.

Now as the bright flame from the oak burning in the fireplace lighted the room and the ironclad door was bolted, they finally felt safe from the threat of Death who had his chance to steal their lives on the battlefield and lost it. Nevertheless, the battle fever and excitement had not subsided yet, so no one was surprised when the subject of death became once more the focal point of their discussion.

"My thoughts are still stuck in the mud of the Mohacs swamps and I reckon that death is not as scary as failure for me," Suleiman solemnly noticed.

Ibrahim was a bit surprise to hear his friend feel so gloomy after such a decisive and historic victory. There were indeed considerable Ottoman casualties, but the Hungarian knights had been totally obliterated. It was now apparent that Hungary would need many decades to produce such a battle-worthy force. On the other hand, the Ottoman Armies seemed practically inexhaustible, as they contained soldiers from many nations, not just one.

"For a human being death is the greatest failure it can suffer in life," the slave whispered, trying to keep his opinion from reaching the ears of any eavesdropper. "A glorious death sounds in my ears like a fallacious consolation, uttered by those who try to soothe the pain of a mourning mother, a widow or an orphan child of the unlucky fallen."

"Yes, but in Mohacs you fought so bravely that even the Janissaries admired your valor, even the ones who few days ago had serious doubts about your ability to lead them. You were fighting as if you were certain Allah shield protected you from any threat of death."

"That's for you, my master, to say now, but I don't know what kind of madness took hold of me. It was as if my natural attention to survival had been put aside by a superior force that pushed me forward."

"It was the hand of Allah!" the Grand Turk asserted with conviction.

Ibrahim Pasha remained silent for a while. He was not the least convinced that his behavior had anything to do with any supernatural force. The more he thought about it the more he realized that his behavior had to do a great deal with his return to the Eternal City. He had fought hard to stay alive and return alive to his home and try his luck for a son. Till then the only times he had taken risks were only with beautiful women he felt he had to conquer to satisfy his ego or to punish their wickedness. Now everything had taken new meaning, another dimension. His exploits should not be temporary but would last long, possibly forever.

"Bismallah!" his lips uttered because this was what Suleiman expected to hear from his loyal Muslim Serasker, but he didn't really trust Allah's intervention. If he had won this battle, it was because he had devise a devious strategic plan. After this victory there wouldn't be many Christian armies in Europe who would dare to take the field in front of the Ottomans. His idea to move his guns in such a way during the battle to crush the enemy central attack by cannon crossfire was truly an important military innovation.

Being a devoted Muslim, a Christian or a Pagan was just irrelevant. His victory was the result of the Ottoman discipline, logistics, strategy and superior armor, and nothing more or less than that. As long as he had these advantages at his service his glorious future was secured.

The Sultan listened to his words without comment. In his mind strange thoughts were lingering too he had never encountered before. His slave had proven in this battle that he was at least as manly and brave as he was, and this simple thought upset his convictions like nothing else. This night he had to stay alone and think over this new development that could change everything he thought about himself too, as in the past there was no way to test his manliness against a submissive slave.

****

The summer was already gone and the autumn's heavy rains filled the empty river banks to the brim, making the return trip treacherous. The Ottoman armies didn't have the patience or the will to fight continuously for an entire year; however, they didn't like to wait for years idle either. The moment the Janissaries had shared the spoils, they started complaining for the Sultan's wish to continue the military activities even thought they were the first to blame him for being inactive. They wanted to go back home before the approaching winter made travelling in the

Balkans a near impossible task.

This argument however was hard for Suleiman to dismiss lightly. If on the way to Budapest they had spent many difficult months on the road during the spring, how long would the return trip take in the winter until they could discern in the horizon the minarets of the Eternal City?

The Sultan decided it didn't make any sense to try to convince the army to leave a strong guard and secure Budapest this year. In a few months the winter snows would fall and most of the soldiers were used to live and fight in much warmer climates.

The trip to the north had been extremely tiresome going through the violent summer storms. This great effort had exhausted every one of them. They couldn't wait to go home, relax in taverns from all the fighting recounting their adventures to friends and children, or enjoying themselves with their wives or pretty Hungarian slaves.

These very sentiments must have been torturing their Master too, because he accepted their suggestions without objection or a second thought. The time for the annexation of Hungary and Budapest had not arrived yet. Thus, the long return trip to the City of Constantine started. Among the many spoils of war they carried home were the two great siege guns Fatih had lost during his aborted try to capture Belgrade, along with three ancient Italian bronze statues presenting Hercules, Apollo and Artemis. Ibrahim Pasha also acquired in his portion of the spoils and two giant bronze candles to adorn the sanctuary of the Agia Sophia mosque.

****

A wise man should know that life is not always full of joy, astounding successes, decisive victories and great feats. God tries to balance sooner or later any existing differences in stature, wealth or success, so that humans are not saturated by undue happiness, adding small or large dosages of failures, pain and sorrows.

As the army was still crossing the mountainous passages among the forest-covered mountains of the Balkans, a herald came in haste. Just looking at his face Suleiman realized the news from the Seraglio was not good. His second son Hurrem had born recently, Abdullah, had died struck by these strange epidemics that swept the Harem decimating the Sultan's offspring.

This piece of news reached naturally also the ears of the Grand Vizier who was handling all the Empire's affairs. The death of any Osmanli male who was a member of the line of success to the throne was a state secret that sometimes required delicate handling.

This time the succession was secure, since there were also other male children available; but, apparently Suleiman was very depressed by the news since Abdullah was the second son of Hurrem, the Sultan's most favorite concubine.

Since Ibrahim had became Grand Vizier and married Hatidge Sultan, Hurrem had secured almost the monopoly of Suleiman's attention. Despite Ibrahim's efforts to point out that Princess Mahidevran was the most appropriate consort for him, the Suleiman seemed enchanted by his slave. She gave him three more sons, Abdullah, Selim and Bayezid to only one daughter from the Tatar Princess. It was as if Mother Nature was serving Hurrem purposes.

It wasn't wise to try to interfere with fate, and perhaps it could be even dangerous to create a conflict. Suleiman was not only his master, but also a man. It was entirely his choice to spend the nights with Hurrem, and no one could do anything about what the Sultan's pleasure was. During his youthful years, he had taken advantage of a similar weakness and now it was not fair to complain if his master's choices did not coincide with his.

If for Ibrahim nobility and royal blood were of great importance, an easy explanation existed. He was the son of a fisherman and it was "natural" for him to try to seek union with royal blood for his children. On the other hand, the Sultan had the sacred blood of Osman traveling in his veins, so it wouldn't hurt to dilute it somewhat with the blood of a Christian slave of low descent.

Tonight what was really important was to become useful once more and encourage his friend who would be very depressed by this unexpected death. As he walked into the Sultan's tent, he found his master silently sobbing. He dismissed all the servants to protect his master's reputation and rushed to offer his condolences. Now Ibrahim was not just his slave and friend, but also a close relative, and his superior status afforded him more liberties and obligations. He could invade even into the deepest corner of the Sultan's mind and probe his feelings, fears and worries.

"Someone must have put a curse on my family," the Sultan grimly asserted. "Few years ago a vicious rumor was circulations that Hurrem was responsible for my other sons' deaths; I had almost believed that my beloved Hurrem out of her love for her own children might have had something to do with these deaths. However, now Death has carried away one of her sons too, my beloved Abdullah. Allah's Slave is now with Allah to serve him. Despite my glorious victory against the infidel knights, I now feel completely helpless, when it comes to protect my offspring. I'm worse than the lowest slave."

Ibrahim was touched by his sorrow and tried to improve Suleiman's moral by following Valide Sultan's recipe with a touch of ulterior motive.

"You shouldn't complaint for your misfortune. Few days ago with your decisive victory you have surpassed your glorious ancestors. Allah has been very kind with you, because He knows that you are willing to sacrifice many of your sons to achieve your aims in battle. Among all people you are the only one who is so powerful that you can make every wish true. If you have lost one child, you have a harem full of beautiful virgins that wish nothing else but give you as many children as you desire."

"You may be right, but right now I only wish to cease living and meet the sons I have lost in Paradise. The power I possess is just an illusion since I cannot even save the lives of my children."

It was apparent the Sultan was suffering from great

depression and the sorrow from his son's death surpassed any previous loss. Unconsciously he was expecting Allah would reward him for his victory, but instead he was severely punished. If he wished to cheer him up he had to try another approach.

"Your faithful subjects have entrusted their sons to you and are ready to die for your glory; thus, you have no right to behave so weakly simply because you have lost a fine young boy. You are the Sultan and your duty is to keep the empire you have inherited in balance. Your son's loss was a great mishap that has saddened not only you but your people too. Thus, now you have to do your best to make your subjects happy again with an equally great beneficence, or sadden your enemies even more with another victory."

"It's easy for you to give me advices, because you know your child is safe in his cradle."

"I wish I could soothe your sorrow by offering you a son of mine, but I have none yet to give. I know that every father sees his sons as an extension of his self, so even one thousand sons of slaves could not replace the one you lost. Every son that comes into this world has already the father's dreams written in his heart and only he can make them true. Thus, the only good advice I can give you is this: If you still love the mother of the son you've lost and think she is not responsible for this grave loss, give her another chance to make you a son to replace the one you've lost. The only way to balance death is with a birth, and only the woman we truly love can accomplish this divine feat."

This last suggestion seemed to strike a sensitive chord, as the Sultan gradually relaxed and closed his eyes to sleep. Tomorrow was another day and under the sunlight everything always looked different.

****

The arrival of the Ottoman armies to the City after the great victory in Mohacs was not celebrated with a long artillery barrage of the cannons along the Great Walls, or with week-long celebrations and festivities, as usual. Only the cannons of the

Edirne Gate were heard announcing the arrival of the Sultan, but their thunder sounded different this time, as the low clouds and the falling rain muffled the blasts and turned them into distant sobs.

Hurrem had been informed about the Sultan's approach and listening to the distant thunder realized Suleiman would be arriving soon; thus, her worries grew in bounces how she would be treated after the child's loss. This was the first time she had one of her children suddenly taken from her warm embrace, carried away through the solemn side-gate for the Harem's dead and given to the undertakers. She was not yet used to the idea that a certain part of her flesh she loved and cherished would be separated from her forever.

She was still young and fresh and inside young women the flame of life is strong, helping them to accept death much more easily than men. Nevertheless, Abdullah's demise was a serious blow that had exhausted much of her energy.

She had to go through all the heartaches of the sickness without the support of a husband by her side. She didn't even have a relative to help her sooth her soul from the pain of her loss. In her mind the idea that while her son was dying, Suleiman and Ibrahim were feasting kept coming back to torture her. This sinful relationship she had hoped would end after Ibrahim's marriage, during the war had grown strong once more. This affair should have to stop as soon as possible; however, to achieve this outcome, she had to control her nervous tension and avoid a new anger outbreak and a setback. To win the battle she didn't have to be stronger than her opponent, but more resilient. Victory was a game of unbending will and time was by her side, not Ibrahim's.

****

As Suleiman entered his quarters he found the Chief Black Eunuch waiting for him. The slave humbly conveyed Hurrem's plea to see him as soon as possible. It was a clear violation of the Harem's rules, as no one had the right to ask something from the Sultan unless given permission. Besides the etiquette breech, he had no wish to see anyone and most of all Hurrem who had been proven an unworthy mother; so, he left the slave waiting to increase his mistress growing tension too. The Persian book on the correct behavior of a Prince had plain enough instructions. A Prince should never concentrate his attention on a single woman or man, because gradually he would become accustomed to their moods. A scale could never achieve balance, if it was loaded by a single weight no matter how light it was. A Prince should have at least two choices to be worthy of his higher status.

Without a word he motioned his pages to take his clothes off and prepare him for a soothing visit to the hammam to wash away the campaign dirt. He closed his eyes and let himself to be indulged by the massaging fingers of his eunuchs. The last stage of his return home had been a torment as everyone was in a hurry to enter the Eternal City and get in touch with his friends, lovers or families.

He had the same urge with his soldiers, but Hurrem was not the first in his list of priorities. First were his precious children and then his mother. Hurrem after this loss was ranked last, but now she was trying to bypass everyone else in a race for his attention.

He tried hard to push his mind in another direction. Ibrahim's suggestion on how to try to fight the fear of Death had returned. Inside him his ancestors fought for supremacy. At one side his grandfather Bayezid the Saint with his infinite trust to the words of the Prophet pushed him to invest the loot from Hungary in building hospitals for the sick, refuges and feeding stations for the starving poor and the needy. At the other corner was his father Selim who had slaughtered more Muslims than any Christian king, but doubled in the process the empire he had inherited without spending a single golden piece in the name of Allah.

If whatever Ibrahim told him about all gods was true, then Allah did not intervened in peoples' lives. Thus, everything was for Him just games He played as the Olympian Gods played before Him entertaining themselves with the troubles of human beings. If this was how the world was made, what was the meaning for him to try to follow the Prophet's words? What was the Quran's worth with all its rules written down with golden ink to last forever?

Until then the life of every Ottoman was governed according by the Quran, but even he, the sole protector of the Kaaba, could see that few of these rules written down hundreds of years ago were pushing many of his subjects into misery. Ibrahim was justified to say that a wise ruler could not govern the world just by following the rules of his father or grandfather. Was it possible that the Prophet might also be proven wrong in few cases?

If this was true, then his father was right, starting wars against Muslims and Christian alike. Selim had showed no respect to the Caliph of Mecca who supposedly was the descendent of the Prophet, and brought him tied up in chains to Constantinople along with the holy relics of the Prophet. Was this the message his father was sending him from the grave? Should a Sultan do as he pleased, if his acts were good for the Empire he had inherited?

Of course, if religion could be used to his advantage, it would be foolish to abolish it. He had to find some spare time soon to discuss all these important matters with his friend. Ibrahim's opinion had been very useful up to now, much more than any judge or member of the clergy. Now that most of his tension and fatigue was gone under the steam, perhaps it would be pleasant to have a chat with him for the rest of the day, but then he remembered Ibrahim's final advice. For a wise sovereign, the best way out of a recent disaster was a new creation, and with this thought his flesh was awakened once again.

Many months had passed since the night he had last enjoyed the flesh of a woman. It had been with Hurrem, and another son had been the fruit of this union, Bayezid. Before him Mahidevran had produced a daughter, Raziye, and before her Hurrem another son, Selim. No one could say that he had not try to be fair; but still Allah had his preferences and offered sons too openhandedly to Hurrem. He was a mighty Sultan, but he was pious too, and should not fight against the will of Allah for as long as he could.

Somehow Hurrem's face slipped back into his mind; but he was angry and did his best to expel it using the face of his other favorites as a weapon. However, even Mahidevran had failed to erase it despite the fact she had the most exquisite features. In all his tries Hurrem's zephyr eyes pierced the heavy clouds of the steam, as they were intimately associated with his most intense moments of pleasure only she knew how to provide. There could be no other explanation. Unquestionably she was not the most beautiful woman in the world, but she was the most skillful he could find; by now he had realized there was none more desirable for him.

Somewhere on the globe every day a new woman was born that would eclipse all others. This is how Allah wished the world to be, so young men would have something better to look forward to. For him Hurrem had been the most attractive, because she was his slave and knew how to keep him smiling and content during his illness. She was also the only one who didn't seem bored listening to his poems. Every other woman in his harem simply pretended to hear them, so that he was not offended and seek another company. Their obvious aim was to use him and become pregnant, so that they would secure a future full of luxury.

On the other hand, Hurrem seemed to enjoy simply being with him in bed as if his undivided attention was her sole goal in life. She always had something interesting to say or add to his poems, even if this was just an unusual harem event, a violent quarrel, a sentimental affair or a clandestine sexual act between two concubines she had secretly witnessed. It was very hard for him not to get excited listening to her tales, and then even harder to resist her charms. Come to think of it, since he met her, she was getting pregnant practically every year.

It was an accomplishment that pleased practically every subject of the Empire. It meant the Ottoman dynasty was here to stay, offering prosperity and security to all its subjects. A slave could not ask for anything more these hard times, when hunger and plague decimated the populations that bloody wars had spared. Gradually Hurrem had become necessary not just for pleasing him, but for changing his disposition and extinguishing his tension.

Since his father's death, the fear of death had been his constant companion. One look at the mirror and the jaundiced color of his face was good enough to convince him he was next on the Death's list; nevertheless, she had a unique but very effective way to entertain his fears. She was giving him sons. It was unusual, but she was the right person to make him now forget the sorrow of his lost son. Was he still the Sultan of her heart, as she used to call him?

Love could take many forms for a Sultan. It could become a pleasurable submission to someone else's desires, or it could turn into a forceful punishment of your lover's audacity, faults or naughty behavior. With Mahidevran it was mostly submission to her flawless superiority, while with Hurrem it was mostly unbending punishment for all her sinful acts. He was unaware of any moral discrepancy, but her lustful behavior triggered his suspicions, especially during the months of his absence from the Seraglio.

He motioned a page and ordered him to convey to the Chief Black Eunuch that he would be pleased to see Hurrem tonight.

****

She must have been waiting in a room inside the Selamlik, possible in the Kapi Aga's quarters for his invitation, because very few minutes passed for her to make an appearance at the steam bath's entrance. He was still naked lying on his back on the jade pedestal of the dressing room, waiting for the slave to spread perfume oil on his body.

She looked pale and in her eyes he could sense also a lot of tension. She was angry, but her anger contained also a lot of fear. The death of her child had wounded her confidence. She was not untouchable any more by the illnesses that had degraded her female opponents. She had realized that Death could come and take her away too any moment he liked, and there was no one who could protect her, not even the mighty Sultan. The gates of her castle had been pierced in the same way his defenses were breeched when Sultan Selim had died unexpectedly leaving him the next in line; but it was a false alarm. The visit of Death had been for one of his offspring. In some strange way this was a relief.

An instinctive reaction was to open his arms and embrace her. That very moment he felt that Allah's will was for them to spend the rest of their lives together. He sensed her flesh was cold and this could be something more than the fact his flesh was still burning from the touch of the steam. It was an unexpected state for both of them, because normally whenever she came to meet him, she was the one burning with passion. She was usually so hot, that a single eruption of passion was not enough to make her fully content. She wanted more, much more.

Was this the secret of her fertility? He couldn't really tell. Despite his many concubines he was ignorant about the ways a woman's body reacted to the male stimuli. The only principle he knew was that for everything there had to be a reason and only he and perhaps few wise men had found the proper answers.

He was aware how bitches behaved when they were in heat and how differently mares behaved toward a stallion. For a mare in heat one stallion was more than enough, but for a bitch there was practically no limit to her lust. Hurrem was unquestionably a mare that gave him each year stallion after stallion, so he would be mad to banish her from his harem for a misdemeanor.

On the other hand, she had to learn how to behave properly. She had to learn her position and how far her authority could reach in the limited time a fighting Sultan could spare for his pleasure. He knew well the heartaches his mother had suffered and he was a fair man who tried to find the perfect balance among the multitude of attractions life offered him so openhandedly.

Even now she tried to dismiss his page from the room with

a node; but the slave was well trained and ignored her command. Inside the Sultan's quarters Suleiman was the absolute ruler. The rejection of her authority increased her anxiety. If in the presence of the Sultan she couldn't even dismiss a servant, what were her chances to dismiss a Grand Vizier?

She waited inactively to hear some kind of greetings, but the Sultan continued to ignore her presence until she had performed the prescribed rituals. She had to prostate in front of him and to kiss the end of his caftan. He was nude at the time and she had no caftan to kiss, so he extended his hand; but she ignored it. She simply kneeled in front of him and bent her neck.

He felt she had shown enough respect under the circumstances; so, he dismissed the page who was massaging him. The ritual now allowed him to talk to her, but he had to be stern, so he asked her grimly:

"What other good news from the Harem do you wish to announce to your master?"

"I came to offer consolation to my Master too for his grave loss," she claimed with a curious tone that could well be considered as submissive; but it could also contain traces of irony, as the word "too" was double-edged. He felt his anger growing for her audacity.

"You better explain to me why my precious son died in your hands."

"It was the will of Allah. He died as painlessly as a candle blown by the wind. I could do nothing more but watch him die."

"Since the day you entered my harem, I have lost three sons."

Even though she was locked in the harem, she didn't fail to hear the rumors circling in the City streets that she was a witch who had used black magic to win the Sultan's heart and soul and make him a servant of her will. She knew much better what the truth was. She was a professional enchantress who knew her erotic trade well. The magic she used was her sumptuous lips. She simply knew how to use them better than any Princess, and this time she had a well-prepared answer to this accusation.

"Since I came into your harem I gave you four sons and one daughter. None of your concubines have offered you more than me. If I have somehow neglected the son we've lost, then you are also responsible for choosing to leave and fight Allah's wars. In every war there are bound to be casualties, and a very dear casualty may be the cost of a great victory of Allah."

Suleiman became more complacent when he was praised and she knew that well. Now he was even weaker because he was naked. This was one weakness all men shared unless they were eunuchs. She also knew her arithmetic was impeccable and two of his other sons lost were other result of his other concubines' faults.

They had not been severely punished, but simply rarely invited to the Sultan's bed to offer a trace of variety to his exquisite taste. Suleiman was very eclectic and she knew it. He was nothing like his intimate friend who was in love with unrestricted love making. He was a slave of every human being that needed relief from the desires his impeccable looks stirred. Ibrahim was openhanded with his flesh as much as Suleiman was with his presents. The rumors claimed that Ibrahim had returned from Egypt with a considerable number of black slaves.

"Extreme power was never welcomed in Allah's Paradise. You know very well that if it was up to me, I would have never left my children all alone, especially if I knew they were sick. However, the son of Selim Khan has the obligation to make the dreams of his father true, so that his hopes his sons will make his dreams come true are realized too."

Talking abstractly about dreams was a clear sign the Sultan had forgiven her. Now it was just a matter of time for her to take the upper hand, and she was well familiar with the necessary approach. She had to let her lips do the talking.

"This dream will surely come true, if the father makes the right choice for his heir."

Suleiman realized the goal of her insinuation and pared her blow.

"All my sons have the blood of Osman in their veins. They

will all be proved worthy of their ancestors."

This obscure assertion was not enough to please her.

"Everyone knows the sons take after their mother."

Her trap was now well set for him to fall in, and he did without too much thought.

"Ottoman Sultans become the sons who resemble the father," he said and he meant it.

"If this is true, then, your proper heir must be Mehmet. He is exactly like you. He has the color of your hair, your eyes and he is as sensitive and refined as you. He has also started to compose beautiful poems."

Suleiman just realized the trap he was in, because of the consequences of his own words.

"There is still Sehzade Mustafa who is the oldest. He is also a very fine boy and a brave fighter, as every one of his teachers assures me."

It was what Hurrem expected to hear to inject her poison to the last drop.

"All his teachers are very wise and Ibrahim Pasha also wise too to choose so trusty teachers. One has to be completely blind not to see that. You know well I'm not blind. I can most clearly see the resemblance. Every time I see Mustafa's eyes, they remind me of your father, the cruel Selim Khan. He looks as much of him as if he was his son. If he ever becomes the Sultan, he will conquer the world. I'm sure he will, but is this really what you wish from your son? Your father was not a happy man because of his ambitions. He wanted to conquer everything in sight, but excessive greed does not lead to happiness. Do you know what kind of rumors the White Eunuchs spread?"

"No, I don't! I don't care much about rumors unless they are facts."

"Who can say after a year what is a fact and what is not. There are liars who will deny everything they did, and your father is dead to confirm their claims."

"What do these rumors claim?"

"They claim that making Ibrahim the keeper of your hawks

was his reward for services rendered; but, who can ever hope to prove such an audacious claim? What happens behind the Seraglio doors will always remain a secret and you know it better than anyone. For instance, rumors also claim that I have earned your preference by secretly giving you to eat pieces of female hyena glands. Would you believe such a ludicrous rumor? Of course not; but if you send a spy this in the rumor he will hear even now in the Spice Bazaar. These devious merchants will say just about anything to make lots of money by selling dearly any rare oil they can find."

"This is indeed a crazy rumor."

"Yes, it is, but you have to admit that what they say about your favorite slave makes a lot of sense. He is just too ambitious and he will deny nothing to gain a higher post. Everyone also knows that father during the last few years preferred the charms of pretty boys more than any woman's. They even say, he died in the arms of a eunuch. Thank Allah you are not like him. You have plenty of Princesses to choose from and only one favorite slave. This means you are a better man than your father or your grandfathers, and no one can deny it after your exploits in Belgrade, Rhodes, and Hungary. These days no one dares to question your manliness. Perhaps it is now the right time to step back and let Ibrahim Pasha take all the chances with a war away from Constantinople. A wise sovereign should know that sooner or later a failure is bound to happen. You shouldn't be the one to carry the burden of a defeat. Let Ibrahim bear it and break his back rather than you. After all you have to admit that he is so eloquent and skillful with his lips he can turn even a defeat into a momentous success."

Suleiman was reluctant to agree, but he had no energy left to argue against a statement that was true to a great extent. His health was so unsteady, he couldn't bear the heartaches of a campaign. His silence gave Hurrem the chance to continue undeterred.

"Who does Ibrahim Pasha think would be your best heir? Whom does he praise more?"

"He praises all of my sons, but Mustafa most of all. It might well be because he is the oldest and has already proven his worth during his hard training as a Janissary."

"This is indeed an explanation that makes perfect sense, but who can say if this is the right one? You are a man and you are good for fighting, but I'm a woman and I can understand much more than a man's lips can say. I know how to read a man's eyes. Do you want me to prove it to you? I can read what a man wants even with his eyes closed. Why don't you close your eyes and let me show what you desire most of all right now? Isn't this the best proof that I know how to read a man's eyes and how to fulfil it?"

****

He had to admit she knew him well enough as if he was her slave. He could never say no to any offer her lips would make. They were simply too sumptuous and skilled to be denied for long. She was simply the very best and a Sultan should never settle for second best.

Military expeditions created a great deal of tensions, and he had been many months under severe stress that clouded his judgment. He owed to himself as a wise sovereign to relieve any wishes or feelings that could affect his ruling. Perfect balance was his goal and Hurrem was the best person to set his mind straight on the most important question an Ottoman Sultan could ask. Did he like women or men most?

As his mind became clearer after the passing storm, he could now plainly see Hurrem's arguments were perfectly logical. He still remembered the lust he read in Selim's eyes that fateful day when he saw his favorite slave for the first time. He also remembered his advice to have this particular slave castrated. It might well be caused by his desire to turn Ibrahim into a eunuch and use him for his pleasure instead of Menekse and Asphodel who were clearly inferior specimens missing Ibrahim's superior wits.

Unquestionably Ibrahim had grown up and was considered now as the most handsome man in his Empire. Even back then he was a most desirable underage slave to own, and the events in the Avret Bazaar had proven the full extent of his charms. Men were willing to die to possess him. He had won the ownership of this slave because of his father's extreme authority and the terror his ring inspired. If he was just another customer, the bidding might well have ended with a duel of the two last buyers to the death. It wouldn't be the first night that blows or stabs had been exchanged during a spirited bidding in a slave bazaar. Men became extremely aggressive when it came to win the favors of such a blessed male slave.

A beautiful woman stark naked was not a sufficient warranty of the amounts of pleasure she could provide and Mahidevran Sultan was such a case. She was too proud to surrender completely to the desires of a man as she was. She was a Princess after all not a professional enchantress who made her living this way. Providing a man with ultimate pleasure was an art a woman had to learn, but to learn an art a woman had to have talent and devotion to her trade. If for Mahidevran love making with the Sultan was a duty, for her it was sheer delight and she was willing to show her man how much he pleased her and become proud for his performance.

On the other hand, a naked male slave could hardly find a way to hide the truth about the pleasure he felt making love. Perhaps this was the reason Selim tried so hard to turn Ibrahim into a eunuch. The attraction between them was simply too much to bear, and a Sultan had no good reason to limit his excesses. Selim's reign was too short and his absolute authority too great to be denied.

Nevertheless, this clandestine affair belonged to the past and nothing good could come out of searching it now. If Ibrahim denied the rumors, there was practically no way to find out what had really happened between his father and his slave. Selim Khan back then possessed the destinies of both the master and his slave.

"Ibrahim is just one of my counselors. He can only make suggestions. I'm the one who makes the finally decisions,"

Suleiman pronounced gravely.

"Indeed you are the decider, but to reach the right decision you must know all the facts. Since you are the Sultan, I'm sure you have the power to find the truth, if you so wish. Sultan Selim as far as I know when his lover Sinan Pasha was killed he had two favorite eunuchs. One was executed, but the other is still alive serving faithfully your slave Ibrahim Pasha. Why don't you ask Asphodel what had really happened."

"And why should I care about what really happened?" Suleiman exploded his tension. "If I was to believe every rumor I hear from the lips of eunuchs about your behavior, then I would have sold you back to the slave bazaar."

"That would have been a wise choice, if you were foolish enough to seek purity in the commodities sold in slave bazaar. Pure virgins can be only noble women and proud Princesses, my only love. Nevertheless, only total fools seek virginity in a courtesan like me. Wise men seek intense pleasure, and I believe you have found exactly what you've sought. You can enjoy pleasure and be proud for your sons too. I was indeed the wisest choice your mother could have made."

"It's true that I never had any reason to complain about inviting you to my bed. You have always exceeded my wildest expectations."

She didn't have to hear much more to realize that Suleiman was still under her spell. Now she had to turn back into an obedient concubine with only one thought in her mind, how to offer her master what he needed most after a war and a son's death, a state of nirvana.

"Sometimes I wish you were not seeking only pleasure in my arms. I am much more than a prostitute, I'm also a mother and an educated woman eager to offer you the best advice possible, because I'm the least selfish counselor. All I wish is to secure the proper future for my children as you do. I'm their mother, and if you choose one of them as your heir, I promise you all the rest will become his to command. My sons all love each other so much they would be more than happy to follow your

61

heir's orders and desire nothing more than that. They are my sons, so they know how well they will be rewarded by being loyal to a mighty Sultan."

****

He had to admit she could read better what was in his mind even than his consciousness. After a long expedition away from the comforts of the Seraglio pleasure came first in line; but soon after when sobriety took the place of plain animal lust, other priorities surfaced. He had lost a son and Hurrem was the best woman to replace his losses. They both knew this was true. Now it was up to Allah to prove Suleiman was still His Shadow.

She was now fully convinced it was perfectly safe for her to put forward her plan.

"If Mustafa is like his grandfather, I wonder what kind of measures you can take to save your precious throne from a usurper," she said posing a rather rhetorical inquiry.

"All my sons are wiser than that. They are not greedy to fight for my fortune. They will take only what I offer to them."

Hurrem was a very shroud judge of characters. She immediately realized that the Sultan's tone of absolute authority was more wishful thinking than solid reality. Her experience with many male children had shown her that the fact she had many sons was a good reason for them to develop competitive natures. On the other hand, many times in his sleep Suleiman had woken up drenched in sweat, a clear sign of having nightmares. She didn't have to think much to decide what the source of terror was for the son of Selim.

She had felt too his terrorizing glance and she knew she wouldn't dare to refuse him anything he might felt like asking. If she was ever invited to his bedroom, her only chance for a better future was if Selim desired to treat her not as a woman but as a eunuch. This was the reason why she did not refuse Gülfem's plea to take her place, even though at the time she was terrified with the idea Selim would eventually find out the switch. Nevertheless, she owed most of her luck to the Kislar Aga who did his best for this dangerous deal to go through.

Surprisingly so, Selim didn't get angry, and that said much about his character. He was probably very flattered that one of his son's Kadin had grabbed the opportunity to pay him a visit to make sure her only son would survive. She was a mother and she would do the same to save a single son of hers.

When Gülfem came back the next day, she was the only odalisque she chose to discuss her escapade and what she heard made a lot of sense. Selim may have been a raping beast, but a Seraglio concubine could very easily put him to shame. Gülfem despite her gentle nature after her long neglect was a dormant volcano that could please even the most violent man. It was a sign Selim's preference to eunuchs was not the result of a female shortcoming or male boredom. Selim was simply getting too old to be feel like the conqueror of a much younger concubine. His preference though had led to a strange twist in favorites, as women lost much of the importance they had gained when Bayezid became Sultan and eunuchs got the upper hand.

In her ears the rumor that there was an old eunuch conspiracy brewing in the Top Kapi sounded too obscure to be believed; but it wouldn't hurt her to investigate. Black eunuchs were very susceptible to bribes and since she gave birth to the first of Suleiman sons, she had plenty of money to spend each month and many presents to give away to make a greedy eunuch talk.

****

"Indeed my sons are very patient and obedient because they are blessed with many of my virtues. They think a lot before they act. Of course, I have no idea how exactly Mustafa behaves. I only know he is Ibrahim's favorite; so, I have to conclude he is too greedy for power for comfort. Ibrahim is indeed a man of many virtues, but usually Allah balances out great virtues with great faults. I don't know much of him, but everyone inside the Harem knows how attractive he is and how lusty. You know him for many more years than I do, so please tell me is he as lusty as they say?

63

Everyone else I've asked says that you shouldn't trust him even with a female cat. What's your opinion? Would you trust him to sleep inside the Eski Saray for a single night?"

"No; but let's say that I trust my Harem even less than him," the Sultan cautiously replied. "Money talks, and eunuchs are much more greedy than Grand Viziers to put their heads on the line for ill-gained riches."

It was a moment of triumph for Hurrem. Breaking the barriers of trust between friends was a critical victory. From now on she simply had to pour once in a while a small drop of poison in Suleiman's mind and let it act. The glass had cracked and the crack could only grow.

Suddenly Suleiman felt the threat growing and tried to promptly extinguish it.

"Ibrahim Pasha has been very loyal to me. He has carried out successfully every difficult mission I have given him. In few cases he was even more successful and competent than me or my father. He pacified Egypt with the least amount of bloodshed possible, so the revenues have grown larger than ever before," he pronounced. "Happy people work harder than scared ones."

His tone was strict, trying to stop her from discussing this subject any further; however, for her every path lay suddenly wide open. She simply had to appear as submissive as she could to retain the advantageous position she had gained.

"No, I don't believe these outrageous praises. For me you will always be the best man of all," she reassured him, and as if she was angry for his praises for a man, she turned her back at him; her instinct led her to follow the paths that led to her master's heart Ibrahim had opened.

"But, now I'm tired arguing. Could you please scratch my back? I'm sorry, but I don't feel comfortable to ask such a favor from any eunuch of yours. Few of them are more aggressive with a woman than even Selim Khan. You won't believe all the stories I hear in your Harem. They may have lost their pride, but have grown long tongues, skillful fingers and tiny fists. There is no woman in the Eski Saray who can refuse a good massage after a hammam, not one, trust me!"

She knew well enough that her slim waist was an open invitation for any man. Subconsciously it was a definite sign of fertility males found very hard to resist, but for him this sudden turn was an unmistakable sign of weakness. It was a maneuver comparable to Ibrahim's strategy at Mohacs. The Akinji had carried it out to perfection, attracting the heavy cavalry towards the concealed cannons; but she went a step further to excite once more his interest. Her brilliant idea to compare his father with few eunuchs was a master stroke that came out of the blue with the power of a thunderbolt.

"How do you know that?" he murmured still stunned by her audacity.

"The Harem holds many great secrets, but no secret can survive for long inside a harem for long. Your father was always the most favorite subject of discussion in the Harem. He had become naturally the measure of comparison, and not only of his vigor; but also of many other virtues he supposedly possessed, if you know what I mean. If you don't believe me, ask Asphodel. I'm sure he knows much more than I do about your father. They used to go to the hammam together all the time, and submissive eunuchs have an eye for naughty details. Asphodel can also fairly judge your father against your favorite too. From what I hear, they also use the hammam together. I wonder why my suggestions about using concubine attendants in your hammam has slowly faded away. Is it because there are simply too many eunuchs in the Seraglio and you have to find them something to do? This is one way to be likable, but I feel it's not the best. Concubines should be used in the hammam and you know it, and this problem can be solved only if your Harem moves to the Seraglio. And it's not only me who says so, but you are simply the last man to find out the truth, as usual. "

"What do you mean by that?" Suleiman asked.

"Everyone knows the eunuchs are your best spies inside the Harem; but have you ever heard of a Eunuch condemning another Eunuch? No, of course not. If they did, then you might have found out that since Selim's era there were eunuchs who were not truly eunuchs. They were fakes. I don't know who is responsible for this travesty, all I know is that the black dancers you offered to your Damat have now been renamed Black Eunuchs inside Ibrahim's Palace for his pleasure. After his return from Egypt, many more Nubians have arrived to serve your sister's needs. Of course, I know that in this palace the sole responsible is your beloved favorite, as much as in the Eski Saray the sole responsible is the Valide Sultan; however, only you are responsible in your Selamlik, and any kind of shortcoming will now reflect badly in your legacy, not Selim's. In my mind, the more eunuch Nubian slaves a harem has the more chances exist few true men have sneaked-in escaping detection. After all, the Ayin prescribes that only eunuchs should judge other eunuchs qualifications and choose the very best ones to serve in the Saraglio."

She had said enough for that day and with a touch of distaste she got up and left the dressing room leaving her clothes behind. As she walked slowly towards his bedroom, she looked behind her back several times to make sure he was following her the same way a stallion follows a mare. A mare in a similar case would raise her tail, so she followed her animal instincts and pulled her long hair away from her back to her breasts. A woman's long hair was a powerful tease for any man. To show her respect for the words of the Prophet, she twisted her hair and then placed it at the top of her head to get it out of the way once and for all.

He was following her step by step as if he was mesmerized by the spectacle she offered.
Reaching the edge of the bed she stopped and turned around for her Parthian arrow.

"I'm your mare. Please ride me to your heart's content, my proud stallion," she begged him and as she stood at the edge of the bed and prostrated to an unknown god who was still reluctant to answer her prayers; but if Allah was reluctant to descent to Earth and give her all that she asked for, His Shadow wasn't.

In his mind now her conquest was complete; but in reality this was the initial stage of her plan. Her victory could not be complete unless she was sure she had drained his lust to the last drop, following her mother's wise advice. When a man was aroused, his brain became momentary numb. Then, any woman worthy of her gender could explain the unexplainable to her husband, as her surrender to his lust was the best way to prove her loyalty and put all his suspicions to rest.

She had discover one more reason that this natural phenomenon was so. If a woman could perform this ritual of trust as many times as she needed to exhaust her man, then naturally the man would make the mistake to assume that she was as exhausted as he. However, this was the greatest male illusion of them all, as an exhausted man was incapable of cheating, while female exhaustion was a temporary phenomenon that normally lasted less than a few draughts from a shisha mouthpiece.

****

Normally it is a very rare occurrence for two minds to reach simultaneously the same conclusion. It is rare because one of the problems is that each human mind has its own point of view. A portion of the differences is also due to the different experiences each human has. In Suleiman's mind Hurrem's passion was a clear sign she was still a slave in love with her master; but in her mind he was her slave, as he needed her much more than she needed him. From the moment she had born a son, her future was secured to a large extend. Now, his weakness became more apparent as his male vigor gradually deteriorated into a standstill.

She waited a little more, and as his breathing beat receded to a steady murmur, she left the bed and walked to the window. It was almost midnight now and the young moon had not the strength to light-up the night skies. The Bosporus Straits in the distance looked like a black river slowly running between its banks forced by a force as mysterious as Time. It was a physical barrier she had never crossed, as all these years locked in the Harem she had spent many hours staring at it, but she had never the permission to cross it and set her foot on Asia.

She was locked like a bird in a golden cage its master kept feeding to enjoy its singing. As a bird she could enjoy everything life had to offer but the pleasure of flying. Under these circumstances, many birds would simply refuse to eat and die, but her life was not her own. She had her children to look after before caring about her needs.

Her mind free of all bonds of decency and oppression traveled once more to Ibrahim Pasha. He could cross the Bosporus Straits as often as he liked, and as a Grand Vizier he had his own boat with twelve oarsmen to command according to his will. His slim figure wondering on the shore in front of her window was still vivid in her mind. Perhaps, now her time had come to claim her rights as a vital member of the Ottoman hierarchy, and the freedom to leave her footsteps on the sand next to the eternal stream of Time.

****

The Grand Vizier one day after his victorious return, did not waste much time and erected on three white marble pedestals in the middle of the Hippodrome Square, the three pagan, naked, bronze statues he had requisitioned from Budapest, as if he was a Byzantine Emperor, a proud testimony of the magnificent victory.

When the local Muslim clergy complained to the Sultan his immediate superior that he was restoring the symbols of the pagans, Ibrahim with his usual diplomatic tact replied that his audacious gesture meant the exact opposite. His decision was to show to the people that the Olympian gods and heroes could not protect even their statues from captivity. Allah, the only mighty god, had captured these three frail opponents and carried them as slaves to His holy city as loot, an undeniable proof of His superiority.

In private quarters he was even more eloquent. These three statues have lost their divine powers long ago first to the power of Christ and then to Allah. This is the reason why the fanatical Hungarians had captured them and exhibited them in Budapest. Now the time had come for Islam to show to the world that it had become the most powerful force on Earth. Unfortunately, he had not found any statues of Christ in Budapest to loot, so they had to wait till they captured Venice and Rome to bring back all the treasures the Crusaders had stolen from the palaces and churches of the Eternal City.

This was what looting your opponent's capital meant. It signified your enemy was too weak to defend his most praised possessions. If the king of Hungary had golden coins in his vault, it was not as powerful message if the Ottomans took them and stored them in their vaults, because the people could not see them and judge the full extent of their victory. This was the reason why he had taken also the great candles and exhibited them by the mihrab (sanctuary) of Agia Sophia to show his strict devotion to Islam.

"These statues have no true value to any living faith today, as the gods and heroes they portrait cannot stir any feelings in the hearts of anyone or inspire a resurrection of paganism. Posting these statues is a clear signal to everyone that Islam is all-mighty. If the Seih-Ul-Islam was complaining, then the Christian Patriarch should complain even more; but he remained silent most wisely. He knows that Europe is full of similar statues of Olympian gods depicting their human virtues, and no Christian sovereign has ever complained, because they all felt that any such statue commemorates the victory of Christ over the pagan gods. Now that we have conquered New Rome, it's time to leave behind a monument of our historic victory that would last forever and ever."

Despite this logic, the Sultan remained still skeptical.

"The human body is the most important of Allah's creations. Man should not try to challenge or mimic His creations."

Ibrahim had an answer for his worries.

"When a man is trying to mimic Allah's creations, he does

nothing more than what your children do when they play with their wooden swords. They try to mimic you, so when they grow up they can become better warriors than you. Exposing these statues to your subjects will teach your subjects how beautiful the human body can be. It is simply hypocritical for them to worship the human body naked in the Avret Bazaar, use it in their bedroom for their pleasure, and not admire it in a public place."

"Yes, but we wouldn't like to see a statue of Hatidge my sister naked in the At Meidan and drunken Janissaries touching it," Suleiman stubbornly insisted.

"This is true as long my wife is young and beautiful; but when she grows older I wouldn't mind admiring a naked statue of her in my palace depicting how she looked when she was young to remind me what treasures Time has stolen from me."

"Then perhaps I should ask an Italian sculptor to come over and make a statue of you."

"No, you don't have to do anything as expensive as that. Use your imagination and envision yourself as Apollo, the protector of the arts, and me as Hercules. Then, you may admire our statues every time you come to visit me and your sister Artemis. If ancient statues have a secret power is that they allow us to compare the living with an ideal. Who could ever blame you, if by admiring the statue of Artemis you can even dream of Hurrem?"

****

Erecting the bronze statues was a minor problem between them and by ridiculing the issue Ibrahim had pressured the Sultan to forget it. However, in other circles where religious affairs and superstitions were still important, Ibrahim's audacious act stirred grievances and murmurs that grew stronger as days went by especially among the Muslim clergy.

The most serious reaction came from a satirical poet who dared to write a couplet about the new Abraham who had raised the same idols the old one had abolished. This audacious act greatly angered Ibrahim because his name was Abraham too in

Arabic, as plainly as Suleiman meant Solomon.

He knew well enough that every attempt to modernize the Eternal City or spread new ideas that might agitate the average man was bound to be opposed with uncommon vigor especially by the Muslim population who was mentally the most conservative one. Their beliefs were restricted into the pages of a single book and would never change till the end of time. This permanent state of stagnation was enough to infuriate him.

His argument was perfectly logical. Could the entire human experience fit into a single book? Was the human evolution going to stop dead on its tracks? Human knowledge had to constantly grow and improve living conditions. It was the growth of knowledge that had allowed Mehmet Fatih to overpower the Roman Empire, and had been very easy for him to convince the Sultan that guns were the main reason Fatih and Selim Khan had been such great conquerors and Suleiman too. Without guns and gun powder the Belgrade would have never fallen, the Knights of Saint John in Rhodes would have never capitulated, and Mohacs would have been another Ottoman disaster in the hands of the Hungarian heavy cavalry charge.

In the Eternal City the answer to every question was sought by the Muslim clergy inside the pages of the Quran and since the beginning of their relationship, he had tried to show to Suleiman that his search for the absolute truth was ill conceived, because truth changed even slowly and imperceptibly every day the sun rose from a different point in the East and set in the West.

****

Ibrahim was not a philosopher. He was a down-to-earth realist. He had experienced the effects of evolution during his short career. If today he was the most powerful man in the Empire after the Sultan and had six horsetails in his banner to the Suleiman's seven, everything could change in an instant, if any of his follies ever reached the Sultan's ears. If he had been a nobleman of Venice who had demolished a hostile army as clearly as he did and brought treasures to adorn the capital, he would be considered as a splendid public benefactor. Here in the Islamic capital of the Ottoman Empire he had been rewarded with ridicule. Every praise said in his favor after the Mohacs victory had now been forgotten. It was unfair, and this grave injustice made him lose his temper for the first time.

This sneak assault on his dignity could not be left unanswered, because It could turn into a riot in the same way a single snowflake could turn into an avalanche. The mind of the mob had not forgotten his shabby origin. He was not just a slave, but the Sultan's favorite. When he became Hasodabashi, the rumor he was a eunuch the Sultan used for his pleasure was created and he had to marry Suleiman's sister to prove he was a man.

In the old days as a page he had no way to react to every gaff and insult. He had to pretend he had heard nothing and forget all these ironic smiles in men's faces when they saw him following the Sultan along with his other servants and eunuchs; but now he was Serasker and Sadrazam (Grand Vizier) and he had to put a stop to every malicious rumor. All the power of the Grand Vizier office was a reflection of the Sultan's absolute authority; so, he had to defend the dignity of his office and protect the Sultan for the wisdom of his choice.

The poet was arrested, flogged and hanged by the neck from the plane tree of public executions in front of the Orta Kapi. From this moment on Ibrahim and Islam would be separated by the blood of the poet the same way the Bosporus separated Europe from Asia.

****

Hurrem did not wait for long to put a new plan into action. The moment she felt Ibrahim's star dimming, she took advantage of this unexpected turn of events and sent one of the women of her court to ask Valide Sultan for a hearing. The winter was gradually approaching its end and with the arrival of spring everyone was in a better, more agreeable mood. Spring was the season the world was reborn and the right time for a novel suggestion.

Till that very day Hurrem had no complaints from the Valide's behavior. Whatever riches and authority she had acquired till then, it was because of Hafsa's permission or toleration. Nevertheless, as she grew older her patience diminished and the feeling Hafsa would always have the final word became an unbearable offense to her personality.

Everything had to be executed according to the Seraglio strict rules and traditions; but she was a Russian. She was born and raised on the endless steppes of the Ukraine. Now she was locked up in the Harem for many years, separated from the rest of the world by high walls and impassable gates well-guarded day and night. In fact, from the moment she became Suleiman's favorite and had conceived his first son, the security measures became even stricter, as her significance for the Sultan's happiness and prestige increased tenfold.

Her only chance to get out of the Eski Saray was when the Sultan informed the Chief Black Eunuch that her services were needed in the Seraglio; but even this short trip with the carriage did nothing to sooth her soul and relieve the tension her slavery created. Watching the world from behind a curtain was a torture, because it was not allowed for her to stop the carriage and take even a simple walk and mingle with the crowd even surrounded by the Janissary guards. Then, when they finally reached the Seraglio, the security and isolation became even greater since she had now to cross three gates to reach the Sultan's quarters.

When the Chief Black Eunuch had brought her in the Harem for the first time, she had the impression that the Sultan or some other nobleman would simply enjoy her for a while and let her free with a good reward for her services. However, soon her mission became clearer and the great duration of her training meant she was destined to have a longer career as a mother.

In the Harem most of the concubines considered her very lucky to have so soon secured a comfortable future; but this oriental mentality was completely alien to her character. She was not the kind of woman who would be content spending all her life next to a single man. As long as she had not a child, she was not so closely watched because there was no intimate connection with the Sultan; however now she could not go anywhere without the company of her courtiers, even inside the Harem or the Seraglio. It was this combination of female companions and male guards that was so restrictive. She was now a person of importance intimately connected to the Sultan, and she had to protected like a precious Byzantine icon. Even a hand that might touch her inside the Grand Bazaar crowds was a fatal offense against the Sultan's property.

To have a clandestine affair with a guard, or even a eunuch was practically a child's play, but having as female companions younger concubines who would love to find out even a single wrong step of hers made any kind of naughty act practically impossible. To condemn her for infidelity meant almost instant death for her and a glorious career opening for the informer. The fact she was the mother of a son made no great difference, when the Sultan's honor was at stake. In any case, after a certain age all sons were separated from their mothers early on to be educated properly like capable princes and mighty warriors.

This entire winter had been extremely frustrating as the weather gradually deteriorated news from great festivities and long celebrations in Ibrahim's palace reached her ears. As a Grand Vizier Ibrahim had to entertain every foreign diplomatic mission at certain intervals that became even shorter when the war with Hungary became eminent. There was an immense amount of information that had to be mined this period as in war every diplomat became a spy.

Obviously the Sultan didn't fail to attend any such occasion, and Hatidge Sultan was also present by her husband's side. Nevertheless, Suleiman had never considered the possibility of taking her along. For him she was just a convenient combination of a mother and a whore.

On the other hand, what she heard about Hatidge's behavior was that she was using Ibrahim as a mare uses a stallion. The rumors claimed that her interests were much broader than a man, any man could sufficiently fulfill. She had become a widow very early in her youth and her long isolation from the natural environment of a Princess had forced her for a while to seek happiness in the arms of her female attendants. Habits were hard to change, and as her husband became more and more preoccupied with the war effort, she did not hesitate to claim the rights of her superior social status.

Hurrem had felt many times the same way, but being the favorite of the Sultan had practically isolated her from any other source of love, pleasure and tenderness inside the Eski Saray. During a war who would dare to try to disgrace the Sultan?

She had spent many nights trying to give a reasonable answer to this question, as the noise and the music from Ibrahim's festivities reached her ears whenever a strong easterly carried the commotion all the way from the At Meidan to the Harem at Bayezid Square.

Perhaps she could have waited a little longer, if the previous afternoon she had not noticed on the Grand Vizier's boat from the Sultan's window, Ibrahim and his bride following the current that circled the Saray Burnu towards the Marmara Sea on their way to an excursion to the Prince Islands. Something had to change in the Harem, so she could escape too from her golden cage, and after the Sultan the Valide Sultan was the only one who could perform this miracle.

Hafsa Sultan's friendship and support had cooled down considerably after Hatidge's marriage and her mutinous attitude; however, during Abdullah's sickness and especially after his death, she had fully supported her. The rumor that she was bringing bad luck to the Harem was nothing more than a malicious gossip that had probably originated from Mahidevran's audacious courtiers who were constantly following from a distance her every move. They were much more annoying than Asphodel who was Ibrahim's top spy in the Seraglio.

No one could be absolutely sure where, how and whoever originated a rumor in the Harem, as many times interests coincided one day and the next day opposed. Yesterday's friends could become today's enemies and she had to be extremely careful in all her actions.

A climate favoring suspicions and conspiracies existed in the City of Constantine since the days of the Roman Empire. The fact the Ottoman Empire had incorporated many Byzantine nobles, raising them to high posts because of their abilities, had infected the Muslim nobility with the virus of intrigue. They didn't have to try hard. Intrigue was in the blood of every Oriental and solving mysteries was the way to survive on the entire Asia Continent.

Nevertheless, this time Valide Sultana's reception was much warmer that she might have expected under the circumstances after Abdullah's demise, and they spent few hours discussing cordially several issues, ranging from her children's education and health to the various other subjects women around the world discuss when men are not around to listen. The atmosphere had gradually warmed up further as Hafsa Hatun had made arrangements to treat her guest with a variety of sweets and pastries, from fruit preserves to baklava, and sherbets chilled with ice carried from the Mount Olympus in Bursa. A mother's joy is always to see her son happy, and Hafsa was wise enough to discern that her son happiness had the name Hurrem.

They could be talking casually over inconsequential issues for hours if Hurrem had not tried to turn the subject to Ibrahim's magnificent receptions. Hurrem knew Hafsa had never participated in such a festivity and imagined there might be some resentment. It would be advantageous, she noted, if similar celebrations were also staged in the Seraglio, inviting the nobility and the high officials of the Empire to warm up the relations between the Sultan and the various members of the Ottoman hierarchy. After all they were all in the same boat.

Unexpectedly Valide Sultan became very pensive as she tried to discern where exactly Hurrem was aiming at. She knew well that organizing such a meeting from scratch required many months of preparations since simply the distance an official had to travel to attend would take weeks; therefore, only significant rare events like a great victory or a marriage were sufficient reasons to be celebrated at this high level.

"I didn't know that," Hurrem humbly confessed, "because I have never been invited to such an event besides Ibrahim's marriage. I find this omission strange for the favorite consort of a Sultan," she complained, but it was the wrong thing to mention that very day.

Hafsa's face changed expression at once and her smile was erased. If Hurrem had prepared a good excuse for her behavior back then, now it was useless. Hafsa's explanation was devastating to her ego.

"If you are referring to Hatidge's presence, you shouldn't forget that she is a Princess and you are still a slave who has other more important duties, namely to make my son happy and content. If any one of my son's consorts was to be invited this would be Mahidevran Sultan who had noble blood in her veins and is legally married."

Hurrem lost suddenly her smile as her feelings were deeply hurt. From that moment on, Hafsa would be considered as an opponent exactly as Ibrahim.

Hurrem felt there was nothing more left to say after this insult and very upset with her face red from anger she got up and started to leave; but the black eunuchs guarding the door well trained didn't move. She wanted to depart at once as a gesture of displeasure, but the Harem's etiquette simply did not allowed for such liberties. Hafsa had not given her consent for the slave to depart, as anger against her master was a feeling unacceptable for any slave; thus, the door remained firmly closed, and Hurrem had to bow deeply in front of Hafsa Sultan and utter an excuse for a sudden headache to be dismissed and allowed to return to her quarters.

She practically run the distance through the corridors, and when the bedroom door was closed behind her safe in her cage Hurrem burst into tears. Inside the Eski Saray she could never become important. The Harem was not the love nest she yearned. It was a just a nursery for the Sultan's children and a luxurious bordello housing the various Sultan's whores. Valide's reasoning was very clear. The Sultan could not be seen in public with a whore by his side. Her presence would simply offend the other legally married guests!

She had to change strategy at once. This visit could potential turn disastrous. Hafsa may consider her as too obnoxious to remain the Sultan's favorite and try to change his mind. The easiest way would be to send one night another concubine to his quarters.

As men matured they became very unstable creatures. If Suleiman ever became jealous of Ibrahim's conquests among women, and Hafsa Sultan sensed this change of mood, she could easily find many slaves capable of attracting the Sultan's eye in the Avret Bazaar and Galata notorious back streets. She simply had to give an order to the Chief Black Eunuch, and in a matter of days the proper woman could be found. The war had provided the slave market with plenty of northern women to choose from that exceeded in beauty anything that was available in the Harem, as her dominance in Suleiman's heart had practically eliminated the need for a harem innovation; however, this state of negligence could change in a flash.

Damned wars! They could change conditions suddenly and without warning. Her only source of security seemed to be her children. Soon she decided this was not true. Beside Hafsa Sultan, her future depended on other people too. One was the Chief Black Eunuch she could bribe, and then was Ibrahim Pasha. Could she really manipulate any of these two?

Her plan to eliminate Asphodel had to wait for a more opportune moment when Ibrahim Pasha was at war.

****

When Hafsa Hatun informed her son of Hurrem's complaints, he didn't fail to ask Ibrahim's advice on this issue. There were few rumors that had reached his ears lately, and he needed to test Ibrahim's fidelity. His close friend and favorite was too attractive to women, was the very essence of this rumor, and his constantly increasing power and prestige was acting as powerful stimulant inside the Harem walls too. Too many concubines were asking Ibrahim for favors, and the best way to repay such a rich man for a favor was by a favor in return.

Suleiman was no fool. He knew that jealousy was behind these rumors, but for a Sultan being extra cautious was a virtue essential for his survival.

Ibrahim didn't wait long to give him a useful advice. Women were always complaining, he remarked. It is in their nature, and Allah was very wise to make women this way. Men were too involved in their violent fantasies of eternal conquests, and women had to do their best to put men's dreams in order. Dreams were good only if they had some connection to reality and improved living conditions, he noted. By complaining women were responsible for the progress of humanity. If men were left alone, they would spend all their time hunting wild beasts or fighting other men to prove their masculinity and conquer more women even by force.

Trying to make more children and improve their living conditions was every woman's duty. A woman was like a firefly illuminating a man's path to prosperity and happiness. As long a woman complained to her man, it meant she loved him and his children. Even if Hurrem wished to socialize, it was simply to make sure she was still as attractive to him as ever. Inspiring jealousy was a useful weapon to every woman, so he shouldn't chastise Hurrem for her audacious requests, but let her enjoy some more freedom to show her he was confident their relationship was secure. Fireflies should be left free to roam to offer a bit of magic in a man's night.

Ibrahim's suggestion was contrary to Hafsa's who suggested he should keep Hurrem under a tighter leash. Suleiman was expecting this kind of conflict. His mother was always too protective for her one and only son. If he had listened to her advice, he would have sold Ibrahim back in the Avret Bazaar, and lose a valuable aid. If he had listened to his father, he his would have castrated him and turned him into a eunuch full of hate for master.

Despite their love and care, parents didn't always have the correct opinion because they were too conservative and resisted changes. This was as much in their nature as glowing bellies in fireflies. Ibrahim's example was useful, but as a wise Sultan he should be more critical. Firefly light was erratic. It went on and off, so following it was not always easy. A safer approach for a Sultan was to leave fireflies free to roam, but keep a close eye to what they were doing. He had many spies in his service. Two more wouldn't make much difference.

This period he was too busy with the preparations of the new expedition this year to be concerned personally with such trivial matters. Hurrem's complaints were one more case where the eye of a woman was focused on insignificant details failing to cover and analyze sufficiently the greater picture. A warrior Sultan was not allowed to become sidetracked by trivial questions like which the most beautiful woman in the Harem was, or what kind of dishes should be offered in a banquet. These issues might be important for a woman locked in the Harem, but were totally meaningless for a man destined to become a world conqueror. These days his main thoughts were how to secure the supplies he needed for the next expedition into Europe. His plan was to go back and secure Hungary, because when the Ottoman armies left, the King of Spain had managed to take back many of the Sultan's gains. This year the needs were even greater, because the army had to become even stronger to complete the new tasks that were laid out in the time between.

****

Hafsa didn't fail to recognize in her son's reply the words of the Grand Vizier coming out from the Sultan's mouth. She didn't have to pose any more questions, because all these details were military secrets only her son and Ibrahim ought to know. Her son was plain enough. She had to limit her concerns only as far the limits of the Harem and not one step further. Since Ibrahim was clearly involved in this decision, her son wouldn't like to

80

appear weak in front of his Serasker by commencing negotiations. If there was any hope of moderation from strict military discipline, she had to approach Ibrahim in an appropriate, personal way.

She had a good excuse. This year the funds spent inside the Harem had been reduced, as the taxes to the public had been greatly increased. Ibrahim had to be the one responsible for any serious cuts in expenditures and the message was clear. They had to get along with what they had; so spending money on any new purchases was very hard to explain and accept. Her plan to seek for Hurrem's replacement had to be shelved for a while.

She was not an unreasonable woman. Ibrahim Pasha was right. People shouldn't feel they were heavily taxed for the Harem's prosperity. Similar impressions would affect the soldiers' fighting spirit. They were fighting to the death so that Islam could reach the four corners of the world, and to be successful everyone had to contribute according to his ability. The shepherds had to offer part of their herds, the weavers part of their fabrics for uniforms and tents to be tailored. The blacksmiths had to produce more arms or horse shoes, the tanners more leather for shoes and furs for the winter, and the farmers more grain and hay for the animals of burden, horses, camels, donkeys and sheep.

Soon caravans were expected to arrive from Africa and Arabia that carried 50000 camels and even more horses for the needs of the army. The warriors would arrive last, as having many soldiers camping idle outside the city walls was a foolish practice. She needed only to be patient for few days more. This confusion was about to end quite soon, as the long trip to the north was going to start sooner than anyone expected, so everything had to be ready by Saint George's holiday. He was the protector of the Army since the days of the Romans, and there was no need to test the popular beliefs with unnecessary image changes. Incorporations were safer than subversions or replacements. The name of the game was evolution not revolution.

It was clear from the eloquence of his arguments that the Sultan had very competent and sophisticated advisors not only in military matters but also in economics. Hafsa felt she would appear stupid to argue against her son or Ibrahim Pasha on these subjects; so she simply acknowledged her total ignorance on these strategic issues and wished her beloved son new successes and eternal happiness.

On her way back to the Harem she decided to take a stroll around the Great Bazaar. It was the mirror of the social trends. What she saw was indicative of the general mood. The jewel and the rug shops were practically empty, as very few had money to spend on trinkets. On the other hand the saddlers and the blacksmiths were working at full swing. The most were forging new swords, knives and battle axes, while few were producing barrels and assembling muskets. She didn't know too much about armaments, but her eye was immediately caught by the shining breastplates and helmets. Her son was sincere. The Empire was getting ready for battle, and it had to be another critical confrontation. Her worries seemed now trivial and insignificant; nevertheless, she was still a woman and didn't fail to take a closer look at the fabric stores and the local slave market.

As the money became scarce, the expansive fabrics were getting cheaper and the slave girls greatly outnumbered the boys because of the war. The balance of Allah was leaning against women these days and she had to adjust accordingly her wishes. She went in and bought some brocades and silken fabrics for herself.

She had an excellent excuse. She was getting older and she needed all the help she could find to keep her spirits high. The visit at the slave bazaar had not improved her disposition. Seeing all these pretty girls in line waiting for a customer to mesmerize and save them from the toils of slavery had spoiled her mood. They were so cheaply prized and so beautiful that most free girls did not have a chance securing a husband. Wars created great opportunities for the men that survived.

Now she could understand Hurrem's eagerness to get out and live her life as long as she was young. After securing the favors of a Sultan and having few children, what else could she expect to get out of life? Now she was old enough to know that becoming a Valide Sultan was not such a great prospect. It meant that the Sultan, your husband, was dead and that you couldn't marry again. You could only give orders and make arrangements about how someone else would become happy. Giving orders was just an easy way to fight off frustrations and boredom by transferring them to your subjects that had to carry them out.

She could certainly get dressed or bathe, but sometimes she was bored to death carrying out the daily Harem's routines. Few other times she became even desperate. She would rather go out dressed like a whore to find out what kinds of men she attracted.

Hurrem probably felt the same way. Offhand she didn't wish to go to bed with any stranger. She simply wished to read the desire in his eyes. Her need for a man was more for her brain than for her body. This was probably one of the reasons Ibrahim was so attractive; but now that he was married to her daughter, she was not a whore to keep on going after him. By going once with him, she had the excuse that as a mother she couldn't let her daughter marry a total stranger. She had chosen her late husband Selim and she was feeling guilty for her failure.

A woman could find thousands of excuses to explain her slutty attitude. Hurrem was right. It was very difficult for a woman to accept she would taste just one man in her entire life. Perhaps meeting diplomats was a good way to meet interesting men from far away places.

The Ayin tradition did not allow a Valide Sultan to marry again, but said nothing about having few affairs. Perhaps this was the only advantage for any concubine to become a Valide Sultan; but to enjoy an advantage you had to earn it. Without risks there were no rewards.

It was easy. She simply had to wear the ordinary clothes of a hard working woman. Around the Grand Bazaar there were many caravansaries. Was it a random occurrence? Was it the result of the need of foreign merchants to have a dwelling close to their place of work? It was difficult to judge, but having many travelers in a certain part of the city had created the need for local merchants to provide besides shelter and food, also temporary wives. Perhaps as a Valide Sultan she had to investigate this social phenomenon.

She went out one of the Grand Bazaar gates and followed the crowd streaming downhill towards the harbor. There were indeed many caravansaries and locandas in this district. It had to be a district where women were cheap because she was approached by many men with naughty suggestions. Few were even using their native tongues. Seeing her carrying a parcel with fabrics, they suggested they had much better merchandise to offer her at a better price. Something kept her from following them through the entrance of Han. Was it a sign of self-respect or of diminishing lust and procreation drive caused by age?

She couldn't really tell because getting older was a once-in-lifetime experience as everything else. She took a back street that would take her uphill at the direction of the Harem. She had seen enough and felt several times the urge of the Devil to follow her instinct rather than her logic. The Christians believed a God existed who guided you to virtue and a Devil who tried to push you towards sin. Muslims had combined this divine dyad into one, Allah who was the source of both good and evil. Muslims were wiser in finding divining excuses.

Few streets further away a handsome young man with blond hair approached her and suggested she followed him, so he could show her precious merchandise she had never seen before that only he imported in the Eternal City. He had blue eyes. When he claimed that for her she would make the best possible price, she simply could not resist Allah's will.

He was right and indeed the price he asked was more than fair for few moments of happiness. He was young and eager to please himself more than her. He took her for a frustrated wife in search for a paid lover anyway, and the customer was always right inside the Grand Bazaar. He led her to a rug storage and politely asked her to feel the velvet's softness of a silken rug on a pile on her chick. She leaned over the pile of rugs as he pulled her kaftan over her head to make her feel blind of her total disgrace. There was no reason for her to resist or complain. Her disgrace had to be complete as half measures were not fit for a Valide Sultan.

She gave him more than he asked, because he had given her much more than she had hoped for. When she left, he promised her that he would always be there, if she needed few extra yards for her dress. He was cute trying to cover up his trade, but the merchants all around him knew his trade and laughed at her expense. She didn't care. All they could see were her eyes, and the Prophet had been very wise on this issue. No man could recognize a woman only from the color of her eyes.

When she was back inside the safety of Eski Saray, she felt that having absolute power meant to be oblivious to what anyone else said about your conduct. She was the first Sultan's Kadin who had earned her Valide Sultan title. Actually she had achieved a bit more than it was allowed by the Ayin. She was not only the master of the Eski Saray, but also of a free young man with blue eyes. Ibrahim had been a good teacher. He had taught her how absolute authority could make weakness look like strength. Now she couldn't contain her euphoria. She had finally exorcised Selim Khan from her memory. Now the only pair of eyes yearning for her flesh she could see was blue, and she couldn't have enough of this magnificent feeling for any woman of being full of a man's most precious essence.

War created indeed marvelous opportunities for fulfillment not only for the warriors but for everyone else who stayed behind.

****

This time the Ottoman Army was greater than ever before since the Empire was also greater and richer than ever before. Adding lands and people to the Empire was a way to grow even bigger during the next war. Few more conquests in the East and West and the Ottoman Empire would exceed even the Roman Empire during its hay days.

The Serasker had as a first target the reoccupation of Budapest, the capital of the Huns, but bad weather along the way through the Balkans caused a delay and the city was found empty, when they finally arrived there in midsummer. Then, the new task was revealed, the conquest of Vienna. It was the capital of Austria and the city from where the army of the enemy had originated the drive towards Budapest. Capturing Vienna would secure also Budapest. Vienna was also closer to the heart of Europe and few days marching to Venice. Vienna had to fall in Ottoman hands if they ever hoped to conquer Venice.

Venice had only marches and its fleet as protection and ships were no match for heavy artillery; but the Ottomans had to be adequately prepare, as the Venetians were still the rulers of the waves. The Ottomans had to sink their fleet first, and this was a task even Fatih had failed to achieve inside the Golden Horn and left the Venetian and Genova ships escape from the trap rather than face a naval defeat in the midst of a land victory.

The strategic plan was sound enough. A Muslim army could not attack Venice having a hostile Christian Vienna at its flank, and one could not attack Vienna having the Austrian army in Budapest. Suleiman was very pleased with the progress. This battle plan was essentially Selim's. He had decided to conquer Venice first and then Rome, and Suleiman was proud to set it in motion. However, because of the bad summer weather it was already September, when the Ottomans reached the walls of Vienna. By now the Roman King Charles had enough time to repair the fortifications and supply the city with provisions for a long siege, but there was no faster way to reach Vienna. It was simply too far away from Constantinople.

One additional unexpected problem this year was the fact that because of the summer rains the heavy siege guns were stuck in the mud and were left behind. Nevertheless, even without the heavy artillery the siege progressed according to plan with the light artillery and the underground mining. Day after day the walls weakened and finally a section collapsed, creating an opening wide enough for eighty Janissaries in line to go through. However, even this crack was not wide enough. Despite the repeated efforts and valiant attacks the enemy created a second line of defense inside the city with muskets and guns which the Janissary failed to pierce despite several attempts resulting in heavy losses.

Ibrahim tried to elevate the army's moral by offering rich reward in gold to every trooper who broke the enemy lines, but the army failed to deliver a victory at the last moment. The defenders were simply more determined to fight it out to the last man than the Janissaries who had other options. It was a test of will and the Christian fighters won the day. The Ottoman troops had to retreat one step away from victory, simply because it was too late in the season and winter snowstorms were approaching.

King Charles, the one the Spaniards called Roman Emperor, was also concentrating new armies to attack the besiegers from behind the same way the Hungarians had done before, when they routed the armies of Fatih in front of Belgrade. It was a lesson the Ottomans had learned well, thus Suleiman and Ibrahim decided to retreat in order, looting Austria as much as possible to weaken the enemy so that next year they would have an easier task. It was clear this struggle was going to be a test of will and endurance rather than valor, and the Ottoman Empire was by now the most powerful in the world and the most united. Vienna was saved for the moment, but its future looked grim.

The Ottoman army reluctantly took the way home. To celebrate the Christian victory over Islam, the Austrians created the croissant buns for the first time to demonstrate by eating them their contempt for Islam. On the other hand, Ibrahim who left last decided to free all the captives. It was a gesture meant to weaken the enemies resolve to fight to the death next year.

He also sent a message to all the citizens in Vienna. He assured them that Suleiman had not come to Vienna to steal their fortunes. He simply wished to meet the King of Spain face-to-face to test his valor, but the king was not as brave as anyone thought and didn't come even to Vienna to defend it.

Although the command of the army was not entirely in his hands, Ibrahim Pasha was blamed for this setback. Nevertheless, Sultan Suleiman defended Ibrahim's efforts, and to change the sober mood he spent part of the loot to organize victory celebrations in the City. He recognized that the logistical problems of an expedition so far away from Constantinople were hard to solve effectively, and Ibrahim was not responsible for any omissions, but the unusually bad weather. The Ottoman Empire had started suffering from the same problems that had put an end to Roman expansion. Its borders were so extended that its enemies had multiplied and united against it. The Ottoman armies had to travel far to reach its borders, so by the time they reached the enemy the months left were too few to achieve a decisive victory by attrition, as staged battles on land were a recipe for another Christian disaster like Mohacs. To achieve its strategic goals the army had to camp and pass the winter far away from home in strange countries and this could potentially become dangerous as the enemy knew the local terrain better. Feeding a vast army for six months created also logistical problems, if the enemy was decisive enough to destroy the local food production. The Christian Europe was saved, but this was a fact only Allah the Knower of all the Great Secrets had realized at the time.

****

The arrival of the winter in the Eternal City was hardly noticeable as the weather was exceptionally mild for the season. The Bosporus streamed to the Aegean Sea the icy waters of the rivers of Russia and the Danube as if it was a raging river, but this cold stream exiting the Dardanelles met with the warm currents from the South and had to fight hard for supremacy. It was a desperate battle of the elements that filled the air of Constantinople with dense mist that stuck on the people's skin forcing them to discard any heavy fur, and winter outfits in favor of lighter raincoats.

After many months of separation and hard fighting, a woman's embrace was the proper refuge where a fighter could hope to find enough harmony and bliss to erase the hardships of the war from his memory. In this battlefield Hurrem was an incomparable companion of any physically and mentally exhausted warrior like Suleiman.

The Sultan arriving in the Eternal City couldn't resist her attraction, and instead of going all the way to the Seraglio and invite her, he decided that it would be much easier to go directly to the Eski Saray and knock on her door. Then the next morning, visiting his mother would be just any easy stroll through the Harem corridors.

Hurrem must have heard of the army's arrival from all the drum beatings as the Janissaries marched and she had made all the necessary preparations for the proper reception of a frustrated soldier. Her body was as naked as the day she was born and her sweat formed shinny droplets that glinted in the moonlight as if it were stars.

Suleiman immediately remembered the fireflies in the garden and the words of Ibrahim. The fireflies were now glittered before his eyes, tumbling one after the other on her skin faithfully following every curve. The woman had succeeded with her body what Allah and his shadow could not. The fireflies had lined up like Janissaries. The divine message was clear. Her flesh had brought order into his universe.

Suleiman clenched her flesh and pulled her onto his and suddenly all the fireflies on her belly at once disappeared. He kissed her lips and she reciprocated the kiss by biting teasingly his lips. He was happy and he had not extinguished her passion with his for many long months. That evening the silky pillows and bedsheets on Hurrem's bed were not wrinkled. Suleiman took her standing on her two feet, as he had once seen a steed take a mare in heat.

****

Everything happened in front of the Kislar Aga eyes who was left standing like an ebony statue lost in the shadows not daring to interrupt the pleasure of his master. He never regretted what he saw and learned.

Hurrem was unwilling to resist for long his bold aspirations. During this evening visit the master had interrupted suddenly her alluring dreams bringing her to the reality of a slave;

89

but every odalisque kept a piece of herself entirely of her own. The only precaution she took was to keep her mouth tightly closed at the time of her liberation, so that her lover's name could not escape and reach the master's ears. She was not really a witch, but she was taught well by her mother that if you want to bear more boys than girls, you have to keep your man away as long as you could endure the torture.

****

Hurrem's new pregnancy did not passed unnoticed by her main rival. Mahidevran's frustration for the loss of a son and the birth of a daughter was too much to bear. She had done everything she could to replace the loss but in vain; so one day the two rivals met face to face in a corridor, Hurrem giggled ironically to enrage Mahidevran; but the Princess attacked and scratched her face, screaming that she was nothing more than "sold meat."

At the time, Suleiman was absent attending military exercises at the plains of Edirne; but, when he returned, he became so furious that his offspring could be endangered by such foolish maiden's quarrels that he wanted to put Mahidevran inside a sack full of rocks and drown her into the Bosporus, as it was customary for all the concubines who had made a very serious crime; but Ibrahim stood firmly by the Princess' side to extinguish the Sultan's anger, avoiding a terrible crime.

He had realized the Sultan enjoyed tales and parables and he was quick to invent one.

"My master," he argued, "you have many fine mares in your stable. Few are good to bear stallions, others are better for parades, few are brave enough for battles, and others are resilient for long marches. It is unfair to waste one such precious animal simply because in a tight stable one mare happened to kick another out of jealousy, even though you may now believe she has passed her prime. This unruly mare is still useful to raise her colt, and she will accomplish this important task much better than anyone else. If your mares fought each other, it was your mistake for keeping them all locked=up together under the same roof. Therefore, I suggest you keep the one you like to ride most often close by, and send the other to another stable together with her precious offspring to calm her down."

The Sultan's fury quickly receded and he laughed heartily with the comparison.

"You are right!" he finally noted. "It is unfair for my son to lose the care and love of his foolish mother. I will send them all the way to the empty palace in Manisa as soon as Mustafa is circumcised. This would also be a good warning for every other mare in my stable. Even though you are no Turk it seems to me you know much more about how to treat mares than me. Perhaps I should appoint you not only as my Hasodabashi but also as the master of my stable."

This was a curious commend coming from the lips of the son of Selim and Ibrahim was quick to respond.

"For this position you already have your Kislar Aga and for nothing in this world I would wish to pay the high price of this position."

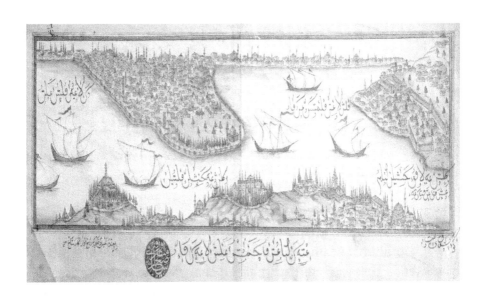

Chapter 12

In the Palace of Ibrahim

*'And one of His signs is that He made companions just for you
so you can find peace within'*
(Quran, Sura XXX, 21)

Ibrahim became more concerned that anyone else after the Vienna debacle. He had realized that despite appearances, if this issue left unattended, this setback had the potential to become the source of great adversities to his meteoritic career.

Even if he was not truly responsible for the outcome, he was the Serasker in charge of the entire Ottoman army.

Of course, this was not the first or the most serious military setback. Sultan Mehmet Fatih had several such setbacks during his reign, but he managed eventually to erase them all from people's memories. All he needed too was to be diligent and do his best during the next campaign against the King of Spain. For the time being nothing was irrevocably lost as the laurels from his victory of Mohacs were still fresh.

The celebration for the circumcision of the Princes Mustafa, Mehmet and Selim was a useful occasion for people to enjoy themselves, and the Imperial Treasury to spend some of the Hungary's loot to promote domestic peace.

The weather was fair and people had crowded the streets celebrating, as all the Sultan's heirs were traditionally very popular. They represented the future of the Empire and there was no reason for anyone to worry about the future. For the Muslims the ceremony of circumcision was comparable to the Christian baptism, and these joyous days the celebration splendor surpassed even Ibrahim's wedding. Once more parades of elite army units, acrobatic shows and displays of wild animals in cages were organized, following the old traditions of the Roman triumphs. However, the Ottomans were wiser than the Romans. Thus, the Sultan offered not just bread and spectacles, but delicious meals to improve the general mood and people's confidence after the setback in Vienna. This delicate operation was concluded with great success, and there were many reasons besides the obvious.

In the recent past the Ottomans had faced much worse debacles, when Mehmet Fatih reigned, and they were able to fully recover soon enough and captured the cities of Belgrade and Rhodes that had resisted. If the walls of Vienna had resisted, it was the wet weather that had prevented the arrival of the siege guns. The Ottomans had to show patience and perseverance and perhaps next summer Vienna would fall, if this was what Allah willed.

The last evening of the celebrations, the Sultan sent a messenger and invited Ibrahim to his quarters. It was late and the At Meidan was empty as the street cleaners did their best to remove all the remaining garbage from the public celebrations and symposiums. Ibrahim was a bit annoyed by this informal invitation. It was a bit late and he had other plans. He would rather spend a quite night in Hatidge's arms, but the Sultan, the happy father of Sehzade Mustafa, shouldn't wait. He followed promptly the messenger through the narrow crooked streets around Agia Sophia to a tiny gate of the Seraglio Walls he didn't even know its existence.

The moon was still high upon the skies, illuminating the grass and shedding thick shadows of very old plane trees from the Roman days. The servant went ahead first and knocked on the gate. Heavy steps were heard inside and then the sliding noise of an iron bolt, before the gate opened with the annoying creaking sound of a brand new hinge that no one thought of spending few drops of oil for the common serenity. In the growing opening a fully armed Mute Executioner appeared well-informed of this invitation who with a node motioned them in.

Ibrahim's heart shuddered as he knew Mutes were the favorite executioners of Sultan Selim. Did Suleiman intended to keep the family tradition? Was this unusual invitation a death trap and the end of the line for him? If Selim was still alive, then he would be killed to make the next Grand Vizier and Serasker more efficient; but Suleiman was not like his dreaded father.

The instinct of survival pushed Ibrahim to turn around ready to start running for dear life; but he knew this was not a solution. His face was well-known and it would be a matter of time before his arrest. Fatih and Selim had created a very efficient network of spies and traitors against anyone who displeased the Sultan.

He becalmed his emotions by reconsidering his mistakes that played a part in the Vienna debacle. During last year's expedition, he had annihilated the Hungarian army in Mohacs and entered peacefully Budapest. This year the Ottomans had recaptured bloodlessly Budapest from the Austrians and besieged Vienna unsuccessfully.

Suleiman was a fair sovereign. It was almost self-evident Ibrahim was a very efficient leader and second to none, well-worth becoming Grand Vizier and husband of the Sultan's sister. Nevertheless, human logic cannot always conquer emotions, and as they strolled on the winding paths of the Enderun Gardens, every shadow looked alive and every tree trunk a hiding place for a Mute Executioner armed with a deadly lasso.

Instinctively he reached for the knife tacked in his belt. His logic dismissed the idea of a valiant defense of his life or integrity. The Mutes always acted as a murderous gang. With the knife tucked in his belt he could probably wound one or two, but in the end someone was bound to sneak from behind and set his noose around his neck. Then, all would be lost, as without breath his strength would abandon him. Then the Mutes would have all the time in the world to torture him to death, revenging their losses.

Thank God, nothing he feared happened in the gardens and they soon arrived in front of the Arz Oda, the Seraglio's Reception Hall. Suleiman was different than his father, and seeing him was still pleasurable. Unwillingly, Ibrahim let a sigh of relief. The Sultan seemed totally oblivious of the worries his sudden invitation had created. Instead he was very gracious and pleasant and he had made every arrangement this meeting to be an enjoyable experience.

It was a warm night and even the silken shirts felt warm and stuck on their sweat. Cool sherbets were promptly served and two black servants did their best to make a draft by swinging two immense fans made of black and white ostrich feathers. Ibrahim's discomfort did not last long, as the sherbet and the air drafts soon cooled his skin. From the very beginning the Sultan made his intentions plain enough. He needed someone to talk to and his mouth was full of questions. Before anything else, the Sultan asked his opinion about the new secret gate.

Now Ibrahim could come and go whenever it pleased him. He could also use this gate to come straight to his apartments unnoticed, without having to pass through the Bab-i-Hamayun, the Orta Kapi and the Gate of Felicity.

Ibrahim didn't answer directly the question because the Sultan's choice of secrecy was annoying. He was a slave and he was not ashamed of his preferences. He could see no good reason for secrecy; so he replied boldly with a question of his own.

"Does your beloved concubine know of this secret gate? She could use it sometime, when she wants to visit you unnoticed."

"No women should not know all our secrets and our wishes," the Sultan calmly replied.

Ibrahim realized this secrecy was another sign of weakness towards Hurrem. The Sultan should have realized by now that this sort of weaknesses made him look as pitiful as an opium addict.

"Of course they shouldn't know, and I'm not sharing everything I do with my Princess either; but tonight when I left her lying in bed, I didn't hide the identity of my host. My Princess knows who my master is and why I have to obey promptly his call. I hope my magnificent Sultan does not need any permission to invite in his bed room any one of his slaves, because even I, a slave, do not have to ask anyone each time I wish to invite a friend to my palace."

The Sultan's face showed immediately his displeasure, and dryly replied:

"I'm afraid that your marriage experiences are not as extensive as mine. Women behave quite differently than men, when they are in love. They are exceedingly sensitive especially in springtime, and under the moonlight sometimes they have the ability to change roles, and the slave becomes the master. Such a night even a Sultan may choose to assume the role of the slave, because this is his pleasure; nevertheless, this metamorphosis does not last long, and as soon as the moon sets and the sun rises up in heaven, everything finds his place in the world the way Allah wishes."

From the tone of Suleiman's voice Ibrahim realizes this kind of discussion could lead only into tensions that would not be to his advantage; so he rushed to change subject. He asked the Sultan whether the preparations of the festivities had pleased him; but he was somewhat surprised to hear the Sultan reply to his inquiry with a question.

"I would rather hear of your impression of the celebrations, so tell me: **Which festivities were more majestic, the circumcision of my sons or your marriage to my sister?**"

It was a question that puzzled almost every citizen of Constantinople, as comparable amounts of wealth were spent. However, the true message of Suleiman's question was that in his heart the seed of jealousy had grown roots. It was a development that could turn dangerous if left unrestrained. It was one more sign that Hurrem had managed to excite the competitive nature inherent in every man.

At least in his mind it was relatively simple to justify this new development. Besides his inferior position in the Ottoman hierarchy, everything else from brainpower to personal attraction and from health to physical strength was in his favor. Since Suleiman was intelligent, this apparent superiority would sooner or later manifest its presence and he as a slave should do anything in his power not to aggravate this reality, but try instead to extinguish it on every occasion even with sheer flattery. Fortunately by now his intellect was more than equal to the task, and could turn a difficult situation to his advantage with a magnificent reverse. He was not about to let a concubine poison his friendship and undermine his position, and his master should be taught a valuable lesson that for the good of the Empire he should let him free to exercise his authority without interference. Compared to this advantage the Sultan's pity jealousies had to be restrained.

"I would rather not answer this question, because I feel I might cause displeasure to my Master," he replied submissively.

"Are you so conceded to believe that the will of a Grand Vizier is more powerful than his Sultan?" Suleiman said with growing apprehension.

"My Sultan knows well that my obedience to his will is an

unbreakable rule during my entire career. Therefore, if he feels that his slave must hurt his feelings, then his slave must obey and tell him what every man in the Eternal City has realized these days. **My marriage was the most splendid celebration ever performed in the entire world through all the eras!"**

This audacious reply was not what the Sultan expected, because it amplified even further his growing jealousy. His grey eyes suddenly darkened as if he was Selim the Grim, but the Grand Vizier had the talent to offer the unexpected.

"What exactly do you imply? **In your marriage I didn't see as many troops parade in your honor. Much fewer free meals were served to my people, and fewer guests came to offer their respects and presents; so now tell me which celebration do you consider more magnificent?"**

Ibrahim didn't appear worried by this clear demonstration of displeasure and his apparent calmness aggravated even further his master. He was expecting this burst of anger and he had the proper medicine to counter it; so he continued his explanation undeterred.

"Everyone knows that the magnificence of a celebration does not depend on how many soldiers, horses or wild animals locked in cages have paraded. Magnificence does not also depend on the amount of food distributed or the number of guests invited, but solely on who was the most important guest who honor it. **In the celebration of your sons' circumcisions the most important and powerful guest was a slave named Ibrahim Pasha who was once the guardian of your hawks and chambermaid, a man you have decided to honor his abilities and made him your Grand Vizier and Serasker to serve, prosper and grow your empire. On the other hand, my wedding was honored by the most magnificent sovereign of the world, Sultan Suleiman Khan, the Shadow of Allah, Master of All Ages and the Universe, Protector of Islam, Guardian of Mecca and Medina, Keeper of Damascus and Cairo, Caliph of the Highest Gate and Custodian of the House of the Pleiades, and this is the only reason why my marriage was incomparable to any other celebration ever from**

now to eternity.”

It was a powerful stroke that reversed the Sultan's displeasure and turned it into sincere admiration. Now the Sultan could do nothing but praise his gifted slave.

“All these years you have served me, I have never regretted my decision to buy you, even though sometimes I wander if you are too clever for your own good.”

Even in this enthusiastic reply there were traces of displeasure; so Ibrahim had to behave even more submissively.

“I will never regret the day I became your slave, and I will always pray to Allah to make me even wiser, so that I can serve my master even more efficiently,” the slave declared; but, despite all these pleasantness, both men's feelings had been hurt.

There was clearly a constantly growing sense of displeasure in the Sultan's mind that was very difficult to measure or reverse it, as by becoming more efficient the Grand Vizier would on one hand benefit the Ottoman Empire, but on the other hand would belittle the Sultan's role in this growth. This tension had not reached a critical point, but it had started to affect the Sultan's decisions and personal relationship. Perhaps his best option now was to meet once more with the Valide Sultana. Together with her female mind it might be possible to find a practical solution out of this developing crisis.

Nevertheless, quite unexpectedly the Sultan became gracious once more and nodded to a White Eunuch waiting for orders and he soon brought along two water-pipes. It was clear that the he tried too to find ways to reduce the tensions and smoking hashish was now his pleasure. Smoking in silence gradually the wrinkles in their faces relaxed along with the nervousness that had caused them.

“I have to admit that several times you Greeks make me wonder how you have fallen so low and became our slaves,” the Sultan noted.

“It's difficult to recognize these days who is Greek and who is Turk with all this blood mixing that has occurred through all these years, and I'm not the only one who has decided to share my blood with a Turk. Our two nations have many special virtues they could share to our mutual advantage. We all know that in the past during the days of Sultan Orhan, Greek blood entered the veins of your breed in the same way many centuries ago Greek blood entered the veins of Roman Emperors. It is natural for any conqueror to mate with the vanquished and the Roman and the Turk conquerors of Greece were no exception; so in the end no difference will remain in bloods, and only superficial differences, like the language, the customs or the religion will remain that mean practically nothing. What happened between the Romans and the Greeks will eventually happen to the Turks and the Romans."

The Sultan didn't seem very pleased with this answer and after few minutes of silent contemplation he firmly replied.

"Mixing the blood with our slaves has been a Turkish privilege, but no one knows if as a result of this mixing the slave will acquire the virtues of the master, or the master the weaknesses of the slave. As an Ottoman Sultan it is my duty to make sure that my race retains the virtues that made it a world conqueror."

"This is your duty, indeed; but for the human race to move forward, there must be a divine way that helps the children to select the best virtues of their parents. This is why your son Selim has hair in the color of his mother, and Hatidge Sultan the color of your father's eyes, while you have chosen the gray color of your mother's eyes that makes you so attractive. It is very difficult to explain the reasons for all these choices, but I'm sure it is the proper one, because there could be no progress, if the children became exactly as their parents."

Despite the conciliatory spirit of Ibrahim's position, Suleiman insisted on his racist, conservative opinion.

"The blood of Alexander, Caesar, Augustus and Constantine must have been watered down inside the Greek veins, otherwise the City would never have fallen in the hands of Fatih like a ripe fruit, and we would be still your servants and missionaries. As far as I know from the horses the best children take after their fathers the stallions, not their mothers the mares."

Ibrahim decided he had to go along with his master's point of view despite his objections; so, he didn't hesitate to convey the spirit of submissiveness and amplified it with a pretentious smile.

"I am not very familiar with the horses' ways; so, it may well be so. However, I'm very happy you have chosen the color of your mother's eyes that remind me of clouded skies rather than the abysmal darkness of the grave of your father's eyes. The Ottoman's have indeed the ability to make the best choices among their subjects, and every capable Sultan of the House of Osman has followed this recipe of success. It is much easier to convince the people to follow your orders, if you can make them believe that you are willing to share your blood with them. The conquest of a nation by another is not complete until the moment it feels proud to say that they have common ancestors. This is actually what happens now as the boys of the Empire are most eager to become your servants and the girls to bear your children. The end of your magnificent empire will come the moment your subjects cease to call themselves Ottomans and start to behave like Greeks, Serbs, Albanians, Hungarians, Arabs, or Bulgarians as they did before."

Bypassing this honest effort Suleiman seemed uncommonly unbending.

"Blessed by Allah who made us Turks so strong that we have no need now to convince anyone by begging. My breed was born in the steppes and we roam the Earth with our horses in every direction of the horizon as we please. We have become one with our horses and thus in our race the stallion not the mare is what makes the critical difference."

Faced with this persistence Ibrahim decided he had to change the subject of the discussion as he was approaching dangerously the level of the Sultan's intelligence.

Since he was young he had noticed that with all people there was a certain level of intelligence for each individual that he simply couldn't exceed no matter how hard he tried. As he approached it, he became increasingly persistent in their views. It was one of the critical characteristics of the Turkish race the Romans considered as barbarians, and he had learned in the Seraglio School various ways to overcome it. Arguing against the Sultan would make the matter worse. It was a much better tactic to play with his weaknesses.

"When I received the invitation of your magnificence, I suspected that a pleasant surprise was stored for me to reward me for the great success of the celebration."

The Sultan was confused by this unexpected change of attitude; so he tried to gain some time with a question:

"The celebration was indeed magnificent and worth of my three sons. What kind of gift would please you?"

Ibrahim smiled with confidence.

"I was actually expecting several belly dancers to wait for us. Boys or girls wouldn't make much difference for us true Ottomans. After all, the circumcision is a ceremony meant to honor the male gender in every expression."

This bold request put the Sultan almost in a state of panic. The only thought he now had was how to apologize for his oversight.

"I didn't really expect you had become so quickly so bored of my sister's charms," he said with cheeks blushing by an indiscriminately mixed wave of anger and shame.

"You should know me better than that. I will never stop being attracted to your sister for as long as she desires me. Nevertheless, even your sister has included in her dowry few pretty young slaves to keep her company, when I'm indisposed, or when she is bored of our everyday routine. A magnificent Sultan like you surely deserves something out of the ordinary such a special day like this. You are not a slave after all obliged to be content with whatever your master thinks you deserve."

The Sultan fully realized the insinuation and tried to explain his choices.

"That's not how I feel right now and all men don't have the same needs all the time. For the time being, I don't feel the need to invite any other woman in my bedroom. After the war, Hurrem has changed dramatically. She is like a new woman. She makes me feel as if we have just met."

"I'm very happy to hear that because I'm not just your slave, but your closest friend too. Hearing of your happiness pleases me too. I pray to Allah this kind of happiness lasts forever, because sometimes we are obliged to change our choices and priorities, when we discover they had led us to dead end."

Suleiman thought he had discovered a weak point inside Ibrahim's arguments.

"If this is so, then perhaps I should try also to eliminate all my weaknesses that are causing me problems," he remarked, but Ibrahim had led this discussion to a predetermined point he had planned when he started it. Returning to the old familiar state of a slave's total submission, he replied with the soft tone of voice of a trusted page.

"If my master thinks that his relationship with a trusted slave is a weakness, then he has every right to seek elsewhere more devotion, support and tenderness. From the very start this slave's only wish was to be used by his master like the pillar gardeners use to support a young tree until its trunk grows strong enough to face the turbulent winds that will eventually blow in every being's life. This is the reason why I felt we should be tied so closely and strongly with me following you every step of the way to glory."

Suleiman liked the allegory and his face relaxed so much he even smiled. Ibrahim subtly took advantage of this disposition change and continued his speech in the familiar tone of a trusted adviser.

"Your blood is noble and in your life you never had to fight hard to gain the pleasures you enjoyed. Your biggest problem was what kind of pleasures to choose among a great variety. My life was different, and I always had to fight every step of the way to rise from fisherman to Grand Vizier. Now, because of your kindness I have many slaves, even with black skin, I can give orders and seek the pleasures I desire; but being a slave for so long, I know well that freedom is the ability of choosing what pleasure the next moment will offer me."

"I had enough of idle talk. What would you like to choose tonight?"

The sound of the Sultan's voice indicated his patience was about to be exhausted, but Ibrahim had become an expert in talking his way out of every difficult situation, and there was no one in the Ottoman Empire equal in this task.

"I am in a difficult position to ask what I wish right now, because I don't want to put my powerful master in a difficult position not be able to provide it."

This was indeed an audacious statement in the face of any Ottoman Sultan, doubting the omnipotence of the Shadow of Allah; however, Ibrahim had become Grand Vizier by knowing when the right time to be bold had come and when it was advantageous to behave submissively.

"I cannot think of anything that is right now beyond the reach of a Sultan besides resurrecting the dead," Suleiman replied with supreme confidently.

"I never intended to put in doubt the awesome power of my Master, and I'm not as devious as Salome to ask the head of a Saint after I dance; but, sometimes superior strength is not enough. A man must also have the desire to move mountains."

Suleiman realized he was entering dangerous grounds, as his slave had some idea in his mind he was still unable to guess. This slave had found a way to make his own wishes appear as worthy rewards.

"I know I should not try to pass judgement on a Sultan's acts. After all he is the Shadow of Allah upon the Earth. Thus, I will simply repeat the words that have reached my ears from many mouths, and my master will decide how he should act upon these news. Many people said these happy days that a Sultan should not spend all his time with only one slave. He has an entire harem and should divide more justly his precious time, so no concubine feels wronged."

"I'm aware of these complaints too, but they are

unfounded. Hurrem has ceased to be another concubine of mine the moment she offered me so many healthy children. She is now much more than my consort. With the will of Allah she is my most intimate companion; so I must be fair and reward her in the same just way I have rewarded every other slave who has exceeded my expectations performing his duties. I have two Kadin that have offered me a single son each, so it is only fair of me to make Hurrem my Kadin now that she has provided me with four male offspring. A Sultan should not be a heartless warrior. Besides wisdom, he has to have also heart and soul. I'm not a silly young man any more chasing women. After all these deaths of children that happened within these walls, I would be foolish to ignore how important every child is for the future of my empire. If this marriage is against the Ayin of my ancestors and bothers few souls, it's not the Sultan who must change his mind but they are. The world around us changes as years go by; so, old traditions have to change too. We all have to learn how to adapt to the new realities. There is no way we can deny the fact we have aged, and we have lost much of our interest for lusty women and intimate friends. Now our children are the most important elements in our lives. I'm afraid we are approaching the age where logic should take command of our emotions."

Ibrahim remained silent trying to fully comprehend the implications of the Sultan's last statement. It sounded very much like the trivial comments one could hear sitting in teahouse enjoying a water-pipe full of hashish. Suleiman was doing just that looking much older and weaker than he really was. He was not feeling at all the same way even though he was of the same age. The flame inside him was still too strong to be contained with his only child. There had to be another reason for Suleiman's change and he had to find it.

"Don't be so pessimistic. We are not that old by any means. We are now right at the top of our male vigor. This coming spring we will prepare for a new campaign against Vienna, and when we capture it, you will feel differently. I'm sure among the captives I can find a German maiden capable of tickling your appetite. It's too early for us to start talking about our heirs. We are still men and they have just been circumcised."

He did not lie. This was how Ibrahim felt. He yearned for every new pleasure his mind could create. Hatidge had not quenched his vital thirst. She had actually doubled it. Her close attachment with her black slave had been a challenge. Basmi was insatiable as much as he was. Their match had been perfect. The slave was too eager to ignite in him a new round of debauchery the moment the Princess had enough of him. Then, she would put the pressure on him until she had his last drop of desire.

If this was a well-thought plan of the women in his harem or purely coincidental, he couldn't discern; but the truth was after his marriage he didn't feel the same need to run after licentious women. Everyone else might think he was completely faithful to his wife, but the truth was a bit different. He was content with his wife and her possession. For how long this feeling would last only Allah knew.

Suleiman's case was clearly different. He had an entire harem full of very attractive women. He also had two beautiful Kadin, and of course the formidable Haseki Hurrem. His master and friend neglected everyone else besides Hurrem. This implied she had to be the truly insatiable one, the one who made Suleiman feel like an aging man. Their brief encounter was now a hazy memory. She had used him back then to gain his support and in the same time she had offered her body to make him believe he had nothing to worry about his relationship with his master. Her attitude was the result of simple arithmetic, the friend of my friend was my friend too. Thus, she had instinctively taken advantage of the male illusion that no harm could come from what you possessed. She had to be behind his marriage with Hatidge too. She had realized he could never belong to her for as long as he was the Sultan's possession; so, she didn't mind at all sharing him, if a princess had priority in using him.

Hurrem was for considerable time a member of the Sultan's harem; so, she must have known most of his clandestine affairs. There was nothing naughty that could remain a secret for long. This abominable custom of having eunuchs black and white as intimate servants was the root of this problem along with the laziness caused by affluence, and the habit of perfect cleanness. The eunuchs, if they so wished, could easily discover who slept with whom. They simply had to combine all the bits and pieces of information that reached their eyes and ears.

There were always young pages opening gates and doors, and there were always eunuchs serving in the two distinct hammam facilities for men and women. Behind closed bedroom doors, no eunuch knew exactly what happened; but if these meetings were combined with visits to a hammam, the truth could be easily revealed.

In his palace he also had many black and white eunuchs. If someone was willing to spend enough money, he or she could easily follow every intimate relationship flourishing within its walls. He hadn't thought much about these facts yet; but if he so wished, he could ask Asphodel about what was going on with the Sultan and Hurrem.

The eunuchs had been very frank with him from the very beginning. There was a eunuch conspiracy inside the Seraglio, and for anyone to find out the secret he sought, he only needed to have enough silver coins and the intelligence to make the right questions to the right eunuch. His associate Asphodel was the right eunuch, and he had more than enough money to reward his sincerity. He didn't feel bad about posing any kind of question, because he was the Grand Vizier and on his shoulders fell the weight to look after the prosperity of the Ottoman Empire. In this supreme post he didn't need to be submissive to anyone but the Sultan. Thus, he felt totally justified expressing his most secret wishes to his master.

"I don't want to hear from your lips that we have reached the age of logic, because I still feel inside me the flame of desire for you. This evening you have invited me to your bedroom and passed me through a secret gate as small as the eye of a needle. Since I am your slave, you can do with me as you please, but this coming Friday you will be the most honored guest in the splendid palace you gave me as a present for my services. And this time you will enter from the main gate as majestically as every Sultan deserves; but I have to warn you that inside my palace all my guests have to follow my orders and be treated as it pleases me, not them."

Despite his slave's assurances of the exact opposite, that night the Sultan could not say no to any of the slave's demands, because after so many years both the slave and his master had gradually developed the same kind of weaknesses.

****

Early next morning, Ibrahim woke up first, as he had the most to lose, if he was not careful. He left the bed quietly not to wake up the Sultan, got dressed all alone without the help of any eunuch, and left retracing the same path he used to arrive. Then, he went straight to his palace and searched for Asphodel in the most logical place he could think of, the male section of the hammam. He was indeed there and looked very happy to see him. They had too much to discuss and not too much time to waste to do it.

Asphodel had aged too as much as the Sultan, and his demands were modest and limited to expensive presents. Ibrahim was by now well aware that every human being tried to find ways to satisfy its hunger for pleasant experiences, and all sorts of human associations had been formed to quench this need. There was no need to ask questions about how Asphodel performed this essential task. He seemed content and this was a welcomed piece of information. He must have found happiness in the arms of another handsome lover.

As Asphodel talked, soon it became apparent he was still among the most conniving eunuchs and this was perfectly logical, as only in this way a weakling could survive in a world where only the strong and powerful could demand openly the satisfaction of their desires. Asphodel knew everything. He only had to ask the right questions.

Hurrem had been loyal all this time as anything else would

be suicidal. Since she had become the Sultan's favorite, everyone followed closely what she was doing. Asphodel could not answer for the Chief of the Black Eunuchs, because he was Hurrem's most trusted servant and kept his mouth shut about her.

On the other hand, the Sultan's two remaining Kadin had joined forces and paid handsomely for any information involving Hurrem; but they were wasting their money. Since the moment Hurrem became pregnant for the first time, her behavior had been impeccable.

"What about before her pregnancies?" Ibrahim asked full of curiosity.

"She did nothing out of the ordinary every concubine fresh in a harem wouldn't do, as far as I know," Asphodel replied indifferently.

"Is there anything else you consider worth telling me?" Ibrahim insisted.

"What a eunuch considers important may be different than what a Grand Vizier seeks."

"How is Mahidevran getting along? Is she complaining for moving to Manisa?"

"How should the most beautiful woman in a harem feel sleeping all alone month after month?" the eunuch replied with a condescending smile. "Every true man in this Seraglio should feel ashamed; but thank Allah I'm not a true man willing to put my life in danger for a true woman."

"And how about the Valide Sultan? Should true men be ashamed for her misery too?" Ibrahim asked in good spirits.

"Hafsa Sultan is quite content, I trust. She spent in Manisa most of her time, when her son was away fighting. They say she has started building a mosque and a hospital in Manisa, so I suspect Allah the Merciful will pardon all her sins."

"What kind of sins the Kadin of Sultan Selim might ever have?" Ibrahim asked rhetorically.

"I'm just a poor eunuch. This is the kind of deadly serious secrets only a Grand Vizier should try to find out."

"Then tell me! I command you."

"Sometimes it is much more pleasant to hear secrets from the lips of the sinner. Why don't you take a trip to Manisa? The fresh air will do you good."

****

Asphodel's reply didn't carry much weight in face value, but being careful and vigilant paid good dividends in the Seraglio. Asking him what he meant would make much more harm than good; so Ibrahim decided he had heard enough. As a Grand Vizier he should pay more attention to the state affairs rather than listening to the malicious imperial Harem gossip.

He was indeed lucky. Hafsa Sultan was back in the Eski Seraglio these days and making an appointment to meet her was not even required. He was not just the Grand Vizier of her son's empire, but the husband of her daughter. They had simply too many issues to talk about and look after. This is the impression he got seeing her forget the strict Ottoman tradition as soon as he entered her chambers. Her first reaction was to send all her chambermaids away.

Another Grand Vizier would kneel in front of her and kiss the corner of her caftan, but he was the husband of her daughter and the father of her granddaughter. There was a blood relationship now between them and as a Tartar she valued blood more than anything else.

They both stood in a state of uneasiness, trying to decide what to do next. She had much more self-confidence than him and she opened her arms. No matter what had happened in between, he had been her lover for a night and she hadn't forgotten how good she felt being treated with tenderness and respect for the first time in her life.

He didn't waste a moment more and embraced her tight as if she was his wife. It was a strange unfamiliar feeling he had never felt before with any woman or man in his life. The memories of their first intimate contact were now too hazy to be recalled in every detail; but he still recalled he had been unconsciously a bit vindictive at the start. Hafsa Sultan was then the widow of Sultan Selim the Grim after all; however, soon enough she managed to soften with her tenderness his resolve to hurt her. She was the first woman of authority who had treated him not as a slave but as a man. He didn't have many delusions in that respect. Despite his recent onslaughts into the Harem, he was not yet a true man. His entire life had been a transition from a man's lover-boy to a man, and Hafsa Sultan has played a very important role, perhaps as crucial as her daughter Hatidge who had given him a child of his own.

She placed her lips too close to be denied. She was eager, warm and tender, but not desperate for a man's touch. He was the Grand Vizier, the right hand of her only son, and he was in no mood to deny her any pleasure she might desire to feel content. He only wished to hear from her lips an invitation, but she was too busy proving to him that nothing had changed between them. She had decided their love-making would be the best renewal of their trust.

It was much more than that. It was also an expression of her gratitude for helping her son achieve his dreams and prove he was as good as his father Selim and his great grandfather Mehmet Fatih. Perhaps she was also grateful for making her daughter happy and giving her a grandson, because as his hands reached her bosom, she simply melted away and pulled him down on the rug.

****

When he came back from the enflamed domain of passion and replaced the velvet of her skin with the silken threads of Anatolian rug, he felt the evening chill seep gradually in his flesh. The wood burning in the fireplace had withered away, and from the window the dark blue reflection of the Bosporus water combined harmonically with the cobalt blue shades of the Iznik tiles of the wall veneer. Nevertheless, this change from warm to chill was more than welcomed. With women, even with his mother-in-law he always had to keep his cool. Now he could not resist the urge to tease her.

"I didn't expect such a warm reception, but I'm very pleased to realize that nothing has changed between us. Unfortunately, time has a way to wither away human emotions."

She was not the least upset by his tease; in fact, she accepted it as gracefully as she could under the circumstances. She got up to assume a higher position, and fixed her messed up clothes to regain her lost decency.

"Don't be obnoxious. It's not becoming of you. You have earned a great deal by being submissive. Don't change the recipe of your success! The House of Osman does not appreciate a 'no' as an answer. Anyway, I wasn't as desperate for a man as you might think. If I pulled you on the rug, it was because my bed was fixed to perfection. We are surrounded by spies and we must be very careful even of the tiniest detail. I hope you are careful too with all your escapades. If I wanted to tease you, I could keep you waiting at the reception hall for an hour; but I'm wiser than wasting an hour of having the most attractive man of the empire doing his best to please all my moods."

"I'm sorry, but I did my best to show to your Highness that our desires were mutual."

"Yes, indeed they were common. After so many years of loneliness, I yearned to taste every drop of your passion. We women are very inventive, when we seek pleasurable but also contraceptive ways to get the best out of a good man."

"I'm very happy to find out you have still high praises for my talents."

"You simply don't know how happy I was for knowing you so well all these years. For a woman becoming a widow is like she has suddenly become a virgin again. If I was not the Valide Sultan and you my son-in-law, I would not hesitate to invite you for a month in my Seraglio in Manisa; but I was what I was. For inspiration our subjects need chaste role models that know how to keep up appearances than promote weaknesses and lust. Now, please tell me! Does my daughter treat you right as you deserve?"

"I have no complaints from her Majesty."

"Yes, but you don't say too many no's, if the right occasion arises."

"No, I don't. I just can't. It's both my weakness and my strength. When I'm facing an attractive human being, you are a selective aristocrat, while I'm an indiscriminant populist. I feel it is to my advantage to become one with my opponents. It must be a characteristic of my Roman blood that needs new strength even by incorporating barbarians."

"I presume you are still emotionally involved with my son too."

"I wouldn't bet against you on this particular subject; but I can assure you it's nothing more than a typical master-slave relationship. He orders me and I obey. There is nothing more than an intimate friendship that gradually is getting older and more balanced."

"Yes, I know this feeling. What I don't know is who will eventually be the slave and who the master."

"Is this so important? As you know, making love is the greatest social equalizer. Your pleasure was always my pleasure, and so it should be forever for all the imperfect Allah's creations who believe the perfection of happiness is split in two symmetric parts."

"Yes, and so it should! By having trusted friends, we can always fall back to for support in case we fail. Loyal friends are giving us strength to advance on unfamiliar paths. Nevertheless, my son has recently developed a tendency to behave more like a slave than a master with women. It is a tendency that may be proven fatal for the House of Osman, if it finally prevails."

"It will become fatal to whom, if I may ask."

"This is not too important, since my son has many heirs; but I wouldn't like to lose either one of you. Am I too presumptuous, considering you also as a precious piece of property?"

"No! You are the Valide Sultan and you have every right to be greedy about slaves."

"Yes, but I have to be careful too using men for my pleasure. You simply cannot imagine how meticulously spies examine all my clothes."

"Why?"

"There are few vixens who would like to steal my position and push me out of my son's heart by degrading the level of my morality."

"Hurrem Sultan is the only one I can think of. Are there many more?"

"She is unquestionably the most potent one; but there are several other weaker ones who would like to see the House of Osman in ruins. Envy is part of the nature of every human being. Human beings simply cannot bear the truth. We are equal only in the eyes of Allah residing far into heavens, not our own judging our existence from up close."

"Ancient Greeks believed that justice is blind. Maybe Allah is blind too to grand us His impeccable justice; but, personally I don't think this is so. I trust Allah favors beautiful women."

"Is this the beginning of a new flattery attack?" Hafsa asked with a long smile.

"Have you aged so much to be impervious to flattery? I don't believe it. You are as attractive as any concubine residing these days in the Eski Saray."

"No. I'm not! In fact, recently I need as much self-confidence as I can find. All my lovers are younger than me. A poisonous tongue may say you have spoiled me; but I know it was all my fault. You have shown me only what I had missed in my entire life before meeting you. Then, it was simply a matter of time for me to find ways to get what I needed to be happy in this life. All it takes is few coins, secrecy and discretion."

"And what about pure love?"

"That's indeed a necessary ingredient, even if it is an illusion. There are simply too many kinds of love around us. I know motherly love for sure because I have experienced it; but I was foolish enough to use many wet nurses for my children. They loved my children too almost as much as I did, I'm sure. Probably I loved them a bit more; but the intensity of a feeling does not make it unique. Selim Khan loved me too, because I gave him a worthy heir and many nights of passion. I bet he loved his eunuchs too, because they made him more times happy than I did, even in a different way. Deep inside there is a selfish reason why we love other people. I believe the reason is that their presence make us feel more complete. Our children are of course the most important beings in our lives, much more important than even our parents, because children represent our future in our minds, while parents are our past. Right now I need you to take care of my future, while making my present brighter every once in a while."

"I could bring more happiness into your life, if you need it."

"No, I cannot chance it! It's simply too dangerous for both of us and the Empire too. We simply have no right to put everything at risk just to satisfy an ephemeral passion. When it comes down to the rug, all men are equal. They all offer a woman the same illusion that she is doing her best to propagate the species. Her pleasure is Allah's reward for all her noble efforts. It's too bad all people don't feel the same way, especially our selfish sons."

"Asphodel told me just this morning that few people regard your visits to Manisa with suspicion."

"Asphodel is a very conniving person. In the end he will meet the same end as his brother; but I bet he is a spy of yours in the Seraglio."

"He is indeed under my confidence, but I'm sure I could find a replacement, if I had to. Silver coins are very useful in this respect."

"Yes, indeed they are useful, if you are after information or pleasures; but they cannot replace the thrill of love. By the way, do you have anyone spying on Mahidevran?"

"No! Should I? As you know, now I'm the Grand Vizier not the Sultan's Hasodabashi."

"No, you should not spy her formally; but as a relative you should visit her yourself more often. I'm sure she will be very glad to see you. I hear she is kind of desperate these days. After her outrage, she has fallen behind so badly in the race for the throne, no one knows what she might do to secure more supporters for her son."

"Do you have any suspicions of a conspiracy?"

"I'm the Valide Sultan. I have no use of suspicions. I need facts. I have a good spy among her maidens. She is very competent. For instance, she told me all the details about your experiences to the greatest detail. Be careful Ibrahim! Women in harems are too conniving for any man to handle, not even a clever man like you. You might fall victim of your desires, if you are oblivious of what happens around you. Few men are too proud to forgive and forget even when you have offended their honor blindfolded."

Ibrahim was simply stunned by this revelation. Hafsa Sultan was right. He was simply too naïve to believe that a frustrated woman would let a servant of hers taste the forbidden apple, while she watched.

"Who is your spy, Zarafet or Yabani?" he asked instinctively.

"I do not intend to disclose the names of any of my spies to anyone. It wouldn't be fair to them or useful to me. If I made this disclosure, is for you to realize that in the Seraglio we are all under suspicion and therefore under close scrutiny. Mahidevran is still too important for my son. Who knows if her other chambermaid is not a spy for the Sultan. Actually, if we assume that he has discovered just one of Mahidevran's escapades, it would surely explain his devotion to Hurrem, a cheap Galata dancer that now has assumed the role of the devoted mother."

"That's impossible! If Suleiman knew of Mahidevran's escapade, he would have executed the villain."

"No, he wouldn't. You simply don't know how conniving the Osmanli breed is. As long as you service them competently, they will keep you alive, trying to get the most out of you. Don't forget our customs. Our ancestors came out of the steppes. We are not crazy to discard a half-squeezed lemon that still has plenty of juice."

"That's a very fitting allegory. It explains practically everything," Ibrahim admitted.

"Yes, it does explain a lot; but you haven't explained to me yet, why did you let yourself to be used for pleasure today? It was the second time, so it was definitely a sin. What are you going to think, when you come face to face with my daughter? Will it be the usual excuse of every slave that he had no other option but to obey? We both know it's a damned lie in this case. I never gave you any order; so what comes into my mind is that you did your best to disgrace the House of Osman. Is this the true motive? Try to be as sincere with me as you can. Inside the Harem my authority is absolute; one scream of mine and the Black Eunuchs will be here to strangle you to death."

"Would you discard a half-squeezed lemon that still has plenty of juice?"

"Yes, because I'm a Tatar not an Osmanli. I follow my instincts; so, try to be more sincere with me than you are with yourself. Anyway, today you are all squeezed up already."

Ibrahim suddenly realized that Hafsa Sultan was not in a playful mood anymore. She was serious, and she had assumed once more the role of the Valide Sultan, forgetting all the frustrations of a neglected concubine. What she was asking was a question he had also posed several times on himself and gotten different answers depending on his mood at the time.

"I had entirely different feelings each time we met. The first time I was feeling like a slave and a vindicator, exactly as you've described. Back then, your daughter was nothing but a spoiled brat, a widow so extremely frustrated for a man that she was willing to use any good looking slave for her pleasure. She simply could not bear watching her consort have so much fun and do nothing about it. This must be a very common feeling among masters, isn't it? Screw well the housemaid and her mistress will surely follow."

Hafsa couldn't resist a smile, even though she might have fallen victim of a similar trend.

Nevertheless, seeing him smile in return, she became serious once more.

"I'm much more interested to hear your excuses for today's debauchery," she urged him.

"Today I knocked on your door because malicious rumors had reached my ears. Our wisest Valide Sultan supposedly goes regularly to Manisa to combine charities with pleasure. It was my duty as a Grand Vizier to seek more detailed explanations."

"That does not make sense. Even if I was so sinful, this would hardly interest a Grand Vizier feverishly preparing for a new military expedition in a few months. I'm sure there is much more than that, so much passion in a coldhearted statesman cannot be explained so easily."

Hafsa was once more in a good mood as if the entire discussion was turning her gradually on. This realization helped Ibrahim to relax his tension and become even more open.

"Actually, I came here today because in the back of my mind was the fear that in Manisa there was a better man than me."

Hafsa suddenly burst in laughter diffusing all the previous tension.

"I got you scared for a while, didn't I my dear, honest lover? Building tension and then releasing it, is another good recipe to get the best of your subordinates. It is a trick Sultan Selim has taught me long ago. Isn't it strange how we take advantage of every piece of knowledge we collect throughout our lives? Sometimes I wonder if it would be as useful for my daughter to know everything there is about you. Who knows how she will take advantage of this intimate knowledge to control you whenever she feels like it?"

"I believe some facts should remain hidden from all of us at all costs, so that we have a reason to keep on living. Complete honesty is a perilous practice," Ibrahim noted.

"Maybe you are right, I'm not always sure what to reveal and what to keep a secret. For instance, do you think that a woman in my position wouldn't be interested to find out whatever my husband did with all his lovers? I'm sure that by now as a Grand Vizier you must have realized that if spending a lot of money is not a problem, one can find everything there is to know, if he knows who and what to ask."

"Should a Grand Vizier waste his precious time to investigate the charitable activities of a most efficient Valide Sultan? I'm sure she is following the established tradition, a modest mosque with one minaret, and a 'kuliye' institution including a hospital, a caravanserai and possibly a sumptuous hammam to steam away every possible sin."

"Have I missed something important in my kuliye?" Hafsa asked with a naughty smile.

"Yes, you have. You haven't said anything about a secret place where the frustrated widows of our dead soldiers can meet their lovers."

"And you have a great idea about yourself. You think that missing you has turned me into a cheap temporary wife. Well, for your information, I'm still a Valide Sultan and choose carefully my associates. In fact, I'm very picky which man I use for my pleasure. Most men will become exceedingly proud of their accomplishment and start bragging. I cannot be too careful these stormy days. One false move and the boat may turn upside-down. It is too dangerous to let many people know of your most intimate secrets. One good lover is enough for me, or perhaps two. After all a Valide Sultan should be a model of chastity for her people."

"You still haven't told me his name. I could find it, if I was really interested."

"Yes, you probably could, but you shouldn't try. He is a very proud man and his pride would make our relationship difficult. Forget what I've said! It's for the best of all of us. If I were you, I would invest your precious free time in controlling Mahidevran's passionate explosions. She is a young woman and sometimes she acts violently out of impulse. We don't want to have to repair a total mess. Few people, when they become angry, try desperately to spread their misery all around them. We must keep Mahidevran's envy under control anyway possible for the sake of her son, and the optimum solution is to prove to her without the shadow of a doubt that you will support her son. I'm sure you know the way to be convincing. You have used it on me and Hurrem and it worked. For a woman it's usually enough to risk your life to please her."

"I have the feeling you are gradually becoming a devious, manipulating female too."

"Yes, I am and I have always been. It's part of a woman's character evolution. As she grows older, she becomes more deliberate as the urge to procreate resides in the background of her mind; but please forget all about me! You still haven't told me how you will feel, when tonight you'll take my daughter in your arms. I don't believe you will simply restrict your thoughts to unfair comparisons, the field I should surely lose."

"You are right once more," Ibrahim admitted after a momentary silence. "I don't wish to hurt your feelings, but physically your daughter is more attractive than you. It is mentally where you are incomparable. You are much more open-minded than her."

"Flattery is a good way to get out of a bind; but it's simply not good enough with me. I know exactly who I am and what my weak and strong points are. My other lover has been very useful in this task. Despite what you might think he is not a male beast. He is much more spiritual than you. Chatting with him has been a revelation."

"Thank you for this hint. There are not many men like the one you describe in Manisa. By the way, in my mind one of your most potent charms of your daughter is her lesbian tendencies. Catching her in the arms of her black consort, has been a powerful motive for me all along. They know it and they take advantage of my weakness every night. Now I don't have to catch them on the act. Licking their lips in my presence is enough to drive me mad with desire and they know it. I simply cannot resist the challenge to bring them both back on the path of virtue."

"You are a very unstable personality, my dear son-in-law. You are in love with lovemaking and this insatiable desire is very invigorating for anyone who comes close to you; but a strong point can easily turn into a weakness, if someone decides that you have become expendable. Setting a trap for a greedy personality like you is a child's play. If I was to tear up my clothes and start screaming 'Rapist, rapist', the Black Eunuchs would promptly dispose of you, no question asked. When they attack, they are even more reckless than the Mutes, because they have nothing to fear of losing. I have tried to curb their urge to strangle unfaithful concubines like rats in the Bosporus Straits, but I'm not sure what they will do in every occasion. They are like mad dogs during feeding time."

"Would you order them to do that in my auspicious case?"

"No, of course not, at least not yet! You still haven't told me what you are going to feel, screwing my daughter tonight," Hafsa insisted in a pleasant mood.

"The truth is that when the candle is extinguished, every woman is transformed in my mind into a greedy beast I have to seed to create a better world. The virtues I have acquired from my parents are not enough, so I must struggle hard to improve my children. If mating with you has been a sin, I simply have to erase my last sin with a good deed," Ibrahim claimed with supreme confidence.

"I was right to insist for a truthful explanation. Now I have a good excuse to erase my sin with a good deed too," Hafsa said and raised her hand for him to kiss to indicate that his visit had ended at this point.

She was right once more. All good things had to end sometime, as humans have the tendency to repeat pleasurable moments to the point they became boring habits. It was one of Mother Nature's provisions that plagued the human species, pushing it always forward to seek the unknown rather than be content with the familiar, a dangerous trend that could eventually lead to perilous paths. However, instinctively he felt Valide Sultana had the upper hand today, and she had to be humbled for their relationship to achieve equilibrium.

"Perhaps one day you may decide to confide me your reasons for letting me use you for my pleasure the very first time," he requested as politely as he could under the circumstances.

"I will not keep you waiting a moment longer, my dear son-in-law," she replied in a teasing disposition. "I'm the Valide Sultana and I have the right to enjoy the best of everything the moment I feel the urge to do so, because when I was younger, I spent the best years of my life, raising the Shadow of Allah what he is. I know you are probably the cockiest man of the empire, but if you know of anyone better than you, I would be most grateful if you were to deliver him to my door. Then, I might not have to travel all the way to Manisa each time I feel lonely like hell locked in the Eski Saray."

He had to admit that somehow, she had managed to turn the table once more at the very last moment. She was indeed a well-trained female fit to become a Sultana, and she was perfectly serious. In her mind slaves were instruments she had no moral hesitation of using them for her pleasure; but on the other hand, in his mind making love with his master was the best way for a slave to reach the illusion of equality.

He got up from the sofa and followed her suggestion like an obedient slave of her will.

"Please convey my greetings to Mahidevran Sultan. Make sure she understands we are both at her side in this conflict. Of course, it's nothing personal. My grandson Mustafa has the better blood in his veins. It's impossible that the sons of a whore will not be affected by the treacherous blood of their mother. Hurrem has the mentality of a slave and she has no scruples, just like you. My son must be blind not to see that. Now there is nothing a loving mother can do but look for another more worthy mate for her son, especially if she feels guilty for her previous wrong choice."

"If this is your final decision, I suggest you put your plan in action as soon as possible. Your son is dangerously approaching the point of no return. His illness is slowly seeping all his male vigor, trust me! If this critical point is ever reached, it would be impossible for any woman or man to stir his heart."

"I believe you because I have felt this way too. When a

good man thinks he is going to die, instinctively he tries to enjoy for the last time all the real thrills he has experienced in his life, before he enters the realm of illusions. Despite all his faults my Selim was a good man."

****

Finding an excuse for a Grand Vizier to pay his respects to the Kadin of a Sultan was more easy than he could have ever imagined, and the help he received from the Valide Sultan considerable, because she was the one raising the point to Suleiman that his son's education needed attention. She suggested that as long as Mahidevran was there with Mustafa, Suleiman should keep his distance from Manisa to avoid any unpleasant scenes, especially now that Hurrem had three living sons. Thus, Ibrahim's suggestion to volunteer came at a very opportune moment.

****

"I wonder which tail wind blessed by Allah has brought you to my quarters?" Mahidevran Sultan inquired with a long smile, when he had completed all the ceremonial greetings prescribed by the Ayin for the occasion.

Ibrahim seemed hesitant to respond, as his ears were still full the Hafsa Sultan warnings about spies, and the Princess was surrounded by her two most favorite courtiers. Sometimes silence was the most eloquent way to describe the urge to express your thoughts; so Ibrahim simply stared at her slaves and did not reply.

"You can talk freely in front my courtesans. They would give up their lives for my sake," she declared, however, despite this announcement, Ibrahim decided he had to postpone any attempt for complete exposure and sincerely expressed his most secret motivations.

"All this time I was fighting the infidels, I have missed all of you so much that now I have to fight hard to resist the urge to embrace both of your courtiers and suffer the consequences of my disgraceful act," he confessed boldly. "I simply cannot sleep unless I find out which one of them has pleased me more during the most exciting day of my entire life.

It was an audacious and unexpected declaration that took all three women by surprise. Now it was their turn to silently collect their thoughts and find the proper response.

"How dare you come into my harem with such incredible demands? My consorts are also my most trusted friends. They are free women, not slaves I can order. Has springtime stolen your wits?" Mahidevran exclaimed and her complexion blushed like a spring rose.

"No, it's not the spring, but the need to find out which one of your courtiers desired me so passionately that inspiring day in the hammam. Since you are their trusted friend, it's up to you to decide the right price for their services. I'm willing to pay anything they ask to relive such an experience."

"We have no need for your money. Suleiman Khan has provided handsomely for me and my son. I have all the means to support two loyal friends without asking them to do errands."

"It's not money that is at stake, but my happiness. Since that day in the hammam all I see in my dreams are few unique moles and two delightful dimples on one impeccable back that stole my heart. Perhaps you don't know what exactly I'm talking about, but I beg you to hear my story carefully and without any interference to decide justly how this mystery should be unraveled for my sake. Then, I promise I will explain to you how a eunuch can offer so much pleasure to a princess he massages."

He had said enough to push Mahidevran into a corner. He was almost certain both courtiers knew all about the first hammam incident; but during the second encounter no courtier was present. If the Princess did not submit to his blackmailing plea, he still had plenty of details to reveal about this second incident none of her courtiers knew anything about.

Sultana's confusion exploded after this new demand and almost mechanically she waved her consorts away. They followed reluctantly her command, as their interest for the crux of this discussion had blown out of proportion by then. Progressing from housemaids in a harem in Manisa to concubines of the Grand Vizier in the Eternal City was an enticing prospect for any woman, but it was also clear Mahidevran Sultan was a liberal master they were not eager to lose unless they had to.

When the door had closed behind them, Ibrahim did not waste any time beating around the bush.

"I'm sorry if I have offended your authority in any way; but there is no way I can keep silent anymore. I'm in love with you, and I cannot wait for the moment the Sultan releases you from his favor to ask him for your hand."

"Now I know you are mad," Mahidevran exclaimed quite alarmed. "As long as he is alive, the Sultan will never allow any other man to touch me. I have given him three children fruits of his passion in the pious Constantinople, not ancient Rome or degenerate Venice."

"Do you think I don't know that probably my desire for you will never be fulfilled? But one day comes when a man must open his heart and let the woman of his dreams know exactly how he feels and let her decide how to respond. This is the kind of decisions a civilized man cannot take by himself. Civilization started when a man decided that making love to the woman of his dreams is thousands of times more enjoyable than raping her just once or twice."

The word "raping" sent sparkles to her eyes, instigating the primal fear of every woman in existence; however, Mahidevran was not willing to be intimidated by unrealistic threats. She felt perfectly safe in the Harem, so she promptly retaliated.

"And I must tell you that if your ex-widow bride cannot satisfy your lust, you can always use one of her chambermaids or even one of mine or maybe both. The Harem rules do not clearly prescribe such an orgy as a sinful act, but they also say nothing against it. We all also know that the Holy Quran says a good Muslim should treat slaves as any other member of his family," Mahidevran noticed with an imperceptible smile.

"Do you really think I could drown my insatiable passion for an Ottoman Princess with a slave, or perhaps two, since it's too great to bear it passively without going mad by desire?"

By now Mahidevran knew well where this discussion was going and boldly displayed clear sings she was thoroughly enjoying it.

"And I'm really surprised if an Ottoman Princess of impeccable education in various harem practices is incapable of fully satisfying a Christian slave of the lowest birth, considering that two low slaves have managed to stir your heart so profoundly according to your admission."

"This is the exact nature of my complaint, and I'm very glad another well-educated member of the Ottoman nobility understands so deeply a newlywed's problem."

"You are not a newlywed. As far as I know you already have a child from this coldhearted woman, as you describe her. This is an undeniable proof that at least for one night your match was ideal," Mahidevran replied fully recovering her disposition after his bold declaration.

Ibrahim was well aware that a man has to offer ample time for a woman to analyze all the implications of a naughty proposal, as few women may be less imaginative creatures than few men, but they are surely immensely more practical and have a sharp eye for crucial details. For a sexually frustrated woman hungry for the love of one man, the passionate offer of another man could not pass unnoticed or be rejected offhand. After all, such a rejection was according to Homer the cause of the Trojan War.

"Yes, indeed that single night our desires were mutual and ideally consumed; but is one night or maybe two enough to fill the life of a man or a woman with enough satisfaction to last for a lifetime? I don't know how other men feel, but for my open heart this is clearly impossible. I need at least few nights a week of over-feasting to satisfy my fervent desires for the woman I love. Is this too much to ask? I'm indeed a newlywed compared to others and this is the reason I came to you today with my humble petition."

"What kind of petition is that? I'm a bit confused and I don't wish to get the wrong impression. Your audacious declaration of your sinful urges has left a lot to be desired."

"I'm glad you've reached so easily the true essence of my outrageous demand. I know well enough that my humble lineage cannot compare with the impeccable nobility of yours; however, nobility is an old tradition that hasn't started from nothingness. It was created with the proper mixtures of bloods that allowed men and women to perform great deeds in the past that once was the present. In this way, the humble origin of few men like me, a descendant of fishermen, can be promptly eradicated, if a son of mine becomes a nobleman because of his exceptional virtues. I believe this is the exact reasoning that has enticed an Ottoman Princess and a daughter of a magnificent Sultan to marry me, a Grand Vizier of humble origin, and give birth to a fruit of our momentary passion. A worthy child from a noble breed is enough to change the world, not just improve a low family status, don't you think so?"

"Indeed I do and I have already been blessed by a worthy son capable of great deeds. I don't think I need a second one. This is what the Ayin prescribes after all. More male children will only increase the chances of a disastrous civil war. Is the Grand Vizier of a different opinion?"

"This Grand Vizier believes the Ayin indeed favors quality rather than quantity; but Allah has cursed the human species with greed. Once or twice even for an entire life is never enough. This is actually the true essence of my request from the moment our union is inconceivable. Since my bride is raising extreme demands on her single chambermaid, is it too much to ask your excellence to offer me the services of one of your two mesmerizing consorts for as long as it takes my desire for you to end? I'm sure the Ayin does not prohibit such a temporary loan. In fact, I would be willing to pay handsomely for either Zarafet or Yabani for even a more permanent arrangement, if you ever decide to part with their services out of boredom. My noble wife has repeatedly hinted that for the sake of our marriage I should enrich my harem with as many concubines as I desire, removing from her shoulders a portion of the burden of my weekly satisfaction. After all the word 'Vizier' as you well know means 'the one who carries the burden' in Persian."

It was a very unusual demand Mahidevran didn't expect to hear. At the moment she was under the impression Ibrahim bold declaration involved only her. This new request put her in a state of complete confusion, and the Grand Vizier took advantage of her bewilderment to make a new demand.

"Could we be alone for a while; let's say for a full hour behind locked doors to talk freely without any interruption? I wish to make certain detailed inquiries, before I can decide which one of these two impeccable courtesans of yours I should choose for my harem."

This new demand startled the Princess even further with its audacity. Ibrahim was taking excessive liberties with her property. This was clearly unacceptable and Mahidevran's face blushed once more in anger; but Ibrahim became so bold he dared to put his finger on his lips insisting on her silence.

"Hush my noble Princess. In this Seraglio also the doors have ears. We don't want to give the wrong impression we are fighting over such insignificant matter, when in reality we have nothing of any importance to share but our loneliness."

"I am perfectly willing to keep my silence and forget anything that happened in any hammam, if you are willing to forget it too," the Princess suggested. "Hot steam is a magical substance that seemingly can turn any woman into a whore, or a eunuch into a stallion. In fact, a eunuch massaging me once revealed to me that hot steam can even turn a man into a woman and reversely, liberating even the most unconscious desires hidden in a human soul."

It was a very curious statement that puzzled Ibrahim for the first time that day.

"Yes, such a divine transformation might be possible; but I do not know if steam can erase completely memories the same way it can cleanse skins. Indeed, I can I still remember every marvelous moment we shared that magical day. Actually, a week ago Hafsa Sultan revealed to me what a frustrated Princess can do out of sheer desperation. She was aware of the tiniest detail, because one of these two pretty maidens of yours is her spy. My eyes were closed shut at the time, so I have no idea who it was; but I'm sure you know better than anyone else. If you wish to regain the right of your privacy from now on, I have no objections accepting this devious spy into my household. The experience has been truly unforgettable and since then an object of intense fascination. I don't mind having a spy in my household, because she will be not the first or the last. Anyway, I have nothing to fear of such a female spy, because my relationship with the Valide Sultan and her daughter is now better than ever."

"What is this supposed to mean?"

"It means that they have both realized I will do everything within my power for the Ottoman Empire to grow and prosper," Ibrahim explained in general rather than specific terms.

"Then you must have also realized by now that my son Mustafa can be the best Sultan ever, when the right moment comes," Mahidevran remarked exposing what was her main motive.

"Perhaps he can be great when he grows up and becomes a man, but I believe now it's too early to talk about a new Sultan. Suleiman is still an impeccable warrior of the faith, and I'm proud to serve the Empire under his leadership."

"Yes, but from what I heard he has shared his most recent triumphs with you. Everyone knows that the brilliant strategic plan that led to this astounding victory was your inspiration."

"Yes, the Sultan has done so, because he knows I'm not too greedy to claim a bigger portion of honors than what I deserve. In a sense, without appearing too bold, I can claim that I'm almost as fair in my claims as the Sultan is, and I'm always perfectly willing to limit my appetite to whatever dish he doesn't wish to consume himself."

"I don't understand exactly what you mean, but I'm not a greedy person too. I'm perfectly willing to share my husband's property. Nevertheless, I'm not willing to let anyone steal what rightfully belongs to my precious son."

"I can sympathize with this modest point of view, and since I'm just a slave of the Sultan's household, I'm perfectly happy to satisfy whatever demands any member of his household makes on me," Ibrahim noticed suggestively.

"Today you are talking in riddles and I cannot clearly discern where you are aiming at. I am a mother, and I have great responsibilities for both my surviving children. As a mother I wish the best for them, but sometimes Allah's will is different than ours and many worthy candidates for honors have been bypassed by inferiors, when their day of judgment finally arrived. I will do everything in my power to make sure this will not happen to my children."

"Everything is too strong a word. It may raise suspicions if it reaches the wrong ears."

"For the time being as the Sultan's Birinci Kadin I have enough money to satisfy even the most greedy judge. How much do you think it will take to change an unfavorable opinion?"

"I don't think who will seat on the Ottoman throne will ever become a question of money. It's an issue the Sultan who has almost absolute power will eventually settle."

"Yes, but there are few trusty advisers he consults to make up his mind. You are one of them, perhaps the most important."

"The Sultan has honored me indeed with his trust and has raised my income to towering heights. Perhaps this is his way to make sure no money offers could ever tempt me to act against the interests of the Empire; but we all know that gold is not the most precious commodity a man and a woman can exchange. Love is!"

"I'm glad to hear that. If the interests of the Empire are your sole concern, then I'm certain you will give your support to my son, when the time comes."

"Indeed I will, but your son is not the only one who needs to be judged. Your conduct is also under detailed scrutiny. Hafsa Sultan is worried you might behave in an improper way out of frustration for the injustice that has befallen upon you as a result of Hurrem's star rise."

Mahidevran raised her eyes to his level and offered Ibrahim a warm and meaningful smile.

"I'm not entirely sure what the Valide implied; but you may reassure her that since I was exiled in Manisa I have stopped taking unnecessary risks, unless the offense against me exceeds the limits of my endurance; but even then I still do my best to behave like a Princess and a Kadin of a victorious Ottoman Sultan. I'm sure Valide is fully aware that I was perfectly within my rights as a Sultana to beat an obnoxious slave that behaved as if she was my equal. Nevertheless, for a faithful woman like me it makes no difference whether I'm surrounded by spies or not. My behavior will be impeccable in any case, because I still wish to see my son on the throne. Only then, as a Valide Sultan, I might decide to take my chances and take revenge for all the years of neglect I had to suffer for my son's sake. Then, as a widow I might even ask my Sultan son for his permission to be wed to another man more sensitive to the needs of a noble woman than his departed father. Now please tell me as an experienced adviser. Am I uncommonly lusty as a Sultan's Birinci Kadin or are there few measly concubines much lustier than me?"

Ibrahim couldn't find anything more to say. Mahidevran had made clear she was going to behave properly, taking no chances with men. This was to be expected under the circumstances; however, she had advanced one step further. She had hinted that the moment she became a widow she would relax the strict morality standards of Ayin and seek another husband. Her insinuations about the desirable virtues of this imaginary man she had left vague; but if a man was wise enough to read between the lines, he would discern that her comment about sensitivity was plain enough. Was this a subtle invitation for a conspiracy to eliminate Suleiman from Mahidevran's life?

It was not such a far-fetched suspicion. In the Muslim world, it was common practice for a widow to enter the harem of the brother of the departed. Sultan Suleiman had no brother, but he had very often referred to Ibrahim as his brother. Was she trying to entice Cain to kill Abel? He simply couldn't leave before knowing how far this Tartar woman was able to push her grit against Hurrem; so he remained seated on the couch.

Of course, even if Mahidevran asked him plainly and cleanly to kill Suleiman to win her heart, he would never dare to attempt such a perilous plan. For as long as the House of Osman remained victorious, no one would even think of removing this dynasty from the throne of the Ottomans. Perhaps for a noble woman the offense of seeing her legal husband in love with a unscrupulous whore was too much; however Mahidevran was a Tartar. She was not born in the Ionian Sea. In his mind the most balanced type of revenge was an eye for an eye; everything else seemed excessive. On the other hand, it was very dangerous practice to imagine that everyone was thinking as fairly as he did. The women the Sultan had chosen as consorts were too violent and crude for his taste. Perhaps, it would be wiser to keep his distance from both Mahidevran and Hurrem for as long as he could not guess accurately their reactions. Jealousy was sometimes a state close to lunacy. Thank Allah Hatidge had not a jealous bone in her body.

"Suleiman is like a brother to me, so I will never stop honoring him, dead or alive," he replied as casually as possible, having to bear the pressure from Mahidevran's penetrating eyes.

"You are a very wise adviser, Ibrahim Pasha. I had simply forgotten how close you and the Sultan feel for each other. For a wronged woman like me, it is very comforting to know that if my morals ever slip lower, a strong hand will be there to keep me from falling. One whore inside the House of Osman is enough."

"Allah is All-Wise and knows exactly what we need to be happy much better than us. If it is Allah's wish for you to become a widow, then the door of my household will always be wide open for you. This is what true friendship means after all. When your friend is at dire straits, offering him a helping hand even before he thinks of asking," he proclaimed.

"I feel exactly the same way about all my friends. I feel I

have to please them as much as they are willing to comfort me," she replied, and got up, but surprisingly she motioned him to remain seated because she had something more to add that would please him.

"By the way, a trusty Kadin who still belongs to the House of Osman has revealed to me long time ago that in Constantinople, there are not just despicable whores and faithful wives. There are also many frustrated wives that can occasionally relieve their frustration by becoming temporary wives of common men of their choice in the caravansaries around the Grand Bazaar. As a Grand Vizier of the Ottoman Empire can you substantiate this dubious rumor?"

"Yes, I believe there are, because the human species has the tendency to always find new ways to go around strict laws and unbending rules to satisfy its primal functions, hunger, thirst, or procreation. I don't know if this audacious custom has been transplanted also in Manisa, but to avoid any malicious gossip I have decided to reside in a Han rather than putting your impeccable reputation in danger."

"I sincerely appreciate your discretion, and I will always be grateful. We Tatars always keep our promises and pay back handsomely in due course all our benefactors."

"Is that so? I was actually surprised not to receive a present for my wedding from you. I was actually so foolish, I considered this omission as a sign of jealousy; but I was obviously wrong."

"No you were not wrong. I was actually mad at you for not asking me to say a few good words in your favor to your master, while Hurrem had been so persistently praising your virtues. However, later on when I asked the right people, I decided that it would be better to keep my reputation intact rather than mimic a cheap whore."

"Who did you ask about me? It's important to know who is spying on me."

"Don't tell me you don't know! He is so obvious. He even tried to blackmail me after our last encounter inside your palace hammam. He was most willing to reveal the identity of my rapist in exchange for my submission; but he failed. I have not been raped by so many men to be totally oblivious of the best one yet."

"You are flattering me immensely."

"When a woman is flattering a man, she is always after something, and you know what I need most from you. To avoid any misunderstanding I need your total support for my son."

"I didn't expect that from Asphodel. He is always so submissive."

"If you think so, you are for a surprise. Eunuchs may behave submissively to a man, but with women they are most aggressive and try to take advantage of every moment of weakness a woman may experience to dominate her."

"But what can they do to a woman in the sorry state they are?"

"You are so naïve sometimes, it's really scary. Wake up before it's too late. Eunuchs are the true inventors of every kind of perversion. The best option a man has is to imitate them. Sultans are complete fools to employ eunuchs to guard the chastity of women, and don't forget to report what I told you to your master Suleiman Khan. This is why Sultan Selim was so fond of them. Every night they had a new trick to teach him."

"Do you know why Sultan Selim had your name in his lips the moment he died?" Ibrahim asked, taking advantage of the Princesses' extreme urge for sincerity, but it was a serious mistake.

Mahidevran's eyes darkened as her impeccable face turned at once by anger into an ugly grimace.

"How could a Tatar Princess know what kind of perversion this terrible beast had in his mind just before he died?"

****

Leaving the Manisa Palace, Ibrahim went straight to the kuliye construction site. It was much more extensive than any previous buildings devoted to the memory of a Sultan's Kadin. Hafsa was indeed a powerful Valide Sultana worthy of Selim Khan.

She was simply careful enough not to offend his authority as long as he was alive; so her mosque was considerably smaller than his. This intelligent choice had allowed her to keep her son alive.

Now that Selim Khan was dead, her influence was even greater than her son's in certain domains where women had the first word. The fact she had provided her son with Hurrem was a testimony to this undeniable fact. Now the remaining charity buildings showed she had entirely different temperament than her cruel husband. Becoming a widow, she felt nothing but tenderness for all the needy men.

However, this view of reality raised certain questions. Selim Khan must have chosen his son's two legal Kadin, Mahidevran and Gülfem. Was politics the sole consideration to these two choices? Did Asphodel knew much more of this selection process? Was his indiscretion the only dubious issue in Mahidevran's past Asphodel had discovered? Was it possible Hurrem had mined sensitive information about all Selim's clandestine activities through Asphodel? If Hurrem was able to blackmail Asphodel and forced him to talk, how could this eunuch resist the pressure of the Sultan, the moment he found out of his secret knowledge?

There could be only one answer to Asphodel's activities. Sooner or later one night he would die as discretely as his brother did. The only question was who would take first the responsibility and Hafsa Sultan had already versed such a solemn prophesy.

As his mind started a wild run, new questions popped into his mind. How Asphodel had managed to become Mahidevran's intimate masseur that day. Was he exercising the skills of this trade or was he trying to seduce the Tatar Princess? In such an exposed position she had no easy way to react to his advances.

His audacious thoughts were interrupted by the appearance of Sinan among the unfinished walls of Hafsa's mosque. Was it possible the pious dervish who had found a way to put a widow's urges under control and stir them to a virtuous path? Mimar Sinan was most certainly a handsome man. Even he felt attracted to his masculinity and his impeccable morality several times during the Egyptian expedition. He was in command of an important mission that period and this position of power precluded any kind of expression of carnal weakness from his part; but, with a woman a position of authority had entirely different function. A Valide Sultan had the right to demand anything from a Janissary, even to shed his blood in her name. Normally Hafsa Sultan would have much more logical demands from a Janissary, and many Janissaries were notoriously obedient to every widow's demands.

Mahidevran had accused him of extreme naiveté and he still felt offended. The root of this problem was not his character, but the overall climate of absolute terror inspired by Selim, where natural urges of everyone else were threatened by death. How could a frustrated woman spend her entire life in seclusion, restricting till eternity her divine urge to procreate? How could a newly liberated widow avoid excesses after his death?

If Hafsa Sultan had chosen Sinan as her lover, how could anyone object to her choice? Ottoman women had the right to choose the best mates to bear the best warriors of the faith. They should also reward Janissaries for their incredible valor in battlefields. This was the patriotic thing to do for the prosperity and growth of the Empire. Hafsa Sultan had all the makings of a saint and she should be worshiped by all women the moment she entered Allah's paradise. His position was now very simple. He would refrain from any indiscrete investigation his nosy attitude might suggest. Both Hafsa Sultan and Sinan were his friends, and he should do his best to promote their happiness by his discretion.

He was not truly naïve. He had simply decided that few of the Harem secrets should never be revealed. His oath as a Grand Vizier did not contain any promise for extreme nosiness. Unquestionably there would be few people that would surely claim he had chosen this discrete approach for his own benefit, but they were wrong. The absolute authority of the Sultan was responsible for the existence of secrecy, and every piece of truth that could potentially harm the Empire should be kept a secret for as long as possible, especially during a Holy War.

His behavior by few Muslim religious simpletons may be considered hypocritical, but in his view the frustrations of a Kadin could affect the choices of the Sultan. Suleiman had shown that he was too emotional in similar cases. He was willing to execute a Princess for attacking an odalisque he considered his favorite. It was the wrong kind of attitude because a Prince Heir was not responsible for the frustration of his mother. The Sultan was responsible for all his Kadin. As a Grand Vizier his duty was to make sure the throne was occupied by the best possible Sultan. For as long as Suleiman was a competent leader the question who was going to be the best heir didn't interest him. Only if Suleiman became mortally ill, the problem of succession might concern him too.

****

He greeted Sinan as if he was his brother. He was a devoted Janissary who shared most of his views. Sinan knew better than anyone the weaknesses of the human species, and did his best to eliminate every possible ill effect. This was the prevailing view expressed by most Janissaries. They had abandoned the comforts of their families and enlisted in this elite corps, with the sole hope that the Ottoman Empire would surpass the Romans, and they were willing to sacrifice their lives or their integrity to achieve this sacred goal. Every benefit they enjoyed doing their hard duties was the reward they enjoyed for their valiant deeds according to Allah's will. The moment they suspected the Sultan, Allah's Shadow, deviated from this holy mission, they felt obliged to question his absolute authority.

His views did not coincide with a Janissary's. He was more flexible and refined. Weakness were not always bad for the Ottoman Empire. All women even the most powerful and authoritative had few moments of weakness. If a man could exploit them for the good of the Empire, this would be a patriotic act. Mother Nature acted in mysterious ways. Mustafa was indeed a formidable heir, but for every great man Mother Nature was willing to create an even better one. In this sense he fell perfectly within the laws of Nature to try to impregnate another Princess with the hope his son would grow to become an even better Sultan than her son. In the Manisa Palace a pregnancy could easily remain hidden, if there were no Osmanli spies.

Suleiman was following closely his father's illogical methods by refusing Mahidevran Sultan who had been so successful with Mustafa to have a second son. This kind of behavior was unnatural and detrimental for the Empire. What was needed was a more flexible law that the strictness of Ayin. The Empire was in great need for able men. If the Sultan's sons were able leaders, they all should have a place in the pyramid of command. Executing them was a waste of superior manpower. Unquestionably, Selim Khan had wronged Hafsa Sultan in many ways, so divine justice had to be administered, as a frustrated Valide Sultan as dynamic as Hafsa could do much harm, even more than a Kadin out of control.

Ibrahim chose to ask only for the progress of the Hafsa Sultan's mosque and nothing more than that. The Sultana's authority should remain untarnished, because at the moment she was the only person who could put some sense into her son's emotional mind. Suleiman was too blinded by desire to recognize the dangers the Empire might face, if one of the sons of a whore became a Sultan. Such low quality, and greedy specimens would surely fight civil wars to rise to the throne. A Sultan's greatest virtue was discipline and purity of purpose, and Mahidevran's character was adorned with both these virtues.

****

Mahidevran was true to her word. In Manisa the harem restrictions were practically nonexistent for a Sultan's Kadin out of favor. The same night he heard a knock on his door. He unlocked it and let the hooded visitor come into the darkened room. Undoubtedly she was a woman, and under the hood she was wearing a yasmak that allowed only a pair of black eyes to glow in the light of the oil-lamp.

The visitor rushed around the room, blowing out the one after the other the candles until the only dim light entering the room was the moonlight that came through the intricately laced curtain, shading the narrow ironclad window that made the small caravanserai rooms look very much like a prison cell.

In the deep darkness her slim figure became visible only as she passed briefly between him and the feeble moonlight. There were not many pieces of furniture in the room, so he sat on the bed and waited for her, but the next moment she was lost in the shadows. This room was unfamiliar and he didn't venture a determined search for the elusive Tartar Princess or her lusty courtiers. He simply waited her touch with anticipation, and his patience was soon rewarded. He felt the warm flesh of a woman seating on his lap and the bittersweet scent of Mahidevran invading his nostrils.

He never suspected he could become excited so easily, but Mahidevran was the kind of woman that could excite a man beyond limits with a single glance. He felt a determined push and he fell on his bed without any resistance. She took command of his night garments making sure he was completely naked as she was before she made intimate contact. Her attitude uncovered her Tatar lineage, as she sat on top of him gave her command of all his senses besides vision. Soon however it became apparent she did not try to assert her status superiority. She may be extremely frustrated, but at the same time very eager to please.

She searched for his lips in the darkness and he was too eager to pull her even closer. She didn't resist, but instead she grabbed his hands and offered her breasts to his sensitive fingertips. It was right then when he realized he had been tricked once more. This firm pair had never fed a child. Was Mahidevran trying to make a fool out of him, or did she wish to offer him a taste of her virgin past? Women were simply too complicated for a man to fully discern their motives, and the Princess had a reason choosing this kind of trickery for a second time in a row.

An enslaved man like him had to simply accept her offer and try to make the best each time, exactly as the formidable

Valide Sultan had shown him. He simply had to behave very submissively each time a female being of superior social status tried to used him for pleasure. This time he had to do his best to find as much as he could from this lusty slave and the caravanserai bed was the best battlefield for him to exert his mental superiority.

"I would simply love to have a lusty woman like you living in my harem," he acknowledged trying to wake up the whore hiding in the slave's mind; but he got no reply as this was the kind of offer this particular slave must have heard many times every time she strolled through a Grand Bazaar looking for fabrics or leather.

He simply had to offer a much better prospect to win her over to his side.

"Can I hope for a daughter that looks like you?" he added trying to wake up the motherly instinct in her. However, she still remained silent perhaps trying not to reveal her identity and continue this charade in total darkness.

When women tried to make him feel like a fool, he became angry, but this was the wrong time to try for more. The slave had other priorities. She wanted to please and be pleased before anything else. Then, she might consider more seriously any proposition he was willing to make. She was justified to behave this way. Every kind of intimate relationship created in the Harem had to be based on a search for exceptional pleasure.

This time he was not going to let her go the moment she had her fill. When she tried to jump off the saddle, he held her waist with an iron grip.

"I want a daughter that looks like you, Yabani!" he insisted.

It was easy for him to guess her identity. Mahidevran was a fair mistress, and this slave was nothing he had tasted ever before. The perfume trick had been good enough for a tease the first few moments. Now, using her name he had put an end to her trickery, but by then he had captured her fascination.

"Why do you want a daughter from me? All men seek

women that can give them boys," she murmured.

"When a man is in love with a woman, he always seeks a baby that looks like her."

"A Grand Vizier in love with a courtier? That's hard to believe," she argued whispering in his ear.

"Yes, but it's true! The world has changed. It is now upside down. Even a Sultan can fall in love with a dancing slave," he argued and she laughed finding his wit rewarding.

"These are not the right days for me to have a child. If you wanted a child, you should have tried harder with my mistress in the hammam; but after losing a heir of the throne, she is not in any kind of mood for another pregnancy with a commoner."

This had to be a slip of her tongue, but it made finding the spy much harder. Yabani had the complete trust of her mistress or at least of her sister Zarafet.

"I can sympathize with her sentiments. Losing a son leaves a deep wound. Thank Allah she still has one more worthy boy to comfort her."

Ibrahim had achieved at least one goal. He had discovered one good reason Mahidevran had resisted the temptation, a proper reason Hafsa Sultana did not know.

"My mistress needs no comfort. She is one tough woman. She grabs whatever she needs whenever she needs it. If she needs a child to be happy, there are many men in the Manisa who would be more than happy to aid her, if you know what I mean. You are just one of them. I'm not a Princess, but I can find better men than you, if I had to. The Janissary Corps is the place for a woman to look for adventures; but what is proper for a courtier is not good enough for a Princess. As long as the Sultan is alive, my mistress is determined to keep her reputation intact. Hurrem would be delighted to discover even a blemish. She has such a nerve! Imagine a sold meat becoming the judge of harem morality."

Yabani was a tough woman too just like her mistress. She didn't beat around the bush. It was a rather easy task for any woman to discern the object of his fascination.

"Too bad the Sultan does not feel the same way like you do. Then, there would be no danger for the throne to fall into the wrong hands."

"Yes! It is a pity this Sultan does not resemble his father. Sultan Selim was a true man."

"Yes, he was. This is what everyone who has met him said. He was so manly even men fell attracted to his vigor."

"I'm sure you have a good reason to say that," Yabani said with a strange smile making him blush. "Don't be ashamed!" she added. "A slave has no options to resist, when his master insists. With a courtier like me it's different. Sultan Selim didn't have to insist to conquer any woman, because every woman wanted a child from him. Too bad I was not lucky enough back then the night he took my virginity."

It was a revelation that took Ibrahim by surprise, and Yabani didn't miss to take advantage and increase his bewilderment by a new revelation.

"Don't be startled. There is no beautiful woman in this Harem that had not tasted Sultan Selim's vigor. Do you really think that a man like him would let a pretty virgin slave slip by? What would be the meaning of being a Sultan then?"

"Hurrem is indeed a very beautiful woman," Ibrahim challenged her intelligence with his indifferent manner.

"People say you are a very clever man, but sometimes you are exceedingly naïve. Sultan Selim has never offered a mate to his son before testing her skills. Do you really believe he would lead such a whore to his son's bed without seeing the effects she had on his only son, the heir of the Empire? No, Sultan Selim was a very deliberate and devious man. He had the ability of discovering every hidden talent and weakness in every human being he employed to achieve his aims. They say he had inherited this talent from his grandfather, Mehmet Fatih. He always acted in complete secrecy, inviting his lovers in isolated kiosks guarded by Mutes away from his bedroom where eunuchs could witness his orgies. So ask yourself if he would think twice to invite Hurrem for a few dances and then try hard to find reasons for her to deny him when his son was more interested in you. Hurrem was simply too bored of him when she chose to exchange places with that silent river of lust, Gülfem. I'm certain he had tested you too, before he made you his son's falconer. All things considered, you are not such a difficult man to analyze your urges or your motives. You are practically an open book."

"Yes, but this book has a nice cover. All things considered, since you are so experienced in these matters, what do you think is my greatest talent?" Ibrahim asked in a teasing disposition.

"All things considered, I consider you a born pleaser; but what kind of pleasures a man can provide to a man like Selim is very difficult for me to judge. I'm a woman after all and I have different needs for any man to gratify."

"Did I gratify you?" Ibrahim insisted.

"Yes, tonight you made me feel like a Valide Sultan or a Princess," Yabani replied turning the tables on him.

It was a dangerous development, but he was truly naïve not to suspect that a bit of news as exciting as his conquests as an Odabashi could remain a secret for long in a harem full of bored women. When the door closed behind a visitor only the intricate details remained a secret in the Harem or the Selamlik. With a man a Sultan's possibilities were more capricious than with a woman, and half an hour of isolation was enough for a vicious rumor to grow roots in the Seraglio. The Sultan's Selamlik was made to promote lust among its visitors, lust the Sultan could exploit; but lust was like a dangerous illness. It was contagious as all slaves were extremely ambitious to improve their prospects inside the Seraglio. Now without great difficulty he could surmise what was going to happen the moment he left. These three vixens, the Princess and her twin slaves would get together and share all the information Yabani could provide from her experience.

He didn't mind for this development. Being promiscuous was an essential virtue for success in the Seraglio. It essentially meant you were practical, immoral, and you had high goals. In such a challenging environment, no one should expect something from nothing.

"When did it happen with you and Sultan Selim?" he inquired.

"Stealing my virginity was actually a very easy task for him. When Mahidevran was presented to him as a bride for approval, he motioned me and Zarafet to stay. He didn't even ask for Mahidevran's permission, and that made her awfully angry."

"And what did she do?" Ibrahim asked with aroused interest.

"She told him that we were not her slaves and he had to ask our permission to use us."

"And what did he do then?"

"He laughed at her face and told her that in his Seraglio, he didn't have to ask permissions from anyone. In there he was giving only commands in accord to his wishes. Sooner or later she would also be asked to stay behind, when everyone else had left."

"Did he ever raise such a despicable demand?"

"For us Tartars this outrage is customary. The Khan has every right on his son's concubines he bought out of his purse, but this is not something you should ever discuss with the chambermaid of a Sultana. I would never disclose something that may soil my mistress' reputation. My mistress and I have almost the same close relationship that exists between the Sultan and his Grand Vizier."

****

He had to admit this day had been monumental in his life, almost as much as his experience in the Avret Bazaar. It has practically changed his entire scope about life. Yabani had been a revelation. If this was her way to repay for the pleasure he had offered her, he couldn't really say; but making love to a woman was the best way to win her trust. Of course, all the stories he had heard from her lips might well have been a part of a more intricate conspiracy to feed him false information, but somehow Yabani's behavior seemed perfectly sincere. She was a conscientious courtier and had accepted her position in the

Ottoman hierarchy without remorse. She would do everything within her abilities to serve the interests of her mistress. However, since she was free, it was conceivable her behavior might not be as submissive as a slave's.

Could it ever be possible that Sultan Selim had slept with Mahidevran Sultan too? He most certainly had the authority to command and impose his will on anyone he might have desired. Suleiman for some reason was still terrified by the ghost of his memory, and he was the man destined to govern the Ottoman Empire for as long as he was alive. What kind of resistance could a young concubine like Hurrem raise? What kind of stand could a Princess from a vassal state like the Tatars make to the sovereign Sultan, when even an ordinary leader of a clan had absolute authority over all its members? Tatar clans were not organized as democratically as an ancient Athenian assembly.

He had to admit that his mind still operated according to the rules of the West; but even in the West and the Roman Empire there were times when an Emperor exceeded all moral limits. He was educated enough to read ancient historians and know that Caligula had mated with his sister and raped many of his senators wives. He couldn't believe it just yet, but the power of an Emperor in both East and West was absolute in every sense of the word.

Surprisingly it felt good to hear he was not the only one who had submitted to this absolute rule. In the human species no one felt offended, if he followed commonly accepted rules even if these rules defied logic.

He had heard stories of African tribes that cooked and ate their enemies after a battle to gain their strength. He had also heard of few insane Christian monks who lived without women in monasteries, or other convents where women tried to prosper without men. All these extreme lifestyles were clearly dead-end choices and survived parasitically at the limits of the "regular" society that had more humane rules more compliant to common logic.

Naturally, the Christian religion did not have the monopoly

in social madness. There were also Muslim monks, the so-called dervishes that tried to achieve a saintly status by fasting. They also fought along with the Janissaries and participated in every looting and raping raid, trying to convert infidels in every way possible for the glory of Allah. Surprisingly, this was the prevailing logic that was now on the rise, conquering state after state and nation after nation in East and West. He would be insane to try to oppose this general trend. In a sense it was as dangerous as trying to stand in front of a stampeding bull herd. His only hope was to divert its deadly course.

Considering his appointment as a Hasodabashi in charge of a harem full of frustrated women, and the gossip about his relationship with the Sultan, he was practically forced to pick up the glove of every female challenge to advance his career with her support or complicity.

****

After Yabani's visit he decided to stay in Manisa for two more days and nights to be consistent with his plan of finding the spy in Manisa. His door was knocked the second night and another capped woman arrived wearing the same perfume like Yabani, pretending she was Mahidevran. This time he was wiser, he was already naked, and instead of waiting for her to make the first move, as soon as she came close and tried to feel her way on his naked body, he grabbed her arm and pulled her on the mattress. She didn't try to resist him even when he forced her to lie face down; but he was finally fed up with aggressive Tatar maidens. He was a man and on a bed he should have the reins from the beginning to the end. After all now he was the Grand Vizier and she was just a courtier that had to please him to convince him she was eligible to enter his harem.

Without a doubt Zarafet was most eager to please him and show him she was at least as good in bed as a harem trained Osmanli Princess. Early on she discovered how exciting was for him to sense her excitement, so she didn't stop urging him by murmuring in his ear to exploit all her assets, even though

Hatidge would never think of lowering her desires to such a level. It was one more sign the maiden tried hard to offer him every kind of pleasure she could imagine and he had to accept her imagination was uncommonly fruitful reaching easily Basmi's levels.

Asphodel had informed him that all concubines in the Harem were very eager to apply novel ideas, and urged the eunuchs to ask their Janissary lovers how they pleased their women. In this way a constant flow of intimate information from the Galata whores to the Janissaries to the eunuchs all the way to the concubines was created, and consequently a reverse flow of silver coins and presents. Of course, every Harem's silver coin originated from the Sultan's purse, but no one knew how far this flow of silver ended.

Most people blamed Hurrem for every curious novelty, but this was untrue. Hurrem was completely innocent. If she knew some devious tricks, she was not going to tell anyone and especially another concubine. Zarafet had to be involved in this network, and the fact she was so submissive meant she was a trusted member. She was simply too eager to please and every time he exploded his passion, it was one more opportunity to start a new cycle of extreme debauchery. It was a mesmerizing process that seemed it would never end unless he decided to put an end to his thorough exploitation. She was the first woman that made him touch the very end of his endurance, as she pushed him deeper than ever into a profound state of bliss.

Finally, she made him feel like an old man; so he simply had to relax for a while to regain his libido.

****

When he woke up he was all alone, but he had made up his mind. Zarafet would be the right new concubine for him. She also had to be Hafsa's spy. She simply knew too much of what was in style in the Galata harbor and this meant she was in close contact with the eunuch servants that manned the Manisa Palace.

****

The last night in Manisa the knock on the door filled him with great expectations. His heart almost stopped beating as opening the door he come face to face with Mahidevran's perfection under the candle light.

She walked right in and sat on his bed putting his heart on fire with her audacity.

"We have to talk," she warned him. "Do you still want one of my courtiers for your harem?" she asked him.

"Yes, I do! Zarafet will be ideal for me. She is most probably Hafsa's spy. She is so well educated how to make a man happy, I'm convinced she is well-connected with the eunuch conspiracy."

"I believe so too," Mahidevran acknowledged with an imperceptible smile. "She is simply too well acquainted with Hurrem tricks. I wonder if she is also Hurrem's spy."

"Is there something I could do to repay you for this gift?"

"What do you have in mind?" Mahidevran asked retaining her grin.

"I always wondered if there was a way to help you forget," Ibrahim said hesitantly.

"I don't want to forget! I need to remember every detail because every detail represents a part of my dream, and like every human being I have the right to dream. I also like to make my dreams come true like everyone else. Sometimes I am successful, sometimes I may fail badly. Suleiman used to be my dream, but he proved he was not worthy of me the moment he became a slave of that fucking bitch."

"What about me? Have I disappointed you as much?"

"No! You are a much more interesting personality than him. You are much more complicated, so I'm always intrigued to discover what makes you tick. Each time we meet you are different and this is extremely exciting. I bet this was what forced Selim to take you under his wing as a falconer and since then you keep evolving."

"I'm very happy to hear you say so nice things about me. You will always be my dream woman."

"You are lying but I don't mind hearing your lies because you are not lying to me but to yourself. Nothing lasts forever unless it is a dream. Dreams are creatures of our imagination and so are lies. If I let you fuck me as much as you want, soon you will get bored of me and my perfection. Then, you might fall for a slut like Hurrem, and this is something my pride cannot allow to happen twice. You see my dream is not a man. Men are for me just tools to make my dream come true, and my dream is to make my son a Sultan, nothing else and I mean it!"

Mahidevran was truly powerful and her words had a devastating effect on his ego. He got angry and pushed her down on the mattress. He was going to show her that his dream was stronger than hers. He was going to hurt her to make her come to terms with reality. As long as she needed his help for her son, she was going to pay the price he demanded.

He lifted her caftan, spread her legs and entered her without a second word. However, she had a surprising line of defense.

"Fuck me as hard as you can if this is what pleases you, but make sure you understand that this will be the last time you'll have a taste of my perfection. I promise you I will never allow myself in such a compromising position."

Immediately he lost all his drive. He had to think and his aroused passion was a bad counselor. He stopped pressuring her and she was well prepared to push him off her flesh.

"I knew you were a wise man despite your uncontrollable urges. This is most refreshing. It means that if my son becomes the Sultan, I will enter your harem most willingly. You not only know how to appreciate class, but you are willing to pay the price to get it."

And with these words she fixed her clothes and got up.

"Please don't go! Tonight I need you so much I can't stand sleeping all alone. Have pity on me."

Mahidevran smiled at him and her smile was full of the tenderness a woman had for her son.

"Let's make tonight the first night of our formal

engagement. After my first failure, I have decided that a woman should not rush to marry any man without a proper period of engagement. I promise you that whenever I need a man you will be the first in line; but I have to warn you that as long as my son is a Prince Heir I will not conceive another son. Is this clear?"

"It is more than clear, but what about tonight? It's not fair to leave me like this."

"Of course it's unfair, and unfair is not who I am. Now I'm your fiancé and I have certain obligations."

And with these words she went to the door, opened it and walked out blending her black cape with the surrounding darkness. Ibrahim had time just to say "No", but it had to be a magic word, because almost immediately a shadow materialized, and walked in.

Had she decided to come back and show her benevolence to a desperate man in pain? He could do nothing but wait for her decision.

In the trembling flame of the oil lamp he saw a young woman undressing slowly all her inspiring beauty. Only the top of her face remained hidden, but it was enough for him to recognize the unmistakable lips of Zarafet. His fate was sealed. She was going to play with his passion until she was certain it could grow no more. Then she was going to use his flesh for her pleasure. Her eyes black like the abyss said plainly enough that there was no way for him to escape because his will to resist had collapsed the moment Mahidevran left his room. Despite being the Grand Vizier of the Ottoman Empire he was the slave of a slave. Just to be sure he pulled away her masque.

Suddenly her dark eyes brought back loose pieces of a memory lost in clouds of steam and opium. Now he could even taste a man and his sourness, but the past was not always a prelude for the future. He felt the weight of a determined rider who knew much better than him what he needed most. The pain of intrusion forced his eyes open and in Zarafet's eyes read the insatiable lust to use him for her pleasure, even if this became painful to him. It was not the first time he had seen such greedy black eyes; but his memory became suddenly confused as his rider decided to fall on the mattress leaving his back open to assault.

His confusion was further attenuated as in his ears a series of conflicting commands lingered waiting for his total obedience, as the pain he felt shifted turning gradually into pleasures as confused and as intense as the pains originally inflicted.

He suddenly felt a hard slap on his face and opening his eyes he saw the submissive Zarafet turning into an all-demanding Sultan.

"Wake up! I haven't finished with you just yet! If I'm going to enter your harem, I must know how much my master is worth!"

Something very basic had changed in the Ottoman Empire, but he could do nothing about it, despite the immense power of the Grand Vizier and Serasker he possessed! He was still the Sultan's lover, but now women had pushed all the men in his past to a dark corner of his memory. He did not resent this involuntary and somewhat violent change. Women were much more gentle and considerate creatures. They were more like silk traders visited his Grand Bazaar rather than conquerors who took possession of his treasures, even though sometimes they were treating him as if he was their subject rather than their master. Women were humans after all and to be a human meant that in the back of your mind the fundamental principle of this Universe, an eye for an eye, applied.

When she finally let him free to catch his breath, she had one more surprise to spring.

"Who do you think I am, Zarafet or Yabani?" she asked.

"Zarafet, without question," he replied with the cockiness every man has after a long debauchery.

"Are you certain enough to bet your life?"

He wasn't. There were just to many similarities to be denied, but a single difference could lead to absolute confusion.

"If you are not perfectly sure, perhaps you should invite both of us to your harem. We are both bored in Manisa, spying on our mistress. Till now she was perfect and we had nothing exciting to report, but only Allah knows what the future will bring. It would be better for all if both of us resided in your Palace. The rumor says it is the most exciting palace in the City."

Chapter 13

Inside the Harem

*"And if they surrender, then surely Allah is Forgiving,
Merciful"*
(Quran, Sura II, 192)

On his return to Constantinople, Ibrahim was the least surprised to receive the next day a new Valide invitation, but Hafsa was a woman and naturally curious to find out how his visit to Mahidevran's palace had ended. She was also a mother trying to make sure her son was happy and free of domestic problems.

Ibrahim was a slave and his wishes were subordinate to hers; so he told her most of what had happened as it was pointless to try to hide his failure to keep Mahidevran content. In Hafsa's eyes he read the verdict. Since the moment the Princess had failed to keep the Sultan forever a slave of her charms, she was an expendable asset. Anyway, a Kadin really didn't matter much. What was still important in Hafsa's eyes was not Mahidevran but her son.

For Hafsa Sultan Mustafa was indeed an extremely important dynastic asset, because he was such a capable youngster and the perfect heir of the Ottoman throne. It was not just her personal estimate that said so. It was the public consensus. Mustafa should be the next Sultan by popular demand. His esteem among the Janissaries was higher than ever before and their expectations for his glorious future even greater than when Sultan's Selim was the Prince Heir, at least as far as the rumors she had heard. Mustafa was as brave and determined as Selim, but less cruel and more just. He was a pious Muslim, but not a religious fanatic. He had the character of Alexander the Great; but he was more morally correct. He had already started his harem in Manisa, and his mother had chosen wisely local consorts of noble birth. The benevolent doctrines of his great grandfather Bayezid the Saint had been combined by Allah with Selim the Terrible martial dexterity. Despite his young age, Mustafa could compete with the best of the Janissaries on foot and Spahis on horseback, but he had always a kind word to say for his brothers the offspring of Hurrem.

Hafsa knew all these loose pieces of information, as she had eyes and ears in every bazaar and meidan. She could sense now more strongly than ever the rising public interest for her grandson. As years went by, Mustafa had become more important than even her son. It was a natural phenomenon. Future was more important than present for every member of the mankind; and as Suleiman's health slowly deteriorated, Mustafa's youthful appeal became more pronounced, especially among the Janissary who was an elite unit based on dynamic meritocracy rather than static nobility. Gradually, Hafsa's first priority had become how to reduce Hurrem's influence on the ailing Sultan. Perhaps it was immoral sending Ibrahim to seduce her daughter-in-law, but the end justified the means in the Harem, and the frustration of a mother should not demolish the expectations of an entire Empire.

Her plan was simple enough. The Sultan, faced with Mahidevran's resentment, might consider her son despised his father too. An eye for an eye was the most common human reaction. Humans were made to react to an injustice by anger; but anger was a bad consulter.

Hafsa had chosen the most competent man for this delicate mission. She knew well enough Ibrahim had no moral scruples. He was madly in love with love. He would never say no to any invitation to share pleasure. He was not truly a Muslim despite appearances. He was a Greek-Roman Dionysian through and through, a true descendent of a degenerate Byzantine breed, ready to compromise rather than oppose a more powerful opponent like Mahidevran.

If she had not found Hurrem in Galata, by now Mahidevran would dominate so completely her ailing son, it would be extremely difficult to control the Janissaries. Her weak son would have to abdicate to stay alive for a while more. How long would her son survive after his abdication only Allah knew. It would be simpler, if he died peacefully, because if somehow he recovered, the possibility of a civil war would be even greater than when Murat abdicated for his son Fatih, or when Bayezid abdicated in favor of Selim.

In her mind Mahidevran was the most dangerous opponent of her ailing son. She was also the most ambitious Kadin. If Suleiman died, then Mustafa would be the next Sultan and Mahidevran the next Valide Sultan. Her own reign dependent on her son's health. As long as Hurrem filled her son with the will to survive she was her best ally.

Her spy had informed her the moment she came back to the Eternal City, and entered the service of her daughter that Ibrahim had not been perfectly sincere. Mahidevran had spent some time with Ibrahim in a Manisa caravanserai behind closed doors one night. Mahidevran was too shy to discuss many details, but when she went out of his room she was very excited. And when they both went to the hammam, her impeccable skin had few browses, squeezes, nips and bites.

Hafsa simply smiled listening to her detailed report. Unquestionably, if women were to select the next Sultan, Ibrahim would be the chosen one. Even she would vote for him. For as long he was following her orders, Ibrahim would be safe. Mahidevran's debauchery was a useful piece of information she could use if the Princess ever became out of control with jealousy. She had behaved like a cheap whore seeking thrills, but such a behavior was to be expected from any frustrated resident of the Harem. In the Harem a woman to win in a war she had to become more sinful than her opponent. Was this Allah's will or simply Hurrem's malignant influence that had turned the Harem occupants into promiscuous temporary wives?

****

"Why do you think she refused you?" Hafsa asked Ibrahim with a naughty smile.

"She didn't want to get pregnant with me," he replied making her burst into laughter.

"I can't believe you were so naive with that lusty bitch! Are you always so inclined to believe whatever a beautiful woman tells you? She simply played hard to get. Men don't respect the woman they fuck; so, she turned you on and left you cold. It is as simple as that. The flesh you desire so much is her ultimate weapon to force a powerful Grand Vizier to do as he is told at the right moment. Only if she decides you are the only man capable to carry out her plan, she will offer you her flesh in a platter, exactly as I did to make sure you are a true friend of my son."

"And what do you intend to do next?" Ibrahim asked with considerable interest.

"I must become even more devious than her, because I have to make sure both my son and my grandson don't get carried away by their wild ambitions. What else?"

"And how are you going to achieve that? Can I be of any further use?" he inquired assuming that Hafsa might ask him to seduce Hurrem too.

In such an eventuality, he would refuse the dangerous mission, since the jealousy of an Osmanli was just too dangerous to risk. However, Hafsa had never considered such a risky idea.

"When a man fails to perform a delicate task, a woman may easily be triumphant. Nevertheless, you are not totally useless for my plan to avoid unnecessary turmoil. You have experienced in the past the overflowing sensuality of Hurrem; so you are the right man to judge the potential of her new adversary. For me a Russian slave the Kislar Aga discovered in the Avret Bazaar is ideal for my plan. She is young, pure like a flower, and totally oblivious of the art of love making. She is exactly the material an aging man needs to start a fresh chapter in the book of life. If Hurrem is the depiction of sin, she is the model of youth and innocence. Youth is the best medicine to combat the fear of death that are torturing my son. I don't want to flatter you, but if I was just a rich noble woman and not the Valide Sultan, then I would buy few versatile and obedient slaves like you and retire in the countryside to plant my personal paradise."

****

Ibrahim remained silent for a while looking lost for words, contemplating the deeper meaning of Hafsa's rather long introduction. Instinctively, as any common man would do, he had put himself in the described position. He had Suleiman's age, and he had achieved many triumphs within the last few years. What the Sultan had that he lacked were his numerous children; but this was not because of some inherent inability, but simply the result of the affluence of eager women Suleiman experienced since the day of his circumcision.

Despite this disadvantage he didn't feel any kind of inferiority, and Hafsa must have realized that by now he was perhaps the most desirable male after her son in the Empire. She also knew better than anyone else he was almost as powerful as the Sultan, but much more democratic and open to any challenges the female species may pose to his manhood. From a falconer and a Hasodabashi, a bed-companion of dominant men, gradually he had been transformed into a most desirable ladies' man. With the addition of Zarafet and Yabani in his harem next year he could easily have four more children.

Come to think of it, Hafsa was responsible for most of his successes with the opposite sex. She had offered him her daughter and made sure Basmi was also included in this lucrative deal meant to keep his lust under control. Lately, she made sure he was admitted into the Sultan's palace in Manisa, to pacify a determined Kadin eager to take revenge for the injustice she had experienced. He managed that risky task better than any eunuch Hasodabashi, allowing her to use him as her secret lover to sooth her heart from the terrible loneliness of rejected consort. Mahidevran was practically a divorcee; but her husband was cruel enough to keep her in chains for the rest of his life. His life may be now in peril, but he had done the right thing.

Hafsa was a sensitive woman and she had sensed the different way he looked at Mahidevran and did her best for his clandestine desire to be fulfilled. She was indeed a wise Valide Sultana, because in the Harem any latent sensuality had to be satisfied one way or another to avoid unnecessary tensions. He couldn't know how strongly women felt, but he had to admit that Hafsa Sultana had excelled in the task of matching undisclosed desires that could have caused considerable hostilities among the Sultan's household which included two highly frustrated Kadin. The fact she had included herself in this widespread debauchery was not a sign of morality collapse; but a show of strength, and uncommon dexterity and realism equal to the skills of her notoriously devious husband. He was also accustomed to put his Viziers to the test, promoting the best and executing the worst to make the next one perform even better.

The fate of the Empire was just too important to be left to luck, and in this task Hafsa had much more delicate touch than her terrible husband. She was so uncommonly powerful for a woman that she could use a man without being emotionally involved. Despite her immense power, Hafsa had all the necessary ingredients to become a whore, but he was never going to let her know how he truly felt about her. It wasn't only dangerous, but also hypocritical. He was a male whore too in every sense of the word.

The Osmanli were remarkable creatures and this was the reason they had created an Empire from nothing. If Sultan Selim had test him as his son's intimate companion, his faithful Kadin could not wait idle and let him become the husband of his favorite daughter blindly. It was also entirely possible she had convinced the Sultan to raise his next status from falconer to "Hasodabashi" after Selim's demise, since by breaking this unwritten rule, she had made sure everyone in the Harem realized he was a man of confidence who kept his mouth closed and didn't boast for his successes as most men would have done in his place.

Anyway, gathering different erotic experiences was for him a worthy endeavor and he didn't grumble. It was not just the pleasure he experienced, but being desirable was also a great boost to the self-confidence necessary for any man with his immense ambitions. Women were instinctively the most meticulous judges of a man's worth. When they met a man, the first question they asked unconsciously was if this man could be a worthy father of their children.

Now Hafsa Sultana intended to use his help once more to achieve her goal, the ousting of Hurrem from the Sultan's life. If her elaborate plan would work, he couldn't really assert at this point, because he had not seen the slave maiden she intended to add to the Sultan's harem. Nevertheless, Ibrahim agreed that her choice of an impeccable virgin to replace an experienced oriental dancer of dubious morality was logically sound and extremely insightful.

He had to admit that at the back of his mind the primal urge to ravage an innocent girl and impregnate her was still alive despite his stormy past. He knew that logically such a prospect was not an enterprise that was going to offer overflowing satisfaction. An experienced woman was much more capable to discern and comply to whatever desires a new client of her charms might have; but a human mind didn't always follow a logical path. If his mind did, he would be still in Parga, battling against waves and casting nets to catch sardines like his father.

A true man was more strongly attracted by impossible dreams. He didn't know this important truth at the time, but the captain of the pirate ship was much too eloquent to be denied a taste of his youthful charms in exchange for a wild adventure. Of course, the sneaky pirate had lied to him to achieve his surrender; but in the end without knowing it, he had opened new vistas to his imagination by revealing that men could be almost as pleasant as women, and only by combining both types of experiences a man could feel complete.

Living beings behaved like a sponge collecting bits and pieces of knowledge each day. Human memory discarded most of these pieces as useless, but relatively few were bound to become precious transplants into the minds of the new generation. In Parga learning how to swim was a precious experience for any fisherman, but the torrents of life had forced him to travel on land most of his life. On land, riding a horse was much more important for a Grand Vizier and he had adjusted to the demands of his career. Pleasing men seemed now an impractical burden that had to be discarded; but was it so useless if it offered him much more pleasure than swimming?

****

"So what do you think? Is she worthy of my confidence? Will she expel Hurrem out of my son's bedroom once and for all?" Hafsa asked and her words interrupted Ibrahim's enchanting trip in memory lane.

The presentation of the maiden had not followed the usual rules of summoning a black eunuch to fetch her. Instead, with a clapping of Hafsa's palms the bedroom door opened and without any escort, the tall figure of a woman covered with a veil had appeared in the opening. Was it a sign Hafsa Sultan did not trust her Kislar Aga?

The slave bowed deeply to show her submission and moved forward, following Hafsa's welcoming nod. Even though the veil covered her from head to toe, the fluidity of the gestures hinted she was a woman determined to attract the eye of a male by the gentle sophisticated gyration of her hips. The difference with a competent belly dancer was more than evident in this short walk, but for a picky man like him this was not such a clear advantage.

The maiden stopped in front of him at arm's length, following the well-established ceremony of every slave assets presentation.

"Aren't you curious to see how she looks?" Hafsa inquired impatiently, raising the level of activity in his brain.

From Hafsa's behavior it was perfectly clear she was proud of her new acquisition, and she was trying hard for his unreserved approval.

"Indeed I am, and I know that the beauty of a pure rosebud clearly surpasses everything Hurrem can now offer. I'm also sure that under these veils a woman's beauty even greater than I have ever seen lies hidden; however, I'm not sure, if the critical battle will be fought in the field of beauty," he remarked as he simply could not resist the temptation to tease Hafsa for her weakness for carnal beauty.

She was for one more time the proud owner of an attractive slave and she was a promiscuous woman. It was humanly impossible for a powerful woman like her not to test for a few days such a beautiful creature. The least she had to do was to make sure the Russian slave didn't snore sleeping in different positions. He was now old enough to know how exactly this test could be performed; but snoring was just a trifle. Without a doubt, the most sensuous moment was what a woman did as she exploded her passion. In his mind the prefect woman should scream to announce her peak, but too much screaming could give the impression she was pretentious, or even worse that she was a sex maniac. A competent Valide Sultan had to experience everything to be perfectly sure of the most harmonious result.

Hafsa was not an amateur, but neither was he. They both had to play their roles perfectly to retain their dignity of their position.

"I'm not a fool," Hafsa snapped back. "I know better than anyone else that beauty is synonymous with youth and every day that passes makes a dent on a woman's armor. In fact, this is what I'm counting on. My son must be bored to death by now having to see the same aging face every day for so many years. If he is not bored, then he is not fit to be a Sultan or a world conqueror. In my mind the answer to this dilemma is so simple."

Nothing in a human society was so simple. This much he had discovered sleeping with men, women and eunuchs. Both women and men were more than willing, by there were artificial social restrictions, and despite human efforts to acquire the most extensive knowledge some bits and pieces escaped.

"I'm not so sure. An experienced woman has plenty to offer, if she feels like pleasing her mate. Her main attraction is that all her past experiences have turned into valuable assets, providing security rather than risk for her lover. She knows a great variety of ways to please a man, because she has already experiences with similar men. For instance, I'm sure any competent concubine in Sultan Selim's harem could also enchant any Janissary guard," Ibrahim asserted, making sure she realized he knew about her Janissary lover.

If someone needed to keep clandestine activities a secret inside the Seraglio, he or she had to make sure he knew at least as many incriminating secrets of the people who were aware of his escapades. The Valide Sultan knew well of this unwritten rule of safety and she showed her will to forgive his indiscretion with a long smile. If he had weaknesses as any human being, so did she, however, from the moment they had made love, their fortunes were intimately connected. She was in love with Sinan, but he was simply too far away to take care of her daily needs. Ibrahim should know he was not the only man in her life and should limit his cockiness.

She was running the Harem as if its members were her family, and her recent behavior attitude suggested Hafsa Sultan was considering him unconsciously as also a member of her harem. It made no sense for any member of the family to make family secrets public.

"I admit that you are essentially correct, but when we dream, logic resides in the background, and as you will shortly discover this girl is made of the stuff of dreams. Please take off her veils and experience the best of what Mother Nature has to offer to a discriminating man who wants to become a world conqueror."

Ibrahim remained briefly inactive as if he was reluctant to add one more challenge to his load of concerns. He was a married man after all, and it was possible sooner or later all his escapades would reach Hatidge's ears. The fact she was a princess was in his favor for the time being. Being jealous of a pretty slave was below her Ottoman nobility dignity.

Hatidge from the very start had shown she accepted the fact her husband would be a respectable Ottoman. Thus, he had the irrefutable right to be served by slaves whenever she was indisposed. In fact, it was well within the Ottoman tradition for any man to use occasionally slaves of both genders for his pleasure to emphasize his virility. This was the oriental way of thinking, and Hatidge must have had similar experiences from her first marriage. It was probably the period when she became so attached to Basmi. The fact she had offered him the chance to share Basmi was ample proof she was not the jealous type. She had unshakable confidence of her status as a master and slave user, and no slave could put it into jeopardy.

If he wished to become adjusted to the ways of the

Harem, he had to stop thinking the Occidental way. Morality varied depending on the specific direction one was willing to travel in the horizon. In the East all kinds of sensuality expressions were acceptable. Sensuality was what Dionysus had brought to Europe after his expedition to the East according to the ancient Greek mythology. This was his firm belief and introducing Zarafet and Yabani among his wife servants after his return from Manisa had been exceedingly simple. Mahidevran's letter of introduction had done the trick. They were her present for their wedding and they were the most versatile slaves she could find. Their long service as her courtiers was an ample security for any highly selective Ottoman princess like Hatidge.

****

"Where is she from?" Ibrahim asked just before touching her veil.

"She is from the Kuban plains in the east of Ukraine," Hafsa disclosed. "These people are a very interesting mixture of many bloods. They are Vikings as much as Tatars. Perhaps this is why I like her. Isn't that strange? We constantly fight against these Scythes, but at the same time they are the most desirable slaves in the City these days."

"As far as I know before the Russians, the Tatar women were the object of the greatest desires in the slave bazaars," Ibrahim teased her.

Hafsa couldn't resist his teasing strategy and his offer of a gracious compliment.

"Is only my race the main source of attraction for a Greek?" she inquired and he had not failed to please her coquetry.

"No, of course not! Women of superior intelligence have another secret path to enter into my heart besides their impeccable looks."

"Thanks for the compliment, but this is not what a woman wants to hear from a younger man. A woman is made by Allah to bear children and this will always be her main concern as long as

164

can. Thus, the best compliment a man can say to a woman is that he wants to make her the mother of his children."

"That's true, but I'm not an ordinary man. We Romans never favored too many children. We prefer fewer children but of superior intelligence," Ibrahim revealed winning this battle too.

"I should have known that this grand Vizier has a satisfying answer for every question. I guess this is his best asset despite what he imagines women like most on him."

It was clear Hafsa had become now the teaser, but the presence of the Russian maiden restricted the range of his reactions at the moment. Thus, to demonstrate his state of alertness, he stretched his hand and removed the first veil covering everything else.

He had to admit the image that came suddenly into his field of vision was quite unusual for oriental standards. This maiden had a remarkable pair of legs that was even longer and thinner than the occidental standards as presented by the Ancient Greek statues of Aphrodite. This revelation made him more eager to investigate what more was hidden under the veils; so he most eagerly pulled the next shorter veil that revealed a rather limited periphery that matched her long legs, but hid well this oriental drawback by an exceedingly slim waistline, an ideally shaped bellybutton and six well-trained abdomen muscles.

She was indeed a remarkable creature as far as he could see, because oriental women took pride in having loose bellies as a proof of the Empire's food affluence. In Russia the conditions were clearly different and the possibility of famine forced women to work hard on the wheat fields, rather than kill time smoking hashish and devouring sweets in luxurious, opulent harems. He suddenly realized he liked this girl, and pulled away the third veil. Now only her face was hidden and the generous neckline made clear this girl's offspring would be fed well.

It was really strange how a woman's body adapted to the prevailing living conditions, as the primary concern for all human beings was to survive. Only when Mother Nature played with human patience changing the climate, the human flocks had to migrate to foreign lands. In his native land the soil was poor and plains were scarce. His ancestors were forced to seek riches travelling upon the waves. His ancestors were fishermen, but he had sought to secure his prosperity onboard a pirate vessel. He was too young at the time to survive on a fighting ship, and the pirate had chosen wisely to sell him off in a slave bazaar, rather than take the chance of keeping him as a mate. Pirates didn't need mates in the first place. They could grab what they needed in the next port of call or the next loot. His mother had warned him to avoid associating with strange men, but she had not explained the exact reasons for her advice.

Following a mother's advice was the safe way, but for a young man following motherly advices was the feminine way. A man had to follow his rogue instincts even if they led him to dangerous waters. Hafsa was wise enough not to advise her son to kick Hurrem out of his life. Her son would do the exact opposite just to prove he was a man.

He was a man too and he simply had to pull-off the last veil hiding the girl's face. It was immaculate with the delicate lines of her Tatar blood dominating her cheekbone structure. Only her hay-blond hair revealed her Nordic ancestry. Her eyes were tightly closed by her eyelids as if she was afraid to face the lust of a potential buyer.

She was mistaken. She was not for sale. Her future was already decided. She was going to spend all her life within the walls of the Seraglio, watching the sailing ships travel along the Bosporus Straits from North to South and the row boats cross from East to West.

He reached for her hands to make her feel wanted and she responded by opening her eyes to see the face of the bold man who dared to put his hands on the Sultan's property. She was scared for the future; but she shouldn't be, because her eyes were undoubtedly her best feature. They had an emerald color he had only once encountered in his life, as the pirate boat had sought shelter for the night in a small cove of the tiny island of Antipaxos across the Parga harbor in the Ionian Sea. He still remembered well the color of the water as he couldn't resist the temptation to follow his master and take a dive early next morning.

Pirates practically never washed with fresh water even after they made love. They simply took a dive. Fresh water was simply too precious to waste in anything but drinking and cooking. This had been his baptism into a different way of living, as water had a way to cleanse the human bodies from the past, when his body belonged only to him.

His new life in the Seraglio had also started with rosewater and a hammam. It signified the beginning of his new career, when his entire life would be devoted to the pleasure and prosperity of the House of Osman

The flesh of this girl smelled as if she just had a hammam too, before her presentation to her new life, when her entire existence would have a single purpose, inspire with her purity immeasurable lust to the man who would invite her one night to his bedroom.

He smiled at her to show he was a friend and an ally she should trust because they had a common purpose, but she was too scared to take his gesture seriously. It was a clear sign of intelligence. Virgins had to be suspicious of every able man. Their attraction was unconquerable and much greater than any treacherous male's.

He had successfully made the transition between several harmonically combined states of the male gender. He had evolved from a hammam and dancing boy to a Sultan page to a man. These were just words people had created to put tags on other people to eradicate their natural appeal. The fact men held the reins of the society meant they were the ones who had put down the rules. Men were hypocritical enough to use derogatory names for dancing boys during the day and fight bloody quarrels for their favors at night. Allah simply laughed at all the tricks His creations did to conceal the truth; thus, so many lies had been spoken through the ages that no one could now discover the pure truth:

"If Allah had created the entire world from love for

mankind, Allah was a woman. Now the critical question was what exactly Allah's Shadow truly was!"

****

"From the expression on your face, I can plainly see that you cannot find many flaws, no matter how hard you seek for them," Hafsa Sultan teased him with the directness of a skillful slave-trader. "Am I wrong?"

"Indeed I can't," Ibrahim admitted as it didn't make any sense trying to hide his desire. It would be a ridiculous attempt and a childish endeavor in the face of such an experienced occupant of the Harem. There were precious few emotions he could conceal from such a creature that had spent an entire life seeking signs of weakness in a male beast like Sultan Selim so eager to conquer new territories at every available opportunity. "She is an exquisite creature with a beauty that exceeds far beyond ordinary limits. If I was a Sultan, I would be most eager to make her a distinguished member of my harem to bear the very best of me offspring."

"Do you consider her even more desirable than Mahidevran Sultan?" Hafsa asked as indifferently as possible to catch him off-guard.

"Mahidevran is a Princess with noble blood, while she is a wildflower of the Kuban steppes. There can be no comparison," he quickly noted, trying to avoid being squeezed to a tight spot.

"You know what I mean. Which one would you like more to fuck tonight?" Hafsa insisted too vulgarly for a Valide Sultan, but he knew she liked to use vulgarity, when she tried to turn him on.

"This is not a fair comparison, because my experiences with your daughter have been extensive. To be perfectly fair in my judgement, I must fuck the slave many times to to form a balanced view," he replied with a long smile displaying his will to keep on teasing her.

"Stop daydreaming!" she urged him in an equally good mood. "This divine creature is not for your teeth. She has been chosen to bear few more grandchildren of mine; but this will not be her primary function. Her mission is much more complicated and you know it. She is as exquisite as Mahidevran has been at her age and her mission is to liberate my son. He has presently descended to the level of becoming a slave of a slave. What a disgrace for a descendant of Osman! He escaped the attraction of a man of low morality to become a slave of a woman of an even lower esteem!"

If their relationship was formal, Ibrahim should have been offended, but their bond had evolved to something else currently indescribable by common people's vocabulary. It was such a rarity, humans had never bothered to create a word to describe it. He was the husband of her daughter, the lover of her son who had also the audacity to make love his mother-in-law few times. The human language was rich enough to describe separately these three relationships, but the combination of the three was too rare to be honored by a single word. By becoming her lover she had proved her morality was at least as dubious as his or Hurrem's. However, the moment he had married her daughter, while Suleiman had accepted as his own the sons of a whore, Ibrahim was the one who had a small moral advantage.

He smiled to indicate he was not offended by this emotional outburst. He actually didn't mind if his past relationship with the Sultan was magically erased from every possible memory. His main excuse was still valid. He was an inexperienced young slave who was suddenly carried away into the Seraglio, sat naked on the Sultan's lap scared to death of denying any service anyone might require of him. He felt so defenseless in this majestic environment, he would never think of resisting, even if the Sultan ordered a Janissary to rape him in front of everyone to test the extent of his submission or simply have a laugh with his friends at his expense. Fortunately Selim desired him as much as Suleiman and he was saved from utter ridicule.

As long as slaves existed, no one would ever think of questioning the level of their morality. Morality was one of the luxuries of freedom and it always depended on both time and space. Many people in various occasions had performed abominable deeds to survive a tough test of their destinies. Since then he had accomplished much more than a mere survival. Ibrahim Pasha had prospered more than any other slave in the Ottoman Empire in his era; thus, Hafsa was completely justified to ask of his advice. This Russian maiden had to make a similar leap and from the status of a slave reach in one bound the status of the Sultan's "Gözde" or possibly of "Birinci Kadin". She certainly deserved this upgrade. She was a truly remarkable creature much more deserving these titles than Hurrem.

If Hurrem deserved a title, this was of the most unscrupulous woman in the Harem. She had excited his passion just to make sure he was not going to take a stand against her strive to win the Sultan's heart. Their fleeting union had been a bribe. This was her main goal. The fact she enjoyed also using his flesh was an unexpected bonus.

If Hurrem was indeed a dancing girl, as the prevailing rumor claimed, her behavior was fully understandable. Money was not the only motive for their performances. Dancers, when they had collected enough money, could start a more direct kind of employment. They could even buy their freedom, if they wished to, but most didn't. They kept on dancing until their charms ceased to be sufficiently appreciated.

Hurrem was also getting enough pleasure from her domineering Kadin status to keep providing the Sultan with every kind of pleasure he desired to retain her position for the sake of her sons. He was the Grand Vizier and knew well the Seraglio economics. Hurrem was the best rewarded employee, if one omitted a Grand Vizier's occasional share from war spoils. The truth was that since he had risen to this lucrative post, he had more money than he could spend in this lifetime, even if he invited dozens of belly dancers to his bedroom for a brawl. Of course he never did such a disgraceful act, because Hatidge was the mother of his son and by disgracing her he would disgrace himself. It would be the act of a master a slave could not find excuses.

In a sense every kind of immoral act, even murder, was allowed for a human being, if he could find a good excuse for it. Now the fact he desired the exquisite creature in front of him had naturally produced a most believable excuse. She was as beautiful as a goddess, while he was just a weak mortal, seeking to achieve immortality through passionate proliferation.

To keep on teasing the formidable Valide Sultana he asked:

"Now that I have testified on her favor, does Your Majesty want me for anything else?"

He was a bit offended, when she didn't invite him to stay, but the presence of the new slave was an adequate excuse. She was the Valide Sultana and her important post required keeping up appearances. She was supposedly the keeper of the Harem's ancient traditions. This was the reason every concubine in the Harem wanted her to be disgraced and lose face, so that her own sins would also be less severed judged.

Hafsa delayed her answer to test his patience. Having men waiting for an answer still felt good, improving any woman's self-confidence.

"Of course you can make yourself more useful if you wish to help your most intimate friend. I simply cannot offer her as a present to my son. He will then have time to react or resell her which is not a fair deal. A man should not profit from his weakness he should be punished. However, if you offer her use for one night as a token of your gratitude for your master's trust in your abilities during an invitation at your palace, then she will not be his to sell, but he will yearn to use her time and time again. I also suggest you become a bit more devious and turn it to a strictly male event, so that in this invitation Hurrem or Hatidge cannot be included."

Ibrahim was startled by her bold suggestion, but he shouldn't. It was not the first time Hafsa was willing to bend the strict Ayin rules to her advantage. He could now easily discern the advantages this devious plan offered. With Hurrem in the Eski Saray away from the Seraglio the degrees of freedom for the

Sultan would naturally increase. If this freedom would ever be exercised he was not sure. They both had similar freedoms also during an expedition, but Suleiman had never taken advantage of his rights as a victor on the slaves he procured after conquering an enemy city. His excuse was that the Ottomans had invaded foreign lands to civilize their inhabitants by establishing the just domain of Allah in the barbaric West.

The truth was that this strategy had been recently very successful, and many cities in the Balkans had been willing to surrender peacefully rather than fight to the death for the sake of few cruel nobleman who ruled them for centuries. From the moment a certain region was conquered, it became instantly a well-governed territory of the Ottoman Empire the Sultan promised not to surrender without a bloody struggle.

Ibrahim had no good reason to try to modify a strategy that worked. However, here in Constantinople the occasion was entirely different, and a foreign slave had practically no right to deny any service a demanding master might ask.

"I have no objections to your plan, but to offer this pretty Russian slave to my master as a present I have to buy her from you first," he argued as indifferently as he could; but Hafsa was not a common woman and she had already noticed a difference in his tone of voice, when he talked about this slave.

"Indeed this is the proper way to conclude our deal; but you have to promise me on your life that you will not lay a finger on her, before my son makes clear what he plans to do with her," she insisted.

"I'm sure your Majesty realizes that from the moment she becomes a member of my household, accidents might happen that I may not be held responsible. I'm a liberal master and most of my servants are not eunuchs because I sincerely despise this breed. I simply cannot trust them. If they ever betray me, they have nothing to lose but their life," he argued and Hafsa remained skeptical for just a moment.

"As I told you, I most firmly believe that a man should not profit from his weakness. He should be punished. If this is the best security you can offer me, then I have no good option left but to make her a present to my daughter's harem. She can do with her slaves whatever pleases her and no harm done."

"Is she really a virgin? I don't really believe an Ottoman would ever own such a beautiful flower without testing her scent just once."

"Don't judge every Ottoman by your deprived standards. The girl was captured as an orphan infant few years back and raised in her estate by a benevolent widow in Manisa."

"I have heard a similar story many years ago. I'm supposed to be a young slave raised by a benevolent widow in Manisa. Is this some kind of local myth circulating in Manisa?" Ibrahim remarked with a suspicious smile.

"They say there is a seed of truth in every myth. I don't know your story, but I know my son better than anyone else. He is too shy with men; so, I suspect that in your case he sent a Janissary guard to choose the most promising boy. One look at your eyes is enough to know you are not a man who says 'no' or 'yes'. With you everything is negotiable. This is why you are so irresistible."

Hafsa Sultan was diabolically insightful. He was indeed the kind of man willing to be used by a master eager to pay the right price. She was also wise enough to guess that a Janissary had chosen him. Up to this moment he had totally forgotten Sinan's involvement in the selection process more intimate details. He felt a little offended by Hafsa's attitude and sought some kind of revenge. Someone had to humble any haughty woman. This was Allah demanded to keep this universe in perfect balance. Women were bestowed the unique privilege of making children offering men a safe passage to the future. They were the gate to the afterlife, but men had kept control of the key. Hafsa should be reminded of this inescapable fact.

"You are indeed an amazing woman! I'm very lucky and proud you and Mimar Sinan have honored me with your friendships," he noted casually to show her he was aware of her new lover, but she had invaded much deeper in his mind.

"I hope you are not too jealous of our common friends," she snapped back at once as if she was expecting his nudge.

****

Ibrahim went straight to his office. For one more time he had been used and outsmarted by Hafsa, but her challenge was not his main concern right now. Sinan was an attractive man in many more ways than one, but he was not a greedy man like the Sultan. Sinan was a slave of the gate and he was his superior, but he was fully content being his best friend. As he rose in the Ottoman hierarchy increasing his authority his preferences also shifted towards the female of the species. His domination on women became his primary concern. If women desired him, he was immune from the desires his second nature occasionally inspired.

Hafsa had made him Grand Vizier of the Ottoman Empire and for this lucrative present the payment she demanded was minimal. In fact, if the Sultan replaced Hurrem with this Russian maiden his position would largely improve. After such a momentous development even Mahidevran would be grateful, and his friendship with Mustafa would be strengthened. Only his relation with Hurrem would suffer, but under these circumstances the influence of a dancer was too minute for a Grand Vizier to be concerned.

****

This momentous night, even before the sun had set behind the Great Theodosian Walls, all preparations for the Sultan's visit were completed in Ibrahim's Palace.

Earlier on, the cooks had prepared all the elaborate courses designed to satisfy the sensitive palate of the imperial sovereign, and to accomplish this difficult feat the Grand Vizier had borrowed few of the cooks of the Ambassador of France, as well as the chef of a rich Chinese silk merchant. Fortunately, the blooming commerce of the era between East and West, North and South had made Constantinople once more the greatest crossroad on the globe, bypassing Venice, Genoa, Alexandria, Lisbon or Madrid. This critical day nothing had been left to chance, and even the experience of the Imperial Harem's Kislar Aga had been put to good use. He was the City's expert on how a new concubine should be dressed and how to act to attract the eye of a magnificent Ottoman Sultan.

Surprisingly, Hatidge treated her mother's present positively and that said a lot about the Valide's authority on her daughter. The trust between a mother and a daughter seemed absolute, nevertheless, Ibrahim felt he had to explain in rough lines the plan against Hurrem.

With his first words he discerned in her eyes the secrecy of a conspirator.

"I never liked Roxelana!" she confessed with apparent animosity. "Whatever fate Allah has in store for her, she deserves it. Very few people in the Seraglio like her anyway."

She even went so far as offering few precious jewels and expensive clothes to her new chambermaid as a welcoming present. It was the kind of friendly behavior Ibrahim didn't expect. If this was a telltale sign of a growing female conspiracy he couldn't yet decide. He was simply too busy with the preparations; but his instinct had been triggered.

Somehow, by leaving his post to go to war, he had allowed few reins of his power in the City to slip away. Perhaps abandoning the post of the Sultan's chamberlain had isolated him from the daily Seraglio rumors and conspiracies. Regulating which concubine would be the one to visit the Sultan's bedroom each week was perhaps as an important post as that of a Vizier and infinitely less risky. It allowed a vintage point to the Suleiman's daily mood. By becoming Grand Vizier and having to be daily in his office advancing the Empire's foreign policies, he had no idea how life inside the microcosm of the Seraglio progressed.

In the old days when Selim Khan was reigning supreme, Menekse had warned him about the existence of a eunuch conspiracy. These days, harem women had taken the reins from the eunuchs. It was an unanticipated development, but he should have been wiser to foresee it in advance. Selim Khan's preferences had been the main cause for the eunuch's rise to power, but now Suleiman's weakness for women had shifted the balance of power towards the weaker sex. Indeed, the moment the men were marching away to fight in foreign lands, the field was left open for the women to take command of the City. Nevertheless, he had to admit that Valide Sultan had chosen to stir the Harem to a safer course by limiting Hurrem's excessive influence. If the Janissary realized that women were in control of the Seraglio and the Sublime Gate, a rebellion was inevitable.

Hafsa Sultan was a truly magnificent sovereign acting in the background. The moment Selim Khan died with few words at the right moment, she had made him Grand Vizier in charge practically of everything besides the Harem. She was wise enough to recognize the dangers involved if he remained there as a Hasodabashi among so many lusty concubines and Kadin. She could read eyes better than anyone and used his licentious character to control even now the Harem frustration of the two neglected Kadin.

The Kislar Aga had to be her most valuable spy. She had to be the one who had relaxed the strict Ayin rules, allowing any Kadin to go to bazaars and the caravansaries seeking moments of well-deserved relaxation. She was also the one who allowed her son to waste so many hours with Hurrem. Unquestionably, Hurrem had a soothing effect on his disposition, a crucial factor if the Sultan would ever recover from his incapacitating illness; but, Hurrem's overbearing performance in the bedroom had shifted the balance of power in her favor.

He could sense that now, as Suleiman was spending most of his time in his quarters, there was hardly a moment free for them to talk in private. Hurrem had taken advantage also of Hafsa's visits to Manisa to isolate the Sultan from his family even more. He had to admit she had now developed a very subtle approach. Now, she exerted her influence through her children, obliging the Sultan to spend much time with his offspring.

No Osmanli could argue openly against such an investment

of time, but only the future would prove if this was a wise investment from the moment only one of his sons was destined to reign. In this respect Mustafa's superiority was overwhelming as far as into the future as Ibrahim could see. This was a fact even Hurrem must have recognized. Hafsa Sultan had to take measures to save her grandson's life, since making arrangements for a poisonous dish was much easier in Manisa than inside the Seraglio with its strict safety rules.

****

When the Sultan finally arrived in Ibrahim's Palace after a long preparation, the moon had risen high enough over the ruins of the Hippodrome to flood the ancient monuments with its eerie light. The Sultan offered no excuses for this delay since he didn't have to.

Perhaps Hurrem had delayed his arrival, but it was almost as probable the Sultan had waited long enough for the At Meidan to be emptied from the usual crowds of visitors and night walkers. From then on only few drunkards would be still out, coming back from the Galata taverns to their night dwellings within the Agia Sophia district, as in the City no wine or raki was served or legally imported after a strict order of the Seih-ul-Islam. It was a useless gesture he didn't oppose as a Grand Vizier that simply made wine more expensive as the tavern keepers had to bribe the Janissary patrols to look the other way at the City gates.

Taking advantage of human weaknesses was the best way for an unscrupulous man to get wealthy and the Aga of the Janissaries was according to the rumors filthy rich.

Ibrahim was the last man to complain about human weaknesses, as he had learned early on how to take advantage from almost every one of them, even drinking and eating like a Christian. He had many excuses for keeping this liberal stand as the ex-Christian Janissaries were the bravest soldiers and the best guards of the City public order, and opposing the Muslim clergy only troubles could bring to an infidel Grand Vizier.

Nevertheless, being noticed by the Janissary patrols were

177

not what the Suleiman feared most, when he came in sneaking late at night. He wished to avoid triggering new gossip about the nature of his relationship with the Grand Vizier; but in Ibrahim's mind this story had ended long ago. His affair with the Sultan was the result of insecurity that made him vulnerable in a strange environment where even his survival was at risk if he became the object male lust.

At the time he had been as vulnerable as this exquisite Russian beauty who was willing to exchange her purity with a sense of security, even though in the Harem the sacrifice of one's freedom didn't secure anything worthwhile besides a decent place to live, fancy clothes and jewels, and few elaborate daily meals. Life was tough for both men and women in the Eternal City and despite the luxury of the Seraglio there were precious few chances for any woman to reach the age of sixty in the Harem or outside. The great majority of Oriental women were blessed with what he considered as genetic dignity, a virtue that guided their steps throughout life. However, it was relatively easy for many women in the Seraglio to betray their natural instincts startled by a man's external appearance and riches in the same way a peacock's feathers appear more impressive than an eagle's beak. If Selim Khan could be compared to an eagle for the Ottoman Empire, then his son, Suleiman, resembled a peacock.

Indeed, Selim Khan had fought valiantly in many battles risking his life, while Suleiman watched the battles from a safe distance. He knew that better than anyone else, and by now all the women in the Harem were aware of his true worth, as secrets didn't remain secrets for long. The Seraglio walls were full of cracks that let rumors leak out sooner or later. This was another secret that had leaked and it was so important that even his life might depend on it.

When he was young he had taken great chances and surprisingly they all had ended in his favor; but now he was an experience statesman, and he should be more careful with the unexpected changes of fortune. Gradually, he had to put an end to most of his clandestine affairs, because sooner or later something might leak and become a noose around his neck. If in the Orient the honor of a man was so important, it was because most women and men had been slaves some time in their lives.

Allah was All-wise to permit one sin as one sin was just a trial, but more than one was a habit. Bad habits could kill or disgrace you. He knew that well enough since childhood. His father was a habitual drunkard and a shame for his family.

****

The Sultan's arrival in the middle of the night had nothing to do with his magnificent appearances during the day that were meant to impress friends and foes. He came dressed in black, riding a black horse accompanied by only two horsemen from the Spahis Corps, dressed also in black, without any distinguishing detail of their status. To any casual wanderer at the At Meidan they might well be three cavalry men returning home after a night out.

His uniform rang a bell in Ibrahim's memory. Suleiman was wearing the black silken cape he wore when they first met in the Avret Bazaar. Was this a subtle reminder of the origin of their relationship or just a habitual disguise the Sultan used when he sneaked out?

Nevertheless, this time he was also wearing a sumptuous green turban with an emerald broach that unmistakably signified his supreme rank as the Caliph and the Shadow of Allah.

They all promptly dismounted, and the pages led them to the open gate where Ibrahim Pasha was waiting. Right there their paths split as the Spahis pulled the horses' reins towards the stables, while the pages led the Sultan in front of the Grand Vizier to accept the customary greetings and prostrations.

The Sultan was in a friendly mood and waved Ibrahim to stand up with a hand gesture, however, being submissive offered emotional comfort to every slave, and Ibrahim pretended he had not seen the Sultan's waving and kneeled to show his respect towards his master.

When he eventually rose, he led the Sultan inside to an

open but secluded court Mimar Sinan, the palace architect, had designed for summer receptions. It was a rather pleasant night and Ibrahim proposed to sit there under the stars despite the creeping chill of the night.

In this court two soft sofas were prepared covered by thick Anatolian kilims from Konia, while in front of a large round table the Ottomans called a "sofra" was placed in front of them. Soon after their arrival the different elaborate courses appeared in impressive shapes and intricate designs as the imagination of the two international chefs had envisioned. They were indeed successful in their trades and even the Sultan who was always austere in terms of variety of tastes could not resist the culinary temptations. Carnal weaknesses were a most welcomed sign for this special occasion.

"I trust this is the best the West and the East can offer to the Master of the World," Ibrahim claimed with his customary self-complacency; but the Sultan refused to acknowledge; instead with considerable interest combined with dignity he asked Ibrahim all about the Princess' health and he explained that she was absent because her daughter had a serious cold.

It was a feeble excuse convincing no one; but Hatidge's absence was an essential element of tonight's plan success. It had to be a night devoted strictly to men's pleasure, as the invitation clearly stated and women were not allowed to attend. Nevertheless, the Grand Vizier was well aware that behind the ornamented window grills two dark eyes would follow closely their every move.

****

The sofra was cleared from dishes by the pages to open space for the cups of tea and the sweets. Space was also left for fresh fruits and cool sherbets. Nothing was forgotten by his staff and Ibrahim felt obliged to summon the cooks and show his appreciation with generous tips. Then he asked the pages to depart and leave them alone in peace.

From the very beginning the Sultan's attitude had a

peculiar air and he had to find the reason. The least he could suspect was that his recent visits to Hafsa's and Mahidevran's quarters in Manisa had been promptly reported to his master. From that point on all short of suspicions could be formed in a distrustful man's mind, and any attempt to provide excuses would cause more harm than good.

Ibrahim's best option was to treat everything suspicious as meaningless and inconsequential. His visit to the Valide Sultan quarters in private was among his official duties. He was the Grand Vizier responsible for the welfare of every citizen, while Hafsa Sultan was responsible for the female population in the Harem. Keeping all these women content cost money he had to appropriate each and every month to avoid quarrels and discontent.

Visiting Mahidevran was also among his duties as she was the mother of the Prince Heir. His education required also funds from the Imperial Purse. Even if his flares with Yabani and Zarafet ever became known, who could blame him? Courtiers didn't have many chances to show their gratitude to the men responsible for their luxurious living conditions.

As a Serasker he had heard many complains from commanding officers about guards abandoning their posts for an intimate encounter in the Seraglio Gardens, the famous Gülhane; but he never considered realizing the suggested severe punishment of these offenders. It was not just the liberal opinion he had that the love between two people would eventually be beneficial to the Empire, increasing the numbers of the youth population. Despite rumors there were no sworn enemies bold enough to try to harm anyone within the walls of the Seraglio.

Foreigners were entering the Eternal City just to sell their merchandise or buy goods from the Bazaars at low prices, not to harm or threaten any inhabitant. The European nations had a hard time trying to secure what they owned in the battlefields, and raiding the Ottoman domain was now just a distant memory. This was also why he resisted wasting good money on repairing the Great Walls. Times had changed and now the priorities were different, as the safety within the limits of the Empire was guaranteed by the might of the Ottoman armies.

Under the Ottoman rule the Balkan Peninsula had become a lair of aggressive attackers rather than a contested piece of real estate. These happy days enterprising Tatar raids reached all the way to the Vienna suburbs and deep into the lands of the Russ. This was essentially the reason why he could relax and concentrate his thoughts only on Haseki Hurrem and the threat she represented for the existing balanced status quo.

"My Master, if you are aware of something that has escaped my feeble attention, please let me know, and I promise it will be soon at your disposal."

Suleiman didn't raise any exuberant claims and reassured him that everything was according to his wishes. However, after the last cup of tea had been served, his inclination to depart gradually became more and more apparent. The Sultan surprisingly didn't feel relaxed and behaved as if he was waiting to face a new trial. Whatever question Ibrahim posed, the Sultan was quick to add that everything had been carried out to his complete satisfaction.

To prolong the visit, Ibrahim clapped his hands and as if this was a secret code, one of the many side doors opened and two slim female figures appeared in the opening completely covered with long veils that reached the slab-paved floor. The one veil was purple-red like a blazing fire and the other emerald green like a crystal clear mountain river in summertime after a long drought. This sudden appearance startled the Sultan and put him back in a conscientious mood.

It was no clear what Suleiman expected, but Ibrahim was not willing to waste a single moment in fruitless long discussions. He had other, much more exciting plans. He wished this night to be different than any other. Repetitions had started to bore him, and one of his reasons to participate in this plot was to prove to Hatidge his relationship with her brother was following a new path. Tonight he was not staying in the Sultan's tent or in his Master's Seraglio quarters. He was in his private domain, his luxurious palace that was newer and superior even than the Sultan's Selamlik. Tonight his secret wishes were going to be fulfilled not the Sultan's.

"These two maidens are the best North and South has to offer to the most magnificent sovereign of the Globe," he claimed extremely confident he was right, as the two women approached them with the gentle quiet steps a cat approaches its prey.

When they were close enough, they prostrated by the Sultan's feet and demonstrate their submissive intentions by putting their faces at the lowest possible level, right on the Anatolian rug. It was a subtle sign they were willing to be treated like dirt, if this was what the Sultan's pleasure demanded.

Ibrahim knew well the dexterity of Basmi in offering pleasure to a demanding man like himself. She was indeed a proficient courtesan and the times he had spent with her truly long and rewarding. Basmi in absolute terms had been the most meticulous lover he ever had.

As a harem slave from her infancy she had been trained on how to please her master more; but, he was a man with special needs who considered an erotic encounter as an opportunity to satisfy additional emotional needs. Whether he liked it or not, he had many accounts open with the Osman family, and every time he used erotically one of its member in his mind it was a momentous success filling him with pride.

This kind of urge was not effected by his doing. From the very beginning he had been subjected to this treatment, when someone had used him as an object of pleasure to underline his superiority in the power pyramid of the Ottoman Empire. Even Hatidge unconsciously had treated him as a male courtesan; but, through the years he had realized that an erotic relationship expressed many latent features of the existing social structure.

On the opposing end Basmi was a conscientious pleaser and this was her greater asset. Her shiny skin was ebony black and in her mind the trends of many generations of slaves resided as a genetic distillate. If the Sultan chose her, Ibrahim was certain he wouldn't return to the Seraglio before daybreak and Hurrem would be positively furious the next morning, when her spies would reveal where her master had been.

The best scenario he envisioned was something that had never happened before. Two friends sharing two women in bed. It would be a bold scene, but it would have profound implications. It would give him the chance to fully compare their abilities to please women.

He was then rather surprised when he saw the Sultan turning to his Grand Vizier for instructions what to do next with these mesmerizing slaves; so he smiled kindly and suggested the obvious, namely removing their veils. The Sultan should have known what a customer had to do when confronted with the task of judging the assets of a slave. The fact Suleiman had forgotten, meant he had stopped to treat slaves as slaves.

Suleiman followed his hint and pulled first the red veil of the black slave. Under it the shinning surface of well-polished ebony appeared inviting his hand to test its smoothness. Basmi's skin was simply superb as if it was a wooden statue meticulously finished by the expert hands of an inspired African artist. Basmi was once more begging to be touched and her mesmerizing scent reached potent Ibrahim's nostrils reminding him of many good old times.

As the Sultan's hands followed his mind's need to explore more and more, the silken fabric revealed first her long neck, and then her affluent breasts with the blazing-red nipples enhanced by henna dye to set a man's body one fire, leading finally the customer's eyes to a red ruby attached to her navel. The precious stone brilliantly reflected the lively flames of the torches illuminating the palace garden, warning every bold onlooker that his eyes were about to enter a dangerous domain of no return.

Ibrahim knew well this feeling as from the first day he entered her there was no way he would resist coming back again and again to experience the same sensation of being swallowed and consumed by a voracious snake that could never be content no matter how hard a man tried. Basmi was born to be a greedy African goddess of fertility that would keep on demanding more and more male sacrifices with no visible end.

Listening to the prevailing gossip, she was also well-aware of the Sultan's many vices, and offered her wet, fleshy lips shaped like a kiss for his pleasure .

If the Russian girl was Hafsa's choice, Basmi was his. Besides her comparable dexterity, she was completely different than Hurrem. She was a black vixen that could never be satisfied enough by any white customer, and she had no special use of the Sultan's sperm other than to quench her thirst. She knew better than anyone that no child of hers seeded by an Osmanli would ever be allowed to live after birth and degrade the imperial blood of Osman; thus, a Sultan was less mesmerizing than any common man.

The seductive scent of sandalwood surrounded Ibrahim once more. It was an invitation to the unknown deserts of Sudan he simply couldn't resist but had to, as tonight the Sultan had the first choice and he would have to be content what was left. Basmi's eyes were shinning now like lighthouses, guiding a struggling ship after a storm to a friendly harbor.

For the Mediterranean, black flesh was a necessary ingredient of paradise, and the black tint signified this ancient trend of all Arabian races, creating extremely attractive mixtures of skin colors along the North African coasts. Now it was simply a matter of waiting a few moments for Ibrahim to measure the content in Mediterranean blood in the Sultan's veins. If he was him, there was no way he would resist the temptation to extend his hands and grab the two juicy fruits Basmi was proudly displaying as a challenge. She had such a presumptuous look in her eyes, no true man would hesitate to teach her a lesson in humility.

To his dismay Suleiman's behavior showed had simply not a trace of Mediterranean Sea. He was an Asiatic. He didn't even pull the veil to expose the sacred temple of Isis waiting with its gates open between the two imposing and superbly sculptured pylons of her muscled thighs. His attention was instead captivated by the enchanting shimmer of the Russian eyes, piercing the veil and turned his glance towards this unfamiliar slave girl.

Perhaps Hafsa Sultan knew her son better than him. It was not just a coincidence that Tatars had kept invading Russia since time immemorial and had the same blood with Osman that made her a more familiar dish. Suleiman had Turkish blood in his veins and if Russia had immense steppes he could roam on his horse, so did this enchanting slave. She was slim and long and eager to be conquered.

It was an invitation he couldn't resist too. Now, he developed similar urges as Suleiman, as if in his veins the blood of Ancient Greek seafarers run, the men who had landed on the Crimea and the Caucuses first, seeking the Golden Fleece and turning the Black Sea into a Greek lake. Was it possible the Golden Fleece was an ash-blond Russian Amazon?

The Sultan's hand pulled eagerly the blue veil and the fabric slipped gently off the girl's back exposing   the   brilliant softness of her impeccable skin. The purity of her existence materialized with blinding directness, as her blond hair braided into twin pigtails came into view. It was probably Hatidge's suggestion, as her long hair left unchecked would cover with its fluidity the divine glow of her complexion that came next into scrutiny.

If Suleiman selected her, it would be entirely his choice to let this cataract of wheat free to roam on her breasts and shoulders. However, this magnificent specimen had much more to offer to an adventurous man and she didn't hesitate to display it, as she turned around and let the silk follow the hills and deep gorge of her backside.

Ibrahim examined his Master's facial expression and discerned the sparse fog of indecision. The Sultan behaved as if he didn't know what to do next. He simply couldn't find a solution that could satisfy all the imposed prerequisites by this member of the opposite sex. On the other hand the girl, despite her youth, purity and inexperience, had made up her mind. She was going to sacrifice her past and present to win a glorious future.

All young maidens followed the same path when they

faced this dilemma, a clear sign females were practical. Her eyelids expertly dyed expertly by his wife in green-blue shades made her eyes look even greater. Her purple lips half-opened looked like a night flower waiting for the moonlight to open and become pollinated. She was a virgin and her flesh revealed this mesmerizing fact in many ways. There were not just her awkward and fumbling attempts to impress her master with her undeniable, unsophisticated charm, but also her fearful stare that signified her feminine instincts were alive as well as the primal fear instigated by the marauding rapist's presence. Thus, she lowered her glance out of shame every moment she felt Suleiman concentrated his attention on her most intimate parts. It was probably this shame that had turned her chicks red during this close examination, even though she knew there were no faults and she was perfectly suited to become the next Sultan's favorite. Now what was left was for him to extend his arms and welcome her into the bosom of the Osman family.

****

In the past, no Osmanli Sultan would hesitate to offer the chance to such an exquisite flower to bear another heir of the throne of the Roman Emperors, as the momentous success of this family in both East and West was the result of its adherence to the unwritten rules of meritocracy. Superior children were the product of superior parenthood. Nevertheless, this Sultan remained for some unknown reason hesitant and Ibrahim had to find out why; so he took two stems of grapes, one black and one white and offered to his master.

"These two slaves were precious presents of your mother to beautify my harem. Perhaps she thought my harem was not as rich as yours and Allah's command is for the master to do his best for the happiness of all his slaves. However, as your slave whatever I own belongs to you my master too; so now tell me, which one do you fancy more? Red wines have strong taste, while whites have a more delicate bouquet, but they are both capable to make us see the world from a new prospective. Thus, please don't hesitate too much to choose, because we are still young and greedy and we can drink both wines to our hearts content without much fear of a long lasting hangover."

And with these words he pinched one grape from each and offered them to Suleiman's lips.

The Sultan did not refused the offer and hesitantly bit the one after the other, as if he wanted to judge the difference. He then tried to smile, but his blushing cheeks revealed his profound embarrassment, however, after a long period of contemplation he found the words to explain how he felt.

"I'm grateful for your superb hospitality, and I hope the next time you'll come into my quarters as a guess, I'll have few presents as exquisite as yours, so that the people will not say that the Sultan is less rich or generous than his Grand Vizier. However, tonight I'm not myself because of my illness. I came nevertheless, because I didn't wish you to think that I'm displeased for some reason, and now I must be on my way. Since we came back to the City, I feel terrible pains in my toes and tonight the pain is worse than ever before."

Suleiman had nothing more to say and he tried to get up, but his clumsy movements revealed he was indeed in pain. Nevertheless, Ibrahim was surprised by this sudden urge to depart, because he believed there wasn't a man on Earth who would refuse the invitation to spend the night in the arms of these two enchanting angels. The reason for the Sultan's refusal of his gracious offer had to be Hurrem, or possibly some other cause his fertile imagination had not yet grasped. Nevertheless, despite the Sultan's unstable state of mind and body, everything pointed out that a new situation was gradually developing. If a sickness had caused the Sultan difficulties to stand on his two feet, he, as a Grand Vizier had to take the burden off Suleiman's feet, as any inability to participate in a military expedition was a good enough reason for the Sultan to be disposed or replaced according to the strict Ottoman military traditions.

Undoubtedly the present occasion was not the proper one for such a profound change in the Ottoman hierarchy. Mustafa was too young to accept the responsibilities and Suleiman was not fully incapacitated yet. Similar symptoms had also troubled Mehmet Fatih, but he planned new military expeditions until the day he died. The image of an all-mighty Sultan had to be preserved at all cost until the moment Mustafa was old enough to take the reins of the dynasty in his hands.

He graciously motioned the two slaves to retire and they, somewhat offended by the rejection, picked up their veils, prostrated with respect and left walking backwards towards the harem entrance.

Ibrahim clapped his hands twice and a black eunuch appeared from the darkness eager to receive his orders.

"Motion the Solaks! The Sultan wishes to leave," he ordered saying nothing about Suleiman's illness. From this moment on it would be one more state secret Ibrahim had to conceal from the all-demanding Ottoman subjects.

****

The sound of steel hitting a rock was heard as the three horses slowly and deliberately followed the wishes of the Sultan; but soon total silence prevailed as the At Meidan was that night more deserted than usual. It was to be expected as the rumors the Ottoman Armies were to be gathered once more to conquer Vienna, and many families had members that would be soon making the final preparations for this treacherous expedition. After a long period of celebrations and festivities most families had to get together and try to gather strength for a new period of emotional stain and worries that could even end up in a tragic family loss. However, Ibrahim was for time being much more concerned about the results of the crucial conflict of interests he had just lost despite his meticulous preparation and solid battle-plan.

Hurrem had just won the battle despite her absence, and this was the most puzzling aspect of her victory. Unquestionably, the Russian maiden was a superior creature and her purity an additional advantage for every true conqueror. This meant that

Suleiman had somehow lost his edge, and perhaps his sickness was the main reason for feeling so weak that he had not even claimed the rights of the master as he usually did in the past.

For him the answer to this problem was straightforward. Since there was no comparison between the two women and no danger of this clandestine affair to become more widely known, Suleiman should not have hesitated to cut this exquisite flower, and add it to his collection. Was this a sign Suleiman had stopped collecting concubines to produce more heirs? Was he losing all interests for temporary pleasures?

As a friend and a faithful companion of many pleasurable expeditions, the most innocent excuse his mind could generate was that the Sultan's pain was so strong that it overwhelmed every source of pleasure. One issue was uncontestable according to Asphodel's reports. Hurrem despite her expertise was not such a hot item anymore. Her pregnancies had degraded her flesh to the point that if she ever made herself available for a second time, he would rather sleep with Hatidge without a second thought.

The Princess was a bit older, but she was a very elegant and sophisticated woman worthy of every attention, while Hurrem was just a professional dancer and an enchantress of limited worth as a display item capable of underlining an Ottoman Sultan's magnificence. Unquestionably even now, Hurrem could seduce many Ottomans in the Empire, but the reason would not be her looks or her extensive experience, but her power to influence the Sultan.

He went back to the sofa to calm down his excitement and plan his next move. He should not act in haste before all the facts were known and analyzed. The Sultan had tried to subtly explain his point of view and this was a positive development of their friendship. In the past, he had tried to explain that as the years went by, the women in his life would gradually become less important, as his children grew and occupied more of his time, pushing Hurrem to a corner of his mind. Passion was a feeling that didn't last long; then other considerations became more important.

Suleiman was right. Right now his health was much more important than any woman. Ibrahim felt healthy and strong and his mind sought women and pleasures; however, if he ever became seriously ill, then his mood would drastically change as pleasure was gradually replaced by pain and the fear of death. If pain became unbearable, then even children became unimportant or even a nuisance with their greed and wantonness that could reach to the point of disrespect.

Perhaps it has been a mistake to invite the Sultan tonight. Essentially it had been a challenge to his absolute authority, but how was he to know Suleiman's troubled physical and emotional state? The Sultan had not confided his condition to his friend, as his health had to be kept a secret of the state at all times to discourage all the potential enemies. The fact he had kept this secret from him meant he was not blindly trusted.

Now his next course of action was relatively clear. He had to regain his trust by taking the burden off Suleiman's shoulders until he felt better and could stand firm on his feet.

****

Ibrahim was so absorbed by his thoughts he didn't realize someone approaching behind his back until two soft hands closed his eyes and a pair of lips reached for his ear. Then, the familiar scent of oriental spices invaded his nostrils. It was as unique as the woman who wore it. Now that Hatidge had become his wife, he knew all about it. It was a blend specially prepared for her by an expert merchant in the Grand Bazaar who imported the ingredients from distant eastern archipelagos. Potentially, sailors had died fighting the waves for these minute quantities to reach the Eternal City. Come to think of it, it was really insane how far human greed reached to satisfy the senses.

He knew well enough where this subtle introduction would eventually lead. Hatidge had watched the sensuous show the two slaves had put on for the sake of the Sultan. He had also heard his words loud and clear about the best North and South had offered for her brother's pleasure. She also knew these were

191

not just words. By now she knew he was always sincere when he confronted her brother. Between friends there was no space left for lies, as one lie could damage irreparably a friendship.

His wife's lips touched his ear.

"Everything did not go as planned for us tonight, did it?"

"How did you come to this conclusion?" he snapped back.

"The Russian came back crying. I used to be a virgin too, you know, so I know perfectly well how a virgin feels when she is rejected by a man. How cruel men can really be leaving a flower wither away barren?"

Ibrahim was surprised by this emotional outburst, and countered it with a touch of ridicule.

"Yes, indeed. Men are the greatest sinners. They risk their lives to conquer foreign lands, when all that Mother Nature requires of them is to keep women happy."

"Hurrem must be a witch. She has enslaved my brother so completely he cannot perform even his most basic duties as a man, produce worthy heirs for the good of the Empire. As far as I know, Russians are superb fighters."

"The Sultan has more heirs that the Ayin prescribes," Ibrahim argued.

"Then, it is even worse than I thought. The Sultan has no further need for pleasure," Hatidge claimed ominously. "I wonder in what dire straits this would lead the Sultan's harem. I simply cannot imagine a Sultan without a harem, when even a Grand Vizier deserves an affluent one," Hatidge noted with an imperceptible smile.

"I hope this is just a temporary effect that will quickly pass away," Ibrahim replied with a long smile up to his ears. "Suleiman is still young enough. The Harem has simply to wait for a while, and everything will be as good as before, I assure you."

"Women cannot wait, and virgins are the greediest of them all. Back then I was so greedy for pleasure I said yes to an old man my father offered to me to advance his evil purposes. I never forgave him for his cruelty, but I fully deserved this punishment for my unusual lust," Hatidge remarked remotely as if she was talking to a third person.

"Yes, but your fair and just brother corrected your father's mistake in the best possible way," Ibrahim snapped back.

"No one can say in advance what's best. Maybe the next time I go to the Avret Bazaar, a slave blessed by Allah who knows how to play the oud better than you will appear at a reasonable price. Only Allah knows what the next sunrise will bring to us greedy mortals."

Ibrahim couldn't resist a smile. Hatidge's logic was impeccable. All women were immensely more practical than men and their priorities were perfectly clear and well ordered.

"Indeed only God knows what's coming at us tomorrow morning, but we are mortals and we have to be content with what we have at hand."

With these words Ibrahim reached behind her and his hands surrounded firmly his wife's thighs as if they were two angry snakes eager to squeeze the life out of their victims; however, his position was too awkward to impose his will, and Hatidge Sultan perfectly capable to easily escape from his hold with a twist of her slim waist.

"You seem to forget sometimes that I'm a Princess too proud to sow the seeds someone else has planted. After all the best way for a greedy man to forget a dream is to experience it."

****

Hatidge was a remarkable creature. Her first marriage had made her extremely keen in analyzing men. Ibrahim after their marriage had searched deeply in her past and found that her first marriage had been indeed a sad experience. She had been forced in this association and soon the results became painfully apparent. She openly refused her legal husband who sought pleasure in the arms of less demanding women. This was the kind of debauchery Sultan Selim could not accept for long. He found a good excuse and decapitated the man turning his daughter into a mourning widow with two children proofs of her lust. Unquestionably, if Selim was still alive, he would have corrected his mistake somehow. He was not infallible, but did his best not to repeat the same mistake. Indeed he had conquered him just once following piously the words of the Prophet. It was a sincere confession Ibrahim could become a dangerous habit.

Repeating mistakes was a great waste of time that led nowhere. When sexual desires were the cause for a union, the difference in age with Selim would soon become an insurmountable obstacle to their pleasure. Sooner or later, the flow of time would prove that every generation was like a row of armored plates protecting the next row like the scales of a fish. With Suleiman there was practically no age difference, and so was with Hatidge. She was wise enough to recognize that younger women exerted an insurmountable attraction on him. It was a state of mind that as he aged could only grow worst. As long as he was keeping up appearances and paid her a visit as many times as she needed him, she shouldn't ask for more.

On the other hand, his flame with Hafsa would be hard for her to accept if she ever discover it; but his excuse was valid. This affair had started before he met her. If a second or a third excuse was required, he could add that it had started as a reaction to her father's actions. This affair would have ended long ago, if it was strictly up to him; but he was not cruel to spoil an aging woman's illusions that she was still attractive enough to attract a younger man.

He was younger than Hafsa Sultan by fourteen years, but this age difference facilitated their mutual understanding. Making love was the best way for a man to show a dominating woman he was as reliable as an honest slave. Making love under the threat of death gave Hafsa also an even better sense of security his feelings were sincere. Actually, if Hatidge was a logical human being, she should be flattered for him being so loyal to her family and her breed. Only if there was a childbirth, then the situation would get too complicated to handle; but he was certain Hafsa was experienced enough to avoid any such mishap connected to him.

Come to think of it, considering that very few secrets

remained secrets for so long, Hatidge might have been informed of this affair by her consorts and had chosen to keep silent, as any word that escaped would make few dear people feel very uncomfortably. Hafsa was one more beautiful woman a descendant of Osman had neglected in favor of men, and Hatidge must have known how much this negligence would hurt the self-confidence of an attractive woman. Despite bearing Selim's children Hafsa had certain uncontestable human rights on pleasure. She had resisted the temptation for long, but when Selim died, she claimed her rights and he was unquestionably the most attractive man she could find inside the Seraglio. The fact that many other women felt the same way was simply a confirmation of this assertion.

With the female species sexual attraction was acting like an avalanche. When it started it could only keep growing as in the back of the mind of each concubine was the urge to mate in any way possible within the strict limits of the Harem. A male had simply to make a glorious start. Then, from mouth to ear his growing reputation was enough of an incentive for other women to join the ranks of the herd the man possessed. These days he had to pretend he was too busy or too choosy most of the time to avoid renewing the same problem he had to overcome the first day he had passed the gates of the Seraglio as a Sultan's slave, namely too many suggestive looks from all sorts of complacent volunteers.

****

Hatidge smiled sensing his embarrassment expressed by silence, and pressed forward. She had sensed from the beginning the attraction he felt for the Russian maiden. It was not such a difficult task. In fact, she was surprised this dubious plan was not just a cover-up to introduce her into his palace; however, the moment he mentioned the name of her mother, her original suspicions evaporated. Ibrahim was not such a simpleton to try such a trick with her, when it was so easy for her to check its validity.

If she was still a naïve virgin, she might have accepted his word; but she had faced too much deceit in her life to take any man on his word. Her father had used her for his political aims first and then her much older husband followed suit. Two out of two was enough to establish a strict rule in her mind, and she was very pleased her new young husband was an exception. Surprisingly her mother confirmed his story. She was the one who had bought the slave and the original mind who had come up with this risky idea.

When Hafsa explained the reason and asked for her opinion, she didn't beat around the bush. Her mother had every right in the world to be optimistic but she wasn't, despite the apparent attraction of the inspiring maiden. Beauty was not always the ultimate weapon for a woman to take command of a man's heart. Most men felt embarrassed faced with the overwhelming charms of a woman. It was not clear whether they were afraid they might be incapable of facing successfully the challenge, or if they would rather associate with a woman they could dominate. Married life was a struggle anyway, and occupying the battlefield in front of an overwhelmingly stronger adversary was a foolish act to say the least. Only a masochist might wish to be tortured for the rest of his life by the shameful deeds of a cheating wife.

Unquestionably there were men of this kind, but they were the notable exception. The rule was that men instinctively tried to dominate their environment anyway they could. This was the reason men were so proficient in acquiring social power and making money, and then spend it buying the best looking women they could afford in a slave bazaar, hoping that female beauty could eradicate their moral shortfalls and physical ugliness.

Ibrahim knew well how to grow in power and appreciate beauty, but he was the exception. He was handsome like a Greek God, but equally unpredictable. He had such immense self-confidence he could attack any new challenge head on without any reservation. He was a typical fortune seeker. She knew well that in this world without taking chances a man couldn't win; but he also needed luck especially when he chose his friends and his enemies. There was no way a man could make everyone his friend, because when someone won there were other people who lost. Power and money behaved this way. Now Ibrahim had grown so tall and greedy that any more power he acquired would belong to the Sultan.

The Sultan was Hatidge's brother, but she was also Selim's daughter and she valued meritocracy most of all. Suleiman was a forceful and resilient Sultan, but his heart was soft and his health weak. He gave everyone a second chance or possibly a third; nevertheless, his special weakness for Hurrem was inexplicable. It was detrimental for the empire her father had built and she considered her own.

****

"I would never consider the possibility of admitting a slave into our harem without your permission," Ibrahim calmly acknowledged as he had discerned the all-familiar Osmanli sparkle in Hatidge's eyes. "After all whatever I happen to own is yours too."

He did not consider her weakness for exquisite courtiers as a fault or a disadvantage. Enjoying beauty in every way made him also feel stronger. It meant they were not limited by the fixed notions about sins imposed by the "wise elders" incapable of tasting pleasure.

Nevertheless, for every human being the procreation period of its life was more time-restricting than its erotic drive. This was Allah's will or what Mother Nature wished for all her creatures, and it was not healthy to go against your own mother. Finding plausible excuses for all his deeds, even the most doubtful, were one of Ibrahim's better virtues Suleiman greatly appreciated and utilized it for his benefit too.

Hatidge had every right to behave like his Sultan master, but she didn't despite being a princess because it went against her feminine nature.

Hurrem was entirely different. She was a slave and

constantly tried her best to improve her position. He had to admit Hurrem's performance was almost flawless up to now. She knew perfectly well when to be submissive and how to impose firm demands.

Hurrem had realized that instinctively a man did not fear a woman he utterly possessed. In a sense she had used Ibrahim to make sure he wouldn't resist her ascent from a concubine to a Haseki. He wouldn't be surprised if she had also spoken in his favor, when he rose from Hasodabashi to Grand Vizier and later to a mighty Serasker. It was not a small thing for a mother in the Harem to have such a powerful ally by her side. Even making love to him might well be part of her plan. No man would act against the interests of his son, and when a woman mated with two men during the same day, who could say who is the true father of the child?

He had forgotten the dates, but it was quite within reason that Mehmet might be his son as much as Suleiman's. Mehmet was the oldest son of the Sultan by Hurrem and the only other eligible heir of the throne, besides Mustafa. His virtues were almost comparable with Mustafa's, but he was considerably younger. If it was up to him to make the choice, he would most certainly choose Mustafa, because he was a braver warrior, a clear advantage for the war times that lay ahead. On the other hand, Sehzade Mehmet was more sensitive and humane, a better Sultan during peacetimes. If it was possible, Mehmet should reign following the warrior Mustafa in the same way Suleiman had followed Selim the Grim. Empires should rest for a while after long struggles; at least this would be his way of thinking, if he was the Shadow of Allah the All-Mighty.

****

Hatidge's cheeks blushed indicating her husband had read her mind. Without realizing it, she yearned for the Russian maiden too. With her the desire was entirely different. She didn't wish to impregnate her, just to touch her soft, smooth blameless skin, or watch her eyes closing incapable of containing the explosion of passion. For her the Russian maiden was a toy she wanted to caress like her white Angora cat she held in her arms, whenever she felt the need to get in touch with another living being during the long hours when her new young husband sought enjoyment conquering foreign lands and enslaving pretty girls and handsome boys. As she grew up, she had gradually developed a curious taste for lemon sherbets that might have a purely sensual origin. Allah must had been a man with female tendencies, or possibly the exact reverse so He could produce offspring.

Unquestionably, Ibrahim was a fanatic cheater too; but from the moment she knew this affair was not really cheating. It was mainly politics. If he was not so ambitious, she knew she could attract and trap him into her harem. Then, she would share him with her favorite slaves, as sharing your wealth with others was the right thing for any Muslim master to do. This was the Prophet's command for all masters and His words had immense wisdom. Sharing was the best the way to prove you were in complete command of your possessions.

She was an elegant princess and she loved her body. She didn't wish to degrade it by multiple births like Hurrem the slave. Since she already had two daughters from her first marriage and a daughter to satisfy her husband's infatuations with eternity, all she needed now to feel perfectly complete was a single son. If Ibrahim wished to spread his seeds inside the wombs of all the concubines of her harem, she had no objections. As long as he came back to her, it was the best proof he acknowledged her superiority. She needed a companion not a prisoner, and he had to know where she stood in terms of "intimate arrangements" with an Osmanli Princess.

"I will never consider refusing any of my husband's gifts and offend him. I only hope he is not trying to fool me with another "Trojan Horse" like a new, sneaky Ulysses. Only fools hope for the same trick to work twice."

It was a reply that couldn't be misinterpreted. Hatidge was a cultured princess and had none of the insecurities of an ignorant slave like Hurrem. She understood Ibrahim's desires as well as he had realized hers.

"This Ulysses has conquered his Troy long ago and now all he wants now is to spend his remaining years happily in Priam's Palace," he calmly replied.

"I would be most happy, if this exquisite Russian slave can bring the smile back onto my husband's lips every time Hurrem steals it. However, he has also to be aware that any true Ottoman and Muslim must honor all the women in his harem equally, so no one complains or feel cheated."

It was a fair statement worthy of the best Ottoman traditions and Ibrahim could hope for no better offer under the present circumstances. If Suleiman had his Roxelana, he would surely best him with this Russian maiden. This issue might well become another source of complains among the Sultan's flatterers; but he didn't care much from the moment he made a gracious offer and Suleiman rejected it.

Virgins were a valuable asset, but they didn't last long in the Eternal City. Perhaps this was one of the reasons the City had been dedicated to Virgin Mary, but it could also explain why Constantinople had also claimed the dubious title of "eternal". At this moment he couldn't have been happier for being selected as the second husband of Princess Hatidge.

The games Allah played with people's choices were remarkable. If Suleiman had chosen a woman like Hatidge and he married a lusty slave like Hurrem, there would be no problem between them, and the Empire would grow undeterred. By marrying a Princess and the Sultan a slave they had violated the established tradition, and these choices were not easily digestible by the general public. It was "unfair" perhaps as much as his palace looked more imposing and luxurious than the Sultan's Seraglio.

****

The next few weeks passed quickly as it always happened every August in the Eternal City, when the bright summer days withered away one by one along with the sun's daily presence in the skies. Suddenly the first chilly northern breezes had started blowing one night, dissipating in just few days all the summer heat.

Nevertheless, no one complained as the need for a change was the dominate feeling especially among men. It had been a long and pleasant summer, and every fighting man deserved to replenish his vigor for the oncoming holy war against the infidels in Austria the oncoming year. The men had already started to feel restless, while the women blessed the Sultan and his Grand Vizier for their choice to give the troops a rest and them a chance to work overtime to please them. No one knew the true reasons for this peaceful choice, but curiosity was not an Ottoman virtue. Ottomans were a conservative breed, happier when life followed regular, familiar paths rather than novel, erratic ones.

Peacetime was such an occasion when a man was almost always certain the next sunrise would find him still standing erect on his feet. Women were even happier than men, and when the rumor that the Sultan had decided to wait in the Seraglio until Hurrem, who was expecting again, delivered her baby, the public opinion gradually turned in her favor. She was not evil after all and Allah was rewarding her for all her benevolent efforts.

The various midwives that looked closely after her had positively concluded from all the available signs the fetus was another boy. However, soon enough new signs appeared that the delivery would not be an easy one; thus, it made perfect sense for the Sultan to stay by Hurrem's side. She wouldn't be the first woman to die on delivery, and in cases like this the husband presence might make a difference. However, this was not to be. When September came, with the first rain drops that wiped clean the City's streets from every trace of summer dust, the thundering noise from every canon on the Great Walls heralded that Suleiman Khan had another son.

It was one more piece of happy news, but to everyone's sorrow happiness didn't last long enough. Soon rumors slipped through the Seraglio Gates and spread over the City's districts as quickly as a wild fire that Roxelana had brought into this world a boy with crooked back! Of course, the father's happy face didn't show it was a great drawback and named the child "Gihangir", i.e. the Conqueror of the World, but most people smiled ironically at this dubious choice, because usually invalids didn't live so long and within the first year died according to Allah's will. However, this bad omen didn't materialize and the boy lived for many years, at least as many as it enjoyed life.

****

The arrival of a new heir was always a cause for celebration in the Eternal City; however, this time there was no official holiday declared, as the birth of such an inferior son was more of a burden rather than an emotional relief. This prevailing state of silence soon gave momentum to another wave of rumors that his birth was the punishment of Allah for Hurrem's sins. However, everyone knew that sins of this nature demanded the participation of a second party which was very difficult to find, as the Imperial Harem was manned by black eunuchs and guarded by the best Janissary.

When the real world cannot provide a proper answer to a problem, then imaginative people seek answers in the imaginary world. Thus, the Satan of the Christian beliefs was blamed for this misfortune, a clear sign that Hurrem was indeed a witch. It was a rumor that hardly lasted for a week, as the Seih-ul-Islam quickly reminded everyone that all good and evil came from Allah, adding one more puzzle to the City's mysteries. However, gradually the fog of ignorance cleared as it became known the Sultan was also sick, and it was the worst possible explanation for the Shadow of Allah that had failed to appear in public for months.

Thank Allah, Mustafa was growing up, but his deportation to Manisa along with his princess mother puzzled the public opinion for a while, before it became known that this relegation was actually a promotion, giving Mustafa the chance to hone his administrating skills as a governor of the Saruhan province.

It was an appointment that quiet down people's objections to this transfer, since Manisa was customarily the city every next Sultan governed to become educated also in politics. If this was a sign Suleiman's health was deteriorating beyond repair was a controversial subject, but from the moment Ibrahim was in command of the imperial affairs and Mustafa the next Sultan, no one had any firm ground to worry about the Empire's future. It didn't really matter who was the commander of the Ottoman armies. Important was the fact that the preparations for the next war intensified as inadequate preparations were the reasons why Vienna had no fallen. The Grand Vizier has learned this crucial lesson.

****

Ibrahim was the first who visited the Sultan after the new birth was announced and he was the first to find out the hard facts. The Sultan was simply appalled by the news. It was the first time Hurrem had betrayed his hopes at the very last moment.

Surprisingly, the Grand Vizier didn't point the finger at the mother. Since their marriage, Hurrem's behavior was impeccable and he said so. Gihangir's birth had been simply a Mother Nature's mistake and no one was to blame. Seeking escape goats would only add weight to the existing problem. From the moment there were already many worthy sons to take the reins of the Empire, the problem was not real but only a product of ignorant people's imagination. The displacement of Mahidevran to Manisa could easily be disguised as the proper act to support her son in the difficult task of every youngster to become a competent state administrator.

In Ibrahim's mind this unfortunate birth was an Allah's blessing. It was a powerful stroke against Hurrem's growing influence. Unconsciously Hurrem's bosom had ceased to be the safest harbor after the storm this unfortunate delivery had created into people's hearts and minds. Overall, Mahidevran appeared as the final victor; but it wouldn't be advantageous to mention her name for the time being. What the Sultan needed above all were few words of encouragement. The future was still bright despite this temporary setback.

"I cannot claim this birth was a blessing. In fact it will be a long-lasting source of personal misery," he noted in good mood. "But one way to remove its adverse effects is to create a bigger source of misery for your enemies who are now celebrating. To restore equilibrium as the Guardian of the Universal Balance, we have to complete the preparations for the next year's expedition against Vienna the best way possible. Vienna is another virgin that needs to be violated."

It was a racy proposition that in the past would make the Sultan laugh his heart out; but this time it didn't cause even a blink. Ibrahim had to try harder to change pessimism about his future as he didn't have to erase Gihangir from the Sultan's mind, but also his pain from the recurring illness.

"You should not blame bad luck or Allah for this misfortune. Allah tries to keep the balance and up to this moment you have been most fortunate, blessed by many worthy sons. If your new son has a blemish, remember what wise, old people claim. They say such children are blessed with extraordinary luck, and no Turk should ever forget the luck of Timur the Lame who almost demolished the House of Osman. Anyway, this is not the first time that misfortune knocks on your door. In the past for every child that died a healthier was born next. Thus, don't try to carry the entire burden on your shoulders. Go and share your sorrow with Hurrem, and if she cannot bring the smile back on your lips, there are many other women who yearn for your touch. Women are the only creatures that can open the gates of Paradise for us men, and we have to use their unique privilege anytime we have the chance."

It was one more well-balanced advice, and the Sultan had no reason to neglect. He got up and embraced his friend to show his appreciation. He also felt the need to visit Hurrem before facing his mother, as he was almost certain she would put most of the blame on his favorite. The fact his friend blamed bad fortune most of all other factors was a sign he was not Hurrem's most determined enemy as she claimed. Now all he had to do was invite Hurrem to his quarters, as visiting the Harem in the Eski

Seraglio was clearly beyond his present capacity.

****

Hurrem's reply seemed logical. His condition after the birth did not allow any kind of transportation without putting her life in danger, but she promised she would come and see him the moment she had fully recovered. Perhaps, she had a good reason to deny the invitation, but it was the first time a concubine would resist his will and his inability to forcefully react upset him. Now the only person he could turn to was Hafsa, the All-Mighty Valide Sultana.

****

Surprisingly Hafsa Sultan was much more considerate that Suleiman expected. After the usual greetings, she didn't waste any time identifying the problem at least the way she saw it. It was a different but equally valid interpretation.

"My precious son, Allah always punishes the excesses. Hurrem had already given you five perfect sons and one adorable daughter. You should not have asked for more. Excessive greed sooner or later is punished. Hurrem is a woman and with every birth her health is damaged. It was just a matter of time for something like this to happen. Women are not sows or bitches to bear children by the dozen. The Ayin clearly acknowledges that one son from each woman is enough. Now it's up to you to correct your mistake and give this son all the love he deserves despite his looks. Looks after all are most important for women the same way flowers attract the bees. For men other virtues are more important. Gihangir is too young right now; but when he grows older he will show his true worth. For a World Conqueror judgment is the most important virtue of all. It is more important than even kindness, because excessive kindness may lead to disasters almost as much as excessive cruelty. A sovereign must be fair and just above all, and seek the deeper causes of every event. In the bazaars people talk about Hurrem being a witch.

Others claim this sad event was caused by Hurrem's indiscretions with the Jew doctor who examined her; but we all know this is typical Eternal City slander. I'm the Valide Sultan and I know Hurrem's conduct has been impeccable the last few years. I swear it on my life. Whenever the doctor touched her, there was always a screen between them and the Kislar Aga was present. Having always a witness present is a good practice, unless it is a matter of state security as when the Grand Vizier visits me. He is always so keen on military detail it wouldn't be safe for a eunuch to be present. They are so greedy for gold, one should be very careful disclosing any piece of knowledge that can be turned into coins by our enemies, and they are so many and so desperate these days after your brilliant victories!"

It was very difficult for him to find any faults in her logic. In fact, Hafsa's explanations were the most down to earth of everything else he heard. She was practical above all and the fact she didn't use this opportunity to blame Hurrem for the mishap as any other mother-in-law would do was a most critical detail. He was perfectly justified to trust his mother blindly. She was the only person in the world that had no reason to lie to him.

****

The drums of war do not need a real cause to start beating. Military conflicts occur every time one form of human civilization collapses and a new one appears in its place. Right then one system of forces that was in equilibrium up to that point ceases to balance out, and all the elements that kept it standing on its feet till then try to find a new position of equilibrium.

This had happened before numerous times with many empires. Many centuries ago Greeks had stopped the Persian hordes; and more recently the Roman Empire had stood as a dam, protecting Europe and the Mediterranean from the human flood that swept like a flood the Middle East. Now the East had flooded once more and its waves had reached the heart of Europe, Vienna. It was an inescapable fact that the East produced more children. For the time being this mighty torrent had stopped there, but sooner or later it was bound to try its luck once more with another wave of aggression, since no state of equilibrium had been reached yet.

For mystical reasons no one knew humans were mystified by certain numbers and three was one of them; thus, they tried to overcome an obstacle thrice. The first time they focused more on surprise and aggression. If they failed, the next time meticulous preparation was their main concern. If the failed, then the third time their main weapons would be pride and desperation. Fatih had conquered the Eternal City during the third siege out of desperation, but he came very close to failure. He had succeeded, because of the overwhelming odds favoring him. Now Ibrahim was following the steps of Fatih. He had to marshal every bit of oriental strength and resilience to break the resistance of the Austrians, if he wished to secure his flank before he made the final push towards Venice. If Venice fell, then the road to Rome and the Vatican was open. There could be no excuses for another failure, since Allah was on his side.

Ibrahim didn't care much about religion; but he had to admit God was one of the most potent images that could mobilize the masses. For him sacrificing life on Earth to secure life after death in heavens was a ludicrous proposition. Paradise was on Earth and he had struggled hard to taste it here in the middle of the Eternal City on the grounds of the ancient Hippodrome, in front of the Delphi Pillar few steps away from the house of God, Agia Sophia.

Only one piece was missing to make his dream complete. He had to recover the Saint Mark's Horses, the Triumphal Quadriga of Lysippus that the Venetian Doge, Enrico Dandolo, had stolen during the Fourth Crusade. It was one of his childhood dreams, taking back what the Venetian looters had stolen was the only way his world could find its balance.

Suleiman's scope was different. He wanted to reach the Red Apple Tree, Ancient Rome. Their dreams were different, but they were complementary and this coincidence made their bond stronger. Their relationship was not sexual any longer, it was spiritual, and if they occasionally united, it was simply to reassure their minds they still pursued the same goals that pushed them in the same direction, westwards. This was the reason why Suleiman's illness was so crucial. If Suleiman gave up striving because of pain, Ibrahim's dream would also collapse.

The element of surprise that had led to victory in Belgrade and Mohacs was now absent, and had to be replaced by meticulous preparation. If a tree was too big to fall by ax, one had to try the saw; so, every time the weather permitted, the Akinji and the Tatar irregulars started raiding the Vienna suburbs. The peasants, who failed to seek the protection of the Vienna walls, were either killed or captured. This tactic reduced not only the amount of supplies reaching Vienna and possibly the available manpower of the defenders, but also deteriorated the enemy's moral.

Soon these random raids became intolerable, and the Austrian ambassador sought to meet with the Grand Vizier and express his grave complains. For Ibrahim this was a meeting where the mutual intentions could be fathomed. In the past, before every war the Ottomans arrested the foreign ambassador of the enemy and locked him in the Yedikule prison. This was not the first time such a meeting would be held inside Ibrahim's Palace. In fact, his residence was for him the battlefield of choice rather the Divan where any sense of privacy was lost. For similar occasions he had also ordered a magnificent throne. The Divan with its oriental décor was more appropriate for formal ceremonies honoring oriental visitors as the Persians, the Indians, or the Arabs.

The Austrian ambassador was direct. He requested a peace treaty and he was willing to assume the status of a vassal state, exchanging the peace for an amount in gold that could be readily negotiated, if the Sultan agreed on the general concept.

Ibrahim took his time to respond, as he felt the ambassador had still few issues to discuss and few closed cards to uncover. He also knew the effect of total silence on the nerves of an opponent from his experiences with Selim. Finally, he stared at his opponent's eyes and with complete confidence he remarked:

"My magnificent Sultan does not act unless he has asked for my opinion. He trusts my judgement so much that, if I don't agree on a plan, the plan will never materialize."

The ambassador received this piece of information with an imperceptible smile and remarked that the Emperor of Spain was willing to show his gratitude for his support with a most precious present that would most certainly satisfy Ibrahim's exquisite taste.

Now it was Ibrahim's turn to smile full of contentment for this proposal. He got up and walked to the window inviting the ambassador to enjoy the view of the Hippodrome from Agia Sophia to the Sea of Marmara, along the Sea Walls all the way to the Yedikule Castle.

"This view is for me the greatest treasure and there is nothing in the world that could make me betray my magnificent Master. I promise I will convey fairly your proposal to his ears, and in due time invite you to the Divan to receive our reply."

Ibrahim was in no rush to reply as long as the war preparations were not completed. With every day that passed the Ottoman armies were growing stronger and its enemies more desperate to counter the raids; but most of all, any thought of peace was unacceptable at this late stage. After all the preparations it was imperative Vienna to fall. All that remained was to make sure the Ottomans secured the maximum advantage from the ambassador's visit.

****

The ambassador's mission to the Ottoman court was never an easy task. Many ambassadors had been roughly treated by the Janissaries, when the Ottoman Empire was at war with their nations. Few years back the Persian emissaries had been executed in the Yedikule castle on Selim's orders before the conflict with the Shah was resolved on the battlefields. The Ottoman's point of view was that the ambassadors were responsible for the message they carried, and they were not the only ones who felt this way in the Orient. Selim's emissaries had been also executed in Egypt by the Mameluke Sultan.

Finally, after a long period of delays the meeting was to occur in front of the Salutation Gate where the Sultan was to receive other emissaries. During the ceremony the Sultan remained silent as it was customary, while the Grand Vizier carried out his role as an intermediate. The only word expected to be heard from the Sultan's lips was the customary "peki" that meant everything was done with his approval.

The basic concept behind this stance was that the Sultan was the Shadow of Allah and Allah chose to speak to mortals very rarely. Within the walls of the Seraglio, absolute silence was the rule and this tradition had reached an extreme under Selim. He had perfected a secret language using nods called "Ixarett" to communicate with his pages and especially the Mutes.

He claimed that the Shadow of Allah should not use the same words as the beggars, the thieves, the prostitutes or the stinking tanners.

The ceremony started with the traditional address by the Aga of the White Eunuchs.

"Hail Great King of the Thirty Seven Kingdoms,
Ruler of the Lands of the Romans, the Persians and the Arabs!
World Hero, Pride of Space and Time!
Master of the Mediterranean and the Black Sea,
Of the glorious Kaaba and the enlightened Medina
That is unique through the ages;
Of Yemen and of Aden, of Saana and of Baghdad
This Tower of Merit, and of Basra and Al Hasa
And all the Cities of Nusiravan,
Of the Algeria Lands and of the Azerbaijan,
Of the Kiptsak Steppe and the Tatar Lands,
Of Kurdistan and Luristan,
And all the Lands of Rumelia and Anatolia,
Of Karamania, and of Valahia, of Moldavia and Hungary

**And many other Worthy Kingdom and Nations.
Magnificent Sultan and Padishah."**

Then the Grand Vizier came forward and welcomed all the foreign ambassadors to be received according to the daily agenda, avoiding excessive praises. The Austrian one was the last one and this was a blow to the national esteem.

"The Great Sultan, Master of the Roman Empire and Constantinople greets and acknowledges the ambassador of Austria, and wishes him to convey his delight to the King of Spain for his generous gifts."

The ambassador accompanied by two Janissaries moved forward and kneeled silently with respect in front of the Sultan according to the Ottoman ritual.

With an imperceptible movement of the Grand Vizier's eyes the Aga of the White Eunuchs motioned a page to leave in front of the ambassador few golden thread adorned kaftans as a payback for his presents to the Sultan; however, their number and worth was negligible compared to the presents other foreign emissary had received before him that day. It was a sign of displeasure and an indirect offense against the Emperor of Spain who was the overlord of the Austrians that could not be overlooked, but Ibrahim had decided to make it even plainer so everyone in the audience realized that war was eminent.

"With respect to the King of Spain's petition for establishing peace in Austria, we have decided that since he is so helpless to disperse few raiders, my Master and Lord of Constantinople and heir of the Roman Empire will visit Vienna to bring order and prosperity to its citizens."

The constant reference of the Roman Emperor Charles as a King of Spain was another insult, because Charles the Fifth was acknowledged in Western Europe as the true heir of the Roman Empire, since he had under his control not only Spain, Holland, Germany, and Austria, but also the entire Italian peninsula and the city of Rome. However, the only other head of state recognized in the Ottoman court as an Emperor were the Mogul

Emperor of India.

The Austrian ambassador was now forced to respond to this new offense.

"The true Roman Emperor is not powerless, and he could easily teach good manners to few thieves and looters who dare to steal animals under the cover of darkness. We all know that these pity outlaws from Asia are subjects of the Ottoman Empire, so their master Suleiman Khan should be the one who has the responsibility to teach them how civilized people should behave on European soil."

Now it was Ibrahim's turn to set the historic record straight according to the Ottoman point of view with a public declaration that would be transferred by the foreign emissaries present in the ceremony to every corner of the world.

"It is well known even to the ignorant barbarians that ancient Rome since the days of Constantine the Great has lost the distinction of being the capital of the Roman Empire. This privilege was transferred by the Roman Emperors to Constantinople and held there for many centuries until the day our mighty Sultan, Mehmet Fatih, with the help of Allah the All-Mighty conquered the Eternal City and secured it for the House of Osman. That momentous day the Roman Emperor Constantine lost his life, his throne, his imperial rights and all his property. Since then, these rights are held by the House of Osman and no one has dared to claim them. On the contrary, all nations of substance like Venice, Genova, or Ragusa have acknowledged this transfer of rights and paid the proper tributes to the Ottoman Sultan as vassals. The Greeks, the Serbs, the Bulgarians and all the Anatolians that used to be subjects of the Roman Empire have also accepted their sad fates and served faithfully their new masters, fighting valiantly under their command, obliterating any barbaric foreign invaders that dared to step on the lands of the old Roman Empire. It was a wise choice, because under the roof of the House of Osman they have prospered, multiplied and grew in strength so much that they are now ready to reclaim all the lands in the West that belonged to the Old Roman Empire from Spain to Vienna and from the shores of Africa to the Danube and the Rhine. It is Allah's will for Constantinople to become once again the capital of the world."

It was a bold claim and Ibrahim remained silent for a while for the ambassador and everyone present to digest the deeper meaning of this historic moment. The Austrian ambassador tried to object; but Ibrahim raised his right hand to indicate that he had not finished yet with all he wished to say.

"But my magnificent Master was most appalled by your audacious claims on civilization. You and your barbaric sovereign must always keep in mind that all the treasures adorning your palaces in the West are not the creations of your craftsmen, but cheap imitations of whatever you have stolen from the East during the despicable Crusades. I don't wish to become boring by repeating what every civilized man knows, so I will not say a word more about philosophy, algebra, theater, poetry, music, architecture and everything else you are trying now to copy. I will simply say that even Jesus the Prophet you are worshiping as Son of God has grown out of the soil and sand of the Orient."

The ambassador by now had realized the new turn of events and did his best to make sure this visit did not put his life in danger, by moderating his stance.

"We could argue for days without ever reaching an agreement on all these subtle points, but in the end only History can show to our offspring who was right and who was wrong. The problem we are facing now is much simpler to solve. The raids on Austrian soil must stop, and if the Sultan does not acknowledge his duty to put an end to the outrageous acts of his subjects and remains silent, this silence will be considered as a compliancy, creating a state of war between our people. On the other hand, if he realizes he is responsible, my glorious emperor will be very pleased and will reward this admission by covering part of the cost of this necessary rehabilitation."

"History always takes the part of the victor. My duty today is to convey the thoughts of your master to mine and wait for his final reply. However, you must also know that despite me being the Grand Vizier, Serasker, a close friend and the son-in-law of my magnificent master, He does not always choose to convey His deeper thoughts to me until the very last moment. Since He is the Shadow of Allah, He is so powerful that He can to turn a beggar into a King for the Hungarians; however, He is also as temperamental and secretive as Allah who can turn within an hour a powerful tempest into a sunny day. Thus, if he does not trust me, his right hand, to reveal all his secrets, how an enemy as your master can ever hope to be trusted more? If my Padishah has been instructed by Allah the Keeper of All Secrets to stage war, then our guns will speak much louder than my mouth in front of the gates of Vienna, and no one would be so foolish to misinterpret Allah's message. Until that moment you should pray to Allah; so He decides to offer wisdom to your master to comprehend better that gold and magnificent kaftans are of little use as protection against hard steel. This is the reason why we Ottoman give precious kaftans to all our enemies in East and West to subside their greed, but until now, no enemy of ours has managed to collect our swords from our dead warriors on a field of battle. Slave, you are now free to depart and report these thoughts of the true Roman Emperor to the King of Spain."

To be called a slave was the last the ambassador expected to hear at such an occasion and he reacted full of indignation.

"Very well! Now I will indeed depart, but as an honored ambassador, not as a slave. I consider my duty to serve the glorious Roman Emperor, and for performing this duty to the best of my abilities I receive a handsome monthly stipend, my salary, and nothing more or less than that."

Ibrahim was enraged for this subtle insinuation, but he showed nothing hiding his anger under a mask of perfect impertinence.

"Inside the palace of the King of Spain you may serve a master who is so weak not to own slaves; however, inside the Seraglio of my master we all are slaves of his Majesty, because only He, the Shadow of Allah, knows what tomorrow will bring to us. The Yedikule Tower cells are full of fools who failed to realize who their true master is the moment they crossed the Imperial Gate. In the past there were also few even greater fools who lost their heads for disrespectful acts very similar to yours. One imperceptible wink is all that it takes for your head to be severed where you stand. All you will hear would be the whisper of the wings of death; so leave in peace and thank Allah for keeping you alive this day."

This last threat was enough for the ambassador to realize that this audition with the Sultan had ended, so he kneeled and retreated with small careful steps backwards towards the next gate that led him to safety. The two tall Janissaries from Bosnia accompanying him did not have to act as respectfully as he and walked proudly erect.

The war was inevitable in the coming months. His intention was to leave from Constantinople the same night and return to Vienna, but this plan was not what the Grand Vizier had planned. His orders for him was to be followed and delayed at every city he passed along his way by the local state officials, so that by the time he arrived to Vienna the Ottoman Armies would have already taken positions in its perimeter. Thus, when the ambassador finally conveyed his report the war with Austria had practically ended and his report was of no value.

****

It was by the end of April Suleiman's second expedition against Vienna got on its tracks and this time Charles, the Fifth Holy Roman Emperor, was much better prepared. He had resolved his conflict with Francis, the First King of France, and had reached peace with the German Luther Protestants. Thus, with his entire army at hand he could send more troops for the defense of Vienna under the leadership of Ferdinand the First King of Hungary and Croatia and representative of his brother Charles in Austria and Bohemia. Nevertheless, impressed by the enemy's strength Ferdinand decided to resolve this conflict as peacefully as he could by sending more emissaries with offers of greater financial compensations for the military expenses, avoiding the unpredictable results of wholescale war.

The Sultan rejected his offer openly in front of the army by saying:

"The King of Spain wants to fight with us the Ottomans and I with the will of Allah I will accommodate him. Thus, if he is so brave, let's meet in the battlefield, and Allah will reward with victory the bravest army. However, if he hesitates the last moment to face me, he can still show his respect to our superiority by paying the appropriate tribute for a vassal to my Excellency."

Ferdinand was a wise ruler and competent army leader, so he was not foolish enough to face the Ottoman armies in a pitched battle. The Christian arrogance had led by now to many irreversible disasters and the memories of Mohacs were still too fresh. The advantage of holding defensive positions behind improve fortifications should not to be underrated; so, King Ferdinand chose to remain behind the repaired walls of Vienna to encourage its defenders for the oncoming struggle.

However, Suleiman leaving the city of Belgrade didn't follow the trail of his last visit to Vienna. He chose to clear his flank to the West that could eventually lead the Ottomans to Venice. On this path the small but heavily fortified town of Guns that once belonged to the now dissolved Hungarian Empire stood. Ibrahim had arrived there first to put it under siege.

When the Sultan arrived with the rest of the troops, the siege bombardment and the wall undermining intensified. The one after the other twelve Janissary attacks were repulsed with heavy losses. The fall of the town was just a matter of time, but time was short. This failure had also undermined the troop's moral, because this castled town was tiny compared to Vienna. If they kept on fighting to the end, the winter rains and snows would arrive, causing more damage and casualties.

Ibrahim decided it was the right time for negotiations, but the Croatian defenders, Catholic fanatics to the bone, refused to surrender despite the generous terms. It was the right time for diplomatic innovation and Ibrahim was once more successful in saving face.

The defenders in a magnificent ceremony surrendered the keys of the city, and the Sultan to honor their indefatigable courage instead of occupying the town with a small garrison as it was customary, was content accepting the Croats' permission to a small detachment of Janissaries to parade through the streets of the town. Thus, the Croats remained virtually free, simply by agreeing never to fight again against the Ottomans.

Now the path to Vienna lay open, and soon the Spahis and the Tatar riders started looting the Vienna suburbs, challenging the Austrian defenders to come out and fight; but no one dared to come out and risk a staged battle with the much more powerful Ottoman armies. They simply waited behind the walls for the help of the weather, as more German and Dutch troops approached realizing the Emperor Charles promise to his brother King Ferdinand.

Despite the detrimental effect on Christian moral that appeared for one more time inferior to the Muslim vigor, it was a wise military decision, as the Ottomans were not so foolish to start a siege and risk a flank attack by the oncoming enemy. There was simply not enough time till the winter to start bombarding the walls, or risk needlessly more casualties.

It might not sound as valiant, but it was clear that the war with the Austrians had to stop and a stable peace treaty concluded shortly. The news that arrived from the East was also worrisome. The Persians had recovered from Selim's setback and would soon claim back the lost territories. Despite the centuries that had passed the Persians considered the entire Anatolia all the way to the Aegean Sea and the Hellespont as their territory, and the Shiites residents in these lands were their allies. The war in the East was inevitable and there was no way the Ottomans could win fighting simultaneously on two fronts.

****

When the Ottoman armies arrived back to Constantinople after the long and dangerous return trip, the Sultan gave the order for long celebrations for the conclusion of another successful expedition. In fact, it had been a very expensive expedition with minimal material compensation, but the casualties were also minimal, the looting and the slaves that normally covered handsomely the expedition expenses.

Unquestionably, the fact that the enemy had not dared to face the Ottomans on a battlefield was a moral victory, and the peace treaty and the accompanying vassal tribute a second real one; but in general all these results were inferior to the expectations and the public celebrations a good way to make the people forget of this minor setback.

The city of Vienna was saved for the second time and this Christian success was celebrated by baking croissant buns for the second time, despite the obligation to pay the tribute of a vassal to the Muslim Sultan. The Ottomans enjoyed also the profits of the pillaging and the sale of slaves to consider. It was one more indication wars were still profitable, comforting the martial spirit and boosting the commerce. Nevertheless, this particular case where both combatants were victorious was a singular phenomenon, signifying a subtle change of trend. And as an imperceptible change very few were sensitive enough to sense it. For all the rest simpletons in the bazaars it was business as usual.

****

When the Sultan came back to his residence, he found Hurrem, Mihrimah and his sons, Mehmet, Selim, Bayezid, and Gihangir waiting eagerly for his return. With them his mother Hafsa Sultana was also present to congratulate him for another victory.

For any soldier who returns home from the war, there is no reward more precious than seeing his beloved ones waiting eagerly his return. He was alive and victorious and this feeling did a lot to sooth any pain or toils. Of course, it would be even better if Mustafa and Mahidevran were there to greet him too, but their absence had also reduced the tensions inside the Harem. Now Hurrem was the only concubine he needed to visit and this

218

development had simplified his life considerably. Being in constant pain was strenuous enough.

Mustafa was absent, but the news from Manisa was good. Despite his youth he was performing well in his new duties as a governor. This is what at least his tutors said according to Ibrahim's report. However, the news from the Orient was worrisome. The Persians had started raiding the countryside around Tabriz. Soon they would try to recover this city as the bulk of the Anatolian armies had been transferred to Europe, however, now it was not the right time to think of war. It was time to spend time in peace with his children and wife, and thank Allah for his safe return as any other tired warrior.

The next few days belonged to his family members. These would be the days when all the presents would be distributed in the Harem. Jewels, fabrics and home utensils were the customary presents to the women, while the children could expect a horse, few captured, ornamented weapons or toys appropriate for their age. His two older sons Mehmet and Selim were now old enough to practice horseback riding, or carry out weapon-practice, especially archery that was the most significant traditional skill a militant Ottoman Sultan had to master. The immense Seraglio gardens of Gülhane were well-stocked with wild animals like deer, pheasants and wild boars to be used as targets, making archery a very enjoyable occupation.

Till that moment he had not realized how important his children were for his happiness, because he was too young and busy with his personal desires and ambitions, but gradually, as his life settled down, he recognized the value of offspring for his happiness. It was a subtle change that emphasized the importance of the role Hurrem played in his life as being with her occupied the most hours of the day. Gradually she had become more of a companion than of a lover, and she had adapted very skillfully in this new role by taking the burden of many decisions related with the Harem and his children off his shoulders.

It was an evolution that simply followed the tradition his mother Hafsa had commenced the moment Selim died. In the past the Valide Sultan activities were limited within the Harem; but his mother had broken this tradition by assuming charitable projects beyond its limits. It was another natural development as the wealth of his family grew immensely after the most recent Ottoman conquests, as one fifth of the loot ended up in the Sultan's treasure chest. It was just fair for the Sultan's family to share its wealth with its subjects through charities.

His mother had chosen Manisa as her favorite city, where she was doing excellent work according to all the rumors that reached his ears. Building a charitable complex with a mosque, a hieratic school, a hospital, and a public kitchen for the poor, was a customary moral obligation of every benevolent Sultan who wished his name to be remembered not only for his martial ability, but also for his compassion. Hafsa had used part of her monthly allowance to finance this public interest project meant to eradicate whatever sins she had accumulated in her life.

It was an innovation no Kadin in the Harem had dared to undertake previously, but there was no way her only son might object. As a Sultan and the son of Selim, fighting was his primary duty. Ibrahim was not just the Grand Vizier but the Serasker too, so he had other more manly duties. Women were better adjusted to carry out charitable projects anyway. They were clearly much more sensitive and compassionate to other people's needs. With the first chance he got, he congratulated her, and Hafsa Sultan accepted his praises with grace.

"Your father didn't have much time to lose for benevolent projects like this. He was simply too busy fighting, but I know he meant well. If he had not died so unexpectedly, I'm sure he would have carried out much more than I can."

Suleiman nodded positively, but he was not sure Sultan Selim had anything else but conquests in his mind. He considered any beneficiary attitude as a weakness and an attempt to turn public opinion in his favor. Sick people were a nuisance and a dead weight, because they couldn't fight either the infidels or the heretics. The least weaklings a nation had the faster it would prosper. This was practically self-evident. Now his son was a weakling as his pains had never ceased during the Vienna campaign. They simply receded for a while and then reappeared. The doctors had warned him it might well last a lifetime.

Was this a punishment for a sin he had committed, he asked? The doctor simply did not know what to reply to this crucial question. They only knew that his grandfather, Mehmet Fatih, also had it, but it was not the reason he died as far as they could tell. It was a kind of disease that prevented him from walking, so staying in his quarters in the Seraglio would surely reduce the pain and discomfort. Was it possible Allah who always guided the steps of his Shadow wished him to stop fighting the infidels in His name? Was his illness his punishment for all his sins?

Ibrahim once had confided to him that a man could not find answers to all his questions. There were always more questions a man should answer in his lifetime. This was one of the reasons mortals made children. The children were the ones who should try to correct their parents mistakes and avoid making new ones; however, this was also another human illusion as more new mistakes were inevitable in an imperfect world where every law had exceptions.

****

Hurrem was undoubtedly a sensitive woman capable of sensing any change of mood in a man's heart. From the very beginning her greatest fear was that Suleiman would resemble his father. Then, her life would have been hell; but her man proved to be different in many ways.

He despised eunuchs so much he had chosen a true man as Hasodabashi. It was a critical choice that said a lot about her man, the father of her children. She also couldn't have children with a man who one day for some strange reason could start executing them. After all she was born a Christian and saw divinity in every child she made. Her children were the reason for her life. She simply had to found out if Ibrahim was a eunuch or a man, and there was only one way to test a man in the Seraglio, where men and women were so strictly segregated. Perhaps, if she had waited for few months more, she could have found out Ibrahim's preferences, but time was short. She had to have a child and a son as soon as possible. Allah might be a man, but He was also benevolent to women eager to conceive.

The moment Hafsa Sultan announced she had decided to offer her daughter to Ibrahim in marriage was the second milestone of her saga. It meant that Ibrahim was abandoning the battlefield of the Sultan's heart without a struggle. The Sultan might try to escape, but sooner or later he would come back to her bosom to enjoy the kind of satisfactions she only could provide.

When Suleiman returned from the last expedition in great pain, she knew he was in no position to claim his lost sovereignty. He needed consolation most of all, and she was the proper person to provide it; so she came to the Seraglio and never left. The Sultan needed a carrying wife not a haughty Kadin hungry for honors and his attention. Now that she was permanently residing in his quarters, she wouldn't even mind if Suleiman came late one night. She knew he was incapable of cheating her with anyone. She even tried to tease him.

"Now that we have so many sons, my feelings would not be hurt if you went out to meet your precious friend for a Galata visit once in a while. Men need to feel like men sometimes away from their wives," she hesitantly suggested.

"You are not my Kadin. You are the mother of my children," he argued.

"You are right. I'm not your wife. Your lovely legal wife is banished in Manisa, and as she said, I'm just a piece of paid meat. Sometimes I wonder why you have punished her so hard for telling the truth. This was actually the reason I had not tried to defend myself when she beat me up. I am indeed your whore, and everyone knows that. I have accepted this role with all my heart, but I sincerely doubt if my children when they grow up will accept this title without complaint. For the time being they are young and innocent, believing whatever I tell them. Only my Mihrimah is hurt, because she is a woman, and she does not like to think of herself as the daughter of a whore. I have tried to explain to her that all princesses have to accept whoever their father thinks they should marry, but she is still too young and pure to come to terms with these degrading Muslim traditions that have turned her Magnificent father into a pimp."

She didn't have to say much more, because the conclusion was inescapable. It was once more a matter of patience and sooner or later the Sultan would arrive to the proper conclusion. After all it was bad for his image to have his legal wives banished from the Seraglio, while he spent day after day in a courtesan's arms. It was not hard to imagine what kind of an example was Suleiman gave to the men and women of the Eternal City. She didn't have to make it clearer. She only had to drop the proper hint.

"Do you think that when I'll grow old too like your mother, I should build a hospital or shelter for the all women of ill repute in Galata? This district has been left to its fate by all your magnificent ancestors and it's not fair for all their services to Ottoman soldiers and sailors."

"No! This district has always been a place left for Christians to manage. Ibrahim told me it should be left to rot from sins to show to everyone the great moral difference between Islam and Christianity. Being across the bay means that Paradise and Hell should be separated, so that everyone faithful, heretic or infidel knows exactly where he stands," Suleiman replied.

"Ibrahim is a very wise man. I feel very safe he is always at your side giving you advices. I wonder, if he could replace you for a while until you fully recover. I think a little rest is all you need to become the young man that swept me from my feet the first night I saw you."

****

It was quite unexpected, but it shouldn't have been so, because it was the logical solution. If the Persians were preparing for war the next few months and the Sultan was incapacitated, then the Grand Vizier should take command for as long as this weakness lasted. Only if the Sultan's health was permanently damaged, only then the option of choosing an heir for the throne would be considered.

The Sultan was fortunate enough to be blessed by a most capable and popular heir, Sehzade Mustafa, who according to all reports with the guidance of his mother and his tutors was performing excellently in Manisa as a governor. Ibrahim was also a competent organizer and strategic planner to such an extent that only his financing skills could be questioned as he was notoriously openhanded; but still, when the Sultan himself presided one day the Divan, the exact words that came out of his mouth were unheard of:

"From now on and as long as he is alive, Ibrahim Pasha will always serve me as a Grand Vizier and Serasker and his tongue will always express my wishes; thus, his orders must be blindly obeyed as if they were coming out of my mouth."

No one dared to object to this momentous Sultan's decision, because Ibrahim had claimed time after time throughout his career:

"In my entire life it has never been important for my judgement what I desired or what would be profitable to me, but only what was beneficial to my magnificent Master."

****

When this historic decision reached the ears of the average Ottoman no eyebrows were raised, because it was considered fair to keep in your household a faithful dog or a trusty horse until the day it died, and this kind of generous attitude was extended also to slaves that had passed their prime and became a burden rather than an asset.

Ibrahim was still in his prime and had plenty to offer in both posts he possessed in the Ottoman hierarchy. Nevertheless, there were always few men who envied another man's brilliant career and would seek damaging details to degrade his status they couldn't reach. These people noticed that the Sultan's oath was not as binding as it seemed. He had promised that as long as Ibrahim lived, he would be the Grand Vizier and Serasker, and a Turk was not like a tricky Roman. The son of Selim always kept his word.

The next issue that bothered few peoples' minds was a the rhetorical question, namely if Suleiman had rewarded a slave's dedication and ability with so great offices, what a just man should do to for a courtesan who had offered him so many worthy children and looked after him from sunrise to sunset?

Only the kind heart of a just Sultan could find an answer to this question, and it did. Hurrem was the only woman who could give the proper balance to his universe. If his father had ordered him to marry two noble women when he was younger to secure the support of two powerful clans, he ought to marry Hurrem to give the proper status to their children that simply should not be called children of sold meat.

It was a just decision that found wide support. The message was clear, buying a slave gave a man absolute control over her destiny; so you could still use her as you pleased and even turn her into a prostitute for profit, as many Janissaries did. Nevertheless, from the moment this slave bore several children with your blood, you had the moral obligation towards your children to make this blessed union legitimate. It was a logic that made sense to many offenders. One child maybe the result of a momentary weakness or even a rape; but many children testified the existence of a strong emotional bond that could not easily be broken.

All things considered, the Sultan's formal marriage with Hurrem was a novelty that stirred the turbulent waters of the Golden Horn. Until that moment no Ottoman Sultan had legally married a slave. They all had followed the words of the Quran about their Kadin and chosen women of noble descent for their legal consorts. They had also restricted their offspring to one son from a single source, however, the case of this remarkable slave was in a sense unique in many respects. Hurrem may have been a slave, she may have been even a conniving witch; but from the moment she produced worthy heirs, she had earned a special status. This was what meritocracy was all about, exactly as it had happened with the infidel Ibrahim Pasha.

Few people, as it always happens, went a bit further. The Sultan was the Shadow of Allah and Allah could do as He pleased. If he so wished, he could get married not only with a slave, but also with his horse for the good of the Empire. In the old days the Turkman warlords when they died they were buried together with their horses and their wives, to make sure no one else used them and offended their pride. What really mattered for a Sultan was to be able to grow the Empire, and a wedding was clearly a good occasion for celebrations, costly preparations, free meals, and for merchants to become richer. Who could object to money flows out of rich pockets? Poor people had earned the right to object only to higher taxes.

****

The only person that dared to verse her objections to this marriage was Hafsa Sultana. She sternly noticed that the Sultan should give the proper examples of behavior to his subjects. The slaves were meant to offer pleasure to their masters and nothing more than that. Few of his children had already produced children with their own concubines. How should he react if one day a Prince Heir asked his permission to marry a slave and keep her as his sole companion for a life time as he did with Hurrem?

"The slaves are not equal to the freewomen and they have not the same rights," she concluded. "If this ever happens, the Empire will be lost."

The Sultan did not need to think much to find a reply.

"The slaves that serve their masters well should be richly rewarded. This is what my justice demands."

"Who can object to just rewards? I never said anything about giving Hurrem more and more presents or raising her salary, and Ibrahim is my witness; but by making her your Kadin, you will violate the unwritten laws of your ancestors."

"Ibrahim says that the laws of our ancestors must be

change to adjust to the new realities. This is the reason why the Divan is in session each and every week, produce new and better laws."

"If this is so, should I also marry a slave that gives me pleasure?" Hafsa inquired hesitantly and with few words raised the level of tension to extreme.

Her son's answer was almost spontaneous.

"Who is this slave?"

"There is no such slave, my dear. My question is purely hypothetical."

"You shouldn't ask me hypothetical questions and waste our precious time. I have too many real problems to discuss these days to philosophize. Soon we will be at war once more and I have trouble walking on my feet."

"Your father used to say that a Turk becomes nothing when he dismounts his horse."

"Yes, but the doctors say that his grave illness that sent him to the grave was caused by too much riding on the saddle. Even a Shadow of Allah should not try to violate certain limits."

"This is exactly what I also claim. This abominable marriage violates certain firm limits."

Hafsa Sultana had raised a crucial point that put extra pressure to the Sultan's mind. He simply had to find an answer and in similar cases in the past he had resorted to the long discussions with Ibrahim when they were younger and less busy with official duties.

"I have crossed these limits long ago, when I fell in love with Hurrem and made many children with her; but now please tell me, when love or desire is excessive? My father always told me that pleasure is Allah's reward for creating more faithful sons, fighters for His glory."

Hafsa recognized Ibrahim's logic behind these arguments. If she tried to demolish them, then her own actions would also lose their bearings and become sins and wanton acts; so she ceased complaining and kneeled with respect in front of the Shadow of Allah. Her gesture was not ironic. Without knowing it

227

her son had offered her with open hand all the excuses she needed for her actions and she was most grateful. From the moment a sin became common, it ceased to be a sin. It became civilization! From now on many Valide Sultanas would swear on her name and imitate her example, rewarding faithful slaves with her passion.

****

When she came back to the Eski Saray, Hafsa Sultan retraced all the details of her son's arguments. As a mother she had every right to complain, but she was much more than a mother. She was the reigning Valide Sultan, and she had no right to question the judgment of the Sultan. If everyone would question his right to command and set down new laws, then the Empire would crumble. On the other hand, she knew that when pleasure became the ultimate criterion and the basis of a civilization, then this civilization would decline sooner or later.

Pleasure was a necessary ingredient to put humans into motion, but it was not enough. No single ingredient was enough, and if purity and abstinence was adopted as the only way to advance, this path would also lead to a dead end. The correct answer was finding the right mixture of ingredients. Balance was the answer, not unreasonable excesses or one-track minds.

When husband Selim Khan died, her world had collapsed. Other women in her place simply lost their drive and faded away in a room in the Eski Saray; but she had become the Valide Sultan and now her only son needed support. The loss of a father like Selim was too much of a load for his son's shoulders. Selim's behavior had raised questions even for her son's choices. Having many Kadin had been a source of boredom for him rather than joy, as different men behaved differently. Thank Allah, Ibrahim was not a eunuch, he was a man and gradually he became detached and sought women as his consorts.

Then, Hurrem appeared and with her skills Suleiman found himself and having many sons offered him the confidence he needed as a Sultan. She had to be thankful to Hurrem for accomplishing this task. Having sons was the proof the Janissary Corps also demanded to trust Suleiman as the new leader in place of Selim. In a sense, Hurrem was an irreplaceable addition to the House of Osman. If other concubines were in her place, the results may be different. Children died often and for an Ottoman Sultan to bear only daughters would be unforgivable.

Come to think of it, she had done the right thing. She complained to a certain point; but when Suleiman put love and desire into the picture, she consented as any wise mother in her place should since Adam and Eve. She was a widow after all. It was only natural for her to feel desire for vigorous younger men. No mortal should try to oppose Mother Nature.

Ibrahim was the most desirable man in the Empire. He was gifted, attractive and bright, in fact he was brilliant. She had a hard time discerning whether his looks or his brains were what turned her on. She was a sophisticated Princess, so brains were important; but she was also a Tatar, an easy victim of her instincts. She was not ashamed of all her carnal urges. Life didn't stop in the steppes when Tatars left their villages to go for a raid, leaving behind women, children and slaves. Stopping life in its tracks was the greatest sin. This was Allah's secret command to all women that no Quran contained, because it was a book written down by men.

Young slaves were an irreplaceable ingredient of life for both men and women, but there were also limits to the extent of youth a widow should attempt. Ibrahim was simply too young for her. He had his own demons to harness, and they were so many he could never relax. Ambition was just one of them. Women were another, but the list was considerably longer.

She had searched extensively all the evidence, when she first found out of his existence. She had heard too many conflicting rumors to trust her ears. She simply had to find herself which were Ibrahim's daemons, but desiring such a conspicuous man was a dangerous luxury for any Valide Sultan. She simply had to limit her scope to less young, famous and flamboyant candidates. Logic dictated that they had to be Janissaries, because this corps contained the most vigorous, gifted and interesting young men. She also had to avoid becoming a spectacle. Manisa was the right town for an escape and a new start away from the strict environment of the Eski Seraglio, where a Valide Sultan had to become the example of discipline. Manisa was in Ionia, the most culturally advanced region of the Ottoman Empire.

It was a curious phenomenon, but no one in the Harem seemed to object when she announced she was about to leave and spend few months in the countryside in Manisa. These days she didn't even need an excuse as her grandson Mustafa was posted there. All cities of the Ottoman Empire from Bursa to Edirne to Manisa had benefited when members of the imperial family chose to live there. What was a burden for a metropolis was a blessing for a town.

Her lover was wise enough to explain the reason, the Empire to thrive needed balance. This was also the reason excessively large domes collapsed. The size of the dome should harmonically match the size of the temple. Agia Sophia had too big a dome for its size. The Roman Empire had also collapsed because the Christian church was draining the life of the state and the state drained the resources of the people with taxation, as the nobility had become too greedy. As a Valide Sultana she had accumulated too much gold, while many other people starved without work. Her lover was right. He was telling the truth. He was simply too austere to look for a handout. He hadn't accepted any of her presents. He simply appreciated any chance she gave him to work hard, so that both their names would live in posterity.

He had also explained to her what creation was meant to be by Allah's will. Women's role was to make children, boys and girls. Men's role was to build houses, palaces and temples, as Allah had divided the duties of mortals as fairly as He could. He had decided to follow His orders and make as many children as he could, and build as many buildings as Allah willed before he died. He had no use for gold other than pay his apprentices.

He simply needed to saturate his life with work, and gold

was too soft and precious to give life to all his dreams. He needed much more plentiful material and he had found the cheapest of them all, water, rock and mud. His name was Sinan, in other words lance, and he had been true to his name.

****

The marriage ceremony for Hurrem was another important career milestone, and she didn't mind much when she was informed that Hafsa Sultan was the only member of the Osman family who had versed openly her complains up to a point, but in the end she had accepted his son's choices as there was always a limit to what demands anyone could raise on a Sultan. It was the price she had to pay and by now she was rich and strong enough to par every obstacle her mother-in-law could raise.

Hafsa had drawn first blood anyway with her attempt to bring another slave, challenger into Suleiman's life; but in this struggle she had accumulated by now many weapons, her children. She was now strong enough to face any kind of challenge women could pause to her domination. She was so strong she didn't really care if Suleiman fell in love with another younger slave. Her children were simply her long lasting security. They were capable, and Suleiman was too fond of them to follow the example of his murderous father and execute them, while he was still alive. When he eventually died, it was simply up to her to limit their greed and aggression. The Empire had grown big enough to be divided and Europe and Asia were the most obvious two pieces.

This marriage put an end to every other concubine's hopes. Soon enough they would all become a nuisance with their constant complaining, and Hafsa Sultana would be obliged to give them away to other notable harems. Being the favorite wife of the Sultan automatically made her the true Valide Sultana inside the Harem. Every concubine suddenly became her friend as she tried to influence her judgement in her favor and earn few more presents. Soon enough even men would seek to gain her trust, as she was the one who controlled her master's heart.

As she spent most of her time in the Seraglio inside the imperial quarters, only her exit from the grounds was restricted.

Fortunately, the aging Black Eunuch was by now far away from his prime. He was rich enough not to push his luck by taking unnecessary risks accommodating the demands of lusty concubines for sinful pleasures. She had also ceased being excessively lusty after all her deliveries, as her children were too important for their mother to risk their lives. As the Sultan's favorite she was under the strictest scrutiny, according to the commands of the Valide Sultana who was treating her recently more as an opponent rather than an ally.

It was the wrong kind of attitude, as she was devoted to her son's happiness and the prosperity of the Ottoman Empire. She only had a different point of view how these two goals could be achieved. She was a victim of a raid, so she knew well enough that wars was no way to achieve prosperity in the long run. A man should not stay away from his harem for months and hope that when he came back everything would be back to normal. When the husband was away, it was natural for the wife to try to look after her house. If she did worse than him, the household would suffer. If she did better, then the husband's esteem would suffer, and then it was natural for the wife to get ideas her worth was greater than his.

She knew that path too well. When she was lonely, she had felt many times this way, and loneliness was the worst adviser. All sorts of urges filled her mind that no Kislar Aga or concubine could satisfy. Thank Allah this wanton period has passed, and now her mind could use logic to satisfy her needs rather than instincts. Now she felt so secure, she wouldn't get upset meeting Ibrahim and his princess bride. She was not a Princess and she could never be; but from the moment she was legitimate Kadin her children were legitimate Prince and Princesses, securing her status.

"Now that we are all one family, we should start inviting Ibrahim and your sister. I feel embarrassed for not being more social now that I'm not sold meat anymore."

Suleiman didn't understand what she meant exactly, but it had to be something pleasant because she smiled.

"Don't look so startled," she continued. "You simply don't know what it means to be a fertile woman of the world in a harem full of pure princesses and virgins. I'm sure your sister being a widow felt the same kind of pressure. It is practically as bad as being a Grand Vizier among Viziers. The envy you have to face daily becomes insufferable after a while. I'm sure that now we are married, Ibrahim will stop looking down on me."

"Ibrahim never looked down on you! On the contrary he was supportive many more times than not. He simply considered my interests more important than yours."

"This is essentially what I meant. Now that I and my children belong to your household as much as your blood relatives, he must take care of our interests too. His special attention to Mahidevran and Gülfem was scandalous. He did them all sorts of unusual favors, when he was Hasodabashi."

"What kind of special favors did he offered?" the Sultan asked with increased interest.

"They were your Kadin, so they were free to go out whenever pleased them. Do you know that I have never gone out of the Eski Saray Gates since I was imprisoned in the Harem? I didn't wish to trouble you with my complaints, because you had much more important issues to attend to than trying to overwrite the Harem's injustices."

****

Hafsa was very pleased to see Ibrahim, and he had a good excuse for his visit. In the Eternal City he had received a letter from her suggesting to elevate the status of Suleiman's present, the Nubian dancer, to the Harem's Kislar Aga. She noted that such a replacement of the other much more feminine Negro was needed, because Hurrem had complained he had been too talkative about all the Harem's inhabitants sins.

Hafsa spies had also reassured her that the aging Kislar Aga had been very close to Hurrem lately, relaying all sorts of intimate harem gossip. It was almost impossible for a Valide Sultan to know what was happening behind closed doors, but she knew Hurrem visited often Aga's room and locked the door behind her to make sure no one would hear their "chats".

There were many things a woman could do to please a eunuch. This much she had heard, because the rumors claimed many eunuchs often visited the infamous Galata district and spent pretty coins. However, in the case of Hurrem this rumor was simply one more case of rampant concubine imagination. She had always good excuses for every visit, especially after the Sultan's illness. She had to learn new ways to please the Sultan. Was this a hint Suleiman Khan now resembled a eunuch?

"This woman has such a nerve to talk like this about my son! Perhaps what we should do to this Nubian is to have him castrated before he assumes his new post just to be sure."

"I have already thought about such an operation, but I wonder if this is our best option. This Nubian is a remarkable specimen of a man. He is truly gifted by Allah the all-Wise," Ibrahim objected. "If you wish to give such an order, it's your privilege, but in my mind planting such a man in Hurrem's doorstep might entice her to commit an serious indiscretion."

"You are an evil man, my son-in-law. I don't wish to put the life of any of my son's Kadin into danger. This is why I have also overlooked Gülfem's numerous visits to Istanbul Hans or Mahidevran's occasional visits to caravanserais in Manisa. My sole consideration from now on is for Suleiman to choose the best son as his Heir, no matter who is the son's mother or her morality standards. My morality standards have been quite low recently too, but I believe the end justifies the means. It was my low morality and licentious behavior that pushed you to your high post; but, no one dares to say I was wrong, or if my dubious choice had detrimental effects on the Empire's future. If I were you, I would put on hold immediately any evil designs against Hurrem. It's not her who is doing wrong, but the strict Ayin rules. She is a mother that tries her best for her offspring to survive and prosper."

"If you believe so, then please give me your order for the castration in writing, and I will carry it out the moment I'm back in the City," he challenged her, but Hafsa was a Tartar who would never hesitate to castrate any man who tried to rape her with her teeth, but would never decide to castrate a man who had not harmed her.

"I resent such extreme male cruelties," Hafsa proclaimed. "We need good men like him, to keep all the black courtiers happy. Imagine, in few years how many young black slaves we will have without wasting any coins. After all, my son is so involved with Hurrem he will not care, if a frustrated concubine of his bears a darker child."

Despite her dubious claims for low morality, her level of humanity was much higher than any man's. In fact, her "low" morality was because she worshiped so faithfully a man's manhood. He simply had to offer her a good way out.

"Then, let's leave this Nubian dancer intact and test his resolve and ability to govern the frustrated harem of a sick man for as long as the Sultan is unable to perform his duties. If he ever recovers, I'm sure the Sultan will forgive any kind of sin that does not involve Hurrem. I will make sure this Nubian understands as much. Only a total fool would play dice with his life to steal the personal property of the Sultan."

"Your proposal makes sense. Let me think about it some more and I will let you know of my decision tomorrow morning."

****

He was the biggest fool of all. From the very beginning he met Hurrem he had gambled with his life, however, at the time he was not truly a man. He was the sex toy of a cruel Sultan and his son. The feeling he had to take revenge for his humiliation has critically affected all his dubious choices even in the case of Menekse. Even now if he was forced to remain for his entire life the lover of a man, he would prefer death than such a humiliation. Perhaps the way he felt right then was quite different than few years back when he was willing to suffer any kind of humiliation just to stay intact and alive; but a human being was a both spirit and flesh after all. From the moment he had his first child, surviving was not as important as when he was treated as a eunuch. What was more important was to give his children a role model they could use to build their dreams on sound foundation.

Tonight he was playing again with his life, waiting in the dark room for Mahidevran to knock on his door. She was going to claim a gorgeous slave was visiting him eager to please him following faithfully her mistress orders, but it would be a lie. He was now experienced enough to know that the same perfume on different skins smelled differently after it was mixed with a woman's sweat. Only for a few moments his nose could be fooled, not after hours of frantic love. The first time it had happened he had to admit he was fooled, but during the second visit their love was like a tempest that lasted for many hours and the scent was identical.

Mahidevran was a remarkable woman, but faced with the prospect to spend a loveless life as Hafsa had done while Selim was alive, she had buckled under pressure. The third time she knocked on his door she was so weak she didn't resist his rape attempt. If he had insisted he would have never found the will to resist him, but the presence of her courtier outside the door had tipped the balance. She had to sacrifice her ultimate pleasure for the fate of her son.

Tonight she was going to knock on his door to continue this charade for as long as she could. She had to find a compromise between her divine mission as a mother and her primal rights as a young woman. He was too mesmerized to deny her anything she wished, even the riskiest prospect of a new pregnancy. In some way she was right. Suleiman's illness had put everyone's emotions into limbo. The days passed one by one and there was no cure in sight. Time could not wait and life too. New universes had to spring out of women's wombs before their youth had withered away. This was Allah's will and Mother Nature's too.

At last he had found the truth. If a human being was an indivisible blend of spirit and flesh, then simply Allah all alone could not exist. If Allah was the one and only god, he had to be the spirit and Mother Nature the flesh. They were both divine so every child they brought into this world had to be divine too. Humans were mortals and to become eternal they had to keep making children.

He heard a knock on the door. By now he was experienced enough to know exactly what to do. He was naked and as soon the caped woman appeared at the doorstep he didn't say a word. He pulled her caftan over her head and lifted her up to his waist. She was already naked and ready to be pierced. He closed the door behind her and pinned her on the wood planks like a butterfly.

"I want a son from you even better than Mustafa," he ordered her and she said nothing to declare an objection. On the contrary she did everything she could to prove she was not a haughty Princess but an obedient slave he could use to realize his dreams.

He gave her all the passion he got, but she was still hesitant to give all of hers as if she didn't truly believe his promises. He was getting tired carrying her weight, so he led her fall on the bed, but she was not pleased and pushed him away murmuring her complaints in his ear. Was she trying to tease him? No she wasn't! As soon as her long legs were resting on his shoulders, she pulled him closer than ever before.

He didn't even think of objecting her liberties. She was a free woman and knew better than any man which was the best position to conceive a boy. She was Mother Nature and he was Allah and she adored everything on him, because he was also the creation of a woman. As he touched the stars he whispered her name for the first time in her ear as he exploded.

"Mahidevran!"

****

There was no reason now for her to keep on playing the same games. She could only fool herself; but she was brighter than that. She stayed in his room until she sensed he had nothing more to give her. She was a frustrated woman and she had enough of austerity; so she left under the twilight and promised him that she would return the next night, if Allah wished. He told her that he couldn't wait to held his fiancé in her arms once more and promised her that sooner or later she was going to be his new Kadin.

****

"Are you totally insane?" Hafsa Sultan asked him the moment he entered the reception hall of the Manisa Palace. "I've asked you to calm down Mahidevran's loneliness, not to set her heart on fire. Mahidevran Sultan is now in love with you and this can be truly dangerous. Hatidge will forgive you, but her brother will not stand for this sentimental nonsense. You are not the Sultan and you must never forget it. You are just a Grand Vizier and even a cook can easily poison you, if the Sultan so desires. The fact you are alive is the best proof you are still useful to the House of Osman. I suggest you leave at once for Constantinople, and I promise I will do my best to calm down your victim, before it is too late for both of you. Remember my words. There is nothing more dangerous than a Sultan on his deathbed."

"What is your decision about the Kislar Aga?" Ibrahim asked as calmly as possible.

"I think the best option is to follow your sneaky proposal, but before letting him loose in the Eski Saray I have to test his resolve here in Manisa. Thus, I intend to award a generous pension for that feminine son-of-a-bitch to keep his mouth shut, and keep the Nubian stallion under close observation for a while."

"Isn't he a bit dangerous for the reputation of a Valide Sultan?" Ibrahim asked startled by Hafsa's suggestion; but he was totally flabbergasted, when he heard her thunderous laughter and he had to wait for her to recover her composure.

"I have terrorized you, haven't I?" she asked him. "But this is how I felt when Mahidevran Sultan came into my room early this morning asking my opinion for her divorce. I knew you were an unstable character, but this was just a bit too much to digest.

Once I was in love with a man too, but my father brought me back to my senses. Becoming a member of the Osman family has its drawbacks. You are not free to act as it pleases you. You have certain obligations. Your beloved Hatidge is carrying another baby. It might be the son you need to feel complete. With your wife pregnant you have few new responsibilities, the same ones I have for my son and all my grandchildren. In my mind they are my first priorities now, and I'm not going to endanger them even though I wouldn't mind spending few nights with a Nubian slave between my legs. We are sensuous beings, but we all have to limit somehow our sensuality to give the proper example to our children that there certain limits no one should try to cross. As long as my husband was alive, I was a model of honesty and fidelity, but when he died I became very naughty to enjoy the rest of my life like a woman. My son is more civilized than his father and you know it, but you have to forget Mahidevran Sultan for as long as my son is alive. Can you limit your lust for women, or do you need the help of a Nubian slave?"

Hafsa Sultan was perfectly serious and Ibrahim realized that to stay alive he had to obey. He nodded yes and she showed immediately her approval for his choice.

"You are the husband of my daughter and I'm very fond of you, but my blood has priority. If you wish to enjoy my respect and your privileges, don't forget it as long as I live. Now go, fight your damned war, and serve my breed which is now your breed too. Wars are very good for men to forget their fervent passions. In fact, I feel that the more frustrated men are the better they fight; so, leave at once and don't even dare to look behind you."

****

The next war was different than anything Ibrahim had experienced and needed a different approach. In the Orient the weather was bearable most of the year. Torrential rains didn't fall, but lands were bare and an army had to carry extra provisions, like fresh water and hay. Going from place to place was another difficult task as the nations that lived in these parts were very resilient and warlike, and hated every invader that went through even if he had no evil plans. Fortunately, for them, no invader wished to occupy these unhospitable mountains, but simply go through with the minimum of losses. On the other hand in the Orient, there was need to carry heavy siege guns, because there were very few castles to besiege; thus, only the light artillery was useful for a pitched battle.

The season was not right for a campaign in Armenia, so Ibrahim could wait for his new child to be born before departing for his new, bold enterprise against Persia.

****

In Hafsa's mind Hurrem's marriage meant her son was sacrificing her motherly love for the love of a Galata dancer. She had been responsible for this choice, but this was not her initial plan. In her mind Suleiman had to have some fun to clear his mind about what purpose a concubine should play in the life of a Sultan. They were simply creatures fit to produce pleasure and children, and nothing more than that. She had accepted this role as long as Selim was alive, but only when he died she had dared to claim her rights.

In her mind her choices were justified. She was the most powerful woman in the Empire, so she should have the most attractive man as her lover. Anything else was unworthy of her status. She was wise enough to negotiate this privilege in the best possible way. To satisfy Ibrahim's greed, she had him married with her widow daughter. She could do no more, as all her others daughters were happily married, or at least so she thought. It was surely not her mistake that her son was sick and in urgent need of a woman's love to recover.

Every woman didn't have this gift. She was the first to realize this piece of truth, because she had failed to make Selim her slave to the extent Hurrem had managed with her son. Hurrem had been taught by her mistakes, and gave her son exactly what he needed, namely the illusion he was the man of her life; however, her son was not a total simpleton as many people thought. He was devious. He was certainly more devious than her or Ibrahim.

The Grand Vizier was too confident for his own good. He was also too optimistic most of the time when the events satisfied his ambitions. But Ibrahim Pasha was naïve in this respect. He should be aware that everyone in Selim's empire was under scrutiny. She always had the impression everything she did since she was married to Selim was under observation. This feeling had not stopped even the day he died. Suleiman Khan was now the Shadow of Allah and Allah was aware of every event. The fact he didn't act didn't mean he was totally oblivious of the events. He was simply to slow to act because he had to be fair. It was very difficult to be fair, because every action had a motive, but the true motives were difficult to discern the moment the act was terminated.

Common people acted more based on their emotions and emotions easily changed. To judge the true motives behind every act he needed time. Ibrahim, for instance, meant well, but he was too impulsive. If you could endure his momentary audaciousness, you would eventually forgive him the way you forgave a naughty boy who stole candies. This was how at least she felt. He had offended her authority, but in the back of his mind he simply wished to please her and felt she was too shy to ask a slave to do what Selim Khan neglected.

On the other hand, sometimes she felt her son was so emotionally insecure about Hurrem's fidelity that he was trying hard to keep her busy by making her pregnant.

This was just another foolish male thought. For a woman pregnancy was simply a brief inconvenience, while her children a long term investment. As these days Suleiman was incapacitated in the hands of his doctors, she decided that her time was also too precious to be wasted in Constantinople, so she had moved to Manisa. The excuse of her memorial project was good enough for the people, but if someone wanted another excuse, she could claim she missed her oldest grandson, Mustafa.

Since he left, Sehzade Mustafa had grown to become a

young man. He was tall and broad-shouldered. He had dark complexion and a pair of black eyes like his grandfather. It was a remarkable resemblance, but old women claimed that boys very often looked like their grandfather, in fact almost as often as looking after their mother.

In Manisa Hafsa Sultana's mosque was progressing at a fast pace. When it was finished, the workers would concentrate their efforts to the charitable complex that was more extensive but less of a challenging task. With her arrival the family bonds with Mahidevran had grown stronger. Was it simply the honesty between thieves? Hafsa Sultana shared the anger that had led to the brawl and sympathized with her, even though at the time she was very upset with this event as it disturbed the peace and order inside her Harem. Now she had to admit that in certain cases when extraordinary events happen, few people reacted in extraordinary ways.

However, Hurrem was not responsible for getting pregnant once more. It was the will of Allah who pushed her son to violate the tradition. She was fair and she accepted that under extraordinary circumstances she had also bypassed the rules of the Harem more than once. She was not fully responsible, because there were few moments when desires overwhelmed logic. Then, only if a woman was extremely lucky, she could escape the consequences not by design but by chance. Chance was the will of Allah, for everything else the mortals were responsible.

Meeting with Sinan in private was her most fervent desire, but if someone witnessed these events, it would be Allah's will. She did everything she could to be discrete during this clandestine affair by covering her face with a veil and her clothes with a cape. The caravanserai was also remote and inconspicuous, but when she returned to the palace a nosy page might get suspicious of her habit to visit the hammam twice a day. Only whores did that just before the first customer arrived and right after the last. Every other common woman spared the expenses, so for an Oriental woman, being extremely clean meant she was not faithful.

Hafsa laughed at the particular subjects people used. Common and clean had conflicting meanings, and an honest whore was the one who charged the right price for the pleasure she offered. As a Valide Sultan she would never know, if she was as honest as a whore. Younger men slept with her simply for the power they shared not the pleasure she offered. Perhaps Sinan felt grateful for getting this commission, but he was also a Janissary who had sworn to serve the House of Osman with his life. She should not be so hard with herself. Every mortal woman was trying to utilize her time on Earth as best as she could, because no one knew how close the end really was. Everything was so unpredictable that every rule had an exception.

One such rule was that women at her age didn't get easily pregnant, but this rule had exceptions too. When she found the first blood, her feminine mind assumed it was just a coincidence, and when it stopped abruptly, it meant she was possibly pregnant.

She had to make a decision, since if she took her time, her belly would grow, and then after few months it would be no harem secret. Then, it would be rather easy for anyone who knew her to point the finger to the man responsible for this outrage. Sooner or later the news would travel from Manisa to the Eternal City and then all hell would break loose.

It was permitted for aging Sultans to crave for young slaves, but mature Valide Sultans to yearn for young Janissaries was still unthinkable. If her secret leaked, then Hurrem would have a holiday as all her sins would be absolved. In fact, she would rise to a higher moral level, because as a slave she had no control of her destiny, while the Valide Sultana had fallen from the top of the Olympus to the gutter by her own free will.

There was nothing for her else to do but go to a midwife as soon as possible, as asking one of the Manisa Palace doctors to perform the operation was simply too great a risk. Allah had shown great consideration because her new pregnancy had started and could use some secrecy too. After all everything good or bad was Allah's will and no Devil existed as the Christian claimed.

****

It was chilly winter afternoon, when unexpectedly Ibrahim received an invitation to visit the Valide Sultana at the Eski Saray. He was surprised because he didn't even know she had returned from Manisa. She was seating in an armchair by the porcelain stove in the twilight of the flames. She seemed gloomy, but her face lighted up when she saw him. Nevertheless, she did not rise to greet him, as she always did since he became her son-in-law.

Her complexion looked pale and she was not wearing lipstick or any other cosmetic dye, eyeliner or make-up, as she used to hide her wrinkles. Her face was plain as if she was not the Valide Sultana but an ordinary woman. Ibrahim could not discern if she had suddenly aged, or if the lack of cosmetics had revealed her true age; but Hafsa Sultan looked old. With some effort in the dusk he noticed that her black hair had turned gray or even white at her temples; however, the most noticeable change was the color of her lips that used to be bright red like blood and now it was almost violet blue.

The dancing flames from the stove did not help much his eyesight, but it seemed as if her face had dried up. She lifted her hand for him to kiss as she used to and Ibrahim noticed how skinny it was and how weak was her grip. As she turned to face him, the shadows fell on her face hiding the wrinkles, but at the same time her shallow cheeks emphasized her high Tatar cheekbones, making their edges as sharp as a broken marble statue from the pagan era.

He could see now how tough a woman she really was, hiding behind the colorful veil of make-up and seductive lipstick that enticed her femininity. He simply could not believe his eyes and wondered how once, long ago, he was so attracted by her looks, but he was really mesmerized by her abundant overflowing femininity and expertise and his memory had not fooled him. Hafsa was still a gorgeous woman not too long ago when he met her in Manisa, and within few months she had lost every feature that made her stand out from the crowd.

"Is Your Majesty ill," he asked almost spontaneously, and she noted affirmatively, forcing him to continue this awkward interrogation. "What's wrong with you, Your Highness? Your Magnificence looks very pale," he insisted with genuine interest.

Instinctively she tried to rearrange her hair with her hands, but the gesture was left hanging as if her mind had decided it was a waste of time. From the expression on his face she had realized that whatever she did the old sparkle was gone never to return. She was a clever woman and she knew when a man was attracted and when he was impervious to her charms.

"Am I ugly?" she asked hesitantly terrified of an affirmative reply.

"No, you are just too weak and lifeless; but I trust with the proper care you will soon recuperate. It must have been a very exhausting trip. In the winter the roads become a mess. When spring comes, I will give the order to repair the pavement. The roads are the blood lines of the Empire, but with the war in the West, my priorities were different. Soon everything will be back to normal; but don't worry! The Persians will pay for the expenses, not your treasury."

He was talking utter nonsense and he knew it, but he was trying desperately to change the subject that was disheartening. Hafsa Sultana had to be encouraged, because she was evidently suffering from depression. He knew the symptoms quite well, since he had to watch his grandmother decline and die of old age back home in Parga. In her case the cause was a bad fall that broke her hip and left her incapacitated in bed. The injury was not life-threatening, but the possibility she might not walk again had demolished her spirit so much that she refused to eat and gradually faded away into oblivion.

Hafsa Sultana was much younger, but she also suffered from depression, as far as he could see. She had not fallen down, but the fatal wound was there. He simply had to find the reasons for this grave change. It was simply too abrupt to be caused by Hurrem's marriage.

"What has happened in Manisa?" he inquired hesitantly as Hafsa secretive stance was evident.

Instead of a reply the Valide Sultan tried to stand up by pushing hard the armrests with her hands, lifting her torso. It took some time for her to accomplish this task, and when she finally set her back straight it became evident that during the few months of her absence she had lost much of her weight as if some kind of mysterious illness was consuming her flesh.

Her well-proportioned body with her soft succulent flesh, its gentle hills and deep, dark valleys had turned into a flat desert full of dry riverbeds where no seeds of desire could ever sink roots and grow. Gone were also her two harmonic domes ornamenting her back reminiscent of old mosques, and her semi-domes in her neckline that underlined her gender.

The only feature that remained unaffected by this unexplainable dry spell was her gray-blue, misty eyes that stared passed him to the dark void through the window glass.

"Nothing much really; my mosque was completed and the next day I looked at the mirror and failed to recognize myself. The wear of time was simply so overwhelming no mortar or paint could hide, " she replied after a long silence and he realized that it had to be this way with all beautiful women that aged and their charms faded away; but somehow with Hafsa Sultan looked as if it was much more than that.

Since she was not revealing the truth, it would be inappropriate to ask.

"You don't seem to believe me," she insisted.

"No, I believe you! For many years, there haven't been too many lies between us," he insisted.

"That's true, and I would like to keep it this way; so, please stop asking me questions and I promise I will do the same. Our bodies used to speak more truthfully than our lips."

Without another word she sat on a sofa and the empty seat next to her was an open invitation he couldn't refuse. He sat next to her, and her hand reached and touched his that was resting on his thigh.

"If someone told me few years back that you and I would ever become such good friends, I would have told him he is the greatest liar of the Empire."

Despite her solemn looks her words were full of kindness and warmth.

"I don't know exactly how you felt back then, but I never saw you as my enemy. Under the same circumstances, my mother would have behaved the same way as you did. She would resist any invader in the heart of her son," he replied trying once more to comfort her.

"Would she also put her dignity at his disposal?" she challenged him.

"No! My mother is not an extraordinary Sultana. She is an ordinary woman," he replied diplomatically. "She was never greedy, as far as I used to know."

"And her son is a great diplomat who would always try to conquer with a soft word rather than a sharp sword."

"Am I wrong trying?"

"No, but there are always limits to what we should try to accomplish and Allah punishes everyone who tries to cross them even with for a good purpose. No man would dare to punish a woman who tried to bring a child into this world, but I fear Allah did that to me."

Ibrahim was puzzled by this unexpected line of reasoning, because he couldn't fully comprehend what she was implying; so, as he was his habit with religious issues he theorized philosophically.

"Allah's acts often may look harsh, but He knows much more than any mortal, even a magnificent Grand Vizier."

She was amused by his excuse that was an invitation to let him know more about her secrets.

"Sometimes a common man may know much more than even a Grand Vizier, because he has more time to spare and acquire knowledge. Grand Viziers have sometimes many critical issues to attend to, and their time may be limited to a single audition."

"The last time I saw You Majesty I felt that there was no other problems left to solve," he challenged her.

"Wrong! Lusty women are as greedy as lusty men are, only their greed has a different expression; instead of an infinite variety of forms they seek infinite duration," she argued.

"Infinity is a manmade illusion. Women know by instinct that we are all destined to wither away like the waves the drop of a stone in a pond has created."

"Yes, indeed, and this is why I have invited my Grand Vizier to my quarters to let him know that my circle will soon fade away too. But before I'm gone, I have to tell you a few more words and don't interrupt me, because wasting time is the greatest sin for a mortal. Selim was right. You were a blessing for the House of Osman. You were a shiny mirror that reflected all our weaknesses; but beware. Some people cannot handle the truth as well as others. They prefer to live inside the fog of ignorance. My son is one of them. He may be a magnificent man, but he will never be great. Having more children than Alexander does not make you Great. After all who is great except Allah? The rest of us mortals we are all weak and sooner or later our weaknesses will surface."

There was a subtle trace of an eminent threat in her words, so Ibrahim tried to find more of the encroaching danger even following an indirect, diplomatic approach.

"Which is your weakness, Your Highness?"

"The same like yours, my dear son-in-law," she replied with a faint smile. "I still enjoy true men almost as much as the first time Selim used me! Remember my words! You are still young and the flame of life keeps you warm; but, when you grow old you will discover that it is also blinding you, preventing you from seeing that this very same flame has consumed your flesh. In fact, the stronger the flame the sooner the end will come."

Her words sprung a chill up his spine. Instinctively he stared at the flame inside the stove behind the thick, blackened glass. It was withering away too. He got up, took a piece of wood from the pile, opened the glass door and threw it in the fire. Then, he threw one more and one more as the fire sent myriads of sparkles up the chimney. The spectacle provided him the answer to her challenging question.

"The only way I can keep my flame going is to put more wood," he claimed with a suggestive smile.

She never could resist his wits and her smile became wider.

"I guess I could invite you to spend the night with me, but I won't. All good as all bad must pass one day, and this is the hardest test a human can endure, the realization of his own mortality. In few cases this test is harder. I used to be a beautiful woman, and I know this has been a hard test for me; but now that I've past it, I cannot turn back and live in a world of illusions. Attractive women are Allah's weakness and He invites them early in His arms. This is not because of His greed. I believe he is deeply benevolent and cannot bear to see them cry, while they watch their faces become ugly on the mirror."

"Why don't we smash all mirrors then?"

"We certainly could, but the best mirrors for any woman are the eyes of young men. What should we do about those eyes? Blind those eyes that reflect no desire? No! It would not be fair for all the young women who stay behind. Old women cannot be so selfish, when they have spent the best years of their lives utilizing them to create substance for their elusive dreams. I have sinned enough stealing two precious moments of happiness from my daughter."

"Only Prophet Mohamed claims that two tries are a sin. Allah, after two made three, and then four and five, to teach us that only the greed for the infinite is a sin."

"I knew I could count on your insatiable greed for more arguments; but I like you more than you may imagine, so I cannot put you through such a torture. Dying in a lover's arms may be everyone's dream, but it is also a nightmare for the lover who stays behind. The greatest obligation of the old generation is to show to the younger ones that death is a test that can be faced with valor, when life has been so fruitful. Death is a single moment while life is so long!"

Ibrahim remained silent for few moments that seemed like eternity. Hafsa logic was essentially correct; but he owed so much to this woman he simply couldn't bear to leave and let her slip to oblivion. Perhaps he was illusionary, but he had so many unfulfilled desires it was impossible to believe that he could ever reach a state where death would be welcomed. He had a growing daughter and he was looking forward to many more happy moments. Hafsa should also look forward to many similar happy events with her grandchildren, and told her so.

"I'm not so sure my grandchildren will be a source of happiness in my life. My son has been very foolish to have so many sons. One good son, Mustafa, was enough."

"One son is never enough. What if Allah claims him one day?"

"Then, my son could pass the throne to another worthy heir. The House of Osman is not the only one blessed, and you are the best proof of this assertion."

"I am very happy being a Grand Vizier. Becoming a Sultan was never among my dream."

"Then your son will be the right one. He has the blood of Osman running in his veins."

"I don't have a son yet. I have to be patient for a while and try harder."

"Sons are not always a blessing. Sometimes being gifted can become a perilous curse."

"I would not like to risk the life of my son for any throne. I am the son of a fisherman."

"Great families may have humble beginnings. Osman started his quest as a nobody."

"I'm not Osman, and my greatest ambitions have already been fulfilled."

"Then, try your best so that my grandson Mustafa becomes the next Sultan. He deserves it. He is also kindhearted and will never harm any of his close relatives. I have taught him so."

It was a humane request that agreed with his logic too; but every human being had each own logic that focused on its survival. This was how Allah had made the world.

Her eyes turned back towards the flames that were now behind the smoked stove glass livelier than ever. He felt they had nothing more to say that would warm her heart more. He got up only to kneel next in front of her feet and kiss the edge of her caftan. And then he remembered that from an identical stance his bold strive to conquer her had started few years back. The position was identical, but the moments were different. Time followed spirals and even though similar positions were attainable something had changed in between.

Back then her hand had reached to caress his hair, while now it lay dormant. He didn't know how many other men her hands had caressed, but this was not the crucial factor that made the difference. He was different too and his arms had embraced many times her daughter. Hafsa was right. Time was the enemy of beautiful women. His hands yearned to touch other women and Hafsa could sense instinctively his growing indifference.

As he tried to raise his head, he felt her hands reaching and her lips touching his forehead. It was a human gesture full of respect and tenderness that did not contain even a trace of erotic desire. He understood perfectly the message. When Eros was gone, gone was also the urge for creation new universes.

Her lips were moist and left an imperceptible sense of warmth on his skin that accompanied him all the way to the yard; but there a sudden breath of cold air from the Bosporus swept it away. He was never superstitious, but in the darkness he felt the presence of Death. It was so strong this feeling that he hesitantly whispered:

"Who's there?" but he received no reply.

He laughed at the idea, because in the Saray death came silently. Instinctively he quickened his steps, as the tree branches played hide and seek with his imagination creating deadly threats and imaginary mute executioners behind every tree-trunk. It was not just the shadows that looked menacing the wind was creating illusions too as it swept away the falling plane leaves, or stressed the fallen branches that reached his ears like sneaking steps behind his back. Now all he prayed was to arrive safe in his palace on At Meidan and seek shelter in Hatidge's warm embrace. It was not such an unusual urge. Every time he approached Death, he felt stronger the need to make love to a woman. It had to be the way most mortals reacted to regain their lost balance, as Death felt like a powerful hand reaching from a grave to pull him in. In gloomy nights like this he felt the need to touch another human being. If it was a man or a woman, it didn't make much difference in his mind. The scenery was similar, only the actors changed roles.

****

It was not more than five minutes horse ride, but in his mind it lasted a lifetime. He had too many things to settle now that Hafsa Sultana was going to leave the stage. Hurrem was the most probable candidate to occupy her position, unless he could convince Suleiman to invite Mahidevran who was the senior Kadin. No, he was wrong. Gülfem was the senior Kadin and she should take command of the Harem. Besides her seniority and experience, Gülfem had one more advantage as Hurrem was needed in the Seraglio to comfort her husband until his illness receded. Hurrem was a newlywed too and she should not reject a privilege she had tried so hard to earn! Most women were practical after all!

****

He left his horse to the gate guards and rushed through the corridors and up the staircase to reach the second floor where Hatidge's bedroom lay. He opened the door quietly like a thief and heard her breath calm and slow indicating she was sound asleep. Only for a moment he considered to wake her up and tell her the grave news of her mother's condition. This kind of news was communicated best during the day. Then, he noticed that next to her his daughter was also sound asleep, and decided that he should retire to his bedroom.

He had just slipped under the covers when a gentle knock on his door was heard. He gave permission for the night visitor to enter and in the doorstep the Russian maiden appeared hesitantly.

"My master I'm sorry to bother you, but my mistress ordered me to wait for you in case you arrive late. Is there anything I can do for you before you sleep?"

It was a normal question for the night servant he normally employed, but this time the usual page was absent and an enchanting creature from his harem had taken his place. From the sound of her voice the familiar insecurity of an inexperience slave was apparent.

"What has your mistress ordered?" he inquired to test the limits of his wife's initiative.

"She gave me no detailed instructions. She told me that I should obey all your wishes."

Ibrahim invited her in, and she was well instructed to bolt the door behind her.

Her silken nightgown that covered her charms like Bosporus fog was the an indication she was well-trained. He sincerely doubted Hatidge would lower herself to instruct her slave in similar matters. It had to be a project Basmi was the most knowable to carry out best.

As she approached, the candlelight on the table next to his bed slipped through the pink silken threads to reveal all her treasures. It was a revelation her sense of morality instinctively had not yet accepted. She was unquestionably a slave, but from the moment she was admitted in his palace, her mistress had not imposed on her any duties she wouldn't have done in her father's house. Hatidge Sultan had left her free to choose the moment of her deflowering and the proper male.

He had never slept with a virgin, and he was uneasy too; but he needed the touch of a woman tonight to drive away his demons. The slave needed also the touch of the master to feel useful, wanted and secure. Ibrahim had to erase all the insecurities the Sultan had created with his inability to impose his will on one of his subjects.

She came even closer at arm's length as his eyes tried to discern which shadow was real and which an elusive dalliance of the candle flame. It was right then when he remembered this particular piece of fabric. It had the exact color of his wife's wedding veils and the same texture.

Was it ever possible the Princess wished to convey a message lending her wedding dress to slave? It was an intriguing possibility that made his brain gallop with long strides.

Hatidge was a very sophisticated Ottoman Princess. She loved Persian poetry and had a very complicated character that sometimes pushed her into unusual actions an common woman would never consider. She didn't have a single drop of jealousy and was genuinely happy whenever he was pleased by Basmi. She had an impeccable logic that if she was surrounded by happy people, she would be happy too. Was this the reason she wanted him to spend a night with the slave or was her message much deeper than that?

And suddenly a mystifying idea started dancing inside is his brain. Was she feeling guilty for not being a virgin during their first wedding night? Was Hatidge trying to offer him this unique kind of pleasure and payoff her debt? He had to admit that her mother had also a quite unusual way of thinking. Hafsa had used him to get revenge from her cruel, inconsiderate husband, even though she intended to offer him her daughter as a bride. Back then she had also a puzzling attitude. Was she thanking him for helping her son, or was she using him as a male prostitute?

For one issue he was absolutely certain. He simply would not spend the night trying to explain Hafsa's motivation, when she had in his arms a mesmerizing houri to do as he pleased.

The angel smiled. Perhaps his eyes were too eloquent, so he didn't have to say anything. The girl pulled the covers and sat gently on his lap. She was too shy to take off her nightgown, but instead she lifted it up and placed it over his head, removing the last obstacle in front of his eyes to enjoy her nudity and be inspired.

Ibrahim smiled with her innovative spirit that showed her shyness might be present, but it had its limits. She was a slave and a virgin, but she was much more decisive than his wife, perhaps because a slave was more familiar with the process of being looked at than a princess. On the other hand, for some reason he was reluctant to lay his hands on her perfection. As far back as he could remember, beautiful women had always terrified him. Their skin was so soft and the aroma of their sweat so superior than a man's odor. He never could get used to Hatidge's taste, while Basmi was an entirely different dish but equally delicious.

He was curious how the Russian would taste, but she had different priorities. She needed to become a woman as soon as possible. Could she be another wild Amazon eager to steal his sperm to procreate her race?

Women were so complicated they were practically a different species than men, and this slave made her wishes plain from the very beginning. She was not going to be denied this unique experience for a second time. If for him circumcision was martyrdom, for her deflowering was resurrection. An aging personality died and a new one was created in its place, and he was going to witness this miracle all through the night. He didn't wish to miss a single moment; so he focused his senses to all the signals she emitted. She had liberated him from all his fears and at the same time mesmerized him with her witchcraft.

He raised his torso and let his tongue taste her nipples, while his nostrils sucked her scent hastily like a bloodhound. Her kin tasted like milk, or milk tasted like female flesh. These two divine substances were practically inseparable in every woman.

He left his tongue free to roam wildly like a stallion on a steppe. The Russian girl started laughing her heart out. He wondered if she was making fun of him, but he soon realized that his beard tickled her. He took a deep breath and found the courage to dive into her deep-blue eyes. They were staring through him, wandering into unknown worlds her imagination had created for this momentous occasion. Perhaps he was her white knight, or a Tatar rapist; but perhaps he didn't match her ideal lover, because she closed her eyes and pressured him harder.

****

She suddenly became so voluptuous the book with the Persian miniatures should be rewritten. She was his slave, but she behaved as if he belonged to her. She needed more to peak and to get what she wanted, she studied him deeper to find what he liked more.

Her eyes were luminous like sparkling stars, and their glitter made her look in the darkness like a lurking predator. Her excited image brought back Hurrem's memories from few years back. Then, Hafsa Sultan's authority had pushed away from his mind that sinful dancer's image, and next Zarafet and Yabani attractions audaciously overpowered Valide's majesty. Eventually Hatidge Sultan appeared swapping her mother into his subconscious to change place with the ebony luminance of Basmi that was shortly eclipsed by Mahidevran's perfect radiance that eclipsed with one stroke every remnant of male or feminine attraction.

Chronos was very cruel with women. He gave them just a short window to achieve their invaluable mission inside this universe, and then took away almost every charm besides their eyes, always seeking desperately their missing other half to achieve completeness.

He was a perfect fool seeking occasionally the touch of men. It was a bad habit he should try to properly discard, as he had gradually realized there was something more permanent in this universe besides the instantaneous saturation of the senses. Women were a man's only gate to his future.

The elusive promises exchanged during lovemaking had also a temporary and mediocre effect on his pleasure. Now he had discover a new inspiration, as if a benevolent spirit had intervened and showed him the way to the maiden's heart.

"I wish I could have a daughter with your eyes," he

whispered almost to the point of desperation, and immediately she closed her eyes shut as if she was considering ways his wish could come true. And she found them. And soon he could nothing but following the beat of her heart with his body, as they both rose slowly but surely towards heavens.

****

Was he too avaricious to ask so much from a slave? He could see in her eyes he was not. Only once before he had seen hungry eyes like hers, and they belonged to a remarkable man. He remembered the occasion quite well. His palace was being built and Mimar Sinan was anxious to deliver the building on time. The architect wanted to add a marble railing in a balcony and the rough white stone had not arrived from the Island of Marmara because of a storm; so, he couldn't work and create.

His frustration had now much in common with the Russian maiden. He wanted to create also a unique masterpiece and the raw material was missing. It was something like an unwritten law of Mother Nature. Beauty always found ways to proliferate propagating in time even by sheer imitation. Ibrahim Pasha was very glad God had made him attractive too. That made the duty of a slave much easier. He would have hated himself, if she had kept her eyes closed all through the avalanche of passion. Now he only had to wait and see if Allah was so cruel to deny such a humble favor from such a gorgeous creature.

Returning abruptly to reality, he saw her eyes full of tears. He couldn't say if they were tears of sorrow or joy. He only knew that he had never before felt so content in his life, and it was the divine combination of spirit and flesh that had achieved it. Then, something deep inside told him that in his life he would never feel again as profoundly moved, as highly elated. Every moment in his life was in a sense unique and special; but there were few special moments that were worth going through an entire life and death to experience them.

Only the sleep at daybreak could finally calm down his rampaging heartbeat.

****

The mid-noon sun that slipped through the laced curtains and fell on his eyelids was the momentous event that brought him back to reality. Instinctively he looked around to locate the place where she laid. Unexpectedly the woman he found resting at the other side of the bed had black hair flowing down her back. She was Princess Hatidge!

He felt as dearly as if she was his mother who looked like a guardian angel after his happiness, and with overflowing tenderness he caressed her hair.

"I hope now that you have ravaged her so thoroughly, you'll stop dreaming of her every time you hold me in your arms," she teased him and she had guessed correctly; but it was also quite possible she had spent the night behind a mashrabiya screen, watching his explosions to fathom how strong was his passion compared to his desire for her. It would not surprise him the least, if this was the case. In a harem such comparisons among women had to be rather common, as every human being wished to predict his future.

He was not the least upset with this prospect as he would have done the same, if he was ever in the same position. In a Seraglio full of slaves eager to serve, who could blame a concubine who tried to find out how essential his existence really was for her master?

He had to admit that his wife was an amazing mixture of mentalities. One ingredient was the hard reality of the Russian steppes; the extreme economy of resources imposed by the harsh environment that obliged people to share their time inside the limited space of a tent. The next ingredient was the mystic Islamic command for every human being to leave the world more beautiful than it had found it. And finally, a third element was also present that provided the necessary peaceful environment for the creation of any form of human civilization, namely the female admission of the superiority of the male as a leader. Essentially it was a restraining contract that put limits to what was an acceptable behavior. The female would comfort the male provided he limited his violent and rapacious nature with the divine purpose of creating a new universe better than the old one. For Hatidge the widespread feeling of envy among the various female slaves was unknown. She had to utilize all the virtues her man possessed, and when she was incapacitated, she didn't mind to share him with any of her slaves. It didn't make any sense to envy the pleasure a slave offered to her husband when he came back from the war, since she was enjoying the same pleasure all the time he was gone.

Hatidge did not seem eager to disrupt his thoughts with endless chatting. She usually preferred to listen rather than talk, unless she had some profound wishes to express. It was one of the characteristics she had inherited from her father. She didn't have the strength to strike a blow with a heavy sword, but her tongue was always so sharp he didn't feel the cut but still he bled. She must have realized how much he desired the Russian and now with her silence demanded a plea for forgiveness.

He tried to open his mouth and utter excuses and words of love; but she closed his lips with hers. She must have smelled the other woman's scent on his skin and would not stop her assault unless she wiped it off with hers. Could it possible she was as licentious as he?

Her behavior was unusual and soon her lips traveled from his lips to his chess and the even lower as her tongue tasted one by one all the spots she had founded traces of another woman's presence. She simply had to compete step by step with her opponent to experience the results of this singular beastly demonstration of ownership. At least this is what he thought, but he had misjudged her to a certain extend. She was not angry the least. She was only curious.

"Now that Paris has tasted the three goddesses in a row, I'm very curious to find out to whom will he offer his apple?"

However, Ibrahim was not the son of a king. To become Grand Vizier, he had to find the right balance. Her question was more rhetorical rather than real. Nevertheless, he was still a slave and had to respond to his master's request in a satisfactory manner even if he was dead-tired. Unexpectedly, the Princess did not try to make him feel like a slave, and this was what made her so sophisticated. She had considered the entire affair simply as a challenge of her abilities to arouse as much passion as the Russian slave had done before her. For her he was as important as the heavy sword of her father Selim that when it was dull, it needed honing to fulfill its purpose.

Soon he could only breathe-in her perfume, an opium scent brought from the archipelagos to the East of India. He was in love with this scent and could spend the rest of his life immersed in its vapors. His fate was to spend the rest of his life as a slave of the House of Osman, and the sooner he got accustomed to this idea the better it would be for everyone and the Empire too. If he was ever freed from the bonds of the House of Osman, he would love to end his days as deep in the Orient as his feet could lead him, in the Islands of Spices.

The fact she had used the number three to indicate the number of goddesses he had tested meant she might be informed by Hafsa of his clandestine affair with Mahidevran Sultan, even possibly that she was considering his harem as a possible destination in case Suleiman died. The fact she was so casual about it, meant she was not offended if he had chosen Mahidevran as his second Kadin as long as she was his first. For her traditional values this was the proper solution for any Muslim when his brother died and left his harem orphan. Could Hatidge be so magnanimous?

In such a case he might also have to marry Hurrem and Gülfem too.

No she was not as magnanimous! He had simply a too greedy mind full of sinful illusions. However, filling your mind with many illusions was the way a man could hope to keep a frustrated woman somewhat content, turning a multiple orgy with numerous illusions into an all-consuming orgasm of one.

****

Without an apparent cause Hafsa Sultan slipped away one winter night, and whoever searched for a reason why a woman died in the Harem was wasting his time, a very serious sin according to the Prophet's writings. Death was a mystery much greater than birth that can only be solved if one assumed that the same way seeds can grow to become trees, so can trees turn into nourishment for many seeds.

Perhaps Hafsa Sultan had become lonely, living like a widow of her husband's glorious Sultan Selim Khan, as few men claimed. Perhaps her loneliness in the Eski Saray had become even more unbearable as her son stopped visiting her, as few old women claimed. Few younger women even claimed that Hurrem's behavior was unbearable, when she got married and became Kadin of her son Suleiman Khan. However, only Allah the All-Knower knows the complete truth, because very seldom a single reason is responsible for the death of such a remarkable woman. Anyway, women did not go to war to be struck down by a sword, and had no great power or wealth to be murdered or poisoned like men did. Perhaps, Hafsa knew the true reason of her demise, but never disclosed it because she was a proud Tatar to the very end.

Eventually, from all the rumors that circulated in the Eternal City, only one versed by an old woman of ill repute made some sense. She claimed that when a woman spends her entire life staring every morning at her face in a mirror to make sure she is attractive, there comes a day when her image has ceased to mesmerize the kind of men it used to, and creates only words of sympathy for the detrimental effects of Time. And then, she suddenly realizes that the best years of her life have already passed and every sunrise will be worse than the last.

It is exactly this feeling of pessimism that gradually turns into solemn despair as she becomes aware she has lost the ability to create a new better universe than the last and that in this cruel universe Time does not turn back and every moment is unique and unrepeatable. Right then, the cruel Mother Nature often shows a bit of tenderness and pity to one of her more prized creations, and frees her from the prolong torture of old age by sending a violent illness.   This is how Valide Sultana Hafsa Hatun died within a few days by a persistent cold that the knowledgeable doctors said it turned into pneumonia, when her will to resist diminished.

As everyone knows, Death often obeys the wishes of people who truthfully seek His comfort. In the notable case of a Sultan's mother neither the Jewish doctor, not his miraculous medicine had any effect, no matter how hard he tried to save her life.

During the days of her illness, and only when her only son come to see her, her lips opened to a faint smile; but it soon faded away as sometimes even a powerful Sultan cannot force a smile for long. She simply had too much to say and so little time to do it. She tried hard to offer him few words of wisdom and he stayed at her side cooling her forehead with a wet cloth until her mind lost control of her flesh and her flesh lost the ability to restrain the spirit it. Right then with her last breath that sounded like a sigh of relief her indefatigable spirit slipped away to roam in other spaces, even wider than the Siberian steppes.

These final moments by her side were the least a son could do for a mother who had stayed by his side countless nights, when he was young and sick, or when she was worried about the future of the Empire he had inherited. However, whatever a child does for its creator is never enough to repay for its mother's care, because its care lasts for as long she is alive, while her love lasts until her final breath.

****

Hafsa's death was an unexpected blow for Suleiman Khan, and only when he stared at her coffin disappearing underground realized the gravity of her loss. Until that moment he always trusted she would be by his side, giving him advices and encouraging him whenever a family obstacle appeared insurmountable. She was for him a voice he could trust, and no matter what he believed at that moment, her advice was always coming from the bottom of her heart without a trace of malice. Right then he realized that till the very end Hafsa Hatun was ready to sacrifice everything to make sure he would be happy for ever and ever. No matter how hard he tried to remember an occasion she had denied to listen to his problems or give him an advice, he couldn't pinpoint one through his entire life.

The Last Prophet was right when he wrote down that the true paradise was not up in heavens but under a mother's sole. He had never felt as secure as when he was inside her arms. But now she was dead and whatever he did she would never return to caress him, and what was left of her were few elegant clothes she wore, some pieces of furniture she has touched, and few letters she wrote to him that now didn't have the courage to reread them.

Losing both his parents, he now felt immensely lonely, as his old obsession with Death came back even stronger than ever. Even the death of his children had not affected him as much as Hafsa's, because back then he felt capable of making another child stronger and healthier than the last. However, his mother's death was something different. It was unique and unrepeatable. It reminded him that everything had a beginning and an end, and his mother was his umbilical cord with life. Now that she was gone forever, it was his turn to wait for Death's visit, as he was the next ring of the chain that connected the past with the future of the Osman's House.

Her son the Sultan was not the only person who wept for Hafsa Sultana. Her daughter, Hatidge and her husband Ibrahim Pasha owed their happiness to her too. She was one of those people that went through their lives as a fertilizer for their happiness to grow and bloom.

Hurrem, seeing the effect his mother's death had on Suleiman, she rose to the occasion, taking command of his life until he was able to take an adequate hold of his sorrow and depression. Now she was the only woman capable of simplifying his life by taking several responsibilities off his shoulders almost as many as his friend did.

It was a welcomed offer because he was also physically weak, recovering from his illness that kept him in his quarters for many months in a row. He couldn't yet freely travel, but at least he could leave his room and walk to his balcony to watch the ships coming in and out of the Golden Horn or the seagulls flying from Europe to Asia in search of nourishment. It was a most hopeful development that gave him the courage to get over the tragic loss, and the optimism it created was enough to prevent him from searching deeper into the causes of her death.

Hurrem had dismissed at once this idea of a conspiracy, as Hafsa's demise was the will of Allah and no one had the right to question His decisions. No one, not even the Grand Vizier Pargali Ibrahim Pasha, could say whether there was anyone else responsible for her death. The only indication that some kind of secret was present was her refusal to discuss the reasons for the rapid health deterioration, as soon as she came back from Manisa. But in the Eternal City similar deaths from pneumonia were numerous as the air was damp and high fevers often led to serious consequences for young and aged alike.

****

Hafsa's death was a much more powerful stroke than his father's because they had spent together almost his entire life; so the entire world should feel how much it had cost him. It was certainly not enough for his grief to spend three days and three nights at her deathbed, and it was a meaningless gesture to hang black veils all over the City. He had to build something in stone to make sure people would never forget her existence. It had to be costly and impressive, but he didn't care much about money. The money contained in the treasury represented the sacrifices people had done for his family, and as the Quran prescribed every rich man should share part of his wealth with people that had helped him to become rich.

For the common people who considered as a healthy habit to walk in a cemetery and waste their time searching for other people's final wisdoms, a marble slab with names and few dates chiseled upon it, and possibly few kind words was enough. But, for a magnificent Sultan the imperial pain could only be measured by the size of a mosque, a religious school, a hospital, a hammam, and the income of the stores built around it that all together comprised a "vakouf". In this way not only the customers would bless Hafsa Sultana's name, but also the young kids that followed this religious classes in the school.

These were Suleiman's thoughts, as he left the cemetery; but soon the events would prove that without a doubt Allah did not like to see children honoring their dead parents by pilling rocks, but by listening to the wise advises the older generation give for as long they are alive. This was the living proof that vanity can move rocks, while faith can move mountains.

For many historians of the Ottoman Empire Hafsa's death was the date where the fall started, and as it usually happens with all falls a small slip is enough of a cause to spread death and destruction to many worthy but unlucky fellows who happened to be born during such a crucial and violent period. In the cruel universe we live in, sometimes one death is enough to start an avalanche of destruction that can injure deeply the lives of an entire generation.

Chapter 14

In Baghdad

'And for him who kills willfully a faithful of Allah, the punishment is hell'

(Quran, Sura IV, 93)

The Sultan's mourning period was interrupted by the ugly

news that arrived from the Persian boarders. The son of the Shah Tahmasp of the Safavid Dynasty taking advantage of the Ottomans' conflict with Charles, the Emperor of Rome had invaded Armenia, occupying the city of Erzurum. It was the first step towards invading Anatolia from the East. Now the major threat was the occupation of Kurdistan that would practically isolate Syria and the rest of the Middle East from the Ottoman Empire. The strategic passages of the Taurus mountain range had to be protected at all costs. Faced with this imminent danger Pargali Ibrahim Pasha, conveyed the Divan in Suleiman's place to formally decide the long awaited war against the Persian Empire.

The Divan was never in friendly terms with Ibrahim, because it contained many members with religious affiliations that were hostile to the Grand Vizier since the incident of the three bronze pagan statues displayed as military trophies at At Meidan. As long as the Sultan remained neutral in this conflict, the religious fanatics did not have the nerve to oppose openly any of his proposals.

Among the members of the Divan the most important position immediately below the Grand Vizier was the Seih-ul-Islam, the Great Mufti of Constantinople. Then, the remaining posts were occupied by the four Viziers, the Beylerbeys of Anatolia and Rumelia, the Kapudan Pasha, the Aga of the Janissaries and the Aga of the Spahis, followed by representatives of the judges and few Pashas with important military commissions.

The news from the eastern borders had already unofficially leaked, but everyone was waiting for the Grand Vizier's announcement and proposals. The existing tensions were so great that as soon as Ibrahim finished his assessment for the existing situation, one of the four Viziers, namely the Defterdar Iskander Chelebi in charge of the Imperial Treasury, asked for the permission to speak. Despite his name "Iskander" he was a descendant of noble Turkish family. He was also extremely rich having many thousands of slaves in his household, even more numerous than Ibrahim Pasha, despite his inferior position in the

Ottoman hierarchy; however, he had occupied this post by Suleiman's order, and Ibrahim was unwilling to openly oppose him especially during such a severe military crisis.

"The news from the East are worse than anyone expected, and they come at a very crucial time, immediately after our retreat from Vienna. Sultan Selim must be very disappointed in his grave because he spent many years fighting in the East to secure Armenia so Syria. Palestine and Egypt could be secured. The Taurus passages are essential for the spice trade. If he was alive and his Grand Vizier had failed to keep these lands secure, his head would fall."

It was a bold threat Ibrahim could not leave unanswered. The possibility of his execution was a step a bit too far. In his mind the loss of Erzurum was a serious event, but by no means irreversible. The safe retreat from Vienna was also a strategic success as no piece of the Empire was lost. On the contrary, the city of Budapest re-occupied by the Austrians the previous winter, had been recovered and the neutralization of Guns had further increased its security.

"The loss of Erzurum in the East was not my mistake, because at the time we were all fighting in the West under the leadership of our glorious Sultan, so the responsibility for any error we supposedly made must be shared by all of us. Only Allah can be at two different place at the same time, as our all-wise Seih-ul-Islam can testify. Therefore, my only option as a Grand Vizier is now to make peace with the Christians in the West, so I can expel the heretics in the East. This is a necessary step our glorious Sultan Selim Khan, if he was alive, would have surely concurred wholeheartedly. Only fools risk to fight at two fronts. Nevertheless, as our most distinguished Vizier has correctly pointed out, it is surely much safer to be the Grand Vizier and Damat of our magnificent Sultan Suleiman Khan than Selim Khan, because he is more eager to be fair than victorious, and prefers to give a second chance to anyone who errs with good intentions. He is wise enough to know that unintentional errors maybe caused by Allah himself to test a man's ability to recover and persevere.

Our wise Padisah has not withdrawn any of my privileges which means he still trusts me completely more than anyone else in this room. He has also honored me with his friendship and made me a member of his family. This is something I value more than any other honor, privilege or material reward for my services."

Ibrahim considered that he had answered convincingly Iskandar's criticism, but he was mistaken as Seih-ul-Islam decided this was a good opportunity for him to express his allegiance with the Defterdar. As always, he chose to start his speech with a general moral advice.

"Slaves should always behave humbly and restrained. They should limit their ambitions rather than overestimate their importance, as Allah chastises severely everyone who violates the limits set by the Ayin. Until this morning no Sultan has made a slave his closest friend. He simply rewards handsomely every slave who serves his wishes; but if an obnoxious slave dares to think he is equal to the Sultan, **then even a cook can dispose of a Grand Vizier**."

Ibrahim didn't have to listen to anything more to realize that these attacks against him was part of a conspiracy against him. Hafsa Sultan has used the same words and this was an unusual coincidence. At the moment, he could not estimate how many members of the Divan were against him; so, he decided to moderate his stance so that more members would feel free to express their opinion exposing their affiliations.

"I would like to assure our distinguished Seih-Ul-Islam that I have never forgotten from how low status I have risen so high, and that I owe my entire career to the trust of Selim and Suleiman Khan. Everyone in this room should remember that I have begged my Master to cease offering more and more higher offices, because I knew that there are always few evil people who will try to slander me and diminish every deed I have accomplished. It is exactly for this reason that most recently my Master has declared in this very hall that everyone should consider every word I say as if it was coming from his mouth. However, no matter what a wise Sultan say, there will always be few foolish people who envy the good fortune of every successful statesman or soldier and try to diminish his accomplishments, without considering the effort and the sacrifices he made to achieve his high position."

Seih-ul-Islam decided this was a good opportunity to chastise Ibrahim's intimate relationship with the Sultan.

"I know a lot about the sacrifices the Grand Vizier made to tighten his friendship with the House of Osman. I am also aware from the last Vienna expedition that he was the only man who had the right to enter the Sultan's tent any time it pleased him. It is the kind of liberties that is criticized daily in every tavern. I only wish the Grand Vizier would stop boosting for this privilege, because all he achieves is to undermine the Sultan's prestige among the troops."

Ibrahim Pasha had to face in the past similar nasty comments and by then his patience was exhausted.

"I have never boosted for any my numerous successes. I simply mentioned them to all those who doubt my authority. The fact I am a slave of the Gate means that I can take orders only from the Sultan, and every right I have springs from his confidence in my abilities. I may be the Grand Vizier and I have never ceased to obey his wishes as everyone else has done among you; but if one of you is so foolish to disobey our Master, I would like to meet him. When we go to war, a Serasker can find many worthy missions for such a brave, but foolhardy man."

With just a few words Ibrahim had achieved total silence, because everyone knew that even in the era of Bayezid the Saint, any kind of disobedience against a Sultanic order was punishable by death without a trial.

"Does the all-knowing Seih-ul-Islam believes that a Grand Vizier of the Empire should ask for his permission every times something unexpected happens that must be reported to our Master? I hope this Divan is sophisticated enough to appreciate that governing an empire that extends from the Danube to the Nile and from the Ionian Sea to the Euphrates is a much more difficult task than managing a charitable 'kuliye'. Nevertheless, if a member has any objection on the way I communicate with my

Master, he can always express his objections directly to him who has awarded me this special privilege."

"Rest assured that I will do exactly that, as every faithful's behavior must comply to the divine laws of Allah. I must warn you that these laws are especially severe for Christian infidels who may have changed their faith, but still have Christian habits, because sinful people should not be allowed to become models of behavior for our youth," the Seih-Ul-Islam snapped back.

"Everyone knows that I used to be a Christian believer, but one day I saw that Allah is Great like many other Janissaries who now fight for His glory. Thus, as long as more and more young men change faith and become Muslims, Seih-Ul-Islam should be content that younger people know which good examples they should follow. They surely know that the greatest sin of all is when the enemy is at the gates, foolish old people start quarreling about trifles, and so do I. The reason of my invitation today was for us to discuss what we should do to repel the invasion of the heretics. On this issue my proposal is clear. We must not waste a moment more in pity disputes about the past. Instead I must leave as soon as possible for the East with every available Janissary troops, and as I move along more Janissaries and Spahis can come and joint me. The enemy has many spies and when he finds out the Ottoman Army is coming, he will not dare to move south from Armenia to capture the Cilician Gates, but rather stay put and protect the lands he has just stolen from us."

Ibrahim's plan made sense, but the Mufti was not willing to accept it yet.

"The Ottoman Armies must have the Shadow of Allah as a leader, not an infidel Grand Vizier, because then the soldier's moral would be dangerously low."

It had now become clearer that the Mufti of Constantinople and the Empire was afraid that in case Ibrahim was victorious, he would become even more powerful.

"This is not just a religious war between Islam and the heretics. The Cilician Gates do not only lead to Mecca Medina, but also to the grain of Egypt that feeds many faithful in the City, so it is very important that we win any way we can. If there is a shortage of grain, then the mob may revolt, so the Sultan will be more useful here than me to keep the internal peace," Ibrahim declared, but the Grand Mufti of Constantinople was still no convinced.

"No! The presence of a fighting Sultan is more important on the battlefield than in our capital. A Grand Vizier can never hope to replace a Sultan. How can a zero replace the infinite?"

It was a dubious religious argument meant to impress an ignorant audience, but Ibrahim was ready to demolish it without second thought.

"I certainly don't know this kind of mathematics well, because I'm just a slave. All I know is what the Quran says: 'Allah has built the universe from nothing'. Thus, Allah can make a Grand Vizier from just a slave."

After this rebuttal, it was the right time for Iskander to express his objections and change this spiritual subject to something more tangible, money.

"Extreme wealth makes few people feel superior to everyone else, but this is a dangerous illusion for any slave. His fortune is not his, but rightfully belongs to his master."

Ibrahim took his time responding to this new attack. Its intensity showed there was some new source of power behind it. It could well be Hurrem who held the strings in the Seraglio taking advantage of Suleiman's current illness and Hafsa's recent demise. Preparing an army for war was an expensive undertaking and most of Selim's viziers that had been executed was because of financial irregularities.

"In this case I suggest the experienced in financing and Defterdar Iskander Pasha comes along to make sure no financial resource is spent vainly," Ibrahim proposed.

It was a proposition well-received by every other member of the Divan that had remained silent till then, avoiding to be implicated in the dispute. It was a welcomed sign that encouraged the Ibrahim to advance one step further.

"I also suggest that Seih-ul-Islam should join us too, since we will be fighting the infidels, and his presence will be most beneficial to the troops moral. And I now promise I will consider most carefully all his proposals anytime he decides to visit my tent, even during late hours."

It was an pointed addition to a logical proposal that became the object to a widespread discussion among the members of the Divan for a great variety of reasons. It sounded serious enough but there was also a generous amount of irony very few missed, because this Great Mufti was a known pedophile. Thus, the Seih-Ul-Islam was among those who took it seriously.

"The Grand Vizier's proposal has certain merits. The Sultan could eventually join the army the moment it becomes clear the King of Rome or the Venetians are not planning to attack us from the rear. He could also lead the troops collected from the West to Armenia the moment his health has fully recovered. Iskander Pasha should be responsible for every expenditure to lessen Serasker's logistical burden, so he can concentrate his attention only to the progress of the war. However, when our glorious Sultan departs, the Eternal City will be completely undefended. In the old days of the Romans many times, when the Emperor was gone for a military campaign, he left the care of the City to the Christian Patriarch. If this was a successful strategy then, we should follow it now too," Iskander Pasha argued.

"No! Our magnificent Sultan has a worthy son, Sehzade Mustafa, who will gain a lot of experience from a critical post like this commanding the metropolis of the Ottoman Empire," Ibrahim snapped back. "It is an occasion we shouldn't waste and I'm sure the Janissary Aga will agree with me on this issue. On the other hand, religious belief is most useful at the battlefield to fortify the troops not far away behind the front; so, there in Armenia and in Persia will be Seih-Ul-Islam's contribution most valuable. I am sure he is most willing to volunteer his services for the glory of Allah."

It was a powerful stroke that hit its target with vengeance, as the Janissary Aga second Ibrahim's motion. After the Grand Vizier he was the most important member of the Divan in charge of the most valuable unit of the Ottoman army and the state security forces.

Another ally who rushed to support this motion was Hayrettin Barbarossa, the Kapudan Pasha, who was also of Greek origin from the Island of Lesbos. He added that the Ottoman fleet was by now in control of the Aegean Sea, safeguarding the Eternal City from any possible Venetian raid and ready to carry any troops and supplies from Europe to Asia.

After this fortuitous development aligning the armed forces to Ibrahim's side, the two conspirators had nothing more to say. It was the right time for Ibrahim to say the final word with an explicit patriotic note.

"I am very happy we finally all agreed in a winning strategy. It means there is no division of wills, and we are all eager to carry out the great task in front of us to the best of our abilities. When all the Ottomans are united in an aim, there is no enemy in the world that can defeat us."

****

Sultan Suleiman had not a missed a word from this important conference. He was not well enough to attend it in person, but was seated invisible behind the screen in a secret room Mehmet Fatih had built long time ago, when he decided that his presence in the democratic Divan was detrimental to his image as an absolute ruler.

In past time during such a Divan meeting, a commoner, trying to support his petition did not recognized among so many imposing and well-dressed officials who the Sultan was, asked Fatih to show him who the Sultan was in order to address him accordingly. The Sultan was so greatly offended he was inconspicuous among his officials that he never attended again such a conference, but instead had this metal screen built so that he could follow the discussion if he had to, but still be able to terrorize the members with his invisible presence.

Suleiman was now in a similar mood. He did not wish to show how weak he was, but at the same time he had to appreciate how well Ibrahim handled the situation. The final decision the Divan had eventually reached was a useful compromise between the opposing trends.

Ibrahim Pasha in the past had cooperated well with Iskander Pasha, when he organized Egypt, and the financial results were astounding. This experience made this conflict between the two men even more curious. Religious controversies often had their origin into financial claims, but Iskander Pasha was immensely rich, so money was not the object of this unexpected dispute. If he was present, many bitter words would not have been spoken. Sultan Selim had taught him that clashes occurred when there was no superior force present to quench them.

It was now imperative to try to get healthy and make his presence felt.

****

Suleiman's first Persian War was not conducted as a powerful Ottoman invasion in Persian territories similar to Selim Khan's conquests. It couldn't be so because the Ottoman Army this time was not in full strength. Ibrahim had adopted a more cautious approach, because after the first catastrophic defeat at Chaldiran, the Persian military strategy had changed. They were not willing to face the Janissaries and the Ottoman artillery in an open field battle. Shah Tahmasp preferred to stage an attrition war, adopting guerilla tactics in a mountainous terrain and defending from few strongly fortified positions.

An entire year passed without a major battle and slow advances that tested the Ottoman resolve. When finally the Ottoman army reached the borders of Armenia, there was a lively argument between Ibrahim and Iskander Pasha. Ibrahim suggested they should move to the South and threaten Syria and Baghdad, obliging the Persians to accept an open battle in Mesopotamia. However, Iskander proposed to attack the Persian capital Tabriz forcing directly the Persians into battle. This attempt required following difficult mountain trails where Persian forces could ambush the Ottoman units. The local Armenian population also did not trust the Ottomans because of Selim's atrocities and had sided with the Persians.

At last after an exhausting journey the Ottoman army arrived in front of the walls of the fortified Armenian city of Van. The city was built on a narrow peninsula on the shores of the lake Van with strong fortifications protecting the city from the land.

Ibrahim decided to use the modest Rhodes recipe, a combination of threats and promises. With the help of Mimar Sinan he constructed a number of barges armed with cannons, and destroyed the city walls on the lake side. Then, he landed several Janissary units and placed them in front of the dilapidated fortifications ready to attack, but instead of using these ferocious soldiers, he sent emissaries with peaceful proposals. For the benefit of all and to save lives, he gave the Armenian defenders his word of honor that if they surrendered, not a drop of blood would be shed.

The Armenians who in the past had felt on their necks the heavy sword of Selim, surprisingly trusted the words of a Greek who had a reputation for non-violence. They could also see how strong the enemy was and how desperate and fruitless any thought of resistance would be. Ibrahim's wording was also moderate and convincing.

"I haven't come all this way to steal your lands. I have much more fertile plains than your precipitous mountains. I am also not striving to change your beliefs, because I know that God is one. He speaks in many languages and has many names. Only if a man feels like I did that to prosper he has to change his faith, only then I will support his conversion. All I want from you is to become our allies, and stop aligning your interests with our mortal enemies. If you agree, my army of engineers will stay here to protect you, and to help you build better houses, wider roads, stronger bridges, or repair your beautiful temples ."

His friendly attitude convinced enough people to take command of the city defenses and open the gates. When the Ottoman army entered Van there was absolute order and no violent acts and looting were committed. Soon the news traveled to the entire Armenia and many cities followed the example of Van, sparing a lot of lives and cities from utter destruction. It was a great strategic victory obtained at minimum cost over a powerful Christian adversary who in the past had stopped Tamerlane.

After the city of Van, Ibrahim set his sights on Tabriz, but before leaving Van, he instructed Sinan to build a mosque and a kuliye, as acts sounded louder than words. His wish was to turn this troubled region into a faithful ally of the Ottoman state and he accomplished it.

"We must not let the Armenians ever forget that a Greek conquered their land and another Greek beautified it."

****

Tabriz was the summer capital of the Shah and the most beautiful city of Persia. It was so remotely located it didn't need walls to protect it. This was the reason it didn't suffer in any previous occupation. Every powerful army that happened to reach it could conquer it without fight. In principle, if a city's behavior was as submissive as a woman, Tabriz behaved like a whore. The women of Tabriz had behaved like whores too in the past, as the previous time an Ottoman had conquer it, Selim Khan, he had great difficulties convincing the soldiers to abandon it and return to Constantinople.

For Ibrahim wide open cities were worthwhile trophies and Tabriz was built on high elevation and during the summer the climate was cool and pleasant, a good place for the army to rest. Only during the winter it was freezing cold and uninviting. For Selim Khan the most valuable commodities he had earned from Tabriz were the Persian artisans who transferred the art of manufacturing glazed tiles and beautiful pottery to Iznik.

Ibrahim was the last Ottoman who would try to plunder such a marvelous buildings or destroy the beautiful gardens that surrounded them. Tabriz had surrender peacefully with no enemy troops in sight, so he placed few Janissary units inside the city for protection and prohibited the entrance to any other unruly soldiers that might behave like looters. The rest of the army camped outside the city at a safe distance and only higher members of his staff were allowed to reside inside the Shah's palaces.

Living at such magnificent surrounding Ibrahim realized that what was imposing and beautifully made in Constantinople was the work of Roman, Armenian, Persian or Middle Eastern artists decedents of great civilizations, not of Tatar or Turkoman nomad tribes residing in tents. This was the second time after Cairo and Egyt that he felt the attraction of the sophisticated East. It was the same feeling that had pulled Alexander the Great all the way to India.

When he was back in the Seraglio he would try to convince Suleiman to build something as luxurious and majestic as the Shah's palaces, surrounded by artificial lakes and magnificent fountains. With Suleiman's character convincing him would be an easy task. He had to build a magnificent building to house the Divan and then commission Sinan to supply Constantinople with affluent water from the Belgrade forest.

****

Iskander Pasha seeing Ibrahim's military success got jealous and decided to follow his example. He asked for the command of a strong unit of Janissaries and Spahis with the purpose of invading the neighbor land of the Azeri. However, the Azeri tribes were more warlike than the Persians. They lived at the edges of the Caucuses' slopes. The Persians had invaded their lands, but failed to occupy because they were strongly fortified. Thus, Iskander Pasha's attempt to conquer this inhospitable land ended in disaster, when his troops fell victims of an ambush with tremendous losses of almost ten thousands men.

Iskander Chelebi had risked his life and lost it. Together with the keys of Tabriz, Ibrahim sent a complete report of the events and let Suleiman make the decision.

****

278

Ibrahim was not the only one who knew how to report events and many letters were also delivered in the Sultan's hands written by the spies he employed. This expedition was the first time he had stayed behind doing menial work, while his Vizier was conquering lands in his name. The Roman history was full of cases like his where a general had become so successful that he threatened the status of the Emperor. History was one of his most favorite subjects of study when he was a student at the Seraglio School his great-grandfather had established.

All reports didn't touch the same issues in the same way, but it was remarkable that Ibrahim's report was accurate enough. Iskander Pasha had been inexperienced and careless and now he was responsible for the deaths of thousands of brave soldiers. On the other hand, the casualties in conquering Van and Tabriz were minimal. His friend had triumphed, as even his impeccable father Selim the Terrible had captured Tabriz at a cost of a very bloody battle.

Now there was no way Suleiman could stay idle in the Eternal City and let Ibrahim demolish the Persian Empire. His dream was to follow the steps of Alexander the Great. It was the same dream Mehmet Sultan and Selim Khan had, but now this dream was becoming reality in the hands of another man, another exceptional Greek, a man who had started as a slave even lower than Alexander, but had achieved the same aims without shedding rivers of blood.

It was Allah's will that his daydreaming was interrupted by a page who conveyed another piece of happy news. His sister Hatidge had brought into this world Ibrahim's first son. Perhaps the fact Suleiman was gravely ill was the true cause, but somehow this news had made him unhappy. When he bought Ibrahim from the Avret Bazaar, having to celebrate his son was not one of his plans. Now all he could recall that made sense was Ibrahim's words:

"In this world, if our dreams haven't come true, it may be simply because what happened is the dream of another man more capable than us."

Without a doubt Ibrahim was right. He was healthy fighting the Persians in Tabriz, while he was lying in bed unable to walk. Was Ibrahim the true Allah's Shadow?

Was it a coincidence that the next herald who disturbed his thoughts brought in a request of the Seih-Ul-Islam to see him at his earliest convenience?

What did he want besides libel his intimate friend? He simply could not wait to find out.

****

"I respectfully greet my Padishah, Lord of Mecca and Medina, Master of Damascus, Jerusalem and Cairo, Emperor of Constantinople, Rumelia and Anatolia. I pray Allah always guide His Imperial Highness. I know the Caliph's time is more precious than gold, so I will not try to be pleasant with flatteries. My Master knows well that as the Seih-Ul-Islam of Constantinople my first and last priority is the Caliphate and the security of Osman's throne. Thus, I have no fear my Master may misjudge my intentions. I have never envied power because I know human power is an illusion. I am more interested in the eternal glory that springs only from Allah. If a Grand Vizier with one word can relieve a slave from all his taxes, I can relieve with one prayer a sinner from all his sins. Nevertheless, today I didn't knock on your door to discuss how great is the sin of a faithful to stare on the three naked statues erected in the middle of At Meidan, because when a conniving infidel slave prays inside the imperial mosque of Agia Sophia, he may not beg the invisible Allah for forgiveness, but pray to a ridiculous painted caricature made invisible covered by plaster. This is a much graver sin Allah simply cannot forgive or forget.

Also I don't intend to pass judgement on a man's audacity to erect a palace even higher than the Seraglio, because I don't know if his Master gave him permission to do so. I will not also say a word against the very close relationship a slave might have develop with his master, because the words of the Prophet are true and not hypocritical like the words of Christian priests who chastise in churches all men who find pleasure with boys, while after the sunset commit orgies inside their dark convents. I speak only the truth and I feel no shame spending a night with a handsome and educated slave, following the example of Socrates, Plato, and Aristoteles, instead of wasting my time, trying to satisfy a silly woman interested only on cooking, knitting and cleaning, or which luxurious dress she will wear during the Ramadan. For these reasons I pay no attention to all the audacious claims a slave makes in the Divan about his intimate friendship with his master, because I know this is the kind of relationships that make him sink even lower in the eyes of Allah."

Suleiman was getting bored listening to this tiresome, introductory monologue that revolved around what he was not going to discuss; so, he raised his hand to make him pause and gravely remarked:

"I should warn you that the walls in the Divan have eyes and ears; so, if I so wish, I can listen to what anyone says exactly without the need of an informer. Thus, I know that a Sultan is everything and a slave is nothing, but also that from nothing Allah has built the universe, so slaves may eventually become Sultans."

The Great Mufti realized that he had to be extremely careful with which parts of his thoughts should reveal to make sure that the Shadow of Allah would get the correct idea. "I am not Allah to know exactly what kind of secrets every man keeps deep inside his mind. I only try to avoid a plan like this turning few loose strands of malicious gossip into a violent wave of protest by myriads of faithful in the At Meidan. I know nothing concrete, but only that the trend of every human weakness is to worsen with time. Perhaps responsible is the growing despair of every man who sees his days become fewer, and the weaknesses of his flesh grows until the moment, when every desire that has not yet fulfilled becomes a nightmare. Maybe for you being so powerful this way of thinking is unbelievable, because in your entire life you have succeeded in all your endeavors. Honor, victories, power, gold, women and men, all have always been within your grasp. However, who knows what kind of unfulfilled desires a slave may have, especially one who started his journey in life from the lowest possible level?"

Suleiman remained silent contemplating his response. The plain truth was that he also wandered when Ibrahim's ambitions would be saturated. Thus, his interest was aroused.

"I don't have any signs that Ibrahim plans to revolt against me."

The Grand Mufti realized he had just touched a sensitive chord.

"Of course your Majesty has no signs. When a hunter goes to the fields to make love to his bride, he doesn't look around to find the telltale signs of a rabbit; but this does not mean a rabbit is not hiding in the bushes next to him looking for the right time to run away. However, when one sees the tracks of a camel in a desert, then the camel is surely not far away."

The Mufti's face became suddenly so intense that Suleiman felt he should try to comfort him with few encouraging words.

"Don't worry so much about my throne. Even when I go to sleep, I have many hound dogs eager to seek rabbits for my sake."

"I sincerely wish Allah has everything as well arranged as Your Majesty believes, but we Turks should not forget that all nations do not think or behave as fairly as we do. History is full of examples where Greeks lied or betrayed their people to serve their personal interests. Right now Ibrahim Pasha is the Serasker of the mightiest army in the world. In the Divan he claimed that he now believes in Allah.; but now please consider my last and most crucial question. Can anyone trust a man who has betrayed even his God?"

By now Suleiman was well aware that Ibrahim was an atheist who didn't need to believe in any god to find solace. He believed only in himself. Religion was just a tool he used to advance in the Ottoman hierarchy, a tool himself also used to put entire nations into motion. The House of Osman had utilized the Janissary Corps to mobilize all the Christian populations that contained the bravest soldiers, the most able seamen, and the most devious diplomats. This was a fact the Great Mufti did not took under consideration, when he made his wild assertions. He was a hypocrite who tried to discard all the facts that did not serve his purpose.

"Our pagan ancestors have also changed their faith and became Muslims, because it was advantageous at the time. It was the religion of the masters they chose to serve. Ibrahim has done nothing worse than my ancestors did. From the moment we met, he has never betrayed me, and he has always helped me add more worthy nations into my empire. He was by my side when we chased the Knights of Rhodes out of the island, and with his plan we scythed the flowers of the Hungarian knighthood to the ground in Mohacs. According to his report, the Ottomans have just conquered Tabriz, the capital of the Persian heretics, while I was lying on my bed incapacitated. I still have many dreams for the future, and I will need an honest man like him to realize the ones I can't because I'm sick. But even when I become useless as a soldier, I will not stop my quest until I reach the end of my life."

He thought the Grand Mufti would have nothing more to add, but he was wrong. He was silent simply because he was waiting for the right moment to poison his Sultan's mind.

"I trust you are overestimating the abilities of your slave. You are the most competent leader and proved it in Rhodes, Belgrade and Budapest. Your retreat in front of the Vienna walls was not a true defeat. It was simply a retreat similar to the action of a wave hitting a rock on a shore. Sooner or later the wave will come back stronger than ever and turn this might rock into sand; but for the wave to become stronger, it must be pushed by the wind. Only a strong wind can turn a breeze into an indefatigable tempest. This wind is the religion and these days Allah is the strongest wind of all. However, all I hear in the mosques these days is that our glorious Sultan is tired and has left the war into the hands of his Grand Vizier who has never betrayed him up to now. Now please tell me, how many more victories your friend must taste before he decides he is better than you and kicks you and the House of Osman out of the Seraglio?"

Similar rumors about his illness had already reached Suleiman's ears, but he had only considered the possibility Mustafa was the one who might try such a risky endeavor. What the Grand Mufti insinuated was that Ibrahim was an even more dangerous opponent who didn't have to wait to be of age to claim the throne of Osman in the name of his own son.

"Ibrahim is just a faithful dog that will never bite the hand that feeds him," he replied.

The words sounded full of conviction, but the tone of voice was full of doubts. It was what the Mufti wanted to discern to pour some more poison.

"Ibrahim is indeed a faithful dog who has offended your sister by collecting many lusty bitches around him to challenge the fertility of the glorious House of Osman with his offspring. Everyone knows he has appointed as the new Kislar Aga of the Eski Saray a slave you have offered him, offending you. I have no use for Nubian slaves, but if I was given such a present from my Sultan I would cherish it to the end of my life."

This was not a new piece of knowledge Suleiman ignored. It was one of his mother's last acts she had not found time to clarify. He could easily make few wild speculations about the reasons behind it, but he was not in the habit to speculate before he had given the right to a defendant to explain the reasons for his act. Anyway, the only person alive capable of explain this curious event was Ibrahim and he was fighting hard in faraway Armenia.

"If such a slave can satisfy your envy, I'm sure Ibrahim Pasha will be rich enough coming back from Armenia to buy such a slave for you too, if this is what you demand to soften your criticism," Suleiman noted with poisonous irony. "Everyone knows my Grand Vizier would rather negotiate than fight to death with his enemies."

"I'm not his enemy. I'm just a faithful supporter of my Caliph and a vigilant guardian of the Ayin. Now that Ibrahim Pasha has a heir, I wonder for how long he will be fighting for the glory of Suleiman Khan and not for his own son."

"I would be a truly pitiful Sultan if I was afraid of newborn baby, but I have to admit that at the moment Ibrahim has achieved all the goals he aimed at. Should I wonder if in the back of Ibrahim's mind the idea of becoming a Roman emperor is hidden?" Suleiman asked ironically.

"And as a pious Muslim I must declare that condemning a faithful slave to death is a hard decision. It's not something a fair sovereign can decide without a convincing proof of his guilt," the Great Mufti remarked with the solemn face of a judge pronouncing a sentence.

Now he could afford to show moderation, as now it was clear Suleiman Sultan had few doubts to reconsider. His mission had been accomplished, so he calmly continued his thoughts.

"Unquestionably this is a serious consideration, but as it always happens in life, when a treachery is fully realized, it may be already too late to defend against it. It may sound absurd, but when a friendship becomes dependency and subjugation, it is better for an emperor to be surrounded by enemies rather than friends. At least then he knows exactly who to defend against to save his good fortune. Nevertheless, I believe it's still too early to take drastic measures, because there is a war and the Persians may solve this problem for you. On the other hand, it is very regrettable when due to an illness a warrior is so weak that has to wait for his enemies to solve the problem a foe has created. I fear that is cases like this the best solution is to apply the laws of his ancestors. Then, he is not experimenting perilously and his decisions are justified. One must have no guilt feelings, no matter how severe the punishment may be, when he applies the divine Laws of the Holy Quran. The life of an infidel slave is nothing compared to the lives of thousands of Muslims, and the neck of a slave thinner than even a single hair from the Sultan's beard. Civil war among Muslims must be avoided at all costs, the Prophet advises."

The Grand Mufti did not seem willing to stop talking and his shrieking voices sounded like the prayer of a muezzin; however, Suleiman was now bored listening to his advices.

"Mufti, today you have filled my mind with all sorts of negative thoughts. I have now more urgent issues to consider like the war against Persia, a war Ibrahim Pasha is conducting brilliantly in my place. However, just to be sure, in case my health condition improves, I will go and find him. As long as the army is victorious and there is plenty of looting, I have nothing to fear from any conspirator. Thus, I will postpone any decision until this war is over, and I'm back in Constantinople."

Now at last the Grand Mufti realized that it was time for him to go.

"I am very sorry if I have caused unwillingly my Master a bit of sorrow; but my duty is to look after the Shadow of Allah and protect the House of Osman. So, go in peace to Persia to meet your slave, and I will try to find out as much as I can about what he plans to do when this war is over. I greet my Lord and Caliph of Islam, and I hope the next time I see him, his problems may have been reduced by one with the help of Allah."

****

The departure of Ibrahim from Constantinople to the distant Tabriz had its drawbacks. The Ottoman Empire could not be governed efficiently without his advices. The greatest problem that surfaced when he was gone was the arrival of the Barbarossa fleet for repairs. The Kapudan Pasha also inquired the construction of a considerably larger fleet. His plan was to extend the Ottoman Empire from Egypt all the way to Gibraltar along the North Africa coast.

These lands belonged to the Muslims for centuries, but the Spanish fleet of the Roman Emperor Charles was threatening to split them in two. He claimed this spread of land as a heir of the Roman Empire. On the other hand, the local Muslims believed that since the Ottomans had replaced the Byzantine Emperors, these lands belonged to the Ottomans. Creating a fleet was an expensive and risky undertaking for any Turk more skillful riding horses than waves.

Sultan Selim had made the four Barbarossa brothers

admirals of the Ottoman fleet, and this decision had been very successful, as with their aggressive leadership the Aegean Sea had been put under Ottoman control all the way to Crete subjugating all Venetian colonies. But the Barbarossa brothers did not stop there. They turned Tunis and Algeria harbors into their lairs, but the Spanish fleet attacked them and managed to kill two of them. Now the last brother, Hayrettin Barbarossa, was asking for more ships to take revenge and recapture Tunis, but Suleiman was weak and not certain he could risk opening a new front against the Spaniards. Barbarossa had to travel by land and reach Ibrahim in Persia to make the crucial decision.

****

The admiral's trip was beneficial to both. Ibrahim welcomed the pirate with all the honors any Kapudan Pasha deserved. They also exchanged gifts to create a stronger bond, and for every Spanish sword Ibrahim received, the admiral took back in return a Damascene. For every Spanish doubloon made of from the West Indies gold he offered as a present, Barbarossa received a lira made of Nubian gold, and for every roll of fabric captured from Genoese carracks, a roll of Bursa brocade.

It was not the first time the two men met, but it was destined to be the most important. If Selim Khan had discerned the flame of conquest in the eyes of Barbarossa family, now the Grand Vizier had become even more fascinated with the prospects Barbarossa the corsair revealed before his eyes with his bold, adventurous plans for sea conquests around the Mediterranean and the Red Sea all the way to the India Ocean.

Spain had become strong finding gold instead of spices in the West Indies, and this proved there was only one short way to reach Indies and Indochina, to cross the Indian Ocean as the Portuguese did around Africa. Real power laid in ships that could strike everywhere they liked, disembarking Janissaries at will in every beach and harbor far beyond the horizon.

"A true emperor should not limit his dreams only where his horse or his camel could reach," Barbarossa boldly claimed.

"You are right!" Ibrahim exclaimed. "The glory of Iliad must be followed by the thrill of an Odyssey, if the hero wishes to reach safely the warm last embrace of Ithaca."

The very next day he wrote a long letter to the Sultan, explaining in every possible detail why the Ottoman should build a fleet bigger and stronger than Spain's and use it to dominate the Mediterranean Sea and the Indian Ocean. It had to be a raiding fleet capable of striking in many more places than one, create havoc and then leave, before the King of Rome had time to react with overwhelming force, taking advantage of the shorter distances between Spain and Africa. The domination of the Mediterranean was clearly the first necessary step to secure Egypt, Mecca, the Red Sea and finally India. Suleiman Khan would undoubtedly agree with this plan, and after the first victories at sea, the Ottomans should capture Baghdad and then Basra to gain a safe harbor in the Persian Gulf. Such a harbor would be useful to replenish the ships coming from the Red Sea and Yemen, Ibrahim Pasha reassured him full of excitement.

"And what should happen if Suleiman is scared and hesitates? Turks are not made to fight riding on the waves," Barbarossa noted in a very sober tone, and Ibrahim had to stop dreaming and find a realistic answer.

The pirate was neither fool nor a dreamer. Crossing the waves with his galleys he had learned the importance of standing firm on his two feet.

"Our goal is always the prosperity of the Ottoman Empire, and whoever stands in our way should be brushed away," Ibrahim declared with a distinct air of unbending determination.

"Inshallah!" the pirate Admiral solemnly wished.

They had nothing more to say as the walls of a tent had both eyes and ears.

****

Iskander did not waste any time and as soon as he reached Tabriz he sent a letter to Hurrem describing his point of view of all that had happened. He had found out of Ibrahim's report and had

288

to rewrite history to suit his aims. He was devious enough to know that if you say one incontestable truth among many lies, the validity of all your lies is enhanced. The truth was that Ibrahim Pasha had signed the treaty of Van's surrender as Sultan Ibrahim, but the title didn't have the same gravity it had in the Eternal City. For the Persians "Sultan" was simply a title equivalent to "Serasker" or "Pasha". For them the supreme ruler was the "Shah" equal to the term "Padisah" Ottomans used.

When Hurrem received the letter, Suleiman Khan had already left to meet with the Ottoman armies and Ibrahim near the Cilician Gates on their way to Aleppo and Damascus. She decided that a piece of news impressed more if the intended receiver reads it with his own eyes. If Ibrahim Pasha was present during the reading, he could surely convince his friend he had chosen this title for the good of the Empire; but she should not forget to set the stage for the drama with a tender love letter.

"My Master, you absence has already started a wild fire in my heart that cannot fade away. Show mercy for this troubled soul and sent me a letter, so that it can find relief. When we read your letters with our children our eyes fill with tears. You are asking me why I am so angry with Ibrahim Pasha, and if this is Allah's wish and we are reunited, I promise I will explain you. Me and our children wipe our faces with the dust from your shoes."

****

Baghdad fell as easily as Tabriz. It's walls were no match for the Ottoman guns, and both combatants knew it, so fighting for it would be a needless waste of lives. The city was an important strategic post that controlled not only the two rivers, Tiger and Euphrates, but also the traffic of goods from India and Persia to the West.

The Baghdad conquest became once more a good reason for celebrations and the Sultan gave out many presents to all who had contributed to this new series of victories that led from Van to Tabriz and Baghdad. Not only the leaders, Ibrahim and Iskander got rich presents, but also many gold coins were distributed to the Janissaries and the Spahis who fought hard in the mountain passes of Armenia to win these important city-trophies.

Among the Janissaries, Sinan was the most rewarded for his contribution to the fall of Van, the most important city of Armenia and the northern gate to Persia. From now on he would become a distinguished member of the personal guards of the Sultan, the renown Haseki.

The Ottoman army didn't stop its march in Baghdad. It advanced all the way to the Persian Gulf and occupied the harbor city of Basra. This city was to become the gate to the Indian Ocean and an important outpost for a new branch of the Ottoman navy that was quickly formed to control the Red Sea and the Aden Straights.

The Persian reaction to this setbacks came in the mountains of Armenia and Kurdistan, where the most warlike tribes of Muslim heretics had always found safe refuge. It was the kind of guerilla warfare the Ottoman army could never win conclusively, because the regular army had to use the mountain passes, while the rebels controlled the mountain slopes and the high ground, a great strategic advantage for anyone who staged small scale skirmishes and sneaky ambushes. It was the kind of war that created almost daily a report of Ottoman casualties, a minor defeat, or even a serious catastrophe.

Ibrahim blamed Iskander for these failures, because he was the one who started this war instead of making peace negotiations with the local chiefs and warlords. As expected Iskander blamed the Serasker for not fighting hard enough and committing more troops to this cause. However, now Suleiman was present and had formed a personal judgment of the military situation. Ibrahim Pasha was right. The Ottomans should seek peace with the local tribes exactly as his father Selim had done almost twenty years ago.

The conclusion was uncontestable. The city of Tabriz and the region around it were strategically indefensible and so would the Taurus mountains be, if there was no peace with the locals.

The only issue that truly mattered was to keep the Taurus passes clear of enemies and open to the commerce. From the conquered cities only Van, Baghdad and Basra had any value and they had to be defended, because they were controlling important trade routes with the Far East. Baghdad was no more the great city the Abbasids had built. After its destruction by the Mongols of Tamerlane, it had never fully recovered; but its position controlling the two great rivers of Mesopotamia had not changed. To pacify the feelings of the population there was no looting and the Ottoman Army staged a magnificent military parade through the streets. Ibrahim Pasha was not a true Muslim, but pity for the vanquished enemies was one of his more apparent weaknesses. His plans needed loyal, hardworking subjects, not insurgent rebels.

Ibrahim Pasha also knew how to stage a religious miracle to take advantage of the sentiments of the local population. He didn't have to think much or invent the wheel. He simply had to read history. As Constantine the Great had done before him, discovering the Holy Cross that had established the Roman occupation over the Holy Lands for several centuries until the Crusades, he had to discover a holy tomb, and he surely did find one. It was a winning recipe that Mehmet Fatih had also applied with the discovery of the tomb of the Muslim hero Eyup Ansari in front of the Theodosian Walls of Constantinople,

Indeed after few minor excavations, the tomb of Abu Hanifa, a Sunnite Imam who had died in prison when the Persian Shiites conquered Baghdad, was discovered. It was an easy task, because just few years back the father of Shah Tahmasp, Shah Ismael had demolished it. The remaining bones of the Sunnite saint were discovered by the marvelous scent they emitted inside a byzantine sarcophagus. It was a godsend sign that the arrival of the Ottomans in Baghdad was in agreement with the will of Allah. To celebrate this momentous discovery Sinan was commissioned to build a splendid mosque that would celebrate this historic event. And thus Baghdad became the last holy city after Mecca, Medina, Cairo, Jerusalem, Damascus, and Constantinople resting safely in the hands of Sunni Muslims.

The resulting religious fever was so great that no one in Baghdad paid any attention to the execution by hanging of Iskander Pasha with Ibrahim's decree for all his military failures. It was an act within a Serasker's rights, but the presence of the Sultan in Baghdad made this death sentence somewhat awkward. Nevertheless, the Sultan did not show any signs of anger, as similar events were rather common during an expedition, when a Pasha failed to perform efficiently or follow direct orders. In the case of Iskander Pasha the formal accusation was embezzlement of public funds. It was an accusation that was very easy to prove, as Iskander Pasha was the Defterdar in charge of the Imperial Treasury, and the richest man in the Empire. As it was customary in similar cases, the entire fortune of the Pasha was returned to the Imperial Treasury, a measure that pleased sufficiently most parties concerned.

****

Hurrem had an uneasy sleep that night. For many months all the news she heard from the war were Ibrahim Pasha's victories and it was a very frustrating process. As Ibrahim's successes piled up, replacing him with Iskander Chelebi would be more difficult. She had to find a way out, and making the Ottoman fleet even stronger did not help, because it was clear that Barbarossa was siding also with the Grand Vizier.

These were very difficult days as Ibrahim's successes inspired also her own children, triggering their imagination. Thank Allah, Suleiman had joined the Army and Baghdad's capture was also his doing; but what if his illness returned and incapacitate him even more?

Ibrahim would not be the first time a Grand Vizier became so important. Halil Pasha had also become so strong under the reign of Sultan Murat the Second that Mehmet Fatih immediately after the fall of Constantinople had decided to eliminate him by accusing him for treachery and conspiracy with the Byzantines.

Her thoughts were interrupted by a knock on her door. It

was a messenger carrying a letter from Iskander Pasha. It was another setback, a letter from a condemned man waiting execution by hanging, a sentence reserved for the common criminals, not an Ottoman Vizier who should be decapitated. Iskander Pasha claimed he was innocent. He had worked hard serving the House of Osman throughout his life. His military failure was not intentional. It was a stroke of bad luck that could happen to anyone. The one who had been working silently to bring down the House of Osman was Ibrahim Pasha. He was collecting from the very beginning wealth and power, and secretly conspiring to replace Suleiman in the throne of the Ottoman Empire. He was recently signing treaties as Sultan Ibrahim, so that people did not realize what had happen and who was exercising now the true authority in the Empire. This was going to be his last letter, and he was hoping Allah the All-Seer would not let this injustice to continue and this letter to reach her somehow.

Finishing the letter, Hurrem rolled it back and placed it inside the mother-of-pearl inlaid ebony box he used to keep her most precious jewels. These were the last words of a dying man no one could refute, and they were more precious than diamonds or pearls.

****

The winter was approaching and the northern wind in Baghdad started carrying the chill of the first snow up in The Taurus mountains. Soon the Ottoman army should leave the pleasant climate of the Mesopotamia and take the road back to Constantinople. The preparations were almost completed and what still remained was for the Sultan to give the signal of departure.

Ibrahim felt they had to talk in private, and being so close to the ruins of Babylon was a good opportunity to have a stroll away from any inquisitive ears. They both yearned since childhood to follow the steps of Alexander the Great. Possibly the Sultan wanted to talk to him too, because he accepted the invitation with more eagerness than usual. Perhaps the change of climate or diet had been beneficial to his disposition.

As they approached the ancient site, the sun was approaching the horizon, and the midday heat had receded, so that wandering among the ruins of the ancient palaces and the fallen walls decorated with the flying lions and the bearded warriors became almost pleasant.

When they decided to visit the site, in their minds the majestic image of the Hanging Babylon Gardens their imagination had built was still vivid; but as they moved forward, disappointment replaced their initial zeal and excitement. The luscious trees and shrubs they had envisioned were replaced by few palm trees, acacias and tamarisks trying to survive here and there after a hot summer until the fall rains.

The Sultan remained silent possibly overwhelmed with disappointment, and the slave fell the need to express his regrets for this emotional letdown by starting a different subject.

"My Master, I hope that the result of this expedition have pleased you. Alexander's Babylon maybe unworthy of your magnificence, but Tabriz and Baghdad are worthy jewels to adorn your crown," he remarked; but perhaps Sultan's heart was still heavy after his mother's loss, or possibly there was still some discomfort and swelling of his feet that affected his mood.

"As the years go by, I feel that time passes quicker than before. I may have been successful on most of my plans, but I have started wondering what is the use adding more riches, lands and power, when I still don't know how the new year will find me. Is accumulating more wealth a worthy cause for a father, when he knows that his children may become soft, more greedy and less worthy? Are more riches worthier than the company of trusty friends and loving relatives? History has also taught us that unworthy sons usually follow great fathers."

Suleiman looked uncommonly pessimistic this afternoon, and it could well be the result of his illness, the aging process, or possibly a day of low spirits after many days of great successes. Suleiman was approaching the age when both his father Selim, and Mehmet Fatih, the greatest Osmanli conquerors had died.

Ottoman Sultans with the exception of Bayezid, his grandfather had not died of old age. Perhaps this was beneficial for the Empire because younger and more dynamic men took over the reins; but this was one thought he would never communicate to an ailing man. Instead he decided to appear more optimistic and cheer him up.

"Especially you shouldn't complain for your accomplishments. You have many worthy sons that everyday prove they are fully capable of more victories and conquests. Despite few exceptions, you are also surrounded by capable men who can support your sons' quest to make this world a better place to live, and the Domain of Allah you possess even more prosperous."

"It is indeed true that Allah has blessed me with worthy sons, but this might well be a curse in disguise. One day I must pass judgment on all my sons and choose the best among them. Then, all the rest will have to die and the more worthy they are the more difficult it is for me to punish their virtues with death. Above all I have to be fair."

The Sultan's dilemma was valid and it was a problem he had already considered for long since the death of Sultan Selim.

"Being fair is indeed of fundamental importance for every sovereign. You have to reward virtue and punish sin before anything else, and jealousy is not a virtue. Your duty as a father and a Sultan is to choose the best heir and nothing more or less than that. If you are just and your sons as virtuous as they appear now, then the ones who are not chosen for the supreme position should be happy with any position they are assigned to, and try to do their best to carry out their duties. Thank Allah, there are many positions in the Empire where a man can do good and prosper. If they limit their ambitions to this goal, they will not push their reigning brother in the uncomfortable position to execute them. Fatih's law is not Allah's law and should be changed, if it leads to a meaningless bloodshed of worthy fighters of the faith."

"That maybe so, but even though the law is cruel, it is also effective. It gives a clear cut solution to an existing problem that in the past has almost led the Ottoman Empire to ruin. We the Ottomans should not let our empire built with the blood of our ancestors collapse as Alexander's or the Romans, because of civil war. This is a real threat that demands a clear solution no matter how cruel it may appear to the common folks. Only exceptional leaders can perform exceptional deeds. I believe these were your own words few years back."

Suleiman's dilemma was now clear, and having such torturing thoughts might well be partially responsible even for his health problems, Ibrahim silently contemplated, and by being silent and thoughtful gave the Sultan the opportunity to reach a conclusion.

"I simply cannot let everything to chance. When I die, my sons may become jealous and start a civil war instead of sharing fairly all the power and riches their ancestors and I have accumulated. Thus, I have the responsibility to choose a clear cut solution and not let them decide how they will share their good fortune. I simply cannot put the World Order into peril for the lives of few greedy children."

It had become almost apparent that the Sultan, troubled by his illness and natural pessimism, didn't have the mental capacity to try something different, even though it was clear even to a commoner that condemning a man to death before any crime was committed was not an acceptable, humane solution. However, Suleiman had often chosen practical solutions rather than humane. There had to be something wrong in his blood.

Now Ibrahim had a rather clear idea what was in the Sultan's mind. He should try to be practical too and gain the most from the expected developments.

"I can sympathize with your solemn concerns; but it seems to me that you shouldn't pass judgment too soon. If you think your sons are jealous of each other even now, perhaps you should also take into account that they are not the sole responsible for any developing greed. In my mind their mothers are more responsible than anyone else, since they all have grown older far away from your proper care, training and attention."

Suleiman realized where Ibrahim was driving the conversation. Mustafa was the perfect candidate for the throne, and sensing this fact Hurrem had instilled hate in her children's hearts for their older and more virtuous brother.

"It is perfectly human for a mother to think her children are the best and try to protect her offspring," he concluded, trying to dress an assertion with the severity of a universal law.

"No sane man can doubt this logical assertion. It is almost as valid as the fact that a wife can influence greatly her husband too."

"Every Sultan is a mortal man, and has weaknesses as any other man, even if he is the Shadow of Allah," Suleiman argued in vain. "You should know that better than anyone."

"Yes, but the only two moments a Sultan shares with common men are the moments of his birth and his death. Everything else in between is entirely different. You command and the mountains tremble from the galloping horses of your heralds, spreading your will to the four corners of the horizon with the threat of his sword."

Suleiman smiled listening to his last remark, but it was not clear if he was amused or ironic.

"Yes, but few people say that if my Grand Vizier does not agree with my commands , then they are not carried out to completion."

For one more time Ibrahim was amazed with the extend of the Sultan's spies; but he had to pretend he didn't put great importance to what people said; so he smiled indifferently.

"My Master, you know better than anyone else that all the rumors are not worthy of your attention. There is plenty of hate out there, but I'm not the least worried. Love will always prevail in the end. As long as there is love between us, I feel perfectly safe that even if I fail once, I will always be given a second chance. Fortunately, your ancestors have been wise enough to offer a Sultan the opportunity to have four wives and hundreds of concubines. Thus, the opinion of a single wife does not amount more than all the rest, and the view of one concubine less than an one hundred other women in the Harem."

"Hurrem is not like any other woman. She was a concubine blessed by Allah, and this was the reason I decided to raise her to the status of my Kadin reserved only for princesses. It was surely an exceptional decision, but you know better than anyone else that when I'm faced with exceptional beings, I have the wisdom to make exceptions to the ordinary rules. Actually Hurrem was the only Kadin I chose, because the other two were chosen by my father. Every man has the right to choose the special woman of his life. Anyway, both of you exert on me special attraction that for the time being I'm still incapable of resisting. Without anyone of you I fell lost, and this is the solemn truth everyone has to accept."

Suleiman looked perfectly sincere describing his present condition. However, Ibrahim knew that being attached to a certain object with unbreakable bonds meant that also the object was condemned to rotate forever around the other end of this fateful attraction. The prospect of spending the rest of his life going in and out from the Needle's Eye was like having to carry out a life's sentence. For him complete freedom was more precious than gold.

"I would be the last man to deny that my Sultan has more rights than me. In fact, if I had the right to choose the mother of my children, my Sultan should have the right to choose at least two more or even three more Kadin of exceptional status," Ibrahim said confirming his inferiority.

In Ibrahim's mind the possibility Suleiman would allow his two neglected Kadin to take a divorce was still alive; so he decided to take a chance and continued.

"I believe Gülfem Sultan has been punished long enough for the death of her son. It is fair of you to give her a child, because she is still attractive and of a pleasant disposition. When I was your Hasodabashi she never complained for your preference to Hurrem."

"Indeed Gülfem Sultan has never offended me and my choices as Mahidevran. Now that we are discussing choices, do you know why Hafsa Sultan chose your Kislar Aga for the Eski Saray?"

"No! She has never explained the reasons went as far as explaining to me her ulterior motives, so I can only guess."

"And I would be very interested to hear your best guesses and compare them with my suspicions."

"We all know well how suspicious are few women of owning attractive slaves. I believe she was afraid someone or even I might be tempted and neglect my duties to her daughter. Handsome men, black or white are always a temptation," Ibrahim claimed without a second thought, putting the Sultan's suspicions to rest.

Since they were reunited in Baghdad speaking to the Sultan he hadn't tried to have the last word. He could only sympathize with the weak condition of his friend. Suleiman was ill and the constant pain and suffering had a profound effect on his behavior. During the war he had come face to face with similar behaviors of wounded men. It was not the amount of pain they felt, but the duration. A human being could suffer immense amounts of pain, if he knew it was a temporary condition, but losing a hand, an eye, a leg or even a finger generated very violent reactions, because it created a sense of hopeless terminality. A proud but wounded man could not easily accept that he was going to live forever inferior than most of his subordinates. With this kind of thoughts flooding the Sultan's mind, it was dangerous to put additional strain by pressing any of his advantages.

During the entire return ride to Baghdad they remained silent, lost in their thoughts. The sun had disappeared in the horizon and with it a profound pessimism had conquered both of them. The next morning they were destined to follow a parallel course towards the western horizon, and this prospect unconsciously weighted heavily on their emotions. Alexander the Great had died inside these ruined palaces, so now returning to a palace full of intrigue had ceased being a source of joy.

****

The return trip to the Eternal City through the Taurus passages might have lasted for months if the local warlords had tried to resist, but Ibrahim had sent messages to them that the Ottoman Army would have no reason to return, if they didn't revolt; so the Kurds were happy to see them go, and they showed their relief doing anything they could to assist them. However, there were times when even having no problems is a source of depression, as every day passed applying the same routine.

In early morning even before daybreak, they would collect their bags, load them onto the beasts of burden and start riding until midday. Then, they would pray to Allah, have some nourishment and start riding once more until the shadows grew too long, when they would stop, put up their tents, start bonfires and have supper. In view of the early awakening, they also slept early to collect strength for the next day.

They have practically ceased to talk, and something had changed in their relationship. Perhaps the long trip had affected their attitude, turning it into some kind of tiresome daily routine; but it was also possible that their best years had passed, and the people they had met and associated with had consumed out their youthful energy.

There was not much they could add to whatever they had done before, and this realization had transformed the passion for life into a boring routine. Now they had certain roles to play that limited their freedom to do the unexpected.

Suleiman had ceased to talk about his daily problems, and the few times that such an occasion had risen, the Sultan had not followed his advices. It was not clear if this was the result of a growing sense of self-confidence, or if he preferred to keep everything a secret. If this was a telltale sign he had lost his trust in him, or didn't feel strong enough to follow his advice, he couldn't say just yet. After all a slave had to wait for the master to make suggestions first.

On the way back they passed once more from Tabriz to make sure everything was in order and safe from Persian raids. Ibrahim found a letter from Hatidge waiting. Without putting any great emphasis on the event, she revealed that the Russian maiden had produced a child, a healthy daughter. It was nothing much for the Princess, but a great boost of moral for him. Hatidge had stood at the proper level for her status. The fact she had mentioned it to him was a sign she acknowledged the child was his. The fact she didn't complain meant she was not considered it an important event. Her husband legally belonged to her. Her husband had the right to have a harem, and births were a common and happy event for every proper harem. It meant the master had the strength to keep his mates happy.

He was happy too. He was not greedy. He didn't need more concubines than four. He wasn't ready to start a new controversy with his master on who was the most prolific. He had also to be content with the fact he was married to the sister of a Sultan, while the Sultan's Kadin were two Tatar princesses and one slave of inferior lineage.

Hatidge right at the end mentioned that she had missed his touch. It meant she didn't have sought another lover. Basmi was enough for her needs. If she felt depressed one night, she could invite the Russian maiden into her bedroom and exercise her skills by seducing her any time she felt insecure. She was not greedy. She was practical most of all. What she needed was to get close to another human being and feel wanted. With the lamp extinguished all men were identical. Perhaps this motto was valid also for women. What really mattered was the role a human decided to play. In ancient Greek theater there were no women actors, just men who wore the appropriate mask. Perhaps this was the essence of the Dionysian Mysteries. If he was in Venice, he might have already tried to see how well he could play the role of a woman too.

He was a man and had to masquerade to feel secure. Women were more practical. They felt that what they needed to be content was not a man, just a child they could call their own creation. The ancient Greek philosophers claimed women were a different species. A man did not need to understand them, just use them to proliferate. Allah provided pleasure to a man for accomplishing this task. If the child was a girl or boy made no difference. Allah was rewarding men in advance. That was all, and everything else was manmade foolishness.

His wife was indeed a wise Ottoman. Her wisdom was distilled in her postscript.

"My darling, rejoice! Now we have two slaves with emerald eyes we can share. Now that our son is born, I cannot wait to feel you deep inside of me even if it might hurt me later."

Human beauty was an event that should make everyone happy. Proliferating beauty was the best way for every human to make the universe more beautiful than he found it. This was a letter he had to keep always close enough to his heart to read whenever he was troubled about how to act next.

****

The same night when he visited the Sultan's tent he immediately realized something unusual was afoot. There was anger in Suleiman's eyes and the letter he held meant bad news had offended his ears. His first thought was that something bad had happened with his children, but he was mistaken. Death had not visited again the Seraglio. He stood there silent expecting as any other slave to be ordered.

"Ibrahim, do you have any interesting news from Constantinople?" the Sultan asked with stern voice, and when he said no, Suleiman continued:

"I didn't expect from you to keep secrets from me, your lord and master."

The Serasker was momentarily surprised to hear his master's scolding, and didn't know what exactly secret had become public. Through all these years many secrets had accumulated between them, and he was experienced enough to know how to avoid an exposure.

"The only secrets this slave has from his master, are the ones he considers unworthy of his attention," he replied calmly waiting patiently to hear more details about the pending issue.

"I could never have imagined that the Damat of a Sultan

would dare to have children with one of his slaves," Suleiman said in severe tone as if he was chastising a naughty child, making clear that the content of Hatidge's letter had become widely known.

He smiled quite relieved, paying no attention to the Sultan's grim mood.

"It's natural for a slave to try to imitate his master. Imitation is the sincerest form of flattery. Nevertheless, I have taken an oath on the life of my children never to honor a slave more than my Kadin.

The Sultan's position for one more time had turned dramatically from attack to defense. Characterizing Hurrem as a slave was also annoying and demeaning. He attempted to repair his position by another arbitrary assertion that sounded good in his ears.

"I used to believe that one Princess would be enough to satisfy your endless ambitions of women."

Essentially there was a touch of envy in Suleiman's accusation; but it was also apparent the Sultan had not read Hatidge's letter, but got his information directly from Hurrem. Now it was the right time for him to counterattack trying to severe the strings that Hurrem was using to turn Suleiman into her puppet.

"My Princess knows well that my heart belongs only to her; but few nights every month a slave can help a man to avoid violating Allah's laws. Both me and my wife know well that our dependence from the love of our slaves is not stronger than a pubic hair but equally curly."

The resemblance of Ibrahim's statement with the words of the Seih-Ul-Islam was striking. Was this a coincidence or intentional? How could Ibrahim have known what was said inside the Has Oda? However, an attempt to recall all the details of that visit was an issue he would have to face later. What was more urgent now was to give Ibrahim a convincing answer for his claim that he was violating Allah's commands by having only one wife and using her flesh for his pleasure, even during the few days every month when Hurrem was dirty.

"I'm very glad that my slave follows so closely the commands of Prophet Mohamed. This piece of news will silence all those voices who consider his conduct disrespectful towards our Muslim traditions. Nevertheless, I would be much more relaxed, if I was to hear from my sister's lips that she knows all this connections and she wholeheartedly approves."

Hearing these comments, Ibrahim let a sigh of relief. All indications pointed to another personal triumph in the field of verbal confrontations with his friend.

"I'm very sorry to hear that my master does not trust the words of this slave and has to hear the same facts from the lips of his sister. However, a slave's displeasure carries no weight compared to the immense wisdom of his master to start doubting even the written words of his most favorite slave, when they are opposing the written words of his own sister, a true Princess with the blood of Osman," Ibrahim remarked and pulled Hatidge's letter from his chest.

Suleiman could not believe his ears hearing Ibrahim's bold criticism about the validity of the accusations contained inside Hurrem's letters. They sounded as if Ibrahim accused him of lying to him by repeating Hurrem's writings.

Nervously, he extended his hand and grabbed his sister's letter and started reading it, murmuring the words. Reaching the very end his face flashed with anger. He simply could not accept yet the fact his sister had fell so low to be so dependent on Ibrahim's flesh. He had to do something violent to relieve his frustration and the only proper expression he could find was to laugh his heart out.

"If I didn't read her letter with my own eyes, I would never have believed that my little sister is so weak that her pleasure is even more dependent than me on your passionate kisses."

However, now Ibrahim reckoned that the Sultan had intruded in his privacy and had to be reminded that there certain limits in their relationship that had to be respected.

"It is not weakness to keep the people you love happy anyway you can. Happiness is not a tasty pie that has to be divided among people. It is something wise people should try to multiply for their benefit. However, this is not the first time Ottoman women excel men in terms of love. Your mother was another woman who loved me like a son, because I loved her son too."

It was another bold statement that took Suleiman by surprise. Ibrahim's confession that his mother loved him was unexpected. Whenever they were together Hafsa Sultan's behavior had been formal and proper according to the rules of the Ayin. Ibrahim's claim that his mother the Valide Sultan loved him was highly improper and caused another flood of envy in his heart he had to try hard to hide. Ibrahim realized the struggle and tried to clarify sufficiently what he meant.

"Finding true love will always remain an elusive dream for every human, while death a hard reality. To forget the love of a slave is any easy task for a wise Sultan who has managed to forget the loss of so many loved ones already, if he ever decides to will it. However, I cannot see why anyone would try to replace one love with another, when he can enjoy both."

"Love can indeed proliferate among all the people we love; but unfortunately what remains the same is the time we need to share love, and this is why sometimes we have to make painful decisions. What is even worse is the fact that we don't know how much time we have left to divide our time fairly among those we love."

Suleiman's words sounded very grim and hard inside the tent demolishing the tender atmosphere Ibrahim had tried so hard to create. His reference to the Sultan's mother was a mistake he should not repeat again. It was apparent that Suleiman's heart was gravely wounded not only by all the deaths of loved ones he had to suffer, but from his illness as well. The fear of death could not grow roots in the heart of a young man; but as the years passed-by and heartaches accumulated on his shoulders, his heart weakened and the common worries that trouble all people found fertile soil to grow absorbing drop by drop the joy of life.

****

Ibrahim realized that for one more time he had to try to entertain the Sultan's fundamental worries. He knew that in the Orient people found relief in narrating myths that contained some kind of moral wisdom. This was the reason why the Holy Books contained so many myths and allegories that tried to sooth the hearts of simpleminded people.

In the Orient common people trusted that time run in circles and human troubles could find satisfying solutions in wise advises that old people could repeat from generation to generation for the younger generations to apply and memorize, but following old recipes.

He had a different opinion. His experiences had shown that every event was unique, as even two identical pieces of marble had different shades. The substance was the same, but the details it expressed were different to a small or a large extent. He desired many women, but each satisfied a different, distinct need. Hatidge's love was as necessary as bread on the table; but to have his palate content he needed different dishes. Basmi was necessary to wake up his lust, while Yabani and Zarafet were for him as useful as toys. Their love was like exercising his fencing skills. The Russian maiden was the true battlefield he had to fight hard to be the ultimately successful, because she was such a sensitive creature she would be hurt, if she didn't feel she was as precious as her exquisite features demanded.

Mahidevran was as exquisite as her, but she was a Princess not a slave. She needed his love and attention, but only to confirm her superiority. This was why she was playing all these games with her disguises. She was licentious, but she was too noble to accept it. She was also a bit devious trying to present her carnal weaknesses as a sacrifice for her son.

If women improve his self-confidence, the men in his life have always tried to drain it. They pushed him lower, while women tried to reinstate his personality to a higher level. Somehow he needed both men and women to be content because the one effect amplified the other; but even different men had different effects on his mood. Selim's influence had been as grim as death, while Suleiman's love was more like a game of chess.

Sinan was right. Everything was going through a continuous process of development. The lives of all humans went through the same phases. They were like songs sung using the same notes, but the intensity or the melodies were different and the results on moods varied. The same sensation created different results each time. It was like cooking using the same recipe and the same ingredients that created different tastes, if the cooking times were different.

People used the same stones to build new temples, but from the moments their beliefs varied, the buildings their imagination designs came out different. Ancient temples were so full of light, while churches and mosques so claustrophobic they were almost scary.

****

"Only the men who do not believe in their good luck are content to spend their lives wandering in cycles around the same places and people, because they are afraid what the future might bring. Thus, they tend to behave like trees that grow roots in one place; but no matter how strong roots they grow, tempests will eventually arrive or the ax of the lumberjack will knock them down. If you truly believe in Allah use the power He has bestowed on you and change your life before it is too late and your legs cannot carry not even your own weight. A man should not lose a single moment of his life trying to guess the moment of his death. Death most of the time comes to knock on your door when you least expect it."

Suleiman was too depressed to respond and Ibrahim grabbed the chance to finish what he had in mind to say.

"Once when I was in Egypt an old Copt told me the story of a foolish Pharaoh who asked his soothsayers about the day he would die. They told him that he had only ten more years left to live. He got so depressed by this omen he decided to build a smaller pyramid than all his ancestors so that by the time he died, his pyramid tomb would be ready."

Suleiman's eye glittered with interest to hear the end of this story that was so close to his fears.

"In the end even these extreme measures did not seem enough; so, to live a longer life he decided that he should turn the night into day by lighting many candles in his palace. Thus, he started ruining his health by staying awake day and night and stopped eating out of depression for his imminent death."

"And what happened next? Did he die earlier because of his foolishness?" Suleiman asked full of stress.

"My master please forgive me, but my mouth has become too dry. Could you please order a cup of tea for me?"

Suleiman blushed for omitting this traditional Ottoman curtesy, summoned his pages and ordered them to bring some tea, Turkish delights and two shisha. In a hurry the slaves brought in two lighted water pipes of unusual design Ibrahim had offered him as presents in Tabriz.   Soon the heavy scent of opium filled the tent and after few deep draughts Ibrahim decided to continue his narration. He had never refused to satisfy the Sultan's wishes, but he kept for himself the choice of the right moment. It was a tease they both enjoyed until then.

"No!" he disclosed. "He finally wised up, followed normal rules and died extremely old, in fact much older than any of his illustrious ancestors. However, he left behind as a monument of his stupidity a pyramid smaller than anyone else's to remind people what a great mistake is to live your life waiting for death to come, trusting the words of devious scammers who claim they can prophesize accurately disasters, deaths or even happy events."

Reaching the end of the story, Suleiman fell in a state of deep contemplation. Perhaps, Ibrahim was right and no one could predict how his life would end or what kind of mishaps he would have to face in his life. A man's future might well be written down, but only Allah could read it. Perhaps he should try hard to get well and accomplish all his dreams, without worrying if he would have enough time to complete them. However, Ibrahim was very confident of his final assertion. No man before his death could fulfil all his dreams. Few dreams were destined to remain figments of his imagination, and a heavy burden on the shoulders of our children. If every dream could come true, then no one would waste his time making children.

"This does not mean we should limit our dreams. On the contrary, we should make as many and as magnificent dreams as we can, and then make plans how to realize them, even though we know that our lifeline may break the next moment. Whenever you die, your children will take over where you left. Life is not a one man's race. It is an endless relay effort."

Without any facial reaction that would betray his thoughts, Suleiman continued to analyze his fears with the same pessimistic tone.

"As the years slip-by, I catch more often myself devoting more time to my memories rather than make more plans for the future. Even now I remember and become sad counting the years that have passed since the night I made love for the first time."

"These years are not a good enough reason for you to spoil your mood daily. I will start getting desperately sad the moment I will realize that was my final explosion," Ibrahim noted in high spirits. "By the way, you've never told me why you've chosen me that day in the Avret Bazaar, when there was so many pretty girls on sale."

"I always wish to be like my father, but I was never as forceful as he was."

"Why do you say that? Your empire now is much bigger than his, and soon the Mediterranean Sea will become an Ottoman lake as it was when the Romans ruled the world. Then we will build a canal and conquer the Red Sea next, our gate to the Indian Ocean, as your father Selim wished."

"I don't know what my father's dreams were. All I know that he never truly loved anyone, and he was the only ruler of himself till the last moment. He always managed to fight one passion with another, while I'm a Sultan enslaved by his passions."

Ibrahim was surprised to hear of this confession. For him being a Sultan meant that every moment he would be absolutely free to choose how to spend the next moment. He had many similar restrictions. Perhaps the human heart was not ready to become fully liberated. Perhaps, having to fulfil obligations gave his heart the security of the slave who had to obey orders.

"We have much in common; but you shouldn't envy your father. He died all alone away from his children and without the tender hand of a woman to wet his lips with a glass of water. Love is not slavery when there is reciprocation. Love is a game that mocks the fear of death and offering us liberation from our earthly bonds. In this universe Mother Nature tries to create complexity from simplicity; but this is a trial and fail process and all failures have to die sooner or later. Death is the just punishment for every being that cannot defeat time and become immortal. However, time is not the only criterion of success; thus, dying of old age is not what we should aim. It is also very important how much love you have experienced in your life. Love is Allah's reward for the man who picks up dirt and water and molds a new world according to his own rules."

Suleiman's silence provided still the opportunity for Ibrahim to plunge forward with his assertions.

"In this universe, only with synthesis we can make a better world. It is our only weapon to make sure that a little piece of our existence will survive after we are gone, no matter what we are, Sultans or slaves. The paradises priests advertise are good promises only for the weak minds who haven't accomplished anything worthy during their first life, and need a second life to finish what they've started. If a man lived eternally, then his magnificent creations would be worthless, because what really counts is how many worthy creations you can complete in a timespan. Time is the true criterion of a man's worth, and that is why I'm not impressed by the universe magnificence, because Allah who built it is immortal. However, if He really has built this universe in seven day, then I'm truly impressed and kneel in front of his immense power."

Ibrahim stopped to take a breather and tried to discern if his words had made on impression. He saw in the Sultan's eyes the rising fog of anxiety; however, it was too late for him to stop. Today he had to reach the end.

"I'm not afraid of Allah's punishment for all my sins. He takes too match time to react and I'm fully aware of the importance of time in our lives. I believe He will be waiting for me at the gate of Paradise to shut it right on my face. The only thing I'm afraid of is the absolute incapacity of the eternal sleep, the time when all my senses retreat and I don't have the strength even to think. This is how Death must arrive too ready to wipe my memory clean. However, no matter how many times I wake up, he will never stop terrorizing me. I only hope by the time this moment comes, I will have psychologically admitted at least the need for this trip of no return. There is nothing worse than the last moments in the life of a man who waiting the oblivion death brings, he feels that he is departing without leaving behind something really beautiful, a poem, a song, a child, or a palace, something beautiful that didn't exist in the world before him. But today, I feel as happy as Allah who has built the world simply because I have conquered a woman and with her complete approval she carries in her womb an entirely new universe. Thus, if my master loves his slaves and feels that uniting with them they all become stronger, happier or superior, he shouldn't be ashamed because some other people call them sinners or weaklings. The relationship that makes you feel stronger cannot be truly called a weakness, because it is the expression of the force we all should exert to create something new. Therefore, you should never feel sorry for any of feeling of love or desire you once felt, because when your life withers away you, you will be sorry only for the bodies that you failed to enjoy and have been wasted away by Kronos, the cruelest god of all."

Suleiman looked at him in silence, but then whispered softly as if this was going to be his last words:

"My father Selim Khan just before he died he advised me

to turn you into a eunuch the moment I feel my desire for you has ended."

It was the second time Suleiman had revealed the secret thoughts of his father, and it had to be a real threat. He made an effort and smile as if he was considering this threat a joke.

"I became a eunuch the first night we spent together and I have nothing to regret. In my native language eunuch is the page that makes sure his master has a happy sleep. In all these years I never considered the possibility that for some strange reason someday I might lose the means to enjoy our moments of desire. For few moments I may fly away like a butterfly to have a taste of another flower, but sooner or later I will return to get warm by your flame. Please try not to hold me too close to your fire, because I will burn my wings, and then I will have to die."

Listening to his slave's wish the Sultan shivered. It could be the chill of the night that had crept around them, but perhaps it was the breath of Death that kept following them, but that night it had come even closer. They both felt weak to face the threat of the darkness and had to get closer to keep alive the flame that warmed their life for so many years.

That night Ibrahim renew once more the vows of their love, because he knew that the best antidote for the deadly boredom that poisoned his master's heart was slow, deliberate, unrestricted love. He felt asleep hoping that somehow a window of hope had opened that night and would allow them to find a way out from the looming dead end; however, no one could deny that the one after the other all the outlets were closing, like a house whose occupants had decided to immigrate to another town.

****

The days of the return trip passed torturing slow, as most of the army had to advance on foot through mountain passages. Nevertheless, their relationship had slowly considerably improve. Ibrahim by now knew well Suleiman's character. He was aware that if he could spend few days with him without any interference, he could drastically improve the Sultan's disposition. The basic problem in their relationship after their marriages was that they didn't have much spare time to spend together. Ibrahim was simply too busy carrying out his duties, and Suleiman was not often in the right mood for chatting because of his illness. Thus, in the back of their minds as they approached the Eternal City, the prospect of a new separation weighted heavily on their temperament.

Ibrahim didn't mind much for this separation. In general, there were other more pleasant ways to spend his time. For him repetition was synonymous with boredom; but he was also aware that after their close relationship of the past, complete separation might be considered almost as treachery by the ailing Sultan. On the other hand, Hurrem influence would intensify the moment they arrived in the City. Then, he had mainly two options, to keep his distance and face the consequences, or stay by Suleiman's side and bear the constant tension of providing explanations for all his actions to counter daily the most recent accusations. However now with the arrival of his son, he had no option but to keep his distance from the gloomy atmosphere of the Seraglio, wait for developments, and hope for the best.

Arriving in Konia, the old Ikonion of the Romans, Sinan arrived in the camp on his way to Damascus, Baghdad and Jerusalem. He was always a welcomed visitor, because he always had something interesting to say. He had just received a commission to carry out repairs on the old mosques and erect new ones, and he was very happy for his sudden success. Ibrahim was not the only man who deserved his high status. Sinan was even more worthy of advancement, because he was not only an inspired architect, but he also excelled as a construction manager. He was one of the few officials that always kept his promises and his deadlines no matter what unexpected difficulties he encountered; but most of all he was a good and loyal friend.

They had their differences of opinions, but they were all in the theoretical level as they saw life under a different prism. Ibrahim was much more interested in ephemeral and trivial issues, while Sinan in eternal. However, these differences didn't get in the way of their friendship. Their parallel careers were like the mortar that may separate rocks, but at the same time unites them into a more solid entity. They had spent many hours exchanging views since they came back from Egypt, and even if they disagreed more often than not, they could comprehend the reasons for their disagreements. He had become a member of the Ottoman nobility, while Sinan had remained humble and much closer to the common man.

What was most critical was that Sinan understood the reasons why Ibrahim had to make certain concessions to advance. The fact that he was more austere with his choices, and as a result his career was less turbulent, was not a reason to be ashamed or to be proud. This time their meeting was somewhat unusual. Sinan had just left Manisa as Hafsa's Mosques was completed, and Ibrahim was eager to hear Manisa news, and Sinan as eager to relay them.

"Mustafa is a very successful governor," Sinan noted. "He is as just as Sultan Selim. This is at least what I heard in the bazaars."

"What happened to Hafsa Sultan? She got very ill almost as soon as she left Manisa," Ibrahim asked hesitantly.

"She lived a full life. This is what counts. She had to go through the transition of aging all women and men have to face, but she didn't wish to. It was too much tension and something had to give. All beautiful women have a hard time admitting there comes a time when beauty fades away. The more beautiful a woman is the more difficult it is for her to adjust to the transition. Sooner or later Mahidevran will have to suffer too. Then, we will see from what kind of metal she is made of. Let's hope she reaches that age for the sake of her son. She is so foolish she even gave me a letter for you."

"She is no fool. She knows all about you and me. She can judge a man from the way he looks at her," Ibrahim remarked.

"Mahidevran Sultan is a Princess. I have no right to judge her behavior. I can judge only her looks as a man," Sinan replied with an imperceptible smile.

Ibrahim rushed to open the letter that surprisingly was not even sealed, a most peculiar characteristic during a period that extreme secrecy was the rule since the day Sultan Selim rose to Ottoman throne. The letter was extremely short:

"Now that you have a son, protect him from all evil as I do with mine."

"This is a letter that does not say much. It is more like an advice. Have you read it?"

"I didn't have to. She read it to me to convince me my life would not be in danger.

"Did you see Mustafa?"

"No, he was posted in Constantinople most of time while you were fighting in the East; but Mahidevran Sultan remained in Manisa to look after Hafsa."

"Yes, but Hafsa came back to the Eski Saray."

"Yes, she did, when there was no hope of recovery. She wished to die and be buried next to her husband. This is at least what she told me."

"I saw her before she went to sleep, but didn't tell me anything more besides that she was too tired to keep on living."

"The purpose of a woman is to bear children and of a man to seed them. Many people take this divine mission more seriously than others," Sinan asserted.

"Despite whatever you might think about me, most recently I can sympathize with this choice. You may say that I have changed my priorities the moment I found out I had a son of my own."

"Then, the Jihad-el-Akbar must have started for you too. I'm glad!" Sinan remarked with an undetectable touch of irony. "I hope Allah blesses you soon with many more sons that you care to have."

"Inshallah!"

"I must be on my way. I don't wish to keep a Grand Vizier away from his important duties. There are all this devious people who say that his first priority has ceased to be the prosperity of the Ottoman Empire," Sinan noted and started the long ceremony of greetings and prostrations a Janissary had to carry out o show his respect to a Serasker.

"Please, stop that nonsense. I demand prostrations only from an enemy ambassador, not a comrade in arms, a Janissary who holds in his hand the sword of Allah."

"I used to hold the sword of Allah long time ago. Now that I have my sons too, I have laid down my sword and picked up the hammer. My period of destruction has passed. Now I want to build a better world than the one I found."

"I didn't know you had children. As far as I know Janissaries are not supposed to be married and have children. Marriage is supposed to make men softer and less willing to die for the sake of the Empire."

"Yes, that's true, but I'm following the example of my Sultan, the Shadow of Allah, and my Serasker who both have children by their slaves. Such great leaders must certainly know what is best for the Empire."

Ibrahim could not contain the urge to laugh his heart out. Sinan was undoubtedly a Muslim, but he was also Greek to the bone. He didn't hesitate to mock a Serasker or the Sultan whenever he had a just cause to do so. He was a typical Janissary ready to sacrifice his life for a Sultan who promised a better world, but as eager to threaten any Sultan or public official who took advantage of his power and position to make a profit, or simply to violate the oath he took when he occupied his lucrative position.

Of course, there were exemptions to this rule, and many Janissary took advantage of the power bestowed on them to make a fortune by illegal activities, as prostitution, stealing or looting; however, Sinan believed on different principles. For him money was an inferior goal for a man's life. Gold was useless as a metal because Allah had made it too soft. Gold had acquired extreme value that made it a commodity worth steeling. For him stone was hard enough and cheap enough to be used in temples. He had been greatly impressed in Egypt when he learned that all the biggest mosques had been built using stones chiseled many-many centuries ago, when the Great Pyramid was erected. It meant that stone was the best material to build temples and worship god. Gold was good only to make jewelry and gain favors from presumptuous women seeking temporary pleasures.

Since now he had his superior's permission to depart he turned around, rode his horse and waved Ibrahim goodbye. Ibrahim watched him as he rode away towards the first turn of the old Roman stone-paved road that crossed Asia Minor.

Suddenly Ibrahim fell all alone. He was lonely and isolated from worthy friends like Sinan. Becoming a grand Vizier had multiplied the number of his enemies and fake friends who were eager to appear friendly to utilize his power and influence for their profit. In a sense he understood how suspiciously Suleiman felt towards all men in his environment and possibly women too. In high places most human feelings were replaced by pretense that was greed in disguise. Essentially he owed everything to Suleiman's power and love, and without them his life might be horrific. His attractive appearance would have been his condemnation. By now he would have had thousands of male lovers, and no decent woman would wish to have the offspring of a dubious male like him.

From the moment he became Hasodabashi his luck with women had changed in many ways. Many women now dreamed of becoming united with a man like him. A single child by him could change the fortune of any concubine.

He had no doubt that if he tried hard enough, Suleiman would be eventually convinced to offer him as present any concubine in his harem he didn't like. It would be a relatively easy task to convince Hurrem that Suleiman desired this concubine. Then, since Hurrem had such a great control on her husband and was so jealous, she could easily convince the Sultan to offer the concubine in question to his best friend as a present. Women were very conniving in that respect and Hurrem was clearly among the most capable in the art of manipulation of feelings.

He was almost as good if he set his mind to it; but

gradually conniving against this Sultan didn't make any sense, when he had granted him every possible honor. It was dishonorable, as bad as treachery. When he was younger he didn't think this way. Cheating his master almost felt honorable; however, now that Suleiman was ill, any cheating felt like cowardice. It was as if he was siding with the Sultan's enemies. It was also dangerous, and now he had a son to think of. Making love to Hafsa was a brilliant diplomatic stroke, and screwing Hurrem seemed like the right thing to do at the time to show her she shouldn't be afraid of him, because he had no claims on Suleiman's heart. Even for his romance with Mahidevran he had a good excuse. She was extremely frustrated and any kind of indecency would be reported to the Sultan and put Mustafa's future into jeopardy. He simply tried to eliminate any detrimental effects for the Empire from Suleiman's mistake to focus his attention only to a single slave of dubious past. However, sometimes even good excuses didn't work, when jealousy or madness prevailed.

He should have opened his heart and discussed this issues with Sinan, but now he was gone and he was all alone. When he was all by himself he had noticed he could find the best excuses; but Sinan's critical attitude would be useful. Sinan's departure was indeed upsetting his emotions. From the day the pirates had captured him, he was very sensitive during separations. Departing was some kind of death. Many times he had felt as if his parents have died simply because it was impossible for him to spend some time with them. When they returned to Constantinople, he would try to find some time to visit Parga or even better to invite his parents to the Eternal City, since Venice was still in control of Parga and a Grand Vizier could not visit an enemy of the Ottoman Empire without creating all sorts of rumors of a possible treachery by his enemies.

He was powerful, but fragile as well. For the first time in his life he dreamed how freer he would have been, if by some magical way he could resign from his office. It was a mad dream, because he was Serasker in times of war, and resigning was nothing less than treachery. If one of his Pashas resigned his commission during an expedition, he would have no regrets executing him. He was not sure what the Sultan would do in such a case, but it would surely turn him into an enemy of the Ottoman state. He felt boxed in somehow and this feeling of inability to escape raised the level of his anxiety.

To relax his tension he tried to change his disposition by thinking something pleasant. He was very curious to see the color of the eyes of his daughter, or whether his son looked like him or Hatidge. He didn't care about the color of his eyes, but he was eager to see whether his son would have the aquiline nose of the House of Osman. Hatidge had the straight nose of her mother. However, if his son for some mysterious reason looked like an Osmanli, then Suleiman's sons may consider him as a probable usurper, if his son was also bright and capable.

He realized he was getting hysterical. His son was still in the cradle, and he was worried what would happened when he matured. Nevertheless, perhaps he should relay his worries to Hatidge and let her assure Suleiman he had no claims on his throne for his son.

The thought his son maybe strangled by the Mutes brought tears into his eyes; but a sudden breath of wind dried them before they could run down his cheeks. Now all he could feel was that he could not predict the future, but do his best to adjust it to his own wishes.

****

Baghdad may have declined to an insignificant city, but it was the world famous capital of the Abbasids. Nevertheless, the loot was minimal for such a long and hard expedition, so the Army's rejoicing was as minute as the number of slaves. Baghdad was few days away from Persia and many months away from Constantinople. This meant that like Tabriz Baghdad would be impossible to keep for long unless the entire Persia was occupied, a feat the Roman Empire had failed to achieve, and no world conqueror besides Alexander, Genghis Khan and Tamerlane had ever accomplished. Nevertheless, it was an important strategically conquest as it lied on the way to the harbor of Basra on the Persian Gulf and a critical step further towards India.

Other nations like Spain and Portugal had discovered great treasures travelling on the waves to America and the Spice Islands; so, perhaps the Indian Ocean was the next domain where new riches could be claimed by the Ottomans. This was why the conquest of Egypt by Selim Khan was so important. He had died by his dream to reach India was alive in Ibrahim's mind. If Suleiman was sick and didn't wish to continue this quest, he was healthy and able to fight with the Portuguese for the domination of the Indian Ocean, India and East Africa.

All these years the Ottomans were fighting in West and East on land, the Navy of the Empire had not only grown immensely is numbers and vessel size, but it had also found the most capable admiral, Hayrettin Barbarossa. He was a Greek pirate from the island of Lesbos who had changed his faith to prosper. He was the son of a Janissary and the widow of a priest. When Hayrettin was born, Lesbos was a hideout of many pirate ships, because it had man bays and coves where pirate galleys could find safe harbors. It was also very close to the entrance of the Hellespont used by many nations to reach Constantinople and the Black Sea. At the time every ship that went through the Bosporus Straits had to pay a tribute to the Sultan for a safe passage; but from the moment it entered the Aegean Sea it was fair game for the pirates.

When Selim became Sultan he made a deal with these villains to respect all the vessels that displayed the Ottoman banners, but sometimes this was not enough and Christian pirates looted Muslim sea traffic. Some other deal had to be made and Selim agreed to support the fleet of the three Barbarossa brothers, if they could protect the Ottoman ships that went through the Aegean. Soon enough few islands where wrestled from the Venetians, many Christian islands were raided so heavily they were abandoned, and most of the pirate fleets were absorbed by the Barbarossa fleet that was renamed Ottoman

Navy.

This fleet became suddenly so bold and adventurous that when Selim occupied Egypt, the three Barbarossa brothers raided the African coast that was mostly under Spanish control all through Libya and Tunis. When his two brothers were killed by the Spaniards, Hayrettin became so enraged and audacious that he was invited by the Muslim Sultan of Algeria to protect it from the raids of the Spanish fleet. It was then when Selim named Barbarossa Beylerbey of Algiers. However, when Selim Khan died, this cooperation withered away because the new Sultan's attention was directed against the Hungarians in the Balkans. Suleiman was not willing to try his luck in the seas preferring the safer ways by land. In the sea Turks had used other nations as seamen that they didn't yet fully trust.

When the Ottomans tried their luck for the second time in Vienna, the Christian fleet had carried out a diversional attack in Peloponnesus, capturing the castle of Koron that dominated the passages from the Aegean to the Adriatic Sea. Sensing the danger, Ibrahim invited Barbarossa to Constantinople for a conference. Barbarossa arrived with forty ships full of booty as presents for the Sultan. He offered black slaves, Spanish gold, and even wild African animals for the Gülhane Garden as tribute, and a new agreement was reached. From now on Barbarossa would be the new Kapudan Pasha, i.e. the Admiral of the entire Ottoman fleet.

As an admiral, Barbarossa's first command was to give orders to the Constantinople shipyards how the new ships should be built to be able to face up to the Venetians and the Spaniards on the High Seas. The timing was ideal, because the united Christian fleet was now coordinated by an able admiral from Genoa, Andrea Doria, getting ready to strike at Tunis.

In fact, few months after Barbarossa's departure from the Golden Horn, horrible news arrived from Tunis that claimed his fleet had been surrounded and burned inside the Tunis harbor, the city of Tunis captured, and worst of all, that Barbarossa was killed in action.

Fortunately only a small part of the story was true.

Barbarossa had managed to sneak half of his fleet into another harbor along the African coast and most importantly he had escaped at night from the Tunis disaster by land. To take revenge of the Tunis disaster with his remaining ship he raided the island of Majorca taking hundreds of Spaniards as slaves. For Ibrahim it was a sign Barbarossa was the most capable admiral in the Mediterranean Sea and worthy of any support, logistical or financial.

Indeed soon Tunis was recaptured and the united Christian Fleet suffered a great disaster from an immense storm, while the Ottoman Fleet gradually recovered its strength. It was now so strong it could face successfully the combined fleets of Spain, Genoa, and Venice with even chances.

****

Ibrahim returning to the Eternal City was simply too busy in diplomacy to have time to rest or look after his family. Fortunately, Hatidge was a competent Sultana and could take care of the Palace. Her education as a Princess was more than enough to look after her and his fortune. She had taken command not only of her son but also of the Russian slave's offspring she treated as if it was her own. His new daughter's nursery was the second room they visited after Hatidge showed him his son. Was it intentional or instinctive he would never know and at the moment the least of his concerns. He needed the touch of a woman and she knew it. To tease him she told him she had prepared an elaborate banquet in the garden. Few glasses of red wine would clear their minds from every unhappy thought or worry about what the future might bring after such a long separation, and he was more than happy to follow her to this sinful breach of the sacred Quranic Laws.

Ibrahim thought that it was the right time to bring the subject of their son to his wife. To start the subject as diplomatically as possible, he mentioned the Sultan's curious behavior, when her letter arrived with the news about the Russian's maiden delivery. Hatidge heard the entire story before having any reaction, but surprisingly she was more amused by her brother's reaction than worried.

"My brother has no idea what it means to have children. In that respect I'm afraid all your efforts to open his mind have been wasted. Everyone agrees that Allah's Paradise is an immense garden. In spring every tree in a garden is blooming and its flowers shed pollen. If this pollen falls on the right flower, then the flower turns into a juicy fruit. However, despite having so much pollen every spring, there are still many flowers that die even though they are as beautiful and have as delicate perfume as the lucky ones. It is a sad event because this way many fruits are never born, and the people that would eat them remain hungry and have to wait another full year for the new crops. I was lucky enough to be born the daughter of a Sultan, and so your pollen found me, even though I had two more children from another man. As a woman I have done my duty to Allah; but all women are not as lucky as I am. I would be a great sinner, if I denied the same happiness to other women. This Russian was unlucky enough to be bought as a Sultan's concubine. My brother decided for some reason that he desired no more children; but it would be a terrible waste such a beautiful flower to fade away. Her beauty is a gift that could bring happiness to everyone around her, so she should be shared by many. Soon her daughter will grow too even more beautiful than her mother; thus my only concern now is to show her as much love as I have for my children, and hope that when she grows up, she will share with my son as much love as I have shown her. Love is the best fertilizer for more love to grow and our world to become a better place than we found it. No one knows what the future will bring us, but if my brother dares to harm my son, then Allah will take revenge on his children, because hate is the best fertilizer for hate on Earth."

Ibrahim was greatly impressed and relieved listening to his wife's explanations. As the years passed he had acquired also Oriental habits and could listen to Hatidge's narrations for hours. Indeed Hatidge had not finished all she had to say that night.

"Love makes all people better, and if I despise Hurrem's

behavior, it is because she grows worse with time. This is why I have never raised obstacles in your relationship with my brother, because I feel it has been beneficial to both of you. When someone is young he has every right to try every fruit Allah's Paradise offers, and I'm the last woman who has the right to judge a man's weaknesses. Nevertheless, as years go by, I have the feeling that this love of yours for my brother is just an elusive, youthful dream that is destined to rot and harm you both. Love must not be sterile simply because then it slowly becomes a waste of time and effort. Wasting time is a great sin, because it makes our life shorter needlessly, when there are so many other activities that bear real fruits. Dreams are useful because they can help us improve our lives, but if something cannot grow, it's bound to die. However, I don't wish to do anything to wake you up. It's your dream and you have to decide when it's dead enough to bury it. If you need my help, you just have to ask for it, but I don't want you or him to blame me for its failure in any way. Nevertheless, I don't intend to remain passive too; so I will do anything it takes to protect my son, and this means that one day I may decide to leave you, take our son and move away from this Palace and this city never to come back. You see I have my dreams too, and I don't intend to sacrifice not a moment more of my elusive dreams for yours. Life is nothing more but a battle between our senses made to feel and our brains made to dream, and to survive we all have to find a decent balance between our dreams and reality. Through these few years you went away I have dreamed too much and now the time has come for reality at last to get the upper hand. My dear Ulysses, it's time for you to drop anchor in your Ithaca. This is the destiny of every man no matter how many sirens he meets in his travels."

Ibrahim realized that it would a waste of time to seek excuses. It would be much easier for him to show repent than try the feeble excuses he had prepared all these years for his clandestine adventures. If Hatidge had found out of any of his escapades, trying to deny them he would simply anger her. She was born a Princess and her wishes carried much more weight than a slave's who had managed to become a Grand Vizier and a Serasker by obeying someone else's wishes. Eventually he had become the most useful man for the prosperity of the Empire; but now being such, he didn't need to make any more concession.

There were three women Hafsa, Hurrem, and Mahidevran Sultan who could easily ruin him, if they decided to open their mouths and talk. The first had fortunately died, while Hurrem would risk everything, if she decided to tell all she knew about him. Finally, Mahidevran was too isolated in Manisa to become a threat of disclosures. Therefore, he was essentially quite safe, unless something unexpected happened that would open up the Aeolus' sack.

"I am very tired of running away from myself. All I need now is a woman's warm bosom to rest for the rest of my life. Please forgive me. From now on I will taste only what you would care to offer me," he promised with as much sincerity as he could find.

"You are surely a very intelligent man, much more than I am, the Sultan or any other man I know. You have a really devious mind that knows how to manipulate people by saying the exact words they want to hear. Your logic is truly unbeatable; but as you know logic is based on human rules of cause and effect, but Allah rules the world beyond logic, and sometimes something unexpected happens caused by laws we are unaware of. Men also obey to few different laws than women and vice versa. One primal law men do not comprehend is why mothers care so much for their children. You are wise, but it is simply impossible for you to comprehend how it feels to have a child growing inside of you feeding by your blood and when it's born to rely on your milk to survive and grow. My wise and powerful Grand Vizier, do you really believe my mother would have kept any important secret from me? Do you think she would die alone in Manisa, when she had a daughter's warm bosom to rest during her final moments? Of course, an obnoxious man would surely imagine that a widow's sole concern was to return to Constantinople to be buried next to her husband. What complete nonsense! Now my highly intelligent

Grand Vizier please tell me! Would a woman wish to be married next to a man who died whispering the name of another woman?"

Ibrahim was too tired to react after this devastating bombardment of well-prepared accusations. He shouldn't have left Constantinople for so long, but he was the Serasker and had to fight the wars the Sultan couldn't. This was his reason of living, however when men were not around, women had all the time in the world to seek and analyze their flaws and weaknesses. Surely Suleiman would by now under a similar heavy bombardment from Hurrem. Faced on a battlefield with blazing cannons the soldiers didn't have many options. They could keep on attacking, hopping the missiles would missed them, they could run away further than the cannons' range, or lay flat on the ground waiting for the guns to unload their fury.

This last option seemed the best option now, so he closed his eyes and rested his head on her lap to trigger Hatidge's maternal feelings for one last time. If she touched his hair and caressed him, he was safe inside Ithaca harbor.

And she did! After all his cheats, she still loved him and the explanation was staring him in the face. She had born two children of his, and she was not going to abandon him just for being a man. Only if his infliction with Suleiman got out of hand, her threat to seek a divorce would materialize. However, she was unquestionably a Princess with Tatar blood in her veins and he had to feel her whip.

"You men will never learn correctly your priorities. Tonight you belong to Sherenk that gave you a daughter and she has the right to be pleased first. When I feel I need a man I will invite you to my quarters."

"Who is Sherenk? I swear I have never slept with any Sherenk in my life!" he protested.

"My darling, I know you didn't touch her lately; but I did several times to find out why she is so exciting. This is why I gave her also this name I like and fits her perfectly. It means "the three colored" in Persian, as you may recall. When you look at her eyes real closely it's hard to tell whether they are blue, green or purple. Haven't you noticed?"

"No, I haven't. For me her eyes were simply as mesmerizing as emeralds."

"Then perhaps you should be more careful tonight. Don't forget a woman's eyes are mirroring the content of her heart. This is probably why I discerned those purple flames and you didn't. Go! She is waiting for you. A man should never leave a woman waiting, because while she is waiting, she entertains the worst possible ideas about him. Next time a woman is expecting a child of yours, don't forget to come and hold her hand to make her feel you will always be at her side, even if she is about to die. If you fail to do that, she is bound to think she was just a good fuck for you."

****

The Hatidge was right! This was how he thought about women and it was not fair. They all had so much more to offer than just a temporary tension release accompanied by a bit of pleasure. If pleasure was his sole concern, a man could offer him as much. The essential difference was that the woman needed to feel wanted, while a man that he was superior.

The Princess was a noble woman in every respect. She was superior than any slave. There was simply no comparison. This was why she was never jealous for his escapades. She simply couldn't be, because besides Mahidevran they belonged to a different species.

The closer example of her from the animal kingdom was the dominant female in a pride of lions. From the moment she was served first, she would not mind if he was coupling with any other female in his harem. Of course the male lion had the right to use her, but only when she felt like it. Now that she had her fourth child, she had enough of child bearing. More children would degrade her flesh and make her unattractive not only to him but to all her future lovers. They were female of course, because with females she could be dominating from start to finish.

Her children were living testimonies of the moments she had surrendered completely to the wishes of a man. Perhaps this was the reason she preferred so much making love with inherently contraceptives ways. Nevertheless, her mind was so simple. He had sensed that it was governed also by other emotions. For instance, he could not deny that she adored her children and not only her own. She loved even Hurrem's offspring. Initially he was suspicious that she cared only for the House of Osman, but he was wrong. She loved even his newborn daughter by a slave. Her role model had to be different and much more primitive than Muslim morality concerned only with male pride.

He was very lucky he had found her. His position would be unattainable, if she resembled Hurrem. However, she was lucky she found him too. Another husband might be reluctant to bear her weakness for beautiful women. It was one critical point they were perfectly matched, and she was sincere enough to admit it.

"Sometimes I tend to feel very lonely. Then, I become very aggressive and all true women like aggression. Perhaps by naming her Sherenk I violated your rights for being the first, but I don't believe in seniority. I believe on familiarity. All these years I had the chance to know her much better than you. We are a perfect match. She adores authority."

"I love her name. In my ears it sounds like "serene". I have no idea about her singing, but there is no way I can forget the lighthouse of her eyes."

"Then stop talking and show her who is the master of the house."

"I always thought it was you," Ibrahim teased her as he departed.

"This is what you got wrong from the very beginning. I'm not just the master of the house. I am your Sultan and don't you forget it!" She snapped back.

****

Having two Sultans over his head was a bit too much; however, he should have expected that as Hatidge was the daughter of Hafsa. Now she knew all about him and his weaknesses and she was the kind of woman he had to respect. Divorcing her would be suicidal. Nevertheless, he had no urge to claim his freedom and this feeling had to be the result of very skillful manipulation. By allowing him a great degree of freedom, Hatidge had extinguished the urges of a man might to dominate a relationship. The only feeling he now had was that of a jealousy. He was jealous like hell of Basmi. She had to be Hatidge's choice for the night.

He was badly mistaken. As he walked out the door of Hatidge's bedroom he encountered Yabani, and Zarafet waiting. Just to be sure he approached them and hugged both of them passionately. Their skin was smooth, pink and delicious as the skin of every woman that has just come out of the hammam.

He went straight to his bedroom full of anger. He was not the male lion of a pride. He was the drone of a beehive. However, Sherenk was there perfectly armed to calm down all his anxieties. She was real and perfectly willing to erase all his illusions by creating new ones. The harem was a marvelous institution for any male, because it provided him with options and solutions to all his personal problems. However, the man had to acknowledge the fact that the moment he omitted any of his duties his void would be filled some other way, as Eros was undefeatable in battle, as Homer had acknowledged many centuries ago.

Books were the source of knowledge and a man could find answers to every problem he encountered, if he was willing to search into books hard enough. Even if a book was on purposely destroyed, the knowledge it contained would be repeated by the readers of the book. This was probably what had happened in the case of the Bible. Students had read it and when the original copy had been destroyed probably by an overzealous Roman Emperor, new Bibles had sprung up written by other authors who wrote down their point of view.

Writing new stories and allegories had to be a useful process, because every author could add new commandments from his experiences, and thus put them to the test of time. Ten commandments were too few to regulate the human species, and one holy book like the Quran an illusion a simpleminded man had dreamed in the desert.

Love was unquestionably an essential ingredient of human happiness, but sometimes even pain could make a man happy. Simple recipes were simply inadequate to guaranty happiness for all human beings. Tonight a Princess like Hatidge Sultana could never have made him as content as Sherenk did with her unending patience and forceful perseverance. If he had to choose one woman, Sherenk would be the one. Selim Khan was a fool to whisper Mahidevran's name; but then he didn't know Sherenk even existed.

****

In the Seraglio, Suleiman and Hurrem were spending their night of reunification. All their children had been put to sleep in the Eski Saray earlier on, tired by the formal ceremony of the Sultan's return. Even though their children were so distant their thought seemed dominating, twisting around their brains like encaged wild animals. It was simply a matter of time when these animals hungry for power and riches would break free.

"How did you find our children? Have they grown enough during your leave?" Hurrem said, starting confidently the hostilities with an air of submission.

"They are fine; only Mehmet's chick was darkened too much. He is old enough and you will have to find him a pretty young slave to sooth his heart like my mother did for me at his age."

"I don't wish to be blamed for any failure, and Gülfem has no daughters for me to match your mother's choice," Hurrem remarked with a touch of irony. "Perhaps it would be a better idea for you to follow your father's choice of Mahidevran. At least she was the one you honored last with a child. Daughter or son makes no difference. It is the thought that counts."

Suleiman decided that he shouldn't reply to her tease. Replying in anger would be the worst he could do. It would mean her arrow found the target; however, she had more than one arrow in her quiver to pierce his thorax.

"I'm sure you know Sultan Selim had her name in his lips just before he died."

"Yes, I do! Nothing escapes my spies; but don't think much of it because he was drugged to die painlessly."

"Spies are useful, but you also have to use your brain to reach the right conclusion. Have you ever asked yourself why such a pious man would not die with Allah's name slipping through his lips along with his last breath?"

"My father was in a comma. In such a condition a man may whisper anyone's name, even yours."

"That's true, but I don't think my dance had impressed him so much to remember me more than her. I may have the name, but she has the grace. Men simply die to fuck her. Of course, if Gülfem hadn't begged the Kislar Aga to replace me, then it might have been a different story. Perhaps you don't know that he had given the Kislar Aga a long list of all the perversion he enjoyed most, and I had to study it for an entire week. Unfortunately, all my studying was wasted along with my elusive dreams to have a child by a vigorous man like him as so many other married and promiscuous loose women."

"Now that you had your fun making up stories to get me excited, let me tell you that I don't believe a single word you say. Gülfem is the last person that might have consider such a trick. She is as innocent as a lamb. Changing places with you was inconceivable. However, if she had ever told me the same story about you and my father, I would have surely believe it. You used to be very ambitious."

"I cannot ask the Kislar Aga to confirm it, because your mother was wise enough to dismiss him, putting the last nails on his coffin in Egypt; but if you find this naughty story exciting. I can surely add few details that will give credibility to my narration."

"This was indeed a nice try to masquerade your lies as truths. However, I didn't know the old Kislar Aga died in Egypt. I presume this was also an act of my departed mother."

"Don't be absurd. I never said that. We all know your mother died long before his death. I believe he was traveling to Egypt, when he was assassinated. Your mother is completely innocent. If you want to find the guilty party you must look elsewhere."

"I bet this is another case where Ibrahim Pasha killed to protect his reputation," the Sultan remarked in a mocking disposition.

"I'm glad that whatever I say amuses you, but Ibrahim would never kill to protect his reputation. On the contrary, he would do anything he can to appear in the worst possible light. This is why he has accepted as a wedding present the two naughty courtiers that always accompany your precious Kadin, the impeccable Mahidevran Sultan. The man is so audacious, he has built a career by being licentious; but who can blame him. Which fool puts a hungry wolf to guard a flock of sheep?"

"Is this a rhetorical question I should try to answer?"

"No, please don't. I don't wish in any way to embarrass you for your unusual choices. I believe you were forced to the wrong decisions by people who look solely after their own interests. I promise I will do my best to put an end to this outrage. When Gülfem came back from that indescribable orgy in the Marble Kiosk, she described me with great detail what Sultan Selim had done to her, after she finished her mediocre dancing routine. I'm sure you are well aware of all her boring dancing figures; otherwise, you would still invite her in your quarters for your pleasure; but, imagine how unskilled and unimaginative this Kadin of yours truly is, if she doesn't shake her naked breasts in front of the man she is trying to seduce into impregnating her. Praise Allah for your manly father who didn't need a naked boy to sit on his lap to get excited and gave her more than she cared for. Nevertheless, I actually think that getting too close to a vigorous man is not an advantageous maneuver for any naked woman as it is for a naked man, and the reason is the prospective. What is closer looks bigger than it actually is. Ask Sinan, your imperial architect, and he will surely agree with me about this optic law. By the way, this Janissary is a genius. He finds inspirations everywhere he looks. When he stares at me, I'm sure he wants to build twin domes like my boobs. If you don't believe me, go to Manisa and examine carefully your mother's Mosque. Then come back and tell me what has been his divine inspiration after spending several years in that town visiting your palace. However, this night should not be get wasted with useless accusations in retrospect. You have just returned from a victorious campaign that added great prizes to your Empire."

It was an unexpected change that transformed Hurrem from a determined attacker to a submissive ally. Naturally, this abrupt change surprised the Sultan who had assumed a hostile gesture, but he was mistaken. Her aim seemed quite different than his fears.

"I'm very glad to hear your praises. I was afraid Ibrahim's successes might have spoiled your jubilant mood. His performance had been impeccable during my illness."

"Indeed he was very efficient improving his image by enlarging your empire. My fears he might take advantage of your weakness to claim the throne by mobilizing the Janissaries were grossly exaggerated. I was wrong and I'm the first to admit it. If you wish to punish me in any way, I will gladly submit to any painful punishment you might choose to subject me tonight."

"This were hardly my intention when I invited you here to my quarters. I'm simply too tired from this expedition and I wish to relax and recover my optimism, spending some time with my children and you."

"I'm glad to hear you say you need me. All these months you were away I was afraid that you might have encountered a younger slave to fill the void our separation has created in our hearts. You know well enough that I have very reluctantly accepted your participation in this campaign, because your health was still too fragile. On the other hand, I was not blind. I saw your need to appear as a fighting Sultan to counter Ibrahim's rise in the army. Now that he has a son, he has one more reason to rejoice, not only he but also his allies. They are all waiting for your next health crisis to seize your throne."

"This maybe the dream of many candidates, but until they act, there is nothing I can do but be vigilant."

"This is the least you can do, because dreaming is the first step towards treason; believe me I know. All these months you were gone my mind was full of naughty images and you were not my only visitor. Now that you came back alive, I am ashamed for my dreams; but back then my will to resist was many times overwhelmed by the most shameful proposals. Now you tell me whether I should be punished for my dreams or be acquitted by you, my husband. In my consciousness I have sinned and I feel I should be chastised most painfully, so that my brain never again is so weak that allows my flesh to feel pleasure from such a despicable orgy that went on and on for many nights in a row until I was pregnant and lost every drive."

The Sultan remained silent overwhelmed by her revelations. In his heart he wanted to punish her for this unbelievable outrage, but in his mind this kind of justice should remain attached to the ancient Roman principles that only acts not thoughts should be judged.

"Please open up your heart and reveal to me your secret thoughts. Do you suppose these dreams of mine are divine signs that my life will come to an end. Old women in the harem say that men just before they die, a vision passes in front of their eye, the vision of the woman that has pleased them most when they were alive. Do you believe this myth?" she continued.

"Indeed I do and I trust you will be the vision I will see shedding away your veils."

"Sometimes you say the most nice things, the ones a licentious woman like me wants to hear. I wonder what kind of visions women see before they die. Logic says that virtuous women must also see visions of the men who would like to fuck them and for some reason they didn't."

****

What was she trying to do serving him all these bits and

pieces of sinful dreams? Was she trying to confuse him by adding a piece of truth inside a mess of malice?

Tonight she was too confident to let him have all the time to guess.

"Did you like my 'choban' salad? I know you Turks like to cut tomatoes and cucumbers in small pieces and mix them to bring out the flavor. In my country tomatoes represent women and cucumbers naturally men. Gülfem told me that your father was among the biggest cucumbers she had ever tasted. Now please tell me. Was she right, or was she trying to get me jealous for all the stealthy pleasures she experienced by taking my place?"

"If you think you can ignite my passion tonight by talking about my dead father, you are indeed perverted," the Sultan noted close to a violent explosion.

"Indeed I would the most perverted woman in the world, if I ever tried to do this kind of travesty; but unfortunately the devil hides in the details. Women know for instance that men like big breasts and when two women lay naked in a hammam, they secretly compare their breasts. I believe this is a habit as old as the Trojan War. Homer knew that and with his fertile imagination created the myth of Paris and the three Olympian goddesses. It is rather logical to assume that Aphrodite had the biggest breast. Now tell me my Paris: 'Isn't it true that among your three Kadin I have the biggest breast as Gülfem claims?"

"Yes it is, but this is not the only reason I preferred you instead of her or Mahidevran. Is this what you wanted to hear?"

"No, of course not. I was simply testing Gülfem's sincerity, because few women are very conniving. They try to make other women interested in sinful acts to degrade them."

"I don't see what you mean. I'm confused. If I know something for certain is that you are no lesbian."

Hurrem hearing his last comment could not contain her laughter. She was obviously happy with her master's state of confusion."

"Indeed I don't give an asper for any woman's tits,

however, Gülfem claimed that Ibrahim has the biggest cucumber she had ever tasted. Was she truthful? Please tell me because that would explain why he is so popular with women."

"How should I know how women think?" Suleiman complaint.

"I'm sure you know by instinct because you are a man. There are many people who can testify under oath Ibrahim was naked, when you bought him in the Avret Bazaar, and please don't reiterate that damned old story about the Manisa widow. It's a just a silly joke only an idiot could invent. If this widow ever existed and Ibrahim is so blessed, she would never have given him a present to any young Prince Heir. It would simply be too offensive to my intelligence. Do you see now why every detail is important for a good 'choban' salad?"

****

Now he was totally confused. Gülfem was too unimportant to become the final target of such an elaborate shot. Nevertheless, Hurrem had proved to him by logic and without involving a third person witness that Gülfem had been unfaithful to him at least for one night. However, Gülfem was too insignificant as a Kadin to force him to act and take revenge for his wounded pride. Hurrem had asked him long time ago to dismiss his entire harem, and let her move permanently in the Seraglio. In the case of Gülfem dismissing her permanently from his life was the easiest task, because she had no children alive, so no child would suffer from her death.

The problem of such an unheard action was with Mahidevran. She was not only beautiful and desirable, but she also had a son and a daughter. Thank Allah, Ibrahim had advised him early on to send the Princess away to Manisa. Hurrem stories had not implicated her for the time being, but it was conceivable Mahidevran had an illicit affair she knew something about while he didn't. Was Mahidevran Hurrem's final target?

Hurrem didn't let him think. She served him her choban salad on the platter.

"I truly don't care about what Mahidevran Sultan is doing in Manisa behind your back. What I need to know right now is which kind of men I should dream tonight, when you finally decide you had enough talk with a promiscuous woman."

****

Listening to her unending blabber, Suleiman started feeling weird without an obvious reason. She was simply younger than him and had more energy to keeping on talking until he had no more arguments. Consciously or unconsciously she was following Ibrahim's recipe of success in every negotiation, namely exhaust her opponent until he had no mental strength to resist and capitulation was the only way to stop her opponent from arguing.

She must have sensed his exhaustion and decided that it was time for the coup de grace.

"By the way, I've heard your precious Prince Heir had a son in Manisa. Congratulations for your first grandson!"

****

The birth of a grandson normally should be a happy event, but in this case it limited even further his options. His father Selim the Grim had been cruel enough to execute not only most of his sons, but also his innocent grandchildren. Would he ever be obliged to follow this path too?

However, this kind of dilemma looked now too remote to become a serious concern. If he was unhappy with the news instead of being delighted, it was simply because it meant he was now an aging grandfather. Bayezid Khan was also a grandfather, when he lost the throne to his son Selim. Was history going to be repeated?

He still remembered how generous his grandfather had been. He had offered him a horse each and every birthday to force him to become a good rider, and he had succeeded. Perhaps this was the reason his mother had married him with Gülfem Sultan, but she had failed to turn him into a stallion. Then, his father intervened and married him to Mahidevran Sultan who was even more beautiful. Perhaps if he had tried harder to conquer his brides back then, he would have appreciated them more. It was not clear whether Hafsa Sultan or Ibrahim Pasha had chosen Hurrem for his concubine. Hafsa claimed Hurrem was her choice and Ibrahim denied any connection; but it was conceivable they both lied and Hurrem could well have been the choice of the Kislar Aga who was now dead and buried. Hurrem had mentioned his death as if it was the result of some kind of conspiracy. What kind of secrets a Kislar Aga might have uncovered he ignored?

Undoubtedly, it had to be a Harem secret. Someone had made him look like a fool, no doubt. Grandfathers were the best fools of all like Bayezid the Saint who was fooled by Selim, his son the Prince Heir just before he died. It was perfectly logical. Grandfathers were nothing but old fools on death-row.

The terror of death surfaced in his eyes and she read it plain and clear.

"My darling, we are getting old. The best moments in our lives have already passed and from now on our only moments of joy would be the deeds of our children."

It was a pessimistic note that affected him much more than her.

"Rumor arrived recently in the City that Iskander Chelebi Pasha was executed; but I don't want to believe it because he was so faithful to the House Of Osman."

"Yes, he was executed for incompetence. He was responsible for a military disaster."

"I am not very familiar with politics and military strategies to know when losing a battle becomes a strategic retreat and when a military disaster. This maybe my personal problem, because my native language is not Turkish. Few years back I was taught Turkish, but it seems to me Ibrahim Pasha has given new meanings to old words. The setback in Vienna has been called strategic retreat, and loosing Tabriz few months after its conquest is called temporary victory. I also heard that the Grand Vizier signs peace treaties as Sultan, and that now blind obedience is considered as treachery. Soon I'm afraid that the Sultan might be called Grand Vizier."

The Sultan didn't seem to react to her ironic comments as if he hadn't heard her criticisms. However, soon it became clear that he was trying hard to control his violent emotions, as his blood rushed to his face, transforming his face into a terrorizing grimace of ultimate anger. Even the hair on his neck were raised as if he was an enraged wild beast, scaring the hell out of Hurrem as his echoed in the empty corridors of the Seraglio like a distant thunderbolt.

"Damned slave, get lost from my sight!"

However, Hurrem was not impressed anymore by these violent explosions of anger. She had fed this Turkish lion for too many years and considered his roars as an instinctive reaction of a tamed cat of a zoo that tried to convince itself that it was still the king of the jungle.

"I was right after all. Ibrahim Pasha has managed to turn back your Kadin into a slave."

And with these words Hurrem turned around and rushed out of his bedroom. The Sultan's anger was so overwhelming that he didn't notice how the two eunuchs guarding the door did not wait for his command to let her out. It was a subtle sign something in the Seraglio had fundamentally changed.

****

"Did you sleep well?" Hatidge asked him at the breakfast table.

"I slept magnificently. Sherenk was truly the flame I needed last night to revive my optimism. How about you? How did you sleep?" he asked to test her reflexes too.

"Yes, Yabani and Zarafet are indeed a joy and an escape from the ordinary. At the very beginning I thought I could tame Yabani, but it was impossible. She tamed me instead. She made me as submissive as Zarafet. Don't you find it exciting? Our moods are not truly ours. They depend as much on us as a son to his parents; but I'm sure a well-traveled man like you knows as much.

They used to say no man could look at my father's eyes for long, but Yabani has proved to me I am not as good as my father. What's your opinion? I'm sorry for asking, but I have to know exactly what pleases you most, so I can deliver it too. It's the only way a marriage can last for long."

****

The birth of his son was the proper opportunity for Ibrahim Pasha to meet the Prince Heir without raising suspicions. Their meetings were not as often as they should for this reason. The Prince was also very reluctant to get in touch with any state official. He couldn't easily forget the unjustified eviction of his mother from the Eski Saray for beating an impudent slave.

Gradually, their formal relations warmed up and Hafsa Sultan was mainly responsible for this improvement. She was the one who had complete faith in Mustafa's virtues, considering him the most worthy heir of Selim's Empire. Selim Khan was the only Sultan who could claim the title "forever victorious" as he had never left a field of battle with the infidels or the heretics, as even Suleiman had left Vienna walls scared of the oncoming winter and the Austrian reinforcements. To an insightful man like Ibrahim it was almost apparent that Mustafa preferred to be known as the grandson of Selim than the son of Suleiman Khan.

This time his trip to Manisa had a different purpose. It was not a pleasure but a business trip. He found the Prince practicing his archery skills. His accuracy and range was remarkable, and the harmony of his movements indicated a long and persistent practice indicative of extensive Janissary training. He expressed his astonishment for his performance and asked how he had acquired it. Mustafa explained with considerable pride that he had spent an entire year in the Janissary barracks following his mother's advice.

Mahidevran was undeniably a good mother. The best way for her son to acquire the Janissary loyalty was to become one of them. For her it was not enough to hire few Janissary trainers as Sultan Selim had done for his heir. Now the Janissaries were considering Mustafa as one of them. Was the Ottoman Empire ready for a Janissary Sultan? This was the question that might soon need an answer if Suleiman was too ill to fight. He had to admit that Mustafa was even at this young age a better man than either he or his father. On the other hand, he was insightful enough to suspect that Mahidevran's suggestion might be motivated by personal considerations, as Mustafa's transfer to the Janissary barracks had freed considerably her time from her son's supervision. Nevertheless, Mahidevran's secret affairs were not his first priority.

Answering questions was not one among Mustafa's intentions. He had stayed too long isolated in Manisa and his mind was full of questions. His very first one was ironic and full of poisonous doubt. He asked how capturing Tabriz and Baghdad was really a victory, while it was almost apparent they could not be held for long. In his opinion the Ottomans had fell into a Persian trap wasting their resources for dubious causes. Ibrahim hasten to explain to him that with few mortal enemies the war was not decided by one battle. Anyway the Persians were fine soldiers, so according to his opinion what the Ottomans ought to do were convince them they should put aside their ridiculous religious differences and form a strong alliance. The true enemies of both were the infidels in the North, the Russians, the Portuguese in the Indian Ocean, and the pagan Mongols in the East. His plan when he became the Sultan was to fight Persia victoriously for several years to weaken their resolve, and then offer them generous terms for a long lasting peace and possibly an alliance against the Christians and the Mongols.

"In any case, if you cannot have strong friends guarding your boarders, it is sufficient to have weak enemies," Ibrahim tactfully asserted.

Mustafa didn't have any objection, or at least he didn't expressed it, an attitude that might be even wiser. According to all indications Ibrahim Pasha was still the right hand of the Sultan. Enemies and friends all admitted **Ibrahim was a sun that illuminated the skies of the Empire.** As every mortal Ibrahim had weaknesses, but his virtues outweighed his faults.

"Baghdad was just a city, but it was important because it controls the path to Basra and the Persian Gulf. As long as the Ottomans controlled the Mediterranean harbors and Baghdad, the Persians would have to submit to their authority. The traders had to use both Persian territories and the Holy Lands to carry out their commerce from East and West. His true fear was that the sea people from Europe could outflank both Ottomans and Persians. They were the most formidable enemies and for this reason Islam had to unite against the Christians, if Muslims really cared for the final victory.

Religion should be the bond uniting their efforts for the common good, not a reason to prolong this civil war among Muslims. Common people were not truly religious anyway. They all understood the Second Life was a hoax and Paradise was here on Earth and did their best to become happy. He and the Janissaries were the best proof of his assertion. People would be willing to believe in different gods, dress in different clothes, speak different languages as long they could earn a decent living. Survival was every man's main concern and when this was assured, the next human goal was more pleasures. This was what the Janissaries also wanted.

Mustafa remained silent listening patiently to his arguments, but when he finished talking he expressed fluently his objections.

"No, human greed doesn't stop there. Men seek new ideas too; so, they are never truly content with just gold, beautiful women, even Princesses, and luxurious palaces. If a man has one Sultana adorning his bed with her beauty, he will seek a second one. Then, when he conquers the second Sultana, he will not be happy, because he is jealous of the whores the Janissaries use for their pleasure. And when he gets all the whores he can afford, he will seek to buy handsome boys with the loot he secured after the last war. Believe me! I know how a Janissary thinks because I'm a Janissary too. The pleasure of conquest never stops."

"I agree, but nothing lasts forever, believe me. You are

simply too young to know that even your lust will someday end as well as your life. We all try hard to forget this horrific fact, but Death may be lurking just around the next corner. This is something all Janissaries know and that's why they drink so much red wine trying to forget it. However, as a Serasker I must always remind them that death may come even swifter, if they disobey my orders. As long as I can lead them to victory and more looting and slaves, I know I will be safe from their wrath."

"Yes, but as you've said, nothing lasts forever," Mustafa objected.

"Indeed this is how this world was made. I also know that with every new victory I make one more step towards death and disgrace."

"Then, maybe your time has come to step aside and let another Grand Vizier continue your saga. The Ottomans are grateful for all you have accomplished," Mustafa suggested.

"This is also my plan, but when I leave I have to leave peace behind. Till then I have to crush our enemies to make them believe that peace is the best option they have. This is what I have accomplished with the Persians in the East. Now I have to make sure the West will be better off signing a similar treaty with us. Then it would be the proper time for me to resign and enjoy all my belongings. As it is, I already have more riches than I can ever use. I know it is a utopia, but this is how I feel after several years of fighting."

"I wish Allah decides to grand you a repose, but I don't truly believe you will achieve it. You may be tired of victories, but your enemies will never accept their defeats as long as they are alive. You are living a dangerous utopia. Even if all your enemies die, their children will never forget their parent's shame. What was a conquest for you, for someone else it was a disgrace, and he will his best to avenge it. This is how human mind works. People will try to avenge even their most pleasurable moments, if someone convinces them they should feel ashamed for feeling good. Isn't it completely insane how Allah has built the world?"

Ibrahim was suddenly awaken by Mustafa's last comment.

Was it random or was it intentional to show him his past was now common knowledge? For many years he had fought with himself to resolve this issue with general vague arguments that were self-conflicting and led nowhere. A fair man could not accept that all pleasures were honorable, because then whores would appear as the wisest human beings. The sole truth was that there were no universal truths.

Mustafa's words still echoed in his ears. He looked at his face trying to guess how much of his past he already knew. His eyes were as black and threatening as Selim's. He couldn't resist all this pressure, so he lowered his glance. Mustafa considered his gesture a submission to his line of reasoning, but it was much more than that. Mustafa had such a great resemblance to Selim it was as if the grim Sultan had been reincarnated. He was feeling once more as if he was a boy. If Mustafa asked him to take his clothes off and sit on his lap, he would surely obey. His authority was unmistakable. But the youngster had clearly not the foggiest idea of what ideas were circling in his brain. Mustafa had a single concubine, beautiful no doubt, who had given him a son, and Ibrahim was a just another guest, wishing to offer him his congratulations for securing a door to the future. Mustafa was simply too premature on the circle of life, and he had a long way to go to become an all-demanding Sultan like Selim Khan.

He looked very confident realizing that with every day that passed, he was getting stronger, while his father became weaker. Suleiman's illness was an indication he wouldn't have to wait for long before the Janissaries intervened and put him on the throne. This much at least they had in common. Having a common purpose was the necessary ingredient for a fruitful alliance. Now all they needed was to make the decision to cooperate. As the youngster had wisely noted, there was not much time left before a defeat might strike the Ottoman camp. Then his position and usefulness would have been severely depleted.

Unquestionably Mustafa was an exceptional man almost as much as he was. They were not perfect, but they were surely better men than who else was presently available. If they failed to act, their future might be dimmer than their present.

"I have a very beautiful daughter. Now she is too young for you, but in few years when she blossoms perhaps you should consider her as a bride for your harem. I'm sure she can produce many clever children, because even now she is too smart for me and I cannot deny her any favors," Ibrahim proposed out of the blue.

It was an offer that took Mustafa by surprise because it was the last he expected. However, it was a gesture that showed Ibrahim's submission in many ways. Offering daughters to men of the House of Osman meant you were considering them a breed of worthy stallions. This was how Osmanli had been introduced originally to the bloodline of the Roman Emperors. They were the best fighters among degenerated Romans who would rather become monks than defend their lands and women. Finally, it became a routine task to replace them on the throne of the Roman Empire.

Mustafa smiled and his smile was unpretentious and warm. It was a sign he liked the idea the way Ibrahim had presented it. Indeed having bright and brave sons was much more important than having beautiful daughters in the mind of any Turk. If this was a mistake only History was capable of judging. A young man was simply too naïve yet to reach the proper conclusion without having similar experiences.

****

She knew she had to be sincere to gain his trust; so she was forward, almost cruel.

"Do you still remember how it was when you were a free man? Perhaps you don't, but I can surely imagine how many women sought your caresses! When I was a free woman, I could entertain any man I liked too. Becoming a slave I lost this freedom; but the urge is still there, or isn't it? They told me that to become a true slave I should twist my pleasure so that it matches my master's. I bet many masters have used you in ways you didn't approve, isn't it true?"

He blushed. In his mind he was still a man; but he had been humbled many times by white men. Hurrem needed someone she could trust, a man who had something to lose if he did not obey. This was why the old Kislar Aga had to go. He also knew too much about everyone; so he had to die. It was a matter of time when the murderers would strike to erase their shameful moments from the Kislar Aga's memory. Her secrets were too insignificant to force her hand. She didn't have to do anything but simply wait and take advantage of every available opportunity to advance her position.

This specific choice for a Kislar Aga by Hafsa Sultan just before she died looked a bit peculiar. She had chosen a black man many people knew was not a eunuch. Was she trying to keep a Harem full of frustrated women quiet, or was she trying to tempt her now that her Sultan son's health was declining?

Hafsa was unquestionably a very efficiently manipulating woman. She was trying to control everyone by discovering weaknesses she could then use to her advantage. What was most peculiar was the rumor she had used the old Kislar Aga for few months as a trainer for the new one. It was peculiar because the two men had entirely different dispositions. Peculiar events had to be explained somehow and Hafsa's death was a good opportunity for her to learn the ways of the Harem from an expert in survival tactics. His answers would be a good test for his moral values too.

"What did you do in Manisa?" she asked indifferently. "Was it worth the trouble? Speak freely. I am a very liberal mistress."

"No! I didn't learn anything I didn't know already," he replied with an almost identical degree of indifference and I have never punished a slave for taking liberties."

"I didn't know you were such an expert on pleasing noble women."

"As far as I was taught the mission of a slave is to please slaves."

"No! The duty of a slave is to follow orders. From what I heard, there are several lonely noble women in Manisa in search of a good man. I bet the late Sultana must have given you permission to extend your services to any rejected soul."

"Yes, she did; but, it is very dangerous for a slave like me to take liberties with any noble woman without an explicit order."

"Do you mean to tell me that Hafsa Sultana has ordered you to fuck Mahidevran and she refused to take advantage of the offer? I don't believe you. From what I heard this noble princess visits caravansaries regularly."

"This is what Hafsa Sultana suggested, but the Princess didn't show any interest in me. Perhaps she does not like blacks as much as you do."

"What do you mean by this insolent claim?" she remarked sternly.

"Hafsa Sultan has warn me that you like to become intimate with every Kislar Aga."

"Is this all she told you about me?"

"No, she also told me that you are very curious to find out who does what to whom, almost as much as she was."

"Isn't everyone in the Harem? Aren't you?" Hurrem inquired with a difficult to interpret grimace.

"I used to be curious, when I was first admitted. Now I'm going to be the new Kislar Aga. Now I know that I shouldn't believe what I hear. Many people have a lot to gain by spreading rumors."

"That's true; but it is also true that sometimes what happens is much worse than the worst rumor."

"I wonder what kind of rumor will spread now that you have visited my bedroom and locked the door behind you."

"I've told you that I'm a very liberal mistress. I will not punish you no matter what you ask me to do to you. The Sultan is very pleased listening to my wild stories, in fact the wilder the better. Tonight he will be very excited hearing that I have spent two whole hours locked in your bedroom."

"Doesn't get awfully jealous?"

"Yes, he does; but, then he believes me when I tell him that it wasn't real, but just a figment of my wild imagination. There is not much difference between reality and imagination, you know. Making love with a man or dreaming of him is for me almost the same. This is the reason why we often exchanged roles. With the old Kislar Aga we often played this make-believe game; but all men are not the same. This much I know well enough. Have you decided what kind of a man you would like to be with me? I don't have special preferences. I'm very flexible. I have been trained to follow a man's lead, even if he is not truly a man. Now tell me as sincerely as you can. Is being always a man your true preference? With me you have to be sincere, so I know where we stand. In this Seraglio there is too much hypocrisy, and eventually too much hypocrisy may be proven dangerous, because it leads to painful surprises. I'm sure a man with in your position knows exactly what I mean."

****

Asphodel seem pleasantly surprised to receive the Grand Vizier's summons to appear as soon as possible to the Sublime Gate. Such an invitation could change a man's career.

"I'm at your service," he promised the moment he had completed the ceremonial greetings of a Kapi Aga beckoned by a Grand Vizier. From the long smile of Ibrahim's face it was clear he was in excellent mood.

"I'm very happy to see you are in such excellent health," Ibrahim responded to his respectful attitude. "It means that still the people I trust are safe."

"You shouldn't worry about me too much. I was wise enough to make my last will and leave it in the hands of a trusted friend."

"From what I hear this is not foolproof method. Recently a Vizier wrote down such a last testament and was hanged by the neck," Ibrahim teased him.

"That's true! I really wish I had another option, but I'm just a Kapi Aga and my resources are limited. I wish I had someone I could fully trust like your Excellency to tell me exactly what to do every day to be safe. As you know I'm very good in following the suggestions of more experienced men than me."

Ibrahim had to admit that Asphodel had still a flexible mind and he showed his appreciation with a warm smile. Eunuchs were normally treated with contempt, but he was not an ordinary man. Building trust with the Eunuch corps had been a wise all-around strategy.

"Actually, I could give you many advices, if you were to tell me who exactly you feel is threaten you. Is it a concubine or a Kadin?"

"I wish I knew as much. It is more of a feeling than concrete information, more of a premonition than of a tangible fact. With few very powerful men a simple wish in the right ears is enough to make a man disappear. Evil has now the upper hand and no one is safe."

"Do you trust me? Tell me your greatest secret and I will never reveal it. You have my word of honor."

"I have always trusted you even when I wasn't sure you were a man."

"Then, tell me what I need to know to protect you from evil."

"I have already told you. You are more of a man than most people think, and that can be dangerous these days, when women have the upper hand in the Seraglio."

Chapter 14

In the City of the Spirits

'And all who bought doubt for the price of faith
will never harm Allah and will be severely punished '
(Quran, Sura III, 177)

The relations between Europe and the Ottoman invaders
did not change drastically after the fall of Constantinople, and the

enemies of the Roman Empire remained enemies for the Ottomans too. The Pope in the Vatican, and the Holy Roman Emperor Charles the Fifth who was trying to replace the fallen Eastern Roman Empire and expand in Spain, Italy, Holland, Austria and Germany, they both had great interest in extending their reach to the East via the Mediterranean Sea that was still the most important trade route in the world.

In this coalition other countries with similar interests also participated among which the Venetian Empire was the most powerful because of its fleet. Venice was the right hand of the Pope during the Crusades, and had almost never failed to support any venture that promised worthwhile financial gains. However, Venice's support was not without drawbacks, as the enemies of Venice became almost automatically allies of the Ottomans.

When Venice decided to support the last Roman Emperor in Constantinople, Genoa that had an important outpost across the Golden Horn in the Galata district decided to remain neutral, and reached an agreement with Mehmet the Conqueror. Thus, they didn't interfere against Mehmet's attempt to carry units of the Ottoman Fleet over land, bypassing the chain that sealed the Golden Horn. Despite the Ottoman fleet's failure to destroy the tiny Roman Fleet or its Venetian allies locked inside the Golden Horn, its presence forced the last Roman Emperor to remove troops from the Land Walls to the Sea Walls critically weakening the defense around the Romanos Gate.

After the Fall, Mehmet Fatih rewarded Genoa by making her the most favorite trader of the Ottoman Empire while he attacked the remaining fortified outposts of Venice in the Aegean Sea, namely the island of Euboea and Peloponnesus, where he was met with spirited opposition that led to considerable bloodshed even though eventually the Ottomans prevailed. Now after the Christian marine unification, and the cooperation of the Spanish, the Venetian and the Genovese fleets under the Admiral Andrea Doria against Tunis, North Africa had suddenly become the most important battlefield between the Catholic Church and Islam.

The Tunis harbor was very important since the Punic wars between Rome and Carthage because it controlled the passage between Africa and Sicily. Recently the Christians had the upper hand because they controlled not only Sicily and Malta, but they had conquered Tunis too. By keeping Tunis under their control, the Christians would isolate Algiers; on the other hand, if the Ottomans regained Tunis, then they could threaten Malta and possibly Sicily.

Since the Ottoman armies were stronger on land, Tunis had to be supplied by sea, making the Christian fleet indispensable. Since the Ottoman fleet was not strong enough to face the Christians, Barbarossa had to restrict his ambitions only to raids of Spanish coasts to intimidate Andrea Doria from Algiers. It seemed like a hopeless struggle for the Ottomans, unless they found another way out of this deadlock, and they accomplished it using the worst opponent of the Holy Roman Emperor, Charles V, the king of France, Francis the First.

Francis was now the major obstacle of Charles' effort to unite under his scepter France, with Spain, Holland and Germany. King Francis was initially defeated and captured, but was later released with the help of Suleiman's gold. He initially considered the Turks as an enemy of the Christians, but they were too far to be a threat, while Charles' ambitions much closer and more threatening for the independence of France. As France could not use Ottoman armies on the battlefield, Francis asked for gold from his Muslim ally to secure an alliance with the English dynasty of the Tudors against the dominance of Spain, and Ibrahim agreed to set up a closer alliance between France and Ottomans, or the "Lily and the Crescent" as it was called. This was to be a serious blow against the all-Christian alliance of the Holy Roman Emperor, because it revealed the true motives of all Christians. They were interested more in tangible financial gains than mystic religious concepts.

With Ibrahim's return in Constantinople after the Persian wars, the Ottoman diplomacy went through another cycle of development. It was a period when every major nation in the world had established an embassy or a consulate in the Galata district and every day Ibrahim Pasha had to meet with foreign ambassadors to make new treats and conclude new deals.

This subtle transformation of Ottoman strategy from pure violence and military strength to diplomacy and intricate negotiations was considered almost a treachery by many naive Muslim officials and clergy. To them negotiating was a sign of moral weakness and religious impurity. In the past, few foreign ambassadors had received harsh treatment in the hands of few Ottoman Sultans. Many had been mistreated and threatened, several had been imprisoned and few were executed in the Yedikule fortress. Ibrahim considered this glorious era of great conquests had passed. What was important now was for the Ottomans to consolidate their gains though negotiations to achieve peace and prosperity. Their armies had wrestled the respect of all the major European powers; but winning the war was not enough. They had also to win the peace, only then the Europeans would consider them as equals. They had to prosper, innovate, and create their own superior civilization.

Unfortunately during the destruction of the Eastern Roman Empire many creative minds had left the Eastern Roman Empire, seeking refuge from religious prosecution in the West. In the oncoming peacetime, the gates of the Empire had to open, so people could see that the Ottomans were not another wave of Eastern barbarians, but competent innovators capable of proposing new solutions to old problems. They had many skills and valued products they were willing to share and open minds capable of learning and improving many Christian trades.

Perhaps the most striking military innovations were their artillery and musket constructions that had made them the most formidable army worldwide. Now the time had come for sea warfare to point out that in the Ottoman empire many nations were contained, like the Greeks, the Arabs and the Albanians that could match the Venetian, Portuguese and Spanish exploits in the Mediterranean, the Atlantic and the Indian Ocean.

The water was one of the elements Ibrahim knew well

enough, better than most of the other Ottoman officials. For him, the land may appear as the safest way, but the seas, crossed by competent sailors and modern ships, were much faster and safer routes, leading to rapid progress and immense riches. Who finished last in the competition for the sea routes was destined to lose also the race to prosperity.

Suleiman may have been as suspicious for an unfamiliar element as any of his ancestors; but now he had to change attitude as soon as possible, because any delay could be proven very costly. The traditional silk roads from the East to the West were long, perilous and costly as many goods were stolen, when caravans passed through many inland nations that had no other revenues but collect tariffs or steal and resell goods from every passing caravan.

The Ottoman Empire was boarded in the North from the frozen steppes of Russia and in the South by the deserts of Sahara and the Sudan. In the East, any Ottoman expansion was restrained by the Persians and the Mongols, and in the West by the Vienna barrier. The moment the Vienna walls stopped their expansion, all that remained were the sea passages.

In the South, the safe passage of the Red Sea had to be utilized after capturing Yemen to reach the Indian Ocean, and in the West, Tunis, Malta, and Sicily had to be captured. If these targets were achieved, the Atlantic Ocean could be reached via Algiers and Morocco still in Muslim hands. Already Algerian pirates had reached Ireland establishing trading outposts.

This was Barbarossa's plan and Ibrahim Pasha had decided to support it. All he needed was some peace and quiet in the internal fronts. To achieve this respite he limited his friendly visits to the Eski Saray to avoid any conflicts with Hurrem. Now that Hafsa Sultan had departed, and Mahidevran was in Manisa, he had no good reason to visit it, as only with Gülfem he was in friendly terms. However, for some strange reason she had fallen into disfavor.

He tried to delay his visit as much as he could, but the problems kept mounting and he didn't wish to make any arbitrary decisions without Suleiman's approval. The rumor that the Sultan was angry for his decision to sign a peace treaty as Sultan Ibrahim had reached his ears and he was wise enough to avoid a second mistake without proving his worth and fidelity in between.

To be certain that the Sultan was in a good mood, he made sure he was not in pain by consulting the doctors. Then, he sent for the new Kislar Aga to be certain the Sultan had not arranged a meeting with Hurrem that had to be canceled.

The Nubian appeared promptly, but his stance was too arrogant compared to previous times. It had to be the result of his masculinity. He was undoubtedly a fine male specimen, and from the very beginning Ibrahim had few objections to this appointment, but Hafsa had insisted. Since Hurrem had made the initial hint, it was almost apparent he was part of some devious plan. An uncut Nubian in Suleiman's Harem was a double edged knife. Since the Sultan was interested only in Hurrem, the other concubines were in turmoil. A complete and viral man could silence the Harem for as long the Sultan had no use for it. This was probably the reason why Suleiman did not object to this appointment. If the Sultan didn't object, why should he?

Ibrahim was actually rather relieved, when the Nubian moved out of his Palace. Since he was the present of the Sultan, he was probably one more spy. He had post him in the stables, but when night fell and he was away fighting in the East who would know exactly what he did? However, this arrogant behavior could well be a sign of an ongoing Hurrem conspiracy.

The Kislar Aga was still a slave, and usually a slave's confidence was directly related to the importance of his master. Now that Hafsa Sultan had died, Gülfem Sultan should had priority to govern the Harem and the Kislar Aga on seniority. However, the Sultan had not approved this leadership change that left Hurrem as the unofficial Valide Sultana, since her senior Mahidevran Sultan was also in exile. It was a development more like an inconvenience than a real obstacle, since Mehmet Fatih's wisdom had remove the Harem from the Seraglio's vicinity. Living in the At Meidan to go to his office at the Sublime Gate or the

Seraglio he didn't even have to get close to the Eski Saray.

"How often the Sultan asks for your services in selecting night consorts?" Ibrahim asked, but the Aga didn't seem to care to reply hastily. "Maybe you are new in this position and you are not properly instructed, so I have to warn you that I share the Sultan's authority; so I can punish a slave or a Vizier any way I please without asking for a second opinion," he continued in good spirit.

This threat and the air of severity Ibrahim Pasha used had an immediate effect. The slave decided that it was for his own interest to reply as satisfactorily as possible.

"Your Excellency, please forgive my impudence; but my mistress has instructed me not to reveal anything about my Sultan's habits to anyone."

"She is indeed very wise to try to limit unnecessary gossip, but I'm not just anyone. I am the Grand Vizier and Serasker in charge of the Janissary corps. It is my duty to know how well our master feels, when I'm planning the next military expedition; so speak up!"

"Not more than once a week. The last time he asked for my mistress was yesterday."

"Good! Being prompt and truthful in this office can save your life. The last Kislar Aga was impeccable in this position. I'm not the one responsible for his dismissal. If you obey my orders as well as he, you will have nothing to fear."

It was a statement that should quiet down the Kislar Aga's fears, but instead Ibrahim noticed an ironic smile materializing on the Nubian's face.

"Are you doubting my word?" Ibrahim asked ready to renew his threatening tone.

"No, of course not! I am only doubting that Grand Vizier's word can keep a Kislar Aga alive these days."

"What is the meaning of this new impertinence?" Ibrahim asked alerted by this dubious comment by one more member of the Eunuchs corps.

"I didn't mean to be impertinent, but the previous Kislar Aga was murdered on his way to Egypt."

"How do you know that?"

"You cannot hide anything from eunuchs. The Grand Vizier must know as much."

Ibrahim was startled by this piece of information. It was too important to be ignored; nevertheless, going through the deserts of Syria and Sinan was a perilous journey for anyone who looked like a slave and was wearing expensive garments. Such a man was an open invitation to desert brigands, and this Kislar Aga didn't seem capable of offering any resistance. Unquestionably, he must have hired some security guards, but this was not always the proper answer. Many security men indicated a valuable treasure was transported and could even be the villains.

"I didn't know that," he confessed and his admission of ignorance and the entire discussion meant he was not the one who had arranged this execution.

Suddenly an idea went through his mind.

"Since you know so much more than me, do you know whether this pious man passed through Manisa?"

The Kislar Aga showed immediately his renewed interest.

"Yes, he did. He stayed there for several days to teach me my new duties."

"And what have you learned from him?"

"That I should pay great respect to the Sultan's Birinci Kadin, but chastise severely any concubine that does not behave properly."

Ibrahim had to investigate the incident of the Aga's demise, because sometimes inconspicuous events led to important developments. Anyway, it was the issues he ignored that could hurt him; however, pretending he was ignorant could also save his life.

The last Kislar Aga knew much, but he also kept his mouth shut. It was one of those cases where there was no golden rule of proper behavior. Survival depended on luck too. When rules ceased to hold, it meant a chaotic era had commenced. Asphodel was right. His sensitivity had detected this subtle change, but Ibrahim had failed to foresee despite his superior intelligence.

Perhaps human intelligence was not enough. One had to be blessed by the Holy Spirit too to be able to predict your Kismet.

****

Despite the troublesome information about the Kislar Aga death, the fact Suleiman was probably in a good mood was a welcome piece of news. It meant he could visit the Sultan and explain to him his plan for the alliance with France that couldn't really wait for his health and mood to improve. A Sultan whose mood was influenced by a woman's visit was not what the Ottoman Empire need these days.

Suleiman was indeed in an optimistic mood this morning. The moment he saw him he started talking about the good prospects for a new military expedition in Persia. This time they would reach even deeper in Persia than Baghdad or Tabriz. With some luck, if they could force the Persian army into a staged battle, they could smash it once and for all. Then, they could reach the Indus River and open way to the East or go to the North towards Samarkand and the Silk Road to China.

Listening to his harangue, Ibrahim realized that his master was under the influence. If this was the result of the elation Hurrem offered or it was the result of an opium sedative, it was not critical. He simply had to make sure Suleiman was brought down to earth the least painful way.

"Persia is an immense country. It will take many victories to cross it. It is also desolate in many regions, so we will need to carry many supplies to retain our military advantage. There is no way to cross it from West to East in a year."

Suleiman suddenly became extremely irritated.

"Alexander the Great did it, so I can do it too. He burned Persepolis before reaching the Indus River, but I will burn down Isfahan," he claimed.

"Yes, Alexander the Great did it, but then took him several years to smoother out the persistent Persian resistance. He also didn't have to carry guns through mountain passages. It would be even more dangerous to assault Samarkand and enrage the

Mongols. We shouldn't forget what happened to Yildirim Bayezid. The Mongols are the Turks worst enemy. This time the Ottoman Empire may not be so lucky. Last time they were allies with the Romans and didn't attack Constantinople but stopped at Bursa. After such a defeat in the heart of Asia, we will never reach the Eternal City alive. Then only Hurrem Sultan could defend your Harem."

His ironic tone enraged the Sultan. The idea that another man could turn Hurrem into his slave was impossible to digest raw. However, Ibrahim was also in an impertinent mood, since early this morning he had to face the results of Suleiman's incompetence. Selim would never have done so many mistakes or let a woman to manipulate him so easily. Suleiman was red hot in anger, but red hot steel could become even harder, if plunged into cold water.

"What makes you believe that I am not Great. My empire is already greater than Alexander's and I'm not dead yet; so by then it might become even greater. Now it extends from the Atlantic Ocean to Tiger and Euphrates, and from Budapest to Sudan."

However, Ibrahim was now also enraged, because Suleiman was trying to usurp the efforts of all his ancestors. Even he had a significant contribution by turning Egypt into a valuable province of the Empire and in capturing Baghdad for the very first time.

"Yes, indeed the Ottoman Empire is bigger than Alexander's, but you shouldn't forget it belongs not only to you, but also to your father, your grandfather, Fatih and to all your great ancestors. Year after year they sawed down the Roman oak until it fell to the ground."

"I have never forgotten the saga of my ancestors. It is you who lately tries to diminish me and the House of Osman. I don't know the reason, but maybe it is because I'm not a Roman or a Greek but a Turk, and my roots are not in the West but in the East. This is why they call me 'Magnificent' and not 'Great' exactly as they did with my great-grandfather who they did not call

'Great' but simply 'Conqueror' even though he didn't just conquer an famous city built by Constantine the Great, but also established a mighty Empire in the same lands as he had. Isn't it true that the same people blame me for the same weaknesses like Alexander's? Am I inferior because I have many women in my harem and have many more sons than he did? Is this a weakness too? Empires need to expand not only in space but in time too. The Ottoman empire is not only greater, but it will last much longer; so, I rightfully deserve to be called 'Great' much more than Alexander did."

Ibrahim realized that under the Sultan's words his ideas were hidden. It was a good sign. Now he had to reduce the tension with a wish in Allah's name to show he was a faithful.

"I wish Allah hears me now and let all our children grow old and become worthy of the glorious House of Osman. Then, my name will never fade away exactly like yours. In fact, if you become 'Great' then I might be called 'Magnificent' by our common enemies. This is how far my ambition goes."

"Is it true they already call you 'Magnificent' in Venice?"

"Yes, it is, and I can do nothing about it! These devious people will do anything to inspire envy between us; but I want you to know that the greater a master is, the more important his slaves feel. Thus, I am the very first man who wants you to become 'Great' indeed."

"Many claim that you don't really love me, that you were my friend simply to grow rich and famous, so you could build a bigger palace than my Seraglio."

"I'm not as greedy as they are and you know it! I always accepted only what you offered me. I also know that without you I would be nothing. It is also true that my rise looks longer than yours, because I've started from a much lower origin. From a Prince you became a Sultan with one step, whereas I had to climb many more steps to reach where I am now. This is the reason why I'm getting awfully tired of fighting and wasting my time aimlessly in quarrels. I feel I need a long rest even more than you do; but for us to rest and sow the fruits of our labors we must have peace;

so I hope this peace treaty is the last I have to sign in your name."

"You are my slave and you will do exactly what I order you. Soon I will be healthy again and then we will both ride towards the Red Apple Tree, as it was always our sacred dream. Don't forget that you have sworn in the name of Allah to always follow my orders."

"Sometimes I feel as if I'm talking not to my childhood's friend, but to Seih-Ul-Islam. My friend Suleiman knows I have no faith in Allah nor in Christ; thus, no oath of mine to any god is binding me more than my word to a dear friend."

"A Sultan has subjects, not friends. A Sultan must inspire the fear of death to achieve absolute obedience. Only by the threat of death I can convince people to die in my name."

"That's not true, people die more often because of love. We both know several mothers who would kill to save their children, and they are women full of weaknesses," Ibrahim argued.

"Yes, but would you die for my sake?" Suleiman insisted.

"I have risked my life for your glory many times and you know it, and my decision had nothing to do with any oath to any god. God is our invention because we know we are mortals and need some kind of assurance that immortality exists and it is attainable someway. God is a bet we humans need to make to drive away the fear of death from our daily lives."

Suleiman looked tired as this discussion had been problematic almost from the start. Every time Suleiman came face to face with the prospect of dying all his courage and self-confidence evaporated. He had spent too much of his life under the threat of execution.

"Since death is always at arm's length, the moments of our lives are extremely precious and we should not waste them making impossible dreams for unending conquests. During the war, many people die to make our wild dreams come true, and this is not fair. Your subjects should live and be happy for as long as possible; but to be happy we must have peace. Peace is not easy. It is more difficult than war, because peace should last longer to give us time to build. It is also much more difficult to raise your children than kill the children of someone else. In peace even the stronger castles will open wide their gates to buy the goods we trade. Selling is much more profitable than looting, because you can loot a nation just once, whereas you can sell many products to every nation in the world. This is why merchants are much richer than warriors; but for the Ottomans to become merchants, we must have peace and become friends with all nations, even the Persian heretics. Then, we can concentrate our efforts against the Portuguese who control the most valuable trade of all, the Spices."

The Sultan watched him silently but closely. Ibrahim's ideas were controversial but they made sense. While they were fighting in East and West, the merchants of the Grand Bazaar who had stayed behind in Constantinople were amassing immense riches by trading food, arms and all sorts of military equipment. During the war the Tophane district was also busy as a beehive, casting bronze cannons and steel to make swords, battleaxes, knives and muskets. Next to the Tophane inside the Golden Horn were the shipyards, building, repairing and modernizing galleys and all kinds of warships and merchant vessels. All these craftsmen have been very prosperous, without putting their lives in danger.

On the other hand, when the warriors came back from the war, many were wounded or had become invalids. Even the ones who came back unhurt, as soon as the loot was spent, they made trouble, looting the peaceful citizens who had become rich during the war. They all complained and had every right to do so for the grave injustices war had imposed on warriors.

Suleiman's silence was the sign Ibrahim waited to keep talking, explaining his plans. The Sultan didn't have to talk because even if he agreed with what the slave was saying. Talking or arguing was a sign of weakness for a Sultan; but to object he had to find a valid argument, and this was almost impossible when the Grand Vizier opened his mouth. His logic was impeccable.

Ibrahim was wise enough to discuss first the critical issues with the Sultan in private to reach an agreement ahead of time; so that what he announced was in complete agreement with his master's opinion. Nevertheless, lately Ibrahim felt that something had changed in Suleiman's manners. He was silent much more often than ever before, as if he knew in advance that Ibrahim's plans were optimal; however, whenever Suleiman cared to object, his arguments were based more on tradition or the Quran than on logic, and this was the case this time too, when he reached the inescapable conclusion.

"The enemies of our enemy must become our friends. If the King of Spain is at war with the King of France, then the King of France must become our best ally. We should also help him because he is fighting our war and he should win. My spies tell me that soon England will fight Spain for a piece of the New World; so, we must help also England in this war and offer refuge to the English ships in our harbors, so they will offer refuge in return to our ships that will travel to the New World across the Atlantic Ocean through the Gibraltar Gates."

"What you say about France, the Portuguese and Spain sounds logical the way you put it; however, since it involves Muslims and Christians, I must also hear what Seih-ul-Islam has to say before making my final decision," the Sultan said trying to avoid a rush decision.

Suleiman was rather upset and tired from their earlier conflict, and didn't have the strength to stress his brain any further on such an important issue as making an alliance with two countries that had both actively participated in many Crusades against Islam. Perhaps, even Hurrem Sultan might have something useful to contribute, as women were practical and examined certain issues from a different prospective than men. When Hafsa Sultan was alive, he often asked for her advice too; however, Ibrahim had enough of long discussions that led to indecisions and unnecessary delays during times when speed was of the essence.

"It is very easy for me to tell you right now Great Muftis' objections, since I know the Quran as well as he does; but listening to the hazy advices of Prophet Mohammed as he saw the world one thousand years ago is the reason why Muslims keep on looking backward, when all Christian nations are looking forward. If your grandfather Fatih searched the Quran for advices on how to demolish the Great Walls, then he would have never entered the Eternal City, and you would still reside in a tent rather than in a magnificent Seraglio. Without artillery we would have also been buried in Mohacs by the Hungarian heavy cavalry. On the contrary, the Christians always question the validity of the Bible and add new rules to Moses' Laws. At the beginning, the Father and the Son were of the same essence, then the son became a man before ending up as man-god. When this issue was resolved, the same questions were posed about his mother Mary and finally the Holy Spirit. Now they fight whether the Pope would be the first or if it is better for all Christian Patriarchs to be of equal status before Allah.

For us all these issues are meaningless and rightly so; but in reality, the critical question is not what is the nature of a man, a woman, Allah, or a damned pigeon, but if a man can ask questions about old beliefs without the fear of losing his head as a heretic. Many centuries ago the Arabs asked questions about an old book, the Bible, and became undefeatable conquerors in East and West, applying the new rules of the Quran; but now the Quran is the old book and has nothing to add to our knowledge. Now it is not synonymous with change and progress, but with the hysteresis and dogmatism."

The Sultan remained silent and reserved as if he was weighting carefully his Grand Vizier's suggestions. He closed his eyes to rest his mind from all the oncoming external stimuli. Ibrahim's presence that day had been a source of considerable tension. Ibrahim was often a courier of news that were not always pleasant, and recently Hurrem had also changed the sensations she produced from sensual pleasures and lust to mental torture and continuous intimidation. She was adding her complaints against Ibrahim Pasha to the ones of the Muslim clergy enraged by what they called an outrage of an infidel having condemned another Muslim, Iskander Chelebi to death without asking for a proper trial by Muslim judges. Sometimes he would rather see Ibrahim disappearing from sight by divine intervention; however, all these years he had spent in his proximity had made him indispensable for his existence. After so much time his passion may have receded, a victim of repetition, but a portion of his brain was still alive occupied by many pleasant memories from their wild years of youth.

Besides his mother Hafsa who was now diseased, Ibrahim was the person he had shared the most time, much more than his father, his mother, his brothers or his sisters. Besides his sisters that were now residing in distant lands, everyone else connected to his past was now dead and buried. Despite his awesome power he was lonely and isolated on a throne that demanded great amounts of energy to retain as his illness slowly drained his will to live.

He opened his eyes and discovered Ibrahim Pasha was gone. Was this a divine message to test his endurance during the oncoming era?" he silently inquired, but no one answered.

****

It was Friday midday and Ibrahim Pasha found an opening during the prayer to take a ride with his trusted white mare on his most favorite trail along the Sea Walls under the hill of the Saray Burnu, plunging like the tip of yatagan into the Marmara Sea. The execution of Chelebi Pasha had turned the clergy against him, and to be perfectly safe from any unnecessary protest, when he came back from war, he had stopped praying in the temple of Agia Sophia.

Islam after almost one thousand years was still an unpolished religion. It had many common characteristics with the ancient Christians in terms of its purity of thought. He had read somewhere that an obscure Christian, Saint Mercury, had become a saint by murdering a Roman Emperor, Julian the Apostate, in Syria. As Islam became the dominant religion in the Holy Lands, these old customs were reincarnated and assassinations became again a popular trend, as killing an infidel was a noble act rewarded by Allah with entrance to Paradise.

He was the last man deserving such an end, because he was never truly a Christian. Since he was toddler, he had been disappointed by his failure to be granted a golden tooth each time he received communion, as his mother had promised to entice him into strict fasting.

Unfortunately, it was not the only time Christianity had failed him. The many other old Roman myths about the arrival in Constantinople of a liberator Christian Emperor through the Golden Gate had also been proven false, as well as the reincarnation of the half-roasted fish of the Baloukli monastery. However, the most frustrating experience had been his useless prayers for his grandfather to survive after a heavy winter cold. He had prayed and prayed to no avail, despite his mother's promises that the Lord Jesus Christ payed attention to innocent children's prayers. All these Christian broken promises had been proven empty words, and this failure made also the elusive visions of Resurrection and Second Life seemed equally absurd.

As his personal experiences on conspiracies increased, he had recently concluded all these illusions were products of devious, secret arrangements between Roman Emperors and the Orthodox Patriarchs to convince naive people to send their children to wars that extended the lands owned by the Emperor, the nobility, and the clergy. The Patriarch was also producing more believers by promising a special place in God's Paradise for all the simpleminded warriors who fell dead during the ever-present religious wars with the Muslims.

Nevertheless, he had to admit that the Muslim Paradise extravaganza was closer to the heart of the Oriental men than the Christian halleluiah singing pure angels. And his favorite Anatolian poet was correct once more with his very sobering verses:

At night you can stare at millions of galaxies
And in the sunlight at the beauty of friends

dancing in a wedding.
Ask an infant that still has his eyes closed
shut and trust its words.
There are no other worlds and other lives.
All I know are my experiences. It's you the
one who has illusions!

The lively breaths of wind carried to his ears the weeping cry of the Muezzin from the Agia Sophia temple, inviting the believers to pray to Allah for their delivery, and soon after similar voices from every other mosque in the Eternal City arrived as if they were echoes. It was a spiritual experience that helped him transcend from the ephemeral to the eternal, and to truly enjoy it, he laid down on the dry sand and watched the clouds chased by the northerly blasts on the azure skies. It was a fascinating spectacle, as massive formations broke down all the way to infinitesimals puffs as the flew over land only to be reunited over the watery expanses on their way from the Black to the Aegean Sea.

Was it possible the Ottoman Empire was undergoing a similarly violent transformation? Was this a universal phenomenon that governed also his life? Was his existence also in peril, when he led the Ottoman armies over land? Should he seek refuge inside the wooden walls of the Ottoman fleet of his friend and ally Barbarossa the same way Themistocles had saved Athenians in Salamis, when Xerxes overwhelmed Spartan resistance at Thermopylae? Was history to be repeated when he sought freedom from Parga slavery in the arms of a handsome pirate who had promised him their love would last forever only to sell him in the Venetian harbor of the Golden Horn to a lusty Jewish slave trader?

No! Such a repetition was an impossibility. He was not an enchanting boy with blond hair and green eyes anymore. He had aged. No lusty mature male would fall in love with him now. During the years that had gone by, his blond hair had turned into chestnut brown and the mesmerizing innocence of his eyes into masculine hardness, as all kinds of painful experiences had transformed the feminine shades of his weaknesses into an irresistible urge for endless conquests as if he was an Osmanli Sultan. It had to be his competitive Janissary nature that had pushed him on this manly path, or possibly the unconscious realization that male attraction for handsome youths did not last long. Even this morning he had seen the first white hair in his beard. He could ask a page to dye it dark, but he would simply fooling himself.

The unstoppable and irreversible process of creation and wear his friend Sinan had warned him against had started long ago, and the first signs gradually became apparent. Hatidge was right in pointing out that his era of youthful follies was rapidly coming to a close, so he would have to change his priorities as his son grew up. Now his offspring was too young to suspect anything, but in few years he had to eliminate his clandestine visits to the Sultan's bedroom at midnight. What was done, was done.

In this content Hurrem was also within her motherly rights to resent his clandestine relationship with the Sultan. As her sons grew up, they had to be protected from every malicious gossip about their father too. Mustafa, Mehmet and Selim were now old enough to suspect what the nature of his close association with Suleiman had been. He didn't resent his lust at the time, but he had to recognize that day by day his trends had imperceptibly changed. Perhaps, responsible for this change was the fact that his lover had aged because of his illness much more than he had. Perhaps, this was the reason he had sought and found comfort in women's embrace. Perhaps, Hafsa's motherly care had pushed him also on this traditional trail. He was most grateful for her help, because without children the life of every man would eventually lead to a dead end. Now his son was his gate into the future, and he had to keep it open for as long as he could. The more years he survived, the more optimism he would inspire to his children.

Undoubtedly, in one hundred years every person he saw

around him as he strolled on the streets of the Eternal City would be dead and buried. Time placed insurmountable barriers even stronger than the Theodosian Walls. Now he was like the Emperor Constantine the Great tracing the limits of his City. In time he wouldn't be able to walk, he could only dream how his life would be, when his time to die would come. Dreaming was the only way out the prison of Time; so he closed his eyes and let his mind free to dream how his life should end.

****

Behind the latticed shutters two sapphire eye followed his every move; but Ibrahim was too lost in his thoughts to feel the infinitesimal pressure of her eyes.

****

He had to be absentminded, staring at the passing waves that traveled undeterred towards the Hellespont, the Aegean Sea and his beloved Egypt, because he failed to notice the soft steps of a horse on the wet sand; but suddenly a nearby shimmy disturbed his alluring remembrances, bringing him violently from the world of imagination back to reality. He turned around and saw his mare's ears rising and her nostrils sniffing the scent of an approaching stallion.

He raised his torso to face the approaching intruder and saw a rider dressed in Spahis' uniform. He recalled the incident of the Janissary guard, when he was still the guardian of the Sultan's hunting falcons. Since that demeaning incident no one had dared to give him orders what to do. Now that he was the Grand Vizier, the Serasker and the Sultan's brother-in-law he had the way to chastise any guard who would dare to remind him of any strict security rule. Perhaps the uninvited visitor was one of the Sultan's heralds seeking him to do a new errand, but as the riders face was darkened by the shadows of the hood, Ibrahim was unable to look for the visitor's intentions.

"Who told you to spy on me?" he asked suspiciously. "You

should be praying for salvation to Omnipotent Allah rather than sneaking behind a Grand Vizier," he scolded him.

"Aren't you interested to look at my face? I bet you will be convinced I meant no harm," the mysterious visitor replied and put all his worries to sleep.

It was Hurrem disguised as a Spahis. He could recognize her sensuous voice in a crowd. Her tone was warm and friendly as if they had really nothing precious to share. Perhaps she was seeking a truce. The Sultan had ceased for years to be a worthwhile trophy as a man. All he had left worth claiming was his power to command. Now, they were both too rich and powerful to worry about the future. Perhaps, this was Suleiman's plan to reduce tensions. Logically the less envy people experienced, the less passionate and forceful were their attempts for supremacy.

Suleiman was as valuable property as a piece of desert. His illness had dried up every drop of moisture love could use to grow roots. He looked much older than he really was, and gradually he had acquired also the mentality of an old, invalid warrior full of strange ideas.

She must have be feeling hot under her black cape, because the scent of roses he knew so well invaded his nostrils; however, her expression did not show discomfort. After all, their meeting was not casual. It had a purpose. She had chosen to meet him informally despite her apparent inconvenience and possible danger of discovery. Was she trying to disguise her hostile aims under a friendly attitude?

"Why did you bother to approach me here?" he asked with an unemotional exploratory tone to indicate his good intentions.

"Aren't you happy to see me?" she asked seeking for a compliment.

"It depends entirely on your intentions. You never had anything I envied. There is no way you can ever become a Grand Vizier, a Kapudan Pasha or a Serasker. From the first time I met you, I had great respect for your capabilities. I always considered you the best consort for my friend. I don't know what your informers told you, but I never had any objection on you becoming a Kadin. You surely deserved this distinction more than anyone else."

"Do you think so? I have no noble blood in my veins."

"I don't believe in nobility. I believe in meritocracy, and you obviously know how to make the Sultan happier than anyone else. You two are the perfect match!"

"Yes, maybe we were a fair match, but people change over the years. You surely must know as much. You had remarkable successes for many years in a row and I don't mean as a Serasker. I bet you had plenty of grudges to avenge."

"Yes, I did, but revenge was not my strongest motive. No one has ever truly imposed his will on me. Everything arrangement has been the result of sincere negotiation."

"Don't spoil it for me. Long ago I was under the impression I was raping you."

"A woman can never rape a man. This is how Allah wills it."

"Maybe you are right after all; but illusions can often be more pleasant than reality. I'm sure you have felt that with all your Sultanas; but the sheer truth is that a slave can be happy only with another slave. Masters are too demanding and look only after their pleasure. Love has to be unselfish most of all. It has to have no other purpose but to bear children," Hurrem claimed and dismounted her stallion with the remarkable grace of a well-trained Solak.

"I'm not so sure about that. Allah rewards even an honest effort," Ibrahim argued and Hurrem silently giggled, providing him with an opportunity to fathom her intentions. "So, what is the true reason of your visit today?" he next inquired.

"This happens to be also my favorite place to roam; but since I found you here I wanted to express my wish for a peaceful settlement of all our differences. I trust they are all the result of a misconception. I wish to assure you that I have nothing against you. I am only trying to save the lives of my sons. Now that you have a son, you must feel much better than ever before how precious is really a child. Please remember that I have five sons I want to keep alive."

"I have never conspired against your children and I hope you recognize that. My sole concern is if Suleiman is incapable to lead, to choose the best possible Emperor for the sake of all his subjects including me and you. If he chooses Mustafa, then you must teach your sons to be loyal to the new Sultan."

"Worthy sons have a mind of their own when they grow up. What their father wishes for their future ceases the day the sons are circumcised. Then, few sons may decide to do what their concubines wish. Few men have certain weaknesses, don't you agree?"

"Yes, but the future is too complicated for us to predict. We can only hope that when we are gone, our children will be wiser than us and more virtuous," Ibrahim insisted.

"Who can discern what's really a virtue? Tamerlane was lame, but never lost a battle; so, I must keep even my Gihangir alive for the good of the Empire."

"And you have every right to do so. From what I hear, he has grown very fond of his brother Mustafa. To me this is a sign of wisdom."

"Yes, but he loves Mehmet as much. He is a very sentimental boy."

"I'm very fond of Mehmet too. He will grow to be a virtuous man too."

"I didn't realize you were fond of Mehmet. That's very interesting."

"He is a very promising young man. I'm sure as soon as he grows up, the Sultan will find many important missions that fit his talents."

"He always comes up with very strong arguments. I believe he will be a great diplomat like you. He also likes beautiful women. We must find the proper consorts for him."

"I am not very good in choosing proper women. Sometimes I follow my instincts rather than common logic."

"What do your instincts say you should do for the sake of

my son Mehmet? If he is to survive, he needs the support of a Grand Vizier who can influence the Sultan with his impeccable logic."

"To be absolutely sincere, I haven't thought much about Mehmet. If something happens to Suleiman, Mustafa will be my obvious choice. He is not only a capable young man with solid moral values, he has also the proper age. Mehmet maybe a fine boy, but he is still too young."

"Then, let's try our best to keep Suleiman healthy for a few more years until our boy grows to be a man," Hurrem concluded and turned back to mount her horse; however, her last statement needed a lot of explanations, so Ibrahim reached and caught her hand that held the reins.

"What did you mean by calling Mehmet 'our boy'?"

"I think I heard you saying that sometimes you follow your instincts. What do your instincts say about Mehmet. Isn't he a very handsome young man?"

"Yes, he is, but what does that mean?"

"They say there are people in the Seraglio who can read lips. Do you trust this rumor?"

"I've never heard such rumor, but I know Selim Khan had organized a very efficient network of spies that is still operating."

"Then, we must not take any chances with the life of Mehmet. Who knows who could be spying on us right now from the walls. Parents have a great responsibility to keep their children alive, but please don't say anything more, and I promise I will not reveal anything of all I know about Mahidevran's son."

"Mustafa has nothing to fear from us. He is a very virtuous young man."

"Indeed he is; but, he is not her only son. She has at least one more from you. Mahidevran Sultan is a very devious woman, when it comes to supporting her sons. She knows well enough that another son of hers has even less chances to survive than Hatidge's male offspring. In the end according to Fatih's law, only one Osmanli will rise to the throne unless our wise Grand Vizier stops this madness."

"I don't believe you. Mahidevran has no son of mine. This is just a piece of malicious gossip you are trying to propagate to serve your purposes."

"Are you sure? When you fuck a woman with so much passion, then the woman has every right to imagine that your entire existence belongs to her. A wise man like you should know about women that they always try to use the best available male to have their children."

Hurrem simply knew or sensed too much of him. It was possible she was blessed by a remarkable instinct, or that she had access to an incredible network of informers. Conceivably, while the Sultan and he were fighting in the East, the women they left behind could get pregnant and deliver their children in secrecy outside the palaces with the help of midwives.

A woman's pregnancy was a natural process and in villages almost all women knew how to carry out a simple delivery. Only when complications happened, the life of the mother and the child was endangered to such an extent they would ask a doctor to look after their pregnancy. It was also common knowledge that if a woman looked after her figure, she easily reach the seventh month without any visible signs of her pregnancy, when the husband was absent on a warfront. And if the child was healthy enough, many times it could survive even after only seven months of pregnancy. As long as Hafsa was residing in Manisa, Mahidevran could not escape her attention, but when the Valide became sick and departed, anything could have happened considering that Mustafa was not in Manisa, but busy in the capital.

Suddenly, everything made sense, even Mahidevran's later. She had secretly informed him he had another son, but he had misinterpreted her message.

Hurrem fell he was too confused to react to her final message, so she pressed on.

"A man should not expect that he can pleasure himself with lusty women without facing the consequences. A wise Grand Vizier should also be careful where he puts his tugra and his dick.

Now that we are all in the same side, I hope you will keep our meeting confidential. The Sultan must never learn from my lips about any of your deeds. Silence is golden in all harems. There is so much in stake with the lives of our children, we the parents have vast duties."

Ibrahim was dumfounded. Hurrem's revelations were just short of amazing and he had to make sure she was telling the truth. She looked sincere enough when she claimed how important would be to sweep everything under the rug. It was a delicate conspiracy of silence, as everyone knew someone else's mistakes and indecencies. No one was to blame, but the Ayin, and to this conclusion he was the last to object.

The Harem populated by young women, was nothing less than a prison restricting the natural urges of most of its occupants, while stretching the Sultan's capabilities over the limits. Prophet Mohamed's advice was to try to keep everything within the bounds Mother Nature had set, avoiding excesses. Ibrahim didn't feel guilty of any crime. When he was sold as a slave, he was just a boy and now he was a man. He had gone through all the stages trying always to perform to the best of his abilities. He had not stopped being a slave who belonged to the Osmanli family, so he had not the final saying even when he talked to his wife. He could only suggest the best way out of a problem, but the final decision belonged to someone else.

Hurrem was in a similar position with the problems under her jurisdiction. It was natural for her to put her children's safety first, even higher than the interests of the Empire. She had hinted her oldest son alive, Mehmet, might be his son too. He didn't remember exactly the dates offhand; but it was something he could check, as Ottomans kept meticulous records of just about anything that costed money.

The only detail he could recall of the incident was that she had sneaked in his room uninvited, while the Sultan had left his quarters to pray in the mosque of the Aga. Possibly the same was happening now. Hurrem was in disguise, because for a Kadin riding a horse outside the Seraglio walls was prohibited by the

Ayin. However, if the Sultan was sleeping in his room sedated by the doctors, she could surely take a ride with the Kislar Aga's permission. To bribe a Kislar Aga was an easy task for such a powerful Sultana. If Hafsa Sultan was alive, Hurrem would be locked in the Eski Saray, but under these new conditions, she was probably residing in the Seraglio to take care of her ailing husband as any respectable wife in the City should do.

As if she had read his thoughts, she casually noticed:

"When the Sultan has no use for me, I'm sleeping in the Hasodabashi bedroom. I'm the only Hasodabashi he truly needs. Now that Hafsa Sultan is in Allah's paradise, I presume we have no further use of the Eski Saray. What do you think? Wouldn't be better instead of spending all this money for the Sultan concubines to give them away as presents to his friends? It wouldn't be too expensive for Sinan to build few more rooms next to the Has Oda for me, the Kislar Aga and my courtiers, so you can have back your old room to sleep over whenever you feel like it. The Eski Saray is well-fitted to be turned into a university by Sinan."

This had to be a trap surely, or possibly a tease.

"I have no use for any special room in the Seraglio, now that I live so close. It's just a short ride."

"Yes, I know; but sometimes we all get bored and we need a change. It was Allah's wish to bless us with a more lenient Kislar Aga this time. Now, I can ride my horse few days a week."

"Allah had nothing to do with it. It was one of Hafsa's last wishes, blessed be her name forever. We all owe part of our happiness to her kindness," Ibrahim remarked to test Hurrem's level of hypocrisy; but Hurrem had already digest the loss of the Valide Sultan.

"What the Harem needs now is a new more lenient Valide Sultan," Hurrem suggested.

"Do you consider Gülfem lenient enough?" Ibrahim asked with his impeccable diplomatic tact.

"Yes, but she has no son left; so, she has to be eliminated from the contest. The poor woman is so lonely. Perhaps you should visit her more often; in fact, it would be best for all of us, if you invited her to live permanently in your Palace. It's much more luxurious than any villa. If you are not willing to admit her in your harem, the Sultan might decide to send her away."

Hurrem had not lost the chance to make a rather questionable suggestion that would erase permanently Gülfem from the list of the Eski Saray residents.

"It is not for me to decide Gülfem's fate. She is still one of the three Suleiman's Kadin."

"Yes, she is; but, I feel it's time for him to divorce her. Suleiman has no blood ties with her. How you feel for her is much more important for her future. If you can convince Hatidge to accommodate her in your harem, I promise I can convince my Suleiman to divorce her shortly."

"If this is the wish of my Sultan, then who am I to refuse his wishes?" Ibrahim replied trying to avoid this new and unnecessary confrontation in the personal level, when there were much more important decisions to be made; but Hurrem must have considered this separation as a critical issue.

"Are you afraid to ask him? If you are reluctant, then I'll ask him. Then, all you'll have to do is to express your interest for her rehabilitation. Her derogatory behavior make us all look bad and the Sultan's patience cannot last much longer. You know how the Sultan feels. He can be very patient with the people he once loved; but when his patience is exhausted, he can behave very violently and then someone may get hurt."

The threatening tone was more than apparent in her words, and Ibrahim was for the first time alarmed. Hurrem sounded as if she was the Sultan himself.

"I wonder if it will be best for all of us if Gülfem Sultan is banished to Manisa."

"I thought that too, but then Manisa will become the center of dissidence and no one will dare to visit this town and be named a conspirator, not even you. Then, Mahidevran will become frustrated. On the other hand, if Suleiman divorces Gülfem, then no one will pay any attention to what she does. I'm sure you can find a proper husband for her the moment she is released from the Harem. A divorce is much better than drowning in the Bosporus anytime."

Now it was perfectly clear what was the nature of the subtle threat. Ibrahim had to act before it was too late. Was this the reason for this unexpected meeting?

"I don't see why Suleiman might decide to drown her. Gülfem Sultan has done nothing wrong!" Ibrahim insisted.

"Indeed she hasn't according to our level of morality; but I'm not sure Suleiman will overlook so easily few of her racy deeds. As everything else the level of morality depends on how many sins the individual is capable of concealing and I have the feeling the eunuchs know too many of her sins. If I was able to open few mouths, imagine how many a Sultan can, if he ever decides to shed some light into the daily deeds of each one of us. Life is a much more precious commodity than few moments of intense pleasure."

This new revelation was quite unexpected. Was she suggesting that she had made few eunuchs talk in exchange for pleasure? It was not an infinitesimal probability. A woman's attraction had to be in the back of any eunuch's mind. If this was an impossible dream, it didn't mean that human beings were incapable of having similar illusions. He still remembered his youthful dreams of flying like a bird. A devious woman could most certainly seduce any eunuch she liked, if her efforts had a purpose. On the other hand, every eunuch was capable of providing a considerable amount of pleasure to a female lover. He could testify to that from his experiences during his training in the Seraglio School as the Selim's courtesan. What a eunuch couldn't provide to a woman was pregnancy. Suddenly he became very worried. There was at least one eunuch, Asphodel, who knew too many of his most sinful moments.

"You should be going. The prayer will be finished by now," he noticed trying to silence her.

"I am not a slave and Suleiman Khan knows it. I am the mother of his children. Anyway we are not doing anything wrong.

We are trying to find the best solution to a serious family problem, namely, how to restrain a sinful Kadin from making him appear as a total fool."

"A neglected Kadin commits no sin sleeping with a man," Ibrahim noted and winked at her. She is simply trying her best to produce more warriors for the faith and we both know it."

She couldn't contain her crystal jingling laughter.

"Try to win this argument against our Sultan, and I promise you one hundred offspring by next year," she challenged him. "His entire harem will be willing to kill to get admitted in your harem, my dear Ibrahim Pasha."

He had to accept Hurrem was a very intelligent woman, and he was a man who appreciated the intelligence even more than the beauty of a woman. Beauty was common in a harem, but intelligence a rare commodity. Gülfem was an example of a typical harem female. She was unquestionably very attractive, but she was more sneaky than bright, and Hurrem's accusations were accurate. Gülfem was sneaking out too often, and her acts was bound to create malicious rumors undermining her safety.

On the other hand, Hurrem was much more intelligent and kept her urges under control even better than Mahidevran. She knew she was a slave not a Princesses, so the Sultan had absolute control over her and her children's destinies. Suddenly he couldn't contain his passion.

"Will one child be yours?" he challenged her back causing a new cataract of laughter.

"Why do you need me, when your harem is so full of younger and prettier slaves? Many claim that my offspring are cursed because of my greed to become the Sultan's Kadin."

"Nonsense! No woman should be blamed for a man's shortcomings. It's the Sultan's illness that is responsible for his retraction. How can a man be seduced when he is under so much pain? This is what my doctor says and it makes sense."

"Is he the one who suggests I should try my luck with another man? Don't be such a fool. As long as Suleiman is alive, I will not betray him with another man, even if my lover may be as powerful and attractive as you," she noticed with a playful disposition.

"I don't see why not, if the first time was so fruitful. It is Allah's sign we are made for each other."

"You know perfectly well that specific time was just a desperate attempt of a new, inexperienced concubine to gain the support of the Hasodabashi in my favor. I simply had to convince him I was the best available consort of the Sultan and the most pleasurable, and nothing more than that," she cynically explained. "What will be my excuse this time? I have too many sons already," she inquired trying to use his wits to find a logical excuse.

"If I were in your shoes and I was afraid that the Sultan may suddenly collapse, I would try to put the next more powerful man under my spell," he explained and she took her time before replying.

"I don't think this is a good enough reason to lower myself to Mahidevran's level. I know well enough that men like to degrade the women they fuck time after time," she snapped back, but still retaining her teasing style.

"Indeed most ordinary men might do that, but I'm different and my record proves it. I have appreciated so much all the women that have given me pleasure, that I have invited them to join my harem."

"Yes, I know of your record just too well, but I'm not an ordinary woman. I'm too possessive to be locked again in another harem. I need a man of my own. Deep inside I'm still a Christian. When I finish with my man, he is no position to entertain another woman for days. If you don't believe me, ask your friend what he intends to do with the rest of his harem. Are you ready to do the same, sent your Princess and all her consorts to Manisa? If they are not enough to satisfy your lust, try Gülfem instead of me. She is a better match for you. Trust me!"

"I am perfectly willing to admit Gülfem into my harem, if the Sultan asks me to; but I wonder how you are going to repay me for this special favor?" he asked her with a suggestive smile.

"I hope you don't suggest an advance payment here in

front of the Sultan's eyes? This was the most outrageous proposal I have ever heard in my life."

"Extraordinary women tend to accept the most outrageous proposals, when they fit their outrageous plans," he replied with his most seductive smile.

****

The Muezzins cry from the mosque of Sergius and Bacchus, the one the locals called Küçük Agia Sophia because of its shape, brought them back to reality. She had to leave as soon as possible, because after the end of the prayer the Janissary guards would return to their posts on the Seraglio walls. The Sultan would be the next one to return. She had to be back to his quarters before he had the chance to look for her and find her missing.

The time of separation had arrived. He reached for her hand to help her mount her stallion and searched for her eyes that lay hidden under the shadow of the cape.

"When shall we meet again?" he asked eager to discover how long he had to wait.

However, the words that leave the lips of a man are interpreted differently when they reach the ears of a woman. His audacity was well-known, but this time he had violated every previous limit. From the moment the Kislar Aga had become one of her accomplishes, she had no difficulty convincing him of letting her slip out the Gate of Death in the Seraglio, and go anywhere it pleased her, when the Sultan was with the Serasker and the troops. The truth was that she loved to roam freely in the Eternal City outside the Seraglio Walls. Now she was a Kadin, and she had identical rights with Gülfem and Mahidevran Sultan. If they had the right to visit regularly the Bazaars and Hans in the vicinity, seeking forbidden pleasures, so had she; but she still had resisted this risky temptation.

Ibrahim had to realize she was not as weak as the Sultan. Today she had managed to slip out unnoticed, but if their secret meeting became more numerous, the chances were someone would notice her departure and follow her. If she could blackmail the Kislar Aga with the threat of castration, so could someone intimidate her with the threat of exposure. However, she was not a Sultan able to submit to all kinds of weaknesses without fear. She was a woman and mother. The word "never" came up all the way to her lips, but she managed to keep it imprisoned. Such absolute declarations were bounding and forced her to lose lucrative opportunities in a universe that was not perfect. Who knows how their relationship might develop, if she ever became a widow and Ibrahim was still as attractive? In such a case she could enjoy as many attractive men as she liked without putting the lives of her children in mortal danger.

"Perhaps, I might be able to find the proper moment, as you say," she replied trying hard to resist the pressure to submit to his invitation with a more definite response.

The truth was that this invitation had awaken up old memories, when he held her in his arms and her legs wrapped around his waist pulled him even closer. Instinctively with her mind confused by the turmoil of her flesh, she pressed her heals on the belly of her stallion urging it to move forward. The stallion objected to her firm command to get away from Ibrahim's mare and rose to its hind legs, trying to throw her off the saddle. However, Hurrem was not the typical female rider. She had Cossack blood in her veins; so she pulled the reins with one hand and embraced the horse's neck tightly with the other. The pain from the reins in the horse's mouth and its inability to shake off the rider forced it to follow her wishes and expressed its frustration by bursting his anger into a reckless gallop along the road it knew well.

It was a stallion no doubt, but a tamed one, exactly as her master. Suleiman also complained sometimes, but she had no trouble controlling his anger too. The moment she convinced him to dismiss the Harem, she would have nothing to fear from any old mare.

Ibrahim on the other hand was too unpredictable for comfort. The more women he conquered the more demanding he became. Perhaps she could tame him too after few months, but it was also possible he might turn her into another obedient courtier of his Princess. He was not the kind of man a woman could totally control because of his stamina and affliction to men. He was simply too overconfident to propose to her to enter his harem after Suleiman's demise. Perhaps in the old days, when he was the only dashing man in the Seraglio, she might seriously consider such an outrageous proposal. Now, after so many children deliveries, she had ceased to be thrilled with the mystery of childbirth. Few moments of pleasure were repaid by hours of pain and extreme labor, and too many women died in the process. Life was too precious to be wasted bearing more offspring. Her last problematic delivery was going to be her very last.

With these conflicting thoughts she entered the narrow corridor paved with cobblestones to avoid a hoof's slippage during the snowy season. The Kislar Aga was waiting for her arrival and held the horse steady by the reins, so she could safely dismount it. He seemed very worried even though it was not the first time she had gone out for a ride in disguise. She asked the Aga what was wrong, and he explained the Sultan was back ahead of time, because he was in pain. When he asked for her, he had to tell him she was out for a short ride on the shore.

She knew well that from the windows of the Marble Kiosk the Marmara shore was in plain view. If the Sultan was eager to spy on her, he knew where to look; but a little jealousy had never hurt her relationship with Suleiman. It actually enhanced it. She asked the Kislar Aga to calm down his anxiety because everything was under control.

****

She found Suleiman lying on a sofa in the Marble Kiosk. He was in pain with his left leg lying on a pillow, and as usual in a bad mood.

"Where have you been?" he asked her with an angry voice the moment she entered.

"I went for a ride in the Gülhane with your last present. It's a magnificent animal, but he is not used yet having a woman rider on its back."

"You insisted on a stallion. My wiser suggestion was a mare."

"Old mares are good for your friend Ibrahim to ride. I always had an urge to ride young stallions. They are much more challenging and fun to ride than mares."

"Yes, but this makes them twice as dangerous."

"Yes, but on the other hand I have to be constantly on the alert. The moment you lose concentration, is usually the time a wild horse may try to hurt you, isn't so?"

"If the stallion is well-trained, then it must be the rider's mistake."

"This is what I believe too. It's natural for a proud animal to detest being ridden, so the rider must always be ready to impose his will. In that respect, Ibrahim may be wiser riding mares. A mare will never consider throwing even an average rider off her back unless he does something very naughty."

"Naughty is not the right word for doing something clumsy," Suleiman objected.

"Sorry dear, but my Turkish is not as good as yours. I always wondered if Ibrahim's tongue is as skillful as mine. Sometimes he says something about me and I get offended, but perhaps his words might have a different meaning I simply do not know. He is an accomplished diplomat after all."

"What did he tell you most recently that has offended you?"

"Just today he told me that our choices of horses express our inner thoughts better than our lips."

"That may well be true. I see nothing wrong with that. He is a very perceptive man. He notices even the tiniest details that escape the ordinary eye."

"This is why I got offended. As you know my stallion is black. I believe this was an intentional stab for the new Kislar Aga he and your mother have appointed."

"What did this Aga do wrong?"

"How am I supposed to know what he does after he brings me here to your quarters practically every day? All I know is that since he was appointed as I guardian of the Harem I hear no complaints from even your lustiest concubines."

"Then my mother's suggestion was correct, Allah bless her name."

"Your mother was indeed a very practical Valide Sultan with a truly benevolent heart. Young girls should not be denied all the pleasures their beautiful bodies might desire. In fact, from what I hear, the Kislar Aga has no favorites, but invites each one to his quarters for training on regular intervals, so they know the exact day and hour, and are prepared and sparkling clean."

"I didn't know so many details, but I still fail to see what you consider wrong."

"Are you forgetting that in the Eski Saray Gülfem Sultan is also residing? She has also stopped complaining."

"Has he invited her also in his quarters for training?" Suleiman asked with inflamed interest.

"How should I know what he does, when I'm practically every night here by your side?"

"So, what do you suggest I should do?" Suleiman asked with an innocent.

"If you want to find out what she is up to, I could remain in the Eski Saray for a few nights each week to spy on her; but she is clever and might stay in her room these days. If you wish to stop being jealous of her the best solution is to dismiss your entire harem once and for all, and divorce that shameless bitch."

"This is unacceptable. If she is so shameless as you say, as a divorcee she can marry one of my enemies and start plotting against me."

"Then, why don't you drown her in the Bosporus and forget all about her and all her disgraceful acts once and for all."

"What disgraceful acts? Have you seen her entering secretly Kislar Aga's quarters."

"No, I haven't; but I have seen the way she looks at him

and licks her fleshy lips. I have also seen how she rubs her legs and lowers her neckline, when he is around. You are a man and I'm sure you know how a woman in heat behaves to attract a man's eyes. I'm bet you also know where a woman's eyes are focused, when she wants to measure the extent of his passion."

"Yes, I know of all these things, but now tell me why your eyes are also searching the Kislar Aga?"

"Because I am a woman and it is natural for me to be interested in stallions even now that I am a mother and a Sultan's Birinci Kadin. It is not intentional. It is mostly instinctive. For example, I didn't fail to notice that your black stallion was aroused the moment he saw Ibrahim's mare. I had to notice those naughty things, because my Tatar trainer once told me I shouldn't try to ride a stallion when it is aroused; but how could I've known that Ibrahim would come and join me?"

"Perhaps he had something interesting to tell you."

"Indeed he did. He had many things to say that he wouldn't dare to say in front of you."

"Did he make any indecent proposals to you?"

"He most definitely could, if I was just a lusty concubine; but now that I am your favorite Kadin, he keeps his distance. As I've told you, he is a brilliant diplomat and has an eye for the details. He suggested I should name my black stallion 'Muhteşem' (Magnificent); but since it's your stallion I still think it must be you who has all the rights to name it. Was I wrong?"

"This is your horse. You should be the one to choose its name."

"I don't like 'Muhteşem'. It is too long and complicated. I will call it 'Aslan' (Lion) because it's short and it can be heard from a distance. Now tell me what do you intend to do with that whore, when you dismiss your harem."

"I will not dismiss my harem. Every Sultan needs to have a harem, because this is what the Ayin prescribes. But now tell me: Why do you insist on calling Gülfem a whore?"

"I will tell you some other day when you are in a better mood. I don't want to stain my hands with her blood."

"Tell me now! Is she conspiring against me?"

"If I do not know, if she is sleeping with the Kislar Aga, how should I know if she is conspiring with someone as devious as Ibrahim. You are the Sultan and you have all the spies you need to find out everything but the deeper thoughts of your slaves. For this mission you have me. Now look into my eyes and tell me, what I desire most this very moment? If you find it, then I will tell you if this is your wish what Ibrahim desires most this moment too."

The Sultan seemed suddenly very tensed. It had to be a pain from his swollen foot.

"Why you are so tense?" she asked. "You are Allah's Shadow and it's not always proper to give a lusty woman what she wants when she wants it. It will worsen her character. A proper Kadin should know how to wait patiently. Then, she can appreciate more the presents you offer her so openhandedly."

"You are a good guesser. Now tell me what Ibrahim wants right now."

"I promise I will, if you cannot guess it; but I'm sure you are a good guesser too, if you could see his eyes the way I looked at me few minutes ago."

"Was he desiring you?"

"No, of course not; but he should. I looked very sensual riding my black stallion. I don't know if you know it, but for women it is very exciting riding a horse like a man. This is why in the West women are not allowed to ride horses the way men do; but I have Tatar blood in my veins. This is what my mother told me. She was raped several times by a Tatar raid party the moment they found out she was not a virgin, but a woman married to a Christian priest. Come to think of it she might have lost me, if she tried to resist them. Are you aware that resisting is the worst kind of attitude for any woman who is about to be raped. This is at least what my mother told me. From the moment a man manages to spread a woman's legs, she must do her best to please him. Even a savage Hun will not kill a woman who promises him she will always be his to take whenever he feels like it. I don't know it for sure, but I have the impression that the raiding party that took me away, respected my virginity because my mother had been so submissive to their desires. If a man is thoroughly exhausted by a war, the last thing he needs is to deflower a young maiden with a tiny cunt."

"Are you trying to seduce me by any chance?"

"I knew you could read minds even better than Ibrahim, but I have to warn you because you are not just my husband and my master, but my lover too. After my last delivery the midwife has turned me into a virgin once more, but just a bit to make me more excitingyou're your sake."

"Are you trying to evade the issue of Ibrahim's desire?"

"No, I'm just trying to retain your interest for a little longer just before I leave for the Eski Saray. However, since you insist on knowing everything, I must provide you at least with a hint. I sensed that Ibrahim desires one of your other two Kadin. Try to guess who?"

"That's not hard, Mahidevran Sultan!"

"No, you lost! That's a wrong guess, but it's natural for a man who makes guesses to be influenced by his own desires. You may be thrilled by taming wild horses, but I feel Ibrahim is content these days just taming your Princess' courtiers. He desires much more peace and quiet, refined pleasures than wild horse rides. This is at least what my instincts say. This is probably why your father dumped him after a single night as he did with Gülfem Sultan too."

"Will you stop these wild stories about my father and Ibrahim. I have told you many times before that I do not trust wild rumors about Ibrahim I cannot verify. This was one of his terms before accepting my offer to become my Serasker."

"You have every right to think this way for such an intimate friend like Ibrahim. On the other hand, it's perfectly true that the old Kislar Aga has been eliminated on the way to Egypt by someone who wanted to silence his mouth permanently, most likely Gülfem with her secret connections from the caravanserais; thus, you cannot ask him all the questions you desire. However,

Asphodel is still alive and at your service. Ask him about your father and Ibrahim, if you don't trust me, your most favorite and faithful Kadin. In my mind what I say is perfectly logical; but all minds are not created equal and so are horses. A horse can be fast, another may have endurance, a third may be a good jumper, and a forth can carry heavy loads like a Sultan. We all know that your father was very fond of his two eunuchs, and I'm sure you know it too. Menekse was manly, while Asphodel totally submissive. These eunuchs were all Selim Khan needed to fit his moods, the same way Mahidevran and Gülfem fitted your desires before you met me. When Ibrahim arrived at the Seraglio, Selim Khan must have imagined this young slave was a wild stallion in need of extensive training, but his expectations were probably refuted. Ibrahim had been tamed by his previous lover; so he was not much of a challenge for a male beast like Sultan Selim. This is what common logic suggests."

"And how do you know my father was a male beast?"

"You should have seen his eyes, when I finished dancing for you the very first time I was chosen as your courtesan; but by then you had fallen asleep like a good boy and you missed the rest of the show. I still do not know why he didn't invite me to seat on his lap like Ibrahim, while you were sleeping. I was bare naked and quite terrified to deny him anything. I was his slave after all, and I knew my master had every right to use me any way he wished. The old Kislar Aga had warned me that Sultan Selim did not accept 'no' as an answer. It was indeed strange he refused me back then even though he desired me so feverishly. Perhaps he had something even more desirable than me waiting for him, when I left so frustrated by your rejection. As you well know, dancing can be a very seductive process not just for the viewers but also for the dancer. Even though I have squeezed my brain many times since then, I cannot point a finger to any direction. I can only say that Hafsa Hatun was not the lucky one that night, because I slept with her that very night for the first time. She showed me how a benevolent mature woman could comfort a frustrated youngster almost as fully as a naughty man."

"And I suggest you leave my departed mother out of this wild story."

"But why you men are so foolish sometimes? All you care about is penetration, while all that women care is dedication, sincerity, and affection. This was what I desired that night and your mother gave it to me with open hands, so to speak. When I woke up the next morning, I was still a virgin, fully content and clean as a whistle. If your father had summoned for me, I would have to go to the harem doctor to stop the bleeding before visiting the hammam."

"And I suggest you leave also my father out of your imaginative extravaganza. Are you trying to excel Halima in story telling this evening?"

"No, I don't. I only extrapolate on myself what Gülfem Hatun had to endure to make sure her son would not be executed by this cruel man, when the time came for him to depart. Fortunately that beast died suddenly on the road, when he couldn't put his evil plans in motion. Unfortunately her son died too, as we all know; so her suffering in bed was a total waste."

"By mixing truth with lies you cannot turn vicious lies to truth. Gülfem is a virtuous woman you cannot slander so easily with your wild accusations. Even if she did all the orgies you claim she did, and I pressure her to confess, she will never do that because she would suspect I might execute her; so accusing her is fruitless."

"That would be a very unfair way for you to react to the truth. And the truth is that from the moment she wanted to save her only son, she did what she had to do as any other caring mother. I would have done the same or perhaps even more, if the lives of my children were at stake, even though I knew that most of the chances would be still against me. There is nothing that can prevent a treacherous male beast from murdering my children after he has enjoyed me in every conceivable way a despicable eunuch like Menekse can perceive."

"I'm totally confused. How a eunuch like Menekse got involved in this unbelievable myth?" he asked rather amused by her dubious claims.

"You are still a very noble but quite naive man, who trusts all he hears. Every concubine of Selim's harem knew Menekse was not a complete eunuch. He only had his balls squeezed for a while, as most white eunuchs do. Asphodel is exactly like him, but from the very beginning only men can arouse his interest. Eunuchs claim his torturers were more thorough in his case, but who cares? Certainly not I, because I use logic. When your father's lover Sinan died, Selim Khan needed two eunuchs to replace the versatile lover he lost. But even Selim couldn't taste each time whatever he desired, as Ibrahim was proven more submissive that he desired."

"You seem to know much more than me about eunuchs. How come?"

"Every decent woman must be well acquainted with eunuchs to know how she will entertain her loving husband when he ages. What is more important is that Asphodel is totally innocent of any Selim's concubine violation. On the other hand, Selim and Menekse quite often invited concubines and shared them equally, as well as boys. It's very easy for you to test my story and act accordingly. Just ask Asphodel, because from what I heard those four were truly inseparable in all their orgies inside the Marble Kiosk."

"I might do just that and then come to strangle you for all these vicious lies," Suleiman exclaimed with a pretentious threatening tone.

"Please do that, and when you are fully content about my sincerity, invite Gülfem Sultan to your bedroom and use her not as a woman but as a castrated eunuch. Then, you shall know how far your father used her; but please swear me right now in the life of our children that you will not hurt her, because it was not entirely her fault. She was simply trying to save her son as I do, so, please don't hurt her; just divorce and banish her from the Eski Saray for her shameless deeds. If Ibrahim Pasha desires her, he will ask for her. Then, you will know that I'm also telling you the truth about his sickly desires for all your neglected Kadin. I call it sickly, but he may consider it, as noble. If you treat him as a brother, then it is noble for him to keep all your Kadin content, so they don't seek elsewhere comfort in the arms of other men who want to usurp all your precious belongings. I believe this is also what the Ayin prescribes for all Muslim brothers."

"The Ayin prescribes that if a Sultan dies, his harem becomes the property of the next Sultan. He is the only one who will decide how to dispose of all the existing odalisques. I have donated most of my father's women except you that my mother had bought for me."

"And this was a very wise decision indeed. Your mother was indeed a practical woman when the sole question was her son's happiness."

"What is that supposed to mean?"

"It means that your mother was also a frustrated woman, as all women locked in a harem are. I'm also a woman and I know how I feel sometimes, when Allah wants to test my fidelity and sends in my path an attractive young man; but I am quite different than your mother because I'm not just a mother but I also have a man who knows how to drown my frustrations in the ocean of his sperm. I'm sorry I have offended your ears with my foul tongue, but I have to be perfectly sincere with you because you are my master, and you have every right to demand absolute fidelity, sincerity and obedience for as long as you are alive, as the Ayin says. However, when a woman becomes a widow, then her obligations to her dead husband end after few months of mourning. It may hurt to follow the hard laws of the Holy Quran, but when a man dies, his brother has the obligation to protect his harem from falling into the hands of his enemies, or isn't so?"

****

He woke up drenched in his sweat in the middle of the night. Hurrem's revelations were too painful to bear; but as far as he could discern they sounded logical, despite his instinctive urge to consider them as wild accusations. They had created a turmoil in his heart he could endure only if he put them to the test. In the case of Asphodel he simply had to summon him along with two Mutes and ask him to shed away all his clothes.

It would be a rather degrading test for any Sultan to check the condition of his eunuchs. It was one of the Kislar and the Kapi Aga's responsibilities; but Asphodel becoming his Kapi Aga following Ibrahim's suggestion, it had to be the Grand Vizier's responsibility. Was his magnificent Grand Vizier as thorough as he should have been with all his appointees?"

Piri Pasha had the perfect excuse for his tolerant behavior. No Grand Vizier would survive who would dare to object or investigate Selim's habits. Few of the Grand Viziers were very attractive men and few were executed. Piri Pasha was old and he had probably survived because he was the personification of discretion. However, the moment Selim died, he had tried to get rid of these twin eunuchs and had half-succeeded. If he was still the Grand Vizier, surely Asphodel would be dead by now erasing from every human memory his father's questionable choices; but he had intervened by making Ibrahim Pasha his Grand Vizier and Piri Pasha lost his chance to take one more weight off his young Sultan's shoulders.

Ibrahim didn't share his hostile feelings. On the contrary, he had to be in friendly terms with Asphodel to promote him for the Kapi Aga post. Was he trying to hide something damaging from his past? It was a very remote probability, because the simplest solution was usually the best to silence permanently a blackmailer, poison him. Ibrahim must have had something else in his mind to keep Asphodel alive.

He summoned Asphodel and the Mutes as soon as his morning dressing routine was completed.

"Send a messenger to Piri Mehmet Pasha," he ordered him and watched carefully the expression on the eunuch's face.

Hurrem's hint that one could guess a lot by staring into someone's eyes was perfectly logical. All he saw in Asphodel's eyes was happiness and relief.

"Piri Pasha has died. Only his mosque and his tomb in Silivri stands firm to remind us of his passage," the eunuch joyfully revealed.

Suleiman knew well of Piri Pasha's mosque, because he had been invited on its dedication. He also knew his first Grand Vizier was dead; but pretending he had forgotten it was also useful. A forgetful man was a person someone with heavy consciousness might try to fool. He was as forgetful as a camel. He didn't say much, but he never forgot anything said in his presence.

"Yes, you are right, Allah bless his soul. I must have forgotten it. I wanted to ask him something, but you might remember it as well as he did."

"Your Highness has just to ask me and I will reply to the best of my recollections," Asphodel assured him falling to his knees.

"I want to hear only the naked truth; so take off all your clothes and tell me all you know about my father. The more you tell me the longer you'll live."

****

She had to accept Suleiman's illness had taken a heavy toll. He was not the man he used to be when he came back from Belgrade, Rhodes or Budapest. From one victory to the next Ibrahim's role increased and Suleiman's lessened in significance. It was not too hard to see how this would end, if she didn't interfere. Ibrahim was a fool to imagine that conflicts could be resolved without bloodshed.

The Kislar Aga came in and relayed the news. The Kapi Aga, Asphodel, had disappeared. The rumor claimed he had been sent on a special mission to Egypt. His best guess was he was gone to investigate the death of the last Kislar Aga. The two guards had seen him exiting the Death Gate with two Mutes and going downhill towards the Bosporus. Usually this was the gate they used to carry the dead bodies they disposed in the Sea of Marmara; but the guards swore he was alive and looked happy despite his two ominous companions.

She knew she had to be patient. If Asphodel was executed, then the Sultan would have to choose a new Kapi Aga. As long as none was appointed, Asphodel had to be alive. He and the old Kislar Aga were the only members of Eunuch corps she had to fear. They knew practically everything that had happened in the Harem, since the day Selim Khan had disposed of his father. They had revealed only bits and pieces of the past, but she knew how to connect the dots with her vivid imagination without paying excessively to hear every detail.

Logic dictated it was almost impossible for any harem woman to remain in the same room alone with a man behind closed doors without some sort of seduction to commence, because seduction was the odalisque's reason of existence. A second such visit was a sign the first encounter had been a pleasant experience for both concerned. Any longer stay than two nargileh smokes meant the woman was insatiable. She was insatiable and knew well how she felt when she was alone with a man; but she was also a mother and had to constrain her urges to the absolute minimum. Only with a woman she could fully relax and let her mind free to experience the full extent of her desires. When the Sultan was at war, having a Kislar Aga with feminine inclinations had been an unbelievable torture. There was simply so much a pretty, young concubine could do to please an older one. The rest had to be left to imagination.

She shouldn't complain for her luck. There was always a young chick eager to please and be pleased. The Harem was just a luxurious prison for impenitent female sex offenders. The only way to limit the developing lust was to have all women sleeping in the same room. However, few of the women had certain privileges. They had earned the right to some privacy. Hafsa Sultan had made sure she was one of them from the very beginning. At first she couldn't understand the reason why ordinary concubines hated her; but soon enough it became fairly obvious. Seduction was much more enjoyable behind closed doors than under the covers in the common room. It was a privilege she was willing to share, when the Sultan asked for her and her room was empty for an entire night.

Mahidevran Sultan was less liberal because she had her

two courtesans to think of. It was their payment for their devotion. Now that she had also become a Kadin, she had the right to have courtesans too, and she only had to choose the prettiest and the most pleasant to the senses. Now that there was no suspicious Valide Sultan to use courtesans as spies, she was certain her courtiers would be reliable for at least as long as their lives were not threatened by a higher authority, namely the Sultan.

Rampant imagination helped to make living conditions tolerable. If you closed your eyes and dreamed, ugly or mediocre flesh could become attractive, genders could change, and roles could vary or switch to adapt closer to the developing moods.

Now with the new Kislar Aga imagination was practically useless. She had denied herself the pleasure because now that Hafsa was gone for good, she had to be in control of the Harem. If she submitted to his attraction, then he would be in charge, turning her into one more of his submissive concubines. She could read in his eyes the desire to rise to the top of the Harem, but she knew how to curb his ambitions with the threat of castration. She had warned him he should restrain his conquests to the ordinary odalisques. She was the Sultan's Kadin and only if Suleiman died and one of her sons reigned supreme, then she might consider falling under his spell and added to his harem.

To whet his appetite she had described what she liked most on him and asked him what pleased him most to show him they were a perfect match; but she also advised him they should have patience as time run in their favor. However, if he dared to invade her bedroom uninvited and raped her, she would be obliged to demand for both his unscrupulous heads. She had to be cruel not because she wanted to, but to prove she was as heartless as a Mute Executioner destined to survive and prosper in a world where women were treated like dirt by men.

Somehow exercising restrain with men had gradually turned into some kind of pride, as men had always been a source of shame since her first rape. It was a feeling very difficult to explain to a free man who had never experienced such a total loss of control over his choices.

She read in Kislar Aga's eyes complete understanding for this particular point of view. Unquestionably, he was a fine specimen that could inspire both men and women to use him. He was an Ibrahim with black skin. With her eyes and nostrils closed, the sensations would be quite similar; but despite his attraction she had to be patient, as patience fortified her resolve.

Of course, she knew well enough that everything was just an illusion that could dissolve like salt in water, if the Sultan decided he had no more strength to bare the pain. As long as he insisted on living, her illusions of authority and grandeur would survive unscathed.

She was not the only one in the Seraglio enjoying her illusions. Her husband was too, who still imagined he was her first man and possibly her last; but if he was happy and content to live in a world of illusions, she had to cope with reality most of the time. If Ibrahim had managed to elevate his status from a slave to a Grand Vizier, she had to perform an equally hard task and become a Valide Sultan anyway possible. The only remaining obstacle was Gülfem Sultan and her still impeccable image of fidelity to her husband. To smear it, she had to smudge her reputation by creating a scandal; but it would be difficult. Her only hope was Ibrahim's attraction for every pretty woman that belonged to the Sultan, his master.

****

Ibrahim was not surprised to receive an urgent invitation from the Sultan. His first thought was that the Sultan had reached a decision about the peace treaty with France; but soon he realized Suleiman had different priorities.

"I'm considering Gülfem as my new Valide Sultan. Do you have any objections?" Suleiman asked him quite bluntly, and Ibrahim had to think fast to find a suitable answer.

"How could a Grand Vizier have an objection for a matter so personal?" he asked rhetorically.

"You are allowed to have any suggestion in every possible

matter, if the Sultan orders you to; even if the question is as personal as why you are so attracted by one of my Kadin."

"I would never have any problem commenting on such an issue, because the answers are apparent to the naked eye. Hurrem is most certainly your most pleasing Kadin I have ever met, and Mahidevran Sultan the most beautiful woman of her era in the Empire."

"What about Gülfem? Don't you find her as attractive as the other two?" the Sultan insisted for a complete response.

"She is as attractive as they are, but in a different way. If I was to compare these three Kadin with the three goddesses Paris had to judge, Hurrem would be the sensuous Aphrodite, Mahidevran the unyielding Artemis who can renew her virginity after each submission, and Gülfem Sultan the sophisticated Athena who attracts a man like you more with her wisdom and judgement than with her insatiable lust."

"From what I have seen, your harem does not contain such a gifted woman. Aren't you jealous of my superiority?"

Ibrahim was simply too wise to fall into such an obvious trap.

"Most men in the Empire are greedy enough to envy your harem that contains so many magnificent jewels; but envy is a curse only when it is combined with uncontrollable haste and voracity. Envy can be a blessing when it is combined with patience and prudence, because it helps a wise man to become better and earn rather than claim audaciously unjustified rewards. My Sultan has many beautiful rings he likes to wear in all his fingers. However, many times in the past has offered me few of these priceless jewels as a token of our friendship, or as a reward for my services. I was proud to accept all these gifts, but as he remembers even better than me, I have never asked for anyone, and I will never do that in the future, because I know that it's not proper to ask for something a man loves and considers it as an inseparable part of his existence. Therefore, only if a master is so pleased with a slave, it is proper for the slave to accept a gift from him, because then refusing it would be even more serious crime than stealing it. But why is my master asking me all these strange questions?"

"I was thinking of divorcing Gülfem Sultan now that I have no more desire for her. She is a descent woman worthy of a happier future, so instead for letting her free to seek happiness in the arms of a Pasha of mediocre stature, I thought of suggesting her the possibility of entering your harem and seek happiness in your household. You are without doubt the most gifted man in my empire, so her shame for our divorce will be quickly forgotten," Suleiman said and caught Ibrahim unprepared to respond quickly.

"I'm deeply honored by your magnificent present and incomparable generosity; but I'm unable to accept it right this moment as I should. A man's harem maybe his empire to rule according to the will of Allah, but in mine earthly paradise I'm not the absolute ruler as you are in yours. My palace was not built by the toils of my hands, but by the dowry of my bride, so she has the right to accept or reject such an important permanent resident. My Princess has honored me with two healthy children, so she has every right to look after their happiness too. However, I will convey your divine wishes to my Kadin, and I'm sure she will take into very serious consideration your pleasure as well as mine. You are the Shadow of Allah after all, a much more important distinction than simply her brother or her Sultan."

"Your humbleness pleases me considerably, but I would rather have a more definite answer sooner. The Harem needs a Valide Sultana as soon as possible now that my health condition is improving. My concubines are in turmoil for their long neglect."

"I was never aware of such a disturbance, but if this is indeed the case, Gülfem Sultan and her wisdom would be the perfect choice for this post. With her unending endurance she can become the inspiration of patience for all younger maidens. It's not only men who must suffer loneliness during a war, but women too. After all Hurrem Sultan has so many children to look after. She must not be burden by Harem worries too. This is what absolute fairness demands."

It was not the first time Ibrahim had twisted the laws of

Islam to his advantage. He was well aware that recently the Sultan didn't believe a word he said; but, he usually followed his advises because they were well-versed and fitted the moral standards of the common man.

Suleiman went this time a step further. He not only silently accepted his suggestion, but ordered him to convey his decision personally to the Eski Saray, because he was indisposed.

****

Gülfem accepted her new appointment with her inbred grace. She smiled and bowed her neck with an air of submission. Her new position offered her an wide array of freedoms but also duties. If she so wished, she could become a new Hafsa Hatun; but somehow it wouldn't be safe. She had not the same kind of hold on the Sultan. Ibrahim Pasha knew it as well as she, and he diplomatically hinted on the differences.

"The Sultan knows that this post will occupy much of your time; but there was no other trusty Kadin suitable for so great responsibilities. He believes that under the circumstances long experiences and modesty is essential to carry out successfully all the existing challenges."

He was under the impression they had nothing more to say and got up from the sofa, but he was wrong. Gülfem had something more to say.

"And what does the Grand Vizier think on this critical issue? Is modesty enough for a Valide Sultan to earn a harem's respect? I'm sure he knows well that a successful administrator must be willing to soften the edges. Cruelty is not always the best way to impose peace and justice, only hope is. Everyone is willing to bear few restrictions when the hope of freedom is alive. Recently many rumors have flooded everyone's mind inside the Harem that it's going to be dissolved sooner or later. There are even few incredible murmurs that claim the concubines would be offered as presents to favorite Pashas. Is there any trace of truth in all these wild assertions?"

"I am aware of these rumors too, but as far as I know this

is something only Allah knows and possibly His Shadow. I know of nothing more and the Harem is a domain where I have no authority, as you well know."

"And what about me? Few rumors claim I will spend the rest of my life in another man's harem. Is there any truth in this audacious claim? I have to know, because as you know better than anyone for many years I have been neglected, and this treatment made me feel unwanted and vulnerable. You may not know it, but most women lose their self-respect under these conditions and tend to behave haphazardly even though they were raised to the highest moral standards."

"I see no reason for a Sultan's Kadin to feel this way. One look at the mirror will show you that you have not lost any of your charms. In fact, a few tiny wrinkles here and there add an air of sophistication that should be most welcome by every woman of distinction. They are undeniable signs that at least for a few nights she has offered the Sultan a glimpse of Paradise."

"I'm very grateful you think this way. I wish that the next man who will invite me to his harem will feel the same way. A woman's self-respect is just a reflection the way the man of her dreams feels about her. A man makes a woman feel like a whore. When a woman is born she feels like a heavenly angel."

"I always thought that a Sultan's Kadin were heavenly angels. This is the reason why I was always tempted to enter their paradise and serve them faithfully."

"It is widely known that you were a man who always knew how to find the best excuses for his every weakness. Could you please find a good excuse for me to show you now all my appreciation for everything you have done for me?"

****

The news about Gülfem becoming the new Valide Sultan stirred havoc into the Harem. There was a widespread fear that stricter morals would be imposed. It looked as if now a rejected Kadin had become the superior of a favorite; however, the new Valide Sultan quickly ensured everyone that she was a wise and reasonable ruler who was not interested in stirring unreasonable passion that could ignite violent conflicts. What was also most important was that Hurrem's status as the Sultan's Birinci Kadin would be retained with all her privileges. Additionally, all concubines would be permitted to exit the Eski Saray once a week, on Friday, accompanied be two black eunuchs to pray in a mosque and then visit the Grand Bazaar for shopping exactly as any Kadin had the right to do so.

Hurrem had also no firm reason to complain. She had all the privileges of a Valide Sultan but none of the burdens. Was this some kind of Ibrahim's conspiracy to appease her?

It was a farfetched idea, but as a Valide Sultan Gülfem had the right to see Ibrahim as often as she liked for consultations as Hafsa Sultan had done in the past. He could even invite her to his palace, if he was too busy to find enough time to visit the Eski Saray himself.

****

Hurrem woke up drenched in her sweat. Her courtier was gone, but she was not the one who had made her sweat. A nightmare was the cause. She tried to recall every detail of her dream, but she couldn't. Her mind had kept only the most painful. It was pitch-black dark and she was paralyzed. Two strong hands had spread her legs open and placed them on a man's broad shoulders. She tried to scream, but no scream came out despite her fervent efforts only a murmur of protest as he didn't show any respect for her pleas to respect her virginity. He was determined and plunged through, overcoming like a breeze one by one all the points of resistance her soft flesh could provide. However, as gradually his persistence prevailed, her pain turned into pleasure and murmurs of despair turned into loud pleas to continue his quest until she was out of breath.

Encourage by her lack of resistance, he flipped her over letting her to regain control. Perhaps he was testing her state of morality, but she was too advanced to be separated from his unbending will to pierce her once more. No woman had any hope against such violent and cruel man as her invisible rapist. It was then when she felt the presence of the second man who sneaked from behind to have his share of her exposed assets. Now, she had to decide whether this auspicious dream was triggered by an unconscious search in her violent past during the beginning of her slavery, or if it was prelude of a disgraceful future in Ibrahim's harem.

She was involved in a very dangerous game. If she could win, then one of her sons would become the Sultan in the throne of Osman, replacing Suleiman. Soon after, she was going to become the new Valide Sultan replacing Gülfem and move forward even faster than her from where Hafsa had left the torch. The Sultan's Harem had to be abolished, but this was not a task a single woman could accomplish. The only way to total success was for many women to consider it a worthy cause and serve it with the dedication of a fanatic Crusader; but even then final success was not assured. A determined man and few unworthy lusty women could spoil everything. However, her mission was to carry out her duty. As the new Valide Sultan, she would employ Mimar Sinan to build her a mansion along the Bosporus shore. There she would establish her harem. She had already chosen her Kislar Aga, and she had a good idea who would be her Hasodabashi, Ibrahim Pasha demoted back to the status of a page.

However, if she lost the gamble and Mustafa became the next Sultan after Suleiman's demise, it would be up to him to decide how he would take revenge for his mother's long banishment in Manisa. She had read Mustafa's eyes. He was a noble young man and would not try to disgrace her in person; but it was also quite obvious he was going to keep Ibrahim in his high post. Then, it would be up to the Grand Vizier to choose her proper punishment.

Ibrahim was an imaginative man. He was also an insightful person. He must have discerned her insatiable nature. If he really wished to punish her, he would simply imprisoned her in his harem. Then, he would sleep with every other harem inmate but her, year after year. He could even turn her into a Hatidge's courtesan and force her to watch him pleasing her and Basmi. He was that devious and sophisticated torturer.

On the other hand, Suleiman was as innocent as sheep. He imagined that by demanding absolute submission he could dominate all men and women, while in fact what he had earned was at best a feeble temporary superiority. He didn't envision that this way he was only seeding winds that were soon force him to sow tempests. Perhaps it was too late for her to react. Perhaps the die was already cast. It all depended on a vague parameter, Suleiman's health. If it worsened and he lost control of the Empire, everything would be lost along with her sons. They were the offspring of a slave after all, while Mustafa was the son of a Tatar Princess.

Selim Khan had been most truthful when he talked to her about the future of the Osmanli family. If the offspring was in par with their ancestors, then the throne would remain in their hands. However, if the offspring was inferior, it should be slaughtered like sheep during Ramadan for the glory of Allah. Then, the proper heir should be chosen among the Tatar Khans.

Mustafa had Tatar blood in his veins. Mahidevran had already made absolutely clear what kind of blood she had by slashing her face with her nails. If the Princess had a knife, Hurrem would be dead now, but knives were not permitted in the Harem, and food was served well sliced to make sure the daily concubine quarrels didn't turn into a bloody mess.

When she called her "sold meat" the Princess didn't know it, but she had repeated Selim's exact words, when he summoned her to his quarters. She still remembered that horrible experience that night in the Marble Kiosk and his words word for word:

"Take your clothes off and come closer and seat on my lap."

The ominous presence of his two eunuchs left no hope for resistance. Her mother's warning still echoed in her ears:

"If you ever come face to face with rapists, only total submission to their will can save your life. Show them that your purpose in life is to please them and you'd love to have their children. Then they might spare your life. When a man makes love to you, he always has his offspring in his mind. Only if he is sterile, then your life is in danger."

Selim was not sterile, but he made sure she understood he was enraged for her refusal to collect his golden coins. Selim Khan was not a rapist either. With women he was more of a poet. By asking her to sit on his lap, he had let her choose how she would please him. She chose to retain her virginity and he seemed very pleased with her choice and showed his pleasure by throwing few gold coins in her lap to tickle her greed for more. If he was in a teasing mood she was too. She had swung her hips so violently the coins slipped and dropped on the floor to show him she didn't care for money, all she was interested that moment was sheer pleasure.

He got the message, but he had to make sure she accepted his absolute authority.

"You are sold meat. If you wish to ever become free again, you must be frugal and collect every coin or present every man gives you. It's not a gesture of disgrace, but you should treasure every token, so you can buy your freedom one day. A poor slave will always remain a slave. Now show me all you have learned in my harem on how to please an aging Sultan, and I will be even more generous than I was when you whet my appetite with your dancing figures," he promised and he was true to his word, because Selim Khan had never lied since the day he had lied to his father to became the next Sultan. He was sincere and always eager to test the extend of human endurance as any competent leader should to complete a superhuman task.

"In your harem I was taught only how to please a Prince Heir, your Highness; but Allah has blessed me with a very fruitful imagination of what every kind of man needs to feel to enter His own Paradise," she replied totally immersed in a profound seduction mood.

It was a subtle hint she wouldn't mind being used both as a divine houri or a handsome boy also by her master's consorts, if this was what the Shadow of Allah wished to reach a state of total bliss. If this violent Sultan failed to grasp the deeper meaning of her words, the two much more sensitive pages didn't, and used her time and time again until they had no strength left and the Sultan no more loose coins.

When she went back to the Eski Saray she had earned more gold than she was worth in the Avret Bazaar, but also learned a valuable lesson. Gold was not enough for a slave to earn his freedom. The owner had also to concede her liberation. Selim could liberate her, but he didn't. He seemed to enjoy her submission to Menekse's commands too much to let her free so easily.

She also learned that eunuchs were even more insatiable than the Sultan because their lust didn't follow the all-familiar cycle of been triggered, expressed, and finally recede as any other normal male. This had to be the reason why Selim was so fond of them. This was at least what common logic dictated; but, she had not witnessed with her own eyes such a display. Selim was known for his secrecy as many other Osmanli; however, insisting on secrecy meant that damaging secrets existed. This was also what logic dictated.

Slavery was a strange institution. Hafsa Sultan would also have left her free, if only she snored in her sleep; but God had obviously another plan in His mind making her a perfect night companion for men, women, even eunuchs. Her resemblance with Ibrahim was mind-blowing.

Selim Khan and Menekse were now diseased. Only Asphodel was still alive. Mentioning his name was a subtle trick to focus the Sultan's attention on his present and past. He was a White Eunuch and he had almost never visited the Eski Saray. She had no ill feelings for him, because if he had his way, he would have never touched her. Selim and Menekse had forced him to touched her to make fun of him and disgrace her femininity as any other male beast. On the other hand, Asphodel had been as gentle and discrete as a maiden. Too bad he had to die not because of any evil deed, but his intimate knowledge of Osmanli hidden vices.

Keeping secrets was a lost cause inside the Seraglio or the Eski Saray, and the reason was plain enough. One could make money by revealing someone else's secret and money were more precious than human lives or reputations.

She got up and stood on her unstable legs. She felt dirty even though her favorite courtier was exotically scented and clean when she came over and asked if she had any more use for her services. Now her sweat had mixed with the courtiers and formed a magnificent blend of female perfumes. It was one more advantage female lovers offered. She didn't have to go to the hammam immediately after a carnal encounter to wash away all the signs of her sins.

Perhaps, rich benevolent Sultanas should help common women to keep their reputation intact by erecting few more public hammams. Marriage failed often and there was no reason for women to be disgraced for their infidelities. It was not solely their mistake. Men got sick, wounded, or even bored. They were normally the first to claim their freedom from the marital bonds in an era when slaves had become so numerous and greedy for money and promotions like Ibrahim Pasha.

Just mentioning his name gave her goose bumps because he was the best lover she ever had, even though their engagement was so brief. She had fathomed her feelings and she found a single answer. He was the only man who had not treated her as a slave. He was the lover she yearned since she was a virgin maiden in her Ukraine village, but had never found. Suddenly she realized how just his thought had made her wet, and she felt for the first time dirty in need of a steam bath. It was not the cleansing action of the steam she needed, but the touch of another human being that would replace the special man she was missing.

****

It had to be another choice of Gülfem, the new Valide Sultan, a new masseuse with black skin; but it might well be a request of the Kislar Aga Gülfem had decided to grant to gain his full cooperation.

"What is your pleasure?" the young colored girl asked with the typical timidity of a new slave as Hurrem was laying down on her back.

Hurrem despite her superior harem status felt too embarrassed to explain, and simply blushed. She didn't have to do anything more. With the efficiency of an experienced tailor who seeks for special bodily features, the young girl quickly followed with her sensitive fingers all the places where lust could be triggered, measuring the reactions of her naked flesh starting from her ears and ending at the tip of her toes without even a trace of adolescence modesty. When she finished her reconnaissance routine only Hurrem was in limbo about how to react to each unexpected sensation.

On the other hand, the girl was very experienced and as soon as she had covered her skin with generous portions of jasmine oil, she laid on top of her as if she was her lover.

"You need a man badly!" she concluded as if she was a doctor who had just finished her examination to determine the source of a serious illness, and Hurrem expressed her agreement with a long moan.

"Close your eyes and let me become what you need."

****

She asked her to stop, but the slave realized she didn't really mean it. She said it just to retain the rest of her decency as the Birinci Kadin of a Sultan and the mother of his children; but for a slave, even the slave of a slave what was important was to transmit slavery as if it was a deadly disease until everyone was infected.

The slave's desire had much more to do than sheer pleasure. She wanted to turn the Birinci Kadin of the Sultan into her slave who would come regularly and ask for her services as if they were fresh water or clean air to breath. And she achieved all her goals as Hurrem's breath synchronized with hers following the primal, divine beat that matches perfectly breaths and heartbeats all the way to heavens.

＊＊＊＊＊＊

"Where are you from?" Hurrem asked the slave. "I haven't seen a Negro with your kind of eyes."

"I'm not a Negro. I'm from the land of the Tai," she replied with a long smile.

"Where is this Tai land?" Hurrem insisted.

"It is a land much farther than Persia or India. A land where women can become men, if they want to. Did you like what I did for you?"

"I just loved it," Hurrem humbly confessed.

"Then you have no more use of men. Whenever you need a man, you'll just come to me; but you'll have to give me presents because I'm not a slave. I am a servant. I only live here to serve the Valide Sultana."

"I'm a Sultana too so you must serve me too," Hurrem demanded.

"I will serve you only if you give me presents. This is why I serve the Sultana too."

"How much do I owe you then?"

"You owe me nothing. The first time is always by the will of Allah, but the second time is a sin so every sinner has to pay the price."

"What's the price for me?" Hurrem insisted.

"There is no fixed price. It all depends how much you need me and how much I need you. I'm a woman after all and I have divine compassion not just sinful passion."

Hurrem left the hammam fully content for the first time. The universe was truly harmonic if slaves and masters decided to cooperate forgetting their pitiful differences. What was important in this universe was time. Everything else, diamonds, silver coins, or gold was just an illusion, a cheat made to fool people into wasting their time to get them, only to exchange them for the time of someone else. The Tai servant was right. She didn't require gold to sell her pleasure. Pleasure had its own value.

Unfortunately Allah had made the world in such a way that the value of pleasure varied considerably with time as moods changed even faster than weather.

This servant was a jewel. Gülfem must have discovered her in one of the caravanserais she was often visiting to have her feminine desires quenched. Now that the Basra was occupied by the Ottomans the commerce had increased immensely. Did she owe gratitude to Suleiman and Ibrahim for their conquests?

****

An new unfair accusation had recently reached Hurrem's ears. They claimed her last delivery of Gihangir was caused because she was seduced by the Jewish doctor of the Seraglio.

It was a damn lie because he was old, ugly and his back was bent, not because of a hump but of old age. He was practically a eunuch, as he was not aroused touching a woman. The old Kislar Aga had made sure of that before letting him touch the Sultan's Birinci Kadin by the most natural way, his fingers. She remembered clearly this necessary examination to make sure she was pregnant. The doctor had used plenty of oil tickling her to trigger her passion and allow his slim hand reach deeply enough to touch the fetus.

Perhaps he was responsible for damaging the spine of her son, but he would not admit it and lose his life. Only Allah knew what exactly had happened, because none of her relatives or Suleiman's had a hump. It had to be one of these cases where even though no one was at fault, Allah had punished her. The Universe was not perfect. Suleiman was now ill and had no use of her, scared that she was cursed and would produce another invalid child. Fortunately, Mahidevran was stranded in Manisa, too far to take advantage of the opportunity. Only Gülfem was available to comfort him.

This thought scared her to death. She had to prevent such an event as quickly as possible. She had Ibrahim's open invitation, but it was not enough. She had to seduce Suleiman as soon as possible before he had time to invite Gülfem to his quarters.

Thank Allah the Ramadan fest would start in few days and the Sultan was very keen on keeping traditions. Thank Allah, Ibrahim was not. Was it Allah's will to become pregnant by Ibrahim for the second time? Only Allah knew of His own wishes.

****

The peace and alliance treaty between France and the Ottoman Empire was destined to disturb the existing balance of power in Europe. It would be the first time a Christian nation would take sides so openly with a fanatical Muslim empire. In the past, Venetians, this unscrupulous nation of merchants who looked everywhere for profit, had reached agreement with their worst mortal enemies to gain access to all the ports control by the Ottomans, from Alexandria to the Black Sea, but the Venetians had lost all their credibility to all the Eastern Christians long time ago, when they attacked and conquered Constantinople and Ragusa governed by Christian sovereigns.

Ibrahim had tried very hard to convince the French ambassador that the Ottomans were very reliable allies that had never gone back to their word, unless their allies violated the treaties first. He also insisted that Christians lived peacefully in the Empire and had nothing to fear from the Sultan as long as they obeyed the laws. The Sultan was a Muslim as well as he, but this was not a sign of oppression but a sign of religious freedom. Religion had to be a matter of choice. He had made a truce with Allah to become the Grand Vizier in exchange for his Christian faith. If he was foolish enough to break the contract and become a Christian again, then the Shadow of Allah would take his head simply because he had broken this divine contract with Allah. In fact, he suggested the French king should do the same in case a Muslim turned Christian and then betray his new faith. One change of faith should be admissible because no child was free to choose its faith and all followed blindly the faith of their fathers.

The French ambassador had no logical arguments against Ibrahim's suggestions. Human logic was unquestionably with Ibrahim's side, as opening the Ottoman harbors to France would create unmeasurable wealth for the French people. This was as certain as the sun rising from the East. France had tried to occupy the same harbors by force during the Crusades, and now after Sultan Selim's conquests they were offered free on a plate. Of course, the French harbors would be also opened to the Ottoman ships, but Ibrahim was wise enough to point out that Ottoman merchant ships would never dare to approach France as long as Christians controlled Italy, Sicily and Malta. On the other hand, French ships carrying the cross would face no obstacles on their way to the East after this treaty. This treaty was a deal France could only benefit by signing it. The profits were so clear even a child could recognized them; however, the ambassador was still suspicious.

"If the French profits are so apparent, this means the Turks would lose money. Are you a traitor?" he asked mockingly.

"No! I'm not a traitor. I'm a visionary. I'm also a Greek as all Ottomans are not Turks. There are also Greeks, Jews, Armenians, Arabs, Serbs and Albanians. Every one of these nations are sailors and merchants, so they will all profit, if commerce increases. Then, even the Turks will profit imitating our success. Then, the Turks will stop fighting as commerce makes more profits than wars and no one has to die fighting. True wealth is made by workers and merchants, not by fighters and slaves. Paid workers work harder than slaves and history has proved that time and time again. If you have studied history, you must know as much. We the nations who were once the slaves of the Romans know that better than anyone else. The Sultan may think he is a Turk, but in his veins runs Roman blood because most of the women of his ancestors were Roman Princesses or slaves. You are a Roman too, because even the French letters of this treaty are Roman too. This much I'm sure you know even though you pride does not permit you to accept it. In your case Roman men were your grandfathers and French women your grandmothers. And this is the reason you write using Roman letters, while the Ottomans Arabic. Sooner or later the son of Romans will come and change the letters the Ottomans use. It's inevitable, because this is what Mother Nature demands to progress. This is why despite all the objections you raise, I know in the end the French king will sign the treaty, because he is wiser than any French ambassador; otherwise you would have become the King of France."

It was the first time the ambassador had heard a Greek talking like this. Usually the Greek immigrants talked only about the lost glories of the Eastern Roman Empire, but they were mostly of Roman descent, not truly Greeks grown on Greek soil. Greece had been the promise land for many nations thought the ages. It was the naval of the Earth for ancient Greeks. Asia Manor was also the crossroad of innumerable nations each carrying its own beliefs that mixed with the old myths, producing new even more complex civilizations. However, accepting his opponent's logic was not the duty of any ambassador, so the Frenchman had to steer the discussion to more familiar paths, namely religious conflicts.

"You may imagine you are a visionary and perhaps your bold choices may be justified in the distant future, but today you are a traitor who has betrayed his Christian beliefs to serve the Turks the infidel conquerors of the Roman capital. I'm sure deep inside you also yearn for the final victory of the Holy Cross."

However, Ibrahim had crossed long ago the limits of his national identity, his religion or his language. He was also well acquainted with the tricks westerners had played in the past to create divisions between people in the Balkans and Asia Minor since the Roman era. Divisions was the origin of chaos barbarians had used to conquer these blessed lands and apply their kind of order to secure their welfare.

From the very beginning of his career as a Grand Vizier he had restrained any tendency to shed blood, because he knew that shedding blood was the worst obstacle between different nations, as for the human species blood should be revenged by blood. Now this audacious French Ambassador was trying to erase his life's accomplishments with one stroke.

He giggled sarcastically as he did every time he wished to

insult a foreign emissary.

"Our memories are not so shallow to have forgotten what the Frank Crusaders did to my nation. They stole everything, even the golden gates of Agia Sophia. And when Mehmet Fatih came to conquer the Holy City, the capital of the world was just a poor, dilapidated village full of looted ruins of luxurious palaces and magnificent churches. Your compatriots did not respected even the tombs of the Roman Emperors, and the holy relics of Jesus Christ and his Apostles. But God is everywhere and we all know it now; so, if I feel like praying, I can kneel inside Fatih's Mosque that has Roman columns holding the dome, and in Agia Sophia that has still Christian icons under the plaster. I have prayed there many times, when I was still just another slave; and nothing happened; but when I changed my faith and prayed to Allah, miracles started happening. My Sultan made me his Grand Vizier and Serasker because of my wisdom and absolute loyalty and gave me his sister as a wife. He also has Alexander the Great as his life-model and he knows well I follow his message. Nations, rather than shed each-other's blood, should mixed their blood peacefully, and this is what Allah and God wish too."

These conciliatory words of Ibrahim was not what the ambassador wished to hear. His aim was to involve Ibrahim in some kind of treacherous deal that would involve the Grand Vizier in some kind of conspiracy plot against his Sultan.

"I am also a peace-loving Christian and I hope all your wishes come true," he claimed with a submissive tone in his voice. "However, right now your Sultan is an absolute ruler, and every other man is his subject forced to kneel in front of his wishes or lose his head. This is not what we call rule of law in the West; thus, as long as this is the Ottoman law, we will never accept you as our equals. If the Ottoman Empire occupies European lands right now, it is not because of his cultural superiority, but because of the strength of the sword."

"Even the most ferocious lion would lick the hand of the slave that feeds it, when it is put in a cage. For everyone else the Sultan may appear as a wild beast, but I'm the one who has

tame it, so he eats only the food I offer him in my hand. In this Empire what happens is because I will it, and if the Sultan wishes something I don't, then it will never happen."

"This is your personal illusion, because now Hurrem Sultan holds the keys of the Sultan's heart. This is what everyone in Constantinople says, not just foolish me," the ambassador boldly claimed.

"This may be true, but who knows for how long this may last? Right now, besides his heart, the rest of the Empire obeys my commands, not hers; however, we have not come here to discuss and measure the weaknesses of our masters. We have come here under their orders to conclude a lucrative deal that would benefit both of us now as well as in the future, as I have explained. If we fail in this task, our masters would have every right to punish us severely."

With this threat the ambassador was obliged to examine carefully every treaty term. Few of them provided for Ottoman ships to enter peacefully and buy provisions as any other Christian ship at the Mediterranean harbors of Marseille, Toulon and Nice. Of course, French warships could enter the Golden Horn peacefully too, but this was not a profitable concession. "This term will not be signed by my King. Religion is one of the three pillars his throne rests."

"A throne should rest on more than three pillars in case one breaks, and only old men need a cane to help their two legs to walk. However, if the throne of France is so aged and weak, then I am willing to do my best to bolster a shaky leg against any Pope who might think it's profitable to topple such a wise King whose judgement my Sultan trust as much as he trusts me who has proposed this treaty. We are all men of our words, so we can keep the terms about harbors secret. From my side I promise that only the Sultan, the Grand Vizier and the Kapudan Pasha will hear anything about any harbor any of our ships can find shelter during a storm."

This bold suggestion took the ambassador by surprise. Accepting a secret treaty was like accepting his king was so weak he was afraid to reveal an alliance with this witty Ottoman.

"Signing this treaty in secrecy is unacceptable. Every spy in Constantinople knows of our long negotiations by now. If nothing comes out of our meetings, it would mean we have failed to find any common ground. This result will surely embolden our common enemies. We have at least to announce a treaty proclaiming our will to become friends."

Ibrahim felt he was one step before their final agreement, and all the ambassador's obstacles were feeble pretexts similar to the rear actions of a retreating enemy who had been already convinced by the volleys of his arguments that there was no hope of winning the fight. The enemy needed just a great blast more to turn tail, and he had great experience in harmless fireworks as well as deadly cannon blasts.

"If the pylon of religion in France is at stake, then let's give these treaty's public terms a strictly religious context and keep our military alliance for cooperation against our common enemies a secret. Then, no Christian nation will have a valid cause to blame the king of France or my Sultan. In fact, other Christian kings may wish to sign similar treaties with the Sultan and put an end to all the bloody religious wars between Christians and Muslims. Let's just say that the king of France and the Sultan have agreed to protect the religious freedom in all the lands they command from now to eternity."

The French ambassador remained for the first time silent, because he had nothing to complain any more. France had no Muslims for the Sultan to protect, while in the East there were many Catholics who needed protection from Muslim aggression. This were exactly the superficial reasons that had inspired the Crusades few centuries ago. For the time being the West had everything to win and nothing to lose. The only drawback was the peaceful opening of the Mediterranean ports of France to the Ottoman fleet and the neutrality of the French fleet that was anyway too weak to protect its shores.

For him it was a diplomatic triumph unless Ibrahim had something up his sleeve. By now their relationship has gone beyond the limits of diplomacy. He had searched deeply into Ibrahim's past and knew enough to trust his words. Essentially this treaty was like opening a tiny secret gate in the Ottoman bastions similar to the Kerkoporta of the Theodosian Walls the Ottomans had used to undermine the feeble Roman defenses. It was not the total collapse of Ottoman defenses, but a crack that could have potentially unexpected results.

Ibrahim remained silent and silence could well be the sign of a conspirator; so the ambassador was not persuaded to break it. However, Ibrahim was silent because his mind raced forward. There was a war to be fought against the fanatic Catholics of Spain. With these treaty France became an obstacle in the middle of the Holy Roman Empire, an obstacle the Roman Emperor had to fight to conquer it, or use armies to guard it. Barbarossa had also gained a foothold in the West Mediterranean he could use to break the blockade of Malta and Sicily as an easier way to attack Rome was from the South, exactly as Belisarius had used to conquer Rome for his Emperor Justinian.

If he failed to achieve this goal and France ever became a marine force, then it might become a threat to the Holy Lands; but this seemed too distant a threat compared to the present gains. After all, he was leading an empire of many nations, while France was a weakling nation surrounded by Christian enemies.

Triumphs or treacheries were many times a matter of time scale. As far as he could see in his lifetime this treaty was another diplomatic triumph of his administration, but to achieve it he had to convince the reluctant Sultan to put his tugra at the bottom. He could clearly see all his objections, as the treaty put certain limits to his divine authority. He could no longer at least in paper prosecute Christians, but he could argue for days that the greatest threat for the Ottoman Empire were historically not the peaceful Christian subjects, but the rebellious Persian Shiites, the innumerous Mongols, or the barbaric Russians.

According to his expert opinion, the nations in the Middle East had to stop fighting each other and instead cooperate to achieve prosperity. They should also become liberated from the bonds of their overaged holy books that had done much to create conflicts and put limit to people's activities.

On the contrary, in the West people had made their revolution against the Pope and the Bible, and Suleiman had been wise enough to support and save the Protestants from the total extinction the Holy Inquisition had planned for every western heretic. Now the right time had come for the Muslims to make their revolution too and give new meaning to the words of the Prophet. If the Holy Bible was now imprisoned within the walls of the churches, the Holy Quran should also be locked within the walls of the mosques.

The French ambassador was a clever man and an efficient diplomat. Before giving his consent he had put forward another feeble term. He asked for the Sultan to allow one of the churches of Jerusalem that long ago had been turned into a mosque to be converted back to church, so that the French pilgrims had a temple to pray. However, Ibrahim Pasha had a long experience with fanatical Muslims to give this idea a second thought.

"The king of France can ask me for an entire province and I will give it, because it is within my rights; however, a mosque is the house of Allah and only He can give it back to an infidel."

This was his declaration of intend, but the Catholic Church got the permission to establish a modest mission and a temple for religious purposes.

****

The Sultan raised his eyes from the long firman and looked at his Grand Vizier who waited kneeled in front of his majestic throne. All that was left for a new reality to be born in the Ottoman Empire was his tugra, as his top official had assured him. After a long interval of silence and deliberation he asked him looking straight into his eyes all the way to his soul:

"Do I understand correctly that according to this piece of paper, from now on I will share my authority on my subjects with the King of France?"

Ibrahim replied swiftly without a second thought:

"Indeed your Majesty will share as much authority as the King shall on every believer of the words of the Prophet in France."

"Is it true then that if I sign this treaty, from now on all the goods of the Franks will be imported in my Empire without any tariffs?"

"Yes, without a tax exactly as our merchandise will reach French harbors."

The Sultan remained only for a moment silent and then posed another sincere inquiry:

"If Allah has no gains over Christ and His Shadow loses his authority to command his subjects, why should I sign this piece of paper, when only my enemies have something to gain?"

Ibrahim had seriously consider his answer to this question for many days.

"Treaties are planted on the present and gradually grow as time passes towards the heavens. You are very wise to realize that today our commerce with the West is suffering because of the war, and we import more goods than we export to our enemies. However, what is true today may become a lie tomorrow, if we try hard enough. I used to be an infidel and poor as a beggar few years back. Now I'm a believer and so filthy rich that I can buy the best jewels, clothes and furniture from Venice for my household. If Your Highness believes that with every year we Ottomans will become so weak and poor that in the end the Christians will raid our towns, steal our women and rape our sons, then You have every right to tear this treaty to pieces and punish this dreamer. My dream has always been that in the future the Ottoman Empire will grow in strength so much by your brave sons that the faithful will multiply and flood Europe with their children. I also believe that your subjects will built marvelous contraptions, the West will buy with the gold they have stolen from us during the Crusades, and that the people of the entire world will look at us with envy once more as they did before, when they trusted all our prophets and saints, our gods and goddesses, our language and our values."

Listening to Ibrahim's speech Suleiman's face revealed the

raging battle within. His slave's words had deeply puzzled him. His worries were indeed a product of his pessimism caused by the continued drain of courage he experienced caused by the thought of his incurable disease. In the past they had often talked of the possibility of applying certain measures to encourage tradesmen fleeing from the East to the West during the various religious wars between Christianity and Islam to return peacefully to the Ottoman Empire and infuse the trades and arts they had developed and learn in the West, especially Italy and Spain that had quickly developed through trade into the powerhouses of arts, commerce and science.

They were not the first such Ottoman dreamers. Mehmet Fatih had invited the Jews persecuted in Spain to return to the East and the land of their ancestors, and Selim Khan had also moved by force Persian artisans from Tabriz to Iznik to infuse pottery art and decorative tile manufacturing. Nevertheless, persecution and violence were not the best way for the Ottoman Sultans to achieve these aim. People were willing to abandon the land of their ancestors much easier, if the hope for a better life for them and their children was assured.

Constantinople had to become the cultural center of the world as it was when Constantine the Great laid down the first cornerstones for his magnificent buildings. This was Ibrahim's goal when he built his magnificent palace to show how well rich people could leave under the Ottoman rule in the Eternal City. Affluent people needed a safe and attractive place to live their easy lives, and the Bosporus Straits were a unique location in the entire world.

This was the reason why he had tried to adorn the Old Roman Hippodrome with his bronze statues together with the Roman obelisks to show that there was cultural continuity in the Ottoman Empire from the Egyptian Pharaohs to the Greek World and the Roman Emperors to the Ottoman Sultans. His plan was for new churches and mosques to be built to demonstrate religious freedom, and soon after magnificent public buildings and institutions not only for the rich state official but also for the average citizen or even the poor, as Fatih and Bayezid had done. Nevertheless, despite his eloquent arguments the Sultan had remained suspicious of this grand plan. If Constantinople was flooded by rich westerners the local folks might revolt seeing their religious values, customs, and the modest hereditary way of living challenged by infidel foreigners. Then the religious wars could be transferred from distant battlefields inside the Eternal City with catastrophic results. Finally, Suleiman exploded his oriental frustration.

"You Greeks should not hope you can ever assimilate the Turks the same way you absorbed the Romans. We know your tricks all too well. After all you have nothing more to teach us that we don't already know. The time has come for the entire world to kneel at our feet the same way in the past Orient kneeled in front of the Romans."

Suleiman's passionate voice surprised the Grand Vizier. It showed that deep inside the Sultan's heart a hidden flame was burning. However, it was not just Suleiman's patience close to exhaustion. All these years Ibrahim's tolerance for Oriental conservatism was dangerously approaching its limits. Up to this moment he had never lost his cool, but human patience was a glass that drop by drop was filling with complains. Now his glass was approaching its full capacity. Thus, his quick reply was for the first time painted with the vivid colors of anger.

"No one desires to absorb you Turks, because your minds are like the desert sands that can seep all the moisture falling from heavens without the growth of a single flower. We offered you our seeds of knowledge, but no one grew roots and no flower bloomed. We the Greeks are like the busy bees that pollinate the flowers of knowledge of all nations; however, beware that without flowers no fruits can ever grow for knowledge to cultivate your barbaric minds."

Now it was Suleiman's turn to be flabbergasted by this unexpected explosion of the slave's anger. Besides Hurrem, Ibrahim had now commenced his personal revolution, and the Sultan was caught unprepared to quench it. His father Selim was urging him to get up and use his heavy sword to silence forever this audacious mouth that dared offend his race; but, at the same time his mother's hand held him back, raising excuses for the slave's abnormal behavior. Ibrahim had endure enough abuse by Muslims and only twice he had tried to defend his accomplishments against the unjustified charges of Iskander Pasha and the abusing poet.

If the Grand Vizier had exercised his authority against everyone who was abusing him, then half of the City's population would be hanged or behind bars. His mistakes dwarfed compared to his accomplishments. Besides his mother, no one had been so tender on all these occasions, when Death had visited the Seraglio full of vengeance. Thus, the Sultan with a visible effort managed to keep his nerves under control, and Ibrahim felt this struggle and eased his anger too. Suleiman was still his best friend, the man who had covered his nudity with his cape in the freezing Avret Bazaar. He was now for one more time Suleiman's slave eager to serve his master and steer him back on the proper path. He still was the Sultan's most trusted counselor.

"Every morning we wake up, it can be our last, and being a slave or a Sultan does not make much difference when death is near. As every worker who gets up from bed each morning and goes to work as if he was immortal, so must we be worthy of the immense power that lies in our hands. A leader is truly great only if he can overcome the great obstacles that will stop an ordinary man. After all, a peace treaty is nothing more than a piece of paper. What luck can a piece of paper have, facing your mighty sword? The written words are just a dream, an illusion while the sword is the hard reality. Your sword will decide who will be free and who will become slave. Today your ships are your swords and your horses that gallop on the waves to bring your banners to the end of the Earth, much further than the Indus River of Alexander to the Islands of the Spices."

This new Ibrahim's idea flooded Suleiman's eyes with anticipation. With the eyes of his imagination he could see the Ottoman fleet reaching India and the Indonesian Archipelagos where all the spices came from. It was an effective diplomatic stroke that had shifted the subject of discussion from the permanent conflict between Turks and Greeks to spices and possibly the seductive opium trade. However, in the end once more the unending doubts and suspicions of the Sultan regained the upper hand.

"Yes, but as we all know at the very beginning even the Holy Quran was just dreams of the Prophet written on paper, but in the end these dreams were eventually realized and brought the Romans to their knees. Dreams I cannot contain can wreck my Empire too," the Sultan argued; however, now Ibrahim had calmed down his nerves and found promptly a powerful stroke triggered by the Sultan's reference to the Quran.

Religious issues was a battlefield where Ibrahim felt at ease. During the years of his Seraglio training the Quran was the main subject of many courses according to the orders of Selim Khan. Ibrahim had learned by heart all the principal verses that had more moral value than the boring repetitions of a prophet, trying to teach barbaric Bedouins how to behave. He smiled politely as usual. Indeed, surrounded by so many slaves, concubines, eunuchs and spies Suleiman had every right to become suspicious. He had to help his master overcome his conservatism; so he boldly claimed:

"If the Quran is for Your Magnificence an integral part of your Muslim reality, then this treaty is a portion of the Holy Quran too in a very subtle and implicit way!" Ibrahim claimed and this was not the first time he was making an audacious claim and it would not be the first time that he would twist words to prove he was right. The Sultan was well aware of his ability to argue and remained silent avoiding any opposing comment that might be refuted at the next moment making him feel like a fool.

The very first time he met Ibrahim he had felt a strange but unconquerable attraction for his flesh, but as years went by this attraction became more spiritual than carnal. His desires gradually weakened replaced by a mental need for Ibrahim's ideas, especially when Hurrem entered his life, occupying more and more of his daily life.

He could remain silent listening to him narrating stories about magical foreign lands and strange nations, or the various deeds remarkable people from many nations had performed in the past, like Hannibal, Caesar, Attila, Constantine, Heraclius, Nicephorus Phocas or Basil the Bulgar-slayer pointing out that every nation had its own heroes, not just the Turks or the Muslims. Ibrahim during innumerable nights had become his Halima who could talk to him until he fell asleep, soothing his nightmares for thousands of troublesome nights whenever his nightmares kept him awake.

Was Ibrahim now trying to ridicule the words of the Prophet? It wouldn't be the right time as his anger had not completely subsided; but how could he be calm after all Asphodel had confessed about Ibrahim and his father being lovers? Surely Ibrahim had a lot of explaining to do after this treaty was concluded one way or another. Was it possible Ibrahim was right about Quran too? Could a atheist be right and the Last Prophet wrong?

"I know all the words of the Prophet and he said nothing about a peace treaty with the infidels, and I can summon the Great Mufti to prove I am right," he pronounced with confidence, but Ibrahim's ironic smile still persisted.

"I know the entire Quran by heart and I have kept in my mind everything worth keeping and nothing more than that. The second Sura clearly proclaims:

"All people are a single nation"

My dear friend and master, this simply means that every war among people is a civil war everyone wise overlord should hate. However, in a slave's heart a line from the ninetieth Sura is much closer and will always remain imprinted with golden letters. My master may have forgotten it after all these years he spent as a mighty Sultan and his mind is so full of worries, but even he is still obliged to obey it, if he is truly a pious Muslim. Thus, listen to the words of the Last Prophet and sign this treaty because it is what He demands of you."

"And what will make you realize life is an uphill path?

The liberation of a slave!"

Suleiman remained silent, but a tear slipped from his eyes and was quickly hidden between the bushy hair of his beard. Ibrahim's claim was true; so, he summoned the scriber who was much more skillful drawing his tugra than him.

Ibrahim had seen him signing many times and knew exactly what would be soon painted under the treaty terms and the invincible war banners that were an integral part of an Osmanli signature. These military flags were always implanted in the middle of a field full of colorful wild flowers and Anatolian tulips. It signified the Osmanli promise, eternal peace after the Holy War. It was indeed spring, and after a bloody war with Persia peace would finally prevail on the lands of the Empire and it was his accomplishment. It was March and the Anatolian plateaus were already covered with the colors of life, prophesizing a peaceful period only Allah knew how long would last. The die was cast. He had nothing more to do in both East and West and his consciousness was clear. He had done his duty as a human being and his son was going to grow in a better world than he had lived.

The Sultan got slowly up, still holding the treaty in his right hand like a sword.

"It's a sin for the Shadow of Allah to work during the Ramadan. The French king will get my answer, when these holy days are finally over. I will now go and pray for Allah's guidance."

****

The rumor that a peace treaty with France was about to be signed had already spread in the Eternal City along with the most important terms, as it was almost customary to fathom the reactions of the local religious mob, the most fanatical in the

Empire. Ibrahim Pasha had issued strict orders to all Christians to avoid any kind of celebrations for their delivery that could potentially trigger reactions among the Muslim population. His orders were clear and concise. No public protests would be allowed during the Ramadan. The punishment was death by the sword.

Now that the Sultan had decided to sign the treaty, Ibrahim reckoned that it would be prudent to inform Sehzade Mustafa about the agreement. He was a man now, and he should also be convinced about the correctness of this important treaty that he might have to enforce, if for some reason Suleiman was unable to perform his duties as a Sultan in the future.

To save time and avoid any malicious gossip he decided to meet him secretly half way from Manisa in Bursa at the Yesil Mosque and sent him an invitation to that effect.

****

It was in March when the Ramadan started that year and the warm weather warned everyone that the blooming spring was approaching, making the task of following the Prophet's words about abstinence even more difficult. In the evening, as soon as the last rays of the setting sun disappeared, a strange fog started raising from the lead-colored seas that slowly drifted over the tilled-covered roofs of the modest human dwellings in the seven-hill Eternal City all the way to the evergreen Belgrade Forest and the distant shores of the Black Sea.

As the air was still damp and cool, the wood-stoves and the fireplaces were lighted-up adding their smoke to the creeping patches of springtime fog. It was the time when every descent citizen had reached home and locked the door behind him, as it was not prudent for any faithful or infidel to be seeing wondering in the streets. These were the days when the black sheep of disrespectful folks would be distinguished from the white flock of the Muslims.

Ramadan meant for most people that it was the right time to fest not only from food, but also from every other carnal pleasure that dragged human spirit down to the gutter offending Allah, its Creator. Thus, it was much safer to stay indoors rather than soil the good family name of either faithful or infidel, as even the dirty, pork-eating, drunkard Christians had to fest from carnal pleasures, as Easter was also approaching to celebrate the Death and the Resurrection of Jesus Christ. Only when the sun reappeared from the Asian hills of Üsküdar it was perfectly safe for the working class to appear on the streets like industrious ants to commute to their place of employment. Only in the narrow streets of Galata, where only infidel sailors and sinners wandered all through the night till sunrise, there would be still open doors welcoming every Christian worshiper of Satan who found carnal pleasures irresistible even during the holiest days of the year for all religions.

****

The month of Ramadan was Hurrem's favorite season. This year it was not just the spring approaching that made her saps overflowing like spring torrents after a heavy rain. It was mainly the fact that Allah kept Suleiman away from her for many days. Of course, through the entire month she had decided to reside in the Seraglio, and her excuse was quite believable. Since she was his Birinci Kadin, she had to be close to her husband to eliminate any malicious rumor that might spread, if she had stayed alone in the Eski Saray among all the lusty concubines that had not been allowed or wished to become Muslims, and would do their best to seduce her and spoil her impeccable reputation of absolute fidelity to Allah and His Shadow.

Being remote and untouchable was one way for her to keep the Sultan's attention. The other was to be close enough to demonstrate the sinful urges she should restrain for the sake of the Prophet. During this holy month strict fasting made his illness to reside, and this was surely a divine sign that sins were the origins of every human suffering, even if excesses were sometimes inevitable to turn the entire Globe into Allah's Domain of Peace by proliferation. She simply adored reading in his eyes the desire constantly growing as he watched her wandering inside his bedroom wearing transparent "salvar" and low cut lingerie like a cat in heat.

These were the days she felt safe enough to stare at him in a very naughty way, as if she was measuring the extent of his desire, while she let sighs full of passion escape from her ruby painted lips. Then, she would find an excuse to leave him all alone and retreat to the empty Hasodabashi bedroom to let him relax, before her brief visit to his personal hammam, where the White Eunuchs lurked to get a glance at her nude attractions and revive their flesh.

Finally, she had realized another advantage of having eunuchs in a harem. A woman could tease these so-called men3 to her heart's content without reprisals.

Nevertheless, after Asphodel's sudden disappearance, the discipline had relaxed and many young eunuchs in the Seraglio blessed the name of Suleiman for discarding this old relic from the notorious Selim era, despite the resulting degradation of the overall White Eunuch's status. Every change created waves meant to destroy the old command structure and build a new one that would favor the greedy newcomers instead of the saturated old guard.

A rumor had recently leaked that Suleiman Khan had no interest left for his harem, leaving it in the hands of the Kislar Aga. They all knew however that this was a temporary measure the ailing Sultan had taken to avoid a harem rebellion. Soon the news traveled that the imperial Harem was about to be abolished, as there were eyes and ears everywhere, and everyone was by now aware that Hurrem's and Ibrahim's wishes would eventually prevail. On this subject these two wills coincided perfectly so the Seraglio life would continue harmonically.

There were even few malicious rumors claiming Ibrahim Pasha was going to retire, and then only the will of Haseki Hurrem would count in the Seraglio. Till then, no one doubted that if Ibrahim Pasha sought retirement, Hurrem would surely grant his choice as that would mean the next Grand Vizier would be chosen by her to make sure one of her sons would reign. However, since Sehzade Mehmet was still too young and Suleiman's illness had miraculously receded, no wise man was too keen in making so risky long term predictions.

Allah was very careful on this particular point. Long term predictions of human should fail, so only His name would be blessed and not some other sacrilegious crook who tried his luck making wild predictions for the future.

Hurrem was well aware of Kismet, and did her best to control it. Every evening as the Sultan left his quarters to visit the Seraglio mosque together with his Aga courtiers, she would change her revealing clothes for something more sober and strict, so she would be ready to greet him, if he was desperate enough to knock on her door on his way back. Most of the evenings she could hear his steps circling outside her door, but he didn't enter uninvited in case she was not in the proper mood. Usually she was ready to respond favorably to his surrender, but during the Ramadan she had decided that it was to her advantage to resist his advances at least for a while to make sure he understood he was the greatest sinner of the two.

This evening everything seemed a repetition of the past days, however, his steps were not heard outside her door until past midnight, and thus she had decided to get undressed and go to sleep. Suddenly the door opened without knocking and he appeared in front of her with a menacing look. In his angry eyes she saw again the long forgotten illusion of rebellion from her powerful attraction. It meant he had been visited by his Makbil (beloved) Grand Vizier. He seemed ready for a fight, but in cases like this the best policy was to appear submissive and friendly to confuse him rather than offer him a chance to explode his anger at her expense.

She had realized long ago that during his angry moments his father Selim prevailed and Suleiman could become violent; however, it was not required of her to behave totally slavishly, so without following the demands of the Seraglio ceremonies, she spoke to him directly with all the tenderness she could master under the circumstance.

"What kind of heartbreak brings the Magnificent Sultan of my heart into my humble bedroom?"

Suleiman made the mistake to look at her eyes and the luck of desire he read deep in there pushed his male confidence into retreat. He lowered his glance and tried to find excuses for his delayed appearance.

"Tonight I must decide, if I should sign the peace treaty with France or not. Delaying my decision is a clear sign of weakness."

Hurrem knew from other lips how the negotiations had stalled, so she was well aware of the existing conflict with Ibrahim's suggestion. However, the Sultan's appearance was a sign the meeting with Ibrahim had been another formal one, and her appeal was still unconquerable in battle. This increased considerably her confidence to try another tease.

"Indeed it is. If it was not Ramadan, you would have pierced me with your sword long ago. What is your decision? Do you intend to offer the infidels what they so audaciously demand?"

The Sultan felt the need to explain his decision and satisfy her curiosity.

"From now on France will become our ally, while Spain, Genova and Venice will be alone against us in the Mediterranean Sea."

"This is indeed a wise decision, but where did you find the strength to reject the Grand Vizier's wise suggestion and sign the treaty?" she teased him.

"Who told you that Ibrahim is opposing this treaty?" he replied falling in her trap.

Hurrem served him one of her most convincing innocent smiles.

"As you well know, the news arrive with great delay in the Harem, and the last rumor I heard was that there was a serious conflict between you and Ibrahim Pasha for the first time."

Suleiman did not respond to her reply, trying to discover

the deeper meaning of her comment. Hurrem took advantage of this momentary silence to add a bit of poison.

"Do not despair my darling, if the welfare of your Empire has obliged you to change your mind. Even if you lose the entire universe, you will still be the one and only Overlord of my heart," she proclaimed and with these words she lowered her nightgown uncovering part of her breasts, blinding her opponent with the white brilliance of her milky flesh. However, this unexpected peek of the Paradise was quickly terminated, as she covered her nudity once more by raising once more the delicate lace, behaving as if this racy revelation was a mistake.

"My Master, I'm terribly sorry, but my desires made me forget for a moment what day it is. Sometimes, with you I feel like a perfect whore."

This abrupt change from hot to cold ignited an extreme transition on Suleiman's emotions. Hurrem knew that the easiest way to grab a distant apple was to shake the apple tree; so, she laid down and turned over on her stomach like a cat that has caused some damage and needs to caressed to reassure herself that her owner was still interested in serving her vital needs. However, even though her body seemed willing to be conquered, her spirit was still rebellious and her tongue untamed.

"Don't take this strategic retreat too seriously. There is a wide consensus against continuing the war among your subjects. Anyway, only a madman would keep on fighting about what he believes it's right against a powerful adverse current. Here in your arms I feel secure, when I know my world is controlled by such a capable man like Ibrahim Pasha the Great."

Her subtle irony slowly started to have an effect on Suleiman's consciousness and he asked for an explanation for her dubious accusations. Her voice sounded relaxed and sensuous as her hands kept teasing his growing passion.

"My darling, I'm very happy these last few years that because of your illness you have left most of your worries occupying your mind to your slave who is in better condition to solve the daily problems and has stronger hands to fight your battles and conquer nations in your name. This way you can spend more time in my bed till that awful day Allah the All-Knower decides to invite you to the Paradise of all the faithful. It was a very wise thought to let Sultan Ibrahim to conquer Tabriz and Baghdad in your name too. This way I had the indescribable pleasure to entertain you as much as you could stand in my bed for almost two entire years. I trust this faithful slave knows not only how to satisfy you, but he has also discovered what I need to be totally happy. Every bit of gold you've spent in his name was not wasted. Have you noticed that he has never said anything against me during his entire life? A more devious man than you might have suspected he is trying to seduce me, so that the moment you are too weak to defend your throne, I would not react and let him have his way like he does with you. But you have complete confidence in him and me, because, as we women know, all men trust completely only what they fuck. This makes me wonder if Ibrahim Pasha in the future will keep on respecting my desires so fully as he does with yours, or if he will gradually become more demanding and rebellious? After all his total submission during Ramadan can be just a show meant to put us to sleep."

Suddenly reaching the end of her praises she poured all her poison, surprising Suleiman with her audacity. The Sultan didn't believe his ears. What had started as a praise had ended as a mock. This obnoxious Ukrainian slave was making fun of him and his personal choices that followed strictly the words of the Prophet. He felt a sudden burst of anger that sent all his blood to his head, changing his complexion from pale to bright purple as if he had a heart attack. This blood onslaught was so violent that his tongue couldn't express the thoughts of his brain; so, nothing more than a primitive loud growl was born deep inside his throat that echoed past the closed door of her bedroom into the empty corridors.

And then something completely unexpected happen, the kind of a coincidence people usually associate with the hand of God, completely unexplainable by the known laws of Nature. A lion brought from Egypt by Selim locked in a cage in the Sultan's private zoo in the Gülhane Gardens, as if it heard his single cry of despair, replied with a similar roar but infinitely mightier, announcing his own frustration from slavery.

After Selim's Egyptian campaign, this warlike Sultan had found amusing keeping many wild African animals like leopards, lions, elephants, and giraffes in cages inside the Gülhane gardens to be used as trophies during parades after military triumphs exactly as the Roman Emperors had done long time ago. Few of the less dangerous and rare animals like deer, antelopes and wild boars he let loose to use as target practices with his bow and arrows.

This time in the middle of the night, the lion possibly felt like announcing its presence the same way lions do at night in the African savannah, or perhaps expressing his frustration for being locked up away from his natural habitat. Only Allah knew the true reason; but there are always superstitious people who try to find the deeper meaning in quite casual or trivial phenomena that for some unexplained reason are coincidental with equally rare personal events. This way sometimes the weakness of one creature is complimented by the strength of the other and in this way the briefly disturbed balance of the Universe is restored.

Suleiman listening to the lion's roar became greatly disturbed and for few moments his complexion became even whiter than her breasts. In his ears this roar sounded like his father's terrifying growl just before he stroke his victims with his mighty sword. Was his father furious for his attitude and yelled at him from heavens to demonstrate his anger?

As if he was a defendant seeking excuses for his deeds, his lips uttered softly a murmur meant to be heard only by his consciousness:

"Yes, but Ibrahim Pasha has always been my most trusted friend!"

Hurrem realized the right time had come to deliver the final stroke and with the cold voice of the prosecutor she concurred ironically with her master.

"Indeed he has been the most loyal. Who can deny his fidelity? He is perfectly loyal to your blood. One can even say he is addicted like an opium addict. He has served your father, your mother, your sister and you like the most obedient slave carrying out all your demands to the best of his abilities. Has he ever said no to any of your wishes? Were you ever more demanding than your father or more forceful? Were you more resourceful than your mother, the mighty Valide Sultan who was always so manipulating and understanding of all your needs but never of hers? You didn't have to hear what the eunuchs said. You only had to obey to his logic. And Ibrahim has betrayed his breed, his tongue and his god by being loyal to you. His loyalty to Osman's blood is so great that if Allah's hand wipes you and all your children off the face of the Earth, his son will live to propagate your breed until the end of time. Surely such a devoted man will never try to usurp anything from you, because he already shares it."

Suleiman with every word she uttered he felt his will dissolve like butter in a frying pan.

"I have sworn that as long as I'm alive my lips will never order his death. There is no way a just Sultan, the son of Selim Khan, can go back on his word for any reason."

"Indeed he can't because he would lose face; but there are many ways to solve such a problem. If the road to Edirne your stallion knows well happens to be flooded, you can still arrive there, if you ride a clever mare."

"What does that mean?"

"I'm your mare. You can use my lips to raise the sword of Selim from the ground. After all these lips are your most obedient slaves who have never denied to fulfill your wildest desires. They are not going to start now betraying you, if you only decide to swear to me tonight that you will always put my wishes second only to yours."

The Sultan was too deeply in turmoil to realize where such an oath would lead as he had abandoned all his being into her skillful hands.

"I swear in Allah's name!"

It was the signal she expected to make her next move.

"And I swear in Allah's name too that my wishes will always come second to yours and in my bedroom you will always be my one and only emperor. In here even Allah has no hold on me, even if your most secret wish is to turn me into your most faithful bitch during this Ramadan. I know Allah is just a benevolent spirit that resides up in heavens, while your flesh is tempting me like a devious snake to take a bite right here on Earth. You are my Adam, so I must become your Eve tonight. This is Allah's will and I have to show total obedience to his Shadow!"

He soon fell like a drunkard who could not keep his lips from drinking her sour wine, as wine is never responsible for a drunkard lack of balance. His thirsty lips are the ones to blame!

****

She could feel it in her guts that the moment was approaching when all her lifetime dreams would be tested. Her spy had informed her that Ibrahim Pasha was about to leave for Bursa. Bursa was a strange destination for a Grand Vizier these days. In the past it had been the Ottoman capital before Edirne took its place as the back door of Europe. Nothing was there besides few old mosques and cemeteries, and a moderate palace. Its only significance her logic had found was being half-way to Manisa, Mustafa and Mahidevran.

She couldn't discern which of the two would be Ibrahim's destination, but either one was almost equally treacherous. She had to make her move too and make a decision now, because by the time she found out who had an appointment with destiny, it might be too late.

Keeping Suleiman's desire content was very important. The illness had drain the Sultan's energy reserves. The more exhausted he was the less receptive to Ibrahim's charm. Suleiman was her slave she shared with Ibrahim, and such a slave could not serve two masters as Ibrahim could. But by being the ideal slave, Ibrahim had shown his inability to ever become a master. This versatile man was perfectly content serving as many masters as possible.

The old Kislar Aga had confessed to her, Ibrahim had been locked behind closed doors with Hafsa Sultan among his many other visits. Why would a Valide Sultan decide to lock her door in the company of a young man, when no one would dare to open it without her permission? For her the answer was perfectly clear and unique. She was afraid the Sultan might burst in who needed no knocking. The old Kislar Aga despite his normal feminine tendencies caused by his missing balls, had a weakness too as every other human being. He had complete trust in his remaining senses. Faced with a closed door, he was left clueless.

In the Harem an unwritten law reigned supreme. There were infinite shades between a man and a woman, and a woman could play the role of a man, if she found a partner more submissive than she was. In the Harem she was taught by eunuchs to be totally submissive and that made her capable of making even them happy. It was not any special talent she possessed. It was all in her training. Concubines had to be taught how to please an overaged Sultan or even a Sultan who had received a serious wound on the battlefield. It was not such a remote possibility, when all stakes were on the table with a vicious enemy like the Mongols. This was the reason why a Prince Heir had to have children even before occupying the throne. Osman's blood should live eternally even against Allah's will.

Suleiman had Selim's blood running in his veins, but his illness had made him weak. In her mind, right that moment Ibrahim would be the perfect Sultan, because fighting two wars in East and West had exhausted the Ottoman vigor as much as Suleiman's; but for Ibrahim to become the Sultan, Suleiman had to die, and murdering a Sultan was still a risky choice. Rising an atheist to the throne was also an inconceivable option after so many bitter religious wars against the Christians and Shiites. Ibrahim was wise enough to know he had no chances; but if Ibrahim was eliminated as a heir, then Mustafa was the obvious choice of the religious mob.

Mustafa was a fine young man with strong morals. She would never have any hope of manipulating him. She and her sons were doomed. Her only hope of redemption was for Ibrahim and Mustafa to die; but it was simply too risky and too difficult for such an attempt yet. Suleiman by banishing Mahidevran and her son to Manisa had put them beyond her reach. Only Ibrahim was within her reach now as the final crisis approached.

When she was still a concubine, she had heard in the Harem many stories the eunuchs narrated to impress the odalisques with their power and knowledge. These sorry excuses of the male gender were simply fascinated with the Mutes and their ability to impose death on their victims. These expert executioners were supposedly manly and brave; but they never attacked their victims alone or face to face. There was always one or more who sneaked from behind to stab or use the silken cord as a noose to strangle their victims. The Harem eunuchs were too graphic describing the deeds of their lovers they had watched many times in action when Selim was the Sultan. Their victim's face turned blue as the blood flow to their heads stopped, and all their muscles contracted, trying to catch a breath of fresh air. The eunuchs claimed many victims had become wet or defecated during the final struggle, as the Selim the Terrible and his twin eunuchs looked and laughed at this appallingly gruesome spectacle.

Her vivid imagination during these narrations put her sons in this position. No, her sons didn't deserve such a horrible death in the hands of Mustafa who looked so much like his grandfather. This had to be the sorry end of traitors and as long as Ibrahim was loyal Suleiman would never order such a death for his Beloved.

She could certainly feel Suleiman's reluctance, because she was feeling in a similar way. She has used Ibrahim once when he was the Hasodabashi, and he had done all he could to please her as if she was a Princess. Now, he might possibly be the father of her most favorite son too, the one she wished to be the next Sultan the moment he had the proper age and training for this important post. Ibrahim was the best lover she ever had, the only man who had treated her like a human being. Back then he had whispered in her ear many times that he loved her, and that he would be her mate every time she felt lonely and neglected.

Since then she had dreamed him taking her much too often. In fact, she usually closed her eyes every time she made love with someone and dreamed of him instead. She felt no guilt. Almost every concubine or Kadin had similar desires about him, since Ibrahim was the most attractive man they knew. This was what prostitutes did too, when they made love to their clients. They dreamed of their pimp. He was the favorite lover of their dreams.

In this sense Ibrahim was her pimp too and his love was not a sin, as dreams were the only domain of absolute freedom for every slave, an immense range where no master could impose his will. She had no second thoughts on this matter. Kismet was responsible for her becoming the Sultan's Birinci Kadin. Back then if she had failed to inspire Suleiman, Hafsa Hatun had promised her she would become Ibrahim's slave. She was Valide's most skillful tool for the liberation of her son from Ibrahim's unrelenting hold. Suleiman had demolished all her illusions, when he became enchanted with her dance the second time.

As a concubine she had no fervent desires to become the Kadin of a Sultan and lose the slave's hopes for eventual liberation; however, since the moment Suleiman started giving her son after son, she could do nothing but take care of her precious offspring as any proper mother would do, putting her children's life far beyond her husband's existence no matter who this husband was, Sultan, Grand Vizier, Janissary or even farmer.

For most people dreams far exceeded their sober realities. In her case, after Suleiman's incurable illness, reality exceeded her wildest dreams; but becoming the Sultan's Birinci Kadin was not a true blessing. If she had another man's children, then they would be safe from any harm. Now with the blood of Osman running in their veins, their future looked grim. Selim's legacy was a mortal threat for all of them. Mustafa looked so much like his grandfather few eunuchs claimed he was his son, not Suleiman's.

It was not such a wild rumor now that she thought about it. When Suleiman married Mahidevran, he was just an innocent boy, while she was a quite a woman according to the Harem's rumors. They were living in Crimea back then. If Selim Khan truly desired her, he could sent his son for a mission and leave behind his bride unattended.

Suleiman had no harem back then, no Eski Saray, or eunuch guardians of his honor. He was not a Prince Heir either, just a youngster with a beautiful bride. Allah was very lenient in cases like this, if Sultan Selim had visited her just once like the mighty god Zeus. The bride might well be carrying the son of his son after the first night or maybe an entire week of debauchery.

According to eunuch testimonies, Mahidevran was a very voracious Tatar woman with insatiable hunger for true males. If Selim had slipped into her tent at night in Crimea, while she was sleeping, she wouldn't be the one to refuse such a mature lover at the peak of his manhood. After all, back then Selim Khan had not yet developed his abominable urge for pretty eunuchs. Actually this sinful night might well be the reason Selim developing a disgust for women. This was what her logic now suggested as eunuchs were sterile and more than capable to imitate the behavior of a submissive woman in bed.

She had inspected Asphodel for a long time to find out the source of his attractiveness. He was the depiction of a complete male disaster up front, but his backside was in many ways much better than most concubines she knew. He even knew perfectly well how to belly-dance to seduce an Ottoman by swinging his hips. It was almost apparent by the way he walked. All these were telltale signs Selim was a mighty warrior, but also mentally unstable. Even Asphodel was puzzled why Selim Khan decided to send a poisoned kaftan to his only remaining son.

Now everything made sense, even the rumor that Selim Khan called Mahidevran's name and wrote her a letter shortly before his demise. It was natural for every human being to recall the most inspiring sexual experience of its life to die happily, when it realized it was about to die. She had a similar fixation with

Ibrahim Pasha, when he was still her Hasodabashi.

She had no chance in this competition with Mahidevran Sultan. Selim had aged by then and she was just a dancing girl he shared with his two abominable eunuchs. The experience was by no way unique and precious. In the Harem it was well known that whenever Selim was in the Marble Kiosk, he invited all sorts of clandestine visitors not only from the Eski Saray, but from Galata too. He had no use for more sons. He had more than he needed, so killing all sons but one was his most dominant idea in Selim's mind. Probably, Piri Pasha had a list of possible Sultans in case Suleiman died or if he was a total failure. As Selim knew of Suleiman's affliction for Ibrahim, it was quite possible he had prepared another accession if Suleiman was too feminine to lead the Janissaries into battle. This must have been Suleiman's greatest fear, being disgraced as a man and having to face the silken rope of the Mute Executioners.

****

There were indeed too many secrets hidden in the Seraglio when Selim Khan ruled, and few of them might persist even after his demise. It was humanly impossible for any odalisque or Kadin to discover them all no matter how hard she tried. The Harem concubines had access only to only what the members of the Black Eunuch corps knew. The White Eunuch corps was the manly domain, and the most knowledgeable person was the Kapi Aga. As far as she knew many Grand Viziers had been executed unexpectedly; so, there was a rumor that in the end every time a Vizier was summoned to Selim's dwelling he carried his last testament with him.

On the other hand, as far as she knew, no Kapi Aga had been executed, at least until Asphodel's disappearance; but they were all freed from duty with a sizable pension. It was a sign the eunuchs knew too much and they had taken precaution to pass their knowledge along to a suitable no one knew anything about, especially the Sultan. These days, there was no Kapi Aga appointed. Ibrahim knew too much. If he was really as cleaver as he claimed, he must have transferred his knowledge to a man of his complete trust. This was what her logic dictated.

****

Suleiman felt completely exhausted both mentally and physically. She had done all she could to show him that she was the goddess he should eternally worship and her orders should be the ones to follow, not Allah's. It was the first time she had been so oral giving him orders what to do to please her, and he felt too weak to deny not even a single one of them.

It was not such a drastic change for him. Mahidevran was in command from the very first time. Hurrem up to now had been very submissive, and this was her main advantage in his mind. She made him feel like a man, the way an Osmanli Sultan should feel. In a sense she was as submissive as Ibrahim. This was why he needed them both and would never consider killing either one of them. Banishing Mahidevran was not because she slashed Hurrem's face with her nails. It was principally because she didn't show any respect for his property and his authority.

His father had made it perfectly clear. An Ottoman Sultan was worthy of his throne only if he retained the authority to command his subjects. If he lost this asset, he was as worthless as a Turk without a horse. His father was a poet and knew well how to disguise his words to sound good in every ear. In his mind women were pictured as fragile gazelles ready to flee in view of a lion. Men should behave like lions even though there were brave female lions too.

A Turk to be worthy of his gender he had to be a rider, and riders could ride both stallions and mares depending on their mood. On the other hand, Mahidevran Sultan was a Tatar rider, and it was difficult for him to feel like a Sultan with her.

His mother Hafsa Sultan the moment his father died had taken command of his life and offered him Hurrem, a concubine trained to follow the orders even of an overaged Sultan. He was not overaged, but the illness had made him feel and look like an old man. The worst enemy of any aging man was the lack of sleep and the nightmares of losing command over his flesh. He had not lost it completely, but his will to live was exhausted by the pain. Perhaps this was the reason why Hurrem had been so demanding rather than submissive lately. Women have a sixth sense for these changes. The moment a man ceases to be a rider, they jump on the saddle faster than a Tatar, and pay no attention who the horse was. This was one of the secrets his father had revealed to teach him how a man should behave. For Selim Khan being a man was an essential ingredient of every Osmanli Sultan. He had read Roman History and discovered that every time a dubious male became an Emperor, the Empire suffered a period of decline. Then, even a woman could become a better ruler as long as she kept behaving like a man.

Now lying on his bed the old doubts came back to haunt him. When he was all alone, they always came back more pressing than ever before. Having a human being sleeping next to him exorcised his nightmares in a way he couldn't understand. Perhaps this was the reason Sultan Selim had always these two damned eunuchs by his side at night.

This night when he crossed her doorstep he had nothing naughty in his mind, but she had seduced him and turned him into her slave and a petty sinner. Now that he was all alone, he sought reasons for his total surrender and being a sick man was the most obvious one. From the moment he had resigned his command into her hands, he was not truly a sinner. He had become a slave following orders, but a slave felt no guilt for his sins. This was an issue Ibrahim had been most convincing explaining long time ago. Only when a human being was free to act as it pleased, Allah could raise the issue of morality. As Ibrahim logically explained to him, for every human survival was the ultimate concern, and from the moment this survival was threatened, it was fully justified to be cruel, bloodthirsty, barbarous, even inhuman.

He had experienced this dramatic change when Asphodel narrated in great detail what happened between his father and Ibrahim and his two eunuchs. He had become momentarily furious enough to make a nod to the Mutes to silence him permanently, and they did!

He had to be very strict and thorough that time. This eunuch simply knew too much, and he was not in any condition to handle the truth. It was simply too devastating and a mighty Sultan should not allow a eunuch to demolish his world. The truth was something like the Ariadne's thread; however, although it was supposed to lead safely through the Labyrinth of lies to the exit and salvation, in his case it led directly to the man-eating Minotaur.

He didn't trust fully all Asphodel's narrations. He was an Osmanli Sultan and Osman and his ancestors had become emperors by guiding the faithful to their death for the ideal of building a better world for their children. To accomplish this monumental task they had to steal lands and enslave enemy nations who behaved like sinners and teach them how to be virtuous. As long as there were sinners, there would be enemies for Islam to conquer, and faithful had to die for this holy cause. This was what his father Selim had taught him when he was a child.

However, Ibrahim proclaimed that sin was a human invention to justify the punishment of the sinners by looting their treasures, raping their women and enslaving their children. To have sins you had to believe in a god who issue few strict orders sinners would be unwilling to obey despite the threat of a divine punishment because they were weaklings.

During a battle, the greatest sin was to be dressed with the enemy's uniform or holding the wrong banner. This meant that whatever he did with Hurrem during the Ramadan was not really a sin. It was a momentary lapse into insanity.

Now that he had put his mind in order he could go to sleep and totally relax. He closed his eyes and waited for the Sleep to conquer all his senses. Sleep was his salvation, it was subtle as the woman of his life that had ravaged his flesh as if he was a damned infidel.

****

Ibrahim was mentally exhausted. Seeking acceptable explanations that made also financial sense to a pious Muslim for every term of the treaty had been a heavy burden. He was so tired, he failed to realize he was asleep and still thinking of viable arguments.

He tried to get up, but he couldn't. Was he put in chains by the Sultan's guards? He tried to move his hands, but they were tied securely somewhere he couldn't discern in the dark even thought his eyes were wide open. Even the flame of the lamp by his bed was extinguished, so he couldn't tell if he was still on his bed and not locked inside a sunless prison cell. Recognizing the familiar softness of his mattress, relaxed his fears. He was safe in his bedroom and someone had blown off the oil lamp and drawn the heavy curtains to keep the moonlight from reaching his eyes.

The sound of a soft breath reached his ears next, as if someone was lurking in the dark. Then he was able to discern a second breath, and then a third or possibly a forth as soon enough of his hearing became overwhelmed with delicate sounds that remind him of leaf rustling. He could follow the noise of one leaf to its source, or maybe two, but as more leaves rustled both the sounds and their origins got confused. If the sounds were truly leaves, he was in the middle of a forest. His blood froze by the thought he was surrounded by Mute Assassins, but he quickly discarded the idea as his personal guards of his palace were devoted to him and would not let any assassin sneak in without a fight. Nevertheless, as time went by, he was becoming convinced he was stalked by predators and could not defend himself.

Suddenly the floor planks cricked and the soft sound of silk rustling coming from his right side revealed that one of the predators had decided he was weak enough to be devoured. He was completely at his captor mercy, and this unsettling thought awakened the sensation of the trapped animal he had once felt, when he tried to wander inside the hold of the pirate ship and measure the treasures these Ottoman bandits had stolen. Back then the thump from a closing hatch signaled his life had drastically changed. It was a sound that meant his freedom to choose was lost as well as his moral values. From a human being suddenly he had become merchandise to be sold to the highest bidder. He didn't know much back then, but the customers were very demanding to get their money's worth most of all.

He still remember how foully the hold stunk back then, but this time his nostrils were flooded with an enchanting blend of oriental perfumes he failed to recognize no matter how many deep breaths he took. Only women could smell so divinely, and his discovery was soon proved convincingly as an unknown female laid on top of him offering her nipples to his hungry lips to suckle. The smell of milk became unmistakable, giving him a vital clue dispersing with one stroke all the devils surrounding him in the darkness. He whispered his best guess, and her name sounded as a prayer to a benevolent god.

"Sherenk?"

He heard several subdued giggles from all around him, but he was much more delighted to feel the soft skin of a woman's belly on his lips seeking desperately the wet touch of his tongue. He couldn't resist the attraction and left his tongue free to taste the delicate favors of an excited woman as he wondered far below her naval into the valleys and shadowy forests the Prophet had promised to all his believers.

He heard her moan and then a powerful cry as if she was a Byzantine vicar seeking to attract pious believers from the wilderness to his empty temple. He could not refuse her supplication until she was pleased sufficiently to let her body fall next to him exhausted.

He was ready to abandon all his existence to the arms of Morpheus, when the familiar scent of opium blended with oriental spices from the distant islands of the Indian Ocean made its appearance, displacing with its vigor every other invader of his nostrils. His lips declared their independence, uttering hesitantly her beloved name: "Hatidge?"

However his plea for confirmation was again frustrated, as her lips were too busy igniting his desire for a second time. Soon enough he had nothing more to give as the pain from her teeth was divinely transformed into unmeasurable pleasure by the Goddess Aphrodite.

She had to remain close-by on his other side, because Isis came to her aid, adding sandalwood mixed with the powerful scent of dark skin to the seductive atmosphere. Trying to defend his command center from the determined attacks of a savage was another lost cause; so, he unconditionally surrendered surrounded from all sides by relentless female vixens that took turns enjoying the warmth of his flesh like moths circling a campfire. Only when she got what she needed, he tried now to utter her name full of conviction:

"Basmi!!!"

"No, Basmi will be next. You're wrong for the third time," the voice of Hatidge replied lost deep in the darkness.

He had nothing more to give. They all recognized that, so they lighted up the lamp again to prove they had tricked him. Hatidge was so sincere she was almost blunt.

"My darling, you may think you need such a luscious harem, but in reality you are such a simpleminded beast you cannot discern a Princess from a slave, when you are excited. In the dark you have failed to recognize even the color of a woman's skin or her personal preferences. On the other hand, a woman is so competent lover, she can imitate any other member of her gender, if she so wishes and she is properly trained."

"My congratulation for your expert training. I would have never thought of such a devious trick."

"It was not a trick. It was a test; a bet that you lost and I won."

"I didn't know I was married to such a devious woman able of planning such a travesty."

"I am not the inventor of this sham. It is actually a very common practice in every harem. The master of the household is too eager to please himself that he doesn't notice who his mate is. Only sensitive human beings that are capable of appreciating the differences should be allowed to have a harem."

Now what was left for him to do was to find the strength

to satisfy two excited and sinful women till daybreak, when the Ramadan fest came back into effect. However, his Princess had not finished her revelations. In fact, she was enjoying herself and all her associates in this extremely sensual enterprise, and didn't object when Yabani took the relay baton and assaulted him even further.

"Perhaps, I should warn you that there are certain strange rumors among the eunuchs that a certain strange substance has arrived to Galata from the Far East that can transform women into men, if this is the pleasure of the master or the mistress of a household."

Allah had a way to turn a man's dream into a nightmare.

****

Allah's wishes rarely coincide with the dreams of a human. That night He had decided that the right moment had come for a Nubian woman to realize her dreams of maternity. If her dreams were slightly different, for Him it was not important. Allah was not a racist after all. He knew everything there was to know. For Him the fact a black woman was willing to do anything to please a white man was a sign of desperation. He hesitate only for a moment, because her desire coincided with the greedy passions of an unscrupulous atheist. It was one of the rare moments when the words and the acts of a god failed to coincide perfectly, and a compromise had to be reached that made the universe imperfect. However, these imperfections were just a temporary phenomenon that eventually died out as quickly as the waves caused by a falling rock in a tranquil pond. Absolute perfection is the final state, when the entire universe will become one with God and the mortal flesh will become one with the immortal spirit.

****

When the sun made his appearance behind the hills of Üsküdar, Ibrahim had reached his decision. He had no further use of slaves in his harem, serving his desires. It was much more gratifying to have free women willing to share their precious lives with him. Then, only time would show who was the most satisfying lover, Hatidge Sultan or he. From now one he had to try harder to prove he was worthy of more than one woman.

****

Suleiman Khan closed his eyes and relaxed, relieving his brain from the burden of controlling his senses. He had finally found the solution to his problems, or at least this was his alluring illusion, because suddenly his priceless peace was shuttered to bits, as the stern image of Iskander Chelebi Pasha in military armor appeared through the fog of his unconsciousness.

"Your dearest friend has stolen my honor and my life. Now he plans to steal even my name," he claimed and he dissolved in the mist before Suleiman had the chance to react and seek explanations.

Suleiman woke up drenched in sweat. The eunuch who was stealing patches of sleep standing on his feet by the bedroom door woke up too and rushed to offer his assistance, a new dry nightgown; but the Sultan was too upset to appreciate his gracious services. He yearned much more for answers to the awful nightmare .

The young page was very efficient and listening to his plea he provided an immediate solution. In the Seraglio there was an old man who was getting rich by explaining the dreams of all the Seraglio slaves. Reluctantly Suleiman conceded, and the aged dream interpreter arrived shortly, still confused by the sudden awakening. However, as Suleiman narrated his nightmare the old man's face relaxed. He assured the Sultan that dreams' complexity had nothing to do with power or riches, freedom or slavery. In fact, slaves and eunuchs had much more complicated and wild dreams than any Sultan, Vizier, or Pasha.

"My Master shouldn't be the least worried," he concluded. "Seeing a dead man in your dreams is a good sign. Soon enough a herald will relay a piece of good news to your Highness."

"Bismallah!" the Sultan exclaimed greatly relieved. "But tell me, why seeing a dead man is a good sign?" he then asked, and the soothsayer readily solved the mystery.

"Allah has made the world in such a way that death is just the end of a cycle. When a single old cycle closes, many new cycles commence. This is why a dead man is always a piece of good news for everyone who stays behind alive and keeps on dreaming. Only when a man stops dreaming, only then he should worry because his end is near."

****

Ibrahim Pasha had chosen a good excuse for visiting Bursa. He had to show he respected the Osmanli, and he was honored for the birth of a son who shared the blood of Osman with his offspring; so he spent an entire day visiting the old Sultans' tombs, praying for the realization of Osman's dream. Only after the sunset as the shadows blended with the night's darkness, he went out of the Muradiye Mosque and wandered among the gravestones and sarcophagi of the old Byzantine cemetery that was now shared and populated by the tombs of Ottoman nobles.

Among the Roman and Muslim graves the dark outline of a man appeared. It was Mustafa the Prince Heir and didn't wait for long to inquire with an air of unbending authority.

"Does my father know of this meeting?"

"No! No one knows anything of it. It would serve no good purpose to inform him of my decision to relay to the Prince Heir the most recent developments in the Empire; but, I have an entirely different view. It's part of your training to judge, if a Sultan's decision to sign a certain treaty is beneficial to the Empire's welfare."

"I'm sure a Khan knows much more than what we think. There is not much that remains hidden from Allah's Shadow. His eyes and ears are everywhere. When there are great rewords to be made by serving him, there are always people eager to even risk their lives to earn them."

"I know that well. This is actually why we are here today.

The welfare of the Empire is very important to both of us, as this will be the greatest reward for all our wise decisions."

"I know well enough your good intentions as well as your abilities. I trust you are the most skillful hand my father ever had. You can turn even a defeat into a victory," Mustafa noticed with a friendly smile that disperse the night's chill.

"This is what my friends claim; but my enemies preach that I'm an infidel traitor eager to acquire even more power and wealth than the Sultan."

"I heard as much too, and I have no reason to suspect you wish to usurp the throne of Osman. I always prefer a victory than a defeat, nevertheless, I also know that a competent Pasha cannot win every battle, if his Sultan stays behind locked in his harem."

"Your father is ill, and when a Sultan is not himself, it is better if he does not risk a disaster. It's much better to send his right hand to take the blame for a possible failure."

"There was no failure though, just a lot of lives lost for a dubious aim, capturing a distant metropolis that cannot be defended," Mustafa argued.

"It was not a triumph either though, so few simpletons call it a failure. Different people have different opinions on each matter. It's natural," Ibrahim noticed indifferently.

"That's true. This is at least how I feel too; but I believe if an Osmanli was in command, less faithful would have died in vain."

"It's difficult to predict the conclusion of a military conflict. There are simply too many unknown factors that can go either right or wrong these days, when guns and harquebuses can kill so easily so many brave men in such a short time from a distance."

"A wise diplomat must know how to predict the future better than a Pasha. I trust you most certainly can do as much. This is why I decided such a perilous journey. I wish to know of your predictions on the success of this peace treaty with France. Do you reckon the war in the West can ever be won as easily as in the East?"

"Only if this is the will of Allah," Ibrahim replied soberly.

"Our enemies are as strong in the West as we are in the East. The distances are also too great for our armies to cross."

"Is peace possible between the Christians and Islam?"

"Yes, if this is the also will of our enemies."

"What is our will to keep on fighting for the glory of Islam?"

"We need a respite for our Sultan to get well again."

"For how long this peace might last?"

"Allah is the one who decides how long a war and peace lasts."

"Yes, but isn't also true that when the Sultan is strong we go to war, and when he is weak we must seek peace?"

"Yes! This was the rule in the past."

"What is the Grand Vizier's opinion about peace and war in general?"

"Peace is more profitable than war, but much more difficult to win."

"Isn't true that when the Sultan is weak the Grand Vizier becomes stronger?" Mustafa inquired with a solemn look on his face.

"Yes, it is true! The Empire must retain all its powers," Ibrahim replied without any hesitation.

Mustafa still looked undecided despite this long series of explanations.

"Is it true that if this peace treaty is signed, the faithful will become equal to the infidels?"

"Yes, because this is also Allah's will, according to the words of the Prophet," Ibrahim replied with so great confidence Mustafa didn't consider questioning his assertion.

"If Muslims and Infidels become equal, then what will be the difference between the Sultan and the Grand Vizier?"

"There shouldn't be great differences between friends! Great differences might kill friendships!" Ibrahim boldly asserted.

Mustafa remained pensive. It was apparent he still had few issues to resolve.

"The Sultan must be all-powerful. He is the Shadow of

Allah. Why should the Grand Vizier be almost as powerful as the Sultan?"

"If the Sultan is the Shadow of Allah, then the Grand Vizier should be the Shadow of the Sultan. The shadow of a man does not exist without the man, so a Grand Vizier without a Sultan is just an fleeting image," said Ibrahim looking straight at Mustafa's eyes.

They were as dark and grim as Selim's. He was still a Prince Heir and all the reports from Manisa claimed he was honest and just; but according to the ancient Greeks, justice was blind.

Blindness was a drawback, not a virtue, and following rigid rules blindly was not always the best approach. Rules had to be bent sometimes to achieve the best possible result. This was the rule he had followed to make the Ottoman Empire greater and more prosperous. If following the Quran was enough to achieve prosperity, then the Seih-Ul-Islam should become Grand Vizier and Serasker; but having a diplomat as Grand Vizier had been advantageous in Egypt, Vienna, Tabriz, even Baghdad. Mustafa had to be wise enough to recognize his deeds.

He lowered his glance to show his respect and added:

"The Sultan has every right to choose another Grand Vizier, if he feels I have failed him, but he should know that all my actions were in good faith and for the good of the Empire."

Now it was Mustafa's turn to reach a verdict, and he did without hesitation, because Ibrahim had never failed to support him and his mother.

"Is there something I can do to facilitate the most powerful Grand Vizier ever?" he asked with an imperceptible smile under the faint moonlight.

Ibrahim didn't fall into the trap of appearing too arrogant; in fact, he would be foolish to challenge Mustafa's hold on the Janissary corps. Thus, even though he didn't expect the offer, he calmly proposed:

"It would be best for the Empire, if the Janissaries remained in their barracks and loyal to the House of Osman, until the benefits from the peace treaty become uncontestable," he subtly suggested.

Now the time had come for Mustafa to show his hand, and his reply showed his self-confidence.

"The Janissaries have no other God but their purse. A salary raise can keep them happy in their barracks much better than any direct order from their superiors."

Ibrahim welcomed the suggestion.

"Then, we have nothing to worry about, this god at least is still on our side."

Chapter 14

In Galata

"The price of a kiss is your life"
(Rumi)

Ibrahim's treaty with France changed the balance of power in the Mediterranean Sea. Till then the first power on the waves in the world was Venice. It had the best fleet and mighty castles on the islands of Cyprus, and Crete, in the Aegean and the Ionian Sea shores, controlling the traffic in all the seas along the trade routes of the East. In the Atlantic Ocean, the domination of Spain was almost absolute, while the Portuguese threatened the trade in the Indian Ocean. Something had to be done in the Mediterranean Sea as a countermeasure.

The fear of the Ottomans was always the sea. They felt weak and always in need of infidel crews to sail their ships or fight their wars.

As usual, religion had been an excuse to cover financial interests. Historically Muslims and Christians were rivals. This situation had drastically changed now as France had become an ally of the Ottomans, affecting the mentality of the common people.

The ships of France could now enter major ports of the East, Alexandria, Beirut, Smyrna and Constantinople, even within the Black Sea with equal rights and tariffs with the Venetians and the Genoese. The special monopolies of Venice and Genoa in the Ottoman Empire were abolished. The beginning of the end for Venice and Genoa riches had arrived.

The Venetians up to that moment have been realists adapting quickly to new conditions. When the Ottomans captured Porto Leone, (Piraeus) and Negroponte (Khalkis), and liberated the castles of Methoni and Koroni from the Venetian hold, they soon dashed to kiss the hand of their Muslim enemy to acquire the same privileges as the Genoese. From the first time Ibrahim Pasha had risen to the Ottoman stardom, they understood he was there to stay and from then on he would be the true center of Ottoman power. As a sign of goodwill, they rushed to gain his appreciation and gratitude using flatterers or offering luxurious gifts, and in exchange, Ibrahim Pasha had opened the Eternal City's markets to the products of the City of Venice. Then, as Ibrahim Pasha soon became the object of envy with his luxurious way of living, not only his palace was filled with jewelry, silk fabrics from Venice, and glass artifacts from Murano, but also the

Seraglio, and most of the mansions of the high standing Ottoman officials.

In exchange Venice was supplied with oriental spices, Yemen coffee, Anatolian leather and carpets, and precious stones, wool and silk from India and China. The exchange developed was considered fair for both states; but now, as the treaty threatened balance against the Venetians monopoly on sea transportation, they reacted wasting no time. Without any protest they changed camps and silently joined forces in Constantinople who anyone who wished the agreement with France abolished and Ibrahim Pasha discredited, namely Hurrem Sultan.

At the beginning this traditional approach was initiated with gifts, then with letters, and in end with formal visits of Venetian women to the Birinci Kadin of the Sultan. Hurrem did not hesitate to utilize the influence of this possibly powerful ally. Of course, few obstacles existed in accepting male visitors in the Eski Saray, or her making unauthorized visits outside the Harem. Thus, the Aga of the Blacks Eunuchs became frequent visitor of the Bailo di Venetia Palazzo, the residence of the Venetian ambassador, conveying verbally her plans for the future.

Pargali Ibrahim Pasha was also a frequent guest of the Bailo di Venetia Palace, and these visits added fuel to various scenarios of betrayal. However, in the past these rumors had been quickly extinguished, as the Sultan and the Grand Vizier put forward their plans for the conquest of Venetia and Rome. This project had been put on hold, when the Ottomans were stopped in Vienna and Güns in two separate expeditions; but now the first military priority had shifted from castles and lands to sea and ports. Neither the Venetians, nor Ibrahim had any reason yet to alarm the other camp that something had dramatically changed; so, the relations between the two opponents remained warm and civil, but everyone was opening the other's grave, since the Mediterranean Sea should have a single master.

After his secret visit to Bursa, Ibrahim felt he had to fathom the effects the peace treaty had on the Venetian intentions. It had to be a mutual interest, as the Bailo di Venetia invited him back to a Palazzo reception. The month of Ramadan was the favorite season for such social gatherings, because no Muslim guests were willing to accept such an invitation. Thus, Ibrahim Pasha could move around freely and speak with European diplomats without having to comply with the strict rules of the Ottoman customs and state security.

During the previous years the receptions Ibrahim held in their palace had triggered Princess Hatidge's curiosity. It was an entirely new experience she had never tasted before being limited inside harem walls since birth. Initially she was impressed by the unfamiliar western clothes, the unusual food, dances, music, even the strange languages that reached his ears. So, she did not lose any opportunity to observe everything through the large latticed windows the female harem residents of her palace used to follow the social events.

Soon enough however, her interest fizzled, as her husband stood like the Olympian god among mortals. Even the western music and elaborate but hypocritical dances caused her overpowering boredom. They seemed all so superficially innocent, like the games she used to play with her baby brother. She could not understand what kind of sense made the movements of male dancers, roaming around the female would-be mates like moths around flames. Even the women's dresses with low hemlines, covering everything were incomprehensible if the seduction of the male was the ultimate goal of this performance.

The Christians were the biggest hypocrites, she concluded. How hopeful could a woman be of enslaving the eyes of the man she yearned, if her dance did not offer a taste of the happiness that awaited him, granting him a glimpse of her navel, this heavenly gate of life, reminding him that this common piece with his mother existed inside him forever?

Perhaps, Allah willing, civilization might reach the West after many centuries, but it would be a tough, uphill struggle. Her brother the Sultan was aiming the wrong guns against Rome and the Vatican. Her husband was right in asking him to open the borders of the Ottoman Empire to foreigners. It was sufficient for the West to take a look at the East's bosom just once to admit its superiority. Compared to the reality of the female body, even the most fertile creations of the human imagination were a sorry substitute.

She wished she was allowed to descend down the main hall and dance in front of all these infidels for the sake of her husband for a single night. She was confident that her "arguments" would be far more convincing and reasonable even than the one hundred fourteen Suras of the Holy Quran; but when she suggested it during a reception, Ibrahim refused the offer. He did not wish to hear anything more on this issue. Even suggesting this dancing exhibition to his female slaves was unacceptable. The lusty eyes of his barbaric guests should not touch the skin of the mothers of his children. This racy issue was permanently closed for him. Thus in the end, instead of waiting for Ibrahim to come back to her after such an event, she preferred to spend the nights in the company of their favorite slaves and their children. This was the solution she had chosen to face solitude each time her beloved was missing for long on a mission.

At first she had tried to express her complaints to her husband, but she quickly realized her neglect was not by choice. His duties as a Grand Vizier exceeded his capacities even when he slept inside the Palace. If it was the slave's destiny to serve the Empire, a Princess ought to find a way to fill her night hours with joy. Now that she had born his children, she had fulfilled her obligations towards him as a wife, and she had every right to live her life until he made up his mind to resign from office and return to her side. She had warned him about her intentions in time, but he seemed not to care much about such matters, as if his life was full of other secret delights that sprung from exercising the Grand Vizier's authority.

In the beginning she was jealous of his independence, and had suspicions that another woman dominated his mind and occupied his time; but she quickly learned from her eunuchs that her husband was faithful in thought, and his adventures with other women were only with her slaves. Thus, the only issue that bothered her was his intimacy with her brother.

It was their secret they didn't share with anyone, a secret that only malicious rumors could create. It ought to end sometime soon, because their son was growing. Ibrahim had to be liberated from this passion, and she was willing to share with him not just two but ten slaves. If sexual greed was what kept him few nights away, she would not hesitate to turn their palace into a paradise of Allah full of enchanting houri. Anyway, everything in life was closely associated with numbers. If the attraction of the Sultan was a hundred times stronger than a single woman's, the solution was to provide her harem with one hundred and one gorgeous and submissive slaves.

However, it was clear male greed resided only in men's minds. The endurance of men was much smaller than their overpowering illusions. A woman could satisfy one hundred men, but if three determined slaves united forces, they could bring any man down to his knees, as that memorable night with her mesmerizing slaves had demonstrated. Ibrahim Pasha still had not realized it, but the hour of parting with the Sultan was coming closer day by day as the number of his concubines increased.

That night she had returned earlier to her harem. She had cast a glance on his guests at the beginning of the reception and every one was familiar and boring. Her two liberated slaves, Basmi from the hot desert of Nubia and Sherenk from frozen steppes of Russia were waiting for her to invite them to her bed. They were willing to offer her all the tenderness she needed.

These slaves had never considered even for a moment to leave the palace and look to find a better future elsewhere. In her palace they had found shelter, food, clothes, jewelry, protection, but most of all love, tenderness and understanding, the family they always wanted. It would have been very foolish to risk losing everything for the sake of a fleeting chimera of an ordinary husband in such difficult times, when slaves had become so plentiful because of the war. These two slaves knew how to amuse the melancholic Princess with conversation and gossip, with their songs and games. When Hatidge realized it was midnight and Ibrahim had not yet returned, she stripped and went straight to bed. The two slaves realized what their beloved mistress was missing this evening; so they lowered the flame of the lamp and laid down beside her. The desire for her husband could wait another night to be fulfilled.

****

Ibrahim had planned the reception seeking the opportunity to ask for the Bailo's views on the treaty. Of course, he was not so naive to expect that the seasoned Venetian diplomat would reveal his most inner thoughts; but, he had the hope that even a nervous movement or an eyelid play would betray uneasiness after certain questions.

His people had managed to read the content of the few letters exchanged between the Seraglio and the Bailo Palazzo; but nothing seemed unusual or beyond the standard courtesy of the Ottoman Court. The letters were signed by Hurrem herself, and within its lines contained nothing more than the typical welcoming words for the Bailo's son, who had recently arrived from Venice, and the wish to invite him soon to the Seraglio and introduce him to her sons.

During this reception, Ibrahim had tried to raise the issue by asking with indifferent tone for the health of his son and his plans for a career in the Venetian Embassy. It was a polite inquiry repeating Bailo's similar question about his own infant son; but nothing strange was noticed, betraying the guilty unease of a conspirator. The formal mission of Bailo's son was to get acquainted with the intricacies of Oriental diplomacy, and the young man would be coming to the palace to pay his respects to the Grand Vizier, as every new member of a foreign diplomatic mission was obliged soon upon arrival to Constantinople. This reception was the perfect opportunity for Ibrahim Pasha to meet the Bailo's son under more informal conditions.

Hurrem's letters had excited Ibrahim's interest solely because her unfulfilled wish to meet him had a undetectable tint of conspiracy. The Birinci Kadin of the Sultan was not allowed according to the Ayin to meet an infidel young man especially a Venetian, a potential enemy. Displaying the beauty of any harem woman to an infidel was an unthinkable sacrilege for any pious Muslim. Why would Hurrem utter such blasphemy was his source of worries.

Ibrahim's uncertainty was soon resolved as without much delay a handsome young man of tall stature stood in front of him greeting him with a deep submissive bow to honor his status. The youngster had black hair, and his skin was well-tanned after the long sea voyage that contracted with his emerald green eyes. Was it possible Hurrem somehow was aware with this man's attractive appearance, and tried to take advantage of his naiveté and immaturity?

The chance of her inviting him to the Eski Saray was unlikely, but as the Sultan was incapacitated by the constant torture of his illness, her liberties had gradually increased. It was a subtle sign that when the Sultans went to war, their wives' restrictions relaxed, as they became the most powerful entities in the Eternal City, when the members of the Divan followed the Ottoman armies. Then only the religious authorities remained in Constantinople; but when darkness fell, there was not much any agent of law and order could do. Allah had made the day for the virtuous and the night for the sinful. Who could doubt Allah's wisdom in balancing the world?

****

"How is he? Is he as attractive as they say?" Hurrem Sultan asked with unusual interest the Kislar Aga who seemed delighted by the results of his visit.

"He is a very attractive young man," the Aga concurred with a mysterious smile that ignited his mistress interest.

She simple wanted much more information than the Aga was willing to provide.

"Do I have to offer you coins to open your mouth and tell me more?" she rhetorically asked with an angry voice.

"No, my Mistress. I'm not a greedy man and I have no use of more money to pay for any woman's services," he replied with an air of wounded pride. "As all women are begging to please me. I have no need for anything more."

"Yes, I know all about your conquests. I only hope that Gülfem Sultan will not reveal your deeds to my husband. He is a very jealous man. He will never accept sharing any of his concubines or his Kadin with another man."

"My Mistress knows well that Gülfem Sultan will never open her mouth. She needs me much more than she needs him."

"Yes, I know of all your illicit adventures. You have become the most popular subject of discussion in the Harem."

"Yes, but I keep no secrets from my Mistress. You know everything you need to know before everyone else," said the Aga showing with a short delay the proper respect.

"Then, tell me exactly what happened when you delivered my letter. I'm interested in every detail, even the most minute that looks insignificant to a male beast like you, interested only in women. Was he excited receiving a letter from the Birinci Kadin of the Sultan?"

The Kislar Aga seemed reluctant to reply trying to find the proper words. Hurrem quickly lost patience.

"Speak or I will punish you most severely," she threatened him, but the Aga seemed undisturbed by her threats and took his time to obey.

"He read it, but postponed his reply for a more suitable occasion."

"He is a true diplomat. He has to find out exactly who I am before replying," Hurrem asserted, but the Kapi Aga did not share her optimism.

"No!" he finally noted. "He gave me the impression he was more interested in me than your letter. He asked me where Nubian slaves like me can be purchased in Constantinople. He assured me this is not a going to be a sort visit. He plans to stay in Galata for long, possibly forever. He intends to enlarge his father's residence the moment his father returns to Venice."

"This is why he needs more slaves. He is also young. He will probably need few concubines before it's time to get married. I wonder what kind of women he likes. Offering him few of our concubines as a gift, we will surely win his appreciation," Hurrem insisted.

"If Your Majesty has to really win his appreciation, I suggest you offer me as a present!"

It was a bold suggestion that really took Hurrem by surprise; but she quickly managed to hide her thoughts with a rather neutral statement.

"You know well I cannot do that. You are a valuable piece of the Sultan's property. If you really wish to be traded, you must make a request to a superior authority."

"To me Your Majesty is the superior authority in the Seraglio. If you wish it, it will be done," the Kislar Aga said and kneeled in front of her feet. "To please you I would do anything."

****

After finishing the formalities, Ibrahim asked out of courtesy whether the Venetian preferred living in the East or the West. The young man replied with a slight tremor in his voice that he had not yet seen anything of the Eastern wonders. Ibrahim did not want to leave his question unanswered, and asked once more looking into his eyes:

"I was very young when I started my search, but even now sometimes I am amazed with what I still discover unseen and wondrous. Many years have passed since then, and now I have almost forgotten what I was looking for back then full of naiveté and juvenile impatience. Many claim it was power, few it was pleasure, but I know myself better than anyone and I'm sure it was pure knowledge. You are now almost as young as I was then; so please tell me what a handsome Venetian is searching today in the East. Is it one of the lost Seven Wonders of the World, a new Silk Road like Marco Polo, or something less ambitious and greedy, something more tangible and earthy like carnal passion?"

The young man lowered his eyes. His cheeks suddenly became red from the thoughts that crossed his mind, or perhaps from the strain to find a credible answer.

"The truth was that I am very selective and this is the reason why I haven't yet found what I need in the West, but perhaps my mistake has been so far not looking where I should."

Ibrahim smiled and remarked:

"I'm just a fool who over the years has forgotten what kind of miracles a young man with hot blood in his veins is looking for. Is it love, this eighth wonder that will still be there even when the Pyramids become one with the desert sand?"

Surprisingly, these words brought about the opposite effect on the face of the young man than Ibrahim expected. Instead of dispersing the stress of a response, it made him blush even more. Ibrahim noticing this unexpected expression of embarrassment, he leaned over and whispered in his ear to reassure him of his good intentions:

"Do not be afraid to open your heart to me! I'm a true admirer of all the jewels Venice can produce. Whatever you'll say, my lips will remain shut forever and your secret secure."

However, Ibrahim's lips accidentally or intentionally touched the young man's ear and made him shiver. Once more the young lad was unable to react, and instead made a sharp turn and walked away silent and confused. Never again during the entire reception any attempt was made to approach the Grand Vizier to offer any explanation for his strange behavior. As Ibrahim watched him dashing away, he smiled. He was still lingering in his nostrils the scent of his skin. It had a strong aroma based on genuine musk. After a long time of false expectations and insufferable boredom, he felt once more his body come alive strictly by the power of imagination. As the years went by, this feeling still remained pleasant even though the intensity had become imperceptibly weaker. He had reached a critical age and realized everything in the world of the senses was temporary, even the basic human emotions of love, thirst, hunger, or even sleep. It all meant is body had begun to take the slippery slope towards decent.

He kept resisting the admission he was not young anymore, but his fight was hopeless. Perhaps, this youngster was his last opportunity to relive his youth. He decided his feelings were much more important than continuing this tedious reception that dragged along in an unbearably slow rhythms as if it would last forever. He got up from his elaborate throne he used during receptions and made a nod to the armed officer standing beside him acting as the master of ceremony. He in turn echoed the command to the slave standing behind him, who beat the gong signaling the end of the reception for the evening.

****

Falling asleep, Ibrahim saw the Venetian youngster pop up again shyly in his mind. From the few words they exchanged, he wondered what was the reason he had fled full of shame. He recalled each spoken word and the reaction on the face of the lad. He remembered that the word "love" had brought the blood to his cheeks, and the word "secret" had been the wind that had filled the Venetian sails. He smiled. Being in love with a woman was a mystery for every man, but very rarely a secret that should not be betrayed between men. In his mind a persistent idea wandered around upsetting and kept him awake.

Maybe he was incurably optimistic that even for a moment believed in this crazy idea. It would be truly an unexpected fortuitous turn of fortune. He tried to clear his mind, but the same old weakness, his curiosity, prevailed again.

In the race hope always leaves behind reality. As his last line of defense he brought the Princess in his mind. It took him long to discern her face and her image faded away under the light of the Venetian's eyes that shone like stars. Decisively he left the bed and started walking as hypnotized towards his harem to revive his memory with her image. The dark corridors seemed longer as his anxiety to reach the end progressively grew, but inside this Palace he felt safe. There was nothing for him to fear but the content of his mind.

Arriving finally by the harem gate, he felt a tender feeling flooding his soul. The women had always been the last refuge of all his audacious relationships with men. Hatidge was his Penelope and he was her Odysseus. Parga was also on the Ionian shores like Ithaca, but this Penelope had her door shut and bolted, keeping him away from his Ithaca.

Before leaving, he tapped the door gently. He did not want in any way to wake up his children; but there was no answer. The Princess had an untamed character and she would never become a slave of her husband's memory as Odysseus' Penelope had been in ancient times. He was not a mighty king like Odysseus, and perhaps Hatidge considered herself the superior breed. With a mind full of dilemmas he returned to his bed and closed his eyes. The young Venetian's image discovered the Kerkoporta at the walls of his mind, and gradually one after another overwhelmed all the obstacles it found standing in its path.

****

When Ibrahim reached the Sublime Gate next morning, he felt his confidence rising once again. The night's struggle with his ghosts had exhausted him, but with the first sunlight he saw his world reborn. He had only lost the first battle, but for the time being the war was not yet declared. He left his horse in the stables and took a stroll under the trees that swept every trace of lethargy away from his mind. The trees had begun to grow leaves, but still had not acquired the usual green color. They had a cinnamon tint that resembled the wood that gave them birth; but the air felt as if the harsh winter cold of the Bosporus Straits had been dispersed starting the yearly cycle of life once more. The thought made his step livelier, as if he was not walking but flying over the pavement.

His life had been generous, and he tried hard to find anything he yearned missing from the sum of his choices. The memories of the past night was still fresh in his memory. Maybe if life had been even more generous, he couldn't have endured it. The scent of roses in the garden brought with it the thought of Hurrem, but it was not lively enough to spoil his mood. He wonder what she was thinking too this spring morning. Had she tasted love last night, or was she left sleepless, waiting in vain for her sick husband to honor her body?

Perhaps this was the only still unresolved problem in the lives of most men who had access to food and water. The physical need they felt each day to perpetuate the species through the trap of lust that Mother Nature had built was inescapable. Perhaps the hatred Hurrem felt for him was nothing but the unfulfilled desire of having a child with him.

If this was truly the reason, he was confident everything could change between them in a single night. Then she could gain her tranquility, as the Princess and Mahidevran Sultan had done before her. As their relation was right now, he could feel her frustration and envy, being a beautiful woman he hadn't pleased for so long.

It was not his mistake. He tried to imagine the expression on Suleiman's face, if he dared to suggest something like that, and he spontaneously burst into laughter. The guards of the main gate had started their salute right then, keeping with absolute precision vertical their spears, and were startled by his reaction.

Until then no Grand Vizier had dared to mock their impeccable greeting. Something ought to be done with this Greek man whose impudence exceeded all limits.

Arriving at the office, he saw a large pile of documents awaiting his signature. The secretary already had classified them according to their importance and their deadlines. He started reading them one after the other, giving detailed instructions for the proper actions to be taken. Unexpectedly the door opened, and a herald brought in a new letter and left it in his hands. Puzzled, because the messenger did not know the name of the sender, he opened it carefully and read the contents. It was an unsigned poem that read:

> The moment I saw you my world stopped on its tracks
> And it will never start its journey again,
> Until our bodies are united forever.
> Every night I'll look forward for you to appear before me
> To guide my clumsy footsteps deep
> Where no one has ever reached so far, all the way into

your soul.

The calligraphic Latin letters, ornamented with long tails, were written with great sensitivity, showing the writer's clumsy effort to remain anonymous; but the fragrance of musk that gushed from the paper was so strong it blanked the scent of the roses coming from the Gülhane gardens. What did the young Venetian sought from him? The meaning of the poem was clear, but the thoughts of people were rarely in harmony with their words. These were wicked times and souls were disfigured by greed and violence.

He brought back to mind the behavior of the young man during his reception. It was very hard to believe that someone at such a tender age could be involved in a conspiracy against him. His cheeks had turned red like a virgin girl's after a rather innocent insinuation that identified love with the Seven Wonders of the World. When he was his age, he had sat on Selim's lap as comfortably as if they were an armchair. The pirate had trained him well to please even the most vulgar man, and to be a slave meant he had no choices.

Selim Khan had never talked to him about love as far as he could remember. This was the best indication no tender feelings were involved, just sheer male lust and the urge of conquest. He couldn't remember what Selim had done to excite his interest. The only thing he was sure of was that Selim had not play the role of a man in love. He had to admit that now he behaved with this youngster as if he needed his touch. He had to be in love to think of nothing else but how to conquer this romantic young Venetian. Love was always so closely connected with innocence, it was as if there was immense pleasure for mankind in demolishing innocence.

What would he have done, if a mature man talked to him about love during his tender age? It was not easy to find a definite answer. In the same age he had already made love with Suleiman and the pirate, when Selim invited him to the Marble Kiosk. An experienced man like him must have realized he was not his first lover. Was this the reason Selim had not invited him for a second time? Now that Selim was dead, he would never discover the true reason.

He didn't have the same character with Selim. If he had a pleasurable experience, he would always try to repeat it. Perhaps this was the reason why he was so preoccupied with the conquest of this youngster. Perhaps he wished to play the role of Selim and see how the Venetian would react. It was not fear that forced the youngster to accept his advances, it was no greed either. It might well be an attempt to become the favorite of the Grand Vizier to advance his career in diplomacy. On the other hand, perhaps, what he was trying to discover was not how Selim felt about him, but Suleiman. If this was the case, then after their first encounter, he should invite the Venetian for a pleasure trip in Edirne away from curious eyes.

What was the force the young man possessed that was attracting him so strongly? Could it be the results of an irresistible physical attraction, or another more subtle consideration? The idea that the youngster sought some kind of revenge did not fit his logic. The Venetian was not a desperate slave trying to survive. He was born the proud son of a ruler.

****

Perhaps if that day the Northeasterly wind blew from Siberia, then the windows of his office would be closed, and the scent from the Gülhane roses would not mix with the rosewater of Hurrem's perfume. Maybe then Ibrahim could have discerned the scent of rose water on the paper and then, and his mind would not have been conquered by Spring and the longing for pure love; then perhaps he might have reckoned the true identity of the poet and writer of the lyrics. Maybe then the history of Cosmos might have taken another path.

Those who have a rather blurry picture of the world around them called it Kismet; but actually Kismet is nothing but the infinitesimal effort Allah the Almighty makes to change the fate of a man, as a spark inside the mind of man at the right moment is enough of a light to decide which road to follow towards life or death.

****

Ibrahim read the letter for a second time much more carefully, trying to understand what might be hidden between these mesmerizing words. All these years he had spent being a slave of Suleiman, he had spent countless nights reading and writing poems. There were even few times when the Sultan had asked for his help to cobble together few elegant erotic verses to send to his Haseki; but he had never written a word for him and their love, as if he was ashamed to admit or describe in writing his carnal desires. Every admission of weakness was left to his faithful slave's lips still unable from the time of the Conquest to raise any resistance. However, today was the first time a young man asked him to show him the way of his heart, and this man had traveled to meet him all the way from Venice.

His Ionian homeland was separated from the Italian mainland by a strip of sea, while from the Turk by steep mountain ranges. He might have lost his mind all these years, but his heart that morning reminded him that he was still alive and worthy to be loved all over again by a delicate, young man. His middle-age flesh was still capable of attracting the youth. It seemed strange, but only for him the river of time had turned back; leaving Suleiman lost in his stormy ocean of violent dilemmas.

Ibrahim tried desperately to forget everything and concentrate on the papers in front of him, asking for his signature, but he couldn't even read one. The Divan could not keep him a prisoner within its four walls. Purposefully he pushed aside all the letters waiting for his consent and went back to the magical rose garden separating him from the secret door, the Eye of the Needle. Ahead of him he noticed a blooming cherry tree. It was strange, but he had never been aware of its presence. How something so simple and banal as few lines on a piece of paper could ever become more important than the beauty of a flower. The cherry blossom flavor was blended with the saltiness of the Bosporus. The Spring was not far away.

He next wondered how magically complicated a man was put together by Mother Nature. Indeed a bold look, an enchanting perfume, or a few meaningful words sufficed to transform him in a single moment from a slave of many weaknesses into a fearless warrior that could combat even the invincible forces of the gods. His love for Suleiman had chased away the specter of Selim in the past. Now he felt ready to face again the specter of another cruel Sultan.

****

He went to the stables, rode his horse, and then left in a hurry, galloping through the Gate of the Empire. Only then was able to feel free again. He turned about once more to the beach of Marmara Sea and galloped frantically among the dunes. He had never before wondered alone without his security guards so far outside the Sea Walls.

Spring was the season that birds returned to the northern river deltas to breed and the sand was full of their tracks. After a long ride he reached the first lake in his path, and countless flocks of seabirds rose hunted by the galloping horse, filling the sky from their wings and the wind with their voices. He stopped for a moment and gazed at their flying formations under the clouds. He caught himself envying their freedom, and rushed to wake the most lazy among them, spreading further their flocks to the four cardinal points of the horizon.

The past winter they had been wintering on the Nile Delta and now they had just finished half of their journey to the mouth of the Danube, the Dnieper and the Don. With this thought his jealousy grew even more; but unexpectedly, a distant voice reached the ears, calling him by his old name: 'Dimitri! Dimitri!"

The feeling that he was not all alone startled him; so, he pulled the reins sharply and the white Arabian mare stopped with the elegant footsteps of gracefully dancer.

He searched eagerly around him to find one who was calling him, but the shore seemed deserted and void of any sign of life. He ought to be dreaming, but this dream was so real that he would the oath someone was hiding behind the dunes and played tricks on him. His ears received a new distant call:

"This way! Over here!"

He turned around towards the sun and between its rays and their reflections on the water a human form appeared, approaching him that seemed to miraculously walk on top of the swamp surface. The proud walking style seemed strangely familiar.

"What is our Grand Vizier trying to find in the wilderness in such a hurry, his missing modesty?" a familiar voice teased him.

Ibrahim immediately recognized him. Sinan, the Janissary Imperial Architect, was after him he had not seen since Konia. Instead of answering, he asked a question with the authority of a Serasker: "And what are you doing here in this lake?"

"The Sultan asked me to build a firm bridge here, because the river carried away the old Roman one on the Old Egnatia Road last winter. My job of testing the hardness bottom here is finished. Suleiman Khan must be planning a new war in the West next summer," Sinan replied and with his hand he pointed to the other side of the lake. There in the background near the line of the horizon, loomed between the reflections of the sun and the water a series of arched bridges that look like humps of camels leading the way of a giant caravan. Ibrahim remembered now the question of Sinan and rushed to provide an answer.

"I am also building a bridge these days, but many folks around me prefer to remain separated by rivers of hate, and every evening I go to sleep, they stay awake and mess up what I have accomplished the past day. Since I'm powerless to react, I'm dissipating now my anger by chasing innocent birds."

Sinan smiled for just a moment, but then he quickly turned serious.

"It's very hard work making good bridges, and the most perilous time is when one thinks the bridge is finished and done."

Ibrahim felt his interest come alive.

"What's your impression of your new master, now that with the will of Allah you have a new duty to rebuild once more the Domain of Peace? Is he a better overlord than me? Is he a more demanding customer?"

"There is no tangible threat, just a feeling. The Sultan has suddenly felt the need to order his slaves by his own lips without intermediaries. Few of his orders are foolish; but I am an engineer and I must follow the orders only of Allah, so that my bridge will survive much more than I will."

Ibrahim smiled hearing his words.

"All they teach the Sultans since birth is how to order. The begging is left only for the slaves."

"Yes! The slaves are made to constantly beg for something the Sultan must provide. This is what the world order demands, so they are all happy and satisfied. If one day the slaves stopped begging; then there would be no reason for Sultans."

Ibrahim was quick to reply: "Your words are wise, my friend. The power to rule was from the outset the apple offered by the serpent to Eve and Adam, not love, as Christian fools think and chose to be locked in their monasteries to sanctify their souls. Power is all that can offer you everything, even love."

Now it was Sinan's turn to smile.

"That's not entirely true. I know precious few who marched throughout their lives against the current and finally won power through love."

Ibrahim understood the hint and responded.

"In the hunt for power one can use the sword, words, love, or even friendship; but it's much easier to succeed in this quest, if one can put to work all four in his favor."

"The Grand Vizier is correct once more; but he must not forget that only love can force power to become your slave forever," Sinan added in good spirits.

"Indeed it can do that, but there is no harm done, if one can put to good use few of the other three ingredients too," Ibrahim snapped back, and they both burst into laughter as they strolled by the lakes shoreline.

He was sufficiently relaxed to remember the name his friend used to call him.

"How come calling me you've used my old name. No one has used it for many years."

Sinan turned and looked at him. His gaze reflected the old, familiar melancholy of a slave.

"At first I cried Ibrahim, but your name sounded like a distant thunder and I failed to catch your attention. The name Dimitris can travel farther, when the wind blows on its back."

"That's just a feeble excuse. There must be another reason. You are much more complicated than that. For you nothing really happens because of a single reason."

"Indeed I feel it's important for every slave sometimes to remember who he was, when he was still free to roam around like the wind."

"Sometimes it is better for a slave to live day by day, and forget all about his past."

"No! When a storm is approaching, one must remember where his best shelter lies, and for most men this is their homeland."

And as if Allah the All-Mighty wished to confirm his words, a breath of wind suddenly blew hard, bringing with him a distant thunder from direction he came. It was the voice of the Eternal City ordering him to return.

Ibrahim visibly upset pulled the reins, as the horse scared from the unexpected noise sought his guidance and protection.

"Such stormy days like this I feel like galloping forever until this aged City is lost from my eyes. I want to reach the end of the world, to discover countries no one else has reached before. I've tried many times to escape, but I always turned back as if I was hypnotized. This city attracts me like a magnet and whatever I do, it's impossible for me to escape its attraction."

Sinan remained silent, seeing him departing without goodbye, afraid of admitting they had nothing more to say. He knew his friend's illness had no cure. He was never, not even for a moment, the Sultan's slave. He was the slave of the toughest master, himself; a master which the more he tried to defy and ignore, the more he fell abandoned, cut-off from his people and his creator. Now it was apparent a dramatic moment was approaching, when he would have to face all alone the destiny he had chosen, since the day he decided to escape from the prison of Parga and Venice, and seek his fortune in the Ottoman Empire.

****

When the sunset finally marked the end of the day, Ibrahim's patience came to an end too. Since early this afternoon he had begun the preparations for the night. He had passed first through the cleansing clouds of steam, and then let the skillful hands of his black eunuchs soften his skin with jasmine oil, before it was time to choose a suit appropriate for the occasion. He had to look as young and attractive as possible, as lust simplified human acceptance and made intimacy much easier.

When this long and elaborate preparation was over, he looked at himself in the mirror. The skin on his body had lost its youthful freshness and his flesh had become looser around the waist. A silken belt probably could cover the greatest portion of the effects of relaxation he was going through, since he returned from the Persian deserts. If this attempt of establishing some kind of permanent relationship with the bodily measurements of his youth, he ought to limit the variety of French cuisine he had lately enjoyed on the occasion of the Treaty.

Now, however, it was too late to revitalize the vigor of his flesh. His magnificent appearance had to be the main reason why the eyes of the newcomer had been attracted. Unquestionably, his hair was still dense, even though few patches of white hair had made their appearance. Until now he had not paid any attention, and now it was a bit too late to try to cover them with dye. The Venetian had enough time in the reception to check him over at his leisure. Any superficial change would simply reveal his fears he was not attractive enough.

He was not a youngster any longer and all his acquaintances expected him to be serious even though his heart yearned to be young and recklessly foolish once again. Was this wonton urge to meet the Venetian an unconscious attempt to return to the arms of Venice and the West, breaking away from the embrace of the Orient?

Now it was not the right time for him to try to dissect and analyze his inner thoughts. He was in the midst of an experiment and he had to try his best to reach a pleasant conclusion. Unquestionably, Suleiman's waistline was slimmer than his because of his strict diet and fasting, but his head had turned white, destroying the initial good impression abstinence created by suggesting intense self-control. Getting old was a critical period when even the most beautiful creatures turned ugly, or more correctly, ugliness was another way of describing the effects of old age with the possible exceptions of deformities or mutilations. These was at least his experiences with living in the same house with his grandparents. When he had entered puberty, he couldn't stand their looks or even their kisses or compassionate caresses.

Time was slipping away quickly, and soon he was going to lose forever the ability to enjoy anyone's love, not just his master's. He simply had to hurry. Mother Nature was simply too hard and relentless on her creatures even though his mother would keep on loving him until she died. Perhaps this was the reason ancient Greeks had envision death as a male entity. Men were always connected with cruelty, war or death. The Greek pagans had many reasons to think so. They were much more analytical than the Christians. They preferred to attach a certain single deity to every human trend rather than attribute everything to a single god. Generalizations like this indicated a lower degree of civilization, not a superior intelligence; thus even the Christians were obliged to accept the weakness of their follies by creating thousands of saints, specialized in specific benevolent tasks.

On the other hand, Muslims were still far behind both religions and slowly added local saints to their primitive pantheon of religious illusions. He had to do the same and accept that his face was getting swept by the passage of time; however, his eyes still had the vigor and undeniable brilliance of youth. It was one of the few virtues Mother Nature had left unchanged to lure admirers, but it had been good enough, as eyes were the open doors to his heart.

Although the night was still cold this time of the year, he had chosen to wear white silk underwear because their contact made his skin shudder. He could not help but smile with the racy thought that the Prophet had forbidden all his believers to wear silken undergarments. He was still unable to understand what bothered Allah or the God of the Christians, whether their believers wore something as soft as a woman's caress that kept their bodies warm and awake. Was there any other way besides making love, to achieve the proliferation of the faithful? Making war especially against the heretics certainly was not what the Prophet had in mind, because of the extreme number of the resulting casualties. This was his subtle argument in favor of his peace treaty.

He next chose one of his Grand Vizier special customs, another luxurious gift of the Sultan. It was a kaftan made of crimson Chinese silk with a snow-white pants and leather boots made of expensive ermine fur brought from Siberia. The page had begun to put a huge turban on his head, when Ibrahim cut him short with a node. It was much better to keep his head uncovered in order to pass unnoticed through the streets beneath the usual black cloak of a disguise. This night he did not need also any brilliant jewels to impress his male audience with reflections of power. On the contrary, he ought to look as discreet as every other wanderer on the sidewalks of the Eternal City.

Suddenly his patience for the ludicrous Grand Vizier preparation ritual came to an end. He decided he could not wait any longer to meet the author of the poem and seek all the answers he needed to satisfy his curiosity.

He summoned a page, and sent a message to the Venetian Bailo. They had to meet without delay at his house to talk in private about the new developments in Europe. The time he had to wait for the messenger to go and return from Galata with the Bailo's answer seemed endless, but in the end his patience was richly rewarded. The Venetian informed him that he would be waiting for him promptly, and if it was permissible, his son would also be present to learn of the requirements of diplomatic protocol.

Ibrahim felt his luck was smiling that night. It was an invitation he would not think of denying; so, he slipped stealthily from a back door of his palace and shortly he got lost in the crowd of the pious Ottomans who came out of the Agia Sophia after the evening prayer.

With quick steps he followed the crowd down the gentle slope toward the harbor and the waiting Galata ferries. Till that moment he never could explain why Allah's believers bothered to go across the bay to pray in Agia Sophia, when in Galata there were several very spacious mosques; but then an idea sneaked into his mind that explained everything. They were former Christians who felt that only in the church of Holy Wisdom they could secretly worship their God, even if it was converted into a mosque for Allah. He was not the only one residing in this ancient city who was trying hard to survive with compromises.

From the journey across the Golden Horn or his uphill climb he wished to recall only his fervent excitement. Nothing else was important enough to retain in his memory.

****

Arriving next to the Galata dock, he had to wait for a while to make sure that all the other passengers had left and he was all alone on the dock. This evening he ought to make sure no spy was tracking him. Since the very first night he spent in the Seraglio, every time he visited it, he felt he was under constant observation by a curious pair of eyes.

At the beginning these eyes belonged to Selim's spies, but later when he died, they were replaced by Suleiman's, since spying every person of some importance was the most essential rule of Ottoman security. Allah's Shadow should not end up dead like Alexander the Great before completing his divine mission.

Several times the spy had been a so-called "Bostandji", a "gardener", member of the Mute Executioners. Few other times a white eunuch he had never seen before in the Seraglio, and sometimes they were both. At first their presence had him worried, but quickly he realized they were the Sultan's people responsible also for his safety. From that moment he stopped paying any attention; but tonight it was different. Venice was a determined enemy and such a private visit might well be considered treasonous.

The quick stepping ascent was very tiring, and by the time he reached Bailo's door he was gasping. He paused on the doorstep long enough to catch his breath. He felt that his best years had passed and he was not so young anymore; but he still yearned for wild adventures fit for much more foolish and younger men. This meant his spirit was willing, but his flesh was weak. He drove this pessimistic idea of his mind and beat loudly on the door. The door opened promptly and he quickly crossed the threshold closing the door behind him. Soon it was in front of the Venetian wicked nobleman who played the dangerous role of the Sultan's ambassador.

The Venetians were a strange breed of people who one could be confident of their words only if they were consistent with their interests. From the old days, they had won extensive and lucrative commercial privileges in the Eastern Roman Empire by the strength of their commercial and military fleet; but this was not enough to satisfy their greed; so whenever they could, they tried to rob the Roman lands as privateers; so, in the end it was no surprise that even those who had authority to welcome their help like the Roman nobility, they preferred to wore the Sultan's caftan more than the mantle of the Republic of Venetian Doge. The Ottomans at least had not come to the East to steal, but to stay and build a new empire.

When Fatih's armies stepped on Peloponnesus soil, the old Roman castles, the one after the other, that had fallen into the Venetian hands, Nafpaktos, Methoni and Koroni, surrendered to the Ottomans. It was impossible for fortifications made to withstand ancient sieging machines like the catapults to stand up also against the heavy artillery of the Ottomans that had conquered Constantinople. However, despite these defeats, greed pushed the Venetian to seek mercy from the Muslim enemy and beg for the old prerogatives of Byzantium.

Now that the war between Christ and Islam was gradually moving from land to the sea, it was more than certain the war with the Ottomans would soon begin again. The castles still remaining in Venetian hands, Nafplio and Monemvasia, would soon fall in the hands of the Ottomans, and then the turn of Crete and Cyprus would come, following the fall of Rhodes and the Dodecanese's. No one had to be clairvoyant to predict the grim future of Venice in the Eastern Mediterranean. The castles built on the mainland would fall first, and then the castles on the bordering islands would surely follow.

The Venetian navy being the strong arm of the republic in a single rich city did not have the resources to withstand the manpower and the resources of an empire. One simply ought to wait for a while until the Ottoman fleet grow stronger and more skillful. The old conflict between Rome and Carthage was now going to be repeated. Then, the conflict with the Portuguese in the Indian and the Spice Trade would start.

The local population offered little resistance, because the Venetians had turn the indigenous population into serfs they treated badly. On the other hand, the Ottomans more wisely made Grand Viziers the most able men they could find. The moral conclusion was obvious. The Ottoman Sultans were fairer rulers than the Venetian counterparts.

The first attempt in the Mediterranean waters had been attempted by Selim Khan, and it was more than successful. He was also the Ottoman who stepped first on African soil. Now that Suleiman had appointed Hayreddin Barbarossa, another Greek, as Kapudan Pasha, many experienced sailors from the Aegean coast and islands volunteered to become Ottoman sailors and pirates.

Algeria became first a vassal of the Turks, and then the entire northern shore of the African continent. After the Black Sea, the turn of the Mediterranean Sea had come, and after that the Red Sea would be used to extend commerce to the Indian Ocean. What kind of fate a small city like Venice or tiny nations like Portugal might have, when the Ottomans had now set in motion entire nations from Hungary to Yemen, and from Algeria to Mesopotamia? Venice ought to reconcile with reality, become allies with Genova and Spain and try their best to drive the Ottoman Empire out of the Mediterranean Sea; but could they ever hope to conquer Egypt?

Venice was caught largely unprepared for such an immense enterprise; so, for the time being the only way to share the trade of silk, spices and coffee was to negotiate with the Ottomans. This was at least the advice Ibrahim gave with a friendly smile to the Bailo.

Listening to his words the Bailo made a grimace of discontent. It was not proper, he said, to spoil such a lovely evening talking about the hazy future, when no one but God and Allah knew what kind of day would dawn next morning. Then, he stayed silent for a moment and added with a faint smile:

"The Grand Vizier is certainly right. Indeed what he said so far is the most logical course of events; but nobody could ever rule out that something unique may happen to change the flow of History. Who can really imagine how the world would have been, if Alexander did not die unexpectedly so young, or if the knives of the assassins had not cut the thread of Caesar's life? Even most recently, the unexpected death of Fatih and Selim Khan had changed history. If they had died few years older, maybe Vienna and then Venice and Rome would be in Ottoman hands by now. Our Lord Jesus Christ likes to make great miracle right at the last moment."

Ibrahim listened patiently and silently to his dubious claims, trying to understand the hidden deeper threats. Whenever he listened Christians talking about miracles, he was sure they were approaching the end of their endurance; however, this Venetian official had also talked that night about the deaths of Emperors and Sultans. Did he know something more or was he simply attempting an diversion with such shaky arguments? He ought to find out more if he could; but his thoughts were interrupted by the sudden appearance of Bailo's son, who immediately captured his eye and attention. The handsome young man approached and knelt respectfully before him, lowering his eyes and Ibrahim stretched out his hand to greet him.

"Please stand up," he said in a friendly tone. "The fact you are a bit younger does not mean you should kneel before me as if I was the Pope."

The young man remained silent and a bit embarrassed, and only the Bailo hastened to add that he was the only man in the room worthy of respect for his advanced age. Then, the young man raised his eyes and smiled at Ibrahim, and his attitude showed that he unreservedly agreed with the opinion of his father.

It was the first time Ibrahim had the opportunity to observe carefully his face and did not let it get wasted in vain. The chandeliers made of colorful crystal from Murano emphasized the subtle shades of his green eyes that had escaped detection the previous night in the twilight of his palace. He decided that he should bathe his palace in candlelight, so he could enjoy all shades of colors of life at night as well as he did under the sunlight during the day.

Eros was never a sin to be kept hidden like a thief in darkness. No animal on Earth except the humans was ashamed to mate under the sun; so, the tricky Christians explained the phenomenon by claiming humans were no animals but images of God. He cursed all religions that had deprived people from enjoying happiness and love with their own eyes; but his silence was exploited by the Bailo to add:

"Our philosophical discussion can't end here and now. As you well know, diplomats are the most inefficient traders and their bazaars never end. They always discover something more to ask or to give; but now it's too late for me. Old wrecks have to go sleep early; but the night is still young like you are. If there is a city world renowned for its nightlife this is Constantinople."

And with these words he said goodbye to Ibrahim and closed quietly the door behind him. Now they were finally all alone.

****

Their eyes met again and Ibrahim singled out the tender embarrassment of innocence. It was the hesitation of the youth to overcome the doubts of adolescence and proceed to the uncertainty of the adult world. In his nostrils came the scent of musk drugging his moral doubts. He turned around toward the exit and the pages noticing his determination to leave opened it without delay, as the younger man followed him without hesitation.

When Ibrahim reached the pavement of the narrow street, he noticed the evening mist's veils slipping quietly over the gardens and alleys, covering the way down to the harbor. It was a mystic sign the path back to his previous life was lost, and he ought to seek a new destination higher up the hill. He lingered for a while hesitant, not knowing which way he ought to go; but he soon felt the Venetian's hand slipping into his palm for guidance and protection pressing him to make up his mind. They were in Galata, the most sinful harbor in the Orient, so there were many choices that could fit every possible mood. Should they visit a tavern to watch few dancing boys seducing drunken sailors?

No, it didn't make any sense to waste their time among male whores! It was too demeaning for a Grand Vizier and a Venetian nobleman to associate even for a moment with the Galata underworld. Their taste had to be much more refined; so they walked for a while undecided as the fog kept thickening, limiting their horizon and their choices.

It was getting late and soon the creeping darkness would make wandering a perilous endeavor, as even the Janissary patrols didn't dare to enter this European district after nightfall. Every merchant vessel docked could well become a pirate ship the moment it left the harbor for the high seas, if the captain decided a good profit could be made. With this thought he pulled his partner closer and quicken his steps towards their still undetermined destination.

In Galata Christ and Allah were partners as mosques and churches shared the same sidewalks since the Fatih era. However, after the sunset all temples had their doors shut to protect their treasures from the scum that sought shelter and solid ground in this town from the toils of seafaring and wave crossing. The fog was now thick enough to hide their faces from every possible old acquaintance, but this feeling of complete isolation drained their will to seek much further for a suitable destination. In the fog the light of an oil lamp at the entrance suddenly appeared as the beacon of a lighthouse, inviting them to seek the safety of a harbor. Sensing his hesitation the Venetian decisively pushed the door of a locanda, and they found themselves suddenly in a new world filled with smells of smoke and breath that reeked of raki. It was strange, but they both felt secure in such deprived environments.

Here they were two perfect strangers among foreigners who had never seen before and will never see their eyes again. The Venetian pulled his hand again leading him this towards the reception. Hand in hand they crossed the lobby, trying to be as imperceptible as possible, and least disturbing, while the loud customers of the tavern sitting on sofas around tables, were waiting for the glasses to empty to order a new round.

In exchange for few coins soon they found themselves alone in a room full of cheap luxurious decorations of golden paint. Nothing in there was reminiscent of the palace solid gold amenities and the multitude of servants they were both accustomed, but complete isolation and banality was what they both sought this night. A lighted fireplace to dry their clothes and a warm bed was what they both needed to spend a night away from their previous selves.

Ibrahim turned and looked at the Venetian with an air of apology, but his facial expression reassured him the room was ideal for expressing his desires; so, he sat on the bed pulling aside the cover made of purple glossy velvet. The pure whiteness of linen was a pleasant change from the loud room colors.

"It is awfully hot in here," Ibrahim uttered, and the words came out awkwardly from his mouth.

He immediately regretted the banality of the words that had escaped from his lip spoiling the mystical ritual of the moment. The lyrics were a flower that flourished longer when the eyes were closed, leaving the imagination to run wilder separated from reality; but his eyes opened wide as the Venetian showed his agreement, as he started to take off his clothes one by one as if his white flesh tested the room temperature to determine which were the most comfortable garments he should retain, if any. His emotions soon revealed they were perhaps under greater turmoil than Ibrahim's, because he chose not to speak another word until all his clothes he wore were lying on the floor. Only then he reached for his red, silken underwear he stopped for a moment, perhaps from shame, trying to hide from Ibrahim's eyes all the weaknesses troubling his mind. However, he quickly decided it would be ridiculous for a young man in his late twenties not to have reconciled yet with every desire of his body, and tried to hide behind a translucent thin piece of fabric his feminine nature.

Another stretch of silence followed his bold exposure, waiting for Ibrahim's response. Ibrahim's fingers were more obedient than his trembling lips, as he rushed to prove he was still among the most handsome males of the Ottoman Empire. It was indeed an irresolute challenge between Hercules and Hermes an ancient Greek sculptor had never considered fit to create.

The Venetian youngster was indeed almost as handsome and harmonic as the statues of Hermes that stood outside

Ibrahim's Palace; but far more desirable, because he had reached the peak of his manhood, and his vibrant flesh was ready to sow eternity in a woman's body; so with a gentle blow he extinguished the lamp, leaving only the flame from the wood in the fireplace to illuminate the room.

Ibrahim could not help but smile with satisfaction, watching the face of his next lover painted in crimson shades by shame. He was behaving as timidly as his country that was ready to abandon herself unreservedly in his strong Ottoman hands, but was trying until the last moment to hide his weakness; so he got up and went to the fireplace to pick up a thin piece of wood burning. Slowly he approached the flame to the young body that was lying now on the white linen. This night he wanted all his senses to enjoy the sinful splendor of a masculine body. The lambent light revealed the beauty of the male torso in all its splendor.

"The eyes," he noted, "are the doors to the soul. Without light we risk losing our way."

He lit the lamp again, and the bright light of the flame dazzled his eyes forcing him to close them. From his mind passed images had never seen with his own eyes. It was his imagination that pulled him deeper inside his brain cells to reveal what confronted the eyes of his ancestors during their feasts and symposiums, naked dancers pirouetting that under the sounds of flutes and harps. Between them he discerned Basmi and Sherenk smiling at him with an air of profound condescension, sharing his lust for the flesh of an attractive male.

Opening his eyes he saw the Venetian kneeling submissively in front of his feet, as their mutual fervent passion drew them closer together. There, embarrassment and shame prevailed briefly once more before Ibrahim with a tender caress of his curled hair encouraged the hesitant man to overcome the last hurdle. His lips embraced the wet warmth of his aroused flesh, and Ibrahim let himself be delivered to the island of pleasure by the raging waves of the youngster's passion to experience bliss. Soon enough he could not withstand the pressure and added his heartbeats with a skillful coordination that shook the foundations of his existence.

****

Was this another divine message from Allah? Was he going to seduce and conquer Venice too? He felt his knees melting and fell onto the bed on his back trembling. The coolness of the sheet was a pleasant change that lasted for a while as their bodies gently separated.

All these years his body had tasted enough of slavery and submission, but tonight everything was different. He could now let his imagination free to choose which moment he would let his lips and fingers wander on the youthful body to kiss or touch what he craved most. His mind was even more demanding, eager to make the most audacious proposals.

They should take advantage of this incredible piece of luck. Since Constantinople was so full of spies, the Grand Vizier would use his wealth and power to make sure this was the first and last occasion they met in such shabby surroundings. He was going to buy promptly a descent but modest dwelling on the Bosporus shore, where they could meet discretely every time they felt the need to express the passion for each other. Galata was simply too dangerous for two male lovers to consume their desires time and time again.

The Venetian didn't seem to object to such a solution, but Ibrahim suggested that if this arrangement was unsatisfactory, he was willing to hire the Venetian and make him a member of his diplomatic staff. The excuse almost presented itself. He needed a trusted Venetian spy in Galata to mine information about the movements and intentions of the Venetian galleys.

Venetian sailors were constant visitors of the Galata harbor, but they kept their lips sealed to all Ottomans. Was the Venetian willing to betray his country for his sake, was the subtle question he proposed.

"Do you trust me so much?" the Venetian asked.

"Yes, now I do," Ibrahim replied with enough passion left to signify his emotional weakness for his hesitant lover.

"Yes, but I still don't know if I should trust you. I had few experiences with men before to know that powerful men like you seek variety rather than duration. You are also a married man with two children and a harem, as far as I know. I'm afraid that soon enough you will get bored of me and seek another conquest."

"No! That's not true. You are just what I need to be content."

"Don't lie to me. I know everything about you. I even know of the weakness the Sultan has for your caresses. Are you going to deny him too? You should know that I don't mind having you spend few nights a week in your harem. Women can't make me jealous. It's you mating with other men my pride cannot stand. If I ever I find out you are seeing other men, I swear I will do my best to seduce them as easily as I have seduced you."

It was an unexpected threat, but from his entire behavior the Venetian had shown he was not his first male acquaintance. He was almost as experienced as he was. Perhaps this was the reason he was so blunt and realistic.

"It's not the same. I am a slave while you are a free man. I have to do what my master demands of me," Ibrahim claimed.

"Then you must claim your independence. This what a man in your shoes must do," the Venetian insisted.

"I can only try," Ibrahim promised.

"That's good enough for me; but let's see what how hard you can try. Let's play a game. Let's pretend I'm your demanding master," he proposed and put his arms around his waist. Then he started murmuring in his ear alluring words of seduction Ibrahim tried to parry with a giggle, but the Venetian was relentless, while the defenses he tried to raise were feeble and weak. Ibrahim had to accept that slavery had been too long for him to break off the chains so easily now. He tried to negotiate a truce, but his suggestions were flatly rejected. The Venetian insisted on complete equality and desired to feel the same pleasure he had tasted first.

For a moment they resembled two male lions fighting for supremacy, trying to detach the largest chunk of their prey; but in the end, youth had once again imposed the terms of his surrender. As much as he tried to negotiate, the younger man was adamant and absolute, while he felt weak and exhausted the critical moment. It was the very moment the walls of Constantinople were left unguarded, and as another Dandolo, the Venetian managed to climb over the seawalls of the Golden Horn and commence his total plundering.

The Venetians were not only merchants, they were pirates too. Ibrahim's last heroic resistance was bent and his defenses abandoned. The desires of his conqueror passed triumphantly through the Vlaherna Gate all the way to the sumptuous imperial palace.

The young Dandolo had as a mentor only his insatiable greed, and he did not stop before the Eternal City had delivered all her treasures, even the four bronze horses in front of the church of the Holy Apostles. Only then he released all his passion and fell by his side to grasp a breath of air, while Ibrahim desperately tried to calm down the racing beat of his heart.

Ibrahim's hand reached to touch his lover's chest in the place of his heart. He found it easily, because it was still beating hard as if it was almost ready to bust. He smiled tenderly. It was an expression of gratitude for the portion of himself that had been scattered in each other's heart. The thought that even now he could attract so strongly a youthful body had clouded his eyes.

The Venetian saw his eyes moistened and a suspicion crossed his mind.

"Forgive me!" he whispered, looking guilty. "I got carried away by my strength and went beyond all limits. I promise I will not rape you again. For me you are not a slave."

But Ibrahim had no serious complaints from his lover. He had also been young few years back, and he had felt in his loins the untamed power of youth. He was aware that when this flame was lit by a spark, it could not be extinguished until it had burned every tinder.

Despite his age, he was still capable of scattering thousands of seeds into the wind like a dandelion filling the molds of his desire. Fate and his audacious choices had made him a slave of the Osmanli Sultans. He was supposed to buy the right to live and love with this allegiance. His flesh had been bought long ago for only one thousand silver coins, but he had sold his mind for millions and millions. This would be his excuse for all his deeds the moment of judgment.

It was strange, but when he was finally relieved from the Venetian's weight on his back, he finally felt relieved from all his fears too. He had reached the end of his journey and didn't care anymore about whatever had happened with Selim Khan that night at the Marble Kiosk. Tonight his memory had opened its gates wide open. Tonight he had lost the battle against the young lion, but Eros was truly undefeatable in battle, as Homer had claimed, and Mother Earth always like to close loops with the same magnificence they had begun long ago.

****

As he left the warm bed Ibrahim saw his lover's face saddening so he tried to disperse his concerns with a smile. When he was as young, he had the tendency to stay committed in achieving impossible tasks and had lost the true essence of living.

There were no important roles two male lovers could play in life, no matter how hard they tried to convince themselves they did something meaningful. All that mattered in their relationship was who had the control of the game of ecstasy in his hands. The price he had paid in full tonight for the bliss he received. His precious time had already been transformed into another precious commodity, self-confidence. From the very first moment he lay his eyes on the Venetian's complexion, what he craved for was one last glimpse on himself before permanently saying goodbye to guilt.

All this years he felt shamed whenever he offered pleasure to man, and tried hard to find excuses, and being a slave was the most convenient one that gave him the excuse he couldn't refuse to serve his master's pleasure.

Tonight he had enticed the Venetian into wrestling with him, but from the very beginning he was sure it would be more pleasant if he lost the battle; so after a certain moment he had stopped resisting him and let him have his way to see what kind of passions he was still able to excite in the mind the vibrant flesh of a younger man. Now he was perfectly content because the Venetian had ravaged him so completely. This was a part of himself, no woman could satisfy and up to that moment the list of female conquests he had tasted was sufficiently extensive. Now, he was in position to believe every fantastic detail Menekse and Asphodel had revealed to him about his past.

With his perseverance to realize his illusions of magnificence, he had achieved a truly impossible task. He had become Grand Vizier, Serasker and Damat of a Sultan; but in reality he was made by Allah for a much more vulgar mission. In all his life he had strived to become an angel, the carrier of noble thoughts, but in fact he was content only as a devil, the instigator of sinful thoughts. He was a human being that claimed he had divine aims, but in fact he was no better than a Galata whore. This was probably the reason why he was so attracted to Hurrem and neglected the divine harem of a splendid Ottoman Princess just to visit a cheap Galata locanda with a younger Venetian.

Greeks and Venetians were never made to be content as conquerors or owners. They were always traders, and everything, even their hearts, was a commodity they should trade for profit like everything else. Perhaps the war with Venice was not truly necessary. All he had to do was convince the Grand Turk to change somewhat his bad conquering habits and start trading too.

Suleiman ought to understand that the days of great conquests were gone, and from now on gains would be the result of skillful negotiations and mutual consent.

The skies outside the window were getting lit by the rising sun still hidden behind the Üsküdar hills. After this passionate night of debauchery, they ought to hurry back to decency. As the Venetian grasp his hand trying to pull him back to bed for another round of wrestling, Ibrahim had to be unwavering for their own safety.

"This night" he claimed pompously, "I'd like to keep as a jewel for the rest of my life; but the Grand Turk will always demand of me to follow his orders and no one else's. You should trust my words too if I say that I do not yearn for him, he yearns for me; so, you should never become jealous, because I'm not his slave. I belong only to you for as long as you desire me."

The young man remained silent and pensive throughout their crooked path to the Bailo's residence threshold; but there his sorrow of separation overflowed, and with desperate gesture he hugged Ibrahim tightly and stuck his lips on to his.

"Stay with me forever!" the Venetian demanded next, while he was still confused. "In the harbor is still moored the boat that brought me here. If you wish it, it can take us away from here to other lands the Grand Turk will never find you."

Ibrahim looked at him intensively. Inside his emerald eyes he discerned there the joy of a pirate after a successful raid, but something within him warned that he should not believe his words. He tried to reassure him with a lie.

"I yearned for you so much, I didn't even asked for your name!"

"My name is Lodovico!"

"My lovely Lodovico, if I was ten years younger, maybe I would follow you in your travels to the four corners of the globe. Now it's too late for me. My fate is locked inside the Seraglio; but do not shed a tear because tomorrow night we will be together again," he promised and with his hand he raised the hood over his head.

The black cloth severed the eye contact and only then was able to depart and descend towards the harbor. Step by step his will became stronger eventually, defeating the curiosity that pushed him to take a last look behind his back to see if someone was following him.

****

It was the first time in his life he felt this feeling of completion. Every other time that he had let himself be seduced by the caresses of a man, he had tried to convince his consciousness that he was the last time he submitted to the desires of another male; but until that moment he had not yet succeeded. For a while, he fancied the desire was permanently extinguished after every trace of passion was dissolved; but the moment he came across another handsome man his curiosity was once more enflamed. He had to try again and again as if the repetitions would help him dominate his weakness; however, this time everything was different. With every step he took to distance himself from the source of his yearnings he felt freer than a bird.

He was not sure it was all his fault. Maybe it was the others' fault who during the most critical moments they lost all their strength and will, becoming soft as clay to be mold as he wished. Even Selim with all his bestial savagery had been unable to subdue him and leave him content. Never in his life by making love with a man he had discovered total liberation. Something was always missing, something he would always seek by entering the embrace of the next man. It was some sort of slavery that would extend until he ceased to be desirable.

Only women could fully liberate him, because they made him feel he had accomplished something more permanent and precious than few fleeting moments of pleasure. They could offer him a child, a tangible proof that a part of himself could live forever to conquer the fear of death and utter oblivion.

****

It was still very early morning and the Galata streets were filled with another unfamiliar world coming down to work in the port. It was the time the fishermen returned with their booty, and the first customers to be arrive to the seashore would have the best choice.

Ibrahim stirred the crowd of ordinary mortals, trying to solve everyday problems with the vital energy, wits and skills they possessed. Life had shared fairly the burden. Many backs could not withstand the weight they carried and were bent, while others walked straight, carrying only their own weight. Maybe someday he could also discard the weights that made him crouch, and discard slavery.

Only for few moments he considered the possibility and its consequences. His children would still be secure under the care of the mothers who adored them; so, his legacy was safe. The only issue worthy of consideration was which of the women in his life he needed most. It was the only reflection that kept him wondering all the way home. His Princess always found a way to capture his imagination, presenting each time a novel, unexpected version of her personality. She kept on playing with his weaknesses like a cat with a mouse, until she got tired of the game and then she completely devoured him.

Hatidge was molded and trained since childhood to give orders in all languages, even the fluent language of her body. From the moment she had his child, she had slaves devoted to a single mission, to offer him whatever was required to keep him content. She was as necessary and seductive as the sea that could one moment be rocking his vessel between her lips and the next to swallow it without warning. Many times he had felt drowned into the black abyss of her lustful eyes, but at the critical moment she would let him surface to get his breath, before she sucked the last drop of his essence. His life with her was like an endless journey of Odysseus returning to Ithaca and he like the hero of the myth would face the dawn of a new day with the hope for a new beginning; he would be a slave under her spell no matter how many years would pass.

Basmi was something entirely different, yet somehow the contrasts were also their common points of reference. She was a slave trained to satisfy the desires of her master, but she always managed to take initiatives and waken in him novel desires. It was rare for any slave to try to improvise, but he had no objection to experience something new and he had never left her embrace disappointed. She was exerting on him the allure of the Nile's black soil that invited him to plow and plant the seeds of resurrection. She seemed so fertile that he was unable to deny her every time a second seeding. Then, it was time for her to change face and invite him to search in her desert for the Nubian gold.

On the other hand, Sherenk expressed an entirely different kind of femininity. She was dreamy, almost ethereal. She would always be the virgin that kept unmolested the purity of the first night, and every time he conquered her, she made him feel the exaltation of a navigator who first set foot on an uncharted coast. She was the woman he longed to embrace every time he saw the full moon peeping over the Seraglio turrets. She was like the soft breath of wind that one moment could be caressing his hair and the next to lift him like an eagle up in heavens. It was strange that only with her he felt like a man willing to sacrifice everything to give flesh and bones to his dreams.

He felt truly lucky that he had encountered these three rare creatures in his lifespan and sheer luck was responsible for this success. Each one was limited by Mother Nature, but the three of them together complemented harmoniously his universe of desires. Was he exceedingly greed needing so many women to be content? Actually, few months back he needed more, but his Princess had proved beyond any doubt that his strength was faltering, and few of his intimate consorts had to leave so that they could find all the love they yearned in a younger man's arms.

Conceivably his affair with Lodovico might have been his response to his demotion.

As he went down the slope to the Galata harbor, he wondered what was missing from his life and pushed him to try so desperately to find it. What new kinds of sensations Lodovico had introduced in his life? Was he such an unstable personality that he found ecstasy not in the conclusion, but during this promiscuous act itself, as he demolished common morality?

He promptly decided his risky relationship with the Venetian had to end soon as abruptly as it had begun. He was nothing but a brilliant firework that had reached the end of its trajectory, an instinctive proclamation of carnal independence from the despotism of his mind, like closing his eyes whenever he sneezed.

Lately handsome men had failed to create in him any permanent interest whatsoever. All the attraction exerted on his flesh was just curiosity, as he wondered if a man could provide for him a different sensation than what he had felt before; but each time he came face to face with the same answer, just a fleeting desire transmitted via a pair of lusty eyes eager to taste his aging flesh. He has once again felt cheated by their alluring promises of a man's flesh. His love was like an endless wandering in a barren and inhospitable desert, where he was always afraid he might lose his sense of direction and die stranded hungry and thirsty.

His Princess was right! Such demeaning relationships were not worthy of his time, simply because they led nowhere. He had been fooled once by the promises of a devious pirate mesmerized by the thought he could break free from the Parga prison, where he could never realize his dreams. Luck had proved the pirate correct; but if he had become a star, it was because of his canning, his extraordinary looks and exceptional talents. The pirate had simply sold him to the highest bidder. His only contribution to his own phenomenal success was his initiation to the man's world.

Suleiman despite all the religious barriers he had in his mind should finally realize that their relationship was nothing more than a youthful adventure that had attracted their curiosity what was the true source of pleasure, the flesh or the soul. It was not entirely his fault, if he had welcomed him with open arms as a conqueror. He was a slave after all, the lower step of the human pyramid, but he was desperate to experience life at its fullest. What the Sultan had invested in him, had been repaid handsomely by his time and services. This much Suleiman had already confessed. Only by spending time with him and Hurrem the Sultan could ever be happy.

Tonight he felt he had to clear up mind from all the fears Selim Khan and his eunuchs exerted on him all these years, even if they were all dead and buried. Now that his past had revealed all its secrets and he knew exactly where he stood, the time had come for the Sultan to grant him his freedom. He was finally fed up being a slave. He had reached the state to become the master of his existence, his time, and his pleasure. The end of Ramadan would signal for him the end of a long probation period.

These thoughts filled him with optimism for the future. He would be really crazy to desert the women of his life even for a moment. Lately, in an effort to close the deal with France, he had kept himself away from their attraction. Now even the narrow-minded Turks who surrounded him looked cute in their primitivism. Their behavior was like children's paintings; naive, honest and full of the primary colors of nature, without sensitivities or subtle shades. The creatures that passed in front of his eyes this morning were dressed with a myriad of bold color combinations. The Ottoman world was certainly nearer to reality than the black and white Christians of the West, and it was astounding that the specter of Hurrem still loomed in his mind. He was still as angry with himself as the day of his marriage. He wondered if he was ever able to forget her. Was the Prophet all-wise who spoke of four wives to provide harmony in the life of a man. He did not know why Mohamed had come up with this "divine" number; perhaps it had to do with something as simple as the four points of the horizon, or the four legs of a table; but his life could not find her balance, if he did not conquer her once more.

****

His recollections were interrupted abruptly when a hand touched gently his shoulder. Startled he stopped and looked behind him ready to complain about the disturbance, but facing Sinan, he immediately lost any combative mood.

"It is the second time the fate crisscrosses our orbits during the last two days. What does the Grand Vizier seeks to discover again here so close to my refuge?"

It was a simple question of social interest without any trace of nosy curiosity.

Ibrahim felt briefly embarrassed, as if there was a way hidden truth in his mind could become readable; so, he quickly cobbled a lie: "It was a magical night and I had some free time to mix with the crowds as a commoner, a stranger among strangers."

Doubt cast a shadow in Sinan's eyes, and then the familiar expression of absolute trust settled permanently once more; but even this momentary doubt was strong enough to paintIbrahim's complexion in pink shades. He knew his friend did not believe his words, but an innocent lie was not enough to demolish his friendly feelings. Sinan had fully accepted his weaknesses. He cursed himself for not making a more believable story, but now it was too late to take it back. However, his friend ignored the lie and invited him to rest from a long walk inside the garden of a nearby mosque. Without realizing it, his footsteps had brought him for a second time in front of the Mevlevana mosque. Suddenly he felt awfully tired from the previous night's adventure and pleasantly accepted the invitation to give a rest to his trembling knees.

They passed the iron gate and found themselves within the monastery grounds. He chose to sit outdoors on the marble enclosure built around a cypress's roots. During all his searches as a child he had failed to discover even a single fruit tree in any cemetery. It was a sign that nothing beneficial the dead could offer to the living, only memories.

Sinan smiled. It was obvious he was happy for this fortuitous meeting.

"I don't want to muddy your thoughts in there with our whirlwind dancing all over again. Anyway, it is still very early for us to confront our death and spoil such a splendid sunrise.

"In Ibrahim's ears Sinan's words were heard as if they were an oracle. He wasn't going to die that day. He strained his mind to clear the bad thoughts and find comfortable shelter once more in his rampant optimism. Now that he had taken all the critical decisions, nothing bad could happen to him; so, he tried to change the atmosphere with a joke.

"The best time to meet my death has passed me tonight," he proclaimed.

"And I hope it was a night worthy of such momentous struggle," Sinan replied, participating gladly in this game.

Maybe, he thought, Ibrahim had sneaked out from his sophisticated harem in disguise to take a stroll in the red light district that offered cheap thrills to seafarers. Galata was the most favorite of all the sinful districts of the city, and found no peace even during the holy Ramadan days. In great secrecy even Muslims whose faith was not enough to restrain their carnal impulses fled there to satisfy their secret passions.

Sinan's speculation had not missed reality by much; but Ibrahim felt a little annoyed when someone pocked at his weaknesses. His erotic life had certain peculiarities that violated ordinary morality limits even though similar behaviors were more common in the City than not. This kind of hypocrisy always bothered him; so he cut him somewhat abruptly.

"I put very little value on my weaknesses for certain people. I don't even differentiate them into women or men. We are all so fragile creatures, we may be lost tomorrow as easily as those heavenly clouds above us. The shapes living flesh takes are my favorites, exactly as your weaknesses are the domes and minarets of your mosques. Allah made me with the mission to seek the ephemeral moment of warm flesh, while you seek the cold eternity of stone. Throughout my life, I did not find another way to prove I'm still alive but by love, and I know that when I die, my eyes will miss blooming flowers, slim cypresses, or even your shiny Iznik tiles. As for the heaven and hell we hear inside the mosques of Islam and Christian churches, they both remind me of the hazy visions I see, sucking my hookah that quickly disappear like smoke the moment the blazing coals are extinguished."

Sinan did not seem disturbed by this sentimental explosion, and calmly replied.

"Allah has made the world so that every human being should find a destination. Allah has molded you to comfort people, while my destination is shaping humble stones. Only Time will show whose toils will produce fruits longer."

Ibrahim searched hard to find a proper reply. This morning he felt especially alienated from anything related to ordinary morality or obscure religious commandments.

"Your mosques and temples are nothing more, but expensive monumental tombs of gods who have died long ago. In the end, when humanity will be wise enough to take the next step. They will be ravaged like the Acropolis, the Holy Apostles, or the Pyramids. Only ideas and enflamed desires will live as long as humanity exist, even when the sinful flesh that born them has turned to soil," Ibrahim proclaimed and at first his voice was hostile, but gradually he repented and changed his tone adding the warmth of friendship.

Sinan sensed this change and took the liberty to add one last tip. It didn't passed unnoticed, because it was not tied to any previous discussion.

"The law says that mosques of ordinary people, even Grand Viziers, may have only one minaret. Only the Sultans and Allah in Mecca may have two or more. Nobody knows when the end of his life will come, and even an innocent kiss can cost you your life."

Ibrahim suddenly felt uneasy. It was the second time that Sinan referred to the same subject. Sinan had stirred forgotten images from the past buried in his memory. He recalled that since the first time he met Suleiman in the Avret Bazaar, Sinan was always by his side, all the way from Vienna and Mohacs to Egypt and Persia. He was like his guardian angel. Was it a coincidence, a sign of Allah's benevolence of Allah, or a secret order of His Shadow to protect him? He decided that now it was not as important anymore. Suleiman was too concern with his illness to follow closely all his movements. Anyway, it was too late to regret his mistakes; so he smiled. He needed to open his heart somewhere and Sinan had shown every time he knew how to listen.

"Maybe when I was younger my kisses could fetch a high price. Now, supply these days far exceeds demand. Now only a fool would pay attention to something so trivial that lasts only for a moment."

"Human patience is a glass that is slowly filling up. Eventually a single drop can make the glass overflow," Sinan argued.

"If I remember well, your favorite holy book nowhere claims that a kiss has the power to turn an angel into a devil," Ibrahim remarked and Sinan was in no position to refute his claim.

"Allah's angels are indeed made of pure intellect and are free of any trace of eroticism. They are not like animals made to feel only the power of the flesh. Humans are condemned to live among angels and animals, so they must choose the role that fits them," Sinan admitted.

"Even for a moment I could not live like an angel. Animals have at least the pleasure to sow and grow their children, so they can become better than they are. Only eunuchs can claim the dubious honor to compete in virtue with angels. An angelic world would be powerless to wrestle eternity from Death, the Grimmest Reaper of them all."

Sinan unable to argue he found advisable to issue another grim warning.

"Unfortunately, masters still have the power to turn their slaves into angels."

Ibrahim could now easily reach the end of his reasoning.

"Then our overlords are doomed to behave like animals, trying to make their slaves live like angels. And this is something that all slaves will never forget, when inevitably the time will come to be released from slavery."

Sinan realized the implication of his friend's promise so he added in good spirits:

"My master has shown me many times how to live like a man; so I cannot have another mission in the world but to try to teach him how to live like me."

Ibrahim could not restrain a smile. Sinan was a Janissary and he had been trained to behave in a certain way, as the Janissary Corps had a strict code of ethics. Raising in its ranks meant Sinan had been efficient in his duties. However, somehow he was not the same man any longer. He was undergoing a process of transformation. Unquestionably, he had been following Selim's orders in the past, but now he was gradually turning from a destroyer into a builder. He was undergoing a change similar to what happened to wild trees after they were grafted.

Sinan was acknowledging Ibrahim's contribution to this change. Sinan was also man enough to admit it. Offering him the opportunity to build his palace, he had opened new vistas to his career as an engineer and their travels in Egypt had broaden his horizons. Now the only gift possibly missing from the Janissary's life was the pollen of love. His life should not be wasted. He had to sow children and to vaccinate ordinary people even without them knowing it. Perhaps talented people like Sinan had him as a role model, but being so self-conscious, he had failed to notice it. He was indeed a fool thinking that his deeds passed unnoticed.

Unquestionably, the Ottoman Empire had a Sultan at its tip; but the tip of the sword was good only for piercing. In a yatagan, the Janissary main weapon, the most deadly edge was the curved blade. It was the only part that could slash a chain mail. If a Sultan was great, then the Empire would grow; but if he was weak or ill, then the Grand Vizier could step in and carry the burden. This was his greatest achievement.

He turned his gaze to the few graves stacked on the side of the mosque. They were all threadbare and frayed with blackened tombstones from moisture and decay. Life was a challenge, a thrilling experience as magnificent as a bird struggling to fly; but there were also cosmic forces trying to keep it a prisoner, to force it to crawl like a worm on the ground from one black hole to the next. Only death in the end like an accurate scale could measure the actual weight of every human life, even when the grave had been erased from the memory of the children. It was really a shame that in this world there was nothing else that kept records of the lives of ordinary people who toiled on the soil, apart from some common words engraved on tombstones. How could an entire life of a human being be enclosed in a few words?

Unexpectedly he felt goosebumps and spontaneously looked for the exit iron gate.

"Only the ordinary lives of ordinary people can be exposed in a few words chiseled on a tombstone. For us, the precious few, History will speak much more eloquently. Something inside me says that when our time will come, your stones will be valued more dearly than any of my kisses," Ibrahim pointedly noticed. "History is always written by the masters, and all of them have something of Cheops' weakness; so, do not despair, my friend. Sooner or later the Sultan will appreciate also the value of the stones."

Ibrahim was right, Sinan considered. This was the way Allah had molded people. As Suleiman gradually realized his strength was weakening, and death was approaching, he was bound to look after his legacy the same way his father and mother had done before him. The stone was the best material to challenge eternity and entice people to remember a man's deeds. After the season of pleasure, the era of marble would infect even a magnificent Sultan.

Sinan was few years older than the Sultan and the Grand Vizier, but he was their servant and had to wait for his turn. However, by being older he had an advantage. He knew better than anyone of them what a man would have to face through this transition, when a proud man would have to step down and allow a younger man to take his place. Ibrahim was his friend and patron; so he had to be warned that he was threading on a dangerous path.

The Bailo's palace had always been under the gaze of the Sultan. Any mighty Khan had to be aware who was in contact with his enemies. Ibrahim could easily justify a short nightly visit in a Venetian residence. He did not stay there for more than an hour, but his early bird waking up in a notorious locanda would be far more difficult to explain. Sinan didn't wish to reveal the fact he had been following his master since he left the Seraglio last evening, but he couldn't remain silent either.

"Until the moment a sick Sultan's heart turns into stone, all his intimate friends should keep a safe distance especially at night. Everyone knows that in his harem there is a Sultana who is very jealous of any competitor sharing his precious time with her."

Ibrahim was well aware of the dangers, but he had chosen to ignore them. Suddenly his patience was exhausted too as much as Hurrem's. Hastily he said goodbye and took the slippery slope towards the harbor at a faster pace. Sinan kept looking at him until he disappeared into the crowd slipping down the slope like a mighty torrent. Maybe something deep inside him magically revealed this would be the last time he saw his master alive, and he needed to absorb enough of his precious essence.

****

She was well accustomed by now to surprise eunuchs with her bold inquiries, and the Kislar Aga had no drastically different attitude. In fact, his well-concealed masculinity made him her most favorite tease.

"I wonder what kind of punishment my husband will inflict to a eunuch in his harem when he finds out he is not sufficiently cut. Do you know if this has ever happened before?"

"Yes! It did happen few years back when another Negro Kislar Aga managed, who knows how, to sneak in the Eski Saray and become rich with concubines' presents."

"Yes, you are right! Now I remember. Few eunuchs are simply too greedy for their own good; but I wonder how he did it. Do you by any chance know how this deception was carried out, so it will never happen again within these walls? I have a young daughter who is coming of age, and I must do whatever it's needed to protect her from any nasty surprise. Virgins are very impressionable creatures you know. Who knows what kind of illusive dreams about men an encounter with a naked man might entice."

Hurrem was indeed in a teasing mood, but it was her turn to be surprised by the dubious explanation she heard. According a rumor there were few well-trained men that could exert with their belly muscles exceedingly powerful suction that concealed their true nature.

"Nonsense. It must be one of these farfetched rumors I hear every once in a while within the Harem walls. I won't believe it no matter what you say, unless I see with my own eyes how skillful the Nubian men in your tribe really are," she insisted, and she had the looks of a woman who would not back up in front of any man especially a slave.

"In my village men don't practice such skills. They never try to hide their manhood. On the contrary, we trust that with the women of our tribe our luck will improve as we grow."

"Don't be impertinent with me. I'm the Sultan's Birinci Kadin, and Allah punishes everyone who does not respects certain limits," Hurrem replied with pretentious anger.

"I meant no disrespect, as my mistress is not a member of my tribe. Her skin is also more white than the goat milk she bathes in," the Kislar Aga snapped back winning a giggle full of pride from his mistress that didn't last long as he decided he had enough of her tease and challenged her.

"Allah has made the world so that different tribes have different customs. In my tribe men consider black women more desirable. Their scent is also more attractive for us men, especially when they are in heat. Then, they are truly irresistible."

It was a challenge Hurrem was not in the mood to leave unanswered.

"I don't believe you. I have seen how you look at me when I bathe; so don't lie to me. All black eunuchs I have ever met would love to fuck me, but they can't."

It was a challenge he was not in the mood to leave unanswered.

"Yes, but I can. This is the invitation I read in your eyes."

"Yes, you are certainly a stronger man than me and you could probably force my submission; but if you try to rape me, your head might fall. I despise rapists," she threatened him, but it was more of a challenge, and he was enough of a man to know the difference.

She knew it too, but it was not yet the right time for her to experience his male superiority. Her worst fear with men was that she might get hooked, and then everything she had done to gain her freedom to choose would be lost.

"Tonight I have the craziest fear. I dread a man will find me sleeping naked and will use you me as if I was his whore; but all my servants should realize that I'm not a whore. I also don't like any slave to die because of his desire for my flesh. So please stay guard for me tonight, and I will never forget it. No one who has served me has not been rewarded to his heart content."

****

An idea entered uninvited Ibrahim's mind. He turned back to see if anyone was following him. Inside the early morning crowd that rushed down the slopes towards the harbor, it was impossible to recognize any face. Perhaps, he thought, instead of stopping and turning around so often, it would be a better idea to go through the Perfume Bazaar close to the old Venetian Harbor at the other bank of the Golden Horn. The shops there would be a good excuse, if anyone had seen him wandering in the streets so early in the morning. Then, he would go straight to the Sublime Gate to work just in time for his daily schedule.

Arriving at the bench in front of a perfume trader, he asked for a bottle of jasmine oil without much thought. Jasmin was his favorite scent since the first day he set foot in the Aga hammam in the Seraglio, when Selim Khan was still the Padisah; but unexpectedly the storekeeper looked at him in a weird way, and did not try to fulfil his order.

He felt his mind flare up with anger, as nothing that day went according to his wishes. Nevertheless, he tried to remain calm, because he did not wish to attract the attention of the other customers. He could have easily terrified the merchant, if he uncovered his identity, but this was the last he wished to happen.

"What is wrong with my order. Is there a shortage of jasmine oil?" Ibrahim asked with feigned indifference, and the merchant looked at him carefully from head to toe, as if he was a troublemaker; but he quickly changed his manner when he saw on Ibrahim's fingers his expensive rings. More relaxed then he asked with some concern:

"You must be a foreigner, otherwise you ought to know our all-wise Sultan has recently prohibited all jasmine scents to be sold to true men. You are not a white eunuch, are you?"

"No, not yet. I'm not so old to lose all interest. Why do you ask?"

"You are dressed well, you are very attractive, and you ask for jasmine oil. That's why! Am I wrong?" the storekeeper explained and twisted his brushy moustache like a seasoned Janissary.

"You are attractive too, but today I am in the mood to buy just some jasmine oil and nothing else," Ibrahim retorted flattered by the comment.

Ibrahim Pasha had never visited the Perfume Bazaar to shop, because white eunuchs always bought all the perfumes, oils, and soaps used in the Seraglio. They also bought all the fabrics and most of the jewels the Sultan wore, and he had blindly followed this imperial tradition in his palace too. Unquestionably, eunuchs had better tastes in every item related to pleasing human senses, or at least this was the general consensus in the Eternal City since the Roman days. Until now he had no objection following their fashionable suggestions.

By this short delay in his response Ibrahim gave the merchant more time to provide few more explanations. Recently in the imperial capital, jasmine products could be bought only by women and eunuchs. Sheikh-ul-Islam had warned the Sultan that men lost their male vigor, if they used jasmine oils day after day; so a firman was signed by the Sultan no merchant dared to disobey and put the future of the Ottoman armies in peril.

Ibrahim could not contain a giggle, but seeing the merchant's facial expression to his reaction, he decided that it would be safer if he asked for an alternative legal oil fit for true Ottomans. The seller, rather relieved, suggested cypress oil that was recently very fashionable.

"Why is that?" Ibrahim inquired.

"Don't you know?" the merchant wondered. "Only unsophisticated mountain shepherds do not know that galley masts are made of cypresses!"

****

"What should I do with you?" Hurrem rhetorically asked.

"Cut my head for trying to rape you in your sleep, what else?" the Kislar Aga replied teasing her.

"No, I cannot do that. You didn't rape me. Your urge just flattered me. It was Allah's will to test my fidelity during Ramadan."

"No, Allah had nothing to do with my urge. I was just my response to your open invitation from the very first day my mistress set her eyes on me, her most obedient slave."

"That may not be such a vicious slander as it seems first hand. Long time ago I used to have a Negro master, when I was still dancing in Galata. He was so possessive and violent, there was no way I could refuse to follow his wishes and risk a whipping that could mark my skin forever, ruining all my chances for riches and prosperity. Thank Allah he had also other slaves under his wings and rarely asked for me. I wonder if the late Kislar Aga knew that, when he bought me long time ago. Kismet plays very complicated tricks with the lives of certain people no one can predict in advance. Are you aware of any such rumor about my past?"

"No; but if the late Kislar Aga knew anything, then the Grand Vizier must have also known of them, when he put me in this post to temp you."

"I always thought that the Sultan was responsible for your transfer to the Eski Saray. If what you say it's true, then I must thank the Grand Vizier for this most useful present."

"Everybody knows the Sultan does not do anything without Ibrahim Pasha's agreement. The Sultan has sworn in public that everything the Grand Vizier says comes out of his mouth too. They are very close friends after all, and they used to spend many nights together, talking from midnight till morning. Everybody wonders what they were talking about for so long, but I have a suspicion all they talk is about naughty women. Men are very lusty, and Ibrahim Pasha is one of the worse. You will not believe what my spies in his palace tell me. He is almost as lusty as a Nubian slave. Trust my words! I know of men much more than I know of women. Women have to limit the chances of a pregnancy, after all."

"I trust your advice, but you have to understand that whatever happened tonight between us was an exception, not the rule. The rule is that you are my slave, and you are obliged to follow my orders, not I yours. Then, if I'm fully satisfied with your deeds, I might consider giving you a bonus, when I'm in the mood."

"Trust that I will obey your wishes. For me you are my other Sultan and Allah's Shadow."

"No, today I have proved to you that I'm much more than that. I'm the woman of your dreams; but now cover up your nudity. The Sultan maybe on his way to visit me. Anyway, it's not to your advantage, if I ever become used to your looks."

"Then, it might be better if your Majesty covered her nudity too."

"Yes, it might be, but I'm not yet sure. When I'm not sure, I prefer to do nothing."

****

Half way home Ibrahim changed his mind. It might be advantageous if he talked to the Sultan before anyone else; however, the white eunuchs guarding his door told him that his master was visiting the Fatih mosque for the glorification of the Ramadan ceremonies following a Seih-ul-Islam suggestion. Rumors had leaked that a firman was about to be signed that made Muslims equal to Christians, and he had to display his unshaken Islamic faith.

Perhaps the best thing Ibrahim could do was to meet his Princess. His empty bed must have been reported to her by now. The Sultan should have to wait for him. All things considered, Suleiman was the one who had the patience to fast for a month to ensure Allah salvation of his soul. During his entire life he had never been truly patient. He was not like Sinan. He had to constantly advance and to achieve this goal he was willing to forgive himself for every compromise he had to endure. When he grew really old, he would have plenty of time to regret for his sinful deeds and this was his most frequent excuse.

****

When Ibrahim arrived hastily and panting to his palace, he found Hatidge lying onto fluffy pillows under the garden trees, waiting for his arrival. Spring was arriving and on the tree branches the first leaves were shyly peeping at the warm sunlight. They were still sparse and their shadows did not obstruct sun's warmth most welcomed after a cold winter. At her feet her two favorite courtiers were seated staring at her eyes, waiting to hear her orders; but for some time they were listening only to polite requests. Eros had put the slaves to the same level as their mistress, and she had to ask for their consent.

Amongst the wild flowers that lifted their heads after the first spring rains, his two children played with abandon, making unique creatures of their imagination with mud. Unseen a third baby kicked inside Basmi's womb trying to come out too. It was as if Olympian goddesses walked on the Earth once more transforming mud into flesh and bones.

Seeing their unbending conviction to proliferate, he felt embarrassed by his own weaknesses. He had needlessly lost much of his life chasing illusive chimeras. The only option he had now that made any sense was to reside in his palace by their side to make sure they were protected from the kind of weaknesses that had kept him slave from the first moment he set foot in the Eternal City. His mind flew to the words of Sinan. It was never too late to start war with himself. He wanted to meet and tell him that he was right suggesting he ought to start the great war every man had to win to earn the eternal peace of his soul; but, he didn't feel this need particularly pressing. Tomorrow was always another day.

The voice of his Princess dispersed his thoughts.

"My dear, I hope your bed tonight was not as cold as mine to seek the company of slaves."

Ibrahim stood once again startled and embarrassed in front of her, and the color of shame dyed his cheeks red. In the past, he had spent innumerous nights away from her on campaigns and missions entrusted to him much too often by his master. Was last night's absence a mere coincidence or something more serious?

Her smile gave him courage to answer vaguely: "Always sleeping away from you is a test, a power struggle between daily duty and the pressing desire to get lost in the ocean of your kisses."

Hatidge did not change even for a moment her grim expression, but light suddenly illuminated her complexion. Maybe it was just a thought or a playful sunray had found a path through the foliage.

"As time goes by, I feel greater the need to hear your breath next to my ear whenever I sleep. The tenderness of my favorite consorts' caresses is no longer adequate to fill the voids inside of me."

Ibrahim didn't need to hear much more to sense the nature of her decisions. He also felt that morning his guts flooding by the very same feeling. Unconsciously he let his gaze wander over her expanding body. Inside her was the mold of his future, his son, just as his mother had been his creator. These two precious women were the only gods a man ought to believe in.

He looked into her eyes with adoration. His only hope for freedom was to delay his total submission to an ardent desire for unconditional surrender to her wishes. He turned over seeking help from the other two pairs of eyes that were fixed on his. The two slaves also waited nervously to hear what kind of future was in store for them. He was momentarily concerned, as for nothing in the world he wanted to be deprived of their love.

The Princess easily discerned the cause of his reluctance. In the past he had faced similar dilemmas, but now she felt he had to reach a final decision. She was a Turk and she understood that his numerous adventures were not the result of a secret weakness of her man, but the irrefutable proof of his vital force. It was the force ensuring her that after the most bloody battle, if only one man was left alive, her breed could be reborn from its ashes. He was not raising after all any unreasonable demands, and the wisdom of Oriental women was secretly guiding her steps to paths unknown in the Christian world of the Occident. From similar roots had sprung all the world conquerors Christians in Europe trembled. Her brother had proved unworthy of his legacy. He had fallen prisoner to an unyielding Russian conqueror and sooner or later he would have to face the consequences of his unconditional surrender.

Her smile became wider and it was miraculously reflected on the lips of her two consorts.

"Do not worry! I am not such a foolish ruler to turn my embrace into a cage, and have my favorite nightingale fade away prematurely."

****

Entering his bedroom, Suleiman didn't expect to find Hurrem lying naked on his bed, but his surprise grew even greater when she ordered with a nod the Kislar Aga standing by the door to leave the room. During the past few years, she had earned the special privilege to spend most of the nights of the Ramadan month alone with the Sultan, as the other two Kadin had practically disappeared from his life. The Sultan could find excuses to stay alone with Ibrahim until dawn only through very few nights this month. This year, however, up to that moment it seemed she had lost only a single night, and the excuse of the alliance treaty was credible.

She had gathered up all her hair to look slimmer and less feminine, and she was lying on her breasts to hide most of her weapons; however, this was just a wild guess, because exposing her attractive backside might mean she was in no mood to risk

515

another pregnancy. What was the meaning of the Kislar Aga's presence she didn't appear willing to explain, forcing him to ask for an explanation; but, she brushed aside his request with a tease.

"Are you jealous of a Nubian slave? I don't see anything he has that you don't. The only difference I see is that he is not a pious Muslim, and he has no reason to observe the Ramadan fasting. Poor Negro pagans, you will never be admitted into Allah's Paradise unless you are castrated."

It was clear she was trying to provoke a confrontation, but he was not up to it. His long ride to the Fatih Mosque and back had provoked a new pain attack on his foot. She sensed his discomfort and press forward her advantage. She turned around now that the Kislar Aga was gone, and begun her second phase of tease.

"Which side of mine pleases you more? I have no preference. It's all up to you," she subtly proposed with an elusive air of submissiveness, but quite astonished he failed to reply.

"The Kislar Aga always flatters me that my back side is my best asset, but I'm sure he is not just trying to flatter me. After all black women have bigger asses than me. Mine is more like a youngster's. What do you think? Muslim men have much greater experience than any woman on the subject. I'm sure if your father was here, he would punish severely my audacity, so that I wouldn't dare to ask again such naughty questions. He was a true leader of men and no one dared to disobey him. Please tell me now, has Ibrahim Pasha ever dared to disobey you?"

"No, he hasn't, but sometimes he takes initiatives I don't really concur."

"Then please tell me, have you ever ordered him to sleep with another man to test his obedience?"

"Why should I demand such a thing from a friend?"

"Just to tease him and see if he is as obedient as a slave should be."

"You seem to forget Ibrahim Pasha is my friend and the husband of my sister. Why should I wish to insult him?"

"You have insulted him much more by giving him the Kislar Aga as a slave; but I have to admit Ibrahim Pasha is a difficult man to offend. His consciousness is as malleable as plaster."

"That's true; but if your hands are skillful, you can shape him into a piece of art. There are not many men like him in my empire," Suleiman explained.

"Is this what makes him so desirable to my master?" Hurrem inquired startled by the Sultan's unexpected revelation, but Suleiman refused to be submitted to such a demeaning interrogation.

****

"So what's your final answer?" the Princess inquired resuming her impartial attitude, but her previous confession of interest had been the key Ibrahim needed to break out of a lifelong prison term.

He had to admit her logic was unshakable. Only an insane man would choose a risky exception than the safety of the rule. A Sultan could afford to be greedy because he was the Shadow of Allah and had every right to demand everything; but he was just a human being and should try to be happy just by being a man and the husband of a Princess.

"Then, let's go to Egypt. An Ottoman princess should not have to spend her entire life in Constantinople. The world is full of miracles that wait for her to experience. The ancient Egyptians claimed that following the River Nile to its source, we will reach Allah's harem Eden."

****

"My dear husband, for me it may be enough, if I know that you love me, even when I don't see you every day; but don't you think it would be better for our kids to see how much their father adores their mother? Before answering me, try to remember how you felt, seeing your father surrounded by all these degenerate white eunuchs."

It was a rather unusual question that forced Suleiman to think carefully before replying. He did remember that he felt uncomfortably, but before admitting it, he had to discover what was the final purpose of all these questions.

"Eunuchs were always a significant portion of a Sultan's servants. They may be a nuisance; but my subjects would feel strangely, if they knew their Sultan was surrounded by true men. Eunuch pages are an old Ottoman tradition."

"And I say eunuch pages are very inferior to women courtiers. Women are much more submissive and tender than men. You wouldn't become as jealous, if a courtier was here instead of the Kislar Aga, admit it! In the back of your mind there is always the ludicrous suspicion that a eunuch may one day become bold enough to lay his hands on your Kadin, especially if you don't invite her often to your chambers."

"I have to admit this thought has never occurred to me. Perhaps you are much more devious than me or my ancestors," Suleiman noted ironically.

"Perhaps I am also more frustrated, but if this is so, it is all your doing. I am more submissive to your will than Ibrahim Pasha; so it's natural for any soft plaster to seek skillful fingers to turn it into a piece of art, as you so have eloquently described."

"What are you implying? Has this audacious Negro laid a hand on you?"

"Why are you so eager to pose such naughty questions? Are you so jealous of me that you cannot stand the thought that a Kadin of yours may be inviting lusty black eunuchs in her chambers, when you are not visiting the Eski Saray? If this is so, then you should invite me to reside in the Seraglio, so you can have white eunuchs permanently guarding me, when you are in pain and unable to visit me. Suspicions can make any one's life miserable much more than a temporary sickness."

Now it was clear where she was aiming at. She tried to make him jealous by suggesting the black eunuchs of the Eski Saray were more licentious than the white ones. Her ultimate goal was to reside in the Seraglio, so that she could monitor more directly who his visitors were. Perhaps few years back, this was a worthwhile goal, but since Ibrahim's marriage and the deterioration of his health, he didn't have the energy to be naughty with anyone, not Ibrahim, not even her.

"I was thinking about such a possibility much earlier than you. In fact, asking you to spend the Ramadan month in the Seraglio was a test to see how such a cohabitation might work sufficiently well for both of us. Soon enough this holy month will be over, and then I will let you know how this test has turned out."

"I didn't know I was on trial. If I knew, I would surely have tried to bribe the judge the moment the sun sets," she replied and her eyes sparkled. "In fact, for many years I haven't danced for you. Why don't you ask the Kislar Aga to brink his drum and play for us. Nubians are exceptional drummers too. Everyone knows that."

He knew that well indeed. He still remembered this Nubian beating his drum the night he had offered him to Ibrahim Pasha as a present to trigger his interest for black men. He also remembered his unexpected failure. With his slave friend he had much in common, so he had assumed Ibrahim would be as attracted as he had been by the shimmering black flesh and its seductive dancing figures. However, Ibrahim had surprised him, and still he couldn't really say if he was more attracted to his sister or to the higher social status the marriage with his sister offered.

"That's an excellent idea. Why doesn't he dance with you? I have seen him dance and play the drum at the same time. He is an excellent dancer," he proposed to pressure her.

She had to realize he knew much more than she thought. Of course, he was not Allah to know what exactly she had in her mind; but being His Shadow his knowledge was quite extensive. The rumor was that Ibrahim had used the Nubian as a Black Eunuch in his harem. Turning the Nubian into his Kislar Aga was his mother's suggestion, and she was his Valide Sultan responsible for his harem. She must have been aware of the slave's exact physical condition, as a Sultan was simply too important to be concerned with a slave's manhood.

Hurrem suddenly got worried. Her tease had suddenly got out of hand.

"We don't need him, after all. I wish to dance naked for you, and I would feel embarrassed, if I had his eyes staring at me, while I try hard to excite you."

"Why, he is just a eunuch and he must have seen you naked many times before in the hammam," Suleiman noted indifferently.

"Yes, indeed he has; but he has never seen me dancing. I have few new figures in mind that only my husband should see. I'm his Kadin and it's his privilege. He should not share it with a page, because this will make his Kadin feel even cheaper than a concubine. Is this how you want the mother of your sons to feel tonight?"

He had to admit she was good in finding good excuses; but her effort was adding fuel to his jealousy. There was a scent in the air that smelled of debauchery, and he had to find out sooner or later. Sooner was better, because his patience was coming to an end.

"No, I don't wish to offend you as much as I didn't wish to offend Ibrahim Pasha with my present. I was only testing you. Why don't you get dressed, and then I will invite this Aga and ask him to dance for us naked. Have you ever seen a eunuch dance naked? People who visit Galata say it is quite a spectacle. Their moves are as exciting as any female dancer's."

Suleiman seemed impatient to reach a conclusion. He was essentially challenging her. She was confident she was a much better dancer than any damn eunuch, but the Kislar Aga was a blessed male. She could always argue she was not aware of the fact and blame Ibrahim for allowing an uncut man to enter the Eski Saray. Hafsa Hatun had made this proposal to make her life difficult, but she was dead and buried, while Ibrahim was alive and quite active. This test might turn to her advantage after all.

"Are you sure he is completely cut? There are all sorts of eunuchs these days. The rumor says that he was made impotent by Ibrahim Pasha, before turning him into a Kislar Aga, but who knows exactly what was his final decision. As everyone knows, Ibrahim Pasha is a very forgiving man who hates spilling blood; so, he may have just squeezed his balls like a pig. If you like the spectacle, you may watch him dancing naked, but I promise you will keep my eyes closed, so I will not be offended. After all it is Ramadan and I must keep my dreams pure."

He had to admit she was very clever. She could twist every issue and turn it to her advantage. This time she had transformed her ordeal into a test of his purity. Seating next to him, she could easily reach and test the effect the Nubian's dance might have on his flesh. Life had suddenly become very complicated, but a Sultan had to know as much as possible to be safe from any form of conspiracy. This had been Selim Khan's final advice. He had to be aware of the existing reality and then act accordingly, because by the time a conspiracy materialized, it might be too late to save his throne. This had to be his first and final concern.

****

She had to admit that when he was under pressure his will was strong enough despite his illness. He watched the Kislar Aga sensual dance half-naked, calm and secluded, smoking his nargileh with Olympian calmness. She had to admit also that the Kislar Aga was a great dancer that could have an illustrious career in a Galata tavern too; but talented or extremely endowed people very rarely failed to be noticed in Constantinople, when they were under the public eye.

Beautiful slave women were mostly bought and turned exclusively into concubines of rich Pashas and merchants, but young men could pursue different careers. If they had an impressive and ragged physic, they were bought by the Sultan and normally turned into fearsome Janissaries. However, if they were both attractive and intelligent, they were turned into pages, or eunuchs serving the Sultan. Ibrahim had managed better than anyone else. Besides his diplomatic and military talents, the reason was probably his utter submissiveness at the very beginning. She well-aware this was just a front he had used to become Suleiman's Hasodabashi. When he was sure of his status, he had changed his appeal and many members of the Harem fell for his charms, even few adventurous eunuchs.

Ibrahim had become a legend in the Harem, but the moment a man become a legend, it was very difficult even for her to discern the truth from the exaggeration. Her mind operated according to her experiences, and she had to admit a woman could not remain for long in the same room with Ibrahim, without getting few very naughty ideas.

Suleiman was a man, but it was clear he was attracted to men too. She could see it with her own eyes that despite his calmness, the Aga's sensuous dance had an effect on him. What she didn't expect was that the Chief of the Black Eunuchs was also aroused by his own dancing.

It had to be the result of his tribal past. For him most of the dances he performed were to expose his assets to the females of his tribe. Then after the ceremonial dance, the lust generated was used for a good cause, the proliferation of the tribe.

She had supposedly her eyes closed, but by seating on the left side of the Sultan, she could open her left eye, when she felt curious enough. Suleiman had his eyes half-closed too, but his excuse was obvious. In the nargileh bowl a pinch of opium was added. After a while she became so excited she asked for a few deep nargileh draughts to set her imagination free too.

****

When she came back to her senses, she was laying naked on the Sultan's bed. The Kislar Aga had disappeared like a genie in a bottle. She was not used to opium, since Hafsa Sultan didn't allow any Kadin that might get pregnant to smoke narcotics. She used to say that her grandchildren had to be born bright and alert.

The grandmother had done her best, but their father had failed them. It was not entirely his mistake. The gout crises he experienced were hereditary and had no cure. When he was in pain, opium offered a relief. She needed a relief too from the excitement of the Nubian. All his dancing figures had one goal, turn the women of his tribe on. This was what he tried to imply jumping up and down at the very beginning. When this goal was achieved, he had started moving his hips bac and forth to project the obvious implications. He was a man after all and had to impress even the most attractive and discriminating virgins of his tribe. Compared to them she was a pushover. During the Ramadan, she was aroused even by the thought.

It was very fortunate the Kislar Aga had departed. She had an instinctive fear, Suleiman could sense the true extend of her excitement almost as accurately as she could measure his.

"I must have fallen asleep. Please, come lie next to me. I feel terribly lonely. Who took my clothes off?"

"Who do you think?" he asked her with a teasing attitude.

"You, of course! Who else would dare to touch me?" she replied full of confidence.

"No, I didn't do this menial duty. I have servants for this kind of duties," he calmly explained. "I bet my Kislar Aga has undressed many times not only you, but most of my concubines in the Eski Saray and perhaps my wild Tatar Kadin too."

He was playing cat and mouse with her for a change and he was thoroughly enjoying it. To pretend she was not aware of the difference between a man and a eunuch would offend his intelligence, so she didn't make that mistake.

"Yes, he has! Why shouldn't he? He may be a slave, but he is a man too. He has shown great compassion for all your concubines through all your crazy wars. Most of them have lost all hopes to become mothers. Only a very cruel man like you would deny a woman the possibility of having a child. How don't you let them free to find a man, any man? For many of them even a Nubian slave would make a good father, if you were willing to let them free to do as they please. If I were you, I would empty the Eski Saray from every concubine by the end of the Ramadan. They are all too rapacious for you and too old to please your sons. Mehmet and Selim will soon become of age, and then we'll need many empty rooms for their harems."

It was fairly obvious she was trying to change the subject from the presence of the Kislar Aga to Ibrahim's infidelity. It was unfair for him to start blaming her for the Nubian's presence in his harem, because he had already admit it. He was also the one who had tried to make him the Kislar Aga of Ibrahim's Palace. His only excuse was that he was the Sultan and the Shadow of Allah. Only Allah could judge him on his way to the Paradise; but now he was still alive, so even Allah couldn't blame him for anything.

"I know of a better way to empty the Eski Saray, if I so desire. I can send all these unhappy concubines to the bottom of the Bosporus," he threatened.

"Yes, you most certainly can do that, but then you would be a cruel murderer, not the benevolent Shadow of Allah. I believe you have to be fair and sincere with them. They have done nothing more than me or you. You were the one who allowed another man to undress me. Why did you do that? Were you trying to disgrace your loyal Kadin?"

"No, this was not my intention; but I had to see with my own eyes how familiar was the Kislar Aga with performing this difficult task."

"And what's your impression?"

"He is very efficient in undressing women. You haven't lied to me on this subject."

"I have never lied to you. You know that. You simply have to ask me exactly what you need to know; but be careful not to offend my feelings. I'm still the mother of your sons."

"What's that supposed to mean?" he asked with aroused interest.

"It means that whatever you do to me, my children will seek vengeance."

"Are you threatening me?"

"No, of course not. How could a slave threaten the Shadow of Allah? I'm simply stating a fact. We are a family, so whatever I do to you, my children will take revenge on me too. This is what a family is all about. Ask Mustafa how he feels about his mother, if you don't believe me."

She was surely audacious and out of control, but in principle she was right. Almost all of his sons had her blood, and they all adored their mother who had earned their respect.

He was sickly and was approaching dangerously the age when his father and Mehmet Fatih had died. Women normally lived longer than men. This was another fact of life. If he executed her, soon he might be forced to execute his sons too. Then, he would have to face Mustafa and Mahidevran, and they were much more formidable opponents than Hurrem. He was cornered, and had to make concessions, for the sake of his legacy.

Hurrem saw the first signs of capitulation with the explosion of anger in his eyes. If the Vienna walls had forced his retreat, she could surely complete the same feat with her flesh.

"Why don't you seek the advice of your Grand Vizier? I'm sure he will convince you that your suspicions that perhaps I have permitted your Kislar Aga excessive liberties on my body are just another figment of your imagination. You may not realize it, but sickness makes men weak and weakness erodes a man's self-confidence. Then, all sick men start to imagine the women they love and who care for them are having affairs with their closest friends. Men are so imaginative sometimes it's scary. If you need reassurance of my love, all you have to do is to use me for your pleasure tonight, as if I was your whore. This Ramadan has lasted too long."

No man could stand up and face such a combination of arguments. She could also play the role of a prostitute better than any woman in his harem even now when she had stolen five children from his loins to achieve numerical superiority.

****

Hatidge Sultan appeared surprisingly accommodating to her husband.

"If this is your decision, then go to the Sultan tomorrow morning and tell him you need a long leave of absence. If he refuses to grant it, tell him that I had a nervous breakdown after finding out of your common affliction and asked you for a divorce. He will surely understand that we have to go on a trip to work out all the problems in our relationship."

Ibrahim was puzzled with her suggestion. Was she so deviously clever or was it a subtle threat to make him make up his mind?

Her reply was not exactly what he expected.

"Only if you intend to keep on seeing this handsome Venetian, you should consider it as a threat. As it is now, it is nothing more than an excuse for my brother, and I'm sure it will work out fine. He is very considerate, when it comes to members of his family he knows they love him. My mother was the best example. I'm sure he knew of your long visits to her quarters. He is also aware of your most common excuse, solving sensitive matters of state. Sometimes I wonder who are you trying to fool. If you cannot fool me, what kind of chance you think you have against the Sultan. If he so desires, he can get the most out of anyone with the treat of the Mutes. No one is willing to play dice with his life these days, do you?"

****

526

Suleiman seemed so weak after her thorough exploitation, Hurrem decided it was the right time to push him a bit more. She had to strike the steel when it was hot to make it harder. From the moment he had accepted the remote possibility the Kislar Aga had a taste of her flesh, the Sultan would not react to the next revelation.

"When tomorrow morning Ibrahim Pasha comes asking for your signature on the peace treaty, don't forget to test how deep his concessions to the Venetian demands have gone. Was it just a kiss, as the rumors claim, or something naughtier? Ibrahim Pasha is so submissive to your orders, I sincerely do not know, if he didn't act always following faithfully your sensations. Men are so easily convinced to surrender everything and there are no consequences after nine months. This is probably why men visit steam baths so often. It is also the reason why all diplomates belong to the male gender. You men simply love the negotiation process."

"What exactly do you mean?" he dared to ask with a trembling voice.

His weakness was now evident to a naked eye. The only issue that was still lingering was if his exhaustion was the result of his illness or her debauchery.

****

In his troubled mind confused thoughts and mixed feelings roamed unhindered. He was deeply shocked when he heard the daily report of the slave who followed the Grand Vizier's every step for many years. He described the visit to Bailo's palace and his departure, the entrance to the inn and finally the Venetian's passionate farewell kiss. What else had happened behind the walls he could see only with his imagination, and he could not accept it.

On the other hand, he had absolute confidence in his spies. No one would ever dare to tell such a lie, risking his head for a bribe. What now he ought to digest, was that Ibrahim had violated the unwritten oath that each slave is loyal and serves only his master. He had been for a few hours the slave of another man who was younger and much more attractive, and by now he might be swayed to start another relationship. The way the Venetian had stolen the kiss at the threshold without paying any attention to the eyes of passers-by could mean nothing else.

He simply could not accept the new reality that loomed threatening his future.

****

Hurrem interrupted once again his thoughts uninvited and her words sounded as unbending as if she was leading a charge of the ironclad Christian cavalry against him. If she was not present this morning, it might have been easier for him to push the spy's report behind him. As it was now he couldn't pretend nothing happened, and she knew how to hurt him more, so he would never forget the insult.

"I'm not the least surprised by Ibrahim's behavior and so should you. This man is completely unreliable and unfaithful. You have to do something to put him under control unless, of course, you want Ibrahim and your nephews with Greek blood to finally get their hands on the Osman legacy and ruin your family's good reputation."

Suleiman felt the blood pressure rise inside his temples, but he couldn't react or explode his anger. He had been betrayed and he had to do something about it. This was the meaning of Hurrem's glance even though her lips said nothing, waiting for his decision that never came. However, she simply could not contain her anxiety any longer and took control of the situation with another bold stroke.

"I wonder what would have happened to me if you burst one night suddenly into my bedroom uninvited and found me naked in the arms of my Kislar Aga. Would you look the other way pretending nothing happened, or would you take your mighty sword of your father, and cut both our heads for our despicable betrayal?"

It was clearly a rhetorical question he felt he didn't have to answer, but she wouldn't accept such a compromise.

"What kind of excuses would you find for our licentious behavior? Was it because springtime make women and men more voracious than normal? Was this just another case of mistaken identity quite common between black slaves and white sluts under the cover of darkness? No, of course not! These would have been the excuses of commoners, not a Grand Vizier and a Serasker. I suspect he would claim that it was simply another case of long and tiring negotiations, when a sign of good faith more intimate than a signature had to be provided to seal the secret agreement. Everyone knows that treaties between nations have a lot in common with marriages. They can only be legalized by a passionate kiss at the end of the ceremony."

She was hitting hard and he should expect that. His relationship with Ibrahim had offended her time after time, so many grudges and unrealized hopes had accumulated through the years. The fact his meetings with him had become sparse did not mean much for her. The sparseness might well be a sign of aging or the effects of his illness that deteriorated his overall attitude, turning him gradually into a loner and a hermit.

Ibrahim was unquestionably alive and well, and his raunchy attitude signified his need to seek fulfillment in the arms of other men. There was no way for him to deny this fact. His illness had effectively aged him, and his lover had no patience to endure for much longer this separation. Hurrem was not unreasonable or audaciously profane making these comments. Was she warning him that if he didn't get well soon, she would follow Ibrahim's example and seek another lover?

No matter how strict the measures of security in the Eski Saray were, it was always possible for an inmate of a prison to seek pleasure in the arms of his warden. Ibrahim had no similar restrictions and last night he found fulfillment in the arms of younger man rather than his, a painfully plain case of betrayal. From an early age he was brought up listening everyone talk about the sacred blood of his generation Osman, and how it circulated in his veins going from father to son unaltered, the same way the blood of a stallion reached its colts without mixing with the blood of the mare. Now that he was older, he had doubts and Ibrahim was the man who had raised them, arguing many times about mules.

As far as he knew, if a mule was born by a mare, it was big and strong like a horse; but if a female donkey was its mother, then it would grow much smaller than the father, but resilient like a donkey. This was a clear sign the mother's blood and womb had too much to contribute.

Were his sons destined to become slaves like their mother or world conquerors like him? Was Ibrahim's son a true son of a Princess and the true heir of Osman's blood? The birth of Gihangir was a sign his sons had ceased to bear his marks; but it might as well be a sign he was getting old and had to be replaced by a younger stallion; otherwise, the Osman stable would suffer. Ibrahim's betrayal could mean nothing else that a conspiracy was brewing.

Ibrahim was the most distinguished man and had the greatest self-confidence in the Ottoman Empire. Hurrem had every right to push him into making a decision. Ibrahim had betrayed his religion too by becoming a Muslim; but for him Islam was just a front, a tool to use for achieving his goals. His preference for Mustafa was also well-reported and his frequent visits to Manisa in the past were well-known. The excuse of giving lessons of administration to his presumed heir too feeble to be believed at face value.

He turned and looked at Hurrem zephyr eyes. What would be her response, if he died prematurely? Then, Mustafa would enter triumphantly the Seraglio, and claim all his possessions. Even Ibrahim had a claim on his throne through his son. None of his sons besides Mustafa could resist the claims of a magnificent and powerful Grand Vizier. Even if he didn't die but was incapacitated, the Janissaries would have no difficulty or moral doubts putting in jail in the Yedikule Castle any Sultan unable to lead them into victories. During the last riot, he was able to control their wrath only by striking the leaders with his sword on horseback. If today the same riot occurred, he would be unable even to ride a horse.

It was questionable what his beloved Kadin would do, if he was locked in a cage like his great-great-grandfather Yildirim Bayezid. Who would she have to serve wine or dance naked, Mustafa or Ibrahim Pasha? Ibrahim was without a doubt the most mature and immoral. His mother had denied the vicious rumors that Hurrem was a Galata dancer, when the Kislar Aga had bought her. She had assured him these claims were manufactured by the Tatar supporters of Mahidevran Sultan. Ibrahim had also pledged she was the daughter of a priest; but somehow the Kislar Aga who could ascertain the validity of all these claims had mysteriously disappeared.

Who was responsible for his demise, his mother, Ibrahim Pasha or perhaps Hurrem?

However, this was by now a meaningless old tale that had turned into a legend. Hurrem had made plain, he should not dare punish her without creating animosities with his four sons. Even his daughter Mihrimah he adored would surely turn against him, if he drown her mother in the Bosporus. He realized he was now all alone like a bear surrounded by hungry wolves. None of them had the capacity to deal the death blow, but if they all agreed to cooperate, they could easily topple him from the throne with the help of the Janissaries.

He read the answers to all these questions on her face. It had the identical expression during Ibrahim's wedding, when she removed her veil and offered to dance to entertain them. Back then her offer was not solely for his eyes. She wanted Ibrahim Pasha to see not only the color of her eyes, but her firm belly, her navel she kept hidden till then for the eyes of her master. A lot could happen during such a performance, if a dancer from a Galata tavern truly wished to attract the attention of the customers and men had drawn swords to earn favors.

Ibrahim used to invite many times dancers from across the Golden Horn, when they were young to entertain them during his nocturnal visits. It was a child's play for any such dancer eager to make few coins more to lower her salvar to allow a man's eyes to get a better glimpse of her buttocks or shake her breasts so hard to set them free from the confines of the brazier. From the moment certain women saw the shimmering of coins, they were willing to do just about anything to secure an extra tip from a delighted customer.

He was young and naïve at the time and he had asked many of them why they preferred dancing half-naked rather than marry a man, even a Janissary, and they all have told him they were trying to feed their children in difficult times. Would Hurrem do differently in their place?

Suddenly he felt anger and grievance drowning him. Only his mother he could trust, but now she was dead. Everyone else was like a jackal circling a sickly lion, trying to grab a piece of his prey. He ought to give everyone a lesson and show them he was aware of their tricks.

He looked at Hurrem with hatred. She was also like everyone else and she ought to go to the executioner too; but, as he saw with his imagination the splendor of her eyes extinguished, this horrifying picture somewhat softened his anger. He looked instead for excuses. He hadn't see anything with his own eyes, but only with his mind. He was Allah's Shadow and Allah the Benevolent waited after death to pass judgement. He ought to wait at least for his suspicions to be realized in her singular case. The presence of the Kislar Aga in the bedroom raised suspicions, but it was not a definite proof of infidelity.

However, his friend was guilty of treason and there were credible eyewitnesses of his guilt. Ibrahim's punishment would be the warning for everyone else who could not restrain his behavior by the context of the written and unwritten laws of men. Now all he had to do was choose the proper punishment for each one, so no one would claim he was unjust; but the Prophet Mohamed was not helpful in that respect. Stealing was unquestionably a sin but stealing a loaf of bread to feed your children was not enough of a crime to be punished in Hell.

Ibrahim many times before had raised the point of divine justice during his atheist claims. Allah's justice was too simpleminded to be considered divine, as even the pagan Romans applied much more sophisticated laws and punishments. If Allah had created flowers with such divine scents, colors, shapes and textures, why humans shouldn't have more intricate laws than just too extremes, Paradise or Hell?

The Shadow of Allah had to be fairer than the Romans. He first had to put Ibrahim on trial and then decide his fate depending on the findings. This was at least what Seih-Ul-Islam would do in his place. He immediately rejected the idea. Ibrahim Pasha could not be tried in public. His crimes were too personal, obscure and dishonorable to become widely known. For the time being most of them were mere suspicions; but even mentioning the possibility of a conspiracy could incite a Janissary rebellion.

****

Hurrem read the hesitation and the change of heart in Suleiman's in eyes. His feelings and unconquerable passion for the same gender was clouding his judgment. Suleiman's health was weakening day by day, so she had to act in his name.

Suddenly an evil idea crossed her mind. It was truly an ingenious idea worthy of an exceptional mind. What common minds call divine enlightenment, in reality it's just the necessary discontinuity in the smooth flow of thought, whenever the human mind fails to provide a solution and reaches a dead end. Simpleminded people could not escape the dead end, while brilliant minds could reach the solution the same way a thoroughbred stallion could jump over an obstacle insurmountable for a humble donkey.

"If I were you, I would be patient for a few more years to see, when he'll become bold enough to ask for his harem your only daughter."

He saw in his eyes she had hit the target. It was humanly impossible for Suleiman not to picture in his mind the image of Mihrimah in the arms of his lover. This combination was unbearable; but she had not yet said the last word. Now that his imagination wandered outside the harbor, she could more easily lead it where she wished.

"Do not imagine that I want you to punish him because I envy Ibrahim for sharing you with me every time he sneaks in the Seraglio through the small garden gate," she said. "This is an old story that after so many years does not amount much. Back then I was too young and unsophisticated. Now I know you are a man, and you can spread your seeds wherever you please like a true Ottoman. Besides, a slave can never raise such claims against his master."

Hurrem stopped and watch carefully if his anxiety had grown, and then took courage to continue her attack.

"Do you believe in dreams?" she rhetorically asked, since Muslims believed that an angel had visited the Prophet and dictated the Koran.

He nodded affirmatively and she was so pleased she had captured his undivided attention she confessed: "Recently I keep on seeing the same terrifying dream. This is why I don't feel safe unless someone is guarding me. I wish he was you, but tonight you were not available, so I had to invite the Kislar Aga to extinguish my fears."

"What is this terrifying dream?" he asked since he was often tortured by nightmares.

"I was only trying to put an end to my torture," she humbly confessed making a brief pause to prolong his agony for more details. "The nightmare actually started on the first night of

Ramadan and continued till last night. Every time I close my eyelids to go to sleep after my nightly prayer, I keep on seeing the same awful, degrading dream."

Her allusion brought immediately into mind his dreaming of Chelebi Pasha, and Hurrem realized her words had hit a sensitive spot in his mind, so she continued more confidently her narration to its conclusion.

"During Ramadan each night I have been seeing your dear friend sneaking in my room in the Eski Saray, wearing woman's clothes and jasmine perfume. Each time I freeze out of fear and stay still, unable even to flicker my eyelids; but he takes advantage of my passivity, and rips one by one all my clothes without giving any importance to my pleas. Then, without any rush, as if he enjoys his every move, he lies bare in front of me ready to pounce on top of me like a wild beast; but right then luckily I wake up, dripping sweat from anxiety. However, every time I see this dream, he comes closer and closer with red eyes blazing with passion. Last night he was at an arm's length, so if no valiant nobleman appears to stop him and protect me, this coming night he will surely get what he wants, and then how could I face my master, when I know that deep inside me another man has infected my body with his sperm? Of course, I realize that all this may be just a troubled dream of a woman who was forced to sleep for many nights alone without feeling inside her the fluttering wings of a lovebird; but people say that sometimes dreams have the power to warn us about oncoming events that no matter how foolish they seem in daylight, no one knows what's in store for us at nightfall. Who can really assure me that my dreams are nothing but the hidden desires of another man, who in his sleep has found unguarded the backdoor of my mind and ravaged it? This is the reason why I'm asking you to punish him once and for all, so that I will not dread each night you are not sleeping beside me in the Eski Saray that I might wake up at sunrise and find the traces a lusty intruder inside my womb."

Finishing her lively description she seemed content with her deed, but still Suleiman was skeptical. He wandered if every detail he had to listened to was truly a prelude of the future, or just the nightmares of his favorite Kadin that had their source in her own secret desires for his magnificent lover. Yet her narration was so lively, that unconsciously he sought to reach for his sword to protect his honor from a fictional creature lurking in the shadows of his mind.

"Do not look for your heavy sword my lord," she noted with subtle irony. "There have been many years since you could cut down Janissaries heads to protect my honor. Now everything you try to lift seems too heavy, and you have to think a lot before you can make a decision to use it. Why should you be in a hurry after all? if one has sufficient patience to wait for Allah's actions, all problems are eventually solved by themselves. Then again, perhaps you should ask the opinion of a respected Mufti, or the king of France or even of the Venetian Bailo if you should punish a bird for its audacity to steal seeds from your garden during the winter. The world around us as we age is constantly changing for the worse. Perhaps the time has passed when a man could earn kingdoms with his mighty sword. Maybe now everything precious we yearn may be achieved more easily by the creeping power of weakness. Instead of demolishing walls by their cannons, now your Janissaries dig burrows beneath the walls and trust the stone weight will do their job. What's the use of your bronze cannons, my dear Suleiman? There have been rendered useless! Soon bronze statues will decorate your mosques, exposing the new gods bare naked. I will be your topless Artemis, you will have turned into Hercules, the model husband, and Ibrahim will look like Apollo the musician, so that throughout the City faithful and Christian infidels may stare at out nudity and mock us incessantly with their vicious, obscene graffiti."

The last accusation was like a knife that tore the veil of mist before his eyes. Now he could clearly discern that none of the slave's deeds was accidental. Everything had its deeper symbolism. The balance of his Universe had been gradually eroded and there was only one way to regain it again. On the other hand, a Sultan should never become a liar, because he was the Shadow of Allah. Now, he had to seek the Grand Mufti opinion on every religious matter.

Hurrem could not restrain a smile of contempt listening to this recipe for bypassing this emotional dead end.

"It's no wonder Ibrahim has climbed so high, when all around you there are so many foolish advisers. A donkey that carries sacred books on its back, will always be a donkey," she ironically noted, but she quickly changed her expression to that of a caring mother and added:

"My darling, I'm sorry! Needlessly you have become very tense once more, seeking solution to an aged problem. Why don't you take a nap now, and let me think it over. I'm sure I can find a practical solution that will keep your oath intact. I'll leave you now, because when I'm near you I simply cannot think of anything else."

****

For an effective Grand Vizier visiting the Sultan immediately after a concubine's visit, was an old and useful method, and in Ibrahim's mind Hurrem was always a concubine made mainly to please his master. In his mind the fact she had made four more sons was irrelevant as long as Mustafa was so competent; however, this morning the Sultan responded negatively to his request of an audience. The Sultan was not feeling well, but he was hopeful that after sunset his pain would recede. Actually this delay might be useful. The Venetian lad loomed suddenly as a threat, even though their separation had occurred with the best possible terms. However, if Hatidge was aware of his naughty adventure, so could the Sultan. In his schedule the Venetian might be a fleeting affair, but an overzealous Sultan might seek revenge for his slightly soiled honor.

What was more important was what kind of stance the Venetian might keep, and last night it had become obvious the lad was very sentimentally unstable. He simply had to leave Constantinople for a while and posting him to a notable position as a state official was the optimum way for everyone to relax. He called the scriber and dictated one more firman. He had to authority to sign it, but he decided at the very last moment that signing a firman when Suleiman was at hand might not be the best option. The Sultan had to become aware of his painful decision too to appreciate the fact their relation was still the strongest bond of all. However, Suleiman was in great pain. Ibrahim could see that even from the threshold of his bedroom; but it was simply too late for him to retreat. The die was cast.

"What was so urgent? Did the Bailo had something thrilling to propose?" Suleiman inquired with a trace of irony.

"Indeed he did, and I'm sure it would be to our advantage for us to accommodate all his wishes," Ibrahim Pasha noticed raising the level of the Sultan's tension.

"What's the meaning of this assertion? In my ears it sounds like another unacceptable concession," the Sultan snapped back trying hard to keep his nerves under control.

"It means that we might have to bribe him to keep the Venetian fleet locked in the Adriatic for a while, so that we can move few ships from the Mediterranean to the Red Sea," Ibrahim explained stunning his master.

"And why Venice would wish to do that?"

"Because I've spent almost an entire night with Bailo's son trying to convince him we can still remain in friendly terms. I have to admit he is a remarkable young man, not just a pretty face. At first he tried hard to gain more concessions, but in the end I managed to offer him a position in Valahia in return for a secret treaty of neutrality. From the very beginning I knew the Venetians are not great fighters, but just skillful traders. Everything they do has to lead to some kind of profit. I have brought the firman of his appointment for you to sign, because for them a Grand Vizier's signature means nothing, even if under my name I write my title, Grand Vizier, Serasker, Kapudan Pasha, or even Sultan. They are always very well informed and know better than anyone else who has the true power in Constantinople. All they needed of me was a kiss to display my friendly sentiments, a strong handshake was simply not enough."

Suleiman was astonished by this revelation, but he still had few questions to ask.

"Have these Venetians noblemen become so degenerate to have negotiations concluded in Galata taverns and bordellos?"

"Yes, indeed they are and we should be as conniving, when secret deals have to made. It is well known that prostitutes have a way to soften any hard male objection."

He had to admit that Ibrahim Pasha had a way with words and could transform even a treachery into a noble deed.

"I wonder if I should meet this remarkable young Venetian too. I simply have to know everything there is about the character and moral values of every Ottoman official I send to Valahia. I need no scandals or treacheries so close to our borders."

"Indeed you should meet him," Ibrahim admitted without a second thought, "even though you can always punish him severely, if he dares to betray your trust or possibly mine."

"Yes, this is exactly what I will do, after any sign of treachery or audacious behavior. He is not the husband of my sister after all. He is just a clerk who works for my interests and a salary should be enough for his services."

"Indeed he is not your Makbil; but if he can prove he is worthy of your confidence and succeeds in all the tasks he might face, you can always marry him with your daughter Mihrimah. He is a very gifted young man. This would be the kind of marriage that her mother might like too. From what I know she is very interested in every Venetian jewel she can lay her hands on. By the way, how does your majesty likes the name of Iskander? As you well know it means "Alexander". Isn't it a good name for my son?"

****

Slowly but surely the events had force her to make even painful choices which under normal circumstances she would postpone, if she could help it; but time always moved forward and delays could be proven costly or even fatal. Ibrahim Pasha had been either too greedy or too desperate to try to make his revolution at this particular moment. He should have shown more wisdom or more compassion for the ordeal his master was going through. Indeed the Venetian affair was a trifle that would be overlooked under normal circumstance. If he desired Lodovico so much, they should have been more careful and meet secretly in a Grand Bazaar Han. Such a meeting would surely pass unnoticed there. If she was he, she would wear an inconspicuous garment and use one of the palaces backdoor entrances leading to the Grand Bazaar, as she had occasionally done in the Eski Saray. She wouldn't put everything in danger by visiting the notorious Galata district where spies galore. The Grand Bazaar was only few steps away. There his presence could be more easily explained by purchasing a present, while Galata emitted always the foul odor of conspiracy with all these conniving foreign embassies and consulates hording its streets.

She had to admit the Venetian was a most attractive man and elegantly dressed that could make many women fall for him; but she was more clever than that and much more reserved. Perhaps, her reputation was also better than Ibrahim's, or an European man would never consider flirting a Sultan's Kadin to test her morals; thus, these conditions kept the meeting strictly within professional limits. She was expecting he would ask some kind of favor in return, but soon enough he made clear the meeting would be the only reward he sought.

Damned fool! She had come prepared for much more than that, but he didn't display any tendency for a quick conquest. If all European men were like him, how come Vienna didn't submit to the Janissary attack? She couldn't think of anything else but that it had to be another miracle of Christ. She simply had to find exactly what had happened behind the closed doors, and the easiest way to do that was to mimic the invitation and draw the conclusions. She did just that and her conclusion matched Kislar Aga's. Women were not Lodovico's cup of tea.

****

Unquestionably Ibrahim Pasha was wise enough to suspect it was a trap. To succeed she had to make sure the letter appeared sincere and genuine; so she wrote:

My one and only love,

Tonight I will wait once more to watch with the eyes of my imagination your shadow slip through the garden to visit your master. I can feel your pain of submission better than anyone else; but I cannot offer you any relief unless you are willing to make the first step. If there is still left a spark of passion in the fire I once saw burning in your eyes, come, cut my chains, and make my dreams reality, if only for a single night. Forgive me if I have tried to harm you few times, but jealousy makes me lose my mind thinking of you night after night, year after year.
This holy month he never asks for me, so you can have no excuses. If you keep on denying me, you should know that Death will be my next lover, because I cannot stand spending another night serving his wishes. Every time he invites me to his bedroom, it's an endless torment. For me, now there is only one choice. Loving you or death.

Your eternal slave...

****

Reading the content of her letter, the Sultan became upset even though she had assured him it was just a lie. It was an invitation only for the eyes of the Grand Vizier written by the hand of his favorite Kadin he would recognize among thousands of others; but there was also a separate note written by her hand, warning him that it was a fake invitation she intended to send to Ibrahim to show him how loyal his slave was. Now it was entirely up to him to decide, if he should send it or not. If Ibrahim replied in writing, she promised she would deliver also his answer for him to judge the full extent of his "loyal" friend's treachery.

The letter looked indeed like a trap rigged to catch the traitor of his honor and trust; but there was something hidden in her words that worried him. It was not the idea of a trap itself that upset him, but the bait she had used to attract the prey. The very words betrayed a well-hidden desire, so this attempt of suggesting a meeting was a smokescreen to hide her devious deceit. He wanted to forget or find excuses for Ibrahim's acts, but Hurrem insisted on her challenge. She was pressuring him to make a decision, but a Sultan should not be blackmailed.

He called the scriber and dictated his own message. He simply couldn't write something too explicit or emotional. The invitation had to be polite and casual as usual, because any piece of paper might be lost or misplaced. It was an invitation for supper like many others for many years. The text should not initiate any suspicion. Now all that was left was to find out which of the two invitations the slave will honor.

When the scriber finished his mission, he read the letter one more time before releasing it for delivery. His invitation was too pressing, whereas hers much more liberal. Ibrahim could visit her any time he pleased until the Ramadan's end; but, there was nothing he could do soften his request. He was a Sultan destined to order, while she was a woman made to be patient. If Ibrahim knocked on his door tonight, he would have to find good excuses for many invitations in a row to prevent Ibrahim from accepting hers another night; but what could these excuses be without arousing suspicions? There was no trace now of any unfulfilled passion. His heart was shuttered. He was just another ordinary man with limited participation in life's palette of pleasures. Lodovico had simply shattered his monopoly rights of the master.

****

It was late afternoon when Ibrahim received Hurrem's letter. Not much time had passed since he and his Princess had finished supper, and all that remained was to conclude another Ramadan night was a courtesy visit to his harem. Since his return from the Divan early afternoon, time had passed with torturing slow rhythms, as they all were waiting for that very special moment of sexual relief. Thus, he examined carefully the wording, and concluded It was definitely a last desperate attempt to lure him to his death. Hurrem should have known he had walked throughout life with logic as his only guide, not rampant sentimentality.

Her writing style was too familiar. He had often helped the Sultan compose poems for his beloved during their early years together; but this was not the only task the Sultan could not carry out alone. If Suleiman was not eloquent enough to find the right words, for him it sufficed to recall her eyes and the words found themselves how they should be laid down on paper.

He brought the letter to his lips and a delicate scent of roses reached deep into his mind and made him drunk. It was her irrefutable signature. Effortlessly the lyrics of his favorite poet, Rumi, found the way to his memory, but as much as he tried to remember the entire poem, ultimately only one verse kept wondering in his mind:

"Today I feel so dizzy, I cannot distinguish the rose from the thorn."

He was almost as puzzled as the poet this very moment. If this letter ever reached the hands of the Sultan, it would mean her death; but she had dared to write it. She might have become desperate facing the prospects of Suleiman's gradual carnal demise, and despair was always a bad adviser. On the other hand, perhaps she was trying to obtain a written proof of his betrayal to support the arguments against him, and the charge was old and well-established after eons of Roman conspiracies: "He had Roman blood running in his veins."

The Kislar Aga awaited motionless like an ebony statue to convey his reply. It was an indication he expected to carry back a written letter. With a nod he dismissed him with empty hands. In the Aga's eyes he read deep disappointment for his failed mission. Perhaps sending the Kislar Aga in such a trivial mission had also a secret symbolism. She was willing to share him.

As if the Nubian could read his mind, he asked full of submission:

"Is there anything else I can do for Your Excellency?"

Of course, if they were alone in a deserted island, their relationship might have taken a different course, but in a crowded city like Constantinople, other people put down the rules of engagement. The Nubian was still a slave with limited ambitions compared to him. His skin was also black, and that meant a lot in this magnificent locality. He was a fine specimen that within a Sudanese tribe would earn him a high status even though his ancestors were not noblemen.

He suffered by the same drawback, but he had struggled hard to improve his status all these years; however, the Nubian was not as lucky. His spirit was not appreciated as much as his flesh.

"Yes, you can! Please tell me: Have they turned you in the Harem into a eunuch?"

Maybe for him this question had the air of human interest, but for the slave was an insult he couldn't leave unanswered. The Nubian was proud and had suffered long enough in Arab hands.

"No! See for yourself exactly what kind of man I am!" he proclaimed with pride.

****

The slave closed quietly the door behind him. Eventually, resisting the temptation had to be the correct decision. It was safer remaining uninvolved in these perilous power games Hurrem's crooked mind had staged. This woman was devious indeed and would leave no stone unturned to disgrace him. Suddenly he became very angry. After all, she had no right to interfere with his happiness. He was happy indeed, because for the first time he had found the strength to withstand the demands of an audacious female. The only thing he had to do the rest of the night was to discover what kind of surprises Allah had in store for him, when he crossed the threshold of his beloved wife's bedroom.

His ears the voice of Muezzin came uninvited, inviting the faithful to celebrate the end of another trial day of their faith. He was an infidel, but this night even the unbelieving Christians in the Eternal City would comply with the commands of Allah to contribute more warriors to the armies.

A bang on the iron glad door added to his worries. A messenger had arrived with a letter from the Sultan. Nearing midnight was the only time Suleiman sought his companionship in the Seraglio; so he was not too surprised by this invitation. His master seemed oblivious of the Prophet's teachings once more. They had drunk innumerous times red wine before going to bed in the past, as Bacchus was always the most favorite pagan god in the Thracian shores of the Bosporus Straits even after the Muslim Conquest. They both needed an excuse to behave like pagans. Tonight he would rather spend some quality time in his harem, but he was still a slave and he could not deny this invitation, so he had to find excuses. It would be a good occasion to explain even further the auspicious Galata events after few glasses of red wine.

Despite appearances, Suleiman's message timing had filled him with a burst of optimism. The Sultan still needed him after midnight, and suddenly the need to obey the will of his master became even more pressing. Maybe the jealousy he felt for his immodest love affair with the Venetian lad had played a role.

Suleiman was reluctant at first to sign the firman for Lodovico's appointment in Valahia, but when he mentioned all the advantages this action had in neutralizing any possible reaction by the Venetian fleet to the signing of the peace treaty with France, he finally conceded the Ottoman Empire needed a long period of recuperation to recover its vigor and stage a war in the Indian Ocean. Concessions had to be made as after the recent conquests, many more Christians and Jews in Syria had become Ottoman subjects.

He didn't wish to wait for long to wake up his servants; so he wore himself a white kaftan adorned with pink pearls. His eye fell on the knife, Selim's old gift. It wouldn't be a bad occasion to remind to Suleiman their first night; so, he shoved it into his girdle. Some drops of jasmine scent was all he needed to be fully prepared. This night would be the last time he wore this notorious perfume with its dubious side effects.

Next he rushed to the Princess' door, showed her the letter and explained what had happened. It made no sense for her to wait for him, but he promised that before sunrise, he would be back in her arms. In her eyes he saw the irrefutable signs of disappointment, but she said nothing more than a friendly greeting.

"Give a kiss from me to my brother, your all-demanding master," and when she finished, she closed his lips with a kiss that made his blood rush to boost all his senses, making the separation even more difficult; but there was nothing else he could do other than follow the messenger rushing back to the Seraglio.

It was not far, but they had to go through all the dark corridors that led to the throne room. Closing the garden door behind him in his ears still echoed Hatidge's last words:

"Remember that no matter what happens, you are still the man of my life and I still remember who you really are. Our dreams of liberation can wait for one more night."

The idea that in every turn might the executioners might be expecting him with silk loops and sharp daggers was not something unusual for him. He was accustomed to this possibility almost from the first night he spent in the Seraglio. It was the ultimate horror that accompanied the throne of the Sultan as the Roman Emperors before him, and it seemed this fear had soaked the very stones of the dilapidated Grand Palace in this exact location and raised once more in a different style. Only the shape of the building had changed through the centuries. The stink of fear remained the same.

****

With the eyes of imagination Suleiman Khan traveled all the way to the Eski Saray. His Kadin must have already arrived there and sent her message with the Kislar Aga. Now she was anxiously waiting for Ibrahim's reply; so, he quickened his pace to reach the Has Oda first. From an early age he had learned the importance of arriving first on the battlefield and win the sword of Osman, because the second runner was destined to die a horrible death. After the illness his life was not worth living most of the time; but there were few precious moments with Hurrem that kept him waking every morning. After his illness, he didn't even dare to think how Mahidevran Sultan would treat him. The Tatar princess was simply too proud to marry a man who could not ride a horse. The myth claimed Tatar women were descendants of the Amazons. Amazons killed their mates the moment they realized they had been impregnated.

Actually, walking was much more painful than riding now; but there was no way to reach the Has Oda on horseback through the winding corridors. He cursed Mehmet Fatih for his choices. The Seraglio had a floorplan as complicated as the mind of its owner; but his mind was also by no means straight and simple. For him to survive it had to be complex, and make sure he had taken all the necessary measures to rule and guide the vessel to a safe harbor.

There was no way a man could comprehend a woman; so he had to be constantly vigilant. Reaching safely his throne, he asked for the Kapi Aga. He was foolish not to have placed a spy in her chambers just to be sure of her loyalty. Gradually, she had become a critical portion of his survival. Without her he had no reason for living, if Ibrahim ever abandoned him.

****

Soon enough the black slave from Nubia arrived. He carried no letter. Ibrahim hadn't bothered to write her not even a single word. Her letter was a trap and he must have realized it; but, still not responding to the invitation by a Birinci Kadin was certainly demeaning.

She asked the Aga if he had anything more to report. He said no, but his eyes were shimmering. He was lying and his wide smile and pearl-white teeth spelled fluently his lie was not important; but, she was curious enough to seek answers, and he was too weak to deny anything from her majesty. He was another man foolish enough to challenge her supremacy with such a meaningless blackmailing. Today, she was so angry, she didn't care for anything else; but at sunrise her disposition would most certainly improve, when she found out how badly the Sultan had spent the night.

She never expected that she would feel this way, but suddenly she caught herself feeling better every time Suleiman was in pain. Being married was a very complicated human relationship. Even being a slave was simpler; so, to exercise her authority she dismissed the Nubian. Somehow ordering around attractive slaves made her feel better about herself.

****

It was relatively easy for Ibrahim to recognize the signs of extreme discomfort on Suleiman's face. It was certainly the wrong occasion to raise the subject of a long visit to Egypt. He had decided this would be his better approach, a short leave of a few months to entertain his Princess and forget all the heartaches of the Baghdad expedition. Then, he was going to ask for an extension, and then a second one. By then the Sultan would have found his replacement, as there were many talented men coming out of the Seraglio School occupying the posts of the minor Viziers. If he couldn't choose, he had certainly few good suggestions. The School was under his direct supervision, and he had spent many hours teaching the next generation of Ottoman officials the art of diplomacy. When others had built an empire on mosques and superstitions, he had chosen schools and knowledge. This institution was going to be his legacy.

****

As the door closed behind her husband, Hatidge could not help it her eyes were clouded by tears. Till the last moment she had hoped Ibrahim would find a plausible excuse to avoid visiting the Top Kapi palace that night. It was now clear her husband would always remain a slave, always willing to kiss the caftan of his master rather than risk a revolt. He was like a faithful dog that ran to welcome his master shaking his tail. Neither her kiss could hold him firm, nor the emerald eyes of a slave, nor the ebony skin of another. Perhaps the only solution left was to go on a long journey, taking with her everything that was dear to him, his women and children. Maybe if Ibrahim lived alone for a while, he could find the strength to face himself and the scent of jasmine still lingering in the air could now make her change her mind.

"Tomorrow morning we'll start packing. This town does not fit us anymore," she said and her voice was as expressionless as her grim father when he was going on a new campaign.

The slaves at her feet nodded affirmatively, but in their eyes she read the difficulty of realizing such a tough decision.

****

"I have asked you to leave," she yelled at him, but the slave gave her no indication he intended to depart.

"What are you trying to prove by disobeying me? That you are a man? Keep in mind this can change very quickly, if you stop doing what I want."

She sounded very ominous, but Aslan seemed impervious to her threats. Somehow he was able to acquire insolence from an unknown source. It was not difficult for her to guess the source of his inspiration. It was her weakness, but for her plan was to succeed, everything had to change. As if he was already gone, she started getting ready to sleep.

He was up to the task and followed her lead, discarding one of his clothes for each one of hers.

"Do you really like so much what you see to test my resolve?" she asked him with a vulgar tone of voice that had no trace of anger for his insubordination. On the contrary it was full of promises.

The Nubian nodded his head affirmatively, denying her the pleasure of listening to his capitulation. This was not her plan. She had to turn him into an obedient accomplish.

"How often do you see me naked in your dreams?" she inquired indifferently.

"Not as often as you see me," he responded boldly to her challenge.

She didn't get upset, as dreams were common traps for every slave.

"Are you afraid to see me often!" she said playfully. "Black slaves have the right to dream the gate of Heaven too, but only a Sultan can cross it as often as he likes."

This Nubian boldness was intriguing. She knew men well enough to realize this was the result of the primal pressure to procreate, but she was still hesitant, if she should offer his reward in advance or after the completion of his mission. Since she couldn't make up her mind, she decided to be patient and conservative. It was better for her slave to live for a few hours in the world of his dreams and expectation; so she slowly crossed her legs to inform him of her decision, but he showed that tonight he was not going to display his normal submission. Instead he sat at the edge of her bed, cradled his head between her legs, and took a few deep breaths to saturate his lungs with her scent.

This was at least what was her initial plan; but he was much more devious than that, as she soon discovered. He was testing her scent and her resolve to resist and found it lacking. He was right. She simply could not resist the primordial flood that slowly overflowed the dam her mind had raised. With the last drops of her resolved, she tried to pull his head away, but she couldn't. Her fingers slipped on his hair. Was this the reason Negro slaves always kept their hair so trimmed? As a reply to her futile attempts, he forcefully pulled her thighs open, reminding her of the first Tatar rapes; but he didn't want to prove he was an irresistible conqueror. He did his best to show her he was just a servant of all her secret desires and nothing more than that. She decided that perhaps, the moment she had managed to subdue the first explosion of his passion, she could explain to him what would be his next mission.

****

It was very difficult to discern if the Sultan's tension was because of his illness, or the disconcerting news of his leave of absence. All he had to say was a simple "why" that gave him the opportunity to express one by one several reasons he considered convincing enough. The first one was that now with the peace treaties he had signed in Europe and Mesopotamia the probability of war in two fronts seemed remorse. It was one reason Suleiman quickly dismissed with an argument stolen from his book of tricks.

"War comes when it's not expected. At the moment I have no other Serasker who can replace you."

"Mustafa is a very competent soldier," Ibrahim argued in vain.

"Yes, my son is a brave soldier, a good swordsman and a fine marksman with bow and arrow, but that does not make him my best Serasker yet. He has to mature a bit more before attempting to lead an entire Ottoman army to victory."

"I was even younger, when you made me Serasker," the Grand Vizier argued.

"Yes, you were indeed younger, but as we both know you were an exception. Even Selim Khan would be proud of your courage and canning. If you were mediocre, then I would have sent you back to Parga to fish long ago."

This piece of friendly praise dismissed most of Ibrahim's worries. If his first argument had failed, he could raise many more without great difficulty; but he had to be sure first the Sultan did not consider his request as an opportunity to accompany Lodovico to Valahia.

"Your denial fills me with pride; but it will surely disappoint my beloved Princess. She cannot wait to visit Egypt with me and see the Pyramids and the Red Sea," he revealed as indifferently as possible, but Suleiman had prepared a devastating reply.

"Let me worry about my sister. If you want to truly please her, try to devote more nights to her in your palace."

"Should I go now?" Ibrahim inquired a bit upset by the Sultan's intervention into his personal life.

"Yes, you may go. Tonight I'm more tired than usual. Perhaps tomorrow night I will be a better company."

****

Ibrahim left the Seraglio rather relieved. His relationship with Suleiman seemed intact. The Sultan had also shown consideration for his rather auspicious affair with Lodovico. He behaved as if he was trying to forget the event. He had also shown some interest for its effects on his marriage. A scandal would be damaging for the throne, and any damage on the Serasker status would surely affect the fighting spirit of the troops, especially the Janissaries who were offspring of infidel parents. It was unquestionably a very wise attitude coming from a competent ruler that put the good of the Empire much higher than his personal feelings.

Undoubtedly the Sultan still considered him as his possession, and his flick with the Venetian a personal insult, but conceivably he was treating the entire incident as the action of a sentimental fool. Suleiman was correct. Sometimes his actions exceeded the generally accepted rules of decency; but he was exceptional and extending the commonly accepted rules was one of the rights every exception had. It was the only way the human species could ever evolve.

****

Hatidge didn't say much next morning. On the surface she treated his early return as an expected, natural development that might not have resolved the underlying issue, but on the other hand she did nothing to add to the existing overall stress. Ibrahim felt obliged to relay her the news about Suleiman's refusal to grant him any form of dismissal. After all, besides Hurrem, Hatidge was the only person who could make Suleiman change his mind with a brief visit. She had proved once more she was a true Ottoman Princess worthy of her noble blood.

Despite his mental superiority, he had to admit his overall attitude was as common as that of the ordinary folks strolling on the Galata streets or around the Golden Horn docks.

Hatidge had the discretion to say nothing offensive, but what bothered him more than the ironic grimace in her face, was the expression in Sherenk and Basmi's eyes. It was relatively easy to disappoint a Princess, because of her exaggerated hopes; but it was hard to disappoint a slave. Fortunately there was still hope a workable solution might be found the coming night. Maybe the coming night was another chance to drastically change his life, but there was nothing in the world he had not tasted, from the euphoria of victory and conquest to the shame of a defeat and the submission to the wishes of the victor. Nevertheless this emotional saturation gave him courage. His life was about to close one more long cycle of maturing. This moment was as important as when the privateers had ripped him forever from his home town.

Life was a spiral whirling nonstop around centers of attraction controlling the life of every individual, but this image of stability was elusive. Every moment could become the beginning of another cycle around a different center of attraction.

Since he was admitted in the Seraglio, his center of attraction had been Suleiman. Lodovico's appearance had put this cycle through a test. If he had chosen to follow him to Valahia, this cycle would surely break apart; but he was not ready to try something so desperate and put in danger his status quo.

Hatidge year after year had tied him down even more with her courtesans and children, reducing his choices. He had to choose now what to keep from his old self, and what to leave behind. If Lodovico was a slave, he could buy him to reside in his palace. Then his happiness would be complete.

Few moments passed before he became aware how weak his character truly was, going after every man and woman who showed him some interest. In this crooked path something would always be missing. If Lodovico was his slave, then after a while his eyes would fall on another man, and in Constantinople many attractive men were available. The Janissary corps was still a magnet for ambitious, gifted men. In fact, in his eyes even the Kislar Aga became more and more attractive day by day. He had become a challenge and a worthy trophy from the moment he became Hurrem's lover. He had started feeling like a greedy Sultan who could never be content with what he had. Perhaps the fact his life had started in the inconspicuous Parga, a port on the Ionian shores, was responsible for his dubious trend of character; but greed could also be weakness of his race that had found refuge at this isolated place.

Suleiman was farsighted enough to suspect he had deep in his mind the desire to rival his power and have everything within his grasp; but on the other hand, if Suleiman insisted on keeping him by his side forever, then he should make this small concession. After all he was not interested in long term relationships, only brief subjugations. At least in this respect they were entirely different. An Osmanli would never release his hold on a conquest. Wherever his foot stepped, he would never retreat; but he was another species. He was undoubtedly an expert on strategic retreats and honorable concessions benefiting all. He was a trader by nature.

****

There was nothing more he could do this time. His messenger to the Bailo's palace brought him back the bad news in the form of a personal letter with the a Venetian embassy seal. The Bailo was rather eloquent in his letter, explaining briefly what had happened. The Sultan's firman was clear. The situation in Valahia was deteriorating and the presence of a competent Ottoman official essential for the retentions of this rebellious region. Lodovico had to be on his way by the end of the day, or face dire consequences.

Only one issue was still vague. What would be these consequences was another serious issue he had to resolve that might need more time than usual; so an early evening visit to the Seraglio might be to his advantage.

****

Suleiman's eyes focused for a moment on the ornamented knife Ibrahim carried in his belt and his mind flooded with another serious concern. Surely, this was not the first time the Grand Vizier wore arms in public. It was part of his Serasker uniform; but it was late at night, and no one would see it and become impressed with such a dubious exposure of military armor. In the past Ibrahim had often entertained him, explaining all the tricks he used to intimidate foreign ambassadors, and how important it was for a Grand Vizier to appear as threatening as possible, when he made negotiations with the enemies of the Ottoman Empire.

The ambassadors were humans too, and it was impossible not to consider every time he became angry the possibility he might potentially stab them in his rage. Perhaps this was Ibrahim's ultimate aim now. If his goal was to make him feel insecure, fortunately the letter of Hurrem had warned him of what might happen, and he had taken the measures. Until this matter was resolved, he would keep the Keeper of the Sword, Rüstem Bey from Croatia, always by his side. A Sultan could never be sure, how obediently his slaves would behave in each case.

"I didn't expect you to visit me so early this evening," Suleiman remarked. "Has a new problem appeared?"

"No, everything is under control in the Empire. I simply realized that you need to see me more often than in the past; otherwise, you wouldn't have refused my request for a short trip to Egypt to make sure there are no problems with pilgrim traffic to Mecca."

"You didn't tell me this was the excuse for your trip there," Suleiman ironically noted.

"You know that if I want to convince anyone for something, I can find a million excuses."

"Yes, I know it all too well. I also know that if an opponent does not concede, you can even threaten to stab him with your knife."

Ibrahim smiled slightly listening to Suleiman's remark.

"Yes, I could do that. I could even stab your guard too, by the time he draws his yatagan, if I am still quick enough. Yatagans and knifes can become rusty, if one does not use them often enough. Actually this knife has not been used for many years, since your father gave it to me as a present, if your memory has not betrayed you."

As the Sultan recognized the knife, his anxiety defused, and the tone of voice softened somehow; but it was difficult for him to forget, so he added: "My memory has not suffered as much as my legs, so I will not forget the Galata taverns for a while, and how licentious are the men who visit them during the holy month of Ramadan."

Suleiman had to make sure Ibrahim realized that repairing their relationship would be very difficult; but Ibrahim was more clairvoyant and imaginative than in recent times. Instead of seeking brilliant arguments to express his excuses, he used the verses of their favorite poet:

"When I'm with everyone but not with you, then I'm lonely.
When I'm alone with you, then I'm with everyone."

The Sultan looked at him a bit startled. It was a response he didn't expect, so he was unprepared to refute it. Ibrahim had responded as a subjugated slave not a cunning conspirator who had come that night to steal his life and his wife, as Hurrem's dream suggested. The most singular infraction, besides the Lodovico affair that was still troubling him, was Ibrahim's intention to name his coming son Alexander or Iskander, exactly as he had seen in that awful nightmare. Nevertheless, with few words his friend had forced him to abandon most of his reservations. The intensity of the last few hours and the long fasting had exhausted his energy.

During springtime his illness always worsened, but the words of the poet influenced him as a strong red wine for both his troubled body and mind, relaxing his stress and lowering the defenses of his mind. However, it was still too early to start drinking on an empty stomach. He was feeling hungry and he needed first some nourishment to replenish his stamina before a long duel; so, he flicked his fingers and the servants began to bring in trays with a fastidious supper. The electrified atmosphere of a brewing crisis for the time being seemed dissolved.

The Sultan showed his preference for the traditional roast lamb, while Ibrahim who as usual had not fasted at home, he was content with a few fruits. For some time they both remained silent. During their lives they had spent many nights chatting until morning, but now it seemed as no one knew what kind of pleasantries to say, thus gradually through the silence tension found the chance to return and intensify. On both faces it was evident their friendship was not going to be the same from now on.

In the Sultan's mind the same thought kept twirling. It was impossible for him to understand what had happened and Ibrahim had sought refuge in another man's embrace and the very next day to ask him for a leave. All these years he had tried to prove to the slave how precious was for him their moments of intimacy. He had tolerated without protest even a woman to come between them, and uncomplainingly he had paid for the grand wedding of his beloved; but nothing was enough to satiate the hunger of this greedy slave.

"I always wondered why my father was so generous with you," he nervously inquired.

"I wondered that too for a while," Ibrahim admitted. "He was so stringy and threatening with most people that I was also surprised at the time, but not anymore."

"What have you found out?" Suleiman anxiously asked.

"Nothing definite, but after so many years, I'm now wise enough to know that few harem secrets will never be revealed. If his two favorite eunuchs were alive, then I might have satisfied my thirst for knowledge. All I may now say is that Allah had different plans, and He is omnipotent," Ibrahim remarked indifferently.

"Now that you've mentioned his favorite eunuchs, why do you think my father tried to kill me with the poisoned shirt?"

"Selim Khan didn't really tried hard. If he so wished, you would be dead by now. He always got what he truly wanted," Ibrahim replied letting himself into a trap.

"And he always liked you more than he liked me. I always felt it, so don't try to deny it," Suleiman added ominously and Ibrahim felt the door of a trap closing. However, after so many years he didn't mind releasing some of the pressure he felt, holding deep in his heart so many secrets.

"No, I will not try anything so foolish. Now, we are both old enough to handle the truth. If he indeed had stronger feelings for me, it's probably because he desired me, and carnal attractions sometimes appear stronger than anything else; however, the turmoil they create it's for nothing, since they deflate much faster than they inflate. Your relationship with your father is lasting till this moment, while his passion for me didn't last more than a single night. This was the kind of man your father was. He was thrilled with a conquest only for as long as it lasted."

"Did he conquered you too?" Suleiman asked just to be sure for the validity of his suspicions via a full confession.

"Don't ask silly questions. How could he do that? I'm a free spirit, remember."

"Yes, I have realized that long ago, but this is not exactly what I meant."

"Yes, I know; but these are silly questions. After so many years, it makes no difference either way. What really counts today is how we will feel tomorrow for each other."

"Yes, I may sound silly sometimes, but I am your master; so, when I demand an answer, I must have it on the spot."

"Then, let's just say that he was not the first or the last man in my life. A mighty conqueror like Your Majesty has to realize that sometimes surrendering can be even more pleasant than conquering," Ibrahim humbly confessed.

Suleiman didn't seem the least surprised by this revelation. Deep in his heart he knew the truth long ago. He was now too thoughtful to ask any more questions, and Ibrahim grabbed the opportunity to explain his point of view.

"I was not to be blamed though. Back then I was just a slave destined to serve men or women in a hammam. This was going to be my career, as the slave trader had told me. Having a Prince Heir buy me was an unbelievable stroke of luck; but

Padisah Selim had the power to squash me like a bug, if I failed to please him as much as he expected."

"I realize that, but you were not the reason he tried to kill me. As far as I know, he could have you any time he wished to," Suleiman pointedly remarked.

"Who could deny Selim anything?" Ibrahim admitted as if he talked to himself.

"I wish I was as powerful as my father, but I'm not. I'm a weakling waiting to die. Perhaps, this was the reason why my father tried to kill me to save me from all this misery."

Ibrahim suddenly realize how deep were Suleiman's wounds. Having a constant source of pain could make any life, even a Sultan's, utterly depressing. Pain was the most direct way for Mother Nature to point out to any being that it was inferior for as long as the pain lasted. If the pain lasted for months or years, then it was easy for a man in pain to draw the conclusion life was not worth living. Nevertheless, Suleiman had not reached this precarious state yet, as he was asking too many questions that had no meaning for a man on his death-bed.

"Do you think, my father slept also with Hurrem?" the Sultan asked him indifferently, and this change of his tone of voice was a great surprise for Ibrahim. "From what I can still remember, she had been a very sensuous dancer that night."

"Don't torture yourself asking questions that can never be answered. I was in love with you at the time and cared for no one else. We had spent an entire month together in Edirne back then. He could invite practically anyone of your Kadin to his chambers, when we were gone, and no one could deny Padisah Selim anything. Sinan Pasha became a eunuch to earn his favor," Ibrahim argued. "But who cares now who made love to whom after all these years? The past exists only in our memories."

"I care! I'm now Allah's Shadow. I have to pass judgment to all my subjects, and I must be fair," the Sultan declared and in his voice Ibrahim felt Selim's freezing coldness.

He had to do something to change this gloomy atmosphere that smell of death.

"This lamb seems delicious. I wonder if I should have some too. The doctors say that after a certain age we should all stop eating meat, but I don't think we can. Eating meat has been implanted so deeply in our brains, I don't think there is any way to uproot it. What do you think my master? Could you stop eating lamb, if this was the only way to improve your health?"

****

As Ibrahim exited the Gülhane Gardens through the tiny gate, he had a long smile written all over his face. Suleiman's behavior had been exactly what he should have expected.

If Alexander the Great had conquered Babylon Suleiman had to conquer it too. In a way he felt the same urge too. He had slept with him so many times before, one more wouldn't make much difference. It was a feeling most whores would share, but their feeble excuses were valid for him too. He had to earn a living, and people had done much worse than that just for a loaf of bread. In this occasion he felt strongly that one way to convince the Sultan to let him go to Egypt, was to show him how immoral he really was. This trick had also worked his father. It was one of the many eunuch secrets Menekse had revealed to him. No Osmanli would consider keeping an odalisque for more than a night, if he discovered she was not truly a virgin.

Selim's favorite eunuchs did not wish to lose the Sultan's favor, so during his night visit to the infamous kiosk, they had thoroughly sedate and degraded him to their heart's content. However, Ibrahim had no way to know, if this was true or not. Now, the only concern that matter was if Suleiman has ceased to consider him as a precious jewel or just a trinket he would be willing to discard and let him go.

Hatidge would be furious now, but women were made by Allah to sympathize with this kind of slutty behavior. Allah was not responsible for such a sin. It was the goddess Aphrodite. She was

561

probably responsible for his dubious tendencies too. Ancient Greeks were indeed much wiser. Mars and Aphrodite were brother and sister born by the same father Zeus, as closely related as life and death. Christians, Jews and Muslim were very naïve, imagining that a single god was responsible for everything. With one stroke they had eliminated all these intimate relations among the Olympian deities, and were finally left with mysteries only science could unravel; but until then, they were left clueless. He was much wiser than that. Human minds worked on the basis of associations. To arouse the interest of a lusty man, he had to do nothing more than start licking a roasted suckling lamb bone in front of his eyes.

Now in his enterprising mind there could be only one explanation. The Sultan was content with his behavior; otherwise he wouldn't invite him for tomorrow night too. The Venetian incident would be soon forgotten, if the Sultan was assured he would be his for as long as he wished. Hatidge had to realize that being a Princess and the Kadin of a Grad Vizier meant she had to put few limits to her greed too for the good of the Empire.

****

"You may not believe it, but I have enjoyed our conversation immensely last night," Suleiman assured him as Ibrahim deeply prostrated and kissed the corner of his caftan to demonstrate his total obedience. "I spent the entire day thinking about you and my father. It was indeed very difficult to draw the correct judgment before you came up with a profound concept I could have never thought, if I was all alone. A suckling lamb is delicious. This is how Allah made it; so it's not the lamb's fault, if a wolf is sneaking into a shepherd's sheepfold to steal it. And who could blame a single lamb, if a hungry wolf pack has the same urge? In fact, a lamb's advocate could even claim that Allah who made lamp so delicious is responsible for creating a sense of unity within a pack wolves. Isn't that so my wise Grand Vizier?"

Ibrahim had to confess that he had not considered yet this exact point of view; but rather than seeking for quarreling arguments, he would rather spend the night discussing more pleasant issues. If the Sultan was reluctant to let him visit Egypt, his slave should wait for him to get better. Then they could all go to Egypt and take their Kadin along too. A pleasant trip would be beneficial to all, even to the Egyptian populace that would consider such a trip the proof of the Sultan's acute interest for their prosperity. Without much thought he suggested so.

****

In the Sultan's face Ibrahim read this time few traces of mistrust. The man was so unsure of his condition that his mind created all sorts of suspicions. Was he trying to lure him away from Constantinople and open the road for a Mustafa coop? If he was ill, this dubious trip would give Ibrahim one more chance to prove his superiority to all his subjects along the way. He would travel carrying with his entire harem, while he would have to face all of Hurrem's challenges. Such a trip would be just an appalling nightmare for him.

****

"Do you really believe Selim Khan has also invaded my harem like a hungry wolf?" Suleiman insisted leaving in Ibrahim's hands the task of extinguishing his fears.

"Why do you think he would act in such an audacious manner?" the Grand Vizier asked unwilling to enter in such a dangerous discussion.

"Because I know now that when men get older and approach the dreaded state of incapacity, they try to have a taste of everything they have missed during their youth," the Sultan replied well-prepared and vigorous for a long discussion. "This is actually the best excuse I found for your naughty behavior too."

Now Ibrahim was in a bind. If he tried to refute the Sultan's suggestion, he would effectively destroy his best excuse, as Suleiman had already admitted. The Sultan had suddenly become proficient in raising the kinds of arguments the Grand Vizier would use in his place. It was a frightening prospect, because then he might have no further use for his services. He was worried, and suddenly his stomach felt empty. He didn't have any for supper, imagining the Sultan would have ordered another sumptuous suckling lamb dinner; however, in the Sultan's eyes he couldn't discern tonight even a trace of lust. He was either too exhausted by the pain of his illness, or Hurrem had used him for her pleasure earlier. She was a Christian too and she didn't care much for all this Ramadan religious nonsense.

****

It had gradually become crystal clear the Sultan had conceived a devious plan he carried carefully step by step. For the time being he couldn't discern what the next step would be; but it was comforting Suleiman was not as violent man as Padisah Selim. By now in Suleiman's position Selim he would have called the doctor and turned him into a eunuch. For some mysterious reason he was spared and this should be considered as a sign of weakness. Ibrahim had to take advantage of this fault any way he could; so he got up.

"My Princess is waiting for me. There is one more night left till the end of Ramadan and she simply cannot wait."

"But she has to wait. My sister is not as promiscuous as you imply to have no patience. She is an Osmanli Princess. After all she has all these fabulous slaves to use, if you aren't in her harem to contain her lust. She has born four children altogether. She needs no sons carrying Osman's blood too. Hurrem has born all the sons the Empire needs for the succession."

Ibrahim was further surprised adversely by this comment, and tried to change the subject.

"Indeed Hatidge has several pretty courtesans and you are well aware of how attractive they are. If I remember correctly, they were also yours to use, but you declined. I still cannot believe your heart could be so hard to refuse my offer that night," Ibrahim snapped back.

"Yes, indeed my heart is hard sometimes. In a world full of weaknesses the Shadow of Allah has to be hard enough to pass judgment. Tonight you'll spend the entire night with me. You'll be my prisoner until the Ramadan's end. This will be your sentence for all your sins. Then you will be released to follow your bride's harem to Egypt never to return, if this is what you wish. This is my promise and the son of Selim never lies. This much at least I know you know."

****

Ibrahim felt relieved. The Sultan had invited him to stay in his chambers in his old familiar room he used, when he was his Hasodabashi. Suleiman must have pleasant memories from this period of their lives. After all these revelations he could not hope to be set free. This entire charade meant he had decided to let him go after the end of the Ramadan. Suleiman had finally realized it was not fair to keep a slave he could not use for his pleasure. His presence by his side would be just a painful reminder of their glorious past that could never be repeated. Their relationship had rotted away and the best way for the Sultan to seal from the creeping rot that could poison and degrade everything in its path was to let him go.

Maybe after spending few years in separation their friendship could grow again free from any trace of lust that had led it to a dead end. He had to admit that his old zeal to please was exhausted, and the Venetian had been just a failed attempt to seek a replacement.

Suleiman had finally realized that giving orders was as pleasurable as receiving them. Every possible path gave a human being a chance to discover parts of himself he never knew existed.

When exactly this urge for discovery would end for him, it was not clear; but clearly the illness had put an end to Suleiman's youthful explorations. His youth had abruptly come to an end, and the slave should not be alarmed by its suddenness. He had the same age, but he was healthy; so, he felt as bullish as ever before.

The doors of his room were locked, but he was confident later that night his services would be in demand once more. The Sultan's disposition had greatly improved with the discussion, and it was extremely difficult for any man to dissolve all his weaknesses so quickly.

****

When the door opened, the sun was already high. He had slept like a log. Drinking red wine on an almost empty stomach had been too much for his constitution. Thank Allah Hatidge had offered him few sweets with his cup of tea just before departing. She insisted and he had not refused her offer at last. Her argument was too naughty for his taste.

"A man should never make love on an empty stomach."

Tonight her offending comment was grossly unfair, but there was no way to prove her wrong. He had slept with a man behind lock doors, but only Suleiman could testify at his behalf if the intermediate door was bolted too after he went to sleep. A slave was never allowed to do that in case his master needed his services. Actually he thought in his sleep he heard the nob of his outside door turning at night, but he couldn't be certain who it was. There were White Eunuchs guarding the Sultan from every possible harm that may have checked this minor unguarded door, if it was locked from the inside. It was not.

Indeed this door opened and a eunuch brought him a tray full of delicacies from the Seraglio kitchen. Mehmet Fatih had decided that the best security was to have a single kitchen preparing food for everybody. When there were so many people present, an evil man would find very hard to slip some poison in any plate. Selim had made sure he ate in the same wooden plate as everyone else and the same meals as every Janissary.

Experience had shown a Sultan could be as safe, if his food was prepared by a single cook he could trust. This cook should not only be a competent culinary artist; but he had to have many children too. Their lives was the best security the Sultan had, and this safety measure was effective. Children were the greatest hope for the redemption of any slave.

Suleiman had smiled under his moustache, when he promised his Grand Vizier that after the Ramadan's end he would be free to leave with his harem. Now he knew why. His son would remain in Constantinople as a hostage. Now he was curious enough to ask about his son the moment he saw the Sultan, but his intermediate door was still locked.

****

Hurrem could not contain her anger. Her spy had just reported Suleiman has spent every night this week isolated with his beloved brother-in-law. No one knew what was the reason for this unheard outrage, but the Kislar Aga was bold enough to dare giving her advice. She shouldn't complain. Everything pointed out that Suleiman's health was improving. Soon enough he would be once more on the saddle, leading his Janissaries to new victories.

She knew a woman could never hope to lead the armies of Allah, but she was also aware Ibrahim Pasha could carry out this task better than anyone else. This was the essence of the rumor that slipped through the Seraglio walls early in the morning. There was not a single soul in the Ottoman Empire that would complain, if it learned that the two friends had spent the night together, planning for the next expedition. There was even a wild rumor that Ibrahim Pasha had tried his best to convince the Venetians not intervene, if the Ottoman fleet came out its lair to put an end to Venetian occupation of the Ionian Islands and Parga his birthplace.

She knew well enough Suleiman was not fit to ride on any saddle. He was too weak even to invite her to his bed. The rumors were not founded to reality, but it was easy to see who would benefit from similar rumors, Pargali Ibrahim Pasha. She simply could not wait any longer. She had to act decisively before it was too late. As far as she knew according to the Ottoman traditions, the Grand Vizier was the man who held all the leads. Piri Pasha had secretly invited Suleiman to come and claim the throne of Osman the moment Selim had departed.

She knew better than anyone who Ibrahim would call, Sehzade Mustafa. Then, Mustafa Khan was going to invite Mahidevran Sultan to the Seraglio and make her the new Valide Sultan. These were well-established ceremonies and Ottomans respected traditions; so the moment Mahidevran Sultan came to the Eski Saray as Valide Sultan, her fate was sealed. From the moment Mustafa decided to execute his sons following the tradition, she was nothing but the new Sultan's property and Mahidevran hated her guts. If she couldn't succeed in killing her, she was going to do her best to disgrace her. If the Tatar Princess had her way, she was going to put her in a sack and damp her into the Bosporus.

The sad truth was that only Ibrahim could save her. If Suleiman died, for a few days he would be the acting Sultan in the Seraglio. He might invite her, reject her, or even kill her. Her best option was if Ibrahim decided to admit her to his harem, but possibly Hatidge Sultan hated her too and would not concede turning her into a belly dancer. What a fall for a Sultan's Kadin!

****

Hurrem was the last visitor Hatidge Sultan expected to see at her door step, but she was known for many audacious acts.

"Is Ibrahim Pasha in? I heard he is visiting the Sultan many nights in a row, and I'm very worried what might have happened to my husband. He was too weak when I left him almost a week ago," she explained even though no explanation was required.

"You are always welcomed in our house," Hatidge replied graciously, and showed her to sit the empty spot on the sofa next to her.

"I'm very happy to hear it, because I possess nothing you may envy. Recently, even my husband's love is fading. Now the only thing I care deeply is the survival of my sons. I may have many sons, but each one is too precious to me to lose."

"No one is threatening your sons. Certainly not I or my husband. He is very devoted to his duties and as you may know, he is not keen on Ottoman tradition. He will do his best to stop this madness; but it's not up to him. If Allah wills something to happen to my brother, then my husband will make sure the best man rises to the throne of Osman. This is his pledge to me and my brother too. However, the Sultan even in his dying bed retains much of the awesome power of Allah's Shadow. Hopefully, my brother is wise enough not to leave for the last moment his most important task of any dying Sultan, leave the throne to the best man fit for this post."

"I realize that, but from the moment Mustafa becomes the next Sultan, my children are in mortal danger."

"Nonsense! Mustafa is a fine young man. If he becomes the Sultan, he will make sure your children find the place they deserve. Every Sultan needs men he can trust by his side."

"I wish the issues in question was as clear and forward as you presume, but we all have weaknesses that force us to act secretly to fulfill them. I'm sure that even you, a distinguished Ottoman Princess has felt awkwardly sometimes. Most people have very limited options and do what they are asked without complaint, but I'm different. I do what I feel it's right. I simply cannot follow orders unless they suit my fancy. This makes me look too capricious in the eyes of few men, so they detest me," Hurrem explained.

"My husband is not this kind of simpleminded man, I assure you. You have nothing to be afraid from him as long as it is for the good of the Empire."

"Then, I wonder if it's for the good of the Empire, if we become good friends," Hurrem inquired as she had skillfully manipulated the conversation to fit her aims.

"Who can argue against such a noble accomplishment," Hatidge wondered with a touch of irony that was noted, but Hurrem didn't seem to mind.

"Mahidevran Sultan would mind! I'm as certain as that soon noon is approaching," Hurrem claimed in anger; however Hatidge was much calmer than she might have expected and looked at her as, if her mind was travelling elsewhere.

"I'm not like Mahidevran Sultan either, so I cannot say how she might react. She has given birth to just one son of my brother, while you have offered him five young lads. In my mind this makes you equally precious as you are."

Her answer made clear it would be hard to trigger any kind animosity in Hatidge's heart. She had a sumptuous palace to live and raise her children, a distinguished husband who could pull Suleiman by the nose. Now Ibrahim had also the power to raise and lead armies into battle.

"I wonder how Ibrahim Pasha feels on this issue. Is he here? I would surely appreciate, if he was to assure me that he feels the same kind way like you."

"No, my husband is not here. He spent the night in the Seraglio. He must be planning a new war with the Sultan."

"Aren't you jealous your husband has spent the night in another bed?"

"What good would my jealousy do? I don't think anything I could do will make him change his mind. He always does what he has set his mind on doing well in advance."

"I couldn't live with a man who does not care how I feel. Suleiman was also like this at the beginning, but now he has changed. Now, he shares all my concerns and acts accordingly. How is Ibrahim treating you? You are an Osmanli Princess after all. He must show respect."

"He does respect me as much as I respect him, but the Sultan is his main concern as it should," Hatidge replied trying to appear as indifferent as she could to a practically complete stranger who tried to invade her privacy; but this was not what Hurrem had come to hear.

"I can read in your eyes how much it hurts to have a husband as desirable as Pargali Ibrahim Pasha. We have much in common, and all our children are in grave danger. Men simply cannot feel how much it hurts to bring a child in this world and sympathize with us. They are wild animals; so they try to treat us like animals too. At least you are a Princess. You and your children live under the same roof with their father, just as the members of any descent family should."

"I sympathize with your toils, but there is nothing I can do with the Sultan," Hatidge retorted, trying to end an embarrassing conversation; however Hurrem wouldn't accept her brush-off and reached to touch her hand.

"I'm sure you can do much more than that. Suleiman is your dear brother. This ordeal cannot last long without someone getting hurt, seriously hurt, and from the moment blood is spilled no one knows how it might end."

"Are you trying to scare me?" Hatidge responded to her emotional outburst.

"No, I'm trying to warn you that things are not as clear as they seem to be. Something terrible is brewing. I wish I had something more to say, but how can I explain a premonition or a hunch?" Hurrem noted and squeezed her hand.

"What exactly do you want me to do to calm your fears?" Hatidge retorted to her plea.

"Visit your brother as soon as possible and try to calm his anger any way you can. I suspect Ibrahim's behavior has troubled him deeply, and no one knows how he might react to his new ridiculous flick with this licentious Venetian youngster. I know that for your husband is just one more adventure, but my Suleiman is dying and the response this affair may trigger may easily get out of hand. My husband is an overly jealous male, and sometimes he responds just like a spoiled brat who is losing his most favorite toy."

Hatidge contemplated for a while before delivering her final answer.

"I'm sorry, but there is nothing more I can do. It is a personal matter, and they must solve themselves any problem they might encounter. There are not children anymore. They are grown-ups. They should have stopped suckling their thump long ago."

"Yes, indeed they should; but have they stopped, really? I sincerely doubt it."

****

Despite the adverse effects of his unexpected detention, Ibrahim looked relaxed and confident. Without a doubt, his fleeting affair with the Venetian had certain beneficial effects too. The sensation he was still attractive enough to attract the attention of a younger man was just one of them. There was no human being who didn't like the feeling of being wanted.

"You look very revived this morning. It has to be the effect of spending a sinless night. The Prophet must have been right at least in one of his assertions," Suleiman acknowledged after the traditional morning greetings.

"The Last Prophet has been right in much more than one thesis; however, if he is wrong in even one, then he is not a messenger of Allah but an impostor, Your Highness."

"Have you found this fallacious assertion by any chance? I would be very interested to know it," Suleiman snapped back.

"Indeed I have, but it seems to me that you have already known this fault and corrected it," Ibrahim replied with his usual confidence, a clear sign his old self was back with vengeance.

Suleiman had to admit that few years back this was the kind of Ibrahim he admired, confident, aggressive, and snappy. Somehow through the years his edge was blunted, but today he was as attractive as ever. It would be awfully hard to punish him for his last severe disloyalty; however, on the other hand, if a child was not punished severely after each misbehavior. then it would repeat the same fault later. This was a very serious dilemma he faced besides the obvious restriction that the punishment should fit the crime.

Was he seriously considering the possibility to leave even this indiscretion unchecked? If he had to, he could easily find a very good excuse, the same one he had used when Ibrahim committed his first offense. If Allah didn't punish a naughty child immediately after the act, why should he? As time went by, he could find even more excuses, and then his anger would evaporate. After all, it was dangerous to make critical decisions under stress.

"Why don't you give your master a taste of your wisdom? I'm sure my entire Empire will benefit."

"For a man to be happy one good woman is enough," Ibrahim Pasha revealed putting on a face as sober as Seih-ul-Islam. Despite the tension between them, Suleiman couldn't resist a good laughter.

"If this is indeed so, then one man should also be enough," he retorted.

"This is also a fair and valid limit a wise man should always keep, avoiding dangerous excesses, your Highness."

"Am I to assume that you have repented?" the Sultan inquired still eager to add an excuse in favor of the defendant.

"Not necessarily! In fact, I am proud for my audacious act, since the best way for a man to recognize his limits is to surpass them. Allah has made us humans this way, so we must not doubt his wisdom," Ibrahim audaciously argued, trying skillfully as usual to turn a grave mistake into a good deed.

"I thought you claimed few moments ago that the Prophet was wrong. How could you be right in both assertions?" Suleiman argued confident he had found a logical discrepancy.

"It most certainly can, my Lord. The Last Prophet was correct when he gave that limit, but since then women have made great strides, while we men have lost a great part of our superiority. I'm afraid now we are just about even."

"Does that mean you also intend to dismiss your harem?" the Sultan inquired still doubting what he heard.

"Yes, when I leave for Egypt with my Princess, I will leave my children behind in the care of the rest of my harem. Having so many women at my disposal has been a grave mistake and Allah had punished my greed already by sending me a Venetian angel as a messenger."

Ibrahim was trying to turn another of his faults into an advantage. Suleiman could see that plainly, but he couldn't but admire his inventiveness.

His intimate friend had a remarkable ability to attract attention. He had unconsciously sensed that from the very beginning, when they met in the Avret Bazaar. With his financial affluence he enjoyed he had bought for a menial amount of silver this remarkable slave who had repaid him a million times. He had to accept the fact that other people around him could also be attracted by his slave and would try to take a bite from this tasty piece of meat. As long as Ibrahim considered him his Master and obeyed his commands, he shouldn't resent the fact other men or women might use him too. Allah was benevolent after all, and forgave every sinner who sincerely repented.

****

Ibrahim Pasha could read in his master's face that the Sultan was gradually softening his resentment for his misbehavior. It meant he still considered his existence useful despite the price he had to pay. He hadn't been too costly. If he had submitted to Selim's advances few times, it was not too critical, because it was the result not of a sinful character, but of survival instincts. If the gossip about his frequent visits to Bursa had also reached Suleiman's ears, his excuse was adequately valid. He had to make sure that a gorgeous female like Mahidevran kept her urges under control, limiting any adverse comments of the locals to a minimum.

Beauty for a woman was a blessing, but it could easily become a curse. If he couldn't display his intelligence, he was depressed. It had to be the same with stunning women too. The most beautiful flowers had to attract bees and become pollinated, even though the fruits they produced were not as tasty as others less appealing to the eye. If the Sultan forgave this indignity, then his adventure with Gülfem was inconsequential indeed. The poor woman had been punished for life for losing a son, but it was hardly her mistake.

Life conditions for a married woman rejected by her husband were hard enough. After such a momentous event, many married women had chosen to live clandestine lives. With their hopes for normal family life shattered, they had become temporary wives of other less demanding men. This was their just revenge for the cruelty of their husbands, and a fair penalty for their husbands' failure to meet the terms of the marriage contract that demanded the proliferation of a family. The Prophet had put special emphasis on the sexual satisfaction of all his believers, hoping this way they could overcome in numbers their infidel opponents. It was a critical issue Christians had not seriously considered, when they preached abstinence as the proper way for a believer to reach Allah's Domain, the Kingdom of Heavens. Nevertheless, this was not the way few women treated the subject, considering satisfaction a worthy goal by itself, matching the greedy male point of view. Hafsa Hatun belonged to this category, but Haseki Hurrem was more enterprising, and tried to achieve both goals simultaneously. She was as greedy as Suleiman and thus a trophy worthy of his attention.

At the very beginning Suleiman had been wise not to pay special attention to Hurrem's untidy past compared to the different kinds of pleasure she provided. After all she was also just a slave as much as he was, and the rule of slavery was that a slave's assets should be exploited in every possible way, as the slave had no inherent morality rules his master should care for.

Suleiman was grossly unfair blaming him for infidelity. Sharing slaves among friends was a very common trend in Constantinople. If someone should complaint this was Princess Hatidge, not her all-demanding brother. These were the rules he would set for his subjects, if he ever became a Sultan in Egypt. He would reestablish the word of the Prophet that all the faithful should seek all the pleasures of the Kingdom of Heavens on Earth too.

****

Suleiman remained silent for a while, contemplating his next move. Mating with youth had to be a common trend that guided both men and women in their respective choices. It was a very attractive prospect, because psychologically it created the illusion of immortality. It was also the hidden desire everyone had experienced, while he was too young to seek complete sexual fulfillment and had to spend few years in the precarious state of abstinence.

It was difficult to decide when these sudden urges had first originated in his heart; but he suspected his father's unrestrained sexuality was the main cause. When he was still a young lad, he had watched secretly Selim as he mated with a lusty concubine, and was surprised by what a courtesan would do to please her mate. This had to be also the reason why he found Hurrem so attractive. Her attraction was contrary to the Prophet's advice, no doubt; but Allah had not decided, if he should punish him or not for his excesses.

Nevertheless, as he grew older he realized that his father did not restrict his lust only to women. He invited also attractive Janissaries into his quarters, and even built a special pavilion on the Bosporus shore for this purpose. He had never witnessed personally such an encounter, but the rumor was that Sinan Hadim, the young Grand Vizier, was more than just a friend of his grim father. He had watched them though looking at each other eyes in a curious way.

If his father was punished by Allah with death for his weakness towards eunuchs, he couldn't say, but unquestionably his two obnoxious lovers were a burden the welfare of the Empire could not afford after Selim's demise. Piri Pasha was right in his verdict for death sentence. They had to die before uncut eunuchs became a fashionable accessory for the Ottoman nobility.

A Sultan's ultimate duty was to provide the most attractive and useful image for his subjects to imitate. His father had never gave him such an advice, but he was wise enough to realize his obligations as a distinguished sovereign. As he grew older, his torturing worries that his time on the throne might not be long enough to give him a taste of everything there was grew from day to day. If his illness was a warning that death was approaching, he should surely act decisively to restore balance in his account.

Despite his age he was still curious what kinds of sensations were left to try, and his illness had made this urge quite acute recently. Ibrahim had been submissive to all his commands, but it seemed that with the Venetian Ibrahim had deviated from his old self for some reason. Perhaps this was also an aging affect similar to the side effects of his torturing pains. When he was in pain he could not really move and needed to be pampered by his servants. It sounded as an easy excuse, but he became very submissive when in pain. Come to think of it, pain or the fear of pain was what made all slaves submissive to their master's will.

He was so curious to experience new ideas and so eager to renew his interests, he decided to play around with the lyrics of a poem to hint the slave. They were not his words, but the poet's, who through the Sultan lips expressed his secret desires in a covert way:

"Tonight I feel so dazzled by desire, I cannot distinguish the rose from the thorn."

At last after so many years of hesitations he had crossed the limits too, claiming the slave's singularity.

****

In Ibrahim's ears this verse sounded peculiarly. The same words had been twisting in his mind the entire night. Was it possible their thoughts followed somehow the same path?

If he had any doubts, they were quickly dispersed, as Suleiman subtly expressed his secret thoughts assuring him of his desires with a friendly smile:

"Our favorite poet is an inexhaustible source of delicately phrased excuses."

Now even the reasons for his master's unexplained jealousy became clearer.

****

In Ibrahim's mind this last comment had a trace of irony. It was a sign that raised again his concerns. He had not failed to notice that in the spacious bedroom there were no more servants. It was a clear sign Suleiman had decided he would be the one to serve him. Some other time this issue would have caused him great joy, now, it was quite indifferent. He would have preferred if it was possible to find a viable excuse to return to his palace. As the prevailing atmosphere was developing, this evening had nothing else to offer to both but sheer boredom. Reciting poetry has ceased to excite both long time ago.

"A roses always imply a beautiful woman, and as usual, beautiful women have been excluded from this occasion," Ibrahim noted nervously.

Ibrahim felt unsure for the outcome, as the poem had few ambiguous verses. He would rather use his words to clarify his position.

"Master, please tell me. What will hurt your dignity most, if a stranger tries to steal your property, or if you sin, stealing his possession?"

This riddle appeared to have such an obvious answer, Suleiman didn't have to think much to reply.

"That was a foolish question. If someone steals my wealth, I will become very angry. This is why I loathed the thought you spent a night in a Galata locanda with the damned Venetian!"

"Then you should forget all about him. In Parga your pirates stole a very precious Venetian property long time ago, so now a representative of Venice came to claim it back."

The Sultan became suddenly too overwhelmed by his emotions to react. Ibrahim was a truly priceless jewel as long as he was in his service. Losing him would be really an irreplaceable loss he would surely regret. It was to his best interest to accept Ibrahim's skillful request for redemption. His best approach was to continue in a field where he felt more confident, poetry; so he noted with a friendly smile:

"Roses remind me indeed of women. Their lips are as inviting as rose petals."

Ottoman platitudes and clichés were always for Ibrahim sources of boredom; but this night he was forced to endure uncomplainingly Suleiman's wisdom claims. To entertain the boredom and divert banality he added another comment to make his master feel safe:

"Indeed they are, but the fruits of roses are too sour for our sensitive palates."

For the Sultan a rose was always connected with his beloved Hurrem, so the words of Ibrahim sounded as an insult; so he continued his effort to lead the discussion where he aimed.

"Yes, but their seeds are useful if your dream is to grow of a garden full of roses."

Ibrahim had enough of this discussion. Long ago, he had learned most of Rumi's poems by heart, but now his patience on listening to more Rumi repetitions was exhausted, so he showed his will to submit:

"As you so wisely said before: Our beloved poet is an inexhaustible source of delicately phrased excuses."

"Yesterday I was clever, so I wanted to change the world. Today I am wise, so I am changing myself," the Sultan boldly claimed, and Ibrahim was now faced with the task decipher successfully the Sultan's verse.

Suleiman had a strange smile on his face. Was he teasing him with his Rumi riddles? What was the meaning of his claim "changing himself"? What did Rumi meant with his secretive claim? Was Suleiman influenced by Sinan's teachings?

Probably Rumi was an old man when he wrote this poem. Pious old men approaching the moment of death, sought redemption from their creator for their sins to secure a place in Paradise. Suleiman had to believe he was close to death to promise he was going to change. He had the same age with the Sultan, but he was still healthy, attractive, and very much alive, so he had no reason to try to change anything in his life. He was still a slave, but he lived a successful life full of gratifying experiences. On the contrary, the Sultan was now sick and in pain. It was natural for him to put all his hopes in an attempt for a radical change; but what kind of transformations this change would include? This was the puzzle he was now facing.

Ibrahim always believed that the genius of man was not measured if he was just capable of finding the solution of a problem, but how quickly he reaches the correct conclusion. Intelligence was measured by the reduction of the time wasted. Even Rumi had a verse to that effect and Suleiman used it to give him a warning:

"For every sin there is an apology, only the wastage of time is inexcusable."

He examined carefully Suleiman's facial expression. It was tense and with every passing moment his impatience grew. It was obvious the passage of time weighted heavily in his mind. For some reason he feared he would be dead by sunrise, so he urged him to hurry. He was sure he could find the solution to any problem, but as the time left was getting less and less, he struggled harder to find the proper solution. He was still confident the solution was already in front of his eyes. All that was left for him to do was to clear the fog clouding his vision and see it. The very thought that back in his palace three gorgeous women waited impatiently for his return, while he was forced to seek for solutions of dubious riddles of a sick man on his death-bed infuriated him; but suddenly his logic showed him the way to the heart of Sultan's problem.

The true solution of a problem should satisfy all available conditions, even the most insignificant from the beginning to the end. He remembered the Sultan's words. He had said: "Our favorite poet is an inexhaustible source of delicately phrased excuses." And before that another strange verse: "Today I feel so dazzled by desire, I cannot distinguish the rose from the thorn."

Unconsciously his mind sprang the next verse of the poem, and his lips uttered the words by themselves:

Love has made me so dizzy this evening, I cannot distinguish
which of the two is the lover and who the beloved.

At last he had unravel what Suleiman was too ashamed to express in his own words. Now that he had found the lead, there were abundant signs that should have revealed the final conclusion. The fear of his terrible father and his weakness for his mother was just two causes. His attachment to Hurrem was nothing more than the need of every man to find a substitute of his dying mother to take care of his need for affection. Even the cruelty he had shown to captives after his victories was nothing but the manifestation of the hatred he felt for all those who were unable to resist and succumbed to the overwhelming power of their conqueror.

Suleiman needed many women to feel like a man; so his caring mother had assembled an entire harem of attractive creatures to offer him the confidence he lacked, but it was not enough to prove his manliness. His mother had failed; so Suleiman had tried his father's recipe. He had come to the Avret Bazaar to buy a male slave. If women had failed him, perhaps a man was what he needed.

His father instinctively had sensed the problem and tried to solve it the only way he knew, replace the woman's tenderness and submission with a young man's. Selim was well familiar with man to man relationships; so he tried his best to train his son's slave and make him learn the eunuch ways, but he had made a poor choice for a student. Instinctively he had chosen what he desired as a courtesan, an exceptionally gifted man. Fortunately for Suleiman they had much in common. The slave was young too and had also a tough time deciding which was the proper role he should to play in life to be content. He had also an open mind like the master and had to try everything too, before making a sincere commitment. As a slave he had been trained to behave submissively to stay alive, and so he did in every occasion at the beginning. However, as his status improved and his authority increased, he simply had to try also his luck as a ruler. As the Ancient Greeks had said, it was natural for the strong to rule and for the weak to endure.

The match of interests was almost ideal for many years, but for any inquisitive master it was impossible to pass an entire life among slaves without exciting his curiosity to try even once their kind of pleasure. In the end the conqueror and his slaves would become one. They were like two rain drops that yearned to be joined into one, because only then Mother Nature could find her lost balance. A slavery could end only when a new one commenced.

******

Ibrahim's gaze focused on Suleiman's complexion. It was crimson from the shame of a conqueror who had lost the final battle and couldn't bear the agony of defeat. The master had heard the last verse and understood the slave had guessed his secret desires. Now the both realized what was bound to happen, but felt reluctant to make the first step towards their future. The only danger the slave now faced was if his master could not look on himself in the mirror and live from then on without any alluring illusions about who he really was. Maybe it was difficult for a descendant of Sultan Osman to realize that from now on he ought to satisfy the desires of a slave in order to retain the security of the slave's presence by his side.

Ibrahim had experienced this transition when in a single night he had relinquished the masculine freedom to choose; but for him it had been relatively easy to change his ways back then because he was young and undecided. Suleiman was mature and the change would take great time and great effort. His state of mind was also unstable and perilous, almost as difficult as for a grown man who was suddenly turned into a eunuch.

Ibrahim knew that feeling all too well. Such a change was riskier for a mature man than for a young boy. It could even prove impossible to bear, as many men went crazy in the process of changing personalities. He knew that well enough because many times he had also faced the prospect of losing his manhood, when Selim Khan was still alive and threatening. However, Selim was not the only danger. In the Janissary Corps, during a battle similar phenomena of violent castrations battle wounds were not rare, so several times he had faced similar mental tortures. He was also aware of other Janissary who had buckled under this pressure and chose volunteer castration to get rid of this fear once and for all and fight valiantly for Allah.

If he had not taken the last step, it was because of the tender care of all the women in his life, who as if they were precious allies, they gave him the boost of moral to continue his fight, even though few battles were lost in between. In the end his war had to be won.

Now there was no doubt that Hatidge's decision to ask the Sultan to make him the Beylerbey of Egypt was the correct one. Life in the Seraglio had become so complex that even his own mind was pressed hard to find viable solutions every day.

The City also had nothing more to offer him. Galata's roads were slippery and full of all sorts of traps and temptations. Even the most virtuous man could be tempted one night by the Devil. The Muslims were wrong, The Devil existed, but it was not as powerful as God, because he appeared only in human form and took advantage of human weaknesses. He knew Devil well, because he had fought against him many times. Sometimes the Devil had the muscles of a man, and few times he stared at him with the zephyr eyes of Hurrem.

This woman was indeed the Devil for him always full of seductive promises, while at the same time she was an angel for his friend, keeping the man in him content. Unfortunately for Hurrem he was the Devil who tried to lure her beloved husband to disgrace, threatening the lives of her sons too.

Tonight the Sultan had taken the last step and asked his help to change, but tomorrow Hurrem might lure him back in her embrace. If he was free, he could solve all these problems by escaping, but he was a slave and the Sultan was the only one who could set him free under the law. His eyes were slowly drawn towards the abyss of total submission. There they met Suleiman's eyes and were experienced enough to know what was hidden deep in his master's mind. With a magnanimous gesture he ordered the last page to leave. He and Suleiman wished to be left alone. The servant, well-trained looked at the Sultan expecting his orders, but he remained passive as if everything that happened was according to his will. He had made clear the Grand Vizier spoke with his tongue and his words were as precious as pearls from the Indian Ocean. At last, the persistent gaze of a Grand Vizier forced miraculously the pending issue. Now they were alone and to be certain the great secret did not leak, the Grand Vizier went and bolded both doors. The old charade of the all-conquering House of Osman had to continue till eternity.

****

He stretched out his hand and straighten Suleiman ruffled hair. The Sultan opened his eyes still blurred and sluggish after the ecstasy of passion. In his dreams Ibrahim had seen scrambled and unsorted bits of the past and the future. He saw pious Muslims passing for thousands of times through a backdoor, praying under the dome of Agia Sophia; and then curious Greeks slipping through the eye of the needle searching deep in the Seraglio for its secret treasures, during a marvelous dream that had turned many centuries into fleeting moments.

Then, he suddenly realized that Time was playing games with him, trying to lure him to his death. When Time was present, ordinary mortals shuddered counting the moments left to live. In an instant his final decision was molded. Now that he had learned the truth, he could no longer be involved in the same power games. To retain his sanity he had to leave the Seraglio in a hurry, take along his children and his harem, and make a new beginning away from the Osmanli madness. He had to change too, as no longer grabbing bits and pieces of life from the table of his master was enough to satisfy his insatiable hunger for life. Without the freedom to choose life had no meaning.

"I have to leave!" he said firmly and saw the Sultan's eyes clouding with tears. At the beginning they both had hoped their friendship would last forever, but it was Allah's will everything from pain to pleasure to have an end, and the last Prophet had expressed so plainly that even a Bedouin lost in the desert should keep his hopes alive and seek redemption in the paradise of an oasis.

"Even this will eventually pass," the Last Prophet claimed as only death lasted forever.

"No, you cannot leave me just yet. You have to stay here till sunrise in the next room. I may need you later. This is all knew to me," the master explained, and the slave was well aware how the master felt; the need of every human being to feel desirable was inexhaustible.

The slave's heart gamboled with the thought that now he was suddenly the master. He had been a slave of several masters in his life and he was well aware that a master had the right to say I'm bored. Then the slave had to seek another master. He was free, at last, so he went to the Hasodabashi bedroom and unlocked both doors before falling asleep.

****

Returning to the Eski Saray, Hurrem felt like a prisoner freed for just a moment and then put back in chains. She was desperate and her apparent inability to liberate herself from the torture of submission to the Sultan's will filled her mind with pure madness. She had only one way out of this endless slavery. She asked the Kislar Aga to appear as soon as possible.

He came rushing like the Sultan's black stallion. He was perspiring and tried hard to catch his breath. All men were most desirable at this excited state. They were as if they had just finished satisfying their lust for the first time and tried to recover their strength for a new venture, but she knew she should tease him for a while to help him on this task.

"You made me very happy last night. I'm sure you have noticed it, but it takes great patience and training for us to achieve the state of perfection when two souls become one, and know instinctively what the other half needs to achieve the state of bliss. Last night was just the first of your new magnificent future. Are you ready to follow me in this path? I would be very glad to lead you all the way to fulfillment."

The Nubian slave smiled and licked his sumptuous lips to show his agreement as words were not always the best way to convey emotions.

"Good! This is what you must do next tonight and I'm sure you are man enough to do it. I bet all the men in your tribe had to kill a man to earn the women of another tribe. I'm afraid there is no other way for you to convince the woman you desire that you are worthy of her favors. A man or maybe more have to die for your children to be born. This is the way Mother Nature has found to make sure the best man wins the right to seed children. You told me long time ago your given name was "Lion"; so do what lions do to prove their worth as kings of the jungle. Life is a jungle anyway, and the weak must perish for the strong to rule."

****

Hurrem was terrified seeing the Sultan bursting into her bedroom at daybreak not like a conqueror but as a fugitive. Few hours had passed since the Kislar Aga had left for the Seraglio to carry out her orders, but since then he hadn't come back to tell her what had happened. His task was difficult and the risks were considerable. Difficult tasks needed resolve but also flexibility to be carried out successfully. She knew that all along; so her instructions were vague. Much more important was to make the Aga understand what was her major problem. Ibrahim should be stopped from interfering with her intimate relation with the Sultan.

The sun had risen and in the dim light she saw clearly despite her slumber and quickly understood who was chasing Suleiman. Ramadan had ended and his remorse was for feeling so weak and incapacitated. It meant the Devil had not decided yet to leave them alone. He constantly had to interfere stealing pleasure from his master on every occasion. Some other night she might tease her husband for a while to fill him with lust before serving him the pleasure he sought, but her instinct urged her this daybreak to be generous. She had to finish the voyage through the Ramadan test as an ideal companion full of understanding.

The Sultan striped quickly and slipped under the covers with closed eyes waiting for an experienced slave to satisfy every urge his male lover had left yearning. He watched her body language fill his mind with elusive promises he could not resist even in this dilapidated state. The pressure raised inside him during the night had to erupt somehow. He laid in bed beside her, while his fingers searched and found her nipples; but she pushed his sweaty hands away and resolutely, turning her back to him. Her almighty laughter filled the air as he searched feverishly to find the door he sought to explode his passion, but the exact origin of laughter is sometimes hard to locate in a human being. For instance, it could be the joy of victory in the eternal struggle for supremacy between the sexes, or an invitation for a confused desire looking for a path to sneak into her heart.

Laughing or crying may have also their source deep in the heart of man; but very often they can be caused by just a spontaneous skin effect, as skin is the first obstacle any invader finds in his path. How anyone interprets the natural phenomena is his responsibility and like everything else in life one has to suffer the consequences of his or her choices during each and every moment of existence.

Suleiman in the past was always optimistic, even when death was beating on the gates of his Seraglio, as no mortal had never refused granting him a wish. Thus, now he chose the more enjoyable interpretation of the phenomenon and he replied to her laughter with the only way the body of a man knows how to speak, by contact. He had never spent even a moment of his life worrying that the woman of his life reserved a part of her body for someone else or that she did not want to bring another child into this world now that she reigned supreme. Instead he imagined that the entire Allah's universe was made to offer him new, or less familiar delights that would sooth his soul until he entered the promised paradise up in heavens reserved after death for all the pious Muslims like him.

Hurrem reacted to his intimate touch with a sigh that revitalized even further his aching flesh. His hands stroked spontaneously both her buttocks, as if she was his mare. The female instinctively reacted to his command and started galloping. With eyes closed it is much easier for the mind to travel to imaginary worlds where everything is perfect overcoming the restrictive boundaries of reality. This night had awaken once more old memories. She was still a virgin slave who tried hard to find a new balance in her life postponing her less urgent burdens to the future. She had to put an end to her toils as quickly and as safely as possible.

Her frantic gallop quickly surpassed his feeble stamina. His hair on his neck stood up like an angry wolf's. The Allah's world would always contain slaves and masters, as there always would be wolves in lamb's clothes and lambs in wolves' clothes. Hurrem was now the lamb with the exquisite flesh to saturate his refined palate. In his mind her total submission to his desires extinguished all his doubts about this exceptional night. No matter what had happened, a woman could always bring balance to a troubled man of mixed preferences. Ibrahim had raised few very unsettling questions, but as long Hurrem was there to answer them, he was safe.

He plunged his teeth in the soft skin around her neck. Her body leaped reacting to this painful assault and an instinctive scream slipped through her lips that began as a protest, but slowly turned to a soft murmur, revealing her complete subjection to his wishes. It was the subjugation of a cat to the caresses of its master. His desire was so intense that with a few thrusts every drop of desire of his was spent. Under his closed eyelids Ibrahim's image sprang, and as if she had guessed the content of his mind, a cry soft like a sigh, "Ibrahim", escaped from her lips that passed unnoticed through the violent waves of his rampant desires.

****

Her patience was exhausted. As everything else, patience had limits. She simply couldn't go on with her life this way. Sooner or later her secret desire would come into the open. The only solution she could see was if the Devil stopped interfering with her life, putting in question all her life's accomplishments. Now she had become one of the three Sultan's Kadin, but his sheer existence was constantly awakening her shabby past. Ibrahim was a temptation she found constantly more difficult to resist. Suleiman's illness was slowly forcing her to seek replacements. This night the Kislar Aga and Suleiman had come to her rescue, but if his condition worsened again, the she could find no good excuses preventing her to behave as a whore at every available opportunity.

The Sultan's piousness was also another factor and it was difficult for her to decide if it had something to do with his declining health. When people approached their death, it was natural to behave more religiously; but, it was also possible that an illness prevented them to become more sinful. Nobody ever knows what is hidden in the mind of the man each and every moment, and his favorite poet assured her that within a man the entire universe could fit.

Suddenly a distant cry was heard that in her ears sounded like the whine of a dying man. It had to be the distant voice of a muezzin from the Agia Sophia Mosque the wind had brought it to her ears. Soon total silence prevailed as if it was a luxurious bedcover hiding from the curious eyes of a Sultan all the sinful details of a mesmerizing odalisque.

By now her avenging angels of male purity should have finished their task. Her orders were subtle but clearly versed. The Devil should lose his tail, as a devil without a tail in the eyes of Allah would look as pure as an angel.

****

Suleiman was perfectly serene resting on his back next to her all-conquering flesh. In his mind she had been as powerful and devious as Fatih. After many years of resistance, he had to submit to her will; as his illness had devastated every desire for resistance.

Hurrem did not let this opportunity to utter an excuse for her unintentional revelation escape. She stretched and whispered in Suleiman's ear:

Do you think I always know what I must do?
That as long as I breath, I belong to myself?
No! I'm like the pen that never knows
Which word it will be asked to write next.

Suleiman smiled. He was right. The poet had just provided an excuse for everything.

****

Through the thin fog of uneasy sleep Ibrahim felt he was not alone in the room. Maybe if it was still darkness his nightmare would remain hidden. He opened his eyes wide and in the rising sunlight he saw a dark human form approaching with a threatening gesture, holding a sharp razor blade that sparkled as it move closer through the sunrays. It was the Kislar Aga and he was not alone. He had with him several black eunuchs. The survival instinct pushed him to look to find his knife and raise it aggressively for his defense.

He fought like a man, slashing black flesh right and left in despair, and the blood of the raging eunuchs painted the linen red and filled the air with their shrieking curses. He saw the Kislar Aga's knife falling on the floor and his heart was filled with hope; but the battle was uneven and unfair. The slaves would always face unfairly their master, and it was not their fault. A single master had many slaves under his foot.

Soon many powerful black hands kept him completely immobile resting on his back at the Kislar Aga's disposal. He pulled his knife from his hands, and tore one by one all the clothes he wore. He did not stop even when even his silken underwear had turned into ribbons. The Aga picked one and turned it skillfully into a noose. Ibrahim felt the tightness of the delicate silk noose, dividing his body into two pieces. An unbearable pain filled his guts that made him forget even the primal thirst for air. The hanging piece of flesh slowly turned into purple like an imperial Roman toga. The pain reached such a high peak that even the cold steel blade slashing his body was a relief, because it meant the dissolution of pain.

The Grand Vizier watched his dead blood discarded as jet painting the walls, following the rhythm of heartbeats. He felt with it his life slipping away, but the death coming was welcome, because as the end came closer it took away the pain. He collapsed exhausted on the rug as the black hands that kept him enslaved, retreated and swiftly disappeared into the darkness of the corridor.

He knew what the long wait was for. According to the tradition they had to carry the hot oil to seal the wound. Maybe if he was younger he could withstand the new reality; but now it was impossible for him to confront the eyes of the women of his life, or telling his son fairy tales with the feminine voice of a eunuch. With all the strength left in his wounded flesh he got up, opened the door and plunged stumbling through the dark corridors, leaving behind bloody footprints. Soon he realized he was out in the yard. At each step the pain was awaken again, but he had to reach a fountain. The thirst of bleeding ate his guts. He bent down to drink and there he collapsed unconscious on the pavement.

Through his mind scattered images passed rapidly, as his senses tried to recycle pain with old memories. Time had turned back many years. It was strange now that his quest was all over, he did not feel any grudge against anyone. All through his life Allah had tried to give him a lesson, but he had isolated himself, plugging hermetically eyes and ears. From Selim Khan he had learned there were forces in life no one could overcome, no matter how exceptional he was. Many times, Suleiman's behavior had revealed that even if he resembled his mother, deep inside his ideal was to behave like his father. Even the kiss of the

Venetian conveyed a secret message. It was the kiss of Judas, the final salute of all the men he made happy with his body.

On the other hand, few days ago the women in his life had offered him a helping hand urging him to escape even at the last minute, but he was greedy and had postponed taking the drastic decision; but the future moved sometimes slowly and others rushed on, and then there was nothing even the most powerful men could do soften the blow.

Even Hurrem had sent him a message he had declined to answer. Perhaps, if he had accepted her offer, Suleiman would be now in his position.

He had not pay attention even to the words of his favorite poet, Rumi, and who had solved all his toils with his licentious dervish lover by stubbing his lover's heart with a knife. It was his bold advice that only with a knife one could cut away his weaknesses once and for all.

He always had the hope that in life everything was unique and unrepeatable. It was his last and fatal fallacy. The mind of a man, if it was left free, it could travel all over the universe; but this was not Allah's wish. Man may have discovered fire. In the future he may even grow wings; but he would always seek refuge in the past, because the memories were the attraction that would keep him forever a slave of his feelings.

He had made many strides in his life jumping from one orbit to the next, assuming that everything he wished for was attainable, but he was wrong. There were orbits that were inaccessible and forbidden to a mortal during his lifetime. They were kept in reserve, waiting to be expressed in the future; as the human greed of each generation surpassed all the old ones.

Eventually he could not complaint to Allah. He had been a Ramadan sinner through all his life and He had punished him when His patience was exhausted. He had warned him inside the Galata mosque what would be his end. He even sent also his messenger, Sinan, countless times to warn him to start early the great war with himself, but he never paid attention to His words.

It was remarkable that his life in the Seraglio ended today as surprisingly as it had once begun. All efforts avoiding fate was futile and his life circle was ending without him being able to escape from his predetermined orbit. All he had finally won was that in his last moments he could close in his heart all the precious moments of his life that his mind had chosen to keep alive in his memory and relive once more the highlights of a long journey.

He opened his eyes wide and looked at the sky as even the brighter stars faded away under the sunlight. Suddenly he saw leaning over him a familiar face. Sinan had rushed for one more time to protect him. He started to talk as fast as he could, because he wanted to tell him a lot and he was afraid his time left would not be enough.

"I'm not afraid of dying. I'm used to dying. After all, very passing moment we die and a new man is born in our image. Even when we sleep at night we die, and when we wake up the next morning our minds are reassured by sleep that better days are bound to come."

He made a last effort, as the words slipped with difficulty through his lips.

"Tell my master that dying was my decision, and he shouldn't blame anyone else. His slave has sinned too much for a single life."

As Ibrahim finished all he had to say, Sinan wiped his sweaty forehead. He wished these moments to last forever, and Allah the Benevolent would grant his last wish, if he wished hard enough. He had reached the point of final universal awareness.

As his life ended he had finally discovered and the meaning of death. It was the ultimate dream when infinity collapsed into nothingness, and man could retain forever in his brain the memories he chose. It was up to him now to concentrate his entire life into one moment. Instead of a nightmare, he was wise to let his existence sink into a the emerald lake of a slave's eyes and uttered her name to open the gates of Paradise. Sherenk!

And then, the vortex of a galaxy suddenly opened deep in his mind swallowing all his senses. His long journey to the distant heart of the Milky Way had begun.

END OF THE THIRD VOLUME

ONCOMING FOURTH VOLUME: HURREM

References

1. "Ibrahim Pasha, Grand Vizier of Suleiman the Magnificent," Hester Donaldson Jenkins, Columbia University, Longman, 1911.
2. "Suleiman the Magnificent and His Age," Metin Kunt, Christine Woodhead, Longman, 1955.
3. "Suleiman the Magnificent 1520-1566," Roger B. Merriman, Harvard University Press, 1944.
4. "Suleiman the Magnificent, Sultan of the East," Harold Lamb, Doubleday & Company Inc., 1951.
5. "Suleiman the Magnificent," J. M. Rogers and R. M. Ward, British Museum Pubs, 1988.
6. "Dawn of the Beloved," Louis Gardel, The French Millennium Library, 2003.
7. "The Ottoman Empire 1700-1922," Donald Quataert, Cambridge Univ. Press, 2000.
8. "Sinan," Arthur Stratton, Charles Scribner's Sons, 1972.
9. "The Essential Rumi," Coleman Barks, Castle Books, 1997.
10. "Sufism," James Fadiman and Robert Frager, Castle Books, 1997.
11. "The Qur'an" Translation by M.H. Shahir, Tahrike Tarsile Qur'an Inc., 2001.
12. "Inside the Seraglio," John Freely, Penguin Books, 1999.
13. "The Ottoman Centuries," Lord Kinross, Morrow Quill Paperbacks, 1977.
14. "The Decline and Fall of the Roman Empire," Edward Gibbon, Wordsworth, 1998
15. "Constantinople," Philip Mansel, Penguin Books, 1995.
16. "Istanbul, the Imperial City," John Freely, Penguin Books, 1998.
17. "Imperial Istanbul," Jane Taylor, I. B. Tauris, 1998.
18. "Lords of the Horizon," John Goodwin, Vintage, 1998.
19. "The Ottoman Age of Explorations," Giancarlo Casale, Oxford University Press, 2010.
20. http://en.wikipedia.org/wiki/Bayezid_I
21. http://en.wikipedia.org/wiki/Selim_I

22. http://en.wikipedia.org/wiki/Suleiman_the_Magnificent
23. http://en.wikipedia.org/wiki/Pargali_Ibrahim_Pasha
24. http://en.wikipedia.org/wiki/Roxelana
25. http://en.wikipedia.org/wiki/Ayşe_Hafsa_Sultan
26. http://en.wikipedia.org/wiki/Mimar_Sinan
27. http://en.wikipedia.org/wiki/Mahidevran_Sultan
28. http://en.wikipedia.org/wiki/Hadim_Sinan_Pasha
29. http://en.wikipedia.org/wiki/Raziye_Sultan
30. https://en.wikipedia.org/wiki/Apollo%27s_belt

Printed in Great Britain
by Amazon

26631625R00341